THE HOUSE OF LIGHT

ELIZABETH JAMES

authorHOUSE®

AuthorHouse™
1663 Liberty Drive, Suite 200
Bloomington, IN 47403
www.authorhouse.com
Phone: 1-800-839-8640

First published by AuthorHouse 8/4/2008

ISBN: 978-1-4343-6634-4 (sc)
ISBN: 978-1-4343-6635-1 (hc)

Library of Congress Control Number: 2008900937

Printed in the United States of America
Bloomington, Indiana

This book is printed on acid-free paper.

Front Cover: adapted from The Practicing Alchemist,
an engraving by Rembrandt van Rijn, 1652.

Other Books by Elizabeth James:

Bridges of Time, 1st Books, Bloomington, Indiana, USA. 2001.
Across the Bridge. XLibris, Philadelphia, Pennsylvania, USA. 2004.

ACKNOWLEDGMENTS

The author is indebted to the following authors and their respective texts for providing valuable background information. These are listed chronologically by year of publication so that no preference is shown for any text above the others. The texts are:

- *The History and Antiquities of the County Palatinate of Durham,* by William Hutchinson (Hodgson, Robinson, and Robinson, London, UK, 1785).

- *Harun al Rashid: Caliph of Baghdad,* by Gabriel Audisio (Robert McBride & Company, New York, 1931).

- *Tales of the Arabian Nights*, ed. by H. W. Dulcken (Castle Books, Secaucus, NJ, 1984).

- *Harun al-Rashid and the World of* The Thousand and One Nights, by André Clot (Librairie Arthème Fayard, Paris, France, 1986; English translation by John Howe, New Amsterdam Books, New York, 1989).

- *The World of Islam,* ed. by Bernard Lewis (Thames and Hudson, New York, 1992).

- *Fingerprints of the Gods: The Evidence of Earth's Lost Civilization,* by Graham Hancock (Three Rovers Press, New York, 1995).

- *A Brief Illustrated Guide to Understanding Islam,* 2nd ed., by I. A. Ibrahim (Darussalam Publishers and Printers, Houston, TX, 1997).

- *The Ecclesiastical History of the English People. The Venerable Bede,* translated by Bertram Colgrave (Oxford World's Classics. Oxford Paperbacks, Oxford University Press, Oxford, UK, 1999).

- *Islam: A Thousand Years of Faith and Power,* by Jonathan Bloom and Sheila Blair (TV Books, New York, 2000).

- *History of the Arabs,* 10th ed., rev., by Walid Khalidi (Palgrave Macmillan, Basingstoke, Hampshire, UK, 2002).

- *Polio,* ed. Thomas M. Daniel and Frederick C. Robbins (University of Rochester Press, Rochester, New York, 1997).

- *The Qur'an,* 9th U.S. ed., translated by M. H. Shakir, Takrike Tarsile (Qur'an Inc., Elmhurst, New York, 2002).

Ms. Sharida Hassanali is gratefully acknowledged for fruitful discussions about the customs of Islam. Ms. Laylaa Ali and family are also gratefully acknowledged for providing valuable answers to many questions. Mr. Tony Munari is acknowledged for his expert production of the maps that adorn several pages of this book.

And last, but by no means least, mention needs to be made of the author's participation in the local Writers' Group. The meetings, held twice per month, have been fruitful, productive, and fun. For these interactions, the author is grateful and offers thanks and gratitude to the members of this Group.

Elizabeth James
September 2007

FOREWORD

This is a work of fiction. The story is structured within an accurate historical context. But with the exception of some of the historical characters and several of the historical events, all of the characters in this book are fictional and bear no relationship to any real person, living or dead.

For the most part, modern place names are used instead of the more confusing, older names. The language used throughout the text is English, even though it must be recognized that in the time when the historical events occurred, other languages were used. Other than the occasional common phrases, no attempt is made here to reproduce the various foreign languages as they may have been spoken by the characters in this story.

CONTENTS

HISTORICAL NOTE

A Northumbrian nobleman, Benedict Biscop, founded the Anglo-Saxon monastery of St. Peter at Wearmouth in 674 A.D. on a hill above the River Wear on land given by Egfrid, King of Northumbria.

The Wearmouth monastery was constructed by stonemasons brought over from Gaul and was the first stone-built monastery in Britain. The Wearmouth monastery and its twin monastery at Jarrow to the north, built eight years after the Wearmouth monastery, served as a dual center of learning for most of Britain. The floor was constructed of fine white concrete, and each monastery had a chapel, a refectory, and a private chamber for the abbot. The monks lived in individual thatched huts that stood to the east of the monastery building but within the precinct.

The monastery was built within a twelve-month period and was surrounded by a large wooden rampart that had been constructed with a deep ditch on the outside. A sturdy gate allowed entrance to the monastery precinct. The ramparts' massive fortification was completed in an unheard-of brief period of weeks, rather than months. The protection seemed excessive, but it was known that there were those who would put to the sword any monks or such persons as followed the monks into the new and growing religion.

A cemetery was located immediately to the north of the Wearmouth monastery and within the enclosure. The cemetery was separated into two parts—the lay cemetery and the monastic cemetery. In the lay cemetery, a mix of male, female, and child burials took place. They each were placed in the supine position, shrouded, lying with their heads to the east and their feet either crossed or together. Some of the more prominent members of the community were buried in wooden coffins. The monastic cemetery was reserved exclusively for the monks, who were also buried, shrouded, in the supine position.

Visiting monks and scholars knew of the location of the monastery, as did traders who brought goods to the monks and to the villagers. But other travelers had to know of its existence and be given directions; otherwise, they would pass it by or only find it by accident.

Eight years after the completion of the monastery at Wearmouth, the twin house was founded at Jarrow-on-Tyne, in honor of St. Paul. These two monasteries were so closely connected in their early history that they are often spoken of as one, even though they were really about ten miles apart. Both monasteries were built in the Roman fashion and furnished with glass windows (hitherto unknown in England).

Like Wearmouth, Jarrow was one of the seedbeds of Christianity in the north. The foundation of both religious houses can be traced back over centuries. Both monasteries were centers of learning and religion that were shared by few others, since most religious centers were for prayer only. After the creation of the two monasteries, the abbots had made it known that any travelers who passed through the monastery would be asked for any books that they might carry. Alternately, visiting monks would be asked to bring books as a loan. These books would be copied by the resident monks and returned to their respective owners as soon as possible.

The subsequent rise of the two monasteries with the copies of various texts, some of which described human rather than spiritual affairs, brought a new wave of scholars who wished to read works of philosophy, history, and mathematics. The abbots of Wearmouth and Jarrow reacted with alacrity to requests for rediscovered ancient texts. New translations of Greek and Roman works were brought in by scholars from all parts of Europe.

The Venerable Bede, who had entered St. Peter's in 680 A.D. at the age of seven, remained in the monastery until his death in 735 A.D. "Servant of Christ and Priest of the Monastery of Saints Peter and Paul, which is at Wearmouth and Jarrow" are the words that Bede used to describe himself. During his lifetime, he wrote *The Ecclesiastical History of the English People,* which he completed in 731 A.D. This work is the primary source for understanding the beginnings of the English people and the coming of Christianity. It is also the first work of history in which the A.D. dating system is used.

Bede died in his cell at the monastery in the year 735. Cuthbert, a young monk who was with him, later wrote an account of Bede's death and became St. Cuthbert, as he was known later (the patron saint of the cathedral at Durham). Cuthbert described how Bede finished dictating a chapter of a book that he was composing. Cuthbert reported that just before he died, Bede said, "I have a few treasures in my box, some pepper and incense. Run quickly and fetch the priests of our monastery, and I will share among them such little presents as God has given me."

The monastery suffered greatly from raids by the Danes in the early to mid-ninth century. After the conquest by William of Normandy, both monasteries were restored, though not to their former independence. They became cells subordinate to the cathedral priory of Durham and were thenceforward occupied by a small number of monks. The current site of Wearmouth Abbey is occupied by the Church of St. Peter, which traces its origins back to the abbey.

* * *

It is recorded in the Anglo-Saxon Chronicles that in 787 a.d., "There came for the first time three ships of Northmen from Hordaland [the district around Hardanger fjord in West Norway]; and then the reeve rode there and wanted to compel them to go to the king's town because he did not know what they were; and they killed him. Those were the first ships of the Danish men which sought out the land of the English race."

Thereafter, the Chronicles record many attacks on the eastern coast of England, in which plunder and killing seemed to be the objectives of the sea raiders. Now known by the name Vikings (often translated as "pirates"), they established a kingdom based around a city called Jorvik (modern York), which was formerly known as Eboracum in the time of the Romans.

* * *

The Prophet Mohammed was born in the northern Arabian trading city of Mecca between 570 and 580 a.d. When he was forty years old, he heard the angel Gabriel speaking to him and telling him to start a new religion: Islam. After a slow start, Mohammed made a lot of converts to his new religion. By 640 (after the death of Mohammed) the Arabs controlled most of western Asia, and soon after that, under the rule of the Umayyad caliphs, they conquered Egypt. By 711, the Umayyads controlled all of western Asia except Turkey (which was still part of the Roman Empire), and all of the southern Mediterranean: Egypt, Libya, Tunisia, Algeria, Morocco, and most of Spain.

In 750 a.d., the Umayyad caliphs were replaced by the Abbasid caliphs, and the surviving Umayyads fled from Damascus to Spain, where they founded the Umayyad caliphate of Spain, which ruled Spain for many years. In 762 a.d., the Abbasids moved their capital from Damascus to the new city of Baghdad. Baghdad was soon a large cosmopolitan city, where people spoke Aramaic, Arabic, and Persian.

By the 800s Baghdad probably had nearly half a million people (that is half as big as Rome during the Roman Empire) and was the largest city in the known world.

The Abbasids ruled all of western Asia and North Africa from 750 a.d. until about 1000 a.d. In 1258 a.d., the Abbasid dynasty ended. Harun al-Rashid (Harun the Wise) was the fifth Abbasid caliph. He and his fabulous court at Baghdad are immortalized in the *Thousand and One Nights*.

Born to the Caliph al-Mahdi ("Guided to the right path") and the former slave-girl al-Khayzuran, Harun was raised at court, where he was well educated. Before he was out of his teens, Harun was made the nominal leader of several expeditions against the Eastern Roman Empire. His success (or, in reality, the success of his generals) resulted in his earning the title *al-Rashid*, which means "the one following the right path" or upright or just. He was also appointed governor of Armenia, Azerbaijan, Egypt, Syria, and Tunisia, and named second in line to the throne (after his older brother, al-Hadi).

Al-Mahdi died in 785 A.D. and al-Hadi died mysteriously in 786 A.D. (it was rumored that his death was arranged by al-Khayzuran, Harun's mother and chief adviser), leaving the caliphate open for Harun. As caliph, Harun was a great patron of art and learning, and is best known for the unsurpassed splendor of his court and lifestyle. Some of the stories, perhaps the earliest, of the *Thousand and One Nights* were inspired by the glittering Baghdad court, and King Shahryar (whose wife, Scheherazade, tells the tales) was probably based on Harun himself. The stories are numerous, and many have been lost with time; only, it is believed, a minority have survived.

It is documented that Harun al-Rashid established diplomatic relations with the court of Charlemagne in France. Although the two men never met, the alliance was well recognized. As a result, the Umayyad caliph in Spain never imperiled the extension of the Abbasid Empire west along the Mediterranean shores of North Africa.

Harun al-Rashid had two sons; the eldest was al-Amin ("Faithful"), while the younger was al-Ma'mun ("Trustworthy"). When Harun al-Rashid died in 809 A.D., there was an armed conflict between his two sons. Al-Ma'mun won and became caliph and ruled the empire from Baghdad. He continued the patronage of learning started by his father and founded an academy called the House of Wisdom, where Greek philosophical and scientific works were translated. In 833, al-Ma'mun died and was succeeded by his brother al-Mu'tasim ("Adhering," to faith or God). The House of Wisdom continued to flourish under successive caliphs. Al-Mu'tasim died in 842 and was succeeded by al-Wathiq.

Caliph al-Wathiq was succeeded as caliph in 847 by al-Mutawakkil. Under both these caliphs, internal arguments and rivalries arose between the scholars in the House of Wisdom, but the excellent translations of many Greek texts continued, and these translations were copied and read widely through Mesopotamia, Syria, and Egypt.

Caliph al-Mutawakkil's troubles seemed to start early in his reign, but the difficulties were enhanced when the Vikings attacked Constantinople in 860. Whether or not this was the cause remains unknown, but the Caliph died from poisoning in 861. Over the next five years the throne in Baghdad was occupied by Caliph Muntasir (also poisoned to death in 862), Caliph Mu'tasim (deposed in 866), and Caliph Mu'tazz (forced to abdicate in 869).

* * *

Jabir ibn Haiyan (721–815) was the greatest chemist of Islam and for centuries thereafter perhaps the greatest chemist that the world had known. He has long been familiar to Western readers under the name of Geber, the medieval rendering of Jabir. This is the man who forms the basis for the description for Alric's adoptive father.

Jabir ibn Haiyan was the author of many texts related to alchemy and medicine. Jabir deals also with various applications, e.g., refinement of metals, preparation of steel, dyeing of cloth and leather, varnishes to waterproof cloth and protect iron, use of manganese dioxide in glass making, use of iron pyrites for writing in gold. He described the he knew how to concentrate acetic acid by the distillation of vinegar, and was also acquainted with citric acid and other organic substances. One of his chief contributions to the theory of chemistry lies in his views upon the constitution of metals.

It is impossible to measure the full extent of his contributions to science and medicine, but even on the slender basis of our present knowledge, Jabir's contribution is considerable.

*　*　*

PART I: PROLOG

Map 1: The location of Wearmouth.

CHAPTER 1

Last night, I, Alric of Wearmouth, dreamed again. It was a pleasant dream, and seemed so real.

In this dream, I saw the seashore. The beach had outcrops of rock rising from the sand that sparkled beneath the summer sun. White-capped waves created by the cold sea broke against the shore, and the hissing of the water against the sand and pebbles gave rise to a sound that was hypnotic. The cool wind and the screeching sea gulls broke the reveries of anyone who walked on this lonely stretch of beach.

I awoke and saw shafts of early morning light enter through the narrow space between the heavy curtains. I lay motionless to allow the dream that had filled my mind to disappear as fog does in the early morning breeze. I could hear the sounds of people starting their morning activities. Perhaps it is my age and the feeling of the approach of the scythe of mortality, which brings an end to the life of all men, which allows me the luxury of sleeping later than others! I lay still as I recalled what I had seen in the dream.

It was not the nightmare I had experienced on previous occasions of hot sand and ill-tempered camels.

I could see the monastery standing in its enclosure, perched dramatically on the headland, close to the point where the river flows into the sea. Above the sound of the waves, I could hear the monks chanting praises to God as they went to Vespers, the service that was held in the late evening. The monastery and the nearby village were seen as a lonely, wind-swept religious community. To the villagers, the natural beauty of the headland and the monastery gave them a sense of peace and security. This belied the bustling settlement that had a skilled and highly organized work force.

In the evening, the stones of the monastery infused with pink light gave it a halo effect. The crucifix on the eastern tower appeared as a conduit that connected the monks and villagers with the means to talk with God. On those days, and they were often, when it rained or when the sea fret clothed the landscape in a misty gray cloak, the villagers sought solace there and cleared their minds so that they could see the world afresh.

Thus, in the late summer of that year, seven hundred and ninety years after the birth of Our Lord, all seemed well with the people who lived in the area that was called Wearmouth, but the villagers and the monks were on a constant watch. They had heard tales from traveling monks and traders of sea raiders that had struck at similar settlements within the past three winters. The ferocity of these attacks was the talk of the monastery and village. They sought the treasures of the church and killed without remorse until their bloodlust was satisfied. Animals and goods were taken, and then what was left of the buildings was burned.

This was the start of those dreadful times when the voyages of the sea raiders would sweep along the coast of northern Europe and eventually to the land that lay on the other side of the Western Ocean.

In my dream I saw my twin sister, Hilda. Her straw-colored close-cropped hair rustled gently in the wind and she smiled at me through blue eyes that bespoke of her Saxon heritage. It has been so long since I last saw her that, at times, I often wonder what she really looked like. Is it a true picture of her that I see in the dream? I wonder too if my father and mother were the same as in my dream. The events that brought me to my present situation were so sudden and shocking that I find I must often call the truth to question.

Using the notes I have made over a lifetime that have been collected and compiled into the journal of my life to an earlier point, I feel it is now time that I officially set all of my history to writing and record for posterity. People will come to know of my humble beginnings. They will know that all is not lost when a boy is taken from his home to strange and wonderful lands. They will know that not only pain but also joy can follow when he is taken to places where he can see the likes of which others may never see in one thousand lifetimes.

My story will be a chronicle of the events of my life. I will record it as clearly as I remember it and not distort the truth with my own emotions. I will write my story as a chronicler of the actual events. I will present an accurate account and the means by which I came to live in the *House of Light* that constituted the royal palace of Baghdad and the Great Library. During the later years of my life, the Grand Library became known as the *House of Wisdom* and it was truly so. It was in this time that I was able to rise from the position of captive to apprentice and thence to my present position in which I have been able to make contributions to science and medicine.

I will begin with a few words about the monastery at Wearmouth that I remember from my boyhood. There were painful times and there were happy times, but using my optimistic thought that *for the wrong reasons the right things happen*, I was able to make the best of my life.

I was young when we first heard that the sea raiders invaded the villages on eastern coastal areas of Britain, known as Britannia from the time of the Romans. With much research and hindsight, it seems that the day of my birth was late in the month of June in the year 775 of the Christian calendar; the day of my birth has, I have since learned, been called John the Baptist's Day.

The sea raiders killed and pillaged without remorse. In my sixteenth year they came again. They always appeared out of the morning mists, or *sea frets,* as my parents used to call them, that so often give the sea an eerie look. It was as if this phenomenon were conjured up to protect the raiders from detection. The villagers had learned to protect themselves from the raiders, but one day their best laid plans failed.

That fateful day arrived.

* * *

PART II:
ALRIC'S JOURNEY

Map 2: The journey to Constantinople.

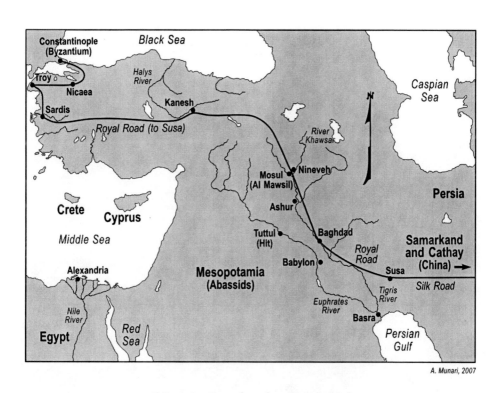

Map 3: Overland to Baghdad.

CHAPTER 2

It was one of those days that frequently typify the end of summer and the time when crops were harvested from the fields. The morning air was cooler, and the newly risen sun had to work harder in its attempt to warm the earth. But the people went about their tasks with fervor.

The fog had cleared. Earlier that morning the chilling raw air had signaled the coming of winter. As day broke, the warmth of the autumn sun had dispersed the gray mist that had enshrouded the coastline.

Alric, a young man in his sixteenth year, and his twin sister Hilda, as yet unmarried—much to the consternation of her parents—were collecting seashells as they walked along the beach. Their blond hair, blue eyes, and fair skin gave away the essence of their Saxon heritage.

Alric, in the custom of Saxon men, wore trousers that were long, loose, and cross-gartered to the knee. These were partially covered by a knee-length coarse woolen tunic, slit from the hips down for freedom of movement. The sleeves of the tunic were long and fitted close to the arms for warmth. He wore a leather belt around his waist. His cloak was a heavy woolen garment cut in a half-circle and fastened at the shoulder with a bone pin. He wore leather boots and, as protection against the cool air, a cloth cap.

Hilda, like her brother, was tall, athletic, and lean, her blonde hair cropped just below her ears. Her clothes were typical of those worn by her mother and other village women and stressed simplicity and durability. She wore a full-length pale blue long-sleeved linen dress under a knee-length brown woolen tunic with short sleeves. A leather belt circled her waist into which she had tucked a knife. Her brown cloak kept out the chill sea air. Her boots were leather and kept her feet warm and dry. Her short hair was tucked beneath the cloth cap, giving her a mischievous elfin look.

Hilda and Alric were like to two peas in a pod. Alric had three birthmarks on the inside of his right forearm. The marks were in the form of a cross, with a crescent-shaped mark below the cross and a star-shaped mark above the cross. At the time of Alric's birth, the marks had been ascribed by the monks as the marks of God that had saved him and his mother from death through the skillful hands of the midwife.

With the onset of Alric's sickness four months ago, the birthmarks had dimmed until his recent recovery that seemed to give the marks a new intensity, as they became highly visible once more.

Ethelbald, abbot of Wearmouth, felt that God had touched Alric and that if Alric had been touched by God, it followed that Hilda was also blessed. As a result, Ethelbald decreed that the twins should consider entering the monastic life and, as if the decision had already been made, decreed that Alric would enter the monastery at Wearmouth and Hilda would enter the convent at Whitby, several days journey to the south of Wearmouth. The abbot noted that the convent at Whitby had been founded by St. Hilda, and further decreed that for Hilda to enter this convent was a sign from God.

The abbot was even more impressed when he discovered that both Alric and Hilda knew the rudiments of reading, taught to them by their mother. Ethelbald's experience was that children did not read unless taught in the confines of a monastery. He saw their reading abilities as further proof that he had indeed received divine affirmation of his choice for their future.

As an introduction to monastic life, Alric and Hilda would study first at Wearmouth to learn the elements of reading, writing, and mathematics, in which each lesson would focus on the integration of monastic training into their lives. Each activity would provide a means of studying God's work and prepare them for a very challenging experience in their lives. When they reached the age of eighteen, they would enter into the formal monastic schedule. At that time, Alric would remain at Wearmouth and Hilda would enter the convent at Whitby.

However, because of Alric's illness, the entry of the twins into monastic life had been delayed. The illness left Alric with minor disabilities. He was not as active as Hilda; he was unable to move quickly, and any such attempt caused labored breathing, and his head pounded from the exertion. The high fever that had confined him to his bed had also sapped his energy, but he was now being allowed to exercise daily in the fresh air. Seeing marked improvement in Alric's condition, Ethelbald decided, after consultation with their parents, that lessons for the twins could now commence. As a result of this, attendance at the formal classes had begun several weeks ago, when, as near as could be determined, they had reached their fifteenth birthdays during the last week of June.

Alric and Hilda were the only two attendees and received the full attention of the monks. Their progress in learning the different alphabets allowed them to learn quickly and apply themselves to reading the Latin and Saxon texts. This, according to their instructors, was nothing short of miraculous. They were provided with scraps of vellum, ink, and sharpened sticks to make their marks and commence the art of writing. One of the older monks taught them the words of the Scandinavians.

Being his first and only pupils, Ethelbald watched their progress with pleasure. He would take frequent breaks from his other activities to attend their classes and help where he could. As they poured hungrily over the writing of the monks that were a part of the monastery library, he would show them drawings of medicinal plants and explain that some of these plants were now grown in the monastery garden.

One day when Ethelbald visited the twins and their instructors, he decided that their progress was sufficient and allowed them freedom for the morning. The thought of a morning away from studies was joyful news to Alric and Hilda. Having finished early-morning duties for their parents, they went to the beach. The seashore always captivated them. They would painstakingly search for anything that was new that had been washed ashore.

This morning, at the request of their mother, they searched for seashells.

Hilda smiled at Alric, relieved at the break from their studies which allowed them to walk along the beach and enjoy the fresh sea air.

* * *

On the cliffs above sat Sighard. He was from a different family and was almost two years older than the twins, having celebrated the day of his birth one week ago.

Ten days earlier the alarm had been raised by Brother Thomas, who had seen three ships sailing to the south. Thomas-One-Eye, as the villagers called him because of an accident cutting firewood that had resulted in a piece of wood piercing his eye, had seen the ships on the horizon and recognized the sails as those used by the sea raiders. There had been no signs of other ships, but as a precaution, the village elders had decided that Sighard should be posted on the headland to keep watch.

Hilda and Alric, knowing Sighard's penchant for interference and believing that he was superior because of his age, wanted no part of his activities. Sighard, unmarried, still lived with his mother and father, and several younger brothers and sisters, in the hut at the east end of the village, but he had his eyes on Hilda as his future wife and, believing this to be a *fait accompli*, would assert himself and command them in their movements and actions. Hilda and Alric avoided meeting him by moving behind the large rocks so that he would not see them as they collected the seashells.

* * *

It was into this cool but tranquil setting that the sea raiders came. They had finished their bloodthirsty activities at various hamlets and monasteries to the south and were returning to their base on the eastern side of the Jutland peninsula. Several weeks of killing and plunder had satisfied them for the moment. As if by chance rather than by design, the commander of the three ships decided to make one last raid. Thoughts of the treasures from the monastery at Wearmouth now fully occupied his thoughts. Neither Alric nor Hilda noticed the ships gliding softly on the white-capped waves behind the headland.

Unknown to them at this time, Sighard was already dead. Had he remained vigilant at his post, he would have lived and been able to raise the alarm.

* * *

CHAPTER 3

The vessels that sailed north to the coast of Wearmouth that morning were the *drakkar* ships, or *long ships*, as the Saxons called them.

Like all Viking ships, they were constructed using the clinker design, in which the ship was planked using one-inch-thick oak boards that overlapped slightly and was held together with iron nails. The spaces between the planks had been caulked with tarred wool and animal fur to make the ship watertight. These planks were also nailed to support ribbing that ran from the gunwale to the keel. The keel was made of one solid piece of oak that gave the ship stability and allowed it to travel straight through the water.

The deck of the ship was four feet above the keel. The space between the two was accessible by one small narrow entry that was usually sealed by a well-fitted wooden cover. There were no sleeping quarters or storage space below deck. Ballast stones were placed along the keel to reduce side-to-side movement of the ship in the water. Crewmen and warriors stored their personal belongings in chests on the deck, and the oarsmen sat on these while rowing.

The ship was sturdy but had sufficient flexibility to withstand the waves of stormy seas and was still light enough to be dragged overland between two lakes or rivers. The bow was tipped with an ornate carving of a dragon's head. The prows or beaks of the ships were colored with scarlet and gold paint that contrasted well with the black hulls and oars. The captain smiled as he recalled the name *dragon ship* used by prisoners. He always removed the carved dragon's head when they were at sea—losing it might be a bad omen.

The sail had been very costly to make, more than the rest of the ship. The women of the Viking settlement had made the linen sail from the flax plant. Small diamond-shaped pieces were woven and then trimmed with leather to keep the shape. All of these had been carefully sewn together to make one large square sail that was as wide as half of the ship's length. The sail was hoisted and held in place on the center mast with ropes made from walrus hide. Once it caught a steady breeze, the ship moved swiftly across the water. If the winds were calm, the oarsmen would take over, but the speed was reduced by half. At night, the captain made sure the sail was lowered. In bad weather, it served as a tent under which the crew slept protected. At times of heavy winds and high seas, the mast could be detached and laid on the deck. Replacing a broken mast would be a major problem.

Meals on board had not been pleasant during this voyage. Most of the food—dried meat, freshly caught fish, sour milk, water, beer, nuts, and cloudberries—had been spoiled due to rough seas, and the men had to live on whatever they could forage.

Each ship was almost one hundred feet long. Thirty oarsmen could swiftly deliver the shallow draft vessels, which could navigate in water less than three feet deep, onto the beach coast or inland along a river. The men who had rested would take their turn at the oars as the others tired.

* * *

Haldor, son of Gorm, a half brother to the king, was a veteran of many sea voyages and battles. He was a tall, strong man who had seen thirty summers. He had worked his way into command by guile and force. He had a craggy face, with a strong nose and high forehead. He sported a scar on the left side of his face from the corner of his eye which disappeared into the beard that ringed his mouth. As he was wont to do, he stroked the scar with a grudging affection when in deep thought.

He had received the scar in his third battle during a lapsed moment when he'd believed he'd had his enemy at his mercy. But the Saxon had quickly taken advantage of Haldor. The swinging long sword would have bit deeply into Haldor's neck had he not stepped back quickly. The blood-soaked blade had cut into Haldor's face, narrowly missing his left eye but leaving some muscles paralyzed because of severed nerves. In spite of the blood streaming from the wound, Haldor had remained calm and, after he'd knocked the Saxon facedown onto the earth, had cut the man's hamstrings. Haldor then left his enemy on the ground, unable to move, and continued fighting, returning later to ensure he died slowly and with much pain. For this, Haldor had been accepted as a hero by his people. By then, his prowess on the sea and on the battlefield was becoming well known and after the death of his father, there being no other claimants for the position, Haldor had been ready to step into Gorm's place and be acclaimed as leader.

Haldor had what some of his men termed a *kingly bearing* in his mail-shirt of woven rings, with his long yellow hair clustering on his fringed red cloak and the bright look of good fortune on his face. His clothes were made for warmth. Under the cloak, he wore leather garments, which acted as a protection against sword thrusts and slashing strokes which could cut into skin and bone. Heavy woolen breeches and under garments guarded him from the cold.

The men under his command were similarly dressed. Their clothing was made by the women of their village. In place of a cloak, some were dressed in furs and sheepskins. The boots and helmets were leather.

* * *

Other than the last raid, Haldor thought, the latest venture had been very successful. They had focused on valuables and had not bothered to take prisoners for use as slaves.

It was these thoughts that brought Haldor back to the monastery at Wearmouth. Perhaps there would be good food that would fortify his men for the long journey home. Perhaps the women would also satisfy his men's appetites!

"Yes," Haldor decided, "we will take on this raid and then make haste for home from this last voyage of the year."

On the out-going journey, the sea voyage between his home and the coast of this new land of the Saxons had been less than friendly. He had already lost two men from each ship when they had been swept overboard into the cold water. They had managed to rescue one of them but he had been in the sea too long and died soon after the rescue.

Haldor looked toward the land. He had heard stories of this monastery and the riches that it contained. The walls to the monastic compound might provide a problem, but where there was a wall, there was surely a gate. Once inside the compound, he did not expect the monks to offer any resistance, and they would die by the sword and axe. The wooden huts that were the dwelling places of the monks would be burned. There was surely a village associated with the monastery. He anticipated that the men of the village would be farmers and tradesmen and most likely not soldiers and foresaw no opposition. The men would be killed, and his crew would enjoy the women, and then they would also die.

It was rumored that books in the monastery library had covers that were inlaid with jewels and golden hinges that held the bindings in place. The golden ornaments that adorned the altar were of particular interest to Haldor. Rumor had it that the gold cross and candlesticks that were placed on the altar were supposed to be so heavy that it took two men to carry them.

* * *

Haldor turned his gaze from the land and quickly surveyed his plunder, which was covered by animal skins and lay in the center of the ship. That autumn he was taking home much tribute and plunder in the form of gold and silver, costly work in amber and jet, ivory, precious stones, and coin that had been imported from other lands. He raised his eyebrows as he realized that the prizes of the Wearmouth monastery could double the value of his treasure. Haldor snapped out of his reverie and brought himself back to the task set before him.

The crews needed a supply of fresh water and food. The journey home in the cooler weather of the late year always gave his men an appetite. Food taken from the villagers would be a great help, and he anticipated a supply of freshly killed beef that they could roast over fires before departing for home. These thoughts made his mouth water.

The river close by the monastery would supply them with fresh water. More important, the beach which sloped into the sea could be approached by his men from the shore and they could move in quickly and undetected to maintain surprise.

He licked his lips as he stared at the rugged coastline as if seeking guidance from his gods.

He signaled to a man holding the steering oar attached to the right-hand side of the ship near the stern. The man moved the oar with little effort and the ship turned toward the shore. Seeing the lead ship change course, the other two vessels followed in that direction and sailed silently and menacingly toward a cove to the south of the river mouth and out of sight of the headland.

He looked around once more at his ship. This was his love, even before his wife and family. The vessel had provided a living for them. They would die before giving up the ship to an enemy!

* * *

Haldor stood contemplating a thought, and a decision came to mind which involved his brother Skardi, who commanded the second ship and was his second-in-command. Skardi was less experienced in battle. Haldor smiled as he scanned the coast thinking of how Skardi would react to his new command.

Like his brother Haldor, Skardi had the killer's instinct and a penchant for survival. Haldor liked to torment his foes and make sure that they died painfully. Skardi preferred to kill immediately, and was a force to be reckoned with. He could handle himself well on the sea, showing much promise as a sailor and warrior.

Before they'd left their home port, Haldor had been uncertain whether or not to take Skardi on this voyage. Skardi, younger than him by eleven summers, was sure he was ready for the raid. Haldor had at first refused, but Skardi's persistence had continued until finally Haldor had relented and decided that only a long coastal voyage and raids would mature his brother.

"Perhaps," he thought, "Skardi will be man enough to take over from me when the time comes?"

* * *

At this moment in time, the crew were resting and allowing the gentle south wind to carry the ship over the water. Haldor looked at his crew with some fondness. They had been through thick and thin together. His men were trustworthy and reliable.

"Yes," he thought, "I have made the right decision and I will be welcomed when I return home." Now he needed to finalize his plan. Haldor relished the thought and smiled to himself. "This will be a good day."

* * *

The fog, now swirling in the north wind, was starting to float away, as the three ships beached and men disembarked. They advanced in silence. As the fog dissipated, the men crouched in silence while Haldor gave instructions. Now he would put his plan into action.

The ships had been three hundred paces distant to the south when they made landfall. Haldor had out twenty of his raiders, under the command of Skardi, as a scouting party, whilst he left another twenty, much to their disappointment, to guard the ships and the booty that was on board. The advance party would detect any sentries and take necessary actions to prevent the alarm from being raised. Haldor and the remaining members of the attacking group would follow; concealment being their watchword. The undulating land offered cover once any sentries were dispatched.

* * *

Sighard grew tired of sitting and watching the sea. He believed he was meant for more adventurous activities than being a mere lookout. Then, with these thoughts in his mind, he made the fatal decision to stretch his legs rather than sit in the cool wind that seemed to penetrate his clothing and woolen clothes.

Sighard descended from the headland and had not seen the arrival of the sea raiders. Their initial approach went undetected as they moved silently through the last remnants of the murky fog. Nor did he sense the presence of the raiders as they walked along the beach toward the monastery. In all, a hundred helmeted men, with long swords and round shields and carrying spears and axes, moved along the beach. They had been told to expect serious consequences for any man whose actions caused the alarm to be sounded. Haldor ruled by fear and intimidation. The men knew that he would keep his word.

At a glance, Sighard would have known they were the feared sea raiders. But he had been distracted by the thoughts of Hilda.

He had learned that she would be on the beach later that morning. Unfortunately for Sighard, Alric was with her. It was his misfortune that he did not remain at his vantage point on the cliff where he would have seen the raiders as they beached their ships and would have given the alarm. But it was not to be.

It did not take the scouting party long to spot Sighard. Seeing him bending over among the sandy rocks, at a point where the waves broke against the beach, they surprised him by coming up from the rear. Before he could react, he was seized by rough hands and his throat was cut.

Sighard fell to the sand as he gasped out the last breaths of his life. The seawater of the incoming tide lapped around his body, giving it an eerie, rhythmic motion, as if keeping time with the music of the waves as they broke against the shoreline.

* * *

Haldor was pleased so far with the progress his men had made. It was still early morning, and his advance guard had dispatched three more sentries at the point of the river crossing. He was disappointed that the fog was disappearing quickly as the sun started to warm the air. But, so far, no alarm had been raised.

He had anticipated that the north wind would carry the sounds of his men in the opposite direction to the monastery and the village.

* * *

Just to the north of where the raiders had landed, Alric and Hilda continued their search of the beach, completely unaware of the events that had cost Sighard and three other sentries their lives. As the last wisps of the gray fog dispersed, they continued their search for the seashells and were so intent on extracting crabs from their hiding places in the rocks that they did not see or hear the raiders as they moved silently along the beach toward the village and the monastery.

"Mother will be pleased," Alric said with a smile. He was breathing heavily as he carried several crabs and placed them in a sack with the seashells they had found. He tried to keep up with his more energetic sister as she moved toward the high cliffs that lay to the north. "But we must return soon," he said.

"Just a little more time," Hilda responded. "Mother knows where we are and Father is busy today, working at the monastery, building a new chair for Ethelbald. We should continue until the sack is at least half full. So we should not worry." The allure of finding more crabs and seashells was too tempting.

They moved into the shadows of the large rocks at the base of the cliffs. Then they arrived at Hilda's secret place, a circle of rocks that formed an enclosure from which they could peer out to sea. This place was special to Hilda. She had discovered it and added to it during the time that Alric had been incapacitated by the sickness that had taken away his strength. She knew in her heart that one day Alric would recover and she would show it to him.

Alric was open-mouthed as he looked at the enclosure, thinking of the effort she must have put into this task. They would sit here for a while as Alric caught his breath and then continue their search.

Hilda had never taken anyone there before nor had she seen anyone in the vicinity of her enclosure. As Alric looked around, the cliffs appeared to rise to the sky, like great megaliths of stone, marking a temple built by some ancient and forgotten people. Hilda loved this area of rocks with the cliffs high above. The fresh salt sea air brought purity to the place. She felt the presence and spirit of the rocks and told Alric all about them as they sat and thought about their next move.

The rays of the sun were already starting to remove the chill from the rocks. Alric smiled at his sister as she took her knife from her belt to examine the blade.

She was troubled as she watched Alric. His sickness had left him weak, but he was, she assured herself, on the road to recovery. Her discomfort came not so much from his sickness but from within her. For the past several nights she'd had trouble falling asleep and when she had, the dreams had come. The dreams were disturbing. There were fleeting images of death and destruction. In these dreams she saw men dressed in strange attire and speaking a language which she could not recognize. They seemed to be men of substance and stature, who spoke to Alric.

There were other issues that had surprised Hilda and occupied her thoughts and dreams. During the time of Alric's sickness, they had found that they could communicate with each other without words and could read each other's thoughts. Their mother and father never suspected this ability in their children. There were many times when they did not speak a word but, mentally, spoke volumes.

Hilda felt that she needed to tell Alric of her dreams. She looked around to reassure herself that no one else was present. Perhaps this was the moment, as they were alone and assured of no interruptions.

"Alric," Hilda said as she looked at her brother, "I have had strange dreams of a faraway land. Now that you are feeling better, perhaps we can talk about them?"

"Oh," Alric muttered perfunctorily and tried to sound interested. He had learned that when Hilda spoke of her dreams he should listen politely, since they were so important to her.

"Yes," she said, "I dreamed that you were in a strange land. I am with you and yet I am not with you."

"That," Alric said, smiling, "sounds impossible! How can you be with me and yet not with me? Is this a riddle?"

"I am not sure but . . . " Hilda began to respond but was interrupted by a sound.

Alric jumped up and started to move out of the enclosure but Hilda tugged at his sleeve to restrain him. "What was that?" she whispered. "Wait!"

She strained her ears, listening intently. A shrieking gull flew overhead looking for food. A tiny crab scampered along the rock seeking refuge from the gull. The northern wind blew steadily, but the sound now was not from the wind.

"I thought I heard voices." A moment later she shook her head. "Never mind," she said, "It was nothing."

She smiled as she tried not to alarm Alric, but she remained suspicious. There was something in the sounds she did not recognize. That often meant danger! She felt uncomfortable. She was sure that she had heard voices or at least a murmur of them in the distance. She decided not to talk any further about her dreams; that would come later. She moved closer to Alric and they started to take stock of the crabs that, when boiled, would make several tasty meals, and the seashells would be used to adorn cloaks.

There seemed to be a hidden message in her dreams, just as, she recalled, there had been meaning in the biblical dreams of Joseph. But her dreams showed conflict and blood. In the dreams, Alric appeared to survive conflicts but he was always surrounded by blood. Hilda decided that God was telling her to protect her brother.

She recalled his recent illness, for there were times when it seemed that the fever would take his life. She had taken on the chores while her mother tended to Alric. Then, when she had finished her work for the day, she would sit with her mother and Alric as they learned to read. They loved to read the books that traveling monks left at the monastery which told of life in other countries.

* * *

On those days when there was little work during the day, Hilda explored the caves that faced the sea, and she became as familiar with the seashore as she was with her own home. She hunted for crabs that had become stranded in the tidal pools and brought them home to boil for the meal table. She knew that one day Alric would join her again and they would enjoy the beach and sea together. This was that time.

Hilda listened again. There was nothing, only sounds of the waves and the gulls, but Hilda's instincts were correct.

The sea raiders were now assembling themselves into an attack formation as they closed in on the village and the monastery. Seeing that a high wall fortified the monastery, Haldor had directed his men to attack the easier target—the village that lay on the cleared land to the east of the monastery.

* * *

Hilda had just finished counting the seashells when Alric spotted the raiders. He was no longer looking at the crabs and thinking of the meal they would make. He was using one rock to chip at another, trying to fashion a stone blade in the manner used by so many of the village men. He wiped grit from his eyes and stood up to look over through the peephole between the rocks. At first, curiosity took over his emotions. Tall men wearing vests and pantaloons made from animal skins were not Saxons, and they were running toward the village, with their swords raised.

The blood drained from Alric's face. He felt a pain in his stomach, as if the milk he had drunk earlier in the morning had turned sour. He was filled with shock and fear. He stepped back, lost his footing on the rocks, and fell onto the sand in front of Hilda. She saw the paleness of his face and realized something was very wrong.

"Alric, what . . . ?" She was not able to finish her words.

The noise of men shouting caught her attention. As she looked through the peephole, she saw them running toward the village. Some of the words were familiar to her ears, as she recalled starting to learn the language of the Norsemen as part of her lessons at the monastery.

"Sea raiders!" she exclaimed. She could hear voices in her own language as the villagers realized their fate. The battle had started.

The alarm was raised by the midden dogs, those half-wild animals that found life in and around the village preferable to that in the wild, where they had to compete with wolves for food and sustenance. Smelling them first and then seeing the strange men approaching the village from the beach as they passed by the base of the monastery wall, six or more of the large beasts charged at the strangers, snapping and growling as they ran. The animals were quickly dispatched by lethal swords. Nevertheless, their purpose had been served.

The snarling attack of the dogs and the yelps that accompanied the bite of each sword brought the attention of the villagers to the raiders. Swords and shields were taken up from the corners of dark huts and were brandished as men and women ran to meet the attack and defend the village. Workers in the monastery ran out of the gate and joined their neighbors in defense.

The noise escalated as Hilda, looking once more through the peephole, could see smoke rising into the clear morning sky. She had to do something, but there was Alric, and she must look after him.

* * *

The attack from the rear took the villagers by surprise, and the slaughter commenced. Men lay dead, many with their eyes wide open in shock and horror. The women, who had, by instinct, chosen to fight alongside their men, also lay sprawled on the ground in the agonies of death.

Hilda knew that they could remain in the enclosure or among the rocks where there were countless places to hide. They might even be able to run to the monastery, where she could leave Alric within the safety of the high walls. She wondered why Sighard had not sounded the alarm. "What about Sighard?" she asked herself. "Probably asleep, she thought angrily, "doing something he should not be doing!"

29

Hilda peered over the top of the rocks, hoping the villagers would be able to drive off the raiders. She allowed her emotions to get the better of caution. Tears came to her eyes as she thought of her parents and friends in the village. A gull, seeing Hilda and Alric dangerously close to her nest in the rocky crag, screeched objections and feigned several swooping attacks on them.

Haldor's men had been ruthless and very quickly slaughtered many of the unsuspecting villagers. After the killings, Haldor was joined by Skardi on the beach as the raiders picked up weapons and shields that lay on the sand near the bodies of the dead villagers.

Haldor looked around and saw the sweeping flight of the gull. He squinted as he looked toward the rocks, thinking he had seen a movement. He called to Skardi.

* * *

Hilda gasped as she realized she had been spotted. Chastising herself, she looked at Alric. It had been a delightful morning and Alric was tired, his energy spent, and he could not run as fast as she. He would surely be caught and perhaps killed. She decided on a course of action.

"Alric, you will remain here and not move. In your weakened condition," she said as she stroked his hair, "you cannot move like I can. I will come for you when this is over."

"But, Hilda . . . " he started to protest. She would not allow him to finish his sentence.

"I will come back for you." She rubbed his hair again and saw the pained look in his eyes. The sickness had weakened him more than he cared to admit. Alric nodded his head. "It will be all right," she said quietly, for his sake. "Stay here and do not make any noise. If you are quiet, they will never know you are here."

Hilda feigned calmness but her insides were twisted in terror. She knew that she had to be strong for them both. She took off her cloak, wrapped it around his shoulders, kissed his forehead, and, with one last look into his eyes, disappeared over the rocks.

Alric clambered up to watch her through the peephole as Hilda ran toward the village. She tucked her tunic into her belt to give herself freedom to run and carried her knife in her hand.

She ran toward the two sea raiders who were approaching the enclosure and screamed at the top of her voice, hoping by some miracle to distract them. As she did so, she noticed one man who appeared to be in command. He was helmeted, tall, and full-bearded. A second man, not as well built as the first but similarly clothed, was at his side.

* * *

The last that Alric saw of Hilda was when she threw herself at the two raiders screaming, "Cowards, the sea raiders are cowards!"

She leapt at the smaller of the two men and thrust her knife into his chest. There was the flash of a sword from the second man and Hilda fell down mortally wounded.

Tears filled Alric's eyes, as he feared the worst. He saw no more of his sister. The raider had turned his attention to his companion. Alric lay in the bottom of the enclosure, tears streaming from his eyes.

He sensed a presence and, fearing it was one or more of the raiders, turned with his fists clenched, ready to give a good account of himself, but there was no one. The shimmering shadows at the other side of the small enclosure seemed to beckon him, and he heard the words: *Do not worry, my brother. In my dreams I saw that you are meant for greatness. Do not worry. I will be with you always.*

Recognizing Hilda's voice, Alric looked at the shadows but saw nothing, and the words disappeared on the wind.

The noise of the fighting continued until the sun was high in the sky, and then, as if by a prearranged signal, all was quiet.

Alric peeped through the rocks and saw the raider as he looked at the dead body of his companion.

*   *   *

In the silence that followed the slaughter, Haldor looked at the body of his brother. He was shocked by the attack that took Skardi's life. He stroked his cheek, as if deep in thought.

He used his foot to turn over the body of the attacker. He knew there was something about this one that seemed different. He lifted her robes with the toe of his boot, raised his eyebrows, and ripped off his helmet and threw it to the sand.

The attacker was a young woman. His sword had cut into her neck, causing blood to flow freely so that it masked her features as she fell.

He looked at Skardi's body once more. His eyes clouded over as he stared at the monastery walls. He stood silent for a few moments and stroked the scar on his face. Finally he reached a decision. The omens were not good. He called to his men, ordered assembly, and informed them they were going home. The resistance, Haldor told the men, was more than he had expected. Fourteen of the raiders had been killed before Skardi had attacked the shield wall from behind. "This," Haldor stated, "is too high a price to pay, and attempting to scale the monastery walls may cost us more. We will return another day."

That being decided, the raiders picked up their dead for the journey home, from which they would be sent to Valhalla, the Hall of the Slain that was presided over by Odin. They would be taken into Valhalla by the Valkyries, Odin's messengers and spirits of war.

He looked at a group of prisoners, all of them women and children, who stood near the entry to the village and were guarded by Skardi's men. He scratched his bearded chin and then looked at his men assembled before him. His eyes darkened at the thought of Skardi lying dead.

"Wait. Put down our comrades. Do what you must!" he said, gesturing with a wave toward the captives. The thought of Skardi's death made him feel deaf to his own imperious command.

By this action, he had lowered the barrier to the final horrific action that was to be perpetrated by his men that morning. As the turned, the plight of the captives was obvious, and the looks on the faces of the women became desperate. The raiders descended upon them like wolves on the sheep fold. Within moments, the screams of the women and children could be heard above the noise of the sea. Even the gulls became silent.

And then it was over. The beach was silent. The raiders moved toward the ships, carrying the bodies of their dead comrades with them.

Tentatively, the gulls took to the air again and shrieked as if in defiance of what had taken place.

* * *

CHAPTER 4

Alric did not know how long he had been hidden when he surveyed the beach through the peephole. It was changed. He could see formless piles on the sand. He needed to leave the enclosure. He recalled Hilda's last words, and he had to find her. His stomach heaved at the thought of his next move.

Picking up his partially sharpened rock, he scrambled over the outcrops of rock, bloodying his hands and knees. He was too sick with fear to notice his torn skin and the accompanying pain as he crawled out of the enclosure and prayed that Hilda and his mother and father were still alive.

His face was ashen, for he knew that prayers were futile as he ran along the beach toward the place where Hilda had fallen. His legs, weakened by the sickness, now found the energy to move.

He ran with renewed strength to find his mother and father and hoped that his vision of Hilda falling under the swinging sword had been only a bad dream. He had to find a way out of this madness. But it was not to be.

The rocks cast dark shadows that made it difficult for him to see safe places in which to step. He moved his head from side to side as he carefully made his way among the rocks. He had followed Hilda's steps when they'd first come here, which had made it easier, but now he was alone. He looked along the beach toward the monastery, his gaze shifting between shadow and suspicion. He cocked his head to one side, listening intently. There was only the sound of the distant surf pounding against the beach and the headland to the south. The wind had eased, and a thick black smoke curled its way heavenward. As Alric gathered his senses, he became conscious of an overpowering smell. It was the smell of burning and a sickening odor that he could not place.

He recovered the sharp rock and held it at the ready, and instinctively squeezed it gently as if it might fall to the sand. This was his weapon; it was not a sword that would gleam in the sun, but it would serve its purpose.

He hurried to the spot where Hilda had fallen. She lay on her back on the wet sand, her face at peace. He thought she was alive until he saw the ugly sword gash in her neck. Her blue tunic was stained with her blood. He looked for the raider that his sister had attacked but there was no body.

"I will return, dear sister, I will return," he said quietly, hoping that she would understand. He continued to make his way along the beach and then inland toward the village. He wondered about the motionless piles on the beach. The only noise was the distant sound of the waves as they cascaded onto the beach and the headland.

He felt the pounding of his heart as he approached the first group of bodies scattered on the ground. They lay dead on the path from the monastery to the village.

Alric started to shake. As he moved closer, he recognized several of the villagers. Their faces grimaced in the agony of death, and he dared not look at them closely. He held his breath, expecting a sea raider to spring from the sand and attack him, but he reassured himself that he had his rock and he would use it if he were attacked. He looked at the lifeless bodies as though he were disconnected from the scene of death.

A movement caught his attention. He froze, and then realized that the movement was out to sea. He looked beyond the monastery and saw the three ships as they were about to disappear below the horizon. He glared at them, wondering if he would ever have the chance to seek retribution. Seeing no hope at all, he turned his mind back to the present.

He walked toward the village, squinting, as if not certain of what he was seeing. He could feel his eyes like hot coals, burning inside, at the devastation and killing that had taken place. It took all of his courage not to flinch.

Some of the women and children had tried to hide where they could, but that had been futile. One by one, the fugitives had been found. The boys were killed immediately, in front of their mothers and sisters. The women and girls, many of them younger than Alric, had been raped and mutilated before being killed.

Alric had never seen horror like this before. He did not understand the reason for the killing. The people of the village were good people. It had not mattered. The sea raiders had done their worst, leaving behind a scene of death and destruction. They had not been able to scale the walls of the monastery, but being vengeful men, they had taken out their passions on the people of the village.

Most of the dead had been mutilated, in payment for daring to show resistance to their enemies. He saw body after body; the carnage terrified him, so much so that he stopped to retch. The village hall and other larger buildings where the skilled tradesmen had worked were burned. Beyond the first huts that formed the village, he found yet more dead bodies. The women had fought alongside their husbands as they had attempted to form a shield wall to hold the advance of the sea raiders, but the attack from the rear meant that their efforts were in vain.

Alric found his mother, her body splayed out on the ground. She had a peaceful look on her pale face; her eyes were closed so as to obscure the horrors of what had taken place. His father lay close by, his life taken by a vicious sword thrust. He had died with his arm outstretched toward his wife as he had tried to protect her. The onslaught by the sea raiders had been too much for the farmer-tradesmen and their wives. Alric moved the body of his father close to his mother so that their hands could touch. This was his last tribute to his dead parents, hoping they would be reunited in heaven. Tears filled his eyes as he knelt beside their bodies.

It was then that it occurred to him that none of the dead were sea raiders. He knew at least one raider had died when Hilda had sank her knife into the man's chest. He had heard stories that they took the bodies of their dead and wounded with them. The former would be given up to the sea, and the wounded, if they survived the journey, would be taken home. If not, they also would have a watery grave in the cold gray waters of the Northern Sea.

At that moment a sound came to Alric's ears. From behind the thick high wall that surrounded the monastery, the monks emerged to tend to the dead and send them with prayers to the afterlife. On the other side of the village, the older men, women, and children who had managed to escape into the forest before the slaughter began appeared from their hiding places.

The monks moved cautiously among the bodies, sprinkling the remains with holy water and chanting the last rites. Alric was at a loss as to what to do next. His parents and sister were dead and the village had been burned. He had no home. Despair took over his body. As he rose from his knees to look toward the sea, he felt a hand on his shoulder. He gripped his rock tightly and prepared himself for action. He turned around ready to confront the person, but as he did so, the grip on his shoulder relaxed and he heard a familiar voice.

"It seems," Ethelbald said, "that the Lord has declared it is time for you to enter into the monastic life." Alric felt the gentle pressure of the abbot's fingers on his shoulder. "You shall live within the monastery

38

walls," Ethelbald continued, "so that one day you will take your vows and become one of us."

Alric nodded, thankful that there was someone alive he could trust and that he would have a place to live.

"Come with me," Ethelbald commanded, and stepping carefully among the remaining bodies, the abbot led to him to a place where the bodies were being assembled for burial in a mass grave at the west end of the village. The body of Sighard had been recovered from the beach. Alric bowed his head in silence as the remains were carried to the cemetery and carefully placed side-by-side on the grass, awaiting burial.

He felt too numb for any emotion, and not wanting to be disrespectful of the dead, he picked up a handful of soil and sprinkled it on to the human remains.

The abbot indicated they should proceed to the monastery. As they passed through the monastery gate, Alric looked back at the outside world. On this sad day of bereavement, he knew his life was about to change.

His life would indeed change, to an extent that he could not have imagined.

* * *

As Ethelbald conveyed his decision to Alric regarding his life in the monastery, Haldor had taken one last look across the sea and scowled as he'd seen the river mouth and the cliffs disappearing from view.

"That damned woman," Haldor's thoughts continued as he remembered Hilda running and screaming toward them over the sand. "She sank her dagger into my brother's chest. And I did not know it was a female until I lifted her robes!"

Hilda's strike had been fatal to Skardi. The blade had passed cleanly between his ribs and entered the heart. As Hilda had struggled to get to her feet, she'd tried to pull the dagger from Skardi's body, but Haldor had been too quick and had dispatched her with a quick blow from his sword.

He scratched his chin and then made a decision that he would avenge Skardi's death. He had seen his brother's blood stain the sand. He continued to stare at the land as it disappeared from sight. He could not forget the look of disbelief on Skardi's face as he'd died. He would take an oath to avenge the death of his brother.

"Next time," he muttered venomously through his whiskered mouth as he stared at the horizon, "you will regret any resistance you make, and you will pay for the death of my brother!"

* * *

The central point of the monastic enclosure that Alric entered consisted of a large courtyard which contained the monastery building and a series of neatly tended gardens to the south, which were ideally exposed to the sun. The enclosure was separated from the outside world by a high wall. On the seaward side, the wall had observation points high above the ground. On the landward side, the wall had two windows and a small but well-fortified gate. The two remaining sides that faced the north and the south were without openings.

The complex contained clay and wattle-walled huts with thatched beehive-shaped roofs that were the domain of each monk. Each hut had a sleeping area, a place for meditation, and a place to work. Ethelbald, even though he was abbot of the monastery, had a dwelling that was no different from any of the others, except that it lay closer to the monastery.

As they walked toward the huts, Alric looked at the abbot, wondering if he should ask his question. "Why does God allow this to happen?" Alric asked.

"We are not sure, Alric," Ethelbald responded, "but God doesn't want you to be sad. He wants you to be watchful lest the raiders return. When you are settled into this house of God, we can talk of what God might require of you."

Alric did not respond. He could not understand the abbot's words or the reason why his parents and sister had to die that day. He looked in the direction of the gate, almost tripping as he did so and thinking that this might be the place where he would spend the rest of his life.

Edgar and Osric, two monks who had been at the monastery for as long as Alric could remember, approached and, at the abbot's request, showed Alric the hut that was to be his home. They proudly explained that he could dwell there for as long as he remained at Wearmouth.

The contents of the hut were simple but functional, and Alric was no stranger to this life, he and Hilda having received tutoring in one of the very same huts. The interior was dominated by a hearth in which a fire had been lit. Smoke curled lazily toward the hole at the apex of the roof. Offset to one side was a bed with two blankets. A table and a chair, on the other side of the fireplace, completed the furnishings. A large candle and a wooden crucifix were the sole adornments of the table. The floor, made of individual stones, was covered with fresh grass gathered from the nearby meadow that lay between the village and the forest.

"Books and illuminated manuscripts and gospels that have been brought from France are kept in the monastery," Edgar explained as he indicated the extension of the monastery that served as the library, "and the library contains more than seven hundred books," he added with considerable pride.

"You will," Osric said, reading Alric's mind, "be allowed to keep goose quills, wooden splinters for making pens, and ink in your hut for copying work when the tasks and prayers of the day have been completed. Then you will retire for a few hours sleep before the predawn hours when you will be awakened by the first call to prayer."

Thoughtfully, Osric rubbed his chin with his forefinger and thumb before he smiled and added, "We do not awake with the sun on our faces."

"We will leave you for a short while, Alric," Edgar said as he and Osric left, "but you will be needed in the kitchen shortly."

They disappeared behind the curtain that hung over the door as Alric, waiting to make sure they were not lingering outside, pursed his lips and frowned. There was one action in particular that needed his attention.

He had sensed that one of the stones in the floor was loose; he had felt the slight movement of the stone when he'd placed his full weight upon it. He pushed it with his foot, and on further inspection, he found that the stone was indeed loose and even removable. Then a sparkle returned to his eyes. Underneath the stone was a cavity which was lined with a piece of animal skin. A previous occupant must have loosened the same stone and placed the skin in there as protection, making it a suitable hiding place for a personal possession. Now, it would become his secret place.

Realizing his need for contemplation and time to adjust, Edgar and Osric watched him each day until they felt he was sufficiently recovered from the trauma of that dreadful day.

Alric was then left to his own thoughts, but his days passed in loneliness, and he made no effort to contact or talk with any of the monks. The shock of the brutal attack weighed heavily on his mind. He was now alone. With Ethelbald's indulgence, he was allowed to walk along the beach every morning. It was Alric's way of recreating his last walk with Hilda.

* * *

Winter was approaching, and Alric pulled his thick robe tighter around his shoulders to ward off the chill. He pulled the hood over his head and walked as did the monks, his head bowed as if in deep contemplation. The memory of that terrible day just a few months before still haunted him. His mother, father, and sister all murdered, and he had nothing by which he could remember them. Their faces seemed to grow dimmer among the mists of memory.

"If only," he thought, "I had something to remind me of them."

His sandy tracks gave way to pebbles that soon brought him facing the foreboding cliffs that rose from the beach as if they were trying to pierce the sky. He never again visited Hilda's secret place. The memories of their last conversation and her command that he remain there that fateful morning were too much to bear. The shadow of the cliffs darkened the area as if trying to hide his memories.

The trees had lost most of their red and gold leaves, since the autumn season was far advanced. The cool morning and the early frost threatened a very cold winter that would bring heavy frosts and deep snow.

On his way back to the monastery, Alric visited the spot where he had last seen Hilda's body. In his mind, he could clearly see her leap at the sea raider and sink her dagger into his chest. Then she had disappeared as the other raider had moved to help his companion. Alric scratched the sand with the heel of his wooden sandal, not sure why but hoping that there would be some sign of Hilda. As if by instinct, he knelt to pray and then yelped in pain. A sharp object below the surface of the sand pierced his robe and cut into his knee.

Alric stared at the point that now protruded through the sand and then carefully exposed the item, scraping away the sand with his bare hands and being careful lest he feel its point again. He stared at the source of his discomfort. It was his sister's knife! Or the weapon that Hilda called her knife. The eleven-inch blade with its five-inch handle lay partly exposed in the shallow depression where it been buried. Just then, the sea flowed into the depression as if to wash the blade clean.

He felt a stinging sensation as the salt water found the cut in his knee, cleansing it from infection.

He turned his back to the monastery walls, picked up the knife, and held it in his outstretched hands. Perhaps the other raider had pulled it out of the man's chest, hoping to save him from his fate. Perhaps . . . ?

Alric ceased to wonder any further. This was Hilda's knife and now it was his. He held the knife at his side and looked toward the monastery walls. He could see the heads of his two guardians, Edgar and Osric, as they peered at him from their observation point. He waved with his free hand and saw them return the gesture. He crossed himself and then made the sign of the cross over the spot where Hilda had fallen.

He turned and walked toward the north, away from the monastery, with the knife in his right hand hidden from the prying eyes of the monks. He did not know what he would do with the knife, but he would need to conceal it under his robe and secure it to his belt when he returned to the monastery gate. He knew exactly where he would hide it later. He would not give it up, as it was now the only remembrance he had of his sister. It would be their secret.

Alric realized that this would be a risky venture. If his secret were discovered, the knife would be confiscated—probably finding its way into the kitchen for use in preparing food—and he might even suffer disgrace for having a weapon inside a holy place. This could be sufficient to cause him to suffer a two-week penance! But the knife was a memory of Hilda's bravery, and no one would take it away. He would keep it always. When he left the enclosure, the knife would be with him, safely tucked inside his robe.

As the days passed, he found an inner peace and often imagined he could hear Hilda's voice as she whispered gentle thoughts in his ear as if in time with the music of the waves.

* * *

It was Christmas before Alric resigned himself to accepting the deaths of his parents and sister. He sensed that Hilda was communicating with him. Her voice came to him as a gentle zephyr of spring. She always spoke to him when he needed comfort or advice. Her voice was as gentle as it had been in life. He even imagined he could see her at times, materializing from the gathering shadows only to disappear and become silent.

Alric accepted her presence and her promise that she would never forsake him. They would remain close, as they had in life. Gradually, Alric started to smile again.

Noticing this change in his demeanor, Edgar and Osric quickly made reports to the abbot. Seeing this as a sign from God, Ethelbald made immediate arrangements for the continuation and intensification of Alric's education.

It was on January 7, the day after the Feast of the Epiphany, that Alric was summoned by Edgar and Osric to Ethelbald's chambers. Edgar knocked gently on the heavy wooden door, and Alric heard the soft voice of Ethelbald bidding them enter. The abbot looked at Alric then nodded to the monks who stepped back to wait patiently at the door.

"It seems, my son," Ethelbald announced as Alric stood before him, "that you are ready for the advanced tasks that will help you with your learning." Alric stood in silence, awaiting the abbot's next words. "If you are to become one of us," the abbot continued, "and be of great use to our house of God, there are further elements of your education that need to commence immediately."

The abbot looked at the two monks and nodded, showing that the interview was over. Without further words spoken, the two monks took Alric to an adjoining room, where his new lessons commenced that very day.

Edgar and Osric taught him the rudimentary arts of reading and writing. He began to learn letter forms using the spherical "O," as was currently being practiced in a country across the sea. This was the letter from which the Roman alphabet took shape. From this simple beginning, he mastered the variants of all letterforms. Within his first six months at the monastery, much to the surprise of Ethelbald and the monks, Alric was fluent in speaking and reading Saxon and Latin, even at a higher level than many of the monks. At the abbot's suggestion, he continued to learn two of the Scandinavian dialects used by the sea raiders.

"One never knows," the abbot explained, "when it will save your life."

Alric maintained his ability to speak his local Saxon dialect. As the months passed and Easter arrived, he became familiar with the various scripts and was accomplished in reading and writing. His arithmetical skills surpassed all other subjects, and he could read, write, and count as well as any of the monks.

He could recite the Saxon and Latin versions of the Lord's Prayer, the Creed, the Ten Commandments, the Psalms, and elementary catechism. Since he had not yet been admitted to the monastery as a monk, he was not allowed to read the Bible because of the fear that the writings contained therein might be too open to misinterpretation in his young mind. He was often frustrated at the form of the lessons. The answers were standard and parroted versions of the scriptures, with no form of interpretation. Alric wondered if he was not supposed to think at all and worried that a monk's life might not be his calling after all.

As summer approached and brought greenness to the countryside, an older monk, Ethelred, who served as the monastic accountant, taught him the mathematics needed in his curriculum so that he would eventually be able assist in counting the assets of their monastery and enter the totals into the records.

Alric continued his studies, along with his other tasks which were a part of monastery life. The days passed as summer turned to autumn and then winter and winter to spring.

The spring had also brought with it people from inland areas where the desolate and frozen countryside had been inhospitable during the winter months. These people believed in the gods of the Saxons, but mostly they worshipped Woden, the head of the gods, and his wife Frigga. The inland people were not as familiar with the Christian teachings as the coastal folk, and the monks welcomed them as they would any new people to convert. There had been many deaths during the past harsh winter. The occasional threat of death at the hands of the sea raiders was less of a threat to those living inland. But a more comfortable living—if that was what continuous toil could be called—in the vicinity of a monastery was always preferable to starvation.

* * *

Just as Alric continued to grow in knowledge and stature, the village outside of the monastery walls continued to thrive over the next year. It even spread beyond the river where the foot-worn track, used by the villagers, meandered and climbed between the fields toward a treeless plateau that overlooked the sea. From this vantage point Alric could see the gray cold waters of the Northern Sea and the monastery that, as a result of further building, looked formidably contained. Stone had replaced much of the wooden and turf structures, and narrow slits punctuated the stone walls. This allowed the monks on watch to view the landscape. Steep thatched roofs were reinforced with slate and protected the monastery from the weather.

Travelers continued to pass by on their way north or south into a world that was seething with danger. Wolves were not unknown in the area. Alric had learned that the people often referred to the sea raiders as sea wolves because of the ferocity of their attacks. This area that Alric came to call his own was small, but from his vantage point he could see the monastery, the village, and the fields spread before him. He knew that a man could walk from one side of the village to the fields in a short time. The only open space lay in the center of the monastery enclosure near to the main door. Here, worshippers could enter the monastery's vaulted interior and raise their eyes to the glory of God.

Against the backdrop of spring planting and promise of the welcome warmth of summer, the months ahead saw visits by wandering friars and itinerant teachers. There were beggars as well as charlatans boasting salves and cures for any or all ailments. Alric spent much of his time among these visitors.

The travelers told stories about lands across the sea where the people spoke strange languages. It was at this time that Alric learned that many of the travelers knew of the land of Angles and Saxons as *Angle Land*, or the word was often pronounced to sound like *Angland* or England.

These perennial travelers were regarded with fascination. Some even attempted to ply magic, but these were considered to be of dubious honor. Others tried to sell papal indulgences, as supposed agents of the pope, which would give the purchaser remission from purgatory. Upon hearing this, Ethelbald threatened eternal damnation upon the souls of the salesmen and upon the souls of those who purchased such worthless and heretical items.

* * *

After one more year and another spring, Ethelbald informed Alric that he, the abbot, was to set out on a journey that would be at least one month in duration. Several days' ride to the north lay the monastery of St. Paul at Jarrow. This monastery was larger than Wearmouth, with a population of several thousand people; the settlement was the largest village in the area. It was a theological bastion and a production center for a variety of leather goods, textiles, and metal objects that varied from ecclesiastical ornaments to weapons of war.

Alric was informed that he would accompany Ethelbald and that this would be a celebration of his forthcoming birthday on June 24, the day of St. John the Baptist.

The abbot was proud of the fact that Alric has made the decision to remain at the monastery as a novice, and soon the time approached when he would take his vows and receive the tonsure. This was the ceremony in which the crown of his head would be shaved in the style of the Roman church rather than in the Celtic style in which the front part of the head was shaved from the brow to a point above the ears.

* * *

CHAPTER 5

Alric spent the next two years of his life quietly and in study at Wearmouth with interruptions for frequent journeys to Jarrow, where he would stay for a week or even longer.

For Alric's inquisitive mind, it was a stimulating time, since the libraries at both monasteries were continuing to grow. He knew that beyond the monastery walls, the increase in the population was causing changes to the landscape. There were the seasonal changes in the patterns of the fields. The ripening crops, rimmed with fragrant flowers, contrasted with those where vegetables were grown. On the road and arterial tracks, carts and people moved along as they went about their daily business. On occasion a horseman might approach the village, causing an alarm to be raised and the specter of the cruelty of the sea raiders to come into the minds of those who had experienced their killing and looting. The villagers had a plan for defending their homes if the sea raiders should ever appear again.

Alric was fortunate that Ethelbald had been insistent that he continue to study languages, and he soon became highly skilled. His fluency in Latin, Norse, and Celtic, as well as several of the languages that had commenced as dialects of Latin, continued to improve.

In late summer, after Alric's nineteenth birthday, the monks and the villagers felt their prayers had been answered, and there was a peace and a happy symbolism in their lives. At that time, the monastery was recognized not only as a center of learning but also as a center of trade.

As such, the monastery drew traders and, unfortunately, men of less reputable businesses to ply their wares. The abbot and his brother monks at Wearmouth, not being men of the world and therefore not wise in the affairs of men, were soon the objects of many nefarious dealings. There were instances of the monks being cheated by the underhanded behavior of merchants who had succumbed to temptation; money being the root of evil, according to the monks.

The monastery opened its doors to merchants every Friday, at which time they were allowed to enter the monastery gardens; Friday also coincided with market day in the village. Not surprisingly, the now thriving village and monastery became even more popular. The exception was Good Friday and those days which coincided with religious holidays. As it happened one Friday, the abbot needed to purchase additional supplies of calfskin for the monks, who would convert this to vellum to replenish their diminishing stocks. On that occasion, the abbot decided he would supervise the purchase and Alric would be by his side to carry the purchased goods to storage.

The merchant who dealt in such items presented the abbot with a sizable tied bundle of calfskin as well as two loose pieces. The top four pieces of the bundle and the additional loose pieces presented to Ethelbald for inspection were of exceptional quality. Ethelbald knew that his monks would be able to produce top-quality vellum from such skins.

Ethelbald nodded his appreciation, commenting on the quality of these skins, and was about to settle on a price when Alric, who could not believe his ears, tugged at the sleeve of the abbot's cassock.

"A word with you if I may, Lord Abbot."

"Certainly, Alric," Ethelbald replied as he turned slowly.

"I suggest," Alric whispered as the merchant strained in an attempt to hear the words, "that we inspect all of the skins in the bundle. And, Lord Abbot, the man is asking an unusually high price."

Looking at the merchant, Ethelbald said, "My young friend will inspect each skin that you have in the bundle."

The merchant immediately became defensive and related how long it had taken him to wrap the bundle of skins, then continued giving numerous reasons why it was not necessary to proceed with the examination of his merchandise.

Finally, Ethelbald held up his hand. "Stop this idle patter," he said. "You have just discouraged me from purchasing your skins and I suggest that you never return to this monastery or village. You protest too much to be an honest man!"

At that moment, Alric felt that Ethelbald took on the appearance and posture of a large eagle looking at its prey as he stared at the merchant with piercing eyes. By this time, several monks and onlookers had stopped to see what was taking place.

"You will remove your stall and yourself from this place," the abbot continued. "And I will see to it that word of your cheating ways is passed throughout this region. You may find that others have no wish to do business with you." A murmur arose from the onlookers. Ethelbald turned to two of the men from the village. "Please escort this man," he said, "his donkey, and his goods to the edge of the village and see him on his way."

One hour later, the two returned, beaming smiles covering their craggy faces. "It seems," one of the men whispered quietly to Alric, "that our friend fell into a mud hole. And all of his skins were ruined. Such a pity! The last we saw of him, he was running down the road trying to find his donkey."

Alric smiled. Justice was simple and it had been served. Alric had proved himself to be observant and, because of his improved skills in mathematics, was asked by Ethelbald to work with the monastic accounts to maintain the monastery spending at an acceptable level.

He did enjoy the ceremony and sacramental symbols of the religious services. During the Mass, the shadows cast by the flickering wicks of the candles danced before his eyes as he bowed his head in prayer. He could hear the disembodied voice of the abbot conducting the liturgy in the singsong tone of ancient Rome.

Alric felt he had much to pray for, in particular for the souls of his parents and sister, Hilda, but he also knew that God's providence had dictated his survival, as it had that of the monastery and the village, which now approached two thousand inhabitants. Crops thrived or failed with the weather or God's indulgence. A dry spring, a wet summer, a damp autumn, long frosts, or a rainy winter could reduce crop yields. A succession of any of the tribulations could lead to a food shortage, with the specter of gaunt, starving villagers gleaning the land for roots, flower bulbs, grass, leaves, and perhaps even an overlooked half-rotting turnip. Such conditions and the constant influx of visitors also brought disease.

Fortunately, one aspect of the new mobility led to a situation that placed Alric on a new track and put the monks in a better position to ward off sickness. As fortune would have it, Ecgfrith, an older monk skilled in the medical arts, arrived at the monastery, ostensibly for a visit on his way to Jarrow, but seeing the thriving community by the sea made it known to Ethelbald that he would like to remain permanently at Wearmouth. Noticing the bright-eyed Alric, who had expressed an interest in medicine, Ecgfrith received the abbot's permission to take Alric under his wing as an apprentice.

Alric formed an immediate bond with Ecgfrith, and thereafter much of Alric's developing character was derived from Ecgfrith. Medical men, such as Ecgfrith, often followed solitary lives giving them time to meditate. Healing the human body was not a simple task, and Alric realized that parroting the scriptures did not help the sick to survive;

they needed to be cured both physically and spiritually. The power of individual thought made Alric all the more determined to follow medicine as his chosen path.

Ecgfrith traveled widely, and he had seen how the body reflected a person's state of health. He believed that breathing the air in the vicinity of the sick and dying could cause disease and sickness to spread. Ecgfrith belonged to a culture that had ancient associations, and he had taken an oath to save lives as painlessly as possible. Medicine was a noble and mysterious craft that he helped Alric understand, and he continued to teach him the use of medicines derived from plants.

This appealed to Alric, who had inherited his mother's habit of reflection, and there was also in him his father's skill and tenacity for carpentry that would enable him to provide for a family. His father had provided a standard of living that was most comfortable. From both parents, Alric had inherited the ability to assemble facts in his mind and make quick decisions.

* * *

As time passed, Alric found himself more settled than he had ever been at any other time in his life. He felt blessed by the knowledge he derived from the books in the monastery library and at Jarrow. He was resolved to become a monk. He would receive the tonsure and take minor orders before the year was out. He would be assigned duties that were in keeping with his skills and the needs of the monastery. He had received Ethelbald's permission to continue his studies in medicine, for he had expressed the desire to become a healer.

"Life as a monk might not be so bad," he thought. "I will learn to heal people's bodies as well as their minds!"

As he walked one day in the bright sun of an early August, Hilda's knife tucked in his belt, his thoughts turned to his future. "At least I *have* a future!" He remembered the men, women, and children he had seen lying on the sand in the twisted agonies of violent death. They had no future. "Why would God allow such a thing to happen?" he asked, looking up at the sky as if expecting an answer. The shrieking of the gulls offered no words of solace. Alric suddenly felt troubled, and his senses told him that the days of peace and contentment would come to a shattering end.

* * *

Alric had just returned from the neighboring monastery of Jarrow, having made the journey as an apprentice to Ecgfrith. The evening meal in the refectory was filled with the somber mood of men with much on their minds. Silence was maintained during the mealtime, and once it was finished, Ethelbald rapped on the table with his wooden spoon to get the attention of his brother monks. All eyes focused on the abbot.

"My brothers," Ethelbald looked directly at each man sitting at the table, "there are rumors of an impending visit from the sea raiders, those foul fiends that last visited this shore almost three years ago. I have heard stories from travelers which told of raids that have been carried out to the south and to the north."

The monks knew that the tranquil days of the past years could not last, but all the same, they were shocked as Ethelbald delivered his news. The abbot had anticipated a deluge of questions, but only silence answered his quizzical look. However, Alric could not contain himself. "Shall we fight?" he asked.

"That is not our nature," Ethelbald responded, "but we must make sure that these strong high walls give us refuge."

"What about the villagers?" Alric's voice was clear in the silent room.

"We shall shelter those we can, but the enclosure is too small for everyone."

"What about a warning system?" Alric continued with his questions.

"I have talked with the elders of the village," the abbot responded, "and we have instituted a warning system that will be in place before night falls."

"I remember the last time!" Alric spoke again, to receive a raised eyebrow from Ethelbald. "There was such confusion everywhere because it is believed that the sentry—" Alric thought for a moment, and then he recalled the name, "Sighard—went to sleep or was not at attentive at his post."

"Alric, allow me to talk with my brothers while you busy yourself in the kitchen." Ethelbald looked straight into Alric's eyes as he continued. "I realize this may bring back bad memories for you, but we will do our best to see that the events of the last raid are not repeated." Alric bowed his head in respect of the abbot's authority and immediately left for the kitchen.

The news struck hard at the villagers. The sea raiders could ruin a village until crops could be replanted and food grown once more. As the news traveled around, emotions of anger and fear gave vent. Some of the villagers were already starting to pack their meager belongings, while others were retrieving weapons from various corners of their homes. Mostly illiterate, desperately poor, and possessing little, the land workers felt they had little to lose and were primed for a fight.

But providence, as decreed by God, played into the hands of everyone. Two days later, three sails were spotted on the horizon moving in a northerly direction. The lookouts waved the warning flags and watched until the sails disappeared. The all-clear flags of a different color signaled that village life should return to normal for the remainder of the day.

At the first opportunity, Alric climbed onto the walkway inside the wall of the monastery and looked toward the sea. I know that you are out there, he thought. He would find them and one day have his vengeance on the men who'd killed his family. He wondered if they would make a return visit to Wearmouth.

*   *   *

The next day, Alric walked along the beach as if drawn to Hilda's secret place. He had not visited the enclosure since that dreadful day when his sister and parents had died. He was so engrossed in thought that he did not see the ship beached a short distance away. His nose detected a scent in the air being carried by a northerly breeze.

The sounds from the distance indicated that the sentries near to the monastery had caught sight of the ship and were raising the alarm. He saw everything as if in slow motion. A line of sea raiders approached him along the beach and close to the cliffs in order to remain undetected. The men advanced in silence as they crept around the rocks.

It was too late. The sea raiders were here. One of them saw Alric and pointed in his direction. After a quick exchange of words, two men started to run toward him.

Alric looked around. He was too far from the monastery. He would be caught before he could run half the distance, and the gate would be locked. He looked toward the cliffs, feeling trapped. Then his eyes caught sight of what he hoped was a way of escape.

He could see three openings at the base of the cliffs. If these caves had an escape shaft that led to the surface, he had a chance. Or perhaps he could work his way into the depths of the cave and find a hiding place until the raiders tired of looking for him and left. After a while he might even be able to break and run for the monastery. He looked toward the two men who were still a good distance away.

Then he scrambled over the rocks toward the caves, unaware that he had scraped his hands and knees on the sharp edges. As he crawled, he mumbled and prayed, wishing that he had gone into the library, as he had planned, or carried out his duties in the kitchen, as needed.

Prayerful thoughts crashed through his mind as he remembered the lifeless body of his sister. He knew he could expect a similar fate.

He was almost at the mouth of the cave that promised him shelter when a helmeted head appeared at the entrance. One of the raiders had cut him off from his safe haven. Alric clutched his robes to free his legs for the fast run to the next cave. After what seemed an eternity, he entered the cave fifty paces ahead of the raiders and hid behind the rocks near the entrance, pressing himself on the ground. He remained still, as if trying to melt his body into the sandy floor. To his horror he saw that the passage, which was to be his escape route to the surface, was partially blocked by a fall of rock. The raiders were close by.

Alric inspected the pile of rubble as best he could. There was, of course, no time and no one to help him clear a way to safety. He stood up but caught his head on a rock that jutted out from the wall, forcing him down. This took precious minutes of time for him to recover. From inside his body, he felt the panic rise, but he knew he must remain calm if he was to survive. He breathed slowly and deliberately to relax his mind and gain control.

After a brief moment, he got up again, found that he suffered no ill effects, and began slowly and steadily to explore the extent of the blockage to the cave. He knew he would not be able to leave his hiding place by the same route he had taken, so he started to move the rubble as silently and as best he could. The cave was much deeper than he had first thought, and if his assumption was correct, this cave continued deep into the rock and had an escape chimney to the land surface above the beach.

He looked around quickly to see if there was anything in the cave that he might be able to use, but most of the rocks were either too small or too big to use as weapons. Although, he thought, picking up a small rock and testing it for weight in his hand, did not David kill Goliath with a small stone? He picked up several more and placed them in the pocket of his cassock, then moved toward the rear of the cave, seeking the way out.

He wondered if the sea raiders were still there. He assumed they would maintain their watch. He turned around and looked toward the entrance to the cave. The sunlight streaming into the cave opening was almost blinding. He crouched in an alcove which hid him from view. Perhaps, he wondered, the raiders might look in, fail to see him, and then depart.

Alric shook his head in disbelief at his own thought. Unless they wished to take slaves, the raiders left no survivors. He also wondered if any of the raiders who had arrived this day had been with the group that had raided the village three years ago and if any of them would recognize him because of his strong resemblance to Hilda. He shook his head in disbelief again. By the time he was close enough to be recognized, his fate would be sealed!

He moved to the back of the cave, cautiously to avoid injury. Once he had maneuvered himself around the bend in the cave wall, he turned and looked toward the entrance again. He hoped he had not been spotted. As he crept deeper into the cave, he heard voices from the front where the pile of rubble lay. He stayed as close to the wall as possible and was relieved that the sound of the voices did not seem any closer. He was conscious of a faint light in the cave.

He stopped on the spot where he noticed the change of light. He could see more clearly, and there were features of the wall that he had not been able to see before. He could not believe that he had found an escape route so quickly. He stared at the ceiling, and in doing so, remembered the approximate position of the chimney at the top of the cliff. He had paced it off from the edge many times, more out of curiosity than purpose, never realizing it would be needed in a life-and-death situation. He waited for a few seconds for his eyes to adjust to the light which glared from the entrance.

Then, he looked up once more and saw the dim gray circular shape just above his head. This was the way to the surface. He had just started to congratulate himself and relax a little when the voices he had heard previously increased in volume. The feeling of panic rose in his throat once more. In an instant, he threw himself against the wall. He tried to retreat back into the cave but knew he might lose sight of the chimney that was his path to freedom. The voices seemed to lose some of their intensity. But the noises in the cave were deceiving. Can they be leaving? he wondered.

He peered around the bend in the wall and saw two men. They took three short steps into the cave, giving their eyes time to get accustomed to the darkness, then stayed near the entrance, heads together as if in consultation. There was no doubt in Alric's mind that they would, sooner or later, come deeper into the cave.

He could see their heads moving, their voices now reduced to a mere whisper. There was only one reason for this; the raiders were making plans to capture him!

* * *

CHAPTER 6

Alric watched the two men intently; one seemed familiar. The bearded face, the strong nose, and the high forehead rang bells in Alric's brain. Still unsure of the man's identity, Alric carefully watched the raider as he stroked his cheek; he appeared to be in deep thought. Then recognition hit! Alric remembered looking through the peephole between the rocks and seeing the same telltale gesture from the man as he had looked at Hilda's dead body after she had struck down his companion.

Haldor and his lieutenant surveyed the mouth of the cave. Alric was unaware that this man was Haldor's cousin, Gunnarr. He felt sure that they were discussing the dangers that lay ahead and making sure they had not been led into a trap. Alric saw Haldor motion to Gunnarr to be silent. He had watched Alric run to the cave and there was something familiar about him. Haldor gritted his teeth. He would have revenge for his brother's death.

The walls cast dark shadows among the stones, making it difficult for him to focus as his gaze shifted from shadow to shadow. He took off his helmet and cocked his head to one side, listening. There was only the sound of the distant surf on the beach behind him. He replaced his helmet, then drew his sword from the leather scabbard and held it at the ready, passing it back and forth from hand to hand, as if deciding what would be his next move.

Alric realized that if he moved now he would be seen and the two men would easily overpower him. He lay low and continued to watch their actions. Obviously, by now the alarm would have been raised and it would be difficult for the raiders to penetrate the monastery precincts and loot any treasure there. There might even be rescuers on the way to fight them, but this would not help him in his present situation.

Alric held his breath as he watched Haldor allow the sword to rest in his left hand and squeeze the hilt, patiently waiting.

"Saxon, I am Haldor, leader of my people and I know who you are!" He shouted into the cave. Alric understood the clear words of the raider's language and the threat they carried.

"You have the look of that girl who killed my brother. I thought I saw two of you in the rocks that day. Now you are mine. Come out, Saxon! I wish you to meet my cousin Gunnarr. I promise your death will be quick."

For what seemed an eternity, Alric remained motionless, hardly daring to breathe. The only noise was the distant whisper of the sea. In the dim light, he saw a smile on Gunnarr's face.

Alric knew now that Haldor had a score to settle and he would pay dearly and painfully for the death of Haldor's brother. The sea raiders loved to inflict pain, and through torture the death of Haldor's brother would be avenged. If he were caught, they would kill him in front of the monastery for all to see what happened to those who resisted. On the other hand, Haldor might take him back to their home base, where others could watch his painful death. Neither plan appealed to him.

As they continued their taunts, Alric decided it was now or never. He would certainly not communicate with them and give his location away. Carefully, and as inconspicuously as possible, he moved to a position where he would not lose sight of the opening to the natural chimney. The surface at the top of the cliff was twenty feet above his head. He tested his footing and decided he could clamber up on a pile of rubble that at one time or another must have fallen from the opening.

His boots were old but had adapted to the shape of his feet, so that he felt he would gain the necessary traction. He needed a secure handholds and footing on the wall and then, inch by inch, he could make his way to the base of the chimney. He tried to imagine it to be a game he had played as a child when he and Hilda, much to the dismay of their parents, had climbed up the face of the cliffs using only their fingers and toes. He looked around one more time to make sure nothing had changed.

The hair on the back of Alric's neck rose as he realized the raiders had moved. He stayed motionless against the wall and watched them as they moved into the shadows of the cave. He checked his belt to make sure his knife was still there. With much relief, he found it.

The sounds of their approach struck his ears. They made no attempt to whisper, now that they felt they had the upper hand. They were unaware that he understood their dialect and expected him to attempt an escape, at which time he would be captured.

Alric needed time to think. The entrance to the chimney was a little higher than he'd first thought. He looked around for an alternative hiding place and squirmed into one of the niches, pushing aside the small rocks and rubble to make room. He pressed himself against the wall, drawing in his stomach and curling up into a fetal position. He folded the robes about his body so that the lightness of exposed skin would not be detected in the semi-darkness. He buried his face in the hood of his robe, leaving only a small opening for vision.

The two men advanced slowly, conferring in their guttural tones, evidently uncertain as to where he had gone. There was silence, and then Alric heard the men breathing heavily from their exertions as they moved over the rocks and rubble, carrying their heavy weapons. The man known as Gunnarr carried a battle axe strapped to his back, increasing his burden even more.

Haldor had advanced even farther into the cave than he'd realized. Alric pressed himself farther into the wall niche, but it was too late. Haldor had spotted him!

Alric trembled as he watched the raider approach. He could see the gleaming eyes beneath the helmet, mocking as if in triumph at his catch. As the man reached into the niche to grab his robe, Alric lashed at him with his foot but the raider brushed it aside and caught hold of his ankle. Without fear, Alric struck at the hand with his knife and felt it strike home. He lunged and struck again, connecting once more with the man's hand.

Haldor grunted from the sting of the knife and withdrew his hand. He could not strike Alric, as he was unable to swing his sword freely in the confined space. He frowned in frustration and retreated to where Gunnarr waited on the other side of the cave.

Alric, now enraged but finding unknown energy, thrust the knife back into his belt, scrambled out of the niche, and made his way deeper into the cave. As he lay there, he felt certain that the pounding of his heart would give him away. He looked toward the entrance to see if the two raiders were still in the cave. He could hear their voices, but the echo from the cave walls masked their words. He heard their footsteps again on the cave floor as they moved in his direction. Their helmeted heads formed a dark outline against the bright sunlight that framed the entrance. Then suddenly four eyes bored directly into his hiding place.

Haldor's eyes narrowed.

Alric felt the raider's eyes, like hot coals, boring into his body, and it took all his courage not to flinch.

"*Hej. Vent!*" "Hey. Wait!" Haldor said to Gunnarr as he realized what he had seen.

Run! Alric's brain shrieked soundlessly. Alric scrambled to his feet and darted farther into the cave over the fallen rock and into an area that opened into a narrow passageway running between the cave walls. He ran deeper and deeper into the cave. Behind him, he could hear the heavy thudding of Haldor and Gunnarr's footfalls. He came to a narrow opening that looked as though it had been cut into the stone and plunged through, falling heavily and scrambling onto his hands and knees.

Over the years the cave floor had filled with rubble and sand washed in by the sea as it continuously pounded the cliffs during the high tides. Openings that at one time had been large were now only low passages. Alric had to crouch to get through, and he hit his head against a stone outcrop. He felt the pain and fell to his knees. Momentarily stunned, he looked back and through his blurred vision saw the dim outline of Haldor.

Haldor was determined Alric would not escape. He had his shoulders through the opening, grunting loudly, and struggled to pull the lower half of his body through the gap.

Alric's brain cried out. *Now!* He wrenched the knife from his belt. He knew his only hope lay in dispatching at least one of the raiders if he was to reach one of the tunnels or chimneys that he hoped lay farther into the cave where they could not reach him. There he could hide in silence.

He saw his moment. The blade flashed as he stabbed downward into Haldor's left shoulder hitting the bone. Blood poured from the wound as Haldor yelled in rage and pain. Using his right hand, he reached for Alric. Clenching his teeth, Alric lunged again, this time aiming for Haldor's neck, but the man raised his forearm, where the knife found its mark.

This time he would not miss! Haldor raised his head but realized it was too late. With a quick upward thrust, Alric plunged the knife into Haldor's throat. The gurgling sound that followed told Alric he had struck true. He stared at the man as his lifeblood ran onto the rocks. He could hear sounds from Haldor's companion as he approached.

Alric continued into the rear of the cave, slithering through gaps and breaches in the walls and pushing his way through narrow openings.

Sometimes he saw patches of open sky above, while at other times he was cloaked in pitch-darkness. In one such place, feeling more secure and invisible, he stopped to catch his breath. But the hunter was not about to give up. Alric had to keep moving.

Finally, he entered a large cavern he had never seen before. Part of the roof had collapsed, and a shaft of sunlight dimly illuminated the space. He looked up at the source of the light, wondering whether it might offer a way out. He tried to climb, but the opening above was a smooth section of rock wall and there was no foothold. He was trapped.

*   *   *

While Alric was retreating deeper into the cave, Gunnarr had carried Haldor's body to the cave entrance. The other raiders, shocked at seeing the body of their leader, questioned Gunnarr, who related what had transpired and the possible identify of their prey.

There were some who remembered Haldor's anger at the death of his brother. It had been even more galling to know that a mere woman had killed Skardi! Haldor had sworn an oath that he would return to this place and take his revenge, and now he too was dead. The raiders saw ill fortune on this shore and began to talk of returning home to present the body of their leader to the gods.

Gunnarr glanced impatiently at his companions but saw the logic of their thinking. Being the closest relative to Haldor, he would assume the leadership for the remainder of the voyage. Not wishing to tempt fate, he looked toward the ship and then back into the cave. "The Saxon should not be allowed to get away with this. Haldor also told me that this man bears a strong physical resemblance to the woman who killed Skardi, perhaps a brother. Whether that is true matters not. The Saxon has killed my cousin Haldor and he must pay for his actions."

The sight of Haldor's body reminded him of the indignity they had suffered. They all agreed to seek vengeance against the Saxon. Gunnarr was pleased that they supported his plan, for to have such a major disagreement at this early point of his newly found leadership would not bode well for him.

Gunnarr pointed out to the men that as long as the ship lay beached in the cove in daylight, they could be easily trapped, and escape might be all but impossible. For the moment, the towering cliffs offered some protection for the ship. He was not familiar with this land that was cursed by his gods. It seemed as dangerous as it was desolate. He had raided the coastal areas many times but had landed on the southern areas that were always poorly defended. In the northern settlements, these Saxon settlers were men of a different breed. They were fighters—just as the Saxon had fought him and taken the life of Haldor.

To kill him would bring favor from their gods, Gunnar concluded his thoughts. Therefore they must do it quickly. Then he spoke to the men. "The man who captures the Saxon will be rewarded when we reach home."

A murmur of agreement greeted Gunnarr's words, and he ordered two of the men to scale the cliffs. Although a short distance, the thirty-foot climb was treacherous and the going was slow for the heavily armed raiders. At length they reached the top and turned to scan the sea. One of them signaled that all was clear. He then turned to his companion, signaled a silence, and pointed to the ground.

* * *

In the meantime, Alric had surveyed his current surroundings and, deciding he had no other choice to reach the outside, he retraced his steps through the cave.

The sounds from within the cave were diminished. He moved cautiously out of his place of relative safety and stood motionless. He needed to find the chimney that would take him to the surface and climb or claw his way to the top. He reached the place where he ascertained the chimney to be and, after recognizing the spot, felt the tension ease from his body. It was then that he heard sounds from above. He paused.

As the sounds became fainter and trailed off into the distance, he reasoned that he was safe once more.

He took a slow deep breath and entered the chimney. He made his way wearily to the surface, clinging to the wall, at times feeling that he could not move. His fingers were cramping but he had to hold on. He was exhausted. His hands were bleeding, and one arm felt numb. There was one more corner to negotiate before he would see the sunlight.

The twists and turns of the chimney had brought Alric close to the edge of the cliff. At the top, he allowed his eyes to adjust to the sunlight before he surfaced, but to his dismay four rough hands seized him from behind and dragged him on to the grass. He could not see his rescuers, but the smell told him otherwise. He had been caught!

His captors, their faces hardened and corrugated by the winds of the sea, laughed as Alric squirmed and tried to escape. He shouted and kicked out, managing to catch one of them in the rib cage. He struggled free from the raider, picked up a rock, and hurled it. The rock found its mark and the man fell to the ground. The strike had opened a wound just above the man's eye, his blood-soaked face making him all the more menacing.

Alric continued to back away and looked for another rock, but a stunning blow to the head from a sword hilt caused him to fall and roll down the slope toward the edge of the cliff. His arms flailed ineffectively as he vainly tried to stop his momentum. He lost his grip on the harsh sea grass in an attempt to hold on to anything that would save him but continued sliding down the slope. The next sensation was that of falling to the beach. Alric's desperate shout echoed against the cliffs and attracted the attention of the raiders below.

Two of them looked up to the top of the cliff, only to have a body fall on them. They struggled to pick themselves up and rid themselves of the falling object.

The two raiders above clambered down the narrow and treacherous route from the cliffs to the beach. In the meantime, Alric had been slapped into consciousness by one of the raiders who had broken his fall. The other man drew his sword to dispatch the still groggy Alric.

"*Nej!*" "No!"

The commanding voice of Gunnarr stopped the action. Alric looked at Gunnarr and caught a glimpse of a bright but dispassionate eye that seemed to weigh him up and found him wanting. Then why stay the killer's hand?

"He seems to have courage," Gunnarr said contemptuously. "Tie him while I decide the form of sport and entertainment he will provide for us, and for those who"—he gestured toward the monastery in the distance—"hide and cower behind the wall."

Alric shook himself back to full consciousness. Now he understood why he had not been killed. Gunnarr would need to plan an appropriate punishment! His painful screaming death would be used as an example to all who dared to oppose them. He saw a smile spread across Gunnarr's face. Gunnarr had dismissed from his mind any thoughts of an immediate departure.

"They will all die," Gunnarr said as he gestured once more toward the monastery. He was a craftsman when it came to killing captives. He was particularly fond of death by torture as a means of teaching a captive and any onlookers a painful and frightening lesson. His last captive whom he had tortured had survived for an excruciatingly painful two days. *This one*, Gunnarr thought as he looked at Alric, *will not die until he is tied to the mast of the ship to Valhalla and burns with Haldor's body. Yes,* he smiled inwardly, *that will be my pleasure!*

Alric was dragged to his feet. One of the raiders seized him by the arms and pushed up the sleeves of his robe. "Gunnarr!" the raider exclaimed wide-eyed, as he held up Alric's arm for all to see.

The others moved closer to see what had caught the attention of their colleague. On the upraised arm they saw Alric's birthmarks that, because of his exertion, were bright red against the whiteness of his arm. The raiders fell silent.

Gunnarr took an uneasy step toward Alric, wondering what had caused his men to behave in such a manner. He took Alric's arm roughly and looked at the birthmarks. Alric, even in his dazed state, noticed that Gunnarr gulped visibly. There followed a discussion between Gunnarr and his men, with furtive looks at Alric and raised voices. Then Gunnarr approached Alric.

"You understand our language?" he asked. Alric nodded groggily. "It seems," Gunnarr said, looking into Alric's eyes, "that you are fortunate to bear the signs of *nauthiz* and *sowilo*—our signs for conflict and success!" Gunnarr spoke of the stylized cross, *nauthiz*, and crescent shape, *sowilo*, which were two letters from their runic alphabet. The raiders considered the rune signs to convey messages, often serious, often magical. "We," Gunnarr said, looking at the men, "believe you may have been sent to us from the gods." He smiled grimly at Alric and then continued. "We will take you to our settlement and the elders will decide what to do with you."

Gunnarr looked around at his companions and, seeing the looks of apprehension on their faces, declared, "Since this captive has the marks of the signs of our people, we will take him with us. We will provide him with sufficient food and water to keep him alive so that he is well enough to face the council."

Murmurs of agreement and anticipation followed Gunnarr's words. He would have preferred to have used Alric as an example to all who watched from the monastery enclosure. "Do you understand me, Saxon?" Gunnarr looked at Alric.

"Yes, I do, murderer."

Gunnarr did not take the response kindly. He hit Alric with a vicious backhand that brought blood to Alric's mouth. "A spirited fellow," Gunnarr snarled as he stroked his knuckles. He was about to strike Alric again when he heard murmurs from the crew.

"Ah," he said as he turned to face them. "I see you think it is bad luck to strike a man with the marks of our gods. He will survive without further punishment, but he will be a close companion to our dead leader," Gunnarr nodded in the direction of Haldor's body, "before Haldor receives the honor due to a leader and passes from the shores of our homeland into the halls of Valhalla on a burning ship."

Gunnarr looked thoughtful for a moment, then added, "The people may even decide that Haldor should be accompanied to Valhalla by a servant. If so, he"—Gunnarr nodded at Alric—"will accompany Haldor." Gunnarr looked around at his companions. Their expressions indicated that it would not take much for them to revolt; his new role as leader was in question. "Now we go home!" he announced.

The raiders' expressions relaxed. They now focused on another goal. They were going home to their families. Alric breathed a sigh of relief as he realized how close to death he had come. He looked in the direction of the ship. It was the closest he had ever been to such a vessel. From what Ethelbald and other monks had told him, these ingeniously constructed ships allowed the sea raiders to make long trips. This one was a fast, slender warship. As near as he could estimate, the ship was about thirty yards long and made from oak. He could see where the boards, secured by iron nails, had been made watertight with tar. There were rings into which the oars could be placed. He knew the ship was capable of making good speed and they would reach the shores of their homeland in a matter of days.

Alric's thoughts were interrupted as one of the raiders hauled him to his feet. In one sudden movement he was slung over the raider's shoulder like a sack of grain. With long, sure strides, the men closed the gap between the cliffs and the ship.

It did not take long for the raiders to push the ship off the beach where the shallow draught allowed it to float unaided in the water. Panting and streaked with grime and sweat, they boarded the ship. The man carrying Alric relaxed his grip for a moment as he boarded the ship, and Alric sank his teeth into the man's forearm. Without a word, he swung Alric around and, momentarily forgetting that Alric bore the rune marks, struck him a vicious blow with his fist. Alric lapsed into a world of darkness.

The raider examined the seeping wound on his forearm where Alric had bitten him. In anger he hit the unconscious Alric once more. Then Alric was thrown unceremoniously into the center of the ship, where he remained unconscious, next to the body of Haldor.

Alric began to sense the movement of the ship, but he was not sufficiently conscious to realize where he was. He wanted to cry out in pain, but he felt utterly helpless. He tried to open his eyes. He could not see the oars, since they were raised against the side of the ship, as if the vessel had sprouted wings. Then he heard the sounds of the oars being placed in position in the rings, a musical note rang out, and the ship began to move. A steady rhythm took the ship out to sea.

Alric continued to feign unconsciousness. He heard only the sounds of oars creaking against the rings as they were alternately raised and lowered into the water.

Then darkness overtook him once again.

*   *   *

As the ship glided though the gray waters, a number of the monks, standing on the high wall of the monastery, watched it disappear into the distance. They breathed a sigh of relief that the monastery had not been attacked and burned. They were congratulating themselves on their own good fortune and for God's protection and were preparing to leave the wall when they realized someone was missing.

Ethelbald looked around at the faces before him, recalling all who were present. He had relaxed, thinking all were present and accounted for, and then his face took on a serious expression as he spoke. "Has anyone seen Alric?" he asked.

To a man, they all looked toward the ship but no one was able to answer the abbot's question.

* * *

CHAPTER 7

It had been Gunnarr's plan to travel in a northerly direction, spend time at the settlement at Dunedin, and then cross the sea to his homeland. For reasons unknown, he decided to sail in an easterly direction and then follow the coastline northward until they reached their home. He would have accomplished this with relative ease had it not been for the freak late summer storm.

It was one of those storms that originated in the Western Ocean and drove with considerable force through the channel that lay between the southern land of the Saxons and the northern part of the land Caesar and his Roman legions called Gaul. The waves pounded the channel mercilessly, and many plying trade between Britain and northern Gaul were lost in the tempest.

The winds suddenly swept upon them from the north. The clash of the southwesterly wind from the Western Ocean and the storm sweeping down from the northern landmass met when the sea raiders were midway between Wearmouth and their home in Denmark. The shallow draught of the ship's keel was designed for speed and the convenience of sailing into shallow beach areas and estuaries. It was not made for fighting an angry sea, and it was not long before the waves tossed the vessel like a cork. The sail was hauled in and attempts were made to stabilize the ship by rowing. But the oarsmen soon grew tired and weary as they battled the tempest.

Alric lay huddled in the stern of the ship near the rudder that had been secured with a strong rope in an attempt to control the ship's motion. He was not tied or restrained—he could not go anywhere in such a storm, only overboard to his death—and lay there wrapped in his woolen robe trying to keep warm in the filthy water that slopped around the interior of the ship. Even his heavy monk's robe, now thoroughly soaked, could not prevent the chill from pervading his body. He had spent the earlier part of the day awaiting his imminent departure from this life. For hours he lay huddled as the storm grew in intensity, either shivering or in a fever. At one point, seeing one of the raiders swept overboard, he had a spark of hope and wondered how many more would meet the same fate.

The ship was uncontrollable as the north wind swept it farther to the south and into the teeth of the storm. In an attempt to remain vigilant, the crew strained their eyes to seek landfall through the darkness and incessant rain. At the same time, they had to use caution lest a dark, ghostly outline in the distance was deadly rocks that would destroy the ship, throwing everyone into the icy waters.

As the ship careened about the sea at the mercy of the waves, water barrels broke free of the heavy timber balks to which they had been lashed and scattered wildly on the deck, splintering wood as they moved from one part of the deck to another. Finally, one crashed through the side of the ship, leaving a hole for the angry, hissing seawater to use as an entry point. The sea poured in with every swell and there was no doubt that the crew were in dire peril.

This was not the pleasant homeward journey the sea raiders had expected. The rain above the ship and the turmoil of gray and gloomy waves beneath had long since brought on tiredness and fatigue. Even these men of the sea found this fearsome and asked themselves why the gods were angry. There were even mumblings against Gunnarr because of his harsh treatment of Alric. They felt that they had angered the gods.

Alric could hear their words plainly, and it became obvious to him that the support that Gunnarr had enjoyed when the ship had sailed from the beach at Wearmouth was no longer evident. He knew that if it had not been for the birthmarks on his arm, he would have been killed on the beach or joined the fish in the tumultuous sea.

One of the raiders cast a glance at Alric. The man made a comment to Gunnarr that he had brought bad luck upon the ship by his treatment of the captive. Gunnarr silenced the man with harsh words.

Alric noted the discontent with unexpressed pleasure. He hoped the ship would be beached somewhere and allow them to wait out the storm. In such a chaotic situation, he may have an opportunity to escape. He remembered Ethelbald's wise words: Patience is a virtue.

He could feel his stomach heaving, and the lack of food over the past day caused him pain, but the heaves brought nothing except the discomfort of his stretched abdominal muscles. He prayed silently as the ship tossed in the gray sea that seemed to welcome it with open arms, promising all on board a watery death.

Alric was surprised to see that many of the men were sick from the constant heaving and buffeting the ship took from the wind and angry waves. He had always supposed the raiders were used to such storms and could bear this discomfort. At that moment, Gunnarr gave orders to bail water to keep the ship from breaking up and sinking. All the crew bailed as fast as they could, even those who were feeling ill; it was a matter of survival. Cold seawater swirled about their legs as they worked feverishly to reduce the chance of the ship sinking.

Gunnarr grimaced at the sea and looked at Alric. The harsh words spat out: "Get a pail and work!" As he watched Alric start to bail seawater, he thought of the spectacle that Alric would provide once the ship was berthed on their home beach. The feeling gave him renewed strength. Gunnarr needed revenge and recognition as well as future command of a ship. Taking the crew home through such a storm as well as a captive for sport and to serve Haldor in Valhalla would get him the recognition he sought, he admitted to himself.

Everyone worked until their arms were numb with the cold. Then, when all seemed to be in vain and the battle with the sea lost, the storm diminished in intensity with a suddenness that deceived everyone, and the sea became calm. The violence that had lasted for several hours was over.

The crew, at least those capable of movement, surveyed the damage. The mast had held, but the sail had been used for another purpose. The keel had sprung several leaks, and the sail had been cut into pieces and used to block the holes. The hole where the water barrel had crashed into the side was taking on water continuously, so much so that their efforts to bail out the water were in vain. Many oars were broken, only about half being fit for use. The fresh water was lost and the only food that remained was soaked with seawater.

Of the sixty men who had originally been on board, fifty remained, and the others had been swept overboard into the cruel sea. Injuries to others as well as sickness made it imperative that they find a beach before the ship floundered on the open sea. They needed a haven where they could see to the repairs, gather food, and replenish the stocks of fresh water without trouble from hostile inhabitants. The men were in no condition to fight, and it was doubtful if they could survive without food and water for another day.

Gunnarr looked around. The sky had started to clear; as best as he could estimate, it was about midday. He looked at the sorry state of the ship and the bedraggled crew. The storm had been relentless; they had to rest.

He could see landfall on the horizon, but their current position was unknown. He knew that the strong north winds had overcome the southwesterly winds and blown the ship to the south. He did not know how far he was off course, so he decided to head for the land to the east.

He even wondered if they had been carried as far as the western edge of Gaul, a great distance to the south of the land of the Saxons.

He freed the rudder from its restraints and set course for the land, commanding the crew to use the undamaged oars. Hours later, they entered a bay that stretched inland between foreboding forests. The crew beached the ship with much relief. Gunnarr knew that the omens of the enterprise seemed dark and sinister, so he took no chances. Using the oldest method known of rubbing two sticks together, he was able to start a fire. Two men cut wood from the nearby trees and Gunnarr fashioned a bow using a piece of the sail as string. He wrapped the string of the bow once around the rod and braced the wooden lath with his foot. With quick movements, he was able to catch an ember in the dry moss and lichens that he had placed around the notch. Then he blew gently into the flame and the fire was nurtured to maturity. From this one fire, four others were started, allowing the men to commence drying out their chilled bodies.

As the fires started to crackle, warmth percolated through the brine-sodden clothes, throwing clouds of vapor into the cool air. Four of the men went searching for food and returned with a freshly killed deer. Another group found fresh water and carried back a plentiful supply. Others had spotted water birds of a considerable size that Alric recognized as geese. The rest of the men collected wood from the nearby forest that could be cut and fashioned to repair the ship in all haste.

Alric focused on the activities, wondering about the possibility of escape. He would try to escape as soon as sleep overtook the tired crew. Even though his stomach was not in any condition to digest the cooked food, he felt that he had the energy to leave the camp when all was quiet.

His hopes were dashed when, after his makeshift meal, the raider who had carried him aboard ship at Wearmouth arrived smiling. Alric thought that perhaps his fortunes had changed. But it was not to be. The man bound his hands and feet with pieces taken from the sail, after which Alric was unceremoniously dumped into the ship, where he rolled uncontrollably and came to rest at the lowest point of the keel. Fortunately, the water that the ship had taken on during the storm had drained away after they'd arrived on the beach. The raider stared at him and mumbled a few threatening unintelligible grunts. Alric's only option was to lie quietly and try to sleep in the discomfort of damp clothes with his hands and feet bound. He lay back as best he could. Every part of his body was stiff with exhaustion, and sleep was a long time coming.

The next morning, before any other work was done, the fires were rekindled. This was necessary to preserve the flames to use in conditioning the wood and making repairs to the ship. For several days, the raiders worked steadily to repair the ship.

During this period, Alric was largely ignored except at mealtimes, when he was grudgingly given a meager share of the food. However, his restraints were not ignored and were checked regularly. He was told that he would relieve himself as the men did on board ship—where he sat—as best he could. The restraints would not be removed under any circumstances. Gunnarr had no doubt that given the chance, Alric would try to escape.

The work continued steadily. The ship was patched and the thick renderings from the freshly killed deer and the geese, which formed the basis of their food, were troweled around the patches to make them watertight. The sail was beyond repair, but Gunnarr ordered that fresh oars be cut and they would make it home by sheer manpower, staying closer to the shoreline than usual in case of an emergency. The skins of the deer that had been killed each day were cut and the insides flamed to remove particles of flesh. As the pieces were each made ready, they were sewn together for use as water skins.

Gunnarr did not take the full precautions of posting a perimeter guard every night. His token guard consisted of four men who, tired from their labors during the day, often slept the night away rather than remain watchful. To all intents and purposes, the camp was unguarded.

In the late afternoon of the tenth day, Gunnarr ordered his men to take water and food. Alric was told to eat and drink also. They would retire early. Alric knew then that the next day they would leave. There was a flurry of activity as the ship was inspected. It was still not as trim as it should have been, but Alric estimated that the condition of the vessel was sufficient to take them north.

There was enough food and water for everyone, but rationing might be necessary. The improvised water skins would not carry enough water for the whole journey, and Alric guessed that Gunnarr would not like the idea of another stop with his partially repaired ship.

As dusk gave way to night and the flickering fires cast a dim light on the sleeping sea raiders, Alric's only companions were fear and despair. He looked around. There was nowhere to go. He tried to sleep, once more trussed like an animal in the bottom of the ship.

In an attempt to chase fear from his mind, he thought about his location. From the direction taken by the ship and the proximity to the Western Ocean, as indicated by the waves, he estimated that they had made landfall on the part of Gaul that jutted into the ocean, which was directly south of Britain. He had read with vigor and excitement the works of Bede, who had served at the monastery of St. Peter at Wearmouth and also at the monastery of St. Paul in Jarrow. Alric was particularly interested in Bede's *Ecclesiastical History of the English People,* which had given him a good understanding of the relationship between northwestern Gaul and Britain.

From these texts, Alric knew that the people of this area were descendants of Gauls, Celts, displaced Saxons, and Romans, as well as renegades from many other lands. There were also, occasionally, visitors from Spain and men who spoke in a strange tongue and who had crossed the strait at the western end of the Middle Sea.

Gunnarr and his raiders treated the land as inhospitable. It was a part of their timeless ritual in which fortunes turned quickly and a master one day could be a slave the next, or dead. They had just been delivered from the storm and they were not about to succumb to an enemy on land. Deliverance was in the hands of their gods.

Naturally, Alric was not about to impart any of his knowledge to Gunnarr. Lying trussed and helpless in the ship, he thought of the simple principle of *an enemy of my enemy is my friend,* and only one conclusion could be drawn by any inhabitants who had observed the activities on the beach.

Gunnarr's decision to forgo the perimeter guards and to strengthen the watch near their camp was an error he would regret.

* * *

Alric tried to free himself, but the bindings still held him tight. He closed his eyes as the sickly odors of filth assailed his senses. The air was heavy and there was no breeze from the ocean to carry away the stench that surrounded him. He could not think. He did not know where he was, since he lay facedown and could not see anything above him. He listened for the creaking of the oars and other sounds. There were none. The ship must be free from the beach and on the sea, he thought. So why am I unable to hear the sounds of oars being used?

He managed to roll over onto his side and open his eyes and looked up to see blue sky. Then the stinking body of Haldor, lying next to him, reminded him just where he was. He could not hear any signs of life. A lone gull shrieked its harsh cry as it flew above the ship. It was free, floating on the air currents in a cloudless sky. He could see the legs and arms of the raiders above him, but they were not rowing. All was silent.

* * *

Alric then heard the sounds of a strange language that he failed to recognize. His lips felt swollen and he wiped his mouth against his shoulder to remove the strange taste. He squirmed around to change his position, and the shock of what he saw drained the blood from his face. The smell of death was real. The raiders were dead and their blood had leached into the bottom of the ship. He turned over and retched but there was nothing in his stomach. He tried to raise himself into a sitting position but rolled against another corpse that was heavy and unyielding. It seems, Alric thought, that Haldor has company! He tried to fill his lungs with fresh air, but to no avail. The still fetid air in the ship made him retch again. He tried to swallow, but his tongue was swollen and dry and caught at the back of his throat.

"*Sabaah al-khair, sagheer as-sin sadeeqee.*" "Good morning, friend."

The voice came to him from above. The words were strange to Alric's ears. He recoiled from the sound of the voice.

"Please," he said to the voice. "Can I have some water?"

There was silence and then Alric heard the voice again.

"*Hal tafhamoon ma aquul?*" "Do you understand what I am saying?"

As if by instinct, he repeated the request for water, starting in Latin and then following up with other northern languages, thinking that the owner of the voice might recognize some of his words.

"Certainly," the voice replied in fluent Latin. "What is your name? But perhaps, first . . ." The voice trailed away as Alric felt the binding around his arms and legs being cut. He attempted to stand but stumbled awkwardly because of the cramp that remained in his dysfunctional limbs. "Wait until I get help and you will have water and food, like the rest of us," the voice announced.

He drew up his knees and put his arms around his legs. They still tingled with the painful sensations of immobility, and he could not yet stand. The odors that surrounded him invaded his nose and throat and burned at his eyes, making them tear. The entire ship reeked. He buried his face between his knees. He could hear the sea slapping against the side of the ship and the soothing hiss of the sea against the beach. For a moment he hoped that he was back on the beach at his beloved Wearmouth, but it was not so.

He could hear other voices, and then two pairs of hands reached down and helped him stand, and he was unceremoniously thrown into the sea. The ship was moored in about four feet of water and Alric was able to stand when he recovered his senses.

He was not to know that the strange language he had heard in the last few minutes had been a discussion of the quickest way to remove the smell from his body and clothes. A cleansing in the fresh saltwater of the sea was the result. Alric heard laughter, without malice, as he was helped from the water by these strange men and taken to sit by a fire. As the flames flickered and the wood crackled, he could feel the warmth penetrating his wet robe.

"Remove your robe or you will catch the shivering sickness that leads to fever and death." Obeying this command, Alric took off the robe and stood dejected in his wet undershirt and breeches.

The voice came from behind him again, but he was still unable to identify the owner. Words were spoken again in the strange tongue, and he was offered a robe. "Put this on and then as best as you can remove those wet underclothes."

Alric did as he was bid, thankful to be wearing a clean robe, and as he sat before the fire, he had a thousand questions. He looked from face to face of the men with whom he sat. They were soldiers. Each man was wearing a heavy cloth long-sleeved shirt, breeches, and chest armor and carried a dagger and a long curved sword in a scabbard. A woolen cloak kept out the cold. The men did not have the usual odor of sweat and leather that was characteristic of soldiers on the move. There was a clean fragrance that made Alric's nose twitch. He saw horses tethered at the tree line, and across the pommel of each horse rested a small circular shield. As he looked at the men, dark eyes stared back at him, returning his gaze with curiosity.

A gentle nudge got his attention. He turned to look at the man who indicated he should stand. It was at that moment that another man approached. This man walked with a proud bearing, and Alric knew immediately that he must be the commander.

He did not know what to expect. If this was the owner of the voice who had spoken to him in Latin, there was hope. During the time he had spent in the company of the sea raiders, Alric had built up a distrust of others who sailed the sea far from their homeland. This man was obviously far from his country. Rather than taking a defensive posture, Alric adjusted his stance to show that he offered friendship. He had nothing to lose and he could not wait to see what this man had to say.

The man surveyed Alric, from head to toe. His companions remained silent; their head attire cast dark shadows on their faces, making it difficult for Alric to see facial expressions.

Alric looked closely at his benefactor. He was, as near as Alric could tell, a man of twenty-five or thirty summers. He was tall, almost as tall as Alric, and indicated a man of strength and power. He was fine-featured with tanned skin and a well-trimmed beard. His hands were delicate and lacked any signs of calluses. He was dressed in a long, cream-colored, flowing cloak. Underneath this were garments made of fabrics that Alric, used to the rough clothing of the Saxons, did not recognize. Alric noticed the handle of a sword that protruded from a scabbard attached to his belt. A head covering, not in use at the moment but hanging like a monk's hood, was attached to his cloak. The stern expression on his face gave way to a smile as he saw Alric looking at him.

"I am Khalil al-Din," he said by way of introduction. The voice! It was the same man who had conversed with him earlier. He noticed Alric's quizzical look. "It is a given name, and the nearest translation that I can give you in the language of the Romans is 'Good Friend of the Faith.' I have been called that for a long time. My official name is Khalil ibn Jabir, Khalil son of Jabir. I command these men," he said as he waved his arm toward the group sitting behind him, "and there are others who are nearby." He looked at Alric firmly. "And you are?"

His hair covering moved slightly in the breeze as he cocked his head to one side, waiting for an answer.

Then, satisfied that he had found out as much about Khalil as he could, Alric announced. "*Alricus Weorosensis sum.*" "I am Alric of Wearmouth."

"Good, we are introduced. For the moment, I will call you Alric. For safety reasons and lest my men have the wrong idea about you, I suggest that you place the knife that you have hidden under your robe on the sand. You can retrieve it later. I warn you that my men have little tolerance for those who would try to injure me." Khalil turned and spoke to his men. His soothing voice sounded calm and reassuring. He turned once more and focused his attention on Alric. "Now, Alric, place your knife slowly and carefully on the sand and make no sudden movements."

Alric did as he was commanded. Khalil reached out and took the knife in his hands, looking at it carefully, as he spoke. "It has a good sturdy blade, not quite as sharp as the ones that we use, but very serviceable. The handle feels comfortable in my hand. This is a good knife, Alric."

Without realizing why, but perhaps because he had seen such actions from the men when they addressed Khalil, Alric bowed his head. The gesture did not go unnoticed among the men and some of them smiled their appreciation.

"Now," Khalil said, showing his appreciation of Alric's gesture, "perhaps we can find out who you are and why you were here with these pirates? But before we start, we will have food and drink to remove the pangs of hunger that come to us early in the morning."

He turned to two of the men. Alric saw the same intense dark eyes that he had seen as Khalil looked at him. They rose and disappeared beyond the tree line, fifty yards inland from the shore. Moments later they reappeared with four others. They were carrying small packets that were distributed among the men on the beach. Khalil spoke rapidly and held out his hand to receive two of the packets and then he turned once more to Alric.

"The food we eat when traveling is light and satisfying and it is not too much of a burden on our horses," Khalil nodded his head in the direction of the trees to where the horses were tethered, before he continued. "You will find in the packet," he passed one to Alric, "mixtures of nuts and dried fruit that will nourish your body without tainting your soul." Alric took the packet, opened it quickly, and pushed a handful of the food into his mouth. "Eat slowly, my young friend. I know that it may have been many days since you ate, but if you take your time and chew each mouthful carefully, you will derive more benefit from the food."

Alric looked at Khalil and then at the men. There was no haste in their eating, such a change from the monks who usually ate a considerable amount of heavy food at one sitting and with much noise. As he ate, he could feel the energy returning to his aching body. The fire had brought the warmth he needed, and he was more comfortable than he had felt in a long time.

When the packet of food was empty, Alric looked around and a question formed on his lips as he pondered what to do with the empty packet.

"Throw it on to the fire." The gentle command came from Khalil. "We do not preserve food wrapping," he said by way of explanation. "Particles of food that remain in the packet will turn bad after a while, and to use the packet again would be to risk our health. We cannot afford to be sick when we travel."

Alric nodded. He did not fully understand Khalil's words but they seemed to make sense. Khalil then brought two goblets of fresh water and offered one to Alric.

"As well as drinking this, rinse out your mouth so that food does not decay and harm your teeth."

Alric followed Khalil's actions of rinsing and then drinking. It was the best-tasting water he had ever had. Khalil smiled as he said, "We have a way of purifying water. We do as the Romans did and add a small amount of what you call vinegar to the water. This kills any unseen small animals that live in the water, and then we filter the water through a prepared jar. The end result is this pleasant-tasting water that you are now drinking. That way, we are able to return to our loved ones in a good health."

Alric drank the remainder of the water, quickly and with much noise. "You eat and drink too fast, my young friend." Khalil observed. Alric looked around at the men who were eating much more slowly and taking the occasional sip of water. "I see," Khalil continued, "that you would like more water."

After the goblet had been refilled three times and the refreshing liquid much enjoyed, Alric smiled in contentment. The feelings of dejection and resignation that had been his sole companions for the past few days were gone, as well as the dehydration that he had suffered from his journey.

He looked at Khalil, who was raising himself up from where they had been sitting. Alric was nudged gently from behind to indicate he should also stand.

He managed to raise himself to his feet.

"You will find our customs different from what you have experienced in the past, and as you stay with us, if that is your choice, you will understand why we are different from you. Now let us walk together along the sand and you can tell me who you are and how you came to be in the situation in which we found you."

He looked at Alric's woolen robe that had been hung on two poles close to another fire. "Your heavy garment seems to have dried quite well, but the stench of death still clings to you." Khalil looked Alric up and down. "We will have to see what we can do for you in the way of alternate clothing. Now let us walk."

He turned to his men and spoke rapidly in his native tongue. A response from one of the men brought a smile to Khalil's face. "Two of my men will follow us," Khalil had reverted to Latin. "They still do not trust you and wish to protect me. Now, you can speak and tell me about yourself."

* * *

CHAPTER 8

Khalil informed Alric that he was the son of a physician and scientist but had chosen an alternate profession to that of his father. He had opted to do military service for the Caliph of Baghdad, eventually rising to a position of command. Khalil admitted that he had sympathy for Alric and was impressed by his education and courage. To Khalil, such a young man deserved a friendly ear.

Alric noted that as Khalil spoke he seemed to be the embodiment of a trustworthy and loyal commander. He was of a calm disposition and never allowed his emotions or temper to influence his carefully chosen words. He told Alric that as one of the Caliph's commanders, he had made war against the enemy of the Caliph and had on several occasions defeated the hated sea raiders whose ships plied the shore of northern Europe and had even ventured into the Middle Sea. From this information Alric realized that Khalil's military tactics were daring, and the bravery and loyalty of his men were undisputed. For a time he had been the Caliph's governor in southern Spain but had preferred military assignments.

For such journeys, Khalil went on, the Caliph's shipbuilders had initiated substantial changes in their seagoing vessels. One such change was the adoption of the *lateen* sail. These sails were triangular in shape and enabled a vessel to sail almost directly into the wind, a feat not possible with square sails. Instead of building ships using the traditional shell-first construction, in which the builder joined planks tightly with fasteners to form the ship's hull, the Caliph's shipbuilders began constructing a skeletal framework first, then attached the planking to the frame. In addition, the ships were not limited to one mast, and each mast carried a lateen sail.

As the Caliph of Baghdad became more venturous in his quest to establish outposts in the western European world, Khalil had assisted by acquiring valuable information for the Caliph's cartographers that allowed them to draw accurate maps. An army might march on its stomach in the western world, but the Caliph's armies marched on knowledge and information.

This made the soldiers and sailors of the Caliph seemingly invincible, and the many of the lands that surrounded the Middle Sea were becoming a part of the Caliph's empire.

The Caliph offered a new culture and standards of living and learning to the conquered peoples of the Middle Sea. These included mathematics from ancient Babylon and Egypt. They had already made possible the concepts of latitude and longitude that helped them navigate the seas and to know their exact location with very little error. The present Caliph, and those before him, insisted that sea captains and commanders be well versed in the basic tools of mapmaking. The Caliph's astronomers had significantly advanced the work of the Greeks in the development of the magnetic compass, something for which Khalil and his peers were grateful.

Alric continued to listen in amazement to this newfound knowledge. Khalil went on to describe how his father prepared extracts from ores that improved the production of metals. He had also prepared extracts from plants that helped patients recover from many forms of sickness. His father's current work focused on the use of a plant extract to cure forms of the plague that flared up regularly in crowded cities. He had introduced the use of thread made from animal gut to sew up wounds and reduce the risk of the wound festering.

Hearing this, Alric felt that Khalil was opening the doors of his mind. He had moved into new surroundings that promised to change his way of life. He felt that an extraordinary journey was beginning, and his world started to look different. He tried to rationalize this feeling as Khalil continued to talk and tell him about more wonderful things. Suddenly Ecgfrith's remedies and potions seemed pale by comparison with the bright, shining future that was held in the hand of Khalil's father. Alric wondered how he could assimilate all of the information.

Khalil was in command of an expeditionary force to the northern parts of the land mass that formed the northern coastline of the Middle Sea. He preferred to gather and assimilate information to take home but, when confronted, would fight. As the sea raiders had already discovered.

Khalil would now be able to acquire knowledge of the homeland of the young man that he had found trussed in the bottom of a sea raider's ship.

* * *

As Alric and Khalil walked and talked, it became obvious to Alric that Khalil was a man of substance. In the same manner, it became even clearer to Khalil that Alric had been educated from a learned community of monks. They both wondered what miracle had brought them together.

Alric found that Khalil had a gentleness about him that was very different to any other men he had ever met, but there was no doubt in Alric's mind that Khalil would be fearsome to his enemies.

His words were very controlled as he asked one question after another. Most of Alric's answers were received without comment, but when he mentioned the slaughter of the villagers and, in particular, the traumatic death of his sister, as well as finding the bodies of his parents, Khalil was most sympathetic, but he had a simple explanation.

"*Insha'allah*", he said quietly. "It means *as God wills it*; we refer to God as Allah," he added. "We must accept God's judgment, even though it may cause much sorrow."

Khalil placed his hand on Alric's shoulder as they commenced walking again. After a moment's silence, Khalil spoke again.

"For the wrong reasons, the right things happen!" he said. "It is a sorrowful time when parents and relatives are killed, but God may have other things in mind for you. Try not to grieve too much, as that will affect your judgment. View all events as the will of Allah and keep a warm place in your heart for your parents and your sister. You will surely meet them again in Paradise, when your time comes."

They turned to retrace their steps, and Alric could see Khalil's men in the distance. The two guards, although close by, remained inconspicuous. Khalil now felt he knew enough of the circumstances that had brought Alric to these shores. As they walked back to the camp fires, Alric noticed that the soldiers were most attentive, ever vigilant. After a few words with one of the men, Khalil looked at Alric and, seeing the apprehensive look on his face, explained, "It seems that a party of riders has been spotted close by, but there is no evidence they had seen my men. My lieutenant, Ahmed, took four men and is determining if there is a threat."

He looked directly at Alric. "I know you fear the appearance of another party of sea raiders and, after what you have been through, I cannot blame you. We have found the enemy very often creeps into position at night. There is a stream a little way inland, and my men are concealed at the most likely crossing place. If an enemy appears, we will take the necessary action."

Then Khalil added, "Come with me so that each of my men who have not yet met you may recognize you and, if there is trouble, you will be seen as a friend rather than a foe."

As Khalil approached the men, they each greeted him by a simple bow of the head. Khalil saw the curiosity in Alric's expression. For Alric, life in the village and among the monks had not been so structured, and loyalty was not practiced to any great extent outside of the family. "We ask for loyalty to the Prophet Mohammed, peace be upon him, and to Allah, may he be exalted, and our soldiers give us a lifetime of loyalty and obedience," Khalil explained.

Suddenly, Alric felt ill and alone. Khalil, ever observant, saw the sadness in his eyes. He placed his hand once more on his shoulder. This gesture did not go unnoticed by the soldiers. This young man was now under the protection of their leader.

A man of some bearing appeared from beyond the tree line, approached Alric, and offered him a drink—the same drink that had been served to the men. It was a sweet tea that had been brewed from black leaves which had been cut into small pieces and placed into a pot of boiling water that sat on the edge of the fire. The man spoke words that were incomprehensible to Alric.

"This is Ahmed, my lieutenant," Khalil said by way of introduction. "You have already met him." Khalil smiled at the thought. "He is the one who nudged you at one time or another."

Ahmed spoke another volume of words that Alric could not understand. "Ahmed is telling you," Khalil interpreted, "that the tea will soothe your troubled feelings. It will not help you forget the tragedy that has befallen you, but it will help you relax. Ahmed also lost his wife and son some years ago, and has some idea of what you may be feeling in your heart. He is also my adopted brother and," Khalil added, "we are very close."

"*Shukran,*" Khalil said to the man, and then he turned to Alric. "That means *thank you* and it is an expression that you may wish to remember."

Alric attempted to repeat the word and felt proud of his first attempt. Khalil conversed briefly with Ahmed and then spoke softly to

Alric in Latin. "You catch on quickly, Alric," Khalil exclaimed. "I think that as time progresses on this voyage, you may learn the fundamentals of our language. But sit, rest, drink your tea, and we will talk of your future."

Alric sat and sipped the hot tea. He was concerned about his future and where it might lead him. The deaths of his family and his sojourn in the monastery had left him with nothing.

The only conclusion Khalil had come to was that finding Alric tied and immobile in the stinking keel of the sea raiders' ship was God's will, and he had been allowed to live.

The question "Would anyone at the monastery miss me?" coursed through Alric's mind. Perhaps not, he thought. And what if they did? What could anyone do? It is more likely they would assume that the sea raiders had killed him and thrown his body to the waves of the cold Northern Sea.

Alric's thoughts dispersed for a moment as he concentrated on the hot liquid. Then he smiled. *If Allah, as they call God, leads his followers so well, he will also lead me to a new life.* The thought made him feel much better.

"You are deep in thought, Alric, as though you are making a decision."

The soft accented voice of Khalil broke into Alric's thoughts. Alric felt a sense of relief; the decision was made. He smiled at Khalil and rose from his sitting position. "I apologize for my omission but I now thank you for rescuing me. I know not what my fate will be. I am in your hands. All I know is that you have treated me with kindness. So, again, I thank you, sir, for rescuing me from a death that would have been so painful that I fear that I would have lost faith in God."

Once again, Alric bowed to Khalil, and Khalil responded likewise.

"Now if I may ask you a question, sir?" Alric said.

"There is no need to call me 'sir.' You may call me Khalil."

"Thank you." Then he added, "*Shukran.*"

"My question, Khalil, may seem highly inappropriate, but I am curious."

Khalil held up his hand, indicating that Alric should pause. "My father once told me that I should never apologize for being curious. That is the way we find out about the world. I am not sure what your future will be, but I recommend that you follow my father's advice."

"How is it, Khalil, that you speak Latin?" Alric inquired.

"Almost everyone in my family has some knowledge of Latin. Ahmed is in the midst of learning that language, so he does understand many of your words. Just as I was at first, he can understand much of what you say, but to speak the words is difficult."

Khalil thought for a moment and tweaked the hair on his chin. "In order for my father to follow his profession in medicine, he felt it necessary to speak the language of the Romans. My Caliph now controls part of the lands the Romans used to call Hispania. We had a need of Latin to speak with the learned men of the conquered people. This land was called *Gaul* by the Romans, and we are on the northwest coast. Since I spoke their language, my Caliph sent me here on his business. But the natives speak a strange language that is beyond me for the moment."

"The natives of this land are now called Celts and their language, Celtic, is known to me through my studies at the monastery," Alric said, then suddenly stood up. "I have enjoyed the tea. I have something to tell you, or rather I have something to ask of you, Khalil. May I request to sit with you?"

Khalil nodded and Alric sat facing Khalil, a serious expression on his face. "I have reasoned that there is no future at my former home," Alric announced. "I ask that you be my guide to my future."

Khalil smiled. "Do you have any idea of what you would like your future to be?" Khalil asked.

Alric noticed that the soldiers who stood nearby were trying to hear his words. He wondered if some of them understood Latin. "Yes," Alric responded. "At the monastery, the monks were starting to teach me the benefits of medicines made from certain plants. I can still remember the types of plants to use for different kinds of sickness. Since your father is a man of medicine and science, I was wondering . . . "

His words were interrupted by Khalil's outburst. "That is an excellent thought, Alric!" He paused, then added, "You realize that you must accompany us to our land, and the journey may be difficult." Alric nodded. "You will have to cross the Middle Sea and then a desert. To do that, you need courage. Do you have the will to make such a journey?"

Alric thought for a moment. In this short space of time, his senses were telling him that Khalil could be trusted. He remembered the comment that *for the wrong reasons the right things happen.* "Yes, I do feel I am able to make the journey and the change to a new life. It is time for me to seek a life of my own."

Khalil signaled to Ahmed, who approached. The two men exchanged words in Arabic, after which Khalil turned once more to Alric. "Ahmed has agreed with me that you should be conversant in our tongue. He has agreed to be your teacher. But . . . " Khalil looked firmly at Alric. "You must understand that you must also teach Ahmed to be fluent in Latin."

"I agree," was all that Alric could find to say.

"Furthermore," Khalil continued, "Ahmed will begin by teaching you our customs. The first of course is how and why we cleanse ourselves on awakening and as required during the day. When we arrive at our final destination you will, providing the Caliph agrees, start learning the fundamentals of reading and writing in our language. From what you have told me, you can read and write in your own tongue and in several other languages?" Alric nodded. "But, I will add, should you fail to grasp the necessary introduction to our language, the Caliph may have other plans for you."

"Other plans?" Alric asked.

"Yes. First, if you fail to master the speech, the Caliph will see little worth in you and you will then be trained as a palace worker."

"A palace worker!" Alric repeated.

Khalil turned to Ahmed and smiled as he spoke in Latin so that Alric could understand. "I do believe that I have caught the attention of our new friend. But it does seem that there is an echo on these shores."

Ahmed smiled.

"A slave," Khalil responded to Alric's question. He saw the concerned look in Alric's eyes.

"I will be no man's slave. My father was born free as was I. No one will take that away from me!"

Khalil turned to translate the quickly spoken words for Ahmed, who stepped forward and patted Alric's shoulder. "He will make a willing pupil," Ahmed said in his own language, "and he has the determination to be successful. He will speak our tongue by the time we reach our home."

Khalil then turned to face Alric once more.

"Since Ahmed has agreed to be your teacher. You must listen to him carefully and obey his commands. At night, you and I will go over your lessons of the day to see how much you remember. It will be good practice for you." Alric felt relieved. "We leave tomorrow morning," said Khalil. "But your lessons commence immediately. Come with me."

They walked together toward the men, whose conversation ceased as Khalil approached. He announced the plan to his soldiers, who looked relieved to be mobile once more. All the while, Alric never took his eyes off Khalil. He watched his body language as it changed with the speech patterns. He would learn the customs of these strange new people.

Suddenly, Alric's eyes were drawn to the large sheathed sword that Ahmed carried from the wooded area where the horses were tethered.

"In our language, it is called a *scimitar*," he heard Khalil's voice. "Most have handles that are decorated with jewels but are not suitable for fighting. This one is unadorned and does not hurt the hand when used in battle."

Khalil spoke a few words in Arabic to Ahmed, who unsheathed the sword and proffered it to Alric. "My brother Ahmed, who has been carefully observing you, has concluded that you are a young man that we can trust. We may meet enemies on our journey and we feel it is appropriate that you should be armed."

Alric examined the weapon, which had been honed to hair-splitting sharpness such as he had not seen before. It had an overall length of three feet, with a functional blade of about thirty inches. The deeply curved slashing blade had the sharpened edge on the convex side. He admired the sword for a few more moments before returning it to Ahmed.

"The sword and scabbard can be attached to your belt," Khalil said. "Ahmed has agreed to teach you swordsmanship! When we reach Baghdad, you must return it to Ahmed. It would be unwise for you, an unknown visitor, to bear such a weapon."

Alric understood.

* * *

Alric's lessons began in earnest. He listened to the soft tones of Ahmed, who pointed to various objects and gave them names. Although this form of speech was new to Alric, he was able to quickly master the simple words. At the same time, he gave the Latin names to Ahmed and offered a few simple sentences that included these words.

Alric noticed that at certain times of the day, one of the soldiers would begin a chant. When this happened, everyone, including Khalil, fell to their knees, heads toward the east, touched their foreheads to the ground, and took up the chant. After several minutes, normal life was resumed.

Khalil explained to Alric that their holy book, the *Qur'an*, ascribed the most elevated qualities to water, as a life-giving, sustaining, and purifying resource. Purification through *wudu'*, ablution, or ritual purification, was an obligatory component of the prayer ritual, and prayers carried out in an impure state were not valid. Thus, Khalil's men were obliged to maintain their ablution for the five daily prayers. When he had first seen the soldiers participate in prayers, Alric noticed that the ritual purification before prayer consisted of washing the hands, the face, the forearms, the head and the feet. This, Alric reasoned, was why the men did not have the usual smell of sweat and leather of soldiers on the move; instead he was conscious of a clean fragrance.

"By doing this," Khalil said, "the believer washes away minor sins, and each drop of water that falls in the hand makes the devil flee."

Alric had recalled the habits of many monks. They were not like this. Cleanliness was not a part of their lives, and they did not wash regularly.

Alric was awakened from these thoughts by Khalil's voice. He turned to see him standing with Ahmed, who held garments for him to wear.

"It is time, Alric," Khalil said, "that you also joined my world by dressing as we do. You will find it much more comfortable than the heavy robe that you wore when we found you and which, I might add in spite of being washed by the seawater," Khalil smiled at the recollection of Alric being unceremoniously thrown fully clothed into the sea, "is starting to smell. Some of my men have commented on it!"

"Because," Khalil continued, "our lands are mostly hot, we dress to protect ourselves from the sun. At the same time, our people also believe that Allah wants us to be covered up. Among these clothes," he gestured to the garments that Ahmed carried, "you will find a pair of loose pants. There is also a tunic that is worn over the pants; this one has been shortened so that it will only reach your knees. There is a large piece of cloth, like the veil our women use, but the men use it as a cloak. It will keep off the sun or the rain and keep you warm if it is cold at night, or hide your face if you did not want people to recognize you. There is also a smaller piece of cloth that is wrapped around the head in what we call a *turban*. This protects you from the hot sun. There are many different ways to wind a turban. Your turban will be wound to show that you are with me and for the moment are to be considered a part of my family."

Khalil looked at Alric's wide eyes. "Do not worry," Khalil added by way of reassurance, "Ahmed will help you dress correctly. However," he looked at Ahmed, "since many hours have passed since morning, I suggest that a good wash is in order!"

Ahmed smiled. Alric looked uncertain.

One hour later, freshly bathed and dressed, Alric felt comfortable in his new clothes. The robe had been discarded—burned, he believed, as there was no sign of it. He spent the remainder of the day admiring his attire and mostly making sure that he did not get his sandals, which Khalil had also provided, caught in the clothing as he walked.

Feeling fresh and clean, Alric luxuriated in the sensation and felt as though he had officially joined Khalil and his men. He looked around and watched the trajectory of the sun as it began its departure from the sky until it was hidden behind the horizon. He recalled a time when the sun had risen several days ago and he had been in another land. Now, he was in a different country, a stranger in a strange land, where he could not even speak the language. He was no longer a novice in the monastery about to take his vows; he now had the ability to start his life over again.

All this has happened in a matter of days, Alric thought. He was tingling with excitement but with some trepidation, since his life had changed so dramatically.

He had no possessions, other than the clothes he wore. He ran his fingers slowly through the sand, sensing the temperature. He allowed it to trickle through his fingers and looked at the darkening sky.

"Being with these men is not a strange life," he declared to himself and to an unseen Hilda. "It is a new life. Even if I never see the monastery and village again, I have already traveled more than anyone else. If they," he thought of the abbot and the monks, "only knew how different things are in this part of the world. My dear Hilda, I am about to start a new life. No matter where I am, you will always be in my thoughts."

I know, the gentle voice responded as he ran his fingers through the warm sand. He smiled as he listened to her words: *And you have no reason to fear the Caliph. He is a wise man and needs someone like you. But there is one you will need to fear. Be on your guard, my brother. Always be on your guard!*

Hilda was still with him, and that made him feel more confident. Her words of caution gave him cause for concern, but that was in the future, and with the help of Hilda and God he would succeed. He looked around at the beach and the men who remained close by; some were preparing to sleep, while others remained attentive.

Alric mused about these things.

He no longer feared the sea raiders who had brought death and destruction to his life twice in the last two years. He allowed his eyes to close as he thought of Hilda. Her life had been taken for no reason at all, other than the bloodlust of the raiders. Opening his eyes, he looked along the beach. Saying a silent prayer, he thanked God for deliverance—or should he thank Allah? He would thank God in his own way.

He could not help but recall the day the raiders first came. It was weighing heavily on his mind. Beneath his blond hair, water welled in his eyes and a single tear rolled down his left cheek. He lifted a hand

and wiped it away. "I am on an adventure, looking for a new life and learning," he said to himself. "And I have found it!"

* * *

CHAPTER 9

Ahmed shook him into consciousness. The sun had not yet risen, but life in the camp had never stopped. Alric did not realize that there had been activity all night. Horses had been prepared for the journey, packs secured, and weapons checked.

Looking around, Alric sought the monks but realized that he was in a different world. This world was one of promise and joy and he felt excited. He no longer had to seek out safety from the sea raiders. He could, within the bounds of Khalil's favor, begin his new adventure. He remembered that one of the books brought to the monastery by a visitor had described the adventures of a long-dead Greek hero called Odysseus, or Ulysses in Latin, who, after the fall of a city called Troy in a far-off land, had overcome all adversity and found peace after perilous times on sea and land. *Could this be my destiny?* Alric thought.

He thanked Ahmed as he got up, walked sleepily to the water's edge, and washed himself in the cool seawater. Now he felt truly awake! The soldiers continued to make preparations to leave and Alric joined them, since he was eager to start the journey.

When the equipment was assembled, the soldiers assigned to cooking duty offered everyone the first meal of the day. Alric thanked them for his plate of food and sat with the men to eat the simple fare of bean mash and fresh corn bread. Alric was not sure how the cooks had managed to obtain the ingredients for the corn bread and he was not about to ask. As he listened to the men talk, he found he could understand some of their words, many of which Ahmed had taught him the previous day. Alric knew that if he could understand the individual words, he would soon begin to be able to translate their sentences. Listening to the soldiers was a great help.

Relaxed and unhurried, he worked with them and resolved he would learn to speak their language by the time they reached their destination. He knew it would take time, but living in a monastery had trained him in the benefits of patience, and so he applied the same attention to learning this new language.

When it was time to leave, Alric was introduced to his means of travel, a small pony with a temperament befitting its rider.

* * *

The ride removed the anxiety he had felt in the camp. His journey had begun and it was too late to change anything.

Alric spent the entire morning observing the landscape. The road they were following was in a fine state of repair and made riding much easier. He thought of the roads in Britain that had not been maintained since the time of the Romans and of the discomfort the travelers had to bear. For the most part, the landscape was scattered with bushes and sand, which soon gave way to more colorful vegetation as they traveled inland to seek water for themselves and their animals.

He rode alongside Ahmed, and at one point Khalil reined in beside him to make sure he was comfortable. There were frequent comings and goings among the soldiers as they patrolled the line. A halt was called to rest and water the horses and for the soldiers to eat a light meal. When they had eaten, Khalil sought out Alric and said, "We will reach our ship soon. So, tell me Alric, the words that you have learned so far."

Alric had foreseen that Khalil would ask him about his lesson. Much to Khalil's pleasure, Alric knew many words and was starting to put them together in twos and threes to form simple phrases. The constant but subdued chatter of the soldiers had, even in this sort time, helped Alric learn some of the fundamentals of the language, much to Khalil's pleasure.

"I see that you have exceeded my expectations," Khalil exclaimed, and he turned to Ahmed. "You are teaching him well, and at this rate he will be speaking our language as he is presented to our Caliph."

"I will work all day and all night in return for your faith in me," Alric offered.

Khalil looked at Ahmed, who nodded to show that he had understood Alric's Latin words.

"Alric," Khalil said, smiling, "you have learned more in this short time than any other person that I have known."

There was a moment of silence so profound that it was as if all had lost their tongues. The whole world seemed to have fallen silent. Alric sat immobile. Khalil looked anxiously at Alric. "Ah," Khalil said suddenly as he realized the reason for the silence. "I see that you have espied our ship. This is the vessel that will take us to our homes."

Alric said nothing. He raised himself in the saddle and looked down into the sheltered cove. There, at anchor, was the largest ship he had ever seen. It was, as near as he could estimate, more than one hundred feet long and about twenty feet wide. It shone in the late-day sun, and the wood appeared to have been polished to a high sheen. The ship had an enclosure or shelter midships with several windows. There was also another enclosure at the stern that was set partially below deck and had portholes at the side to allow light to enter. Below deck there were spaces in the hull where the oars protruded. Because of its position near to the shore, Alric also guessed that the ship had a shallow draft.

He was lost for words, but when he found his tongue the word he sought in Arabic, "big," was blurted out. "But," Alric hesitated, "the men?" he asked, seeing those near to the ship.

"They are the sailors we left to see to the safety of the ship." Khalil paused. "And I see they have not been disturbed." After another pause, he added, "We will sail on the first tide after we have loaded the animals and supplies onto the ship." As an afterthought he added, "We will sail closer to the land because of the horses. They need frequent exercise to prevent the onset of the sickness of the sea. Horses do not recover as we do and may even die if not allowed to move naturally every so often."

He looked at Alric. "Welcome to the first stage of your new life!"

* * *

The next day, half an hour after sunrise, with the horses in their sheltered enclosure at the stern and with a favorable tide, the ship was under way, the oarsmen pulling steadily against the sea. The vessel had two sturdy masts, and each one carried a large triangular lateen sail. A slight breeze started to fill the sails but it was not sufficient to power the ship. Below deck, where the heat was most oppressive, portholes that were cut above each bank of oars were opened to maintain a stream of fresh air and to prevent the oarsmen from being baked like pottery in a kiln.

The chief oarsman beat out a rhythm on a drum using a wooden hammer. The ship moved slowly at first to the pull of the oars. Once beyond the influence of the sheltered cove, the sail billowed and energized the ship. The chief's rhythm picked up as he beat the two wooden hammers, alternating on the leather drum as the ship gathered speed. The oars dipped and pulled in unison to the sound. The captain's voice carried across the upper deck and shouted orders. The helmsman heaved at the tiller and took the ship in a southerly direction.

"Alric," he heard his name, as he stood enthralled, watching the action above deck and peeping through the entry to the lower deck to watch the oarsmen pull and strike in unison. This was so different to the ship of the sea raiders. "Alric, close your mouth lest you catch flies in your throat!"

He heard Ahmed's voice and picked out the words for "throat" and "flies." He turned and smiled, still with the same expression of wonder on his face. Khalil stood with Ahmed surveying the men at work.

"You seem surprised at our ship." Khalil stated. Alric nodded. "Then let me tell you about our ships and our navy," Khalil added. "They sail all over the world. Yes, Alric," he saw the surprised look on Alric's face, "there is a world beyond the Middle Sea and this island that you call Britain. We know from old maps of a large land mass that lies across the Western Ocean. This land spans the whole length of the ocean and can be passed in the south to allow passage into another large ocean. From there, sailing west brings a sailor to Cathay and the eastern end of the Silk Road. With a little imagination and bold navigation, it is the belief of the Caliph's mapmakers that a ship could sail around the world!"

Alric gasped. All he had heard were stories of the world being flat, and if a ship got to close to the edge there was a danger it would topple over.

Khalil seemed not to notice Alric's surprised expression as he continued. "Also, the Caliph prefers not to use slaves in his ships, and we do not use conscripts. We have found that freemen are much more reliable, so the men you see below deck at the oars are free men from many nations who are paid for their work, as are the sailors above deck. They give us loyalty and will also fight as the need arises."

Khalil looked directly at Alric as if to emphasize the next point. "A ship is a team from the captain to the newest oarsman. Slaves are prized for their work around the home and in our cities, but we prefer freemen in our ships. The ships of many other countries that surround the Middle Sea have an insatiable hunger for men to power them. We rotate the men so that those you see on deck will, after a suitable rest, exchange places with the oarsmen, who will then work on deck. And so it goes on until their duty is complete. We do not consume slaves as a fire consumes wood. Our men are not the nameless thousands that you will find on many slave ships, praying for deliverance." Khalil left Alric to ponder over what he had said.

Shortly after they had spoken, the soldiers distributed water to the oarsmen and sailors. The oarsmen were served first because the lives of everyone aboard the ship depended upon their strength. In the style of the Roman legionary, the water was flavored with vinegar, which they sipped from sponges as they rowed. Khalil and Ahmed were also offered water but refused to partake until the crew and soldiers had their allotment. Imitating Khalil and Ahmed, Alric also waited to drink. This action did not go unnoticed among the soldiers and the sailors, many of whom nodded in appreciation of the tall, fair-skinned young man from the north.

After four hours at sea, during which the ship moved under the power of the wind, the same type of nutritious food that Alric had eaten on land was distributed to the oarsmen, who rested their oars along the side of the ship.

Alric suddenly realized that he had not eaten for some time and enjoyed the energy-rich mixture. During the remainder of the day, Khalil and Ahmed allowed him the freedom of the deck. He exchanged words with the crew. His vocabulary was expanding at a stunning rate.

That night, after his daily questions from Khalil, Alric helped the men flush out the horse enclosure with seawater. As happened every night, the horses were given fresh water and feed. That night, sleep came easily to Alric. He lay on a board that was his bed, and as soon as his head touched the wooden headrest, which was covered with skins, he fell asleep.

Alric raised his head just before the sun appeared and felt the motion of the ship as it rocked gently on its journey south. As he turned over, he felt the knife in his belt against his side and took it out. It reminded him of Hilda and her last effort on the beach to save him. As the months had passed, he had come to realize the sacrifice she had made in order that he might live.

Thank you my dear sister, his thoughts went out, and in his mind he heard her response.

You are welcome, dear brother. The whispered words carried to him on the breeze.

He lay on the wooden bed and began to rub the knife using the piece of cloth that Ahmed had given him. It was a simple knife but it was his, and his only possession. He continued to rub the blade, as if it were a talisman that might protect him. Then he heard Khalil's voice telling him that it was time to get up and bathe so that he might be presentable to others on the ship. He placed the knife back in his belt.

As he looked around, he noticed how clean the ship appeared. His bed was the only item that seemed to be out of place. This was nothing at all like the sea raiders' ship, which seemed to collect dirt and foul odors like the village midden.

Alric washed himself with the water supplied by the sailors and then saw them throw the night's refuse overboard. Then each group— soldiers, sailors, and oarsmen—took part in the morning devotions. He noticed that even the sailors from other countries participated in the same manner.

The wind continued to propel the vessel to the south. Alric awoke one morning to find great excitement coming from the deck, and there was a change of attitude among the soldiers and the crew. The chief oarsman shouted commands, oars were placed into the positions for rowing, and the beat of the drum started once more. The ship seemed to fly through the water. Alric noticed that the vessel had turned toward the east and that they were sailing toward the rising sun. He saw the land on the north side of the passage. There was a high rock, the sides of which were sheer and would be difficult, if not impossible, to climb. To the south, the land was more difficult to see.

"Praise Allah," Khalil's gentle voice came from just behind him.

"Are we . . . " Alric sought the word, ". . . home?" he said at last.

"No, Alric, but this is the southern edge of the land where we found you. Some of the ancients called the land to the north and south the Pillars of Hercules. Once beyond this passage, we will be in the Middle Sea that will take us to the city of our destination at the other end of this sea, and from there we will journey across land to our home."

"What about . . . " Alric searched for the appropriate word, "thieves?"

"I think you mean pirates," Khalil offered. "Yes," he said "there are pirates who sail on these waters but at their own peril, and at this late time of the year, they are unlikely to brave the winter seas. Also we navigate at night by the stars and not by the shoreline, so we have no need to approach the shore, where unseen rocks can cause danger to the ship and to ourselves. It will take us several more days to reach our destination."

Alric's spirits soared as he felt the change in attitude on deck. The sailors knew there was no ship swift enough to overtake their own.

In the evening, during refreshments, the jubilation of being in their own familiar waters had infected the crew. The men applied themselves to their daily routines with an additional vigor, and their hearts were lighter. They were going home! There would be shoreline stops during the day to replenish their supplies of fresh water and pick up food through trade or hunting. But the path now led home.

* * *

Alric awakened the next day to a bright sun which caused him to wince as the rays caught his eyes. With difficulty he rolled over and realized that he had slept much later than usual.

He heard the familiar sounds that preceded the distribution of water—the clatter coming from the wooden buckets as water was given to everyone on board. A wet sponge was thrust at him and he looked up to see the smiling face of Ahmed. Alric raised himself onto one elbow and got to his knees. He could see the sun resplendent on a sparkling sea. Ahmed passed a wet cloth to him. "*Shukran*," Alric said to Ahmed gratefully.

"It is late morning. You have slept the deep sleep of the innocent. But now it is time to arise."

Sensing a different tone in Ahmed's voice, Alric arose without hesitation. His eyes were suddenly lit with joy as he noticed that the ship had entered a small bay and that a boat was being dispatched. The crew of the boat made several journeys to replenish the casks with fresh water. They also brought food and other supplies to replace those used on the journey. The captain saw that all aboard were refreshed. The decks were rinsed with seawater, and Alric was told that they would remain at anchor for the night.

* * *

At dawn the next day, the drum sounded and the oars dipped once more into the sea as the next leg of the journey began. There was insufficient wind to fill the sail, so their progress depended upon the power of the oars. The horizon took on a different look and appeared to be dotted with rocky islands that varied in size.

"These are the islands of the Greeks," Ahmed said by way of explanation. "There are many such islands that lie in this eastern part of the sea. As far as we know, there are at least one hundred and sixty-three of them, but less than thirty are inhabited. The Greeks consider these islands to be the homes of their ancient heroes and gods." Ahmed looked around before he continued. "We need to stay alert in case of attack by boats that put out from these islands, but we can outrun any ship that may pursue us."

Raising his arm to shade his eyes from the sun, Alric was able to see the remains of ruined cities that lay at the top of the gentle slopes that, in turn, ran to the sea from the grasslands of the islands. He wondered about the inhabitants of such cities.

Ahmed broke into Alric's thoughts. "We will turn north soon to sail through the straits that will eventually bring us to Constantinople."

* * *

Days later, Alric looked across the water toward a large city that had once been Byzantium but was now known as Constantinople, the city of Constantine. High walls that were being rebuilt and expanded to the west discouraged invasion from the landward side.

Alric knew from what Khalil had told him that almost five hundred years ago, Constantinople had been selected by the Roman Empire to be the new capital, instead of Rome, by the Emperor, Constantine. Built on the west side of the strait and on seven surrounding hills, the city controlled the water channel between the two land masses and gave easy access to the harbor of the Golden Horn. The city had continued to grow, and the population exceeded half a million persons. Recently, there had been frequent changes of the throne after vicious feuds between royal families, and currently all kinds of religious images had been outlawed and this led to much destruction (and much concealment) of paintings and statues.

"Our current Caliph of Baghdad, Harun al Rashid, has recently subdued the Byzantine Empire, and as a result we," Khalil brought his story to an end, "have freedom of movement in and around the city."

As the ship approached the city, Alric had a clear view of the buildings. The city was indescribably beautiful, with excellent, magnificent buildings. He saw circular structures that reflected the light of the sun from their beehive-shaped domes. From Alric's perspective, the city seemed to have streets laid out in the Roman style so that they formed a grid. His eyes took in the panorama and he continued to stare fascinated at the view before him. It was as if he looked at a precious jewel emerging from the blue waters of the sea. As he leaned on the rail of the ship, Alric become conscious of Ahmed's presence.

"I think you are about to ask me about this city, Alric." Ahmed's simple statement took Alric by surprise. He turned and nodded.

Ahmed told him that the people of Constantinople were a varied group of Mesopotamians, Persians, Moors from North Africa, Orientals from Cathay to the east, and a few Europeans. Many were natural enemies, but in Constantinople a fragile truce existed. He added that Constantinople was ruled as a kingdom that was allowed to exist, courtesy of the Caliph, by a previously drawn-up agreement favorable to the Caliph. The city was under the protection of an *emir,* acting as the Caliph's regent, and to maintain law in this political city, the emir was in command of an elite legion of soldiers.

Silks and spices made up a great portion of the trade, but the most prized cargo of all and the most desirable of all commodities were the slaves. All nations that surrounded the Middle Sea prized their slaves. Building projects, working the land, and general house duties required a never-ending supply of slaves. The males who were deemed the most hardy were used in the galleys, and the only way a slave could be released from a galley was by his death.

Women slaves were also used for general household duties, but the most graceful found a different type of life in the harems of the rulers and the nobility. For a slave, freedom was rarely an option.

As he listened to Ahmed, Alric noticed that both land and water teemed with activity. Boats of all sizes crossed from one side to the other carrying men and supplies. On shore, donkeys made their way along dusty roads around the harbor, hauling panniers loaded with materials. Slaves toiled alongside laborers, and craftsmen imported from Sicily were digging ditches, breaking and clearing rocks, cutting stones, erecting walls, and hauling rubble to fill the voids between the inner and outer walls. Pulleys creaked under the weight of their loads, and hammers rang against chisels. Men shouted orders in a dozen tongues. Boys raced from place to place urged on by the voices of their overseers.

Alric wiped the sweat from his brow and caught his breath as he looked out from the ship and tried to take in the sights of the great city. He took a deep breath before the words poured out in a rush. "Ahmed," he said, "this is such a great city, the likes of which I did not believe existed."

Ahmed's eyes clouded but his voice remained steady. "This is the city of my birth."

He did not say any more and allowed his voice to trail off into silence. Unseen by Alric, tears welled in Ahmed's eyes as he remembered the days of his childhood before becoming a soldier of the Caliph. He fidgeted with his dagger, turning it over and over in his hands, then cleared his throat. "It is such a magnificent city. Romans and others have lived here together in peace. And may Allah make it so always."

"*Insha'allah*. As God wills it," Alric responded politely.

Alric was clearly intimidated by not only the size of the city but also the commerce that was taking place before his eyes. He had noticed the change in Ahmed's demeanor, from a lion to a lamb, and he did not understand the feeling that had come over his teacher. He fidgeted and saw that Ahmed was not in the mood for further conversation about the city.

"So, my friends," Khalil's voice broke into their thoughts, "you admire the city. Ahmed, my friend, you are home! There is something you must do?" Ahmed made an effort to speak, but Khalil raised his hand to signal he should remain silent. "After the ship has docked," Khalil continued, "take whatever time you need and take some of the men with you for protection. One never knows what dangers may be lurking in the shadows. Even the Caliph's men cannot be everywhere!"

Ahmed bowed his head in thanks.

*   *   *

There was great jubilation in the city when it was learned that one of the Caliph's ships was about to enter the port. A boat, bearing the harbormaster, rowed out to meet them and to discuss issues with the captain and Khalil. The men drank hot tea on the deck while the stories of Khalil's adventures were told. As the vessel approached the mooring point, the oarsmen dragged the oars in the water to reduce the speed, after which they dropped them into the water, where men in small boats recovered them. After the ship gently nudged the wharf and was secured, the rudder and sail were removed for cleaning, and anyone who, on pain of death if caught, attempted to commandeer the ship would have a vessel that was ineffective.

The ship and the wharf were crawling with activity. As soon as their tasks were completed and the horses corralled on the dockside, the sailors and oarsmen were released from duty and allowed to go ashore. Only Khalil, Ahmed, the captain, his first officer, and the soldiers, who were from Baghdad, remained on board.

Alric watched all of this with great amazement. *It is,* he thought, *truly a magnificent city that lies beyond this ship.*

Two hours later, the crew was allowed to depart, with orders to be available within the week, and since the ship was secure in the moorings, the soldiers relaxed.

Alric sat on the side of the ship, legs dangling. An hour passed, and then another. He waited and watched, curious about the conversation between Khalil and Ahmed.

119

"Ahmed had a wife and a baby son, who, like your family, were murdered by sea raiders," Khalil's voice brought Alric from his reverie. "The bodies of Ahmed's wife and son lie in peace here and he visits the grave whenever we are in the city. May Allah watch over them." Khalil saw the surprised look on Alric's face. "Yes," he continued, "the raiders have even reached these shores. Our mission, when we found you, was to seek out such men and kill them. That we did, and then we also found you."

Khalil looked into Alric's eyes as if seeking questions. Alric thought it prudent to remain silent. He had not known any of Ahmed's background. Other than Khalil, he wondered how many of the soldiers knew of Ahmed's past. The thoughts wandered aimlessly through his mind—a tight maze that was now changed forever. Alric looked at Khalil, who seemed to be able to read his mind, and resolved that he would not mention this conversation to Ahmed; it would serve no purpose.

Alric went below deck and looked at the soldiers who were either sleeping or talking in hushed tones. He exchanged brief nods and smiles with some of the men and words of greeting. Ten minutes later, he emerged once more on to the upper deck, and looked toward the city.

Alric stared at the huge castle which stood as a sentinel over the city, commanding the harbor from the top of a steep hill. He saw minarets and domes. He could see in the distance where the wall began and surrounded the city on three sides, opening up at the harbor to allow entry for the ships. Within the city walls, there were lush gardens and orchards in which was seen a variety of fruit.

Beyond the harbor, he saw a procession crossing the central square. There were two men in the middle, surrounded by others, perhaps thirty in all. They were making their way to a mosque for prayer and were dressed in simple robes. In the midst of the group he saw Khalil and Ahmed.

Alric watched from the deck, but because of the distance, he did not know whether Khalil and Ahmed could see him, but the motion of Khalil's head appeared to indicate he had been seen. Another man walked close to them. He was a tall, proud-looking figure who carried himself with dignity and seemed to have the physical presence that came from a lifetime of command. The procession moved into the mosque and disappeared from sight.

"You have watched the procession to prayers." Alric had not sensed the presence of anyone close by. He turned to see that the captain was leaning against the side of the ship.

"The man with our Lord Khalil," the captain spoke slowly to help Alric understand, "is his brother, and it is known that he has the ear of the Caliph. Whatever he says to the Caliph is taken seriously. Khalil's family is powerful. You know, of course, that the father of Lord Khalil is physician to the Caliph?"

"I knew he was a physician but . . . " Alric allowed the words to trail into silence.

"Our Lord Khalil does not talk about his family's elevation to high positions by the Caliph. They have all made their lives based on merit rather than patronage."

"Captain!" one of the soldiers called. "We have need of your advice."

The captain turned, "I will come." Before leaving to determine what was needed, the captain turned once more to Alric. "You should do well, Alric, if Lord Khalil favors you. He will see that you are presented to the Caliph in the correct manner."

The captain departed, leaving Alric to his thoughts. Alric looked over the side and stared down at the lapping water as it washed against the ship. His thoughts flashed back to life in the monastery. He had not known anyone, except the abbot, who had excelled to such a high position. The abbot told him that favors and patronage were the means to exalted positions. Alric felt sympathy for those who traded in favors.

He would work for his rewards and if they should come, he would work even harder.

These unspoken words lodged in his mind even deeper than he realized. He recalled the words that Khalil had said to him several days ago.

"You, Alric, are not of a noble family, but nobility is not inherited, it is made by actions. Your parents seem to have instilled in you good habits. Indeed, you have an acute sense of right and wrong. Life is measured not by what you do for yourself but by what you do for others. So it is more than the sum of all of its parts! Keep those thoughts in your mind and you will do well!"

Alric stared at the sea, whispering promises to himself. "I will become someone of note. That is my destiny."

These were Alric's thoughts as the heat of the day turned into the coolness of the evening. The streets were no longer crammed with people.

After Alric fell asleep, Khalil and Ahmed returned to the ship and a peaceful silence settled over the city.

* * *

CHAPTER 10

The next morning, the ship was alive with action. Alric was told by Ahmed to make sure he was also presentable. "We are to be officially presented to Lord Asad, brother to our Lord Khalil and the representative of the Caliph in this city," Ahmed said. "Some prefer to call Lord Asad by the title *Emir* in recognition of his status as military commander. In his presence, you had better look and smell clean. Asad is a powerful man. Be on your best behavior!" So saying, Ahmed turned on his heel and left.

Almost one hour later, cleaned and scrubbed, Alric stepped off the ship and followed Khalil and Ahmed from the wharf and up the steps that led to the city streets. The soldiers followed them; Alric realized that this was a major event. At the top of the steps, Khalil was welcomed officially by Asad. This was the same man who the captain had pointed out to Alric on the previous day as being Khalil's brother. When he was introduced to Asad, Alric bowed his head and received a nod from Asad in recognition. Then the group moved toward a main square, Khalil and Asad ahead of Ahmed and Alric, all four surrounded by soldiers.

Whenever Asad moved through the streets, he preferred to walk rather than be carried in a litter, and a crowd would gather. Sensing that the new arrivals conveyed a mission of some importance, the crowd was more boisterous. Children were perched on the shoulders of their fathers, straining for a better view; mothers carried younger children in their arms; and dogs barked. Every window and rooftop overlooking the square seemed to be crammed with people. Alric perceived that Asad must be popular, but he was unaware that his own arrival had spread through the city, and the people wanted to see the tall, fair-skinned, blue-eyed young man from the north.

Oblivious that he was the center of curiosity, Alric looked around and saw that unlike the plain stone, wattle, and thatched-roofed structures of the village and the monastery at Wearmouth, the buildings here were built of stone and clay and had been whitewashed so that they sparkled in the sun. Terra-cotta pots stood at the entrances to houses, spilling flowers in a riot of color. Bees seeking to make the most of the blooms continued their quest for nectar, and the scent of jasmine clung to the air.

They walked along a main thoroughfare from which a maze of streets sprung. The soldiers paid little attention to the crowds of people who thronged the narrow side-streets. Goats, sheep, and children seemed perpetually underfoot. Beggars slept in darkened doorways, alms cups at their feet, while water sellers carrying bulging goatskin water bags did a brisk trade in the sale of the refreshing liquid. The discordant sound of horns and flutes pierced the endless babble of commerce. There was a cacophony of noise, from the neighing of horses, groans of camels, and the bleating of sheep and goats. Adding to the animal noises, vendors hawked cloth and cheap jewelry from shadowy stalls, sipping strong coffee and watching the procession of new slaves with interest. There were nomads hailing from other regions as well as tradesmen from far-off cities and ports. Alric was in awe of the spectacle around him.

Every path and lane had unfamiliar sights, sounds, and smells, as though the city were one large marketplace. Donkeys carried panniers loaded with fresh vegetables, and Alric could smell hot bread, an odor that reminded him so much of home and the monastery, and for a brief moment he forgot where he was.

Alric's awe was overshadowed only by his need to make sure that he was not separated from Khalil, Ahmed, and the soldiers. The chances of such an event were slim because the people had been held back from the main street down which the soldiers marched. He glanced over his shoulder, toward the harbor, wondering if he could still see the ship, but the horizon was filled with buildings and people.

To cater to travel, the city also had a large number of caravansaries. Alric had never seen such centers before, but Ahmed told him that they were common in the countries where people made a living by traveling from city to city. Alric cast his mind back to the visitors who came to the monastery. Most slept by the wayside at night or, for safety, often traveled in groups, and might seek shelter under a wagon if one of the travelers was lucky enough to have one.

"And this," Ahmed announced, "is where we will stay while we are in this city," as he led Alric and the soldiers into the courtyard of one of the most beautiful buildings that Alric had ever seen. Alric looked around. "Lord Khalil will stay at the house of the Emir Asad," was all that Ahmed said to Alric.

* * *

The caravansaries in Constantinople offered more than the usual wayside shelter. They were the most impressive buildings Alric had ever seen. They were areas where travelers, their servants, and horses could find safety and rest along the hard roads of the area. According to tradition, the kitchens of a caravansary had a wide choice of food, to the delight of those who stayed there. This caravansary was no exception.

Ahmed told Alric to wait with the soldiers and he would see to rooms for all of them, two to a room. Alric would share a room with Ahmed. The remainder of the soldiers was being billeted in similar caravansaries close to the harbor. The sailors would stay on board ship; they would not leave the ship in the hands of strangers!

Alric, on the other hand, was a stranger in the midst of the procession, and this pale-skinned, blond-haired, blue-eyed traveler was a rarity for those watching.

Alric and Ahmed ate dinner quietly, from time to time glancing at the mixed company that surrounded them. They felt safe here; the Caliph's soldiers would maintain peace.

* * *

Next day, when the morning sun brought its warmth to the large square courtyard, men and animals were preparing for the day ahead. Sitting on a variety of makeshift seats in the shade, travelers listened endlessly to the tales told by others within the peaceful sound of water bubbling from the fountain in the middle of the courtyard. The cloudless sky promised a hot day, perhaps with the air temperature reaching furnace-like heat.

It was at this time that Alric began to relax. He stepped out onto the upper balcony to take the air, bareheaded and without his outer robe. He rested his elbows on the columned balustrade and lifted his face to the sun. Ahmed came out and stood beside him.

"This is the land I have been telling you about these past days," Ahmed whispered. Alric allowed his gaze to scan the courtyard and examine the nooks and crannies that framed the open space. "Feel free to talk with other travelers," Ahmed said. "They will welcome you into their company." He stroked his cheek. "I have other business that needs my attention. I will return in the afternoon. Do not leave the courtyard!"

"Would you like me . . . ?" Alric could not finish the question before Ahmed responded.

"No, Alric," he said. "This is something that I must do alone."

Alric guessed that Ahmed was going to visit the grave of his wife and son. After he left, Alric spent a leisurely day talking with other travelers, who were surprised that he could converse in Latin as well as Arabic.

From books and travels, Alric had formed the opinion that European cities were large areas built in no particular fashion. From what he had seen and from what he had been able to glean from others at the caravansary, this city was a well-planned settlement with alleyways and back streets and was laid out according to a plan. The inhabitants had imagined the city as a garden encircled with trees. The grand houses built by the numerous titled and wealthy inhabitants were scattered throughout the city and were surrounded by elegant gardens.

Owing to the great number of travelers in Constantinople, the rumor mill was always active. Their stories brought back memories of vanished youth and tales of valor. But life always maintained its normal course after stories were told and retold.

Ahmed returned in the late afternoon and announced that they would be eating dinner at Lord Asad's house. The soldiers would accompany them and also receive the benefits and hospitality offered by Lord Asad's kitchen. This delighted them, for they could indulge themselves on the food of a rich household.

Alric bowed his head when greeted by Lord Asad and received a smile in return. As they were shown into the dining area, Alric marveled at the splendor of the furnishings and tapestries that hung from the walls. He said nothing, having been forewarned by Ahmed that he should speak only when addressed directly by Lord Asad.

In spite of the splendor of the house, the repast was simple, but delicious, and was served in two courses. The first course consisted of cooked lamb with rice, and the second of fresh fruit. The lamb was of a texture and taste that defied description. The one thing that Alric could remember was that it was so tender it could be cut with a spoon.

Frequently he sensed Asad's eye watching him during the meal, and although the conversation flowed, he was not included in any of the discussion. Khalil related to Asad the details of the journey, the discovery of Alric in the sea raiders' ship, his education at the monastery, and his progress in learning the language during the voyage to Constantinople.

Suddenly the voices trailed off and ceased. Alric still remained with his eyes downcast to the table. He had concentrated on the meal while listening to the conversation. He had finished eating and his hands were cradled in his lap.

"Look at me, Alric!" Asad commanded. "I have heard your story. Is this the way it happened?" Asad spoke rapidly.

Alric concentrated on each word. "It is, Lord Asad. Lord Khalil has related to you the details precisely as they occurred."

"I see that you do understand our language. Not that I doubted the word of Lord Khalil and Commander Ahmed, but I was a little skeptical when I heard of your abilities with languages."

Khalil and Ahmed smiled at each other as Alric bowed his head. "*Shukran.*" "Thank you, Lord Asad."

A silence followed as everyone looked at Asad. His eyes narrowed and he fixed Alric in his stare. "You have passed the test," Asad said finally. "You have become fluent in our language. Therefore, on the basis of what I have heard, I am willing to recommend to the Caliph that he accept Lord Khalil's request that you become apprenticed to Lord Jabir. It seems you have a flair for learning that should not be penalized." Asad paused and Alric bowed his head in thanks. "Now," he said, "you may join the conversation, as I wish to hear more from you about your dreams and aspirations!"

At this, the floodgates of conversation opened, and it seemed to Alric that they talked for hours about Britain, the languages that Alric knew, his education in the monastery, and many other subjects that were relevant to his future.

"But," Asad cautioned at they got up to leave, "the future for you, Alric, as it is for all of us, is yet an untrodden path full of wonderful possibilities. You have taken the first step. See that you tread safely on the remaining steps."

Alric bowed his head. "*Insha'allah, Umaraa Asad,*" he responded. "As God wills it, Emir Asad."

* * *

Although it was now night, the nearby streets were as crowded as they had been during the day. There was no curfew, and the fires in the braziers flickered through the night. A full moon provided much light as it hung in the sky above.

The soldiers slept beneath the stars wrapped in their cloaks. The night was pleasant and the lack of blankets and tents for the soldiers was no hardship. Ahmed's men were well trained. They were not given to raucous behavior and were ready to rest after the long sea voyage. Servants moved among them from time to time and provided food and fresh water when needed.

As the men were bedding down for the night, Khalil arrived. Alric suddenly realized why the men served willingly under Khalil and Ahmed. They were true examples for the men, always putting them first; Alric had seen evidence of this on the ship. Even though Khalil and Ahmed had access to more comfortable quarters, they also slept on the ground. Alric promised himself he would also strive to emulate their style of leadership; even though he would never be a soldier, he would cherish these examples.

That night, he nestled in his cloak, and no sooner had his head touched the ground than his eyes closed, and he fell into a deep sleep.

* * *

Shortly after dawn the next day, Alric was awakened. He looked up and saw Ahmed's smiling face. "Time to wake up, Alric. We leave after the morning meal. Once we have crossed the water, we will rest for the first night on the far shore. Then we will make our way steadily along roads that are known to us. Lord Khalil has asked me to tell you that during our journey we will rest at a place called Nicaea. He knows that it is sacred to Christians because of the meeting that took place there almost five hundred years ago in which your bishops drafted policies on some of your beliefs."

Alric eased himself to his feet.

"The cocks have crowed, Allah has received the morning prayers from the men," Ahmed said. "Wash yourself and then eat bread and fruit, but be quick about it." Ahmed pointed in the direction of where the food was available, and Alric quickly followed his instructions.

He looked toward the city, saw the sun rising above the walls, and knew that it would not be long before its rays warmed his body. He had not been given any other instructions, so he decided to wait patiently and watch the developments.

"Allah does not pay wages for those who linger without work." Khalil's' voice was clear in the morning air. Alric turned and smiled.

"What would you have me do, Khalil?"

"Stay by me, Alric, and I am sure I will find tasks for you." He was looking at the preparations for the journey. "I see the excitement in your eyes. Khalil looked at the ground and ran his fingers down his cheek then looked directly at Alric. "I have not yet eaten. Have you?"

"Yes, I have," Alric answered.

"Are your hands clean?"

Alric nodded. Then at Khalil's bidding, Alric took a cloth and placed bread and fruit into it from the tables. He handed Khalil the food. For a long moment, Khalil said nothing as he contemplated the food. Then he spoke. "It will take us many days to reach Baghdad. We cross over the water and then we will follow the coast road to Sardis.

From Sardis, we shall continue our journey to what is called the Royal Road that leads to Susa. This road is very old and will take us along the Tigris River, in the heartland of the ancient Assyrian kingdom. It is believed that the road was planned and organized by the Assyrian kings to connect their capital Nineveh with Susa. The city of al-Mawsil, which you may pronounce as Mosul, is on the west bank of the Tigris River, across from the ruins of Nineveh, and serves as an important stop on the caravan route to Susa. But we will not go as far as Susa. We will leave the Royal Road at Baghdad. Beyond Susa is the road known to many as the Silk Road that leads to lands in the east."

Khalil ate a piece of bread and some fruit before continuing. "I think the Caliph will be well pleased with you. My brother," Khalil did not mention Asad's name, "agrees with me. You have shown a quick ear for our language and you have an aptitude for learning. So this reaffirms my opinion that I should ask the Caliph to apprentice you to my father."

Khalil paused as if thinking about his next words and then continued. "Keep in mind, Alric, that there is no guarantee the Caliph will grant my request, and you must not show disappointment if the Caliph decides otherwise. Such a show of emotion would be very unwise. You must speak only when spoken to and never look directly at the Caliph."

Alric had learned some of the generalities of polite behavior, but he realized that he needed schooling in the details for meeting someone as high as the Caliph. Khalil continued. "During our journey, I will school you in the art of correct behavior. To show irreverence to the Caliph could lead to disastrous consequences." He paused and then added, "For you and for me. Once we start on this journey, Alric, there is no way out. If you wish to leave now, it is your choice. We will make peace and I will make arrangements for a ship to carry you back to your shores. I will ask Allah for his protection when I pray for you."

"I have made my choice," Alric announced. "You have given me a future that otherwise was denied me. I wish to show you what I can do. That is my decision."

Khalil looked pleased. "I did not think I would need to convince you. I see in you untapped qualities that will make you a great man. I am delighted, Alric. You have chosen wisely."

Alric's face lit up. Khalil laughed, showing very white perfect teeth.

* * *

It was mid-morning, and a time when the city bustled with activity, when they departed. The small boat in which Alric and Khalil sat was steered toward the western side of the water channel. Alric was amazed when he saw the number of boats that had been put into service and was even more surprised when he saw the horses. Each soldier would need a horse, and several more would be used as relief animals, while the donkeys would be used as pack animals. There were enough boats commandeered to carry all of the soldiers and the horses across the water but it would take several crossings before all were safely transported to the other side.

Knowing that this would take time, Khalil had ordered the first group to make camp and wait for their companions. Tents were pitched and the men started the general duties associated with camp organization. Khalil had ordered the camp to be created within and around the ruins of an ancient church. The remains of the walls would form a bastion for their defense, should they be attacked. There were no brigands or pirates in the region and Khalil doubted that this would occur but preferred to be prepared and protected.

The sun continued to beat down on the men as they worked. The heat increased, and the water carriers were continuously moving from one group of men to another. Some of the men had stripped to the waist, and their bodies gleamed in the sun. The officers, however, remained in full attire.

"If one is not exerting too much," Khalil explained to Alric, "our style of clothing can keep the heat out, but we also use it to keep the heat in at night."

The sun's power continued to grow in intensity. The whitewashed houses, close by the church, which had earlier in the day reflected the gold and crimson rays, now seemed to bake in the unmerciful heat. The grass crackled underfoot, but the soldiers continued to work. They were going home, and this temporary discomfort was not about to delay them.

Ahmed stayed on the city side of the waterway and departed only when all of the men and their horses had arrived ahead of him, by that time the sun had passed the meridian and was starting on its downward trek.

When evening came, the temperature cooled significantly. The soldiers had all crossed the waterway with their equipment. Horses were tethered, fed, and watered, and the soldiers settled down to their own meal—a thick mutton stew that would put energy back into their tired bodies. The meal was cooked by hired retainers who would return to the city the following morning.

Alric had just lain down on his makeshift bed in the tent he was to share with Ahmed when Khalil appeared at the entrance. Alric had intended to read an old book that Ahmed had acquired. He would need to begin reading more books in the Arabic language if he was to succeed in Khalil's homeland.

"Ah, there you are," Khalil's words broke into Alric's thoughts. "I have acquired a fine horse for you. I also want to put the thought in your mind of choosing a suitable name for yourself in our tongue." He paused as if thinking out his next words. "The Caliph, if he favors you, will give you a name, but a subtle word in his ear beforehand can secure for you one that you prefer."

Alric nodded to show he understood. Khalil withdrew his head from the tent opening and Alric, deciding he was too tired to read, lay down and was soon asleep. It was still dark when he awoke, and he could hear Ahmed's steady breathing.

Alric had seen Hilda in his dream, as clearly as if they had been together yesterday. She was helping him to take his first steps since his sickness took hold and caused him to spend weeks in bed. Her gentle voice that he knew so well was coaxing him to walk again. With each step and each word, he felt stronger. From the forested land to the west, he could hear the birds sing.

In a few days, Hilda said in the dream, *we will walk along the seashore to find shells and crabs in the tidal pools.*

It was during such times that their thoughts seemed to mingle together as one, and their ability to communicate was strengthened. They realized that each felt the pain of the other. When Alric groaned in pain, Hilda did likewise. When Alric smiled with joy, Hilda smiled with joy. They were able to calm each other's fears and treasure this newfound sensation. A super-human bond had developed between them. The dream faded and Alric rolled over to try to get more comfortable and resume his sleep.

"Alric, are you well?" It was Ahmed's voice.

"I wanted to sleep a little longer," he replied to Ahmed's question. "I had a dream about my homeland. It was the same dream I had seven days ago, and once again I awakened before the dream ended."

"After you have washed, we should walk together," Ahmed suggested.

Ahmed arose and, taking up his sword, left the tent with Alric. As they passed the other tents, they noticed that some of the men were beginning to stir, but many still slept. It was as if some mysterious energy bound their lives. This man, Ahmed, with whom he had spent the past several weeks on land and at sea, seemed to be able to read his mind; it was as if some mysterious energy bound their lives.

Perhaps he is so used to me that he knows my mind, Alric mused. Then he wondered if it could be the other way around. It might be he who was transmitting thoughts to Ahmed.

"So, you dream of your homeland, Alric?"

Alric nodded, and as they walked among the tents, Alric spoke of his family. He told Ahmed of the loneliness that he felt since he had been separated from his family. He described the village, the inhabitants, and the monks, as it had been before the sea raiders had appeared the first time. But for the past few days his thoughts had been only of one person—Hilda. "I need to know why she is always in my thoughts, Ahmed!"

"I did not know that you were about so early!" Khalil's soft voice came from behind.

They turned to face him, the light of the oncoming dawn framing his stature.

"Well, it seems Alric needed to talk rather than sleep. And so here we are," Ahmed answered.

"During the time we have conversed," Ahmed continued, "he has spoken of life in his village, where each day was like all the others, only the countryside changed with the seasons. He has also told me of the news from travelers from other cities and countries that stopped at the monastery. It was a pleasant change from talking with the men about horses and the journey."

"You miss your homeland, Alric?" Khalil asked. "But you still wish to make the journey with us?"

Alric nodded.

"You are lonely?" Ahmed asked.

"No," Alric stopped and looked directly at Ahmed, "I feel as if my sister is with me always." He did not offer any other words, but he knew that Hilda's spirit was present, as if she were his protector. He wanted to talk with her, but that had not yet been possible, except for the occasional thoughts.

Khalil's words jarred Alric back to the present. "Everybody feels pain at the loss of someone close," Khalil said. "If she is with you, then you are fortunate. Treasure her memory," Khalil said, "and keep a warm place in your heart for her."

Alric wondered if Khalil really understood. He also recognized that he was feeling something he had never experienced before—the desire to keep Hilda's memory with him forever.

Now he was about to embark upon a journey that would take him to a new way of life. He was excited but at the same time uneasy. Khalil and Ahmed sensed his moods and continued to reassure him that all would be well.

Alric gathered his cloak closer to his body. The first hour after sunrise was the coldest part of the day. He knew that a few hours from now, with the sun at its zenith, the heat would be so great that he would not be able to exert himself lest he burn up. He wondered about his new clothes, then realized they would not be such a burden as his old robe, and after all, he had been able to withstand the cold of the previous dawn.

He was grateful that Khalil had told him that there would be rest periods during the heat of the day.

Khalil and Ahmed needed to see to the business of the coming journey. For the moment, the only things that concerned the soldiers were food and water.

* * *

Alric had a purpose, and it was to learn as much as he could about the different cities of the region. He planned to ask Khalil and Ahmed about everything that he saw. He was overjoyed to see Nicaea, where the first Synod of the Christian Church had been held. As he stood in the old city, he felt a connection to the place.

In the coming days, the daily routine of the journey seemed to make all the days appear the same, with endless hours between sunrise and dusk. They would pass through a land different from any he had ever experienced.

To a body sensitized to cool temperatures and perpetual greenness, this area was strikingly different to Alric. The temperatures varied from near freezing during the night to furnace-like heat during the day. The topography varied from mountainous terrain to lush grassland to desert.

Already Alric's bank of recollections contained images of diversity much more than of any young man who had lived within the protective walls of a monastery.

*   *   *

CHAPTER 11

The rose-tinged horizon gave way to the yellow rays of the morning sun as Alric thought back to the conversations with Khalil and Ahmed, the same thoughts with which he had fallen asleep. He felt happy and contented. He was no longer alone. He had friends in Khalil and Ahmed, although he had no way of knowing what his future would be after meeting the Caliph. He felt optimistic, and in his recent dreams Hilda had smiled on him, as though to give her blessing.

He felt comfortable in his new clothes. He was encouraged to bathe daily and to stay clean. He continued learning the language and had been told that depending upon the Caliph's judgment, he would have access to books. Most important, he was able every day to live without fear. That fateful day when his parents and sister had been murdered no longer preyed on his mind, but Hilda was in his dreams, and her presence and words gave him comfort and guidance.

As he prepared himself for another day. He wondered what sights he would experience—perhaps old ruined cities or new ones alive with people and merchants. He did not want to think about the possibility of being attacked by bandits. He looked again at the position of the sun and hurried his pace.

As the day passed, he remembered he had a number of things he needed to do, one of which was to write his ideas on parchment, lest he forget his thoughts. It was toward the end of another hot day that they rested for the night. Each day seemed to repeat itself, and they all slept soundly after the long journey.

* * *

Their journey had been under way for several days when they approached the beach that lay on the western side of the land. "That is one of the wonders of this journey," Khalil said as he brought Alric's attention to a large hill with the vestiges of the walls of a ruined city visible in the distance.

Alric held his hand above his eyes in the setting sun and scanned the hill. He could see little except for stones and dirt. "May we go closer, Khalil?"

Khalil smiled at Alric's curiosity. "Of course," he responded and looked around. "Ahmed! We will rest for a short while. Send five of the men, please."

Ahmed signaled to those closest to them, and they followed Khalil and Alric. As they approached the hill, Khalil saw the intense interest in Alric's face. "This city," Khalil explained, "used to be visited by people from all over the world. They came in search of trade and found a city richer than any known at the time. Alric, you may have heard of this from your reading at the monastery, if the monks allowed you to read such secular books! This was the city of heroes. Over there on the beach, Achilles killed Hector while Priam watched from the walls."

Alric looked puzzled, and then a light shone from his eyes. "You mean, Khalil, this is Troy?"

Khalil smiled and said, "You have your wits about you, Alric. This is indeed the ruined remains of the city of Troy."

"But where are the high walls and the places where the people lived?"

"You remember, Alric, Troy was destroyed by the Greek kings, Agamemnon and his brother Menelaus. This is all that remains of that once-great city. Had it not been for the Greeks, perhaps the people, loving the land and the city, would have lived here forever," Khalil continued. He looked around. "I see that Ahmed has ordered the men to make camp. Let us return and make plans for food and rest."

Alric said no more. But the thoughts of Troy and its destruction filled his mind. He wondered what treasures of history and information about the old city would be buried under the dirt of the ages.

The next day, Khalil surprised Alric and gave him a pouch that held an ancient Trojan gold coin. A most generous gift. "I found three of these in the fields on another occasion when I passed this city. I carry this one with me. It is now yours, Alric. It is part of your education. Use it to learn."

Khalil saw Alric's eyes widen in wonder and excitement. His desire to travel was still alive, despite having spent many weeks on the journey. Khalil knew his father would see the same desires in Alric.

* * *

At the evening meal, Khalil announced that the next city of note would be Sardis, from which they would take the Royal Road to Baghdad. Alric decided he would broach the idea of keeping a written journal with Khalil. He would wait until they had made camp and eaten and the sun had sunk lower in the sky, bringing to them the coolness of the evening.

Khalil did not even raise an eyebrow in question at Alric's suggestion.

"Since we are on our way home, Alric," Khalil said, "I see no problem with your work as our scribe. However, rather than a journal of this journey, I suggest that you write the story of your life from the beginning of your memory. I think my Caliph will find it interesting.

I know you are not yet fully conversant enough to write in the Arabic tongue, so I suggest that you write in Latin. When the occasion arises, I can have it translated for the Caliph, or he may even wish to hear your own version as you read and translate for him. We will be at Sardis in a few days. At that time we will purchase the materials you need for writing."

Khalil had made the decision. "Sardis," he explained, "is an ancient capital city of this area. In former times, the city lay on a major road system that connected all of the great cities in this area. Sardis has retained its importance, and I know we will find the necessary writing materials there." Alric was thrilled. "I know many people in the city who will help us," Khalil continued.

Alric could not contain his excitement. He had felt a need to talk with others and make new friends, if Khalil permitted it. His spirits soared that evening.

* * *

They arrived on the outskirts of Sardis after four days and, by the time they made camp just outside the city walls, it was too late to accomplish anything that day. Alric spent the night in a state of wakefulness, unable to contain his thoughts about paper and writing. The next day, after sunrise, he washed early and sat in wait at the entrance to the tent that he shared with Ahmed, who was obvious by his absence. The flaps of the tent openings billowed in the morning breeze. The soldiers were already up and about, and the arrival of food from the city, carried by a dozen cooks and led by Ahmed, was a most welcome site.

For Alric, breakfast was an interruption in his plans. He picked and nibbled at the food and suffered in silence until Khalil spoke to Ahmed, "I think we had better go into the city and visit the paper makers before Alric succumbs to anxiety!"

The visit to the city was, to Alric, a huge success. As a result, all of the necessary paper and writing implements were purchased. Khalil was able to buy several goose quills that could be cut and used for writing. He also acquired slim, rounded, short wooden sticks. These could be sharpened to a point and used as a stylus. His ink was a prepared pigment that he could dissolve in water to produce the writing fluid he needed and, for transportation, the pigment was carried in a pouch. The biggest surprise of all was the material that Khalil called paper. Many sheets were bound in a sheaf, which was approximately the thickness of a finger. Four of these were purchased.

Khalil explained that over one hundred years ago, when the Arab people occupied a faraway country to the east called Samarkand, they captured prisoners who were skilled in the art of making paper. They had learned this from others who lived even farther to the east in a country that Khalil referred to as Cathay that lay at the eastern end of the Silk Road.

Realizing the possibilities of this material, caliphs from that time to the present had started manufacturing their own paper, and the knowledge had quickly spread to all parts of the Caliph's world.

"This, I think, will keep you busy for many days!" Khalil announced as they arrived back at the camp and Alric unpacked the materials. "But remember, you must not draw images of sacred persons. That would be against the code of Islam. But you may draw pictures of sites that you see. I suggest you do not draw pictures of any particular person, lest the meaning is misconstrued and your materials confiscated."

* * *

Alric immediately started to work on his writing. Thoughtfully, Khalil had also purchased a package of uneven-sized scraps of paper, which Alric could use for practice before working on the bound paper. He spent the remainder of the day getting used to his new materials.

He decided he would begin with his memories of the harsh cold winter and the joy that everyone in the village felt when the season had passed. The celebration of Easter and the sounds of birds singing heralded the coming of spring. He recalled how they had all looked forward to the warmth of the summer sun that brought fruit to the trees and produced berries on the bushes. He remembered picking berries and his freedom from the leather leg braces and the walking stick. He had the opportunity to ramble in the fields and along the wave-beaten seashore. It was at this time, he recalled, that the abbot officially recognized that he had the correct aptitude to become a monk and that Hilda might become a nun.

He started to write, realizing that some of the memories of his early life were vague. He began his story after his first five summers on this earth. This was the time when he and Hilda enjoyed activities together, often getting into much trouble. Later, they graduated to climbing the cliffs, much to their mother's consternation.

On the first night, Alric wrote with such intensity that the soldiers missed chatting with him. One soldier, who had been designated by his colleagues as the spokesman, sought out Alric. On his approach to Alric's tent, he coughed lightly to indicate his presence. The sound went unnoticed. Not to be daunted by the lack of recognition, the soldier stuck his head through the tent flaps and coughed again. This time he had Alric's attention.

"Yes, Latif," Alric responded.

"We," the soldier motioned his head to indicate his comrades, "wondered if all was well. We had not seen you since the evening meal." Latif looked at the pen, ink, and paper in front of Alric.

"I am writing a book about my life," Alric declared, looking directly into Latif's dark eyes and trying hard to fathom the reason why he was there.

Latif smiled and touched his forehead in a form of salute. "Perhaps you will read it to us when it is ready? Many of us can read but not in the language you use for your writing. We would like to hear your stories."

"I will, Latif, you have my promise. And I thank you and your colleagues for your interest."

Latif walked slowly back to where some of his companions were sitting. They had become very curious about Alric's life, so different from their own, and were glad to hear Latif's news.

As the nights passed, Alric was able to concentrate on his writing, and he was relieved to find that he was able to describe events. Night after night, he continued. Khalil and Ahmed made sure he rested.

Alric remembered his promise and began to read parts of the book to the soldiers; this helped him to recall other parts of his life he had omitted. He learned to carefully dismantle the book and reassemble the pages in a different order, depending upon the additions and insertions he needed to make.

"Hmm," muttered Khalil one night, seeing Alric surrounded by ten of his men, some of whom looked at the book, as if it were some strange object. "This is an important work, and it has sparked interest."

Khalil spoke to Ahmed, who was standing near. "Alric seems to have a talent for writing stories. I am hoping the Caliph will be pleased."

Ahmed smiled. He had already heard segments of the book. "The book describes Alric's personal story," Ahmed commented. "We do not know where or how it will end, but he is keeping the men interested during these long nights."

"Then, my dear brother, he is not writing myths that extend the truth beyond reality?" Khalil asked and then continued: "There is always a certain point in our lives where we lose control of what is happening to us, and our lives become controlled by *kismet*, fate."

"No, Khalil. He is nowhere near finished his work, but Alric's words offer a truth about his past that is commendable. I find that some of the sections about the healing nature of plants are well behind our knowledge, but in others he has ideas that we can adapt and put to our own use."

"That is good, Ahmed."

"His thoughts are clear and unencumbered by preconceived notions. If you pardon my intrusion, I think he will make an excellent companion for your father."

"No intrusion at all, Ahmed, I continue to welcome your thoughts."

Ahmed bowed his head in acknowledgment.

They looked at Alric, surrounded by the soldiers. Alric's eyes shone in the firelight as he spoke softly and with expression. His memory was giving him almost total recall; everything was clear to him.

One of the men leaned over, picked up a stick, and poked the fire, worried that it would not last through the reading. Alric read the names of his father, his mother, his sister, and about the monastery where he had studied.

"In the short winter days," he related, "when it was dark even at an early hour, we spent the time before going to sleep reading, talking about other lands, and wondering if we would ever travel. Mother and father always smiled indulgently at our words, knowing that the chance of travel for them was nonexistent, but they were hopeful that Hilda and I might journey someday. During the long summer evenings, we would all walk along the beach and watch the sunset before we returned to the village."

He continued to read and added the names of the villagers he had known and who had played a role in the story of his life.

* * *

"The Caliph," Khalil said, looking at Alric, "will indeed be interested in your story, but he will be more interested in your ability to record events in detail and with clarity. He has many storytellers, one in particular who pleases him."

Khalil stroked his chin with thumb and forefinger as he thought for a moment before continuing. "Since I left, I have heard of a princess of Samarkand by the name of Scheherazade, a woman of exceptional intelligence, wisdom, and bravery who tells spellbinding tales to the Caliph during the dark Baghdad nights." He looked at Alric. "I doubt that you would replace her, but I would suggest you begin to write about your medical studies to show our Caliph what you know. He will then consider assigning you to a position. Perhaps, and I am hopeful of this, as an apprentice to my father."

"Lord Khalil," by the use of his title, Khalil knew that Ahmed was about to make a request. "Some of the men suffer from minor ailments. And since we do have a medical chest, may I suggest that Alric take charge of the medicines and apply them as best as he knows to the ailments of the men?"

"It shall be so," Khalil said quietly. "Alric," Khalil looked across at him, "you have just been made Keeper of the Medicines. Do as you will and see to the fitness of my men. We have several more days on this journey and I pray that Allah grants us good health. Ahmed, the box, please."

Ahmed sprang into action and returned moments later with two men who carried a box that was approximately three feet in length, eighteen inches in width, and eighteen inches deep. Alric had noticed that a packhorse was used to carry this box, which appeared to be of great weight. After placing the box on its end in the sand in front of Khalil, the men returned to their companions, who would obviously be abuzz with talk at this curious action. Never before had their commander required the medicine box. Ahmed had been its guardian.

"How do you feel about your duty, Alric?" Khalil asked. Alric bowed his head in acknowledgment to Khalil, who smiled. *He is learning,* he thought. "Well, Alric?" Khalil asked.

"You have put much trust in me, Khalil."

"I do that for good reasons that you may one day understand. The most important thing is that you have succeeded in maintaining a good spirit among my men. Hearing your personal story has been interesting. Now let us see what we have here."

Ahmed opened the lock and swung open the heavy lid to reveal the contents. Alric watched intently. He saw that the box was made of thick wood and lined with copper. It held a number of small glass bottles, which contained powders, and packages of wrapped clean bandages. They were arranged neatly on shelves so that the name of the medicine and its purpose were recognizable.

"This is a typical medicine box," Ahmed explained and began a description of the contents. "We have powders to clean wounds and ointments to heal the wounds. We then apply clean cloths to bind them. Binding dirt into a wound causes a man to die in pain. There are medicines to ease the pain of a wounded man and take away the aches in the head, and powders to add to water if we feel that the water needs purifying. We have enough medicines in the box to respond to sickness or injuries for a period of three to six months, our usual time away from home."

After Ahmed's description of the contents was completed, Khalil spoke. "Ahmed will help you so that you understand the words on each of the containers. Now that you have the ability to speak many words in our tongue, consider this an exercise in reading and writing our language." Khalil paused. He seemed to be deep in thought, then he spoke again. "Everyone on this earth has a purpose. Some are born to rule. Others are born to serve. Many are destined for great things. I believe you are one of those destined for great things, Alric. At this point in your life, nothing is really clear and everything seems hazy, as though you are finding your way in a fog. But you are not afraid to dream, and to yearn for everything you would like to see happen in your life. However, you will be whatever the Caliph decides is best for you. In the meantime . . ."

Khalil allowed his words to trail away into the stillness of the night. Alric realized now that his task of looking after the medicine box was to prepare the way so that Khalil could use this as a positive note to the Caliph.

All three were silent for a time; each one content with his own thoughts. Khalil pulled his cloak around his chest to keep out the coolness of the night. Alric thought of the years he had spent in the monastery and the training he had received in the use of medicines taken from plants. Perhaps his dream was to be a man of medicine and healing.

It was Ahmed who spoke. "Tomorrow, Alric, we will continue your education so that you may read and write our language. But for the moment," he looked at Khalil, who nodded as if reading his thoughts, "I suggest that you sleep and be fresh for your start tomorrow."

Alric picked up his book, tucked it under his arm, and bade a goodnight to Khalil and Ahmed. Before he retired for the night, Ahmed found Alric sleeping peacefully with a smile on his face.

* * *

Alric was awake early the next day. Even before daybreak he decided his first task was to read his book! Next came the morning cleansing ritual, then he sat by the light of the fire. The men who were awake had been busy, and one handed him a mug of hot aromatic tea. "*Shukran*," he said, "Thank you."

"I see you are up and about early, Alric," he heard Khalil's voice from behind.

Alric looked up and smiled. One of the men presented Khalil with a cup of the hot tea. Khalil nodded in appreciation and sat next to Alric. The wind had begun to pick up.

"I have frequent thoughts of my dead family," Alric stated. "My book is now my only contact with them. They are memories, but the book seems to give them life."

Alric chose his words carefully. "My words have brought back the memories of the good times and made them seem alive. I have decided to keep this book close by me."

Khalil understood. The wind carried the pleasant odors of food being cooked on the fire. Khalil stood up. "The hot cakes the men are cooking smell very good," he said, brushing the sand from his clothes. "I am sure you are hungry."

"Take these," one of the men said to Alric as he held out a white flat stone on which several cakes were cooling. Alric took two of the cakes and felt the warmth of the meal as he took a bite. It tasted good! He devoured the remainder of the cakes, and before he could ask, Khalil offered him two more. He accepted them gratefully and finished his meal.

New thoughts entered his mind. He could see gardens, the beauty of flowers, paintings, colors, and food, all of which he could not place. It was as though Hilda was trying to communicate her thoughts of this unknown place to him.

Khalil walked away and looked up at the sky. "Allah, I know you see all things and have our futures decided for us," he said quietly. "Please grant me the vain wish that I am right about Alric in that his destiny is one that promises greatness. Give him your protection."

* * *

CHAPTER 12

After leaving Sardis, they moved farther inland, following the Royal Road that ran to Susa in the southwest of Persia and also passed close by Baghdad. The landscape changed from coastal vegetation, fresh sea air, and sea breezes to a desert-like vista liberally covered with rocks. The air was hot and still. Patches of color indicated the presence of a very coarse grass that, Alric learned, was poor fare for the animals.

This is a very strange land, Alric thought as he looked at the barren expanse that lay before him.

The wooded area to the northwest had been lush and green with vegetation. The landscape there had reminded Alric of the fields and trees inland from Wearmouth and to the west of the village, but the sand and the broad-bladed grass were different from anything that he had ever seen.

By midday the blinding sun had made the temperature unbearable. Even the robes they wore were not able to keep out the vicious heat. The air temperature was rising and to continue the journey would have been difficult for the men and the animals. The horses in particular were already showing signs of being affected by the heat, although the donkeys seemed to adjust to the conditions a little easier.

Alric heard Khalil as he leaned over and said to Ahmed, "This heat is unusual for this time of the year. It seems to me . . ." Khalil paused as he looked around, squinting as his eyes adjusted to the bright sunlight. "Over yonder," he said, shading his eyes with his hand. "I think those large boulders should offer us shelter, and if I am not mistaken there will be a supply of fresh water!"

Khalil halted the men and Ahmed went ahead, keeping the horse at an easy trot. When he returned minutes later, he confirmed Khalil's suspicion. The boulder outcrop was indeed a large formation that would provide shade, and there was a small stream with a plentiful supply of water. Ahmed informed them that the boulders formed a protective ring around a pool that was fed by an underground spring, which in turn fed the stream. There was also sufficient shade for them to make camp and take advantage of the protection of the natural walled enclosure.

As they made their way to the rocks, Alric saw two scorpions scuttle away from his horse's feet. Ahmed had shown him a scorpion just after they'd left Constantinople and now he warned Alric that if he should have the misfortune to get bitten by one, the only remedy was to soak a cloth in wood spirits, used for cleaning wounds, from one of the bottles in the medicine chest and hold it to the wound so the spirits could draw the poison from the body into the cloth. Alric suddenly felt very apprehensive about these small creatures.

"And," Ahmed added as he turned toward Alric, "scorpions often make their homes in the rock areas. The men will spend part of the time making sure they are removed from the camp, but that does not mean that they are truly gone! There are those that escape detection."

"Could I see one?" Alric asked.

Ahmed raised his eyebrows and departed, returning minutes later with a scorpion impaled on the sharp point of his dagger. It was a large specimen, about four inches long from tail to the end of its claws. "Here," he said frowning. "Be careful that you do not prick yourself on its tail. Since it has just been killed, I suggest that you allow it to dry out in the hot sun before you look closer."

By midafternoon, the creature had dried sufficiently for Alric to see the body structure clearly. Ahmed kept a close watch on Alric's actions.

"I am fascinated that such a creature," Alric said peering at the scorpion, "can carry poison and yet not infect itself." He looked at the dried carcass. "May I?" he asked Ahmed. Ahmed handed him his weapon, the same dagger he had used to kill the creature. "That is it!" Alric exclaimed as a sack at the end of the tail released a pale liquid when pierced with the point of the knife. "This," he said, "is where the creature carries its venom. The structure of the tail," indicating the segmented organ, "allows the animal to strike its victim with the point." He peered even closer. "It seems," he concluded, "that part of the tail is hollow, allowing the liquid from the sack to flow into the victim."

Ahmed was puzzled. "This is interesting, Alric, but . . . "

"Excuse me, Ahmed" Alric said interrupting him, "but in one of the books that I read at the monastery, the scorpion was supposed to inject venom into the victim by a magical procedure." He bowed his head to Ahmed. "I truly apologize for interrupting you, but I had to find out!"

Ahmed smiled. "Well done, Alric. You have taught me something I did not know. It is good that I can learn from you. And now, may we . . . ?" Ahmed left the question unanswered as he indicated the shade. He looked at Alric and saw the unasked question in his eyes. "Of course you may use my dagger," Ahmed said, "as long as you clean it after you have cut that thing apart! And," he said seriously, "be careful that you do not allow the sting to prick your flesh, there will still be venom within."

Some of the men were huddled, talking in hushed tones, their faces partially covered as though they wished to hide the movements of their lips. Others rested, lying back, with their heads on their saddles. Posted guards watched for the approach of strangers.

The men who saw Alric and Ahmed with the scorpion wondered what Alric was doing. Khalil, having made an inspection of the perimeter, came to sit with Alric and Ahmed and was immediately briefed by Alric regarding the fundamentals of the scorpion's tail. Khalil listened with interest, thought for a moment, and then said:

"My father will have an interest in your observations. He has long puzzled over the problem of a means to get medicines quickly into a patient. He thinks," Khalil pondered his next words carefully, "that the blood serves the body by moving around it. He also believes the heart has something to do with that. He mentioned one day that if medicine could be carried by the blood, a patient might recover much quicker. He never knew how to get the medicine into the blood. You may have an answer for him!"

Khalil scratched his chin thoughtfully, and then continued. "Scorpions are plentiful in the land where we live, and it will be ironic if the answer to the puzzle lay right under my father's nose." Then he added. "I suspect that father will be pleased, and this discovery may also stand you in good stead with the Caliph. Well done, Alric!"

"I think, Lord Khalil, we may wish to take a further look at the guards. The sun is beating down and . . . " Ahmed allowed the words to trail off into the afternoon heat.

"Yes, Ahmed."

They both got up and took four of the men with them to relieve the guards. This would be repeated each hour during the heat of the day.

As they walked away, Alric noticed that Khalil and Ahmed talked quietly, their eyes darting about as if expecting trouble at any moment.

A practice of safety, Alric thought to himself as he remembered the attacks of the sea raiders that had destroyed the village and eventually led him to this unexpected way of life. In the monastery, he recalled that his eyes had always been drawn to the image of Saint Peter, the patron saint of the holy house. In the image, St. Peter stood with a book in one hand, and his other hand was raised as if saluting the sky. The saint had such a peaceful look on his face.

After inspecting the guard, Khalil and Ahmed approached. They both looked serious. Alric rose to acknowledge their presence, wondering if something was amiss.

Earlier in the day, he had overheard some of the soldiers talking about signs and omens, and as they were crossing the river that morning, Alric had had similar thoughts.

"Soldiers often know how to interpret such signs!"

He wondered what this could mean. In the monastery, the monks had taught him to decide which path he should take by observing the ground and the sky. He had discovered that the presence of a certain animal meant that a wolf might be nearby, or a certain shrub growing was a sign of water in the area.

"We are close to a sacred place," Khalil spoke, breaking into Alric's thoughts. "We have made much progress since we crossed the river and we are now within days of Baghdad. Do you see the hills in the distance?"

Alric nodded. From his high vantage point, the land to the south was plain and bare; a landscape of faded brown hillocks and mounds of dirt on the east side of the river rising from the flatness.

"On the right side of the river you can see the buildings that are the city of Mosul. To the left, the mounds of dirt are the remains of the old city in which our Prophet Yunus, peace be upon him, died and lies buried." Khalil noticed the puzzled expression on Alric's face. "I believe that you refer to the prophet as Jonah," Khalil added by way of explanation.

Alric nodded. "Yes, Khalil, he was swallowed by a . . . " Alric frowned as he fought to find the correct Arabic word for "whale" but could not, ". . . large fish, and then before he died, he went to Nineveh to save the city from sin."

"That," Khalil exclaimed and pointed to the hills, which, in spite of appearing close, were two hours ride away "is the remains of the city of Nineveh. The walls fell and the stones are covered with the dirt of centuries, giving the impression that they are small hills or mounds. The southern hill, which used to be part of the ancient walls, is now a shrine to the prophet, who was buried within those walls to protect him from the ravages of time. We must visit the shrine, pay our respects to the Prophet Yunus, peace be upon him, and offer our thanks to Allah for his life."

"Sit down, and let us have tea," said Khalil.

"I will get cups for us," Ahmed added. He soon returned with three cups of the steaming hot liquid.

"Your education now starts here in earnest, Alric," Khalil said between sips of tea. "To this point," he continued, "you have learned our language very well and you are to be commended for it. However, from now on we must be more formal with each other, in particular when others are near us. You have been able to see a part of our culture, but the formalities and protocols will change once we enter Baghdad. It is the nature of our life that we give to each other the respect we deserve. To do otherwise will displease the Caliph."

"If I may speak, Lord Khalil," Alric said quietly, giving Khalil his formal title. In spite of the heat of the day, the hot tea that had been sweetened with honey was invigorating and stimulated Alric's thoughts. "My thanks go to my teacher, Ahmed, who has persevered with me and given me guidance through his words." Alric turned and bowed his head to Ahmed.

"You are truly learning our ways, Alric, and show advances every day. As we are now only a matter of days from the City of Baghdad, it is imperative that you carefully learn our ways and the words of the Prophet Muhammad, peace be upon him. You will start by studying the life of the Prophet Yunus, peace be upon him. His shrine is one to which sick people pray for healing. Guide your thoughts and words in accordance with what you have been taught." Khalil sipped his tea.

"Lord Khalil," Ahmed's words cut into the silence.

"Yes, my friend Ahmed, I am pleased with the progress you have made with Alric. He is a tribute to you and to himself. I assume that you wish to continue to be is teacher?" Ahmed bowed his head in agreement. "So be it." Khalil looked once more at Alric. "Ahmed will continue to be your guide. You will listen to him and obey his every word. Do you understand, Alric?"

"As you wish, Lord Khalil. I am happy that you have appointed Ahmed as my continuing tutor. Perhaps there is another name that I should call him, out of deference for his position?"

"Yes," Khalil's response was immediate. "You shall refer to Ahmed as *mu'al-alim*. You know the meaning of that word?"

"Yes, Lord Khalil, it means *teacher*."

"Good, Alric."

Alric took Khalil's words to heart. His life had structure and purpose now. He took his book of writings from his pouch and passed it to Ahmed, who examined the contents briefly and returned it to him. Ahmed and Khalil exchanged some words in a rapid dialect that Alric did not understand. Ahmed then turned to Alric.

"We find the writings of your life very interesting," he said. "My Lord Khalil has reaffirmed that these will be of great interest to the Caliph, who, as I have already told you, is always willing to listen to stories of life in other lands."

Alric felt proud of his work.

Khalil continued. "Now I will teach you what is really expected of you in terms of behavior and court protocols. We have heard through our messenger system that you will be presented to the Caliph. The manner in which the Caliph accepts you is entirely up to you!"

Alric's eyebrows were raised.

"Ah, yes," Ahmed continued. I see the surprise on your face. We are able to pass messages from Lord Khalil to the Caliph by carrier pigeon. It is fast and efficient. We also have another method that uses riders on fleet horses who work in stages to deliver messages from one corner of the empire to another, with all routes crossing in Baghdad. However, we do not use the riders and horses across the desert. The heat would be fatal to both."

As Khalil and Ahmed started to rise, Alric got up quickly to assist Khalil. He felt Ahmed's hand on his shoulder. His grip was strong and Alric wanted to squirm free but decided to remain passive.

"You must never attempt to place your hand on the person of someone who is above your station in life." Ahmed explained. "That is your first lesson. However, if Lord Khalil requests your assistance, you will give it willingly, without complaint."

Alric said nothing but understood. Khalil smiled reassuringly and touched Alric's shoulder.

"That is a good lesson for you, Alric. There are those who, making such contact, could lose a hand for their efforts. Listen well to my friend Ahmed and you will be prepared. Our country is not like the countries of Europe. We have our customs that follow the teaching of the prophets, peace be upon them." Khalil looked at his men. "And now," he said, "the heat of the day is abating. Let us ride to the city. Make camp, and we shall then pay our respects to the Prophet Yunus, peace be upon him."

* * *

To visit the shrine of the prophet, they climbed to the top of the hill and then, without entering the mosque, entered a guarded doorway that led to a descending passageway lined by large stones that, Alric guessed, had formed part of the original wall of Nineveh. Khalil and Ahmed stopped; Ahmed turned toward Alric and pointed ahead.

"We are close. Follow me," he said.

With that, he began to walk slowly down the remainder of the incline. Alric thanked him in a whispered tone and inclined his head graciously. As they approached the part of the wall that contained the prophet's tomb, Alric felt a sensation he could not explain. As he followed Khalil and Ahmed's footsteps, he knew instinctively he was in a holy place. He bowed his head and fell to his knees, not knowing what he was supposed to do but acting in a way that was most natural to him.

After a few minutes, he felt Ahmed's hand on his shoulder. No words were spoken, but Alric knew that it was time to go. He followed Khalil and Ahmed up the incline. He had not noticed on the way into the tomb that it dipped and rose. The stones that lined the passageway were large and thick. Some were almost the height of a man and at least as thick as a man's waist. The stones were stacked longitudinally and fitted together so well that he doubted a knife blade could be inserted between them. Some even had strange signs cut into the surface.

Alric ran his fingers slowly over them, sensing their temperature and feeling their surfaces. If only he could understand these stones, they could be a road to the past and a treasure of unknown value. Just touching them filled him with wonder. At last they emerged into the blinding sunlight and into the central courtyard of the mosque.

"When you want something, a dream may help you realize your goal." Ahmed's voice broke into Alric's thoughts. Here he was, among the ruins of an ancient city, one that held a great historical past. "The signs on the stones can be read by men of learning." Ahmed said. "If you look closely, you can see that the marks are made up of small triangles. They are the words and letters of our forefathers, who also ruled a mighty empire. Some of our forefathers who wrote these words even pre-date the time of many of your prophets, except the Prophet Ibrahim, peace be upon him, who I believe you call Abraham. Very few men can translate these words, and, it is believed, many of the writings deal with medicine and science. The Caliph has collected many such writings in his library. If the Caliph allows you to pursue science or medicine, I recommend you learn the language of the past. You will hear people speak of the wedge language because of the shape of the marks in the stone that were carved by a pointed stick before the clay was hardened by baking in an oven. We have no words to describe the writing; we merely refer to it as *the writing of the ancients.*"

Ahmed looked at Alric to see if his words had fallen on ears that were receptive. Alric bowed his head. "With your permission, *mu'al-alim* Ahmed, I would speak."

Ahmed smiled at his pupil.

"In private, Alric, you can call me Ahmed. But in public . . . " Ahmed left the words unspoken but the meaning was clear.

"*Shukran, mu'al-alim.*" "Thank you teacher."

"May I suggest, Ahmed, that there are Latin words I would like to use to describe the writing on the ancient stones?" Alric continued. "There is the word *cuneus,* meaning 'wedge,' and another word, *forma,* meaning 'shape.' With your permission, I will make a note in my book to describe the writing as *cunei forma,* the shape of the wedge."

Ahmed smiled. "That is an excellent idea, Alric. I am sure that the Caliph will find your suggestion most interesting." Ahmed's keen eyes spotted something near his feet. He scraped the dirt away to reveal a stone. He looked carefully at the unusual stone showing through the dirt.

"Please retrieve that, Alric," Khalil urged.

Alric pulled the object from the earth. It was a hardened clay tablet of a size that could be conveniently held in the palm of the hand and it was covered with *cunei forma* writing. A corner had been broken off at some time over the ages, but the remainder of the tablet was intact.

"That is yours to keep, Alric. When you can come back to me and tell me the meaning of the words, you will have accomplished your learning of the . . . " Khalil thought for a moment as the words formed,

". . . *the cunei forma* writing as part of your studies. I cannot translate the words, so I rely on you to come to me with their meaning."

Alric bowed his head and placed the hardened clay tablet into his pouch. As he did so, he felt its warmth as it rested against his book. He looked at the pile of dirt that covered the long-lost walls and wondered if there were many such tablets hidden from sight.

"Be satisfied with what you have for the moment, Alric," Khalil's gentle voice seemed to carry on the light breeze. "First, learn to recognize the words, and other tablets will follow."

Alric smiled to himself and nodded in obedience. He patted his pouch, making sure there were no holes through which he could lose the object. He now had possessions in addition to the clothes he wore: his book, the gold Trojan coin given to him by Khalil, and the tablet. He was starting to collect his own personal items. "These will stay with me for the rest of my life," he vowed.

He would learn much from the tablet. He had Khalil's permission, but would he get permission from the Caliph? He looked around at the dirt-covered ruins feeling excited. "This is not a strange land," he repeated. "It is a new land!"

After all, it seemed to be just what he had always wanted—to visit and learn about new places. Even if he never left this land, he had already traveled farther than anyone he had ever known, except Khalil and Ahmed, of course. Although this new country at the moment seemed to be an empty, wind-blown desert with a city across the river, he had already imagined what it must have been like when it was teeming with life. He became lost in these thoughts as he walked toward the camp.

* * *

After they had returned to the camp, Alric spent a long time examining the tablet. He could not make any sense of the signs and fell asleep with the tablet clutched in his hands. Soon, it was morning and the day's activity was about to resume.

At first, his mind could not adjust to his whereabouts. Looking up, he saw Ahmed. He remembered the tablet and, finding it near to where he slept, placed it into his pouch. He would be a man of learning. Perhaps, he mused, one day he would even write another book.

"Lord Khalil has given us permission to spend one day here at Mosul. After you have washed and eaten we will cross the river into the town. Oh . . . " Ahmed continued, "Leave the sword here. You will not have use of it in this city."

Later that morning, he walked slowly through the marketplace with Ahmed. The merchants were assembling their stalls, smiles on their faces and ready to begin a day's work. Alric recalled the merchant-travelers he had met at the monastery. They were all somber men, seemingly with little to smile about and always trying to charge the highest prices to villagers who had little in the way of money.

Alric noticed the merchants being helped by younger men, possibly fathers and sons working together. He realized that he could not have done the same thing with his father in the village. There was limited work and most sons had to work in the fields. Merchants and men with skills were usually visitors to the village. Looking at them brought a warm feeling to his body. It seemed that here, in this land, a man might not be limited by his birth but by his abilities.

When the stalls were assembled, the merchants offered different types of foods, many of which Alric had not seen before. The sight of rich, juicy dates, figs, olives, and multicolored peppers assailed his eyes. The buildings in Constantinople had taken Alric's breath away, but the marketplace in Mosul was even more breathtaking to him.

Alric was surprised to see all types of glass, some of it fashioned perfectly. The sun caught the delicate shapes and colors. The anxiety on the merchants' faces was obvious, as Alric looked closely at the pieces before him. They feared that he might pick up a piece that would lead to breakage. Other merchants displayed gemstones, and yet others sold items of furniture. Chairs, cushions, wall hangings, and intricately woven carpets adorned their stalls.

Alric detected differences in the speech patterns and word pronunciations, which Ahmed explained were variations in the dialect. Even the dialect of Al-Mawsil was a little different to the speech of Khalil and Ahmed. Alric realized that if he was to truly learn the language, he must understand the language variations.

In Ahmed's care, he felt relaxed and unhurried. He realized he still had the accent of the north from whence he came but he would make that disappear in time. Only in that way would he be able to converse comfortably. It would require a lot of patience, but he had learned patience from the monks and Khalil.

* * *

When they had eaten the meal just after midday, Ahmed announced they had to return to the camp. "Lord Khalil has the need to assemble the men and make ready for the journey to Baghdad. We will start out early in the morning. This will be the final part of our journey."

To Alric's quizzical look, Ahmed responded. "This is the last stage, and if we make good time each day and rest the horses at night, we could enter the city in seven days." He looked at Alric. "Do you have any fears?"

"No, *mu'al-alim*. I have placed my trust and my life in your hands and in the hands of Lord Khalil. I will make the best of whatever station the Caliph affords me. I am willing to learn and work. Either is better than the life I once knew or life with the sea pirates or . . . "

"Or death," Ahmed added.

"Yes, *mu'al-alim*, much better than death!"

Ahmed laughed. "You have a good head on your shoulders, Alric. You should have many, many years between here and death."

There was a moment of silence so profound that it seemed the entire marketplace, even the city, was asleep. Alric patted his pouch. "I will seek to improve my learning, and my thirst for knowledge will never cease."

After a brief moment, Alric added, "From what you and Lord Khalil have told me, I will have no choice but to respect the decision of the Caliph, but I do not think I am fearful of him. Lord Khalil and you have encouraged me to follow the path of learning. I believe the Caliph will make a good decision." Alric looked at Ahmed.

"*Mu'al-alim, insha'allah*. My teacher, it is in God's hands."

* * *

PART III:
THE HOUSE OF LIGHT

CHAPTER 13

Alric was sitting astride his horse staring in amazement at the magnificent spectacle that lay before him. The city shimmered in the late afternoon light. The whitewashed buildings gave it a pure and wholesome appearance.

Alric could hear a murmur from the soldiers. The horses seemed to agree with their riders that the long journey was over and muttered their approval in whinnying tones. "This is the city of the Caliph," Khalil announced, the pride showing in his voice, and Alric could see that his eyes sparkled as did the eyes of a child seeing a gift for the first time.

As Alric turned and looked at the soldiers, many of them were smiling with a mixture of relief and joy on their faces. He was glad the journey was over, but now he needed to remember one important detail: only Arabic was spoken here.

Khalil signaled to Ahmed, who gave a command to the men to make ready for their entry into the city. Once he was assured that all was in order, Khalil nudged his horse forward in a slow trot toward the city wall.

Within a short time, my future will be decided by a man I have never met, Alric thought as they moved ever closer to the city. He resolved not to worry. During the last few days of the journey from Mosul, he had been coached well by Khalil and Ahmed, and he believed he knew enough about the city and the Caliph, known to all as Harun al-Rashid, to speak well for himself. Before long, he would know the direction his future would take.

"Are you with us, Alric?" Khalil's voice came through the haze. Alric turned in the saddle and nodded.

"Yes, my Lord Khalil," he said. "I had a few passing thoughts."

"Do not be anxious, Alric. All will be well." Alric felt comforted by the gentle tones of Khalil's voice. "In less than two hours we shall enter Baghdad by the northeastern gate, and a main road will lead us directly to the Caliph's palace. The sight will," Khalil smiled at Alric, "take your breath away."

Ahmed, riding next to Khalil, leaned over and whispered to him.

"*Mu'al-alim* Ahmed has reminded me, Alric," Khalil said, "that the color of your eyes and hair will be a great surprise to many of the people. Cover your head and face so that you do not draw too much attention to yourself. There might be those in the crowd who have very unpleasant memories of men like you who have the northern features. Return the sword to Ahmed and then ride behind us and do not look directly at anyone."

Alric slowed his horse and followed Khalil and Ahmed. He adjusted his head and face covering as two of the soldiers nearby moved their horses forward so that they covered both of his flanks.

* * *

Alric had learned many details about Baghdad from Khalil and Ahmed. The city was situated on the west bank of the River Tigris, was centrally located on various trade routes, and dominated the civilized world. The Caliph's father, *Abu Afar bad-Allah al-Mansur,* had created the city on the precise spot that was known to the ancient Babylonians as *Bag-Ad-Du* and had given the city the name that it now bore—Baghdad. Al-

Mansur had supervised the construction of the city walls using a circle three miles in diameter, thus making Baghdad the *Round City*. It was said that much to the horror of his followers, he had leaped into the moat to be sure that it was deep enough.

The city, with a population of almost five hundred thousand persons, was provided with four gates, the Gate of Kufa, the Gate of Basra, the Gate of Khurasan, and the Gate of Syria.

Each gate was provided with a double iron door, high and thick, of such weight that to close or open one door several men were needed. Wide avenues traversed the city from gate to gate so that each avenue connected a gate with its diagonally opposite gate. This facilitated movement of soldiers from one part of the city to another. The distance between each gate and the next was approximately two miles, measured from outside the ditch, giving the city a circumference of almost eight miles.

The thickness of the walls at the foundation was one hundred and sixty feet but tapered at the top to a thickness of fifty feet. The total height of the wall, including the battlements, was one hundred feet. Around the main wall was an outer wall, thick and high, with a distance of more than one hundred paces between the two. The outer wall had strong towers, and on it there were circular battlements. Outside the outer wall, a high dike had been constructed, and beyond the dike was a ditch into which water was brought from a canal drawing. Within the city wall was an open area built for defense, so that an enemy who managed to breach the wall would have to move through an open space and be subject to further attack.

Inside the wall there were residences for highly placed government officials and officers of the army, as well as for other persons who were required for important business. These were the people who could be trusted to live near to the Caliph. Within this ringed area were the dwellings of the family of the Caliph and those who were close to him.

In the center of the royal residences stood the royal palace, surrounded by a wall. The entrance to the palace was called the Golden Gate, and next to it was the central mosque. The palace was the focal point of the city, and the approach to the palace was impressive. From his studies of Latin, Alric was aware of the saying "All roads lead to Rome," but in the round city of Baghdad, all roads led to the palace. The palace was composed of several enclosed gardens, all leading to the center, where the Caliph's residence was located.

* * *

And now Alric was about to enter this magnificent city. The marketplace that was set up outside of the city walls was a sight to see. It was a strange and stirring sight to behold the number of people who came from various parts of the land with goods to sell, buy, or trade.

Many stood to one side when they saw the mounted soldiers, all wearing the Caliph's livery. No one seemed to notice Alric, as all eyes were on Khalil. Obviously, Alric concluded, he was well known within the city and he was the center of attraction. He rode with a quiet dignity.

In Baghdad, every day was market day. The yells of the vendors, the laughter of children, the scolding or praise of mothers, and merchants and customers haggling could be heard everywhere. There were cries of animals awaiting purchase, traveling bards, musicians, and poet-sellers hoping to attract the patronage of some scholar or noble.

All around Alric crowds were coming and going, shouting and buying, and the air was filled with the aroma of strange foods. There were many food items and goods that he did not recognize. This was very different from the visit to the monastery at Wearmouth by an isolated trader, occurring perhaps once or a month or less.

Alric realized he should not allow himself to be distracted. Khalil led, with Alric and Ahmed riding two abreast behind him. After passing through the marketplace, they rode through the arcade near the gate, which, like the market, seemed to be full of stalls with items for sale and throngs of people everywhere.

Once they were beyond the arcade, Khalil seemed to relax. They had just entered the area where the house of the royal family and prominent citizens were located when Ahmed reached over and nudged Alric's shoulder. "That is where we live," he said, nodding to a group of dwellings to the south of the gate. "We have come a long way on this trip, perhaps farther than ever before. As you become accustomed to our manner of life, you will understand more about the working of our minds and our ways which have led us to this life. Since our lives revolve around the very nature of the decisions we make, all must be thought out carefully."

Just as Ahmed finished speaking, Khalil slowed the gait of his horse so that Alric and Ahmed could draw abreast of him. "We will go to the palace first," he began, "where we will await the Caliph's pleasure. In the meantime, what do you think of our city, Alric?"

"Magnificent!" was all that Alric could think to say, and then he added, "The number of merchants amazed me. There are so many people!"

Khalil laughed aloud. "The Caliph has encouraged the establishment of a merchant class because trade is an honorable career," Khalil explained in answer to Alric's wide-eyed expression. "As you can observe," he continued, "most merchants have their own moveable stalls, although some are fixed or have become housefront stores. The Caliph offers protection to them. Indeed, he also allows trade to be practiced in the home, and women are encouraged to own and operate stalls in the marketplace. Any woman who has learned the craft of her husband or father or has even developed one of her own is eligible to sell her wares. Despite what you may have heard about a harem, our women have always played a vital role in the community, and not only in the traditional roles of childbearing and mother. They serve the community as scholars, teachers, nurses, and many other important activities."

Khalil looked at Alric. "How many of the women in your village were allowed to play such vital roles outside of the home?"

Alric shook his head in amazement.

"You will see," Khalil continued, "that many women cover their heads. We require modesty in both men and women. A woman who covers her head is recognized as having a good moral character and is filled with dignity and self-esteem. The clothing must be loose enough so as not to describe the shape of her body. One desirable way to hide the body is to wear a cloak over other garments. The clothing must be thick enough so as not to show the color of the skin it covers and it must not be showy so that everyone notices the dress. There are mixed opinions as to whether or not the face should be covered. In many cases we leave this to the woman, her husband, or her parents."

As soon as Alric heard this, he understood what he had observed in the marketplace. By the time they reached the palace gate and Khalil had spoken with the guards, the sun began its departure behind the walls, and the shadows lengthened. Torches were lit and cast a much-needed light around them. Alric recalled that when the sun had risen that morning, he had been in another world and looking forward to his future. Now, as it began to set, he was in a city that would be his future. Over the past months, his life had changed so drastically.

He felt the pouch at his side; his book offered him comfort. He ran his fingers slowly over it, feeling its thickness and sensing the words he had written. This was his treasure. He smiled to himself, then looked up and around at the now empty streets, feeling very comfortable. Although his new world at the moment appeared deserted, he remembered how he had seen it when it was teeming with life, and it would start again with the rising of the sun the next day.

When all was prepared, Alric bedded down with the soldiers on a floor above the level of the horses' stalls. It was late and with the weariness of the journey now over, Alric fell into a dreamless sleep.

* * *

Relaxed and rested, Alric awoke at dawn. Khalil had left for an unspecified reason. Ahmed commanded that the horses be given due attention and left with two of the soldiers, saying he had some items that required his supervision. As Alric applied the final brush stokes to his horse, a bevy of attendants arrived with water for washing and bathing and trays laden with food and drink.

Alric spent his time observing the frequent comings and goings in the palace yard. Just before midday, Ahmed returned with clean clothes and instructions that Alric bathe once more. "The Caliph," Ahmed offered by way of explanation, "does not care to meet with those who are in need of bathing. Make yourself presentable, Alric," he commanded. "When you meet the Caliph, you must look your best, and in exchange you may be given something you desire!"

Alric touched the pouch at his side, as if for reassurance. Ahmed observed his gesture. "By all means, Alric, Take your book with you, but have it under your cloak, within easy reach should you need to produce it for the Caliph."

* * *

In an hour, Alric was ready and wearing the appropriate attire. Ahmed returned and smiled with satisfaction at Alric's appearance. "Good," he pronounced. "We will wait in the palace yard until we are called." As an afterthought, Ahmed asked, "Are you hungry?"

Alric shook his head. *Who can eat at a time like this?* he asked himself.

Ahmed continued. "Because the Caliph has decided he will hear you, he will most likely invite you to eat, and you must not refuse. He will expect you, being a younger man, to have a good appetite, at any time of the day!" Ahmed seemed to think for a moment before he added, "You need to cleanse your mind of all negative thoughts." He placed his hand gently on Alric's shoulder. "Follow my lead and you will do well. Bow when I do. Kneel when I do. And keep your face covered until the Caliph commands you otherwise." Ahmed looked across the palace yard and exclaimed, "Lord Khalil returns."

Alric turned to see Khalil approaching in the company of an older man who moved with a grace and stature that belied his age. Ahmed whispered to Alric, "The man with Lord Khalil is Lord Jabir, father of Lord Khalil. Lord Jabir's impression of you will be of some influence when the Caliph determines your future."

Jabir flashed an engaging smile at Alric. Alric bowed his head in respect to the man. "So, you are the one that my son calls Alric al-Biritaanya, Alric from Britain," he said in a friendly voice. Alric bowed his head and remained silent. "I am Jabir al-Hajjaj ibn Yusuf abu Asad abu Khalil. The last two names show that I am father of Asad and Khalil." Jabir looked at Alric. "I see that you understand the names. Khalil told me that you are intelligent and speak our language well."

After a pause, during which Alric was able to adjust his breathing to a normal rhythm, Jabir said, "You may raise your head and look at me. It is perfectly in order to look upon my face."

Alric obeyed. Jabir was a tall, impressive man. His hair and well-trimmed beard, once jet black, were streaked with gray. His dark brown eyes showed an intensity for life. Alric felt comfortable in his presence.

Alric later learned that although deemed, by name, to be of the house of Yusuf, Jabir's early life and origins were shrouded in a fog of mystery. It was rumored that Jabir was born to a wealthy merchant family in an unnamed city to the east. Others said he had spent his adolescence in a city to the south. Still others, less believably, claimed that he was of a line of ancient kings. Reputedly, he had started life as a scribe, being able to read and write at a very young age. "And now, Alric, are you prepared to meet my nephew, the Caliph?"

"I am, Lord Jabir."

"You have the confidence, Alric," Jabir responded, "of one who is sure of himself. You hide your surprise very well, and I like that. I gather you were unaware that the Caliph is my nephew? Well," he added, "he is actually my wife's nephew. I am his uncle by marriage." Jabir allowed his voice to trail away into silence as he looked at Khalil before he spoke again. "My son, Khalil, speaks highly of you." Jabir announced. "That bodes well for you."

Alric felt the gentle touch of reassurance from Ahmed. "Ah," Ahmed exclaimed as he turned around and looked in the other direction, "I see that we have been called."

Alric looked at Ahmed, adjusted his clothing, and then appeared to freeze. Thought Alric, *I am about to meet a man who controls the world!*

There was a moment of silence so profound that it seemed that the palace, the people, and the horses were asleep. Alric could no longer hear the sounds around him. All seemed to have been blocked from his ears. He stood with Ahmed, staring blankly across the yard.

Ahmed looked anxiously at him. All the joy he had seen in Alric's face that morning had disappeared. "Alric, what ails you?" he asked.

"It is just a moment of fear and trepidation, *mu'al-alim.*" He took several deep breaths. "It has passed," he announced to Ahmed. "I am ready, *mu'al-alim.*"

They were approached by a steward who addressed Lord Jabir and asked if they would follow him to a private area of the palace. Jabir nodded, almost imperceptibly. Ahmed looked once again at Alric to make sure he was prepared. Then he smiled approvingly. "Cover your face and head and walk with my son Ahmed," Jabir said casually. "It is better that your face remains covered until the Caliph commands you to show yourself."

Alric adjusted the headdress and face covering and, with Ahmed, followed Jabir and Khalil. As they walked though the palace, Alric noticed a labyrinth of rooms and corridors leading into alcoves, cloisters, courtyards, and gardens. He caught a glimpse of the gardens in passing, which were laced with rose bowers, dotted with splashing fountains, and ornamented with strutting peacocks. Here, he thought, the Caliph and his entourage could stroll, converse, and relax amid a scene that inspired thought.

After what seemed a considerable time to Alric, they reached the entrance to the Caliph's audience chamber. This was an enormous domed room that could hold hundreds of people. The walls of this chamber were covered with heavy red and gold velvet drapes. Plush red and gold carpets with exotic blue designs were spread across the floor, and delicately embroidered cushions lay on each of the chairs. It seemed that every corner flashed with the sparkle of gold and precious stones.

They followed the steward beyond the audience chamber and passed through several enclosures that were private areas in the palace. Alric felt a twinge of anxiety. Each seemed like a maze from which there was no escape. But the refinement of the galleries and gardens increased as they advanced, and the last of the gardens, adjoining the Caliph's residence, was planted entirely with jasmine and fragrant flowers. Their perfume filled the air. Continuing in the tradition of his father, the Caliph had decorated the residence using silks and tapestries.

On reaching the entrance to the throne room, they were asked to wait as the steward whispered some words to the captain of the Caliph's personal guard. The captain then looked at them, recognized Jabir, and with a slight bow of his head motioned them to follow him.

Alric and the group entered the room into the presence of the Caliph. It was an immense room filled with lamps that were fueled with perfumed oil and threw a soft light around the sumptuous chamber.

On this day, there were less than two dozen courtiers present, each dressed in his own splendor, as if trying to imitate the Caliph. The Caliph wore silk clothes and priceless jewelry. Alric learned later that it was he, Harun al-Rashid, who had adopted the comfortable soft slipper with its upturned toe as standard footwear in the palace.

Servants dressed in scarlet silks were strategically positioned around the room. Each held a tall silver staff. Couches covered with silken cushions framed the room. The captain of the guard, in deference to Lord Jabir, bowed his head and retired with the other officers of the household just beyond the entrance to the room.

Alric knew he was the subject of observation. He was the only stranger in the group. He wondered what the Caliph would think when his fair skin, blond hair, and blue eyes were displayed for all to see.

His hands were moist and he was starting to sweat. He did not dare look up, and then he felt Ahmed's reassuring nudge. All Alric could see were the toes of his shoes as they protruded beyond the *jurbah*—the clean robe that Ahmed had given him to wear after his bathing session.

Alric shook himself back to reality. He had faced death. He had been kidnapped by raiders and survived. He had decided he was willing to start a new life in a strange land.

At that moment, all conversation ceased and the room fell silent. Alric felt eyes boring into the top of his covered head. It was the moment of truth! "*Insha'allah,*" he mumbled to himself. "As God wills it."

* * *

CHAPTER 14

Harun al-Rashid, the Caliph, looked at the visitors, then recognized Jabir and smiled. A group of men were seated on cushions around a table, and the Caliph was in the act of taking a large scroll of paper from a cabinet that contained many such items. Each scroll was in its own separate compartment and, as near as Alric could surmise, seemed to be in some form of order.

"Come in," the Caliph commanded as he returned to his position at the head of the table. He turned to the men who sat nearby on the cushions.

"We will continue," Harun said. "I have no secrets from my uncle and my friends," he said in a matter-of-fact manner.

The Caliph's familiarity did not surprise Alric, since Ahmed had already informed him that Lady Amira, Jabir's wife, was his aunt. Harun al-Rashid looked at Jabir. "Please sit, uncle," he said indicating the other cushions placed at a discreet distance from the table. "We shall be finished soon."

Jabir and Khalil sat on the large comfortable cushions. Ahmed nudged Alric and indicated that they should remain standing, behind Jabir and Khalil.

The Caliph turned his attention once more to the officials as they leaned forward and looked at the documents on the table. As they did this, several of them glanced toward Jabir and Khalil and nodded in recognition as they, in turn, reciprocated.

"The important thing," the Caliph said to his officials, "is to make Charlemagne, the Emperor of the Franks, realize how helpful we can be to one another."

As Harun unrolled the document, Alric saw that it was a map; in fact, it was a map of the world. It was laid on the teakwood table, a weight resting on each corner so that it lay flat.

He observed that the men grouped themselves around the Caliph in a specified order. Each man wore clothes of a slightly different style that indicated his position at the table relative to the Caliph. Ahmed saw Alric's eyes focus on one man in particular, and he took the liberty of whispering in Alric's ear: "Abdul al-Warith. He is First Minister to the Caliph, leader of the cabinet, and adviser to the Caliph. He leads this group of men, in the Caliph's absence."

The First Minister stood to the Caliph's right, and another man, of seemingly equal importance to the First Minister, stood to the Caliph's left. Alric heard Ahmed's quiet voice again: "Ali al-Maslawi, a senior minister in the cabinet and also an adviser to the Caliph. He is from Mosul."

As if hearing Ahmed's whisper, the First Minister glanced at the visitors. The scowl on his face showed Alric his displeasure, perhaps indicating he was not comfortable in their presence and that Jabir and his party had intruded upon a very private session.

Alric was curious about the First Minister, who appeared to look directly at him. Al-Maslawi smiled at Jabir and raised an inquiring eyebrow when he saw Alric. He appeared to be much friendlier.

"That document is a map of the world," Ahmed whispered.

Without noticing this interchange, the Caliph continued to speak as he leaned over the map and allowed his finger to trace the outline of continents, seas, and empires. Alric caught a glimpse of the ornate lettering, the bold lines, and the rich coloring. He wondered how much knowledge and adventure lay in drawing such a map, and he realized that the world was a lot bigger than he had ever imagined—much more than his journey from Britain to Baghdad indicated—and there was a lot of the world he had not seen.

"Here, to the northwest on the Bosphorus, lies Constantinople, capital of the Byzantine Empire," the Caliph pointed out. "The Franks are rivals of the Byzantines, and Charlemagne, King of the Franks, is beholden to me for defeating the Byzantine armies and preventing them from driving west into Europe and then into his kingdom."

"And we shall gain from the pressure exerted by the Franks on Spain," al-Maslawi commented.

"Exactly!" the Caliph exclaimed. "The Umayyad Caliph in Cordova challenges the Abbasid administration for authority in the Islamic world. By invading Spain, Charlemagne has drawn the Umayyad forces from the Middle Sea to the mountains that divide Spain from the land of the Franks. It is my hope that Charlemagne will continue to attack the Umayyad armies on this northern frontier until I can deal with their leaders on my own terms." Alric saw Harun smile knowingly. "I have already sent envoys to Charlemagne," he said, "to make overtures of a partnership and continuing diplomatic relationships." Harun stroked the side of his face. "The preliminary word that I have back by messenger is that such an arrangement sits well with the King of the Franks."

Through his limited experience, Alric had always preferred to maintain a prudent distance from great men, a practice he had been advised to uphold by the abbot, for which there should be no exceptions. He had secretly hoped that he would meet the Caliph at some time, but not so soon after arriving in the city.

"I think, gentlemen, we are finished for the day," Harun said as he looked at each individual member of the cabinet. "Our business is done. I have some visitors who require my attention."

The Caliph's poise impressed Alric. As he moved away from the group, Alric was able to get a better view of him. He saw that Harun's face was framed by an immaculately trimmed beard. He wore a silk tunic that was richly embroidered and decorated with a band of silk inlaid with precious stones. A white knotted turban, with a black band which held it in place, gave the Caliph extra height. His clothes fit to perfection and his elegance was impressive.

The First Minister, seeing that the Caliph was finished with the map, moved toward the visitors and was about to make the formal introductions when the Caliph stepped forward to embrace Jabir, who stood when the Caliph approached him. "My dear uncle, it seems like an eternity since I last saw you. Yesterday was it?" The Caliph chuckled at his own humor as Jabir bowed his head. "How are you?" Harun continued. "And how is my aunt, Amira?" Jabir smiled and informed the Caliph they were both well.

The First Minister looked serious and appeared to be deep in thought, with a dour expression on his face. Harun then turned to him and the officials and said, "I have no further need of you."

They all bowed and began to leave. Alric noticed that as the First Minister turned to leave, his expression was malevolent and clearly directed at Jabir. Alric realized that no one else could see this expression on the First Minister's face. Alric's thoughts were interrupted as the Caliph spoke. "Al-Maslawi."

The man who had stood on the Caliph's left turned and bowed his head in recognition. As his name indicated, he was from Mosul in the north, that very city where Alric had ventured into the marketplace to view the people and the merchants' stalls. "I will have need of you later. Wait and I will send for you."

Al-Maslawi bowed his head again. "I will be ready, sire." He and the other members of the cabinet slowly left the room. The First Minister made a point of being the last to leave, gracefully bowing his head as he closed the door. His expression changed now to one of smiling obeisance.

This man, Alric thought, noting the change, is dangerous and can hide his true feelings within a moment.

Harun addressed Khalil, who bowed. "I see, my cousin, that the life of a soldier is good for you."

"It is being in your service, Sire, which keeps me well," Khalil responded.

"My dear Khalil, there is no need to be so formal," he said laughingly at Khalil's response. "As children we were always close enough to be brothers." Khalil smiled. "And," Harun continued, "my loyal friend, Ahmed. Still keeping my cousin Khalil on the right track I see."

Ahmed bowed deeply. The Caliph had not yet acknowledged Alric, who decided to remain silent and unnoticeable with his head bowed slightly, but not too much, since he wished to watch the proceedings.

Alric was in the presence of the man who had his finger on the most strategic empire the world had seen, and would decide if he, Alric, should live as a slave or as a man of learning. Thoughts, questions, and fears galloped through his mind. How would the Caliph receive him? What would be his destiny? Would the Caliph accept him as a person from another land?

"And now, let us sit so that you may tell me of your journey, Khalil."

Jabir and Khalil sat down on the cushions once more. Alric glanced at Ahmed, who indicated that they should remain standing.

* * *

Alric listened carefully to the conversation as Khalil addressed the Caliph. "Great Caliph, we your servants return to bring you news of the mission on which you sent us. We are grateful to have returned to you."

"It pleases me that you have returned safely, my cousin."

Alric's heart was pounding. He fought to control his breathing, as if the floor were rising to meet him.

"Before we discuss your mission," the Caliph responded, "give me more details about this new one you have brought to my court."

Alric dared not look at the Caliph, but he could sense his eyes boring into the top of his head. He could hear Ahmed's quiet, barely audible commands and kneeled with him before the Caliph. Jabir and Khalil remained seated, their heads bowed in respect. Alric learned that blood relatives or those married to blood relatives were excluded from this form of homage to the Caliph.

"I had word from your brother, and my cousin, Asad," the Caliph said to Khalil, "that there was one such person in your company."

Alric's heart pounded even stronger than before, and he felt that it was about to leave his chest. He remembered Ahmed's words that described the carrier pigeon system of passing messages to the Caliph when they were traveling. Alric then said a quiet prayer and strained his ears so that he would not miss any of the Caliph's words.

"Rise to your feet," the Caliph commanded, "and let me see the new one. Ahmed, have him remove his head and face covering that I may look upon him. He may also look at me." He smiled. "I only hide from the protocols of my courtiers!"

Alric did as the Caliph commanded, even before Ahmed could speak.

"Ah," the Caliph smiled, "it seems the new one knows our language very well. That pleases me!" He paused as he looked at Alric. "I see you are from a northern country. Khalil, tell me how you came by this young man. And," he looked at Ahmed, "you, my loyal friend, have my permission to speak if Khalil indicates it should be so." Harun looked at Alric. "You will remain silent until I give you permission to speak."

Alric bowed his head to show he understood as he struggled with his emotions. He felt as if he wanted to shriek something from his seemingly gagged mouth. His eyes were wide with a mixture of fear and curiosity.

He saw Harun's eyes taking in his appearance but did not see the Caliph's nod of satisfaction. As if remembering something, Harun told Alric and Ahmed to sit and make themselves comfortable. The cushions were arranged in a circle around a small table that was filled with a variety of food—cakes, fruits, tasty meats, and a container filled with hot tea. Jabir sat on the Caliph's right-hand side and Khalil sat on the left. Then Harun indicated two cushions on the opposite side of the table for Ahmed and Alric. "Sit closer to the table," he said to Alric, "so that we do not have to raise our voices."

As the knots that Alric had felt in his stomach were released, he nodded and smiled at the Caliph. His smile was returned. This had not gone unnoticed by Jabir, Khalil, and Ahmed, who were pleased with the positive manner in which Alric had been accepted so far by Harun.

There was a hush as Khalil related their adventures in detail leading up to finding Alric and thence their journey to Baghdad. For the first time, Alric heard about the deaths of the sea raiders. As part of their reconnoitering duties, Khalil and his men had found their way to the beach where the raiders' ship had been thrown ashore by the storm. The raiders had attacked without warning or provocation. The fight had been short, quick, and deadly for the raiders. They had been no match for Khalil's well-disciplined soldiers. Those who had survived the first shower of arrows were dispatched quickly by Khalil's men. True to their culture, none of the raiders had asked for mercy and none had received it. Alric felt a sense of vengeance, and he noted that Khalil related with pride that not one of his men had been lost or severely wounded on this voyage. Several times during the story, the Caliph had clapped his hands as a signal for servants to bring fresh tea.

Alric was able to follow most of Khalil's words, even though he and Harun had conversed in rapid Arabic which was colored by a slight accent Alric did not recognize. After Khalil had finished, he nodded to Alric. All was set for him to begin his account of the journey. He steeled himself for the task ahead, focused his eyes, and gazed toward the Caliph as he moved to stand up.

"You may remain seated," Harun said to ease the tension he sensed in Alric. This was Alric's moment. He took the book from his pouch and laid it on the table. "From the size of the book that you carry," the Caliph continued, speaking slowly in deference to Alric, "this may take us quite some time. I understand from what Khalil has told me that you have written the book in the language of the Romans. Other than my uncle Jabir, Khalil, and Ahmed, I have no one at court that is really fluent in that language sufficiently well to translate such works as are written in Latin. My uncle, Khalil, and Ahmed have other duties that do not give them the time to learn to translate. So I find your abilities to read and speak the Latin language to be very interesting. Perhaps it might be useful?"

Alric bowed his head in acknowledgment, though his mouth was dry with apprehension. He took the book in his hands, licked his lips, and started to translate his story. He found that simultaneously reading Latin and translating into Arabic came easily. Easier than he had imagined! All the while, Alric could feel the Caliph's eyes on him as he read. Soon, his voice became strong and clear. There were no tortured sounds that he had feared might occur and embarrass him.

There were no interruptions, and when he finished he could see from the Caliph's expression that his words had been followed. He was delighted with his performance. He arose with a feeling of relief that the task was completed and bowed to the Caliph. Jabir remained seated while Khalil and Ahmed rose and stood on either side of Alric. There followed a prolonged silence during which he remained motionless, the book closed in his hands.

"Excellent," the Caliph's one simple but meaningful word broke the silence.

* * *

By this time, the sun had descended, and daylight was disappearing quickly. Unnoticed as he read from his book, servants had lit torches which cast light into the shadowy room. The flames flickered and swirled, producing tendrils of smoke that curled toward the ceiling and disappeared outdoors through strategically placed vents in the ceiling. The torches flared as the flames consumed the oily fuel. Alric wondered if it was an omen. Even in the flickering torchlight, the Caliph's smile was plain for Alric to see.

"I have been told of your abilities," the Caliph said, "but I needed to witness them for myself. I am pleased with what you have written and related to me. My thanks to you, Khalil," he turned to Ahmed, "and to you, Ahmed, as I understand you have been Alric's *mu'al-alim*. Your efforts in teaching this young man have been well received and, as you can see, he is a good student."

Harun al-Rashid thought for a moment and then clapped his hands. Servants appeared with bread that was still warm from the oven, butter, and an assortment of sweetmeats, nuts, and fresh milk. "Come, tea makes me hungry! Let us eat," Harun commanded as he looked at Alric, "and we will discuss your future. Let us all sit," he motioned to Alric and Ahmed, who remained standing. "I would like to examine your book closely. The words and letters of the Roman writing have always fascinated me. I am very curious about other languages, as I consider them to contain other forms of learning."

Alric looked at Khalil, wondering if he could have direct contact with the Caliph. Khalil nodded, and Alric passed his book to Harun and then once again sat on the luxurious cushion. By this time, Jabir, Khalil, and Ahmed were beaming. In addition to their delight over Alric's performance, they were overjoyed at seeing the fresh bread, which neither of them had eaten since they'd departed from Baghdad almost twelve months before. Alric's eyes devoured the loaf.

187

"*Shukran*," he said as he settled himself onto the cushion. He breathed deeply, catching his breath after the reading marathon.

"Please, my friends, eat! Do not wait for me." By these words, Harun excused his guests from the formalities of only eating when he ate. "I will look at Alric's book and ask questions as we refresh ourselves." Harun opened the book and addressed Alric.

"I see this is paper made here in our country," he stated.

"Yes, Caliph," Alric responded. "It was purchased for me by Lord Khalil." Alric felt relaxed and helped himself to the fresh bread and butter as the Caliph examined his book.

The Caliph then plied Alric with many questions regarding the shapes of the letters and the meanings of the words. Servants appeared quietly and made sure that drinks were poured, and constantly brought silver platters heaped with food. Behind the cushions, now that the conversation was over, household servants and retainers stood quietly. The retainers were large men, wearing white shirts and white pantaloons with a red sash around the waist into which was tucked a massive scimitar. As he ate the dates, Alric regarded his situation very carefully.

"Do you have any other names than Alric?" Harun's words broke into Alric's thoughts.

"I have been called only 'Alric,' Caliph."

"Obviously, you have been educated?"

"Yes, Caliph, the monks in the monastery at Wearmouth taught me to read, write, and understand numbers, as well as to speak and read Latin and the languages of the Celts and sea raiders. They also started to teach me the art of healing and the location of the organs of the body."

"Wearmouth? In Britain? The land across the sea from the land of the Franks? Is that the place of your birth?" The Caliph asked.

"Yes, Caliph."

"Come," the Caliph rose from his cushion and indicated the work table. "Khalil, if you please." They all rose and walked to the table, where Harun retrieved another map from his collection. As he laid it on the table, he said to Khalil: "Trace your journey for me on the map and then Alric can show me where you think Wearmouth is located." They did as the Caliph asked. Harun stoked his chin with his forefinger for a moment. "I have seen men and women of your coloring before, but never this close. Are you all the same from that area?"

"Not all the same, Caliph. Some have darker hair. There are also men and women of my coloring from here." Alric used his forefinger to indicate on the map the general area of northern Europe and Scandinavia. "In fact, this area," Alric pointed to northern Europe again, "was called Germania by the Romans."

"Was it not here where Caesar, the great Roman general, campaigned?"

"That was a little farther to the west, Caliph." Alric pointed to the area that was now occupied by the Franks and had been known as Gaul in the time of Caesar.

"I am also told that you bear signs that have some meaning to us. Let me see." Alric was unaware that the Caliph had so much information about him and was amazed to learn this. He then rolled up the sleeve of his jurbah so the Caliph could see the two birthmarks. "It is as if you were meant to bridge the Christian religion with our faith. Those two marks," the Caliph gestured to the mark that was shaped like a crescent, "are becoming a sign of our faith."

The Caliph paused for a moment. "You have given me much to think about, Alric," he said. He looked at Khalil. "Let us return to our seats for the refreshments."

Jabir and Ahmed had stood silently through the discourse between the Caliph, Khalil, and Alric. When they were all seated at the table, the Caliph sipped his tea before continuing the conversation. "I see, Ahmed, my friend," the Caliph exclaimed as Ahmed reached for more bread and fresh butter, "that you have enjoyed the fresh bread after your travels." Ahmed nodded and smiled. "We have more if you wish, and fresh tea."

Servants appeared instantly, carrying more of the delicious bread and butter and another full container of hot steaming tea. Harun looked at Alric. "In terms of your future, Alric, do you have a preference?" he asked. Surprised at the direct question, Alric felt puzzled, unsure of how to answer. Harun repeated his question. "What would you like to do, if given the choice?"

"Medicine, Caliph." Alric's response was immediate. "I have a passion for healing the sick. Also, being able to cut into a sick person and bring him or her to good health through *chirurgiae* is a dream I have had many times." Alric saw the Caliph's eyebrows rise as he tried to fathom the meaning of the Latin word, and Alric added quickly, "*Chirurgiae*. Surgery, Caliph."

Jabir spoke an Arabic word that was unknown to Alric, and Harun nodded, suddenly understanding the meaning. "Is this so? Surgery?"

"Yes, Caliph."

The Caliph's eyes flickered with interest. "You have ambition, Alric. I like that, but ambition can be a dangerous thing." He looked at Jabir. "Uncle, if you please."

They leaned toward each other, heads together so that the Caliph's lips were masked from Alric. The whispered conversation was serious. "Tell me, Alric," Harun said as he looked directly at him. "Do you fear God?"

"Yes, Caliph."

"Do you fear me?"

Alric took a deep breath before answering. "No, Caliph," he said after careful thought. "But I do fear what you might do to me if I prove to be unworthy."

"A good answer, Alric." Harun leaned forward, his eyes boring into Alric. "What else has caught your attention?" he asked.

Alric smiled as the thought came back to him. "I am fascinated by the language of the stones, Caliph. It is the language that I have called *cunei forma*. The writing of the wedge shapes."

"Excellent! That is where I see you being extremely valuable. From what I have been told, your skill with languages and your ability to learn a language quickly is of great value. Now," Harun paused, "listen carefully."

He spoke a series of words in Sumerian completely at random. There were more than twenty words in all, spoken quickly but clearly. He looked at Alric. "Repeat them in the order I have given you." Harun sipped his fruit juice and nodded at Alric, signifying he should begin when ready.

Carefully, Alric spoke the words in the correct order and pronounced them the very same way. The Caliph smiled at Jabir and nodded his appreciation. "Your instincts were correct, uncle," he said and then turned to face Alric. "Tell me, Alric, do you know the meaning of the words?"

"No, Caliph." Alric felt his face flush.

"No cause for shame, Alric. I was merely giving you the description of your future. It has been suggested to me," Harun continued, "by my men of learning that the language of the stones, the language that you have seen fit to call *cunei forma*, holds the secrets of medicine and science. Therefore, it is my decision that you will be assigned to a guardian. He will teach you the art and science of medicine and surgery and will start you along the path of learning the language of the stones. This language has been known to some of my people for many years, but those with this knowledge are old, and much has not been passed on, there being few suitable candidates."

The Caliph paused to make sure he was being understood. The excited look in Alric's eyes gave him the answer. "You will," Harun continued, "be assigned to a learned man as his apprentice. He will be your master and you will obey him as you would obey me. Lord Khalil and Ahmed will also be watching you to estimate your progress, and they, along with your new master, will report to me. Your new master is my uncle, the renowned physician Jabir, who is the father of my cousin Lord Khalil, the husband of my aunt Amira, the sister of my mother."

Alric could not have hoped for better. He stood up and bowed to Harun and smiled in his appreciation of the Caliph's decision. Sit," the Caliph commanded. Alric obeyed, but felt more like jumping for joy. "You will," Harun continued, "learn the skills of medicine and surgery as are known and then begin learning the language of the *cunei forma*. If you prove adept at the language, you may accompany Lord Jabir on his many travels. You will also try to learn as many languages as you can. I seek additional volumes for the library that I am building only a short distance from this palace. It is my decision that you will assist in the translation of the many volumes that become available so they can be read in the Arabic language."

Alric nodded, barely able to conceal his excitement. "You seem pleased, Alric. Learn well and you will have many years of enjoyable service." The Caliph sipped the last of his fruit juice and looked thoughtfully at Alric, Khalil, and Ahmed. "Do you have anything you wish to add?" he asked.

"No, Sire," they voiced in unison.

"Well, we are finished here. My uncle will keep me informed with regular reports of Alric's progress and work. I will also expect to see Alric here at the palace on occasion so that I may talk with him and make my own determinations of his progress. That is my decision. My aunt Amira awaits you."

"But," the Caliph waved a finger in the air, "before you leave, I have need of your confidence. You heard my conversation with the First Minister and the officials of my government. I have reason to believe that one close to me has made overtures to the Umayyad administration, not so much for beliefs, but to satisfy his own ends. I have my suspicions, but rather than influence your minds, I ask that you be watchful for such a person and help me identify this man." The Caliph's face was serious. "Using your own methods, find this person and report to me. If we reach the same conclusion, we shall act."

The Caliph clapped his hands and a servant appeared. "Find Minister al-Maslawi and bring him to me. There is much that he and I need to discuss. Lord Jabir, I also have need of your presence in this meeting."

* * *

CHAPTER 15

As they walked along the various passageways that led to the palace gate and the outside world, Alric was troubled. Yet it had been a good day. But the Caliph's final warning was disturbing, and the First Minister seemed to be a man who should be watched. There was something about the man that caused Alric to distrust him. The precise reason was not evident but perhaps with time . . .

* * *

When Harun was meeting with Jabir, Khalil, Ahmed, and Alric, the First Minister retired to the private room the Caliph had assigned to him. It was a good time to organize his papers, or so he, Abdul al-Warith, thought. But he was so furious that he was trembling. The Caliph had shown a preference for that interfering fool, Ali al-Maslawi, from the northern city of Mosul.

Abdul al-Warith was First Minister to the Caliph and *de facto* leader of the Caliph's government. In all aspects of the government, he was responsible for policy and, with the exception of the Caliph, was the only person who had the power to enact or cancel legislation. He felt that he should be present every time the Caliph talked with others.

Elizabeth James

Abdul was not a large man, being only of average build. His dark eyes never seemed to lose their intensity. A short, well-groomed beard covered his chin and framed his thin hard mouth. He was a man of conflicting moods, sometimes showing a gentle nature; but there were times he would terrify others by his anger. Most of all, it was his cunning nature that was feared by those who knew him.

He had been dismissed as if he were a mere servant. The more he thought about it, the more irritated he grew. Abdul was furious. He had been sure that the Caliph would include him in all of the meetings, but to be excluded from this one! It was the new one who had accompanied Jabir who had fascinated him the most and made him suspicious. The Caliph had mentioned that he was ready to form an alliance with that other barbarian, Charlemagne, King of the Franks. Could this new one have anything to do with that?

This only made Abdul's humor worsen and he became even more disagreeable. He took his frustrations out on his assistant. The man had only been doing his job but was told he would be dismissed for negligence, have a hand severed for stealing, and even worse, be beheaded for talking too much. On hearing these threats, the assistant decided he would leave for the day. He may be punished when he returned on the morrow, but hoped otherwise.

Abdul had been suspicious when he'd heard of the return of Khalil and his soldiers. The word was that Khalil had been exploring part of the land that lay within the Kingdom of the Franks. Abdul did not like this, especially when he heard that the Caliph had already sent envoys to the Frankish court. He was annoyed beyond measure by the Caliph's insistence on an arrangement with the Franks. He had almost been unable to restrain an indignant comment regarding arrangements with the barbarians. However, he had managed to maintain a difficult silence until he had been ushered out of the room with the others.

He had sat at his desk for hours wondering if he would be called back by the Caliph, but it was not to be. He needed help with some

196

papers, and now that fool he called an assistant had disappeared. Abdul realized that control by fear was one of his own personal characteristics that he enjoyed!

He toyed with the idea of visiting Ali al-Maslawi at his nearby home to give him an attitude adjustment. "What could that fool from Mosul do," he asked himself, "that I, Abdul al-Warith, First Minister to the Caliph, could not do?"

Then he dismissed the idea as being beneath his station. A superior never visited the home of, or made an effort to visit, an inferior. He did not like to miss anything, but he reasoned that there was little to be accomplished by remaining in his office. He extended his arms and flexed his fingers to relax his tensed body. Then he summoned the men of his private bodyguard and left the palace for his house, which was close by, within the city wall. The Caliph had smiled indulgently when he'd heard of al-Warith hiring private bodyguards. The First Minister was of a social and professional station that meant he would be recognized and had nothing to fear if he chose to walk the streets alone. But Abdul had other ideas.

In the area around the palace, a crowd had gathered. The people had collected to welcome back Khalil's soldiers and now had decided to enjoy the cool evening air while making the most of the food that the vendors sold. Their stalls were placed on the outskirts of the palace square and in the gate arcades.

Abdul's mood lightened as he approached his house. The tree-lined avenue held the scent of blossoms to the pleasure of those who walked by. He liked nothing more than this walk, suitably protected by guards in the shadow of the trees. A narrow canal ran along the avenue, giving the First Minister a sense of peace at least. He could hear the soothing sound of babbling water. This was his favorite time; the coolness of the evening after the heat of the day was always a pleasure.

Without a word, he left the guards at the gate to his house and entered his garden. The garden was a delight. Reflecting pools bordered with pebbles were surrounded by beds of delicately scented flowers. Colorful fish, the sunlight catching their movements, darted about the ornamental pools. Those approaching the entrance to the house and gardens were met by the scent of jasmine in the air.

The First Minister did not notice his surroundings that evening as he marched into the house. He went immediately to wash and change his clothes. Feeling more refreshed, he made his way to his study, bright and welcoming, where he recalled the recent events of the day. It was here that he occupied most of his time when not at the palace.

He took care of the royal properties in Baghdad and supervised the collection of the multitude of tax levies on them. He made sure that all of the rents and commercial obligations, as well as fines for petty crimes, were paid to the Caliph's treasury in a timely fashion.

Although most of his duties were carried out at the palace, Abdul never turned anyone away from his house. Visitors were checked by the well-armed guards and allowed access only after they were searched for weapons. The First Minister liked nothing better than private conversations with rich business men and moneyed landowners, often done in secret. Abdul was a whole-hearted believer in having treasure on earth!

They were received in his study only after they had been thoroughly investigated. Money, titles, as well as family blood lines, were all part of the investigation. They were given tea as they sat on fine cushions scattered on patterned carpets of exquisite design. "One never knows," the First Minister had told himself many times, "when one needs a friend."

Satisfied that he had thought out the problems arising from the meeting with the Caliph and his dismissal, they were not so serious that they could not be overcome. He made his way to his day room, which was also his lounge and entertainment room. He sat heavily on the cushions and stared at the old man sitting calmly on the cushion opposite. Abdul clapped his hands impatiently to summon a servant. "Tea!"

The servant, at the tone of the First Minister's voice, disappeared quickly into the darkness beyond the curtains. Almost immediately, a woman dressed in fine silk clothes appeared and set the tea and utensils carefully on the small table between the First Minister and the old man. She placed glasses before them, which she filled with the rich red-brown liquid, after which she placed the pot on a high-standing metal trivet. A low flame fueled by fragrant oil burned from below the trivet.

The woman would take her place behind the curtains and observe the two men through the narrow space between the drapes. This allowed her to monitor the proceedings and then step forward silently to replenish the tea.

The First Minister looked at the woman, grabbed her arm, smiled viciously, and said in an unmistakable tone. "I will have need of you later."

It was a command. She bowed her head in obedience and nodded to show she understood. She trembled, unnoticed by the First Minister but observed by the old man. She knew exactly what the First Minister meant. He would take out his anger and frustration on her.

Her name was Maria. She had been sent to the First Minister as a gift from his Umayyad contact in her home country of Spain. The day of her arrival at the First Minister's house, he had told her she was his to do with as he pleased. If she complained or failed to show compliance, she would be thrown into the street to fend for herself in the seedier areas of the city. He had added that he knew of several soldiers who would enjoy her company.

But Maria was different from any of the other women the First Minister had entertained. She had never attempted to take advantage of her position in his house. He could do with her as he wished and she never complained or attempted to leave. It was almost too good to be true. And al-Warith was determined to enjoy her company, as long as he felt he had total control.

He looked at the liquid in the glass, lifted it to his mouth, and drank the tea. The old man sipped his drink. "It is time," he said to the old man, "to find a way to prevent the Caliph from retaining absolute authority."

The old man placed his glass carefully on the table and looked at Abdul calmly. He spoke in a low voice; his tones were calm and reassuring. "Of course, no one must know this, but I will tell you that the Caliph, true to his forefathers, follows the line of succession. There are those who adamantly believe that the Caliph's successor must be of his line. Do you think it wise . . . ?"

"Do not question my motives," Abdul snarled though his clenched teeth. His frustrations were returning. "I am not talking of a line of succession!" he exclaimed indignantly. "That would put me out of the line of power! I govern the kingdom. I make the laws and I meet ambassadors from other countries. It is only right that the throne should be mine!"

Trying to temper the emotionalism of the First Minister, the old man said, "I advise that you proceed with caution. If your actions are observed, it would leave you open to the most severe retribution." The old man smiled wryly. "Are you more interested in what you perceive to be your future power, or are you more worried about being taken to task over some financial issues? Or even perhaps some issues that involve many women, some of whom were under the Caliph's protection?"

The First Minister disapproved of the old man's words, speaking to him as if he were a commoner or a person of no consequence. He quickly perceived that this conversation had taken a wrong turn, and morality had no place in the discussion. "I advise that you not mention any of my habits again or as sure as you are my father you will suffer horribly before you die!"

The old man picked up the glass and sipped his tea to hide the fear and loathing he felt for his son. Abdul had forgotten the means by which he rose to power and had lost allegiance to his family. The old man looked down as he swirled the tea in the glass, contemplated it for a moment, and then carefully drank the remaining liquid. This man that I fathered, the old man thought, trusts no one. His greed and folly surpassed even those of the man they called Alexander, who foolishly tried to conquer the known world. "Obviously, you do not need help from me, my son," the old man said, raising himself from the cushions.

"I know where to reach you," the First Minister said. "Be available if I call. I may have need of you."

"I understand," he said. He was not eager to be available to his son. "I will await your call." The old man had no intention of putting himself in danger. He had survived several awkward situations in the past and had no wish to become embroiled in another plot. He left without saying anything further.

Each was eager to be away from the other. The old man had not expected to be drawn into his son's scheme, and he had suspected treachery, but not of this magnitude. His son would indeed have to pay the ultimate price if his ill-conceived plot were discovered. However, by promising to be available, he had just arranged for safe conduct that would protect him from the wrath of either side in the forthcoming conflict. He gave himself one week to put his affairs in order and then he would depart for a healthier climate. He began to feel relieved and smiled as he made his way through the streets to his home.

Meanwhile, at his house, the First Minister felt more comfortable. There were many voices on the council, even though the Caliph had been explicit in his appointment of him as a first among equals with the authority to make the decisions. There were those on the council who would form an impenetrable barrier if he were perceived to have thoughts of personal gain in mind—Ali al-Maslawi in particular, the

First Minister thought, who might be thought of by other council members as an unofficial leader of the group.

He rose from the cushions, immediately ordered all of the lamps to be extinguished, and went to the roof terrace to lie down. His head was starting to throb, and there seemed to be flashes of light before his eyes. He did not wish to aggravate his condition by toying with the woman. She would be called later, when he felt better.

He lay on the cushions that had been prepared earlier and started to relax, the pain diminishing. As he looked at the starry sky, he fell asleep and dreamed of untold power, being arrayed in the robes of a Caliph.

* * *

The First Minister was given the name Abdul al-Warith, Servant of the Supreme Inheritor, at birth. As a boy he had been known to instigate serious mischief and watch happily while other boys took the blame. He was born into money and was contented with his situation in life.

At some time during his early twenties, as near as could be told from conversation with others, he'd had a series of dreams. The dreams had occurred every night for a week. Unfortunately, those who'd heard his words—confessions, if they might be called that—had long since died of various mysterious and unknown ailments. Even as a young man, the First Minister did not like to leave a trail!

He'd dreamt that a venerable old man came to him and, with a severe look, reprimanded him for not having made a pilgrimage to Mecca. As a good Muslim, the First Minister knew that it was his duty to undertake such a pilgrimage. He knew he would make the pilgrimage someday, but of late his thoughts had turned to his future. Being from a wealthy family, he had the power of money, but he longed for absolute power. He would achieve this one day. When that day came, he would make the pilgrimage and renew his faith. By then, he reasoned, he could afford to be a *hajji*, one who had made the pilgrimage, and would have so much money that a little philanthropy here and there would ensure his place in the community and, more important, in Paradise.

He'd converted half of his holdings to cash that he'd invested in a series of carefully chosen trade caravans, much to his father's dismay because of the risk. He used the other half of the money to buy buildings, mostly for the land on which they stood, in and around the immediate vicinity of the palace. He reasoned that as the palace became more and more magnificent, he would sell the land at a great profit. He told no one of his scheme and was on tenterhooks while the first caravan was on the road to and from Mecca. He became successful. After several more successes, he was known throughout the city as a substantial man. By that time, some of his close confidants had died from various ailments.

Unknown to many, Abdul had taken a wife when he was a young man. Her name was Kalila, she was the daughter of a Baghdad merchant, a widower, and her dowry added much to his wealth. Being the only child, Kalila would inherit her father's trading business upon his death. But to cover all eventualities, Abdul had already formed a partnership with his father-in-law, Fayyad, and the joint business was very prosperous.

Just prior to the departure of one caravan to Mecca, Fayyad expressed the wish to travel with the other merchants. Kalila tried to dissuade him, but Abdul seemed overly enthusiastic in his encouragement of Fayyad to follow his wish. It was one of those fateful caravans that never reached its destination. An attack by warlike Bedouin tribesmen destroyed the caravan and killed all of the travelers, Fayyad among them. Kalila went into mourning. Abdul was ecstatic. He had just increased his wealth more than twofold! At the first opportunity, he paid the remainder of the fee to the mercenaries he had hired to pose as the Bedouins.

In the meantime, Kalila became suspicious. The failure of her husband to mourn the death of her father in the appropriate manner was, she decided, not natural.

As time passed, she became more convinced that her husband had been involved in the destruction of the caravan and her father's death. Several bags had been delivered to their home, and upon examining these, she found them full of trade items that were supposed to have been shipped in the destroyed caravan. When she confronted Abdul with her thoughts, his response was simple: "I am no robber or murderer. Instead of accusing me of such crimes, you should rejoice with me at the continued success of the business. Silly woman, how long will you continue to mourn the death of your father? You should tell no one of your thoughts. In the wrong hands, they could destroy us."

As Kalila pondered her husband's words, she became more and more aware that something was wrong. Everything always seemed to go his way. She had talked with her friends, without her husband knowing, and heard rumors about her husband's business dealings and associated actions.

Unfortunately for Kalila, Abdul had visited one of her friends for something more than tea and cake. When the woman told Abdul of Kalila's suspicions, Kalila's days were numbered. Abdul made it known that Kalila, because of a recurring tiredness, had decided to journey with a close friend to the coast of the Middle Sea, where she could experience the fresh sea air. Abdul was clever enough to arrange for witnesses to see the two women depart from his house in the company of six well-armed retainers. However, the witnesses did not realize that the two heavily garbed women were actually Bedouin men who had already killed Kalila and her friend, whose corpses were providing fodder for the garden flowers. It was announced shortly afterward that Kalila and her friend had disappeared on the road to the coast. When the bodies of the six retainers were discovered, there were no signs of

Kalila and her friend. Everyone feared the worst. Abdul immediately went into the pretense of mourning to express his sorrow.

From that time on, Abdul decided he would never remarry. He had a better time with the servants than he had ever had with his wife; besides, his wife had been on the point of betraying him.

Thus, Abdul al-Warith had begun his nefarious relationships with women that would not change for the remainder of his life.

* * *

After a further series of financial successes and, surprisingly, no financial setbacks, his journey to Mecca came earlier than he had expected. When the duties of his pilgrimage were completed, he returned quickly to Baghdad, arranging bargains all the way so that his caravans would travel protected and unmolested, whereas the caravans of others would receive considerable attention from bandits. Then, having a desire to see the world, he went to cities spread throughout the Islamic world. His journey occupied four years of his life, in which he had established trading partners. More important, he had made contacts with the Umayyad faction in Cordova and heard their unsettled cries for independence from the Abbasid caliphs.

Abdul was exceedingly careful to preserve his reputation. He refused to admit to himself that in his heart he was a slave to avarice. Like all other covetous men, he was only as honest as his interest obliged him to be. He would be subservient to any superior but would bully those under him.

As his fortune grew, his greed became even greater. The Umayyad family had offered him a high position in their would-be government when the new Caliph, Harun al-Rashid, was either forced to abdicate or died, and the Umayyads were not concerned which event came first!

Abdul made several more trips to Cordova to cement his relationship with the splinter group and had also lined the pockets of several notables with gold so that they would support him, whatever his actions.

After the last visit to Cordova, he felt comfortable about his future. He had been extremely careful to leave no proof of his negotiations and reasoned that his immaculate behavior in Baghdad would bear him out against any rumors.

* * *

When Harun al-Rashid had succeeded to his father's throne as the Caliph, he became the spiritual and secular leader of all who followed Islam. Harun had heard of Abdul's financial successes and, knowing what he planned for construction throughout Mesopotamia, decided that this a man with money and management experience was useful to him. Within the week, Abdul was appointed a financial adviser, and within two years he had risen to the exalted post of First Minister. Before Abdul's appointment, there were several members of the Caliph's governing council who were also considered likely candidates for the post of First Minister. Unfortunately, they either died of mysterious fevers or disappeared as they journeyed across the desert in caravans that were fated to be attacked.

Abdul continued to pander to the Caliph and remove any potential opposition while he feathered his nest with the Umayyads. He managed to cultivate good relations with the Caliph, who listened attentively to his words.

* * *

However, lately and unknown to Abdul al-Warith, suspicions about his wrongdoing had been raised to the level of the Caliph. There were stories that involved the mysterious disappearance of several foreign-born women, and Harun's intuition told him that something was not right!

Baghdad was a city to which not only scholars but all visitors were welcomed, and the Caliph, in an attempt to right the wrongs of the past, guaranteed protection for them. He also decreed that there should be no discrimination against, or misuse of, women. To ensure adherence to this decree, all visitors, servants, and slaves were required to register with the Caliph's police.

Recently, the commander of the police had brought it quietly to the Caliph's attention that the whereabouts of some of the women were unknown; the police could not find any trace of them. They were all of different backgrounds but had one common thread. They had been sent or brought to Baghdad from those parts of Europe under the control of the Umayyad family. With further investigation, the Caliph had come to suspect that through a series of sales that might well be bogus, the women had eventually ended up in the house of his First Minister, Abdul al-Warith.

Unknown to anyone, the Caliph had the First Minister followed. Suspecting this, the First Minister had taken precautions not to step out of line, but he had crossed the point of no return. It was too late to turn back.

The Caliph ordered his police to work undetected and not get too close to the First Minister, lest he become even more suspicious and close down all of his plans. Harun knew that his attention to Abdul's activities was an extremely fine line. Even though he had indulged the First Minister's request and allowed him to employ his own private bodyguards, Harun knew that countermanding his own order would arouse al-Warith's suspicions.

Harun's thoughts had turned to the ways in which he might discover more about al-Warith's activities. If the man, being alone, just needs the company of women, that was his choice, but if he mistreated women and even had them killed, that was an offense punishable by death, even for a minister in the cabinet. Harun had thought long and hard about this and reached his decision with help from an unexpected quarter.

He had received a message that a woman had approached one of his ambassadors as he traveled through North Africa. The woman had seemingly been making her way to Baghdad with the purpose of requesting an audience with the Caliph. When the ambassador had heard her story, he had found it hard to believe. Fortunately he was not a supporter of Abdul al-Warith, and the woman had made sure of that by well-chosen questions before she told the ambassador her story. But she need not have worried. The ambassador was the son of a sister to Amira and Harun's mother, making him a full cousin to the Caliph.

Harun was informed as soon as the message could be carried to him by a relay of pigeons. The woman, Maria, had a simple request, and that was to be lodged in the house of the First Minister to discover the fate of her sister, who had disappeared from that very house two years prior. Maria was tall and elegant, and very much the type of woman that al-Warith sought for his pleasure.

Harun had been loathe to agree to send the woman into such danger, possibly death if his suspicions were well founded, but he had decided to interview the woman to determine if she was telling the truth. Maria arrived with the ambassador, and her identity and visit to the palace were kept a close secret.

Harun grudgingly granted her wish and she was sent as a gift to Abdul, ostensibly from the Umayyads. She was welcomed to Abdul's house and was able to observe al-Warith's activities and to report on any wrongdoings.

Harun had instructed his police to assist her when needed. So far, the danger to her seemed minimal, but indications of al-Warith's brutality gave the Caliph concern for Maria's safety.

It was not the time to take action yet, but Harun knew that he needed to consult his closest relatives and friends—Jabir and his family.

He would not give too much away. He preferred they each reach their own conclusions.

*   *   *

It was into this world of political intrigue, simmering conflict, and skullduggery that Alric arrived. It was far different from the world of the monks. He was a newcomer and was not skilled in the behavior and opinions of the politicians. That was about to change.

He remembered vividly the malevolent look on the face of the First Minister as he was dismissed from the Caliph's presence. Alric sensed that all was not well; that something was afoot.

*   *   *

CHAPTER 16

Before they left the palace, Khalil suggested to Alric that he should cover his head and face even though the walk to Jabir's house was short. They reached the house after only a few minutes. Jabir, being a government official, was superseded in station by his wife Amira, aunt to the Caliph, which gave them the privilege of living in an area designated for a relative of the Caliph.

Alric was astounded at the size of the house and the surrounding grounds. The building was situated inside a large courtyard with a fountain in the center. Beyond the courtyard, there were lush, fragrantly scented floral gardens. As they passed through the vestibule, Khalil and Ahmed dropped their face coverings, and Khalil bade Alric do the same.

Alric's eyes opened wide at the splendor. Colorful carpets hung on whitewashed walls. The marble floors were strewn with heavy plush carpets. Charcoal braziers were placed at regular intervals to drive away the evening chill. Servants bustled about, greeting Khalil and Ahmed, and when they noticed Alric, their expressions turned to open-mouthed surprise at the sight of his blond hair and blue eyes.

Ahmed decided to show Alric the layout of the house. Numerous rooms fed off the central colonnaded walkway that surrounded the courtyard. Each room had a different use, and then Alric detected a delightful aroma.

Ahmed smiled. "Your nose has found the kitchen!"

This room was in one corner of the colonnade, and as they approached, the aroma of roast lamb filled the air. Next to the kitchen was a storage room filled with amphorae. Each amphora was supported by a metal stand, and they were arranged in rows. Ahmed saw the curious look on Alric's face. "This is where the water we drink is rendered harmless," Ahmed said. "River water can cause a sickness of the stomach, so Lord Jabir has the water prepared here." Alric's curiosity increased. "The water is good. Wahid, our house manager, fills the amphorae with water from the well behind the house, and it is allowed to percolate out through the wall of the amphora, where it runs down the side of the vessel into a collector. The process gives the water a sparkling look and fresh taste. In this manner, Lord Jabir keeps the family and servants free from the water sickness."

An older man emerged from the kitchen. He had, by Alric's estimation, seen at least sixty summers. His skin was dark olive and his features aquiline. A smile creased his face as he saw Ahmed.

"Wahid, my old friend, how are you?" Ahmed asked.

"Much better now that you have returned safely," Wahid responded. "And how is Lord Khalil?"

"He is well, Wahid. I believe that he seeks Lady Amira." Wahid looked at Alric. "This young man, Wahid," Ahmed explained, "is from the island called Britain that lies in the northern part of the Western Ocean. The Caliph has appointed Alric to be an assistant to Lord Jabir."

Wahid looked at Alric. "So that means . . . ?" Wahid left the question unfinished.

"Yes," Ahmed responded quickly. "There will be more work and associated smells from the laboratory!"

"This is Wahid," Ahmed explained to Alric. "He served as my guardian to Lord Khalil when he was young and when Lord Jabir was traveling. In this household his word is law, and you will obey him as you obey me and my father."

Alric nodded and said, "It will be so."

Wahid raised an eyebrow.

"Yes, Wahid," Ahmed added, "Alric is fluent in our tongue."

Wahid's face took on a friendlier look. "If you are ready, Ahmed, Lady Amira awaits you in her lounge and she is very curious to meet our new guest!"

Ahmed nodded. He knew that Wahid had been sent to find them after she had greeted Khalil and welcomed him home. They followed Wahid across the courtyard and into the family quarters. The doorway was draped with a brightly colored carpet. He lifted the carpet to one side and announced his presence, then stepped inside, followed by Ahmed and Alric.

They entered a heavily carpeted room lit by tallow lamps hung in wall sconces and in chandeliers that hung from the ceiling. The room smelled of incense that smoldered in cones in the corners of the room. Thick books bound in leather lay on a table.

Khalil was seated with an older woman that Alric knew must be Amira, wife of Jabir and aunt of the Caliph. She was seated elegantly on a cushion and was wearing a jeweled scarf and a veil of white silk. Three young women sat behind her, and they too were veiled. They looked at Alric, and seeing his blond hair and blue eyes, cast their eyes downward and giggled amongst themselves.

"Allah's blessings, mother," Ahmed said once they were in the room. Wahid stood dutifully to one side.

Amira smiled with delight at seeing Ahmed. "Welcome home, my son. I hope that you are well. Khalil has been telling me of your adventures?" Amira raised herself from the cushion and embraced Ahmed, who, in return, kissed her cheek.

Alric was surprised at her diminutive stature. When Amira stood up, the top of her head was barely level with Ahmed's shoulder, and Ahmed was not quite Alric's height! Her jet black hair was flecked with gray and her dark brown eyes gave her a look of mystery. He could not tell her age. Her fingernails were manicured to perfection, and when she turned toward him, there was the delightful fragrance of jasmine which touched and penetrated his nostrils.

"And this young man with you is our guest?" she asked, looking with interest and curiosity at Alric.

Khalil smiled and looked at Ahmed, knowing that his mother's intelligence system, as they called her carrier pigeons, would have kept her fully informed.

"If I may, brother, I will answer that question," Khalil said.

Ahmed nodded his head, smiling. Alric noticed that in the home the formal manner in which Khalil and Ahmed addressed each other was no longer used.

"I sense that you already know of him, mother," Khalil responded, his face creased by a broad grin. "Did not my respected brother, Asad, send you notice by pigeon?" Amira smiled and playfully slapped her son's shoulder before he continued. "This young man, mother, is Alric from the northeastern coast of the island that we know as Britain." He raised his eyebrows. "I am sure that you have already noted its position on the map! Alric came to us by way of sea raiders who had captured him on the beach near his home. I understand they were taking him to their land to be sacrificed."

Alric stood timorously before Lady Amira, wondering what to do and trying to study her without staring. He bowed his head. The young women giggled again but were silenced by a wave of Amira's hand.

"It is my pleasure to meet you, Lady Amira."

Amira clasped her hands with delight as she said, "Ah, you do speak our language. My son Asad had indicated as much, but I did wonder how anyone could learn the language so quickly!"

"Thanks to the efforts of Lord Khalil and *mu'al-alim* Ahmed, Lady Amira, I was able to learn your tongue."

"You have made a good start on the road of culture, Alric. You have learned well and I am pleased," Amira said, acknowledging Alric's courteous words. "I have heard," she continued, "that your homeland is cold and unfriendly."

"That is true, Lady."

"Come here, young man." She spoke with authority.

He approached her, hoping desperately she would not ask him to do anything embarrassing in front of the three young women.

She inspected him closely, much as the Caliph had done, and she asked him to kneel. He could feel her fingers as she touched his hair. Then she asked him to stand so that she could look in wonder at his clear blue eyes. Her manner was friendly, even motherly. "You are such a good-looking young man," Amira exclaimed, "and so tall." She continued her inspection of Alric as she said, "I hear from my son Asad that you are also devoted to learning."

"Yes, Lady Amira, that is true." Alric replied.

There were more giggles from the young women, who were again silenced by the stern look from Amira's dark eyes.

"These three, Abal, Buhjah, and Maha, are my personal maidservants," she looked at the three young women as if daring them to utter one sound, "and they will make sure that you are bathed and clothed in fresh attire." She saw Alric's face redden as he realized what it might mean to have three young women attend him. "Do not worry, my dear. It will all be done under Wahid's supervision, and they will not see your nakedness." The three maidservants maintained a wise and tentative silence. "When you are ready, you will dine with us and we will discuss your future."

"Yes, Lady Amira," Alric responded.

"In the meantime," she continued, "it seems to me that you two," she looked at Khalil and Ahmed, "may also need relaxation in the

215

form of a hot bath. Meeting with my nephew can be very tiring and stressful!"

Before Khalil and Ahmed could respond, Amira added, "Wahid, please see to a bath for Khalil and Ahmed and lay out clean clothes for them. I will choose the clothes for our new house guest." Wahid nodded. Alric smiled inwardly. Lady Amira was in command and everyone knew it! And then," she announced, "we will have our meal."

* * *

Freshly bathed and clothed, Alric was escorted by the three maidservants to the room where Lady Amira was sitting when he had first met her. "Feeling refreshed?" she asked.

"Yes, very much, my Lady. I thank you for your kindness."

She smiled, appreciative of Alric's good manners. "Come," she said as she rose gracefully from the cushions, "I have something to show you." She led Alric to another room that was lined with shelves and what seemed to be an uncountable number of books, all of which were stacked neatly in place on the shelves. "This," she indicated, "is my husband's private library of scientific and medical texts. It is so extensive that he is known throughout the country for his books and learning."

She smiled at Alric's look of awe as he surveyed shelf after shelf of valuable texts that covered all aspects of science. Alric allowed his eyes to roam over the books, noticing that the titles on the spines, as near as he could tell, were stacked alphabetically by author's name. "My husband," she continued, "helped my nephew Harun start his library, which will eventually house more than one hundred thousand texts on all subjects, or so my husband estimates."

Alric stood in amazement. The number one hundred thousand was such that it was difficult for him to understand or visualize; it just boggled his mind.

"Already, scholars and men of science and medicine arrive weekly," Amira continued, "sometimes daily to study the various manuscripts. They are permitted to copy one of the library's texts in exchange for the one they must bring to be copied. The holdings of the Caliph's library may one day exceed those in the famous library at Alexandria before tragedy struck and the Alexandrian library was destroyed." Amira turned at the sound of an arrival. "Ah, my husband is here!" she exclaimed joyfully, placing her hands together as if in prayer.

Jabir entered the room, embraced his wife, and smiled at Alric. "I see that my wife is showing you my favorite hiding place."

"It is very impressive, Lord Jabir."

Alric's throat was dry, and he had to force himself to speak. He had not yet recovered from the sight of such a collection of books in one room. "Now, let us adjourn to the day lounge. It is time to eat," Jabir announced.

As they entered the lounge, Khalil and Ahmed were already seated and awaiting their presence. They both rose as Amira entered the room and sat down only after she had seated herself. Alric hesitated, wondering where he should sit; this did not go unnoticed by Amira. "Come, Alric, and sit opposite to me." Khalil and Ahmed sat on each side of her, "Next to my husband." She looked at Jabir. "I am assuming, dear, that since Alric is your assistant, he is to live here?"

Jabir nodded. "Alric, you must learn to make yourself at home," he said. "My house will be your home."

Alric bowed his head in thanks. The matter of where he would live had not been discussed in any great detail. Now it was decided. *Fait accompli.*

Alric looked at the table as he sat down on the cushion. The plates and bowls were heaped with couscous, bread, olives, fruit, and pieces of tender lamb. His stomach rumbled in anticipation. There had been plenty to drink all day, but he had been so nervous in front of the

Caliph that he'd only nibbled on the food, so now he was ready for a hearty meal.

The servants passed a bowl of freshly scented water and clean towels from one to the other, starting with Lord Jabir, followed by Lady Amira, Khalil, Ahmed, and then Alric. As they washed their hands, the social conversation that was a part of all families commenced.

"By the way, Alric," Jabir's words broke into his thoughts, "since you are considered as one of the family, there is no need to sit on ceremony. Eat whatever you will and do not wait to be invited." Jabir paused. "Tomorrow you begin your new life," he added.

Amira asked Jabir about the health of her nephew, the Caliph.

"He is well, but there is another story that you will wish to hear, my dear."

Jabir looked at Alric. "Alric," Jabir said, "if you would be so kind as to tell your story for my wife as the meal progresses, I will appreciate it."

Alric smiled and nodded enthusiastically. Suddenly, he felt that he was at home.

When the meal was over and Alric had related his story, he felt very tired. Sensing this, Amira had the maidservants show him to his room so that he could retire for the day.

* * *

The next morning Alric awoke from the deepest and most refreshing sleep that he had experienced since the first appearance of the sea raiders. The comfortable bed and the rest had removed all thoughts about the First Minister from his mind. This is, he thought, the first day of my new life!

Alric did, however, wonder about the possibility of meeting al-Maslawi and if he should broach this subject with Lord Jabir. The man was from Mosul, and that seemed to be a good source for the tablets.

Had not one been picked from the dirt of centuries and given to him? Al-Maslawi, Alric thought, might be able to give me information and access to the *cunei forma* tablets or, at least, show me where they can be found.

As he stretched in the luxury of the bed, he looked around. The tiredness from the journey, the excitement of meeting with the Caliph, and his introduction to his new home had brought exhaustion to his body by the time the evening meal had been completed.

The room in which he had slept had been designated for his use only. It was a private area isolated from the other rooms of the house and was situated off the colonnaded walkway that ran around the perimeter of the courtyard.

The walls were covered with rich silks that hung from the ceiling. Plush cushions, beneath a white canopy, formed his bed. The family, under the leadership of Lady Amira, had fawned over him at dinner. Amira's three serving girls, Abal, Buhjah, and Maha, had poured fruit drinks and made sure that each empty silver plate was replaced with a clean one heaped with food.

At every opportunity, they had smiled coyly at Alric, who blushed at the thought of the three of them assisting with his bath after his arrival, but the presence of Wahid had stopped the giggling that always seemed to be present with the young women. Seeing that Alric was overawed by their service, Wahid snapped his fingers and the maidservants retreated behind the fine silk curtains.

Alric had done his best to imitate the eating habits of the family as he took one small piece of food at a time rather than cram his mouth full of the delicacies. He recalled that the eating habits of the soldiers were similar. Mealtimes had been times to rest from the toils of travel and of being constantly on the watch for danger. It was a time to be social with friends.

Dinner allowed the family to talk about the events of the day. Khalil had, with help from Ahmed, recounted the details of their recent trip, in the same way they had told of their journey to the Caliph. Jabir, hearing the story for the second time, listened intently, nodding on occasion, asking questions about events that had escaped his attention during the first telling.

There had been much to relate, and the meal had lasted for three hours. When it was over, Amira clapped her hands, the plates and remaining food were cleared away quickly, and tea was provided.

It had been an exhausting day, and Alric's eyes were heavy with sleep. He fought to stay awake. Amira had then snapped her fingers, and Abal, Buhjah, and Maha had appeared, helped Alric to stand up, and led him to his bedroom under Wahid's supervision. Those were his last memories of the evening.

Alric had only the dimmest memories of being prepared for sleep. He felt refreshed and arose covering his nightclothes with a robe that had been folded and laid on the cushions. Then he made his way to a part of the house that was devoted to bathing and sanitation.

He stripped naked, draped his nightclothes and the robe over a wooden rail, and stepped into a canopied area that, he vaguely remembered, Wahid told him was a shower. A gentle pull of the cord, and water, set to the correct temperature, cascaded over his body in tiny rivulets. This was made possible by several holes bored into a metal container that received warm water from a pipe just below the ceiling. He was pleasantly surprised, since he had expected the water to be cold and had steeled himself for such a shock.

Alric felt energized. He turned around, allowing the relaxing liquid to do its work as it removed the remnants of sleep and prepared him for the day ahead. He used a pumice powder that was provided to clean his skin and a soft-haired brush to scrub away the residual pumice. Then he poured fragrant oils on his head that the water gently spread over his body. He seemed to remember Abal, or was it Buhjah, or was it Maha, advising him that the oils warded off evil spirits and would keep him healthy. He shrugged, pulled the cord, and the water ceased.

Alric stepped from the shower feeling revived. He looked for his clothes and saw that during the time he had been in the shower, towels and clean clothes had been hung on the rail in place of his nightwear. Suddenly, he was conscious of someone standing nearby. As he turned, he was surprised to see Wahid, waiting for him. He tried to cover his nakedness, but Wahid seemed unconcerned.

"Lady Amira requests that you join her for the first refreshments of the day. She awaits you in her day room." Wahid noticed Alric's puzzled expression. "The room where you had dinner last night," he added by way of explanation.

"Thank you, Wahid," was all that Alric could think to say, and then as an afterthought he added, "Should I call you Wahid? Or what do you prefer?"

Wahid smiled. "All servants in the house of Lord Jabir and Lady Amira are accustomed to being addressed by their own given names. There are no slaves in this house. Lord Jabir forbids it."

Alric assumed that the answer to his question was yes, as he dried himself. He talked with Wahid, who helped him understand the reasons for the various types of garments. When he was dressed, he felt ready to meet Amira.

Wahid indicated that he would lead the way, and Alric should follow. Alric felt obliged, still trying to understand the nature of this house. He had heard that slaves were in common use in this country. As he stepped onto the colonnade, the fresh morning air was invigorating. He felt alive!

Amira smiled and greeted him as Wahid showed him into the room. She indicated a cushion opposite, where Alric should sit. "My husband," she said as if to explain why she was alone, "has left to conduct business at the palace, and Khalil and Ahmed have accompanied him. Wahid and my three maidservants will see to our needs."

Alric took a date from the plate that was proffered to him by Maha and regarded Amira carefully. She still retained the benevolent look in her eyes that he had seen the night before. "It seems, my dear, that you have had a difficult time in your young life."

"Yes, Lady Amira, but I think not as difficult as the lives of some. I have been educated and I have had the privilege of learning other languages."

Amira smiled at his response. "You are educated. Now I will ask you the same question that my nephew has a tendency to ask strangers. Tell me, Alric," Amira said, "do you fear me?"

"No, Lady Amira."

She smiled at his response. "And why is that?" she asked.

"Because, Lady Amira, you have the look in your eyes of a gentle woman and I also know this from the way that your son Khalil speaks of you."

"Your answer pleases me, Alric, and I see that with your light hair and smiling eyes you can charm the girls . . . " She stopped in midsentence, as if thinking about her next words, and then she continued thoughtfully. "I do not know if you have been advised accordingly, but let me tell you that you cannot consort with women of our culture. It is expressly forbidden. If you do, and if you are caught, you will be imprisoned, perhaps even executed. My nephew does not make exceptions! Do you understand?" Alric nodded. "You may have a friendship with a woman of your culture but to go beyond that requires the permission of the Caliph. Should the occasion arise where you meet such a woman, I suggest that you talk first with me."

Alric nodded his head again. After the travails of the past months, women had not been on his mind.

"Your eyes tell me," Amira said, "that you are trustworthy and loyal. That is good because if you ever bring shame upon this house, it will be a very sad day for all of us. Now," she said smiling, "that is the end of my lecture. Let us eat fruit and drink juice."

They continued to talk, and Alric found himself laughing with Amira as she listened to some of his stories. He also saw tears in her eyes as he related how close he had been to Hilda, his twin sister. "A regrettable waste of such a young life, but it happens. If you succeed here, as I believe you will, then you will have the world at your feet. My husband has need of someone like you. Not only is he the Caliph's physician, but he translates books from other cultures into our language so that the Caliph can have them in his library."

She frowned, as if deep in thought, as she picked a date from the bowl. Then she looked at Alric and smiled. "Yes, Alric, I see a very positive future for you. But there is one thing that we must do, and it must be done quickly." She paused and then added. "We must give you a name that is consistent with living here. In that way, you will start to be accepted as one of us. Your straw-colored hair and blue eyes will always make it difficult for many to accept you completely. But a change of name will help. Lord Jabir and I discussed this earlier before he left."

Alric was wondering why he should change his name and allowed the thought to register in his brain for a few minutes; then he suddenly realized the wisdom of Amira's words. His thoughts about his future had not included whether or not he fit in, but he was a foreigner. Most foreigners in the country were either traders or people who had been captured by the Caliph's armies. In the latter case, they were slaves.

Amira was silent, giving him time to think. She awaited his answer. She remained settled on her cushion and sipped her orange juice as she waited patiently. She had told Wahid and the three maidservants to leave, and the room was silent.

Finally, Alric's head cleared. He looked at Amira, whose face looked serene. She smiled as she recognized the look in his eyes. "Tell me, Alric," she said warmly, "have your thoughts placed a suggestion in your mind?"

"Yes, Lady Amira," Alric responded almost in a whisper as he felt the blood rush to his temples and fought to regain his senses. "When I first met Lord Jabir he addressed me as Alric al-Biritaanya, Alric from

Britain. I would like to have such a name that reminds me of my place of birth. Can it be done?"

"Yes, of course. My sons Khalil and Ahmed will agree that it is appropriate for you to have such a name." She smiled as she reached over and took Alric's hand in a motherly gesture. He could feel her warmth. "Lord Jabir also suggested that your full name would be Alric al-Biritaanya ibn Jabir. Translated that means 'Alric from Britain of the House of Jabir.' In other words, Alric, after knowing you for only such a short time, my husband has suggested that we adopt you into our household. I agreed with him. You will not immediately have the same privileges as our sons Asad and Khalil but you will be on the same social level as Ahmed, who is very dear to us and who has also been accepted into this house as our adopted son."

"Lady Amira, if I understand you correctly, you are proposing to be my other parents, in place of my birth parents that I lost to the sea raiders?"

Amira smiled and nodded.

Alric turned away so that she could not see the moisture that clouded his eyes. He could feel her attention on him as he gulped back the emotion that ran high within him. He sought to control his feelings as he looked at her. "I am honored that you consider me to be a part of your family."

"Then it is done," Amira responded, and then she announced, "From this day on you will be known as Alric al-Biritaanya ibn Jabir. The permission must come from the Caliph, but I do not see my nephew denying such a simple request from his aunt and uncle," she smiled. "Also, the Caliph does seem to have taken a liking to you. He was impressed during the meeting yesterday."

Alric stood up. "Allah's blessings, Lady Amira," he said, bowing. "Do I have permission to touch you?"

Amira looked at him. He stood so straight and tall and proud. She raised herself from the cushion. "Of course, Alric, and as time goes by, if you feel the need to address me as mother and Lord Jabir as father, we will be flattered."

He approached her shyly, blushing, and placed his arms around her shoulders. Then sobs shook his body as all of the fears and events of the past months ripped through him.

She stroked his hair and whispered, "You are a young man, Alric, and have suffered much tragedy. Let your feelings come out. It is not a disgrace to shed tears for your lost loved ones!"

Finally his body stopped shaking and he was ready to speak again. Amira stepped back and looked into his eyes. He had strength and courage. "My apologies, mother," Amira smiled at Alric's use of the word. "I prefer not to show such emotion. It is not the way of my people."

"You are not to concern yourself with such thoughts. In this house, you will be free to express yourself. I am honored that you shared this moment with me. It will remain our secret." Amira looked intently at Alric. "My dear," she said, "we can never replace your parents who gave you birth and nurtured you through the early years of your life, but we can offer you love and a home. It seems to me that your mother and father must have been honorable people."

Alric's eyes flashed, he nodded, and bowed in gratitude. "My mother took up her own weapons and stood side by side with my father in the shield wall to defend our home against the sea raiders. They gave their lives to protect our home. My sister, Hilda, gave her life that mine might be spared. It is the way of our people."

"Keep tender thoughts in your heart for them, Alric," Amira said as her eyes moistened with emotion. Then she asked, "Your sister Hilda, I believe she was your twin?"

"Yes, mother."

"You must have been close?"

"We were," Alric responded, "and, in some ways, I sense that she is still with me." Alric felt that he had recovered and was back to his former self, reserved and confident.

"My husband will be pleased with the outcome of our conversation," she said as she clapped her hands. Abal, Buhjah, and Maha appeared, picked up the trays, and removed them from the room. "Now," Amira said, "there are things I must attend to. Perhaps you will rest in your room until father returns."

Alric nodded and smiled.

Amira looked at him quizzically. "Can you find your way?"

He assured her that he could and took his leave. As he walked toward the door, he heard Hilda's voice. *She is a good woman, Alric! This is an honorable family.* One word flashed through his mind: *Hilda.* She was still with him! He hesitated, turned, looked at Amira, and smiled.

"Is everything all right, Alric?"

"Yes, mother. All is well." As he walked along the colonnade to his room, he repeated his new name; he liked its meaning. It gave him a feeling of permanence.

"Who am I?" he asked himself when he got to his room. He tilted his head, as he formulated the answer to his own seemingly rhetorical question. "I know who I am," he thought, "and before Lord Jabir returns, I will adjust my thoughts to accommodate my new name. This house is my home. I am thankful to have such a gift. I am Alric of Britain, of the House of Jabir. Alric al-Biritaanya ibn Jabir."

He pronounced the name out loud. It rang in his ears. It had a good sound.

* * *

CHAPTER 17

The next day, Khalil told Alric, in accordance with his father's wish, it was time he started to learn about activities that took place in the laboratory.

Jabir's work with extracts and mixtures for healing was known and appreciated by the people throughout Mesopotamia. The word had spread very quickly that Lord Jabir's medicines bestowed good health on the patient. His results in the laboratory with metals and alloys were also well known, and he provided the Caliph with much information that was used in building projects as well as for military purposes.

"What must I do there, Lord Khalil?" Alric asked.

"Observe and listen well," Khalil said. "My father will explain all things to you, but you must pay attention."

"Does he have his work written on paper?" Alric asked.

"He has written much, but not all of his work is recorded, and that which he has written down is not as organized as it should be."

Alric could scarcely believe his ears. If this was to be his future, he was ecstatic. He intended to learn as much as he could, and perhaps find some means of helping Lord Jabir in his healing work. Anxious to begin, Alric wondered if the first task that he could undertake would be to help Lord Jabir organize his notes and make sure that everything was recorded.

"Well, Alric," Khalil asked, breaking into Alric's reverie, "shall we?"

Alric nodded eagerly. "Where is father now?" Alric asked.

Khalil smiled at Alric's use of the family word. Just as Amira and Jabir had welcomed Alric into the family, Khalil and Ahmed thought of him as their brother. "On the porch at the door to the laboratory," replied Khalil. "He often sits there when thinking about a particular problem. He quietly stares into space as he attempts to resolve some medical problem or wrestle with some other issue."

* * *

They left the house and walked quickly along the colonnade and through a passageway. Once they were in the sunny garden, Alric saw the laboratory. They made their way toward the vine-covered building that stood only a short distance from a sturdy wooden gate that was reinforced with iron ribs.

"That," Khalil pointed to the gate, "is for various reasons, one of which is to bring ores and father's extracts into the garden and thence to the laboratory. Mother will not allow them into the house!"

This was Alric's first chance to look at the garden. The stones of the walkway shimmered beneath his feet as he matched his pace to Khalil's hurried steps. Flowers of different types mingled freely below the shade trees. Alric took great pleasure observing the layout of the garden. The flowers and trees had been planted with care, and the result was a garden that created a sense of the peace and the quietness of nature.

Alric had never seen a laboratory before, and he was unsure what to expect. He had assumed that it would be a room on the colonnade, perhaps not far from his own room. But Jabir's laboratory was not a part of the house. It had been built in a corner of the garden away from the house and colonnade and near the wall that surrounded the house and grounds.

As they neared the building, Alric saw Jabir sitting, as Khalil had said, in a wooden chair on the porch. The chair was placed in the shade of a canopy and, like the porch, traversed the whole side of the building. In this position, Jabir was not to be bothered by the heat from the sun and he could see who approached the laboratory from the house.

Jabir rose from the chair as they approached. He was dressed in plain attire. His jurbah was dark, almost black, and seemed thicker than usual. There were no markings or decorations of any kind on the garment. Alric found this surprising.

"I am dressed this way as a matter of safety," Jabir said with a wry smile as he noticed the look of curiosity on Alric's face. "The clothes that I wear every day will burn easily, and since I am often using the heat burners for my experiments, this garment I am wearing is impregnated with extracts of ores, so it takes longer to ignite and does not flame easily. I have such a garment prepared for you."

Jabir turned on his heel, entered the building, and returned in a few moments with a similar robe. Khalil held the robe for Alric and then he looked at Jabir. "Father, I do have business at the palace, and if you will excuse me I must leave. Ahmed is already there awaiting me."

Jabir nodded and Khalil bade his farewell to them both.

* * *

Alric was ushered into the inner sanctum of the laboratory by Jabir. Unlike the house, there were no elegant furnishings. This was a place of work in which strange substances and extracts were made, tested, and used. Jabir beckoned Alric into a chair opposite a simple desk. He sat down with an air of anticipation and curiosity.

The faint and pleasant aroma of medicines permeated his nostrils. He quickly pulled a cloth from the cuff of his sleeve and sneezed into it.

229

Jabir sat at the other side of the desk and smiled. "Good," he noted. "I am pleased my wife has given you a nose cloth. It means that your sneezes will not contaminate my extracts and medicines. So, you wish to delve into the art of *al khimiya*?" Jabir asked as a way of introducing Alric to the laboratory.

"Yes, father," Alric answered immediately.

Alric decided that the familiar name "father" was in order when they were alone or in the house with family, but a more formal "Lord Jabir" would be more appreciated when in the presence of others.

"Stand up and have a good look at my laboratory, Alric," Jabir offered, seeing the look of anticipation on Alric's face. Alric looked around the large room wide-eyed. Against the sandstone walls of the room stood several stone tables with neatly aligned pieces of equipment, tools, and books. At one end of the room, a furnace had been constructed, and it reminded Alric of the furnaces he had seen in the workplace of swordsmiths and ironworkers. Shelves lined the walls which were stacked with bottles containing colored substances, creams, and potions. There were wide-necked glass bottles that contained, among other drugs, belladonna for reducing fevers, frankincense to cure throat ailments and to stop vomiting, myrrh to relieve headaches and toothaches, tumeric to assist in closing open wounds, and poppy extract to deaden pain.

The floor was constructed of large flat stones; these had recently been washed, as they showed no signs of dirt or grime. Candles stood upright in large head-high candleholders, and other candles were placed around the room in sconces affixed to the walls. These directed the light upward to the whitewashed ceiling, which in turn reflected the light downward into the room.

"I see that my laboratory fascinates you, Alric," Jabir observed.

"Yes, father."

"Now, we will start. It is important, Alric, that you understand that the main goal of my work is to produce medicines that will heal the sick."

He looked directly at Alric as he became very serious about his next words. Alric instinctively touched his nostrils with the nose cloth. "I see that you might observe a slight irritation of the nose, which," Jabir said, "you will get over in time. It is the nature of the extracts in this laboratory that will cause such an irritation." Jabir paused. "However, it is in this laboratory that you will receive instruction from me about the science of medicine and the extracts that we use to cure ailments through the art that is known as *al-khimiya*. Is there something wrong?" Jabir saw the puzzled look on Alric's face.

"Yes, father. It is nothing, but I do have trouble pronouncing your words."

"You mean *al-khimiya?*"

Alric nodded.

"Then say them whichever way you can."

"To me," Alric said, "the simplest way is to pronounce it as *alchemy*. Would that be in order, father?"

"It shall become a part of our vocabulary, Alric." Jabir regarded him with pride and delight. "The essence of this work," Jabir said, "is to discover cures for the various diseases and ailment that are the scourges of this earth. On the other hand, there are those who believe that metals such as lead can be turned into gold. Some think this should be our quest in life."

"Excuse me, father, I have heard of such a quest. But surely that is impossible?"

"Indeed it is, Alric. Others have convinced men in power that the production of gold from lead is possible and it is merely a matter of using the correct procedure. These men are greedy and they want money to satisfy their own ends. I have been pestered in the past to make gold and mind-altering extracts from plants. I must tell you,

Alric, that attempting the impossible dream of converting iron into gold is not a course that you will pursue. Beyond the boundaries that I set, *al-khimiya* is considered to be evil magic."

Jabir rose from the desk and moved across the room to where a large dish sat next to an urn full of water. He poured water into the dish. Alric followed him. "You must wash your hands at regular intervals when handling extracts and medicines," Jabir said as he immersed his hands in the water and rubbed them with pumice that had been impregnated with perfumed cleaning oil. "Transmittal of any of these medicines from your hands to your mouth when taking food can make you seriously ill. In fact, food is not tolerated in this laboratory. There is a place," Jabir nodded to the covered porch, "where we can eat and drink."

When Alric had washed his hands and dried them carefully on the hand cloth provided by Jabir, he was ready.

"This," Jabir said, pointing to a stone table, "is where most of the work of mixing medicines is performed. Here," he indicated a simple balance, "is the means by which I measure the relative quantities that make up a medicine. In the back of the laboratory is the fire and oven that are used for heating liquids and melting substances. The beakers and vessels that you see on the tables are for the liquids and powders that I combine and integrate into the medicines. The large book on my reading table over there is what I call my *Dawaa' kitaab,* or medical book. It is the book in which I record all of my medications, with notes on how the patient fares after treatment. Another book," he pointed to an equally large book on the other side of the desk, "is my *Jiraaha kitaab,* which contains the notes from the times that I have had to apply surgical treatments to patients. It also contains the observations and results of the various treatments that I have applied. Sorrowfully, some of the patients have died, and I make notes accordingly, but happily many have lived! These books are my life. Every year I have the book unbound and pages inserted into the correct places and so they grow. This year, I may have to start another volume for each book!"

Jabir could see that Alric was most interested.

"May I look through the pages, father?" Alric asked.

"Of course, do that while I finish my notes. You may use the small table next to my writing desk. Unfortunately, for one reason or another, you may notice that some of these writings are incomplete," Jabir said as Alric carefully turned the pages of the thick, heavy volume that represented only a portion of Jabir's work.

Alric had heard of such books when he'd begun to work with Ecgfrith at Wearmouth. It seemed that, like Ecgfrith, Jabir relied on the patient's body and state of health to design a cure.

"It is perhaps in this area that you can begin to be very valuable to me," Jabir said thoughtfully as Alric listened carefully, recalling what Khalil had said earlier. "As the days pass, I will start to talk about my work and you can make notes that can, after my inspection for correctness, be added to the collection of my works. In fact," Jabir paused, "this may be a good way to introduce you to my work!"

Alric nodded and looked down at the book as he started to turn the pages once more. He remembered that in the Latin tongue such a book would be called a *Magnum Opus*, a Great Work, or *Liber Vitae*, the Book of Life. Jabir's book was not typical of those that were mired in misleading prose that would force him to stumble through perplexing imagery, fear, and misunderstanding. Alric was particularly intrigued by one of Jabir's front-page statements: "Every person of integrity who practices *alchemy* should keep careful notes and detailed descriptions of the work because memory can be deceitful and fail when accuracy is needed."

Alric felt that he had made a good start by writing about his life and maintaining his personal journal. He had already decided to maintain that discipline and appoint specific times to write about his life with a separate schedule for his work. In this way he knew he could not fail to recall the necessary details of all he had accomplished.

Jabir's written words about integrity and accuracy increased Alric's passion to study *alchemy*. He could feel his heart thumping in his chest in excitement. He would spend his lifetime in pursuit of healing. He looked toward Jabir, indicated that he had finished the book for the moment, and returned it to Jabir's desk.

Jabir nodded, took a flask from one of the laboratory benches, and removed the stopper. "I am led to believe that this extract is," he announced as Alric approached, "to be a new source of health. I have tested it on rats and even on dogs. In small doses it gives the animal energy, perhaps even the ability to survive a serious injury. In large doses, the extract acts as a poison and the animal dies. I have not yet tried it on people, but I suspect that an opportunity will arise in the near future."

Alric's eyes opened wide at Jabir's explanation of the contradictory effects of the extract. Jabir replaced the stopper and passed the bottle to Alric, allowing him to look at the white powder. "You need to be aware of such extracts. An extract that can cure may also kill. Curative agents in high doses are not always poisons, and poisons in small doses are not always curative agents. Remember, alchemy is like an onion: Peel away one layer and there is another layer for investigation that may seem to contradict what you have already discovered."

For the rest of the day Alric watched and listened to Jabir, who was delighted to have someone in the laboratory to teach, and he was equally impressed by Alric's endless questions and thirst for knowledge.

He never mentioned his origins and whether or not he had been born in Mesopotamia. His future seemed secure when he'd married Amira, the daughter of a prominent family, whose sister was the mother of the young man, now the Caliph. But Jabir preferred not to rest on the family name, and continued to find favor with the people by providing soothing salves for wounds, resetting broken limbs, and providing mixtures and extracts that eased pain. One of his patients had died, but Jabir was not blamed for the death.

"It was my own fault," he admitted to Alric. "It was an error in my calculations, as well as a gap in my knowledge at the time. I gave a patient too much of the extract and he died. I made sure the man's family would live in comfort for the remainder of their lives. I shall not make that mistake again."

* * *

Jabir and Alric became so wrapped up in their conversations that they had to be called from the laboratory several times by Wahid to take refreshment. Wahid would not enter the laboratory, for which Jabir was pleased; he might try to tidy up and dust things! They were called several times to the evening meals and finally concluded their business only when Amira appeared and demanded that they finish for the day. They were also reminded by Amira that their clothes smelled and they were to bathe and don fresh robes before the meal.

Wahid collected the odiferous garments as they showered and made sure the clothes were washed and ready for the next session in the laboratory. At that time, Jabir decided that extra laboratory robes should be made available.

* * *

Alric spent the next two weeks at the laboratory bench, an experience that he enjoyed immensely. He learned the techniques of extracting white powders from plants and the means by which spirits of oil could be separated by distillation. In this process, heat was applied to the mixture in a flask; the very volatile components were distilled into a receiver first, and the less volatile components were distilled into another received last or were allowed to remain in the flask. Day after day he thrusted himself into the work. To his regret, there was never enough time in the day. Jabir was only too glad to have Alric's assistance, but Amira kept her eye on both of them to deter any potential for overwork.

Alric's new skills were a mixed blessing. Those who practiced *al-khimiya* guarded their secrets and mysteries to the point of obsession. Jabir was no different. He would never allow his secrets to be available to others. He would rather lose a limb than have another given access to his work. This was one reason why many of his experiments had not been recorded. Now that Alric was his assistant, that would change, and Jabir would have a written record of his work, which would be guarded closely and always under lock and key.

Jabir's visits to the Caliph occupied much of his time, since for the past five years he had been the chief physician and surgeon to the Caliph after the death of his predecessor, who had attended the Caliph's father. Through hard work and diligence, Jabir had become a renowned physician, surgeon, and alchemist.

There were no other alchemists in the city. There had been some at one time, but they had been exposed as frauds and charlatans and had long since departed from the city. Each one had been sent on his respective journey, often suffering from the aftereffects of physical torture and mutilation. Fraud and trickery was not looked upon favorably in the land of Harun al-Rashid.

In addition to consultations by the Caliph, Jabir was consulted by many nobles. His ability to diagnose and cure ailments was uncanny.

With the arrival of Alric, three weeks ago, Jabir had recognized that there came a time in a man's life when he had to choose between what he should do and what would protect his health. They were not always the same. It was time for Jabir to accept the fact that Alric may be his successor.

When he spoke of this to Amira, she smiled. No further words were spoken. She respected his decision. That night, at dinner, the decision was conveyed to Alric. He stood and bowed to Jabir and kissed Amira on the cheek. "Thank you, father, and mother, I am honored," he said, his head spinning with the news. Alric had wanted this to be his life's work, and his wish had been granted. He would not and must not disappoint his father and mother or betray their confidence in him.

Hilda's words came to him once more, softly and as if carried on the gentle breeze of summer: *You fit well into this family, my brother.* Alric felt that as long as he had Hilda's blessing, he would be safe and secure in his chosen path.

"Alric!"

Amira's exclamation brought him back to his present surroundings.

"Let us take refreshments. This will give you pause to consider your decision, since it will affect your life considerably. You may have questions for father."

They talked at length about this, and Alric felt satisfied with all that took place. He ate none of the sweet cake he was offered, merely sipping the juice and eating dates. Jabir and Amira smiled knowingly to each other as they saw the bright look in his eyes and the shine of anticipation and pleasure on his face. Jabir finished his tea and cake, held Amira's hand in a moment of tenderness, apologetically rose from the cushions, looked at Alric and announced, "It is time we went back into the laboratory, Alric. I need to mix medicines for two patients who have a high fever."

Alric jumped up from the cushion, made apologetic sounds to Amira, forgetting in his excitement that he had spoken in the language of the Saxons, and followed Jabir to the laboratory.

Amira recognized his omission but welcomed his exuberance for the work.

* * *

Alric had been working enthusiastically in the laboratory for almost three months. Jabir was a careful teacher and continually instructed Alric in the care that was required when preparing medicines.

He continued to emphasize the importance of his work. "These medicines can save a person's life, and care is required when you mix the individual ingredients, otherwise the medicine may not do its job and the patient will not be cured. As I have said before, too much of one ingredient and too little of another can make the medicine harmful, even poisonous, and the patient may die. This you must always remember, Alric."

Jabir stroked his cheek with his forefinger and then toyed with his beard as he instructed Alric to take extra care when he used the delicate pieces of equipment. Some could not be easily replaced. "The metal pieces cannot be damaged, unless you use a mallet," Jabir added.

Alric looked in wonderment at the glass beakers and flasks that adorned the bench and shelves. The unused ones were sparkling clean, while the used ones waited for cleaning by Ma'ruf, one of the house servants who came in daily to maintain the laboratory in a perpetual state of cleanliness. Alric grew to like Ma'ruf, and they talked frequently.

"Where are you from?" Alric asked after several days of watching Ma'ruf's careful work.

"A place across the sea, south from Britannia. It used to be part of Roman Gaul. I am Celtic by birth."

"I may have need of you as my work increases," Alric announced. "In the meantime, there are some tasks you can perform for me, and I will obtain approval from mother and father before you officially become my assistant."

Ma'ruf smiled and nodded with interest. "If I may, I would like to call you Alric?" Alric consented. "The name by which I was known in my native land is Rufus."

Ma'ruf fingered his red hair, and Alric understood immediately the use of the Latin word. "Lord Jabir and Lady Amira picked out the name Ma'ruf as the closest word in their language to my Celtic name."

Alric looked at the man's red hair. He was aptly named. "I will be pleased to have you work with me, and I will seek permission. But there is one caveat to this."

Ma'ruf looked expectantly at Alric. "Although I know some of your language, I would like you to teach me to write in the Celtic tongue. I will respond by teaching you my Saxon tongue."

Ma'ruf smiled. "It will be done," he said.

Alric then proceeded to give Ma'ruf instructions. "Safety," Alric concluded, "is the watchword." Ma'ruf nodded that he understood. "Now, we need containers of a certain size," Alric said. "Your first task is to find us such containers."

"The most likely place is the kitchen," Ma'ruf replied immediately.

They went to the kitchen at the back of the house, where the head cook listened to Alric's request. "I have such pots in storage. They are the old ones made of iron and some of clay. We now use pots made of copper or glass for most of our cooking."

Alric's eyes lit up. The pots will be helpful," he said, "but . . . "

"You would also like some glass and copper pots?" The cook foresaw Alric's request. "We have spare pots that you may use, but I will have to tell Lady Amira why she may need new glass and copper pots in the future."

"I will inform Lady Amira myself," Alric offered.

*   *   *

Jabir's comings and goings from the laboratory were frequent, but he did notice the friendship that had sprung up between Alric and Ma'ruf. They seemed to be of a similar age and would be good company for each other.

During the times he was absent, Jabir left Alric simple tasks of identifying and mixing ingredients in specific weighed amounts. To assure himself of Alric's abilities, Jabir dissolved each mixture with water, knowing that a specific colored solution would be produced if the ingredients had been mixed correctly. Not one of Alric's mixtures failed Jabir's examination.

Jabir watched Alric work, but he did not fully understand the driving force behind his passion. There were those days when Alric was already present in the laboratory well before breakfast. As time passed, Jabir felt no regrets about having allowed him such liberties. He was working hard, and Jabir was confident that he could start to mix simple medicines with only minor supervision. Preparation of the more complex medicines would require a longer period of time.

"You seem totally immersed in this work, Alric," Jabir observed. "Is there a reason?"

"In my former life," Alric responded, "My choices were to be a farmer like my father, who also worked at the monastery on occasion, or I could have become a monk. In either case, it would not have been my choice in life. This work gives me the chance to heal the sick and save lives. This is what I desire." He thought for a moment before adding, "Even though your books are full of wondrous surgical and medical cures, there is so much that we do not know. I would like, God willing, to expand your volumes several-fold during my time here."

"That is a very notable cause, Alric. I do not know anyone else with such a passion for this work. I can see a maturity in you that I have not seen in others your age. Also I have noticed that my patients seem to be doing much better from the medicines that you mix for me. You will soon be able to accompany me. In the meantime, continue to read my books and we can discuss the various medicines and their use."

Jabir frowned as if troubled by some hidden thoughts, and then continued. "But remember, we do not perform magic. Something cannot come from nothing. Ours is the science of healing; it is the process of increasing the length of a person's life as well as improving the quality of a person's existence."

* * *

CHAPTER 18

As the days passed, Alric was given the opportunity to look at other books on the shelves. He was also given permission to use Ma'ruf in the laboratory and to train him as his assistant.

The books were strange volumes that spoke of metals and salts. At first, he did not understand any of these, but there was one idea that seemed to repeat itself throughout all the books: the manifestation of the truth. In one of these volumes, he learned that the most important text in the literature of *al-khimiya*, or *alchemy* as he tended to pronounce the word, contained only a few lines that had been inscribed recently: "The conversion of lead to gold is not possible with the knowledge that we have." The words were emphatic.

The book of most interest to Alric told stories of well-known alchemists. They were men and women who had dedicated their entire lives to the purification of metals, salts, and mixtures in their laboratories. He learned that solids can become liquid by melting, and liquids can become gases by heating. Other salts and mixtures could be extracted from plants by hot water, which when cooled produced white powders that could be recovered from the liquid and then used in medicines.

"There is much to understand," Alric said one day to Lord Jabir and Lady Amira as they sat at tea, "and it is my goal to understand it all." Alric was becoming more and more convinced that alchemy could be learned in daily life. Jabir and Amira saw that he had spirit and the will to succeed. "At first, I thought it was complicated," Alric continued, "but I can reduce the works to several lines of thought that help me to understand the knowledge." He thought for a moment, and then asked, "When were these books written?"

"Many years ago," Jabir answered. "In fact, some were written many centuries ago. The books contain secrets that will help us heal by developing medicines and surgery to save lives. It is only those who are persistent, dedicated, and willing to study these works in detail who will achieve success. I have sought for such a person for many years. I know now, Alric, you are that person. You can help me decipher the codes of *al-khimiya.*

"But before you start on such a long task, there is one in which I require your help," Jabir said. "I have a copy of a book called *Materia Medica,* compiled by the Greek physician Dioscosrides more than seven hundred years ago." Jabir took two large, heavy volumes from a cupboard and placed them on his desk. "This book is regarded as the authority on plants and medicine. However, I have never been able to read the book. This work is a Latin translation of the original Greek work, and I was hoping that my fragmentary knowledge of Latin would allow me an understanding of some of the contents, but that is not so. This book is written in a form of Latin that is difficult for me to understand."

Alric opened the uppermost volume, looked at several pages, and nodded his head understandingly. "Of course, father, I am not surprised. This translation must have been made by monks in a scriptorium, the writing-copying room of a monastery. I suspect that the translator or translators were not natural speakers of the Latin language. There are so many unusual words on these pages that I am sure the persons involved with this work learned the language of the soldiers. This is a much more coarse and less grammatical language than the Latin of Caesar's works and the other Roman writers."

Alric looked at Jabir, who nodded as he understood what was being explained to him. "Also," Alric continued, "the vellum that comprises the pages is very expensive, and this is probably a type made from calf skin. Although," Alric looked closer at the pages, "some of the pages are made from a coarser material, indicating that the monks may have run out of the supply at times. As you can see, some of the words contain several marks above them. This signifies missing letters, and some words are abbreviated and not marked at all."

Alric looked at Jabir again. "Father, if your knowledge of Latin stems from a study of the classic writers of Rome," Alric continued, "it is understandable that you would have trouble with this pidgin Latin. In fact," Alric continued to turn the pages and look at the text, "I notice that the monks who copied this work have," he looked at Jabir almost in disbelief, "even used some abbreviated Saxon words!"

Jabir laughed. "No wonder I had trouble with my fragmentary Latin!"

"May I use this book, father?" Alric asked tentatively.

"More than that Alric," Jabir's eyes narrowed as he formulated the question. "Do you think you could translate it for me?"

"Into what language, father?" Alric asked, wide-eyed.

"First, I would like it translated into classical Latin that will be of use by scholars in the Caliph's library. Second, as your knowledge and use of Arabic improves, the Caliph would like the book translated into our language to assist other scholars in the library."

"I can do that, father. When do you wish me to start?"

"Immediately, Alric. All writing materials will be provided for you."

Alric nodded and added, "I will do that with pleasure, father. But," he paused, "there is one problem." Alric looked at a page that contained

245

the drawing of a plant. "The drawings may be beyond my abilities . . . " He allowed the words to trail off.

"I understand, Alric. You need not worry. This old book will be disassembled, and the drawings will be copied by those skilled in such art who work in the Caliph's library. You will retain the pages of writing. When all is complete, the old book will be reassembled and retained here for my use. The new one that you produce will go to the library, where more copies will be made."

Alric took a deep breath as he looked at the two volumes; each one was more than a hand in thickness. This was an immense task. "I would like to assess the work involved and even start disassembling the first volume."

Jabir read Alric's thoughts and answered the unspoken question. "Of course, I will send Ma'ruf to you immediately." Jabir saw the smile of recognition on Alric's face. "Ah, yes. Mother and I have noticed that you seem to be forming a bond with Ma'ruf. Your request for him to work as your assistant is granted, as long as Wahid does not require Ma'ruf's services elsewhere. Obviously, you find him a willing worker and he will be given instructions to provide you with whatever you need. First, I suggest that you have Ma'ruf clean one of the stone tables near to your writing table as a suitable place to lay out the pages of the book. The surface of the stone table must be scrupulously clean, otherwise the pages may be harmed."

"I understand, father, it will be done."

Alric was pleased with the arrangement. Ma'ruf, a beaming smile on his face, was delighted when Alric told him the news.

* * *

Alric and Ma'ruf started within the hour. Ma'ruf brought writing materials, the first volume was disassembled, and they set to work.

Silently and slowly, poring over the pages, Alric translated while Ma'ruf supplied writing materials and made sure that the newly written pages were placed in the correct order after the ink had dried. Alric worked steadily, concentrating on the task he had set himself. The occasional scratching of his pen against the paper was the only sound coming from the laboratory.

As the months passed, the work progressed—some days slower than Alric had hoped but much faster than Jabir had dared to hope. After five months, a considerable number of the pages of the newly translated material had been sent to the Caliph's library. Drawings were inserted into the correct places, and the manuscript was made ready for binding. After twelve months from the start of the work, Alric declared to Jabir that the task was complete.

One month later, the original two-volume book was returned to Jabir. The new volumes, each complete with its jeweled binding, were presented by Jabir to the Caliph, who expressed his amazement and appreciation to Jabir and asked him to convey his thanks to Alric.

* * *

Jabir was sitting in a chair on the porch of the laboratory one afternoon; as usual he was protected from the hot sun by the shade of the canopy. The open air offered a refreshing release from work in the laboratory.

I never thought it would come to this, he mused, as he leafed through the pages of a recent collection of notes that were the results of his past year's work on medicinal cures. All of his life, his studies has been focused on expanding his knowledge of science and medicine. He had studied *cunei forma* tablets, and he had unraveled some of the truths behind important questions about nature and medicines, but his studies had taken him to a point beyond which he could not seem to go.

More important, Jabir had been profoundly impressed by the story of the secrets of the *cunei forma* writing. He had heard stories of the knowledge contained in the strange symbols that covered many of these hand-sized tablets. When he had first heard the story, he'd thought it a mere myth, until six months ago. His friend Ali al-Maslawi had returned from a visit to his home city of Mosul and brought back part of a broken tablet as a gift for Jabir. He informed him about another tablet that seemed to possess exceptional knowledge.

"It is said," al-Maslawi had spoken in hushed tones, "that the tablet contains the very secrets that you seek. It is reputed to have been one of several tablets found in the earth under the old throne room of the great king Ashurbanipal. It is rumored that the great king was able to predict the exact time of the fall of ancient Nineveh!" Al-Maslawi had looked thoughtful and then had added, "One of the tablets predicts the coming of a man from the north who has hair the color of gold and eyes the color of the sky."

Jabir had considered this as being no more than gossip with additional embellishments. And then news, courtesy of Amira's carrier pigeons, had come from his son Asad of the northerner who accompanied Khalil.

Then Alric had arrived!

Jabir had hardly been able to contain his excitement. He had canceled all of his commitments and pulled together the most important of his books, and now he sat in the shade outside of his laboratory trying to plan the next steps. Possession of the tablet would be all important.

He knew that under the current circumstances, with the potential threat to the Caliph, it would not be wise for him to leave Baghdad, and that had led him to the decision to send Alric on the quest.

Suddenly, as if by the favor of fortune, Alric appeared from the house and greeted him. "My father," Alric said showing some concern, "you seem to have your mind elsewhere these days. May I be of service?"

Jabir smiled at Alric's smooth command of the language and the formality of the greeting. "I am thinking of asking you to go to Mosul," Jabir answered, "on the advice of Ali al-Maslawi," Jabir looked at Alric. "You remember him?" Alric nodded and Jabir continued. "I have discussed this with the Caliph and he agrees that you are the most obvious person to go to the northern city. My absence in these questionable times would be obvious. Your absence will barely be noticed. But caution should be your watchword."

Alric felt startled but remained calm and did not respond at first. Then he found his voice. "What is it that you require of me in Mosul, father?"

"In Mosul," Jabir explained, "you will meet a man who al-Maslawi says will have a tablet for you. This tablet has words of wisdom that are written in the language of what you have called the *cunei forma.*" Alric listened intently, wondering what was coming next. "I know that you and I have not had the time to go into the details of the *cunei forma* language, but I would like you to spend some time with this man, who is called the Librarian and who will introduce you to the characteristics of that language. The true identity of the Librarian is not known to many. If the nature of his work ever becomes freely known, he will be in danger. There are others who, it seems, realize the importance of the ancient writing. However, the Librarian has, according to al-Maslawi, compiled a list of the *cunei forma* symbols and words that will help us translate and understand the meaning of the tablet. And, if my deductions are correct, there will be others who also have an interest in this tablet. There is the perception that the old tablets offer a man untold power. Learning from the tablets seems to take second place! "

Alric regarded Jabir with excitement and then spoke. "It seems, father, that this is a sinister business that has arisen, but I sense that all will be well. This tablet may be the key not only to the advancement of science but also to the health and well-being of the Caliph. The mysteries of the past should not keep us from discovering its secret. I will do what you ask willingly."

This was the answer Jabir hoped to hear. "I thank you, Alric. It may be a dangerous path that we tread," the muscles in his jaw tightened, "and we will not gain anything by being unprepared. As you know, it is a journey of twelve to fifteen days by caravan to Mosul. I have many resources at my disposal and we should plan accordingly. So we will take the remainder of today to prepare ourselves. Then I will make arrangements that will aid you along the way. It is better that you travel in a caravan. Traveling in a small party of armed men would arouse suspicion and I prefer to keep a low profile until we have a clearer vision of the future. During the journey you will be contacted by a man who will make himself known to you. He will advise you about contacting the Librarian. Also, this caravan will travel by the eastern route of the other side of the Tigris. I fear that the most direct route between the two rivers will be watched.

"Now," he said after a pause, "I must think of the next steps and then we will be ready." Jabir lost himself in thought for a moment, then looked once more at Alric and motioned to the seat on the bench beside him. "Sit beside me, my son."

Jabir still had some doubts about sending Alric to Mosul. The journey could be fraught with danger, and the prize, the tablet which Jabir coveted, could bring danger to his house and family. "One last item," Jabir said seriously. "You must not try to contact the Librarian. He will seek you. He has several homes, one of which, it is said, or so al-Maslawi has indicated to me, is in a hollowed-out part of the wall of the old city. The ruins of old cities descend to varying depths in the hills of dirt. The wall blocks tumbled down over the years, leaving small nooks and crannies, overhangs, and even old guardrooms intact. The Librarian may live in such a place."

Jabir closed the book he was reading. "Books themselves are worth only what is written in them and how they translate to the reader. If they generate ideas and enjoyment, they are worth all of the money in the world. If they generate nothing, they are worth nothing. This book," he gestured to Alric, "was sent to the Caliph by Charlemagne, King of the Franks. The Caliph has given it to me as a present and because of my work in science and medicine." he said.

Alric echoed, "The King of the Franks?"

Jabir nodded. "It is a book of predictions. It is not what I would call true science or medicine, but still, it has some relevance to my work. It talks of the meaning of omens to science and medicine. It seems nonsense, but then the author, whoever he may be, appears to have dabbled in magic and the power of the supernatural. The author seems to have a great spiritual imagination. There is something about the writings in this book."

Jabir paused for a moment then continued. "I have tended to discount the words, but there is one passage in which the author writes about coincidences. I have to say that I found the pages dealing with coincidences intriguing. It is clear that science and medicine, as I know them, are absent from the book, but it has made me realize that having you here could be a coincidence or it may be what the author of this book calls an omen. The key to the whole issue is that the book is well written, so I cannot discount the author as a charlatan. In fact, he seems to be a man of high education. I believe this is a sign," Jabir went on. "You may have been sent to us to be more than just a son of this household."

Alric's interest was increasing each moment. Jabir closed the book and placed it carefully on the bench in the space between them.

"Perhaps my being here is an omen," Alric suggested. "What is it that you require of me, father?"

"I need your help and to swear by the God you believe in that you will follow and heed my words and let no other person know of that which you seek. One mistake could mean death, not only for you but for all of us!"

A silence followed as each one became lost in his thoughts. It was one of those moments when silence was necessary for Alric to focus his mind on and digest Jabir's words of caution. He was anxious because Jabir was worried. As he waited for Jabir to speak, he heard Hilda's gentle voice: *This is how it used to be for us when our father was deep in thought. Be patient, Alric, and all will be revealed.*

Memories of Hilda came flooding back into Alric's mind. He could see them both playing at the edge of the forest, running from tree to tree, hearing her soft giggle, which brought a tear to his eye. He remembered how his mother used to call them for a warm meal of soup and bread when his father had returned from work at the end of the day. These were memories that he would cherish for as long as he held breath.

Reach out to him, Alric, Hilda whispered words continued. *He has need of you.*

* * *

Two hours later, Jabir entered the laboratory where Alric and Ma'ruf were clearing away the equipment. Alric looked at Jabir and spoke. "I have observed, father, that a material that inflames readily when exposed to heat in air can be distilled by heat from this sample of heavy tar that was sent to you from the seepage at Hit, on the Euphrates River."

Alric brandished a glass container of the thick, black, tarry material in one hand and a container of a transparent liquid in his other hand. Jabir examined the liquid and smelled it for effect. "Well done, Alric. I had heard that such was possible. Can it be that this is the Greek fire we have heard about?"

"I think so, father. I have not concluded any tests, but this could be used for peacetime or warfare."

"Most interesting. I would like to leave that for now, Alric, as I have another matter to discuss."

Jabir looked at Ma'ruf, who knew immediately that his attendance was not required. He bowed his head to Jabir and left the laboratory. Jabir waited until he was sure that Ma'ruf had left the immediate area of the laboratory, then he looked directly at Alric. "I have secured a passage for you on a caravan that leaves two days hence. Ahmed will accompany you. You will both be suitably dressed so as not to attract attention. You must be careful lest your fair skin and hair the color of straw give you away!" Jabir exclaimed.

Alric smiled. "I may have the answer, father."

"Surely you do not intend to shave your head and eyebrows?" Jabir exclaimed.

"No, father," Alric picked up a jar of ointment from the table. "When I translated the *Materia Medica*, I was infused with ideas. To some extent we are more advanced in our science and medicine, and I have several ideas that may be of use."

Jabir looked at Alric quizzically.

"The first idea relates to skin coloring. Dioscosrides describes various extracts from plants that left his fingers discolored. A thorough washing removed the coloring from his hands." Alric had Jabir's full attention as he continued. "If you recall, you asked me to test some of your ointments for interaction with each other. This one," he held the jar forward, "is a compendium of the ointments that you asked me to test. I read from the labels that each ointment has its own particular use, varying from treating skin lesions to burns. I have tested all of them, and the results are in this jar. I have selected ointments, depending upon their use, and mixed them. This is the outcome."

He gave the jar to Jabir, who removed the top to determine the odor of the ointment. There was none.

"I made it by mixing . . . "

Jabir listened intently to Alric's description of the preparation of the ointment that was based on an extract from the aloe plant. He gave details of the amounts of each constituent that he had used, the mixing process, and then the final yield of the product.

"But . . ." Jabir began, realizing that Alric had used the dangerously volatile flammable oil.

"If I may, father, I merely used the volatile spirits to bring the constituents into close contact. As the mixture was stirred vigorously, some of the volatile spirits escaped to the air. The remainder I removed by warming to a point above which the volatile spirits are no longer a liquid and escape to the air. As you may have noticed, there is no odor."

"Alric, do you propose that this ointment would color your skin sufficiently so that you would not be recognized?"

"I believe," Alric said, "that this mixture of the ointments will not only protect a person from the vicious sun and perhaps reduce what you call sun sickness but will also add protective coloring to the person's skin." Alric rolled up his sleeve and preferred his arm to Jabir. "And," he continued, taking a cloth, "it can be washed away with a mixture of water and this fragrant oil."

"You have done well, Alric," Jabir commented. "Protection for the Caliph's soldiers from the sun and the ensuing heat sickness is always valuable." Jabir scratched his chin. "So, you are proposing to use it as a skin coloring to give you anonymity on your forthcoming journey, and you will appear, to all intents and purposes, as one born here rather than an outsider from the north!" Jabir smiled then patted Alric's shoulder. "Well done indeed."

He was thrilled at Alric's initiative, and Alric beamed at the compliment. "Now," Jabir commented, "you mentioned that you have ideas from the *Materia Medica*. So far, I have heard one idea."

"Ah, yes, father," Alric exclaimed. "Dioscosrides also missed the possibility that he had created an extract that could create fire and another that could be used as a medicine to relax people. It also seems to me he had tested the medicine, because his notes state that he fell into a sleep where he was aware of what was going on around him and felt compelled to answer any questions very truthfully!"

"And?" Jabir asked.

"I have not proceeded with the extract that can create fire or with the medicine, but as soon as I can . . . " Alric's meaningful words trailed into the air.

"Alric, once this journey north is over, I suggest that you work on these new ideas, but be cautious. You are treading into an unknown area of alchemy." Jabir paused, then said, "Now, you need to make the preparations to leave with Ahmed and we must move with haste. I do not want to lose a day and since you have passage on the caravan, we have made a good start."

Jabir seemed ready to leave when he turned to Alric. "After you have finished here," he said, "please talk with Ahmed, who will describe to you the ways of the caravans. In the meantime," Jabir said as he walked out of the door, "I must get the Caliph updated on recent events."

* * *

The first words that Alric heard from Ahmed were, "You must learn to ride a camel!"

During the next day, Alric spent many hours learning to mount and dismount a particularly surly camel. The animal was not too cooperative and only wanted to grunt, groan, and spit. It seemed to have been born with the urge to poke its nose in out-of-the-way places in search of anything that was of no value. Finally, at the end of a long day, it had decided it would listen to Alric's command and respond to the whip. Alric wondered how it was possible to ride serenely and comfortably on such an ungainly beast. But, much to Alric's dismay, in addition to riding the unpleasant animal, he had to groom and care for it! No one else, Ahmed told him, would care for the camel on the trail, and an unkempt camel may draw attention to them!

Alric pointed out to Ahmed that no decent man should ever have to ride a camel, and he added humorously that in the whole of Mesopotamia, no one could find a camel as difficult as this beast.

As Alric worked with the animal on the second day, it was even more impossible, since it would not stand up for him. But Alric was determined. It was a battle of wills, and finally Alric won.

Ahmed watched in patience, laughing inwardly at the camel's behavior and Alric's determination. "You have established yourself over the rights of the camel, Alric. Now he will behave. But," Ahmed grinned and whispered, "do not tell him we will be carrying pieces of boiled camel meat as emergency rations. He will start his silliness all over again!"

*　*　*

CHAPTER 19

On the appointed day, at dawn, the caravan that had assembled on the outskirts of the city slowly began to move along the road that led from the northeast gate toward the River Tigris. Alric, who was suitably covered with the concealing cream, was amazed at the diverse collection of people. Camels and donkeys were the main means of transportation.

Merchants and travelers had gathered throughout the late afternoon of the previous day, while others had arrived during the night. At a signal from the caravan marshal, a long blast that sounded from a bugle announced to everyone that the caravan was ready to depart.

Experienced camel drivers quickly climbed onto the backs of the sedate animals, tapped them with whips, and offered unintelligible sounds of encouragement, to raise the beasts into a standing position. The camels grudgingly moved and showed their displeasure by a series of grunts and groans as they chewed on the last remnants of an early feeding. Other travelers mounted their donkeys, a contrast to the haughty camels. Those who walked picked up their packages, slung them across their backs, and eagerly stepped out.

Alric and Ahmed, wearing the clothes of merchants and perched on their respective camels, left the city quietly and mingled with the many camel riders. They each had a donkey tethered to their camel for carrying merchandise.

As the caravan set off at a steady pace and wound its way through the quiet city streets, the only sound came from the continually dissatisfied mumbling of the camels.

The group soon crossed the bridge over the Tigris River and moved in a northeasterly direction. As the morning advanced, the sounds of men and women, the cries of children, the argumentative grunting of the camels, and the sound of the eternal wind all mixed as one. The caravan was very much alive.

"I have been this way many times," Ahmed said, "but the desert is so huge, and the horizons so distant that they make a person feel small."

Alric understood intuitively what he meant, just as he had felt when he had looked at the sea from the Wearmouth beach; he had fallen silent, impressed by the sheer vastness of the ocean and its uncontrollable force.

"*Shukran*. Thank you." Alric said out loud.

"You spoke?" Ahmed asked.

"Quietly thanking God for my blessings."

They continued to ride in silence. The caravan slowly made its snakelike way across the desert on the eastern side of the Tigris in a northerly direction. Here, there were places where the route was close to the river, but for the most part the journey was half a day's travel from the river. Their route was a combination of sand and rocks. In some places, the ground was covered with the salt of dried-up lakes. At times, the wind caused the warm sand to blow against their covered faces as the sun beat down on their shoulders. When the sand was too soft, they were forced to dismount and unburden the camels. The ground improved when they were close again to the River Tigris, and the caravan leader chose this as a place to replenish their water containers.

Alric and Ahmed remained alert for any signs of being followed or watched. Over the years, Ahmed had developed an instinct for such activities. On a few occasions, they met a caravan going in the opposite direction. The respective leaders were always ready to exchange information about windstorms and stories about the desert and other travelers they had seen.

At noon the caravan halted and rested for the three hours when the sun was at its strongest; the journey was resumed late in the afternoon.

* * *

At the end of the first day, Alric was exhausted. He had discovered that riding a camel over a great distance was much different from the practice rides he had made, and it was painful to certain parts of the body. After the first two hours, his body had felt numb. That night, he slept soundly in spite of the pain. The next morning, riding across the desert with not another soul in sight for miles except for his caravan was an interesting experience.

Alric's thoughts were interrupted by a signal from Ahmed. Bedouins dressed in black garments, exposing only their eyes, appeared and followed the caravan for some distance. One of the caravan leaders took it upon himself to explain that war between the tribes was a constant series of events. The Caliph had recruited Bedouins to perform surveillance duties along the various caravan routes and to provide warnings about thieves and barbarian tribes. They mysteriously appeared in silence and departed the same way.

Ahmed whispered to Alric that he had no fear of such men, since he was known to several of the tribes. "The Bedouins have eyes like the eyes of the hawk, and they will recognize me, even over this great distance, so you are safe, my friend," he said to give comfort to Alric.

Alric noted that there was a sense of peace in the air.

* * *

That night, the caravan stopped at an oasis. Alric and Ahmed dismounted and searched for a suitable place to watch while the remainder of the caravan arrived. Alric was conscious of his height and, at Ahmed's suggestion, decided to walk with a slight stoop.

The oasis was much larger than he had imagined. It consisted of many wells and date palms. Innumerable brightly colored tents spread amongst them. Men at the oasis gleaned the latest news from Baghdad while the women focused on the bales of cloth brought in by the merchants.

Alric and Ahmed shared a fire with several of the camel drivers. Earlier these drivers had assured the first-time travelers that there was no danger from the Bedouins. One of the drivers had spoken quietly and confidentially his words of wisdom to Alric and Ahmed. "I do not worry about the Bedouins. If I see them, I see them. I do not fear the past, although lessons are learned from past events. If you can concentrate always on the present, you will be a happy man. There is life in the desert, just as there are stars in the heavens. That is why life is to be appreciated for the moment we are living right now."

* * *

During the day, Alric was starting to feel at home in the silence of the desert, and he was as content as he had been in the monastery. Although the vision of the date palms would someday be just a memory, right now it signified shade, water, and a refuge from the threat of attack.

At the end of the day, the silence of the desert was a distant dream. The travelers in the caravan talked incessantly and laughed, as if they had just emerged from darkness and found themselves once again in the world of light. They were relieved and happy, and there was food in their stomachs.

Alric felt uneasy for a moment and mentioned this feeling to Ahmed. There were no guards on duty here, and since they had been taking such careful precautions in the desert, he wondered if this was not too lax. Ahmed smiled and explained, "An oasis is considered to be neutral territory," he said, "because the majority of the inhabitants are women and children. The tribesmen fight in the desert, leaving the oases as places of refuge."

Now Alric understood the joy the travelers felt when, after a day or more of yellow sand and dazzling blue sky, they first saw the bright green foliage of the date palms. These were places where they could rest and feel refreshed without fear.

* * *

The next day they continued north and began to travel faster. The days had always been silent, but now even the nights had also become quiet. It was two nights later, as he was getting ready to sleep, that Alric looked for the star they had followed every night. He thought that the western horizon was a lower than it had been, because he seemed to see stars on the desert itself.

"It is the storm," Ahmed said, "and it will arrive soon." He grimaced.

Alric looked at him in surprise. "How do you know?" he asked.

"There were signs this afternoon," Ahmed answered simply.

Alric shook his head, failing to understand.

It was not until the palm trees stood in stark contrast to the orange color of the evening sky that the strange mysteries of the weather began to unfold. The winds increased in force, and the travelers were pleased that they had set up camp earlier. This effort could take two hours because of the need to unload the burdens of the camels and donkeys to give them a chance to rest before their journey in the morning.

"Remove all the cargo from the beasts, then tie them up," the caravan marshal and his leaders commanded, "and then get into your tents and remain there under blankets."

Only the camp's torches afforded some light in the darkness of the night, and then a sudden gust of wind converted the light-giving torches to stygian blackness.

The wind increased in force, causing moments of instability to men who had been walking outside as they hurried to their tents.

Alric, peeping out of his tent, saw a man go down and roll along the ground, as two others tried to assist him. Camels and donkeys cried in fright as the wind continued to disturb the caravan. Everyone expected it, but no one saw the huge cloud coming from the south. The sand and dust swirled around and around, joining together and hiding the night sky from view.

The travelers endured a restless night filled with dreams of the wind that gave them endless torment. There seemed to be no escape, as tent openings flapped wildly and the supporting ropes threatened to offer the fabric to the wind. Alric and Ahmed lay in the dark interior of their tent, fully covered, to protect their bodies, especially their eyes, from the vicious, stinging sand.

Suddenly, as if by a preconceived signal, the night was still.

The next morning, as the sun rose, Alric, Ahmed, and the other travelers stirred from the little sleep they had gained the previous night. They struggled free from the sand that had invaded their tents and covered their blankets. The sun heralded a new day, and it was time once more to prepare for their journey northward.

Rather than dwell on the storm, which was now an event of the past except for the sand that seemed to be everywhere, Alric decided to concentrate on more practical matters. He and Ahmed had been told by Jabir that in the caravan there would be a man from whom he could learn the secrets of the *cunei forma* writing. Neither Alric nor Ahmed knew this man, but Alric was convinced that Ahmed's practiced eye would recognize him when he appeared. Alric hoped that it would be someone as capable and as trustworthy as Jabir had indicated.

The farther the caravan traveled from Baghdad, the more likely that the contact would approach them. Alric had wondered about the timing, but he knew he needed to be patient. He remembered what the camel driver had said: "I am interested only in the present and I do not dwell on the past." *The man is wise,* Alric thought.

At the end of another day, the caravan stopped for the night to rest at a caravansary that was a roadside inn where the group could recover from the toils and labors of travel.

Alric looked at the building, which had a square walled exterior and a single portal wide enough to permit large or heavily laden camels to enter. The courtyard was open to the sky, and along the inside walls of the enclosure a number of identical rooms, stalls, and tethering bays were constructed for the accommodation of the travelers, their merchandise, and their animals. Ahmed had told Alric that the caravansary would have sweet water for drinking and washing. It would not be the harsh, brackish water that was often found at oases.

"This one," Ahmed said, "has baths, fodder for animals, and shops where travelers can acquire fresh supplies. In addition, some of the merchants who have traveled with us have brought supplies for the shop owners to purchase."

Alric and Ahmed opted immediately for a bath, glad to wash the sand from their bodies, and made arrangements to have a private bath brought to the room that he and Ahmed had rented for the night. Two women of indeterminate age brought the metal bath and placed it in a small alcove that offered privacy. After a few words, the women disappeared, only to return within minutes with two large containers of hot water. These actions continued until the bath was filled with the appropriate amount of water, and then cold water was added to adjust the temperature to a comfortable level.

Ahmed took the first bath and after fresh water had been brought, Alric soaked his aching and sand-weary body in the luxurious water. He had just emerged from the bath and was applying his aloe-based coloring cream to his hands, face, neck, and hair when he realized that Ahmed was missing. He quickly finished dressing and satisfied himself that he once more had the appearance of a native Mesopotamian, and then left the room to search for Ahmed. Turning toward the main gate, he heard the friendly voice from behind.

"Alric, we have a fellow traveler who would like to talk with us," Ahmed said by way of introduction.

Alric bowed his head and the stranger bowed in return. "You are welcome," Alric said but did not give his name.

"I am Rafiq, one of your fellow travelers," the stranger said. "I have been observing you for the past two days. "I believe that you have need of me. Please walk with me."

Ahmed nodded and indicated that they would follow, not yet willing to fully trust Rafiq. This man looked no different from the rest of the travelers. He was of average height and dressed in the same manner as the others, so that he blended into the crowd of merchants in the caravan. He had been completely undetectable.

"You are wondering who I am?" he asked quietly as they walked around outside of the caravansary, giving the appearance of three weary travelers stretching their legs. "You are also," he continued, "wondering if I am trustworthy." He turned and looked at Alric, "I sense that your friend Ahmed does not trust me."

He stopped as if to admire the trees and greenness of the land on which the caravansary was built. Then he addressed Alric. "Lord Jabir said that you were an intelligent young man. So you must heed my words. There is much work to do and no time to waste."

"What do you suggest?" Alric asked.

Rafiq could not tell anyone about his reason for being in the caravan, and rather than arouse suspicion, he suggested that they state that they had been introduced by a mutual friend. Alric was glad that progress was being made; the long journey had not been made in vain.

"Now," Rafiq, said, "to business and the tablets."

"I had not seen the language of the tablets until I came to this country," Alric said, "and so I may need your help in deciphering the meaning."

Rafiq's eyes remained steady. "I do not believe that I can be of much help. There are very few of us who can translate the tablets, and I know only a smattering of the language. However, I do know that some of them hold secrets that have long been forgotten—secrets of subjects such as medicine, science, the key of ancient languages, and above all the key to our heritage."

"Who . . . ?" Alric was about to ask when Rafiq signaled that he should remain silent.

Several women dressed in black robes, which signified that they were married, came to the nearby well for water. Alric noticed that the women barely glanced at them and went about their tasks as if Alric, Ahmed, and Rafiq were not there.

Rafiq continued, "there is a man in Mosul, known as the Librarian, who can read the tablets and he will teach you the meaning of the signs. You will go to that part of the old wall where the Prophet Jonah, peace be upon him, is buried. There you will see many people who wish to be healed by being close to the prophet. The Librarian will contact you. He may not contact you the first day, or even the second day. He will only make contact when he has determined that enemies have not followed you."

Alric said little but listened intently to the instructions. They seemed simple enough. The place of Jonah's burial had been pointed out to him when he journeyed to Baghdad from Constantinople. And Ahmed indicated that he knew the city well enough to find any address.

"I must leave now. It will be fruitless to seek me out, as my journey takes me in another direction. May Allah bless and protect you," were

Rafiq's parting words as he melted into the shadows of the evening. Alric looked around him at the date palms, reminding himself that he was here by the grace of his father, Jabir, whose trust was more important than anything at this time.

"The omens seem to be in our favor, Alric," Ahmed announced.

They sat at the base of a palm tree to observe the last remnants of the day and watched the final arc of the sun disappear below the western horizon as it presented them with a stunning orange-hued display.

Later that night, as they stood looking at the moon and thought about what Rafiq had told them, Ahmed made the suggestion: "You and I can be in Mosul by late morning if we travel alone and forgo part of our rest during the night. The caravan will arrive late afternoon or early evening and I would prefer the privacy of our arrival to the publicity that goes with that of a caravan. We have sufficient dried fruit for food." He looked at Alric. "Are you up to it, brother?"

Alric smiled. Anything that would take time off the journey was worth the effort.

"I think," he responded quickly, "the omens may favor such a decision and," he added rubbing his sore muscles, "that will mean less time riding a camel. I believe it to be a good idea!" Ahmed laughed at Alric's comment.

* * *

Alric and Ahmed left the caravansary under the cover of night, knowing that they had at least three hours before the rosy light of dawn appeared in the east. They prepared their camels and the donkeys. The caravansary guards were not disturbed or their suspicion aroused. Occasionally, a dog barked, but no one, other than Alric and Ahmed, moved in the blackness of the night.

Ahmed knew that one hour before dawn the caravansary would start to come to life. There would be woodcutters carrying wood for the fires to heat the water, camel drivers tending to their animals to make sure that all was ready for the journey, and women going about the preparation of the morning meals for their families.

Even in the darkness, Ahmed was well aware of the route to the north. They were on the eastern side of the River Tigris and the caravansary was set back a little way from the north road. They stopped the camels at the road junction and Ahmed listened intently. His camel grunted as if taking offense at being asked to work in the darkness. He slapped it with the whip and the animal fell silent.

"I hear no one," Ahmed whispered.

They made a steady pace before the sun rose, and within two hours they could see the city of Mosul. The sight gave Alric a sense of relief. They moved their camels slowly but surely toward the city walls that rose above the plain. The walls, the gate, and the palm trees had a golden glow in the early morning sun. As they got closer, the sound of people going about their business came across the sand to them. As they neared the gate, Ahmed looked around warily. The voices of the people were louder.

"We have arrived at a good time, Alric," Ahmed seemed elated. "The streets will be full, and that will give us some anonymity. I know of a caravansary on the southeast side of the city where we will be made welcome with no questions asked. From there, we can easily ride to the part of the old wall where we will have our meeting with the Librarian."

The gate of the caravansary was open and the courtyard empty. The huge interior was surrounded by a two-story building, and all around, above and below, doors opened into the central area from the rooms where the travelers lodged.

A man emerged from the gate house and stared at Ahmed, and then his face broke into a broad grin. "My dear cousin Ahmed," he said quietly, "even under the face covering and the different clothing, I can still recognize you from the way that you sit astride a camel."

Before Ahmed could respond, the man said, "May I beseech Allah that you have not become a merchant?"

Ahmed and Alric's camels, realizing that this was a rest stop, automatically lowered themselves into a resting position. The donkeys, still tethered to the camels, bayed with annoyance at the tension placed on their halters. The camels remained unconcerned of their plight. Alric was pleased that they had arrived at their destination; it was such relief from riding a camel.

Ahmed dismounted first, removed his face covering, and gave his cousin the customary kiss on the cheeks. "Munib," Ahmed said formally, "I present to you my friend, colleague, and brother Alric."

Ahmed indicated that Alric remove his face covering. Munib, shorter in stature than Ahmed and somewhat rounder-faced, smiled at Alric. "Welcome, Alric. Any friend of my cousin is welcome here." And then Munib raised an eyebrow. "Your name tells me that you are not of this land, and," Munib inspected Alric closely, "although you have our skin tone, your blue eyes confirm my suspicions."

Ahmed explained Alric's origins. Then he turned to Alric. "No one, except family, knows that Munib and I are cousins through our mothers, who were sisters. This is our secret for the protection of both of us."

Alric had wondered why Ahmed had not mentioned Munib during their visit to Mosul on the way to Baghdad. Now he understood. "Your secret is safe with me, Ahmed."

Munib looked surprised. "You speak our language very well, Alric," he said. "My compliments to you and to your teacher." In gratitude, Alric bowed his head. "You are a good teacher, my cousin. Now," Munib continued, "I propose that we tend to your animals. A bath will be provided for each of you and comfortable rooms made available for as long as you wish. By late afternoon or early evening, this yard will be jammed with men and animals. A caravan is arriving from the south—

ah," he said suddenly, "I understand you were with that caravan and have left it." Munib paused. "Let me offer you refreshing cool water."

Munib walked to a large stone tank that stood next to the gate. He turned a tap, filled a metal ladle, and passed the water to Ahmed and then to Alric. The cool liquid made Alric feel rejuvenated. "I know, Ahmed," Munib said, "that you have your reasons for leaving the caravan, and that is none of my business. Secrecy will be maintained here. For the moment," he continued, "we shall see to your comfort. Rest, relax, and I will call you for the evening meal and we will dine together in my private quarters."

* * *

Alric awakened suddenly to the sound of loud voices. He was in a state of limbo, not sure where he was until he recalled the bath.

The relaxing bath and the comfort of the bed had brought sleep to his aching body. The bath had been carried into his room by two older women who had lit candles that sent a soft glow throughout the room. The women, without being asked, had added a small amount of lavender oil, well known for its sleep-inducing qualities. Alric had carefully climbed into the bath and sat in the warm water. Thick towels had been left so that he could dry himself, but he decided not to apply the body lotion that the women had left, in case it interfered with his coloring ointment.

Minutes later, wrapped in a clean robe, courtesy of Munib, he had lain on the bed and was soon in a deep sleep, until the sound awoke him. The cacophony filled his ears, and he realized that the caravan had indeed arrived. He looked through the small window which was protected by a curtain. Yes, it was here!

Camel drivers were already tending to their animals. Local men, waiting to be called for paid work, squatted on benches of baked bricks just inside the gate. Merchants bustled about, making sure that their goods were in order as they checked the bales of merchandise, the stuffed saddlebags, and countless other bundles in the process of being unloaded from the backs of camels and donkeys. After all this, the courtyard would also be thoroughly cleaned, in particular the areas where the animals were tethered, and all would be prepared for the next guests.

Dinner that was provided by Munib consisted of an unlimited array of small hot and cold appetizers, *mazza*, which included *hummus bi tahinah*, chickpeas with a sesame paste; *tabbulah*, a salad of onions, chopped tomatoes, radishes, parsley, and mint; and *kibbi*, a ground mixture of wheat and lamb. The meal lasted almost three hours. Munib and Ahmed caught up on the latest rumors, of which Munib was well versed. Camel drivers are known to wallow in the trough of the rumor mill and would regularly pass on to Munib what had happened in Baghdad, and often what was about to happen.

"There is," Munib said looking around as if not wishing to be overheard, even in his own apartment, "word of a great one who would be greater. His name is not known, but I advise that you proceed with caution, my cousin, and you also, Alric." Munib looked into Ahmed's eyes and then at Alric. "Your business here," Munib said, "is for you to know only. I am involved by offering you help. If you need me, I am here."

"It is best at this stage that you do not know," Ahmed added. "It is sufficient that we deal with any danger. But, my cousin, I know that if I need your help, you will be there for me."

Munib bowed his head. Alric remained silent as he recalled Jabir's words before they left Baghdad: "One mistake could mean death, not only for you but for all of us!"

* * *

CHAPTER 20

Alric had been awake for an hour and lay thinking over the plan for the day, until he could rest in bed no longer. He had slept well and had a clear mind. He knew immediately where he was and what he had to do. He was sensitive to his current task and the possibility of discovering the contents of the tablets or at least one tablet in particular.

He sat up in bed and gazed at his clothes that were heaped upon the cushions scattered at the foot of the bed. His first thought was to start going about the business of the meeting with the Librarian. His second thought was more corporal. He was conscious of the ache that invaded his body and that seemed to converge to a climax in his legs. The continuous days of riding on camels and sleeping on the ground and, at best, the nondescript bed of the last caravansary, had given him extreme discomfort. He had an intense thirst. He saw a carafe of water that had been thoughtfully placed on the table by Munib after he had fallen asleep. He got up, seized the carafe with both hands, and drank half of the contents before he bent over and poured the remainder over his head.

A tap on the door caught his attention and he looked up, his hair dripping with water, his pale-skinned face betraying his origins. Before he could speak, he heard Ahmed's voice from outside the door. "Alric, is all well?"

Alric raised his head and made one or two painful efforts to speak before he succeeded in finding his voice. "Yes, Ahmed." Alric opened the door. "Come in, Ahmed," he croaked.

Ahmed entered and closed the door carefully. "I think," Ahmed said, looking at Alric standing in his breeches and undershirt, hair soaked by the watery dowsing, "that I will ask Munib to direct his men to bring fresh water and towels to your room. You can bathe in private and reapply your coloring ointment." Ahmed took in Alric's appearance once more. "Your voice may be suffering from the dryness that accompanies desert travel. Munib suggested it might be so. Khalil and I wondered why you did not suffer when you crossed the desert with us."

Ahmed proffered a small bottle of a clear, thick liquid. "Here, drink this."

Alric wrinkled his nose but took the bottle from Ahmed and examined the contents without removing the stopper. "What is it?" he asked.

"Munib has this prepared especially for travelers. It is made by distillation of the tar from Tuttul. He tells me that his camels and donkeys thrive on it. Drink it."

Alric hesitated for a moment, then drank the thick liquid, and felt the smoothness as it coursed its way down his parched throat.

"Another version of this forms a pure white solid, and we use it for candles. This will lubricate your throat and the lower parts of your body."

Alric noticed that already the coarseness in his voice had disappeared and his throat felt much better. "In the words of *al-khimiya*, Ahmed," he said, "this is unreactive. In Latin, I would call it *parum affinis*, little reactivity."

"Par . . . affin?" Ahmed stumbled in his pronunciation of the unfamiliar Latin words.

"Yes, Ahmed," Alric continued. He felt that he could talk normally again. "I think that is a good name, Ahmed," Alric exclaimed. "We can call it *liquid paraffin*, to differentiate it from the solid material that is used for candles." Alric frowned as he suddenly retreated into the realms of deep thought. "There may be other possible uses of the liquid paraffin," he said, "if it is truly unreactive. Would it be possible for Munib to give me the means by which it is made?"

Ahmed smiled. "Munib did assure me that it was harmless, and I will ask him to give you the recipe."

A tap on the door heralded the arrival of the servants with the bath and hot water. Alric threw on his outer garment, covered his head, and turned away from them while they prepared the bath. Within minutes, under Ahmed's supervision, the bath was ready and the servants left with heads bowed in respect to the Ahmed's commanding voice and stature.

"I will leave you now, Alric," said Ahmed, turning toward the door. "There are several items that I need to discuss with Munib."

Once the door was closed, Alric undressed and stepped into the warm water, where he luxuriated for the next half hour before deciding that he should get ready.

Soon, fully dressed, suitably colored, and covered, Alric tapped on the door to Ahmed's room. "Come in," Ahmed called from within.

Alric entered to find a table laid for breakfast. It was set with a variety of yogurt dishes and pastries filled with nuts and was layered with honey, fresh fruit, and syrup for dipping. To drink, there was orange juice and tea that had the aroma of peppermint.

During breakfast, Munib continued to fidget, as he had since the start of the meal.

"Speak, cousin," Ahmed said authoritatively. "It is obvious that you have something on your mind."

"It seems," Munib began cautiously, as if searching for every word, "that your arrival has not gone unnoticed."

Alric frowned. He stopped eating almost in midbite at Munib's warning.

"Please continue," Ahmed said, as he dipped a piece of fruit into the syrup.

"I had a contact early this morning as I watched my men feed and water the animals. It was whispered communication that came from behind me, but the speaker advised me not to turn around." Munib now had Ahmed and Alric's full attention. "This voice told me," Munib continued, "that the Librarian was expecting you at the designated place."

"When will that be?" Ahmed asked.

"No time was given." Munib shook his head as he responded. "The Librarian will contact you."

"Was there anything else?" Ahmed queried.

"Nothing." Munib shook his head.

Alric relaxed. The news was good.

"That is all, Ahmed," said Munib, and as if in anticipation of Ahmed's next question, he answered, "When I did turn around, the owner of the voice had gone. I was not able to see him to determine his identity." Munib shook his head as if to emphasize the negative aspect of the visitation. Then he smiled and tried to be helpful. "When you are ready, Ahmed, I will have horses prepared for your use."

"Thank you, Munib," Ahmed responded, then he turned to Alric. "I think, Alric, we should play this game, if it is indeed a game. But rather than walk into a situation that is not to our advantage, we should observe who might be observing us."

Alric agreed.

* * *

When breakfast was finished, Munib gave them outer robes that were of a nondescript color, almost the color of the sand in the courtyard.

He also provided them with horses that were equally colorless and looked somewhat forlorn.

"Do not worry, my friend," he said to Alric, who had looked askance at the horses, "these animals will serve you well and will not wilt under the heat of the day." Munib turned to Ahmed. "The saddle packs contain all you will need for a day, cousin. There is fresh water for yourselves and the horses, as well as food for you both and some fodder for your animals."

Munib paused for a moment. "Since you are giving the impression of two wayward travelers, you may also wish to consider purchasing food from a vendor when the occasion arises and use the food in your packs for emergencies only."

"My thoughts exactly, Munib," Ahmed responded.

Ahmed and Alric mounted the horses and thanked Munib as they said goodbye. They rode slowly out of the courtyard, after promising Munib to contact him when they were able to do so.

Although all precautions had been taken to cover their identities and their reasons for being in Mosul, Ahmed still remained cautious. He rode slowly out of the caravansary gate looking about without appearing too obvious. He did not see anyone who aroused his suspicions and whispered to Alric to be on the lookout for any person who seemed to be taking an undue interest in their activities and movements. Alric nodded to show he understood.

He was excited to be at this stage of their journey. He hoped the results of this expedition with Ahmed would outweigh any potential danger. Once they had cleared the gate area, they felt that, so far, all was well.

* * *

For the next three days, Ahmed and Alric spent their time riding around the general area of the ruins of the southwest wall of the city of Nineveh.

Using a different route each day, they paid particular attention to the comings and goings of the pilgrims, specifically looking for loiterers and anyone behaving in a suspicious manner.

To the curious observer, they were just two visitors, absorbing the ruins of the old city, covered by light brown hills of dirt. They ate meals wherever they could find a vendor, and when the air became too hot, they rested in the shade of the ruins, making sure that the horses had sufficient water. This was something that Alric, other than on the journey from Constantinople to Baghdad, had not experienced. His appreciation of Ahmed deepened each day. This was the Ahmed who, with Khalil's support, could disappear for days and return with intelligence and conversation about enemy movements.

Alric listened carefully to Ahmed's words and his guidance. He also realized the reason for the nondescript clothing. At times when Ahmed dismounted and walked ahead to the sandy mound that covered the ruins of the old wall, he would seem to disappear against the background. In fact, the mousy color of the horses also fitted into this scheme of concealment.

On the evening of the third day, Ahmed and Alric visited Munib again, and when they sat down to dinner, Munib announced he had been contacted once more, in the late afternoon, just before they'd arrived. "It is evident," he looked at them both, "that you have been observed. However, the Librarian says he is satisfied that you have not been followed and he will be waiting for you tomorrow." Munib paused and then added, "I was also told to tell you to go about your usual habits of the past days."

"You did not . . . "

"No cousin, I did not see him. Again, his voice appeared over my shoulder from the shadows." Munib shrugged in annoyance. "I thought that I knew the nooks and crannies of the caravansary better than anyone. This one, the Librarian, seems to know my home better than I!"

* * *

The next morning, Ahmed and Alric mounted their horses and followed the north bank of the Khawsar River to the mound upon which was built the mosque in honor of the Prophet Jonah.

They rode, as travelers who had no specific purpose in mind, and within half an hour their circuitous route brought them to the site where they hoped to meet the Librarian. They dismounted and allowed the horses to rest while they, under the guise of requiring water from their supply, looked around. Then from a spot that had been hidden by a slope of the land, a man appeared riding a donkey.

Alric and Ahmed watched him as he drew closer. He passed a flock of sheep and nodded to the shepherds who seemed to know him. "This cannot be the man," Alric exclaimed. "Perhaps we are being observed again."

Ahmed spoke in a whisper. "Have patience and be prudent, my brother."

As the man drew closer, Alric attempted to mount his horse.

"Wait!" Ahmed commanded.

Alric stopped with one foot in the stirrup, the other suspended in the air for a brief moment.

"You, I believe," the man said, "are Ahmed, and you," he looked at Alric, "are Alric al-Biritaanya.'"

They remained silent. Ahmed's hand went to the long, curved sword hidden under his outer robe.

"I am the one you seek." The man bowed his head in deference to them. "I am Alim, Guardian of the Tablets to His Most Royal Personage Caliph Harun al-Rashid. I am otherwise known as the Librarian!"

He tapped his donkey on the rump with a thin cane and rode closer to them, arms open to show he did not have a weapon. "I suggest," Alim said, "that we adjourn to my place of work, where we will not have to worry about being watched. Please follow me."

They rode slowly for almost an hour, careful not to tire the horses in the heat of the day. They followed the mound of earth that covered the old wall of the city. Finally they came to a gap that at one time had been a gate, where the mound was not as high. Alim stopped, dismounted, and appeared to examine the donkey's hooves. As he did this, his eyes swept the terrain for signs of anyone who may have followed them. Seeing that all was well, he suggested that they should again follow him.

Suddenly, Alim disappeared within the mound. Ahmed and Alric, also having dismounted, moved forward with their horses, wondering where Alim had gone, and were surprised when he reappeared just as suddenly. "Bring your horses out of the heat. Quickly! Remove the saddles and tether the horses to the post near to the wall where they can have food and water."

After the horses were tethered, Alim pushed a heavy wooden gate into place. To Alric's surprise, the hinges of the gate were noiseless. He wondered if Alim had used the liquid paraffin on the hinges or at least some similar material made from the Tuttul tar.

"No one can see this place from the outside," Alim said by way of explanation, "since the outer covering of the gate simulates the dirt and sand. To find us, one would have to examine every foot of the walls of the old city, and these walls extend for more than eight miles around the perimeter! Now, let us go inside."

"Inside?" Alric looked at Ahmed. "I thought we were inside!" he whispered to Ahmed.

Alim led them through a door into a large, well-ventilated room that was lined with patterned bricks and carpeted in bright colors. As soon as they entered, he turned and closed the door to the room where the horses were tethered.

"This," Alim said, extending his arms, "is the remains of the old eastern gate to the city. The animals remain in the outer area. This closed-off inner part was formerly a guard house that was built into each of the gate towers. It now serves as my library, dining area, and storage rooms."

Alim removed his head covering. He was, Alric noted, an older man, perhaps of the same age as Jabir. He had gray hair and wide shoulders, and by the way he dressed and spoke, Alric surmised that he was of a noble family.

"In peace I welcome you," he said, bowing his head to Ahmed and Alric, who had, by this time, removed their face and head coverings. Alric could feel the gentle movement of cool air in the room.

And so Alric and Ahmed were welcomed into the historic library by Alim, Respected Guardian of the Tablets to His Most Royal Personage the Caliph, Harun al-Rashid. "Please call me Alim," he announced as he looked at Alric. "I use my full title only on ceremonial occasions, young sir."

Alric smiled. "There is no need to call me *sir*."

"I see," Alim said as he studied Alric, "in spite of the black hair and brown face, you are not of this country as your name indicates."

Alim lit candles, and as Alric's eyes adjusted to the light, they saw the well-stocked shelves. For a moment, his memory flashed back to Jabir's library. Alim's library had the same neat appearance, except for the fact that the shelves were stacked with the ancient fired clay tablets that contained the *cunei forma* writing.

"Will you take water?" Alim asked and saw the concerned look in Ahmed's eyes. "Do not be alarmed," he said, attempting to allay Ahmed's concern, "the water is good." He pointed toward the back of the room where several large sandstone amphorae stood in rows supported by metal stands. "I believe that you may have seen such an arrangement in Lord Jabir's house?"

Alric nodded. Ahmed still looked uneasy. Alim continued. "No one can find us here. The boys will take care of that and they will also tend to your horses."

"The boys?" Alric jumped into the conversation. "Which boys?" he asked.

"The boys who look out for me. These are the children and grandchildren of the people I have helped over the years. They are sworn to protect me, and although you did not see them, there are a least six of them hiding within the dips and hollows that are in the old walls. For that service, I see that they are educated and will one day enter a profession or, like you, Ahmed, become an officer in the Caliph's army."

Ahmed's eyebrows raised in surprise. Alim cautioned, "Lord Jabir, through Ali al-Maslawi, sent me details about both of you. Trust comes from knowing a man's background."

He went into the back of the large room. After a few minutes he returned with a clay pitcher of water and asked them to sit on the seats which were fashioned from sections of the old stone columns dug out of the sand and dirt. He gave a cup each to Ahmed and Alric, indicating that they should help themselves.

"And now to business, but first allow me to explain my need for secrecy." He sipped his water. "As you may gather from my title, I have been appointed by the Caliph as the custodian of any tablets that are found on this site. My main area of business is a building that is situated on the edge of this old city and the city of Mosul. But as you may have gathered, I have another task. That is to separate and preserve in this place any tablets that contain secrets of science, medicine, and even predictions of the future. For this reason, I am known only as 'the Librarian.' There are those who would kill for such knowledge. Remember," he wagged an admonishing finger, "knowledge is power!"

"Now," he looked at Ahmed and Alric, "I have had an uneasy feeling for several months. In fact, I have sensed that I am being watched!" Alim took another sip of his water before he continued. "There have been many times when I was in Mosul that I have glanced behind and wondered about the unexplained shadow or a familiar face that I had seen earlier. A change in the intensity of the light coming through the window of my home had made me wonder if someone was outside watching me. I decided, rather than worry about shadows, I had to take control of the situation."

Alim gave a sigh of uncertainty, then closed his eyes as he contemplated his next words. "All of my life, I have tried to do the right thing by healing people, similar in fact to the activities of Lord Jabir," he said. "And so I talked with those I could trust, and under the greatest secrecy I was able to secure this place."

He looked up at the walls and the supported roof. "Even though I feel safe here, I still believe there is a problem. I have to come and go from here, and that will always be a potential weakness in my secrecy. Hence, my caution!"

They talked for a while as Ahmed and Alric realized the seriousness of Alim's words. They tried to put Alim at ease, and soon they were laughing and joking. After a momentary silence, Alim spoke. "I am convinced that I must be raising some eyebrows again in certain rooms, even in the palace. The rumors of the tablets and their secrets are many, and it would not take long for someone of intelligence to put the thoughts together and recognize the implications of my work with the tablets. That is why I was very cautious in allowing us to meet. I had to be sure that you were not followed here."

"So!" the word burst from Ahmed's lips. "Now I understand."

A worried look transformed Alim's otherwise peaceful face into a mask of uncertainty as he passed his hand through his gray hair. "Ahmed," Alric looked at his friend, "what do we do next?"

"It is my thinking," Ahmed said, "that we may not be able to draw out this person or persons to see who is behind the rumors and the apparent plot against the Caliph." His words seemed to echo in the empty room. "However," he went on, "if the fears of a plot and the rumors are correct, we must be prepared for what may happen. It seems to me," Ahmed continued after a brief pause, "that the person involved and who has an interest in the tablets may have difficulty in attempting to understand the information they contain. After all," he looked at Alim, "other than you, there are not many others skilled in the interpretation of the *cunei forma*."

"So, Alric suggested, "we need to concentrate our efforts and work from a secluded place." He allowed his eyes to sweep around the room. He looked at Ahmed and Alim to see what type of reception his ideas brought to them.

"Then that should be our strategy," Alim agreed, "until you have obtained what you need and can return home."

"That is admirable," Ahmed said, "but I need to see the places where the boys hide and see that they are really to our purpose. I am of little use as a scholar but I am a soldier and that will be my role."

"You trust the boys, Alim?" Alric asked.

"Yes, I do," Alim exclaimed. "With my life!"

They relaxed on the cushions, sipping the cool water and forming a plan of action. Time was of the essence. A low whistle interrupted their thoughts.

"Ah," Alim was immediately alert, "we have a visitor."

He went to the door, climbed on a small ladder at the side of it, and looked through a peephole inset into the wall above. "See for yourselves."

He turned to Alric and Ahmed as he descended the ladder, and they in turn scanned the area for any signs of life.

Two old women were scrounging for scraps and anything that they could salvage from the dirt and sand. They were dressed in ragged black robes, and their clumsy, padded feet underscored their poverty. They struggled as they walked, perpetually bent, no doubt after a lifetime of such activity.

Alric's gaze drifted to the distance, but there was nothing. He looked again, but the old women had disappeared out of his line of vision. A scratching sound on the door brought him back to the present. He descended the ladder and Alim swung the door open to allow the two women to enter.

Alric was alarmed. Ahmed's hand immediately went under his robe to draw his sword. "Ahmed, Alric," Alim beamed, "allow me to present my wife, Masarrah, and my daughter, Nawal!"

The two old women were suddenly transformed. They dropped their black robes to the ground and straightened to stand at full height. Their garments were of delicate pastel shades that had been fully covered by the black robes. Masarrah and Nawal bowed their heads in deference to the visitors.

"They have become well known around the mosque as women seeking a cure for their bent backs, which you can see need no cure. That way we can keep track of the comings and goings at the mosque. And, to my delight," Alim smiled at Masarrah, "I have their delightful company for the midday meal."

In this bent posture, Masarrah and Nawal were able to carry containers of food suspended from belts on their shoulders without arousing any suspicion.

"And now, my friends, I suggest we eat."

They dined at the small table, and the fare that Masarrah and Nawal had brought—white bread, oatmeal cakes containing lentils, and a variety of root vegetables—were most welcome. When the meal was over, they moved to the cushions, which were near the table, to relax.

Alim smiled at his wife. "Any news, my dear?" he asked.

"The caravan brought several pilgrims and there is word of bandits to the north. That is all," Masarrah responded. At Alim's request, Masarrah and Nawal gave details of the various visitors to the city and word of any newcomers. There was nothing to arouse Alim's suspicions.

Masarrah and Nawal cleared up the dishes, wrapped them in cloths, which were then strapped around their shoulders, and dressed themselves once more in the black robes. The reverse transition was complete. They left with as little fanfare as they had arrived.

"My thanks to both of you," Alric said as they left.

He could not see the hidden smiles, but a movement of each head told him that his thanks were appreciated.

*   *   *

CHAPTER 21

Alim was ready, but he was at a loss as to what to suggest Ahmed should do. It was at that moment that Ahmed spoke. "I would like to meet with your guardians, Alim."

Alim surmised that Ahmed intended to determine if the boys were able to provide an efficient warning system. "Of course, please follow me. My wife and daughter also brought food for the boys, so if you can help me . . . "

Alim allowed his words to trail into the silence of the walls, not expecting Ahmed to refuse. As they entered the stairway, he explained the arrangement to Ahmed and Alric. "There is a stairway at the rear of each guard tower. These have been cleaned of the dirt and sand of the centuries. At the top of each stairway there is a cover under which one of the boys hides. He will signal to the others when food is available. Then they make their way here unseen. I will make it clear that you are a friend and they will answer any questions that you may wish to ask. They will welcome the chance to talk with an officer of the Caliph's army. I will be back momentarily," Alim informed Alric.

The two men disappeared up the nearest stairway. Alric could hear the sound of their footfalls decreasing as they ascended. That gave him the chance to look around. The structure was not so much a library and work area, in which each room was filled with shelves that contained seemingly innumerable books and tablets, but also a home.

"I see the look of amazement on your face, Alric," Alim said. having quietly descended the stairway.

The baked clay tablets contained the strange signs of the writing Alric had named *cunei forma*. Alim guided him as they examined the tablets, for there was much that Alric did not understand. One of the tablets he learned was the most important text in the literature of the ancients. "That is the tablet," Alim explained, "that is said to have been written by the great king himself, Ashurbanipal."

"Ashurbanipal!" Alric exclaimed, "Is he not the king who amassed the library here at Nineveh?"

Alric had seen references to Ashurbanipal in several of the books that he had consulted for reference over the past week. From these sources, he had learned that Ashurbanipal had been a great king and was referred to as Asnappar in the Bible or Osnapper in other texts, also Sardanapalos in Greek texts, and Sardanapalos in Latin texts. Ashurbanipal had been one of the most cultured rulers of Mesopotamia, and he was able to read both Sumerian and old Akkadian scripts that were precursors of the Assyrian scripts. And, much to Alric's pleasure, Ashurbanipal had established the first systematically organized library in the region, containing tens of thousands of tablets. As these thoughts flashed through his mind, he was drawn back to the present by Alim's answer.

"Indeed it is, Alric," Alim smiled at his recognition of the name. "He was a lover of learning and established a library of the *cunei forma* tablets. These books," Alim continued as he pointed to the large number of volumes on the shelves, "will help you to understand the words on the tablets. If you require a certain book or a tablet that refers to a particular event, please ask and it shall be delivered to you within moments."

Alric looked around. This could take weeks, he thought. "May I?" Alric gestured toward the shelves in the room.

"Please do, and when you need anything, please call."

Alric looked at the various volumes on the shelves. He wondered how many sheep had given their lives to produce the vellum pages of each book, since each was as wide as the distance from elbow to wrist and twice as long. Bound between wooden end boards and lying flat one upon the other to a depth of four or five books, the volumes could last many decades without damage.

It did not take long before he found a book of great interest. It contained stories of men and women who, like his father, Lord Jabir, had worked the art of chemicals. They were people who had dedicated their entire lives to the purification of ores and plant extracts in their laboratories.

"You find the book interesting?" Alim whispered, his words interrupting Alric's thoughts.

"Yes. It is fascinating to read about the methods by which the extracts were obtained."

"I have here a book that may be of interest to you. It is a translation of the words on a particular tablet." Alim paused as he handed the book to Alric. "My Lord Jabir indicated that you may have some interest in it."

Alric sucked in a sharp breath. How could he have known? he wondered. Ahmed and he had left Baghdad immediately after Jabir's request that they proceed to Mosul and seek out the tablets of Nineveh.

"You seem surprised, Alric. Do you not know that it is written that a fair one from the north would be the son of a noble house?"

Alric's eyes opened in amazement. "You seem to be able to simplify all events in terms of where they have been written somewhere," Alric answered.

"This is a serious mission that you perform for Lord Jabir. Every step must be followed exactly as it occurs."

Alric turned his attention to the book, which was part of a multivolume work dedicated to curing all illnesses. There were sections that dealt with mixtures that delayed aging. But it was the central part that really sparked Alric's interest.

"It is not always easy to find what one seeks. There are many who have read this book and not understood the meaning of the words," Alim stated. "Perhaps words are misread in translation, thereby giving a false impression to the reader."

It suddenly occurred to Alric what Alim meant. "You mean . . . "

"Yes, Alric, that is true. Readers can spend years in libraries reading words that can lead them in the wrong direction."

Alric remembered that Lord Jabir had said it would be good for him to meet Alim so that he could free himself from conventional thoughts. Alric was becoming more and more convinced that Alim was the source of these words.

"Also," Alim continued, "the translations have a fascinating property. A small change in a word here and there can transform a story from reality to myth."

Alric was particularly interested in the original tablet. He thought that, with some patience and with Alim's help, he would be able to translate the original words. This would be a fascinating task, but Alric knew he would require more practice before he was ready. Alric looked closely at a tablet and noted the seemingly countless variations in the use of the wedge-shaped symbols. "Why do they make things so complicated?" Alric asked Alim after examining several of the tablets. "The writing and language of the *cunei forma* are well beyond my understanding."

"Imagine," Alim said, "the secrets that would be lost if everyone was able to translate these tablets. They would lose their value. It is only by persistence and willingness to study things deeply that you will achieve the goals that Lord Jabir has set for you. That is why I am here. I am seeking a true learned man who will help me to decipher the cuneiform codes. You are that man, Alric."

"When were these created?" Alric questioned.

"Many centuries ago," Alim explained.

Alric continued to examine the books and was intrigued by the translations that Alim had written. The *cunei forma* signs had been recorded faithfully by him in a neat hand, along with the Arabic translation of each *cunei forma* symbol. Alim gave Alric paper. "I suggest that, where you can, write the Latin translation of the Arabic words on these loose pages for insertion into each book. You may draw lines on the pages to correspond with those of the *cunei forma* and Arabic so that when laying the pages alongside those in the book, we will be able to match the translations. Then we shall have the translations in two languages."

"May I," Alric looked at Alim, "add the words of my Saxon language?"

"Certainly," Alim beamed at the suggestion, "then we shall have three translations of the *cunei forma*. Through time we shall transfer the *cunei forma* signs to your paper to form a separate book. The Arabic translation is for your eyes only. The Latin and Saxon will be difficult for anyone else to understand. That will be your book."

Alric set to work relieved that his memory served him well. As he looked at a *cunei forma* sign, his eyes caught each detail and fixed it forever in his mind. It suddenly occurred to him that this form of writing was, in truth, pictographic in nature. The sign representing the word for *mouth* was used for *voice* as well as for *speak,* and realizing this, he was able to imagine the sign as it must have originally appeared. He started to make preliminary attempts to copy the symbols onto paper scraps.

Alim, noticing the change of activity, saw the beginning results of Alric's work and marveled at his progress, then nodded his approval.

Alric had been so engrossed in his work that he was startled when he heard Ahmed's footsteps descending the stairway. He had not realized the day was drawing to a close.

Ahmed spoke. "I am satisfied, Alim. The warning system that you have established is every bit as good as you said. You are to be commended on your efforts."

"Good," Alim responded, beaming. "It is time for us to leave here and rest for the night. But first, I suggest that we have a moment of meditation to steady our nerves and a glass of refreshing water as we review the day and the next steps for tomorrow." They had much to talk about. "As you can conclude," Alim said, "we will meet again on the morrow. You know what needs to be done, Ahmed?"

"Yes I do, Alim. We will leave now. I pray that Allah protect you until we meet again."

"*Insha'allah*." Alim responded. "As God wills it."

* * *

Back at the caravansary, Alric had a sleepless night. His body still ached from travel, but at the same time, he was excited to learn more of the tablets. He was perplexed and concerned that he had not felt Hilda's presence for some time. He did not have an explanation, and his thoughts of Hilda would not leave.

As dawn broke and the sun began climbing into the morning sky, he was already up, bathed, and ready for the day. He cast his mind back to the work he had started the previous day and wondered where it would lead. A tablet that seemed to offer untold secrets would be a gift of considerable value. Lord Jabir must have known something about the contents of the tablet, otherwise, Alric asked himself, why the perceived danger and the need for secrecy?

At eight, two hours later, he heard a light tap on the door. Thinking it was Munib, he opened it, but to his surprise, it was Ahmed, who carried a tray laden with fresh bread, olives, and an assortment of fruits and juices.

"Good morning, Alric. I suspected that you would be up and ready, but the look on your face tells me that you did not sleep well!" Ahmed stepped into the room and laid the tray on the table. "Hungry?" he asked.

"Very," Alric responded eagerly looking at the tray.

Ahmed smiled. He had spent too many days on military assignment in the past to know the folly of omitting breakfast. One never knew what the day would bring, and a good breakfast could maintain the body for some time.

"Good," he said, smiling as he looked at Alric. "Food for the body is also food for the mind." Alric looked at the tray. "As well as fruit and bread, I have also brought you some *kibbi* to add a little more strength to your body."

Alric liked *kibbi*, a mixture of wheat and finely ground lamb, which he knew would energize him for the busy day ahead. A light scratching sound on the door heralded the arrival of Munib. He used that form of introduction only with relatives and friends, especially those with secrets to keep. Ahmed opened the door.

"A very good morning to you, Alric," Munib said cheerfully.

The tray that Munib carried bore glasses already containing sugar, and containers of tea and hot water. The hot water container, to Alric's surprise, had a small flame underneath the pot. Munib noticed Alric's curious stare and explained. "This is a little trick that I use to keep water hot, Alric. As you can see, the water pot sits in the holder that has a lower receptacle. We place flammable oil from the tar, which we recover at Tuttel or in some instances from Al-Qayarah that is less than a day's journey from here. We put the oil in the receptacle, light it, and lo and behold, a supply of hot water."

Alric nodded knowingly. He had seen many such heating devices in the laboratory, along with those used by the servants to provide all of the hot water in Lord Jabir's house.

"Munib," Ahmed broke into Alric's thought, "will you join us for breakfast?"

Munib bowed his head and smiled in acknowledgment of the invitation. He arranged the dishes on the table and lowered himself onto one of the comfortable cushions.

Breakfast, as with many of the meals, was a social affair. Munib kept Ahmed and Alric entertained with the happenings at the caravansary and also regaled them with tales he had heard from the various visitors. He had several questions for Alric about Britain and the life Alric had lived at the monastery. Munib allowed some emotion to show when Alric described the attack by the sea raiders. He wrinkled his nose when Alric described the type of food he ate as a child. The plain oatcakes, the vegetables, and the rare occasions when meat, even fish, was added to the diet were not to Munib's liking. He looked at the breakfast platter on the table. The peaches, plums, apricots, and other fruits were delightful. Those had not been grown in Mesopotamia but had arrived along the Silk Road and the Royal Road. Munib gave silent thanks for the blessings of trade with other countries that shared the two roads.

A tap on the door caught their attention. Ahmed sprang to his feet, his sword drawn and ready. Munib signaled to Alric to remain where he was while he answered the door. Ahmed stood in a position where he could not be observed from the outside but he could still see the visitor.

A woman in black, bent over apparently from years of toil and showing deterioration of her spine, stood before Munib.

Without hesitation, Ahmed recognized the woman.

"Please enter, Nawal," he said quietly.

As Ahmed closed the door, Nawal straightened herself to her full height, much to Munib's surprise, and smiled at Ahmed and Alric.

She looked at Munib, wondering if he could be trusted, and she decided to give nothing away in her words. "My father, Alim, will await you within the hour," she said to Ahmed. "He asked that you proceed in the same manner as you did yesterday."

Seeing her hesitancy, Ahmed eased her mind. "This is my cousin," he said, "who owns the caravansary. If you have messages for us, you can rely upon him."

Nawal bowed to Munib. "I must leave now," she said. "I was not followed, but if I stay too long . . . " The words trailed away.

"I suggest," Munib added, "that you take some of this food in a bag so that if anyone should be following you, it will be seen that you were begging for scraps."

Nawal nodded and picked up some of the food. "Thank you," she said. "I will give the remainder to the pilgrims at the mosques, some of whom do not eat regularly." Nawal resumed her bent posture, took the package of fruit, and left as silently as she had arrived.

Munib looked at Alric. "I see," he said observantly, "that you do not carry a weapon."

"I have my knife," Alric said.

To Munib, the knife was a trivial weapon, but he did not know of its history. "Then we must do something about that," he said and turned on his heel and left the room. Minutes later, he returned with an item wrapped in vellum, which he unwrapped to display a knife. "This," he said, "is called a *shafra*." He handed it to Alric. "It is carried in this sheath that is attached to the rear side of your vest, which I presume that you are wearing."

Alric nodded and examined the knife. The seven-inch blade was curved, sharply pointed, and engraved with geometrical lines. The handle was engraved silver which gave the knife balance. He attached the sheath to his belt using the convenient belt clip and placed the knife in the sheath.

"Now my young friend," Munib beamed, "you are protected!"

"Thank you, Munib," Alric responded, and then he looked at Ahmed. "Is it time for us to leave?"

"Yes, indeed, Alric," Ahmed answered. "After the start you made yesterday, I believe that you are anxious!"

"Your horses will be ready in a moment," Munib added.

* * *

In contrast to the day before, when Alim had approached them on a donkey, he took on a different disguise. This time they were approached by an old man, with a white beard, wearing grimy black robes. The man wore an equally unclean turban that sat jauntily askew on his head.

"He has seen better days, despite his present misery and infirmities," Alric said to Ahmed.

The beggar was chanting, "Alms for the love of Allah" as he passed their horses. They were surprised to hear him whisper, "Follow me," and only then did they recognize Alim's voice.

Alim did not speak further or give any indication that he had recognized them until they were safely inside the outer chamber of his workplace. "Apologies for startling you," Alim said once the horses had been tethered and watered and fodder provided in the antechamber to the library. "Cannot be too careful," he added. "Now, allow me to get out of these clothes and clean myself, and we will commence. In the meantime," he gestured to the table, "please help yourselves to water and fruit. I will also make tea when I return."

So saying, Alim disappeared into a room at the back of the library and emerged fifteen minutes later in clean clothes, looking very refreshed. "Now," he rubbed his hands, smiling, "to work! Ahmed, it is your choice. You can remain here with us when we study the tablets or you may wish to be outside keeping watch with the boys."

"No offense, Alim, but I do prefer the outdoors."

Ahmed turned on his heel and disappeared up the stairway and onto the top of what remained of the former gate.

* * *

Alric spent long days during the week that followed diligently working on understanding the meaning of the *cunei forma*. The book that he had started at Alim's suggestion became a record that contained several thousand pictographic symbols and words. For the moment, Alric had no time to even consider the possibility of maintaining his personal journal.

He discovered that cuneiform was used not just as an art form but also for practical purposes such as recording incomes and expenditures of large households, drawing up contracts, and the writing of legal texts, letters, records of public building projects, and records of wars. There were also hymns, prayers, myths, legends, proverbs, and the interpretation of natural and invoked phenomena, medical and mathematical texts, school texts, recipes, and technical instructions.

The range to which cuneiform was used was almost matched by the variety of surfaces upon which it was written. Most commonly, the clay was shaped into tablets, ranging in size from small tablets which could be held in the palm of the hand to very large tablets that could only be held with both hands. Alric was amazed as he considered the depth of knowledge that the thousands of tablets collected by King Ashurbanipal must have contained.

When he took tea with Alim, during a break from his labors, Alim taught him the rudiments of word pronunciation, as best as he knew. They even attempted a simple form of Assyrian speech, after which Alric practiced writing simple phrases. It was at the end of the eighth hectic and intensive day, as they sat drinking tea, that Alim made the announcement to Ahmed. "I would think, Ahmed, that our young friend here," Alim touched Alric's shoulder, "is ready to translate the language of the tablets. Tomorrow," Alim continued quickly before Alric could look up from his tea and proclaim his gratitude, "I will produce the tablet that you came here to examine."

"You mean . . . ?" Alric started to ask. Ahmed smiled at Alric's reaction and nodded his agreement to Alim.

"Yes, Alric," Alim smiled, "that same tablet that was held and looked upon, perhaps with awe, by Ashurbanipal!"

Alric was speechless. He was about to hold in his hands a tablet that Ashurbanipal was reputed to have referred to frequently and kept by his side throughout most of his life.

Alric spent yet another night with little sleep in anticipation of the forthcoming privilege of examining such a prize. It was during this night that Hilda appeared to him. She smiled and gently touched his hand. *It is a while since we last spoke, dear brother, but I have been watching over you and I see that you have found your true joy as you translate the tablets.*

Alric looked at her shimmering form as she materialized. She had not changed at all since that day . . . In fact, Alric thought as he strained his eyes to look at her, she seemed to have radiance about her form. He felt tears well up in his eyes.

Do not weep for me Alric. What is done is done. I am here with you always and I do not sleep. When you wake in the morning, you will remember the details of my visit as you have done in the past. It has been decreed that I will always be with you.

Alric could feel her hand on his head, running her fingers though his long hair as she did when he was recovering from the sickness. *Come brother, do not weep. It is a joyous occasion when I visit you.*

He wiped his eyes with his sleeve and smiled. Then he looked directly at Hilda, his glistening eyes fixed on her face. He now realized the meaning of her words and accepted them with the utmost calm as he inquired: "And now, dear sister, what is that you want of me?"

It was a wonderful moment of silence that followed as they looked at each other. That fateful day of Hilda's death was now in the past, and in future Alric would rejoice in her presence. A burst of joy filled his heart. Hilda knew his thoughts, as he knew hers, and she smiled. She was proud of her twin brother.

His thoughts, in particular those related to the most important tablet that he was about to see, passed between them. "Be aware, my brother. When a great king keeps a tablet close to his side, it may hold terrible secrets. And, if that is the case," she cautioned, "there are others who will be willing to pay handsomely for that knowledge! Remember, dear brother, I can foresee events and will give you warning if there is danger, but I am unable to prevent such things from happening. I am limited in what I can do!"

They continued to talk into the night and they laughed as they remembered the times they had spent together as children. Finally, the vision of Hilda left Alric as dawn turned the night sky into the morning hues of gray and blue.

"This will be an exciting day," Alric announced to the empty room as sleep took him into her arms for the last hour of the night.

* * *

CHAPTER 22

The next morning, Alric and Ahmed made their way to Alim's library, where Alim greeted them and, after making tea, produced the tablet that was of great of interest to Alric.

"So, Alim," Alric acknowledged, as he took the tablet carefully into his hands, "this is the tablet that was created long before the time of King Ashurbanipal?" he exclaimed.

"Indeed it was," Alim replied crisply. He had placed the tablet in its protective linen covering on the table, but before sitting down to examine it, Alric washed his hands, using the bowl of warm water that Alim had thoughtfully provided and dried them well on the soft towel. Then he carefully unwrapped the linen covering. Moments later he held the hand-sized tablet that went back to time immemorial. Alim watched protectively as Alric handled the tablet. Alric needed him to explain some of the different word meanings to avoid misinterpretation.

He was not disappointed in what he saw. The time he had spent studying the cuneiform caused the pictographs to come to life before his very eyes. The writing was a primitive form of the language that bore a closer relationship to the original pictographs than to the later *cunei forma* writing that he had studied for the past week. His original thought was that the language was almost too primitive to understand.

He heard a sound and turned to see Ahmed standing in the doorway.

"All goes well, my friend?"

"Yes, Ahmed. All is well."

"A new caravan has arrived in the city. I will be observing this for any strange or unusual happenings."

Alric thought it strange that Ahmed should constantly wonder about his safety. He continued contemplating the tablet. He reminded himself that this was a very early tablet and was written from top to bottom. In later tablets, the pictographs were written from left to right and were different from the early ones, which were turned on their sides.

"Alim," Alric suddenly asked, "why is it I am charged with this task by the Caliph and Lord Jabir when you are perfectly capable of translating this yourself?"

"The answer is in your initial realization of the correct way to read the tablet. I saw from your actions that you realized immediately the correct manner in which the tablet should be read."

"But . . . ?" Alric tried to interject, but Alim held up his hand to forestall any further part of the question.

"I am accustomed to the tablets written in the time of Ashurbanipal and for three hundred years or so before his reign. That takes us back almost eighteen hundred years. This tablet is two thousand years older and may be from the civilization that we call Akkad, or it may go back to the time of Sumer, which is even earlier. There are no known translations of these early languages. Your work this past week has given you the ability to read *cunei forma* signs, but you have also shown the initiative that was expected of you by the Caliph at the urging of Lord Jabir."

Alim paused as if deep in thought. "And they were correct in their estimation of your abilities. But to continue. My eyes and mind focus on the recent *cunei forma*. Your mind, unlike mine, is not trapped by such conventions. When your flare for language became evident to the Caliph, he realized you could bring a fresh outlook which would be most helpful. Translating the writing on the tablet is not beyond my talents, but the fear of misinterpretation plagues my mind and soul."

"I understand, Alim, but that will not stop us from working together?"

Alim agreed. He was pleased that he would be included in Alric's efforts. He had been given strict instructions that Alric would work alone, if he preferred such a course of action.

"Everyone has their own way of learning things," Alric said. "You have been my teacher for the past week but I apply the learning differently. We are both in search of the meaning of the words. It will be my honor to work with you, Alim."

For the next week they persevered in their efforts to translate the tablet. They worked from early morning until late at night, with the ever-watchful Ahmed guarding the entrance to the library. As the days progressed, they were pleasantly surprised by their efforts. Their character-by-character translation set the mystery of the tablet into the Arabic, Latin, and Saxon languages. They worked with such fervor that Ahmed was beginning to worry about their health and sanity. But finally the task was finished.

The work had drawn on the linguistic abilities of Alim with the new thoughts that Alric brought. The tablet had served as the ideal study to forge a bond between them. During the final two days, they had engaged themselves in a retranslation. This was the only way they could be sure of their findings. Finally, they produced a translation which both felt was accurate. It was the joining of their two minds that gave the translation its particular orientation.

That evening, as was his custom, Ahmed appeared to check on their well-being. He was surprised to see them sitting comfortably on the cushions, drinking tea and talking. "Am I to assume," Ahmed asked, "that you are either completely finished, or have you both taken leave of your senses?"

He could not help but notice the jovial expression on Alric's face. Alric could not contain himself any longer. He dabbed his mouth with his napkin after taking a sip of the tea. "We have done it, Ahmed," Alric exclaimed. "We have done it!"

"Please sit, Ahmed, and take tea with us while we tell you what has transpired," Alim suggested.

Ahmed listened intently to a story that was, to say the least, incredible. "And so," Ahmed began to summarize the story as it had been told, "there were those in ancient times," he said referring to the Akkadians and Sumerians, "who lived even before the Assyrians, who were able to control such power? It does seem incredible, but if only part of the secret of the tablet is true, this is a way to achieve unlimited power. I assume, however, that you are both of the opinion that such power should remain under the Caliph's control, unless he designates others to have this knowledge. We are aware that someone close to the Caliph would use this to his own advantage. He may even try to infiltrate his own personnel into the Caliph's confidence. If the Caliph should lose control of his kingdom, his ability to influence events in this region would be lost forever." Ahmed's voice had remained steady and he showed no signs of emotion.

"An excellent summary, Ahmed," Alim suddenly said. "Now we must make sure this work is safe, and you will need to secure your places in a caravan for the return trip to Baghdad."

* * *

After several intensive sessions with Alim to be sure that their translation was correct, Alric had transcribed the pictographs on the tablet to vellum. He rolled the vellum into a scroll, tucked it inside his inner garment, and secured it to his body with a belt.

After much thought, and to Alric's surprise, Alim relented and allowed Alric to take the tablet to the Caliph. "For without this tablet," Alim reasoned, "the Caliph could presume that the translation is fictitious!"

Alric was ready to return to Baghdad. At Ahmed's suggestion, they decided to travel with a caravan that had recently arrived from the coast.

There was word among the camel drivers that bandits were active in the area, and everyone needed to be watchful. On the second day after leaving Mosul, the hooded Bedouins reappeared more and more frequently, but Alric, remembering Ahmed's words about his good relations with the tribes, was not concerned. It had been almost three weeks since they'd first arrived in Mosul. Before that, it had taken almost a week to travel from Baghdad to Mosul. This meant that their absence may have been noticed in Baghdad. Until the identity of those who plotted against the Caliph was revealed, it would be best not to appear to partake in suspicious activities. If the need arose, Alric knew that Lord Jabir would manage to cover their absence with a plausible story.

* * *

The caravan reached the first oasis without incident. The animals were exhausted, and the men talked among themselves less and less. The silence was the worst aspect of the night, when the mere groan of a camel now frightened everyone because it might signal a raid.

Fortunately, the caravan was a sufficiently large group and had enough able-bodied men to deter an attack by bandits. Ahmed and Alric were more concerned that there might be those among the bandits who had been paid to be on the lookout for them. What better way to find and kill two men for little cause than to blame it on bandits or even on Bedouins?

"We must be alert to all events," Ahmed said to Alric as they ate dates one night during a brief stop at the second oasis. There were no fires, and the moon was hidden behind the clouds. "When I am eating, at times like this, caution is my watchword," Ahmed explained. Alric smiled at Ahmed's somewhat philosophical approach to their current situation.

The leader of the caravan decided that travel both night and day with the necessary stops to rest the camels and donkeys would be advisable. He had been informed that war had broken out between the various Bedouin tribes.

It was six nights later, as Alric strapped himself in position to sleep on the moving camel, that he noticed that the horizon had taken on an uneven appearance.

"It is the city," said Ahmed. "We will be there in the morning."

As the sun rose, Alric awoke to the gentle swaying rhythm of the camel's motion. He could see the walls of the city stretching across the entire desert.

"We have done it!" he exclaimed to Ahmed, who always seemed to be awake.

Ahmed was silent. He knew that they were not yet home, and with the silence of the desert, he was ever vigilant.

"We still have a way to go, Alric," Ahmed responded.

Alric had visions of Lord Jabir's house, the date palms, the garden that signified shade, water, and a refuge from the desert. Yesterday, the camel's groan might have signaled danger, but now it groaned only to show its bad temperament. "Even the animals speak many languages," Alric decided.

* * *

Alric's audience with the Caliph was set for late morning of the next day, and the Caliph had also suggested that Alric be accompanied by Jabir, Khalil, and Ahmed. Harun, not wishing to take any risks, ensured that his guests would arrive without interruption and in safety by sending ten of his soldiers to surround the quartet as they walked to the palace. He had also decided that the meeting would be in the form of a private tea and that no other person would be present. Harun was still concerned regarding the identity of the "one who was close to him" and the plot against the throne, but he needed evidence before he could act with any degree of certainty.

The soldiers had arrived promptly, under the command of a captain, at Jabir's house. Amira invited the men into the garden, where she plied them with cool orange juice and oatmeal cakes with honey. Even in the late morning, the sun beat down mercilessly. The cool drinks and the rejuvenation that the sugar-rich honey gave to the men were appreciated.

The journey, the tension, and the excitement of the tablet had caused Alric to oversleep under the silk sheets in the comfortable setting of his room. He was finally wakened by Amira, who decided she would not allow Jabir, Khalil, or Ahmed near the room lest they disturb him. Alric still felt that he had never left the back of the camel, as the sensation of swaying to and fro in time to the beast's long strides and gentle grunting was still apparent.

As the soldiers refreshed themselves and Alric made ready, Jabir and Khalil had a little extra time to hear from Ahmed about the details of the journey and the visit with Alim, the Librarian.

As they walked to the palace, surrounded by the soldiers, Jabir talked quietly with Alric to make sure he understood the importance of this audience with the Caliph.

"Harun will assign us specific seats so that he can hear each word and see your every emotion as you relate the story. He will value your words. He does not mask his emotions when in the company of family. Above all, be honest and maintain prudent behavior when in an audience with Harun. After all," he took on an even more serious tone, "even though Harun has taken a liking to you, he is a man of mood swings, and sometimes his emotions control his actions. His justice is swift and final to those outside of the family who try to presume too much or take advantage of his generosity. In fact, to my knowledge, your mother, my dear wife Amira, is the only person who can talk with Harun like mother to son. Her reason, she has told me, is that since his mother, her sister, is dead, someone must attend to Harun!"

Alric hoped he would never be in such a position where he felt the wrath of the Caliph! He would heed Jabir's words well.

* * *

They reached the palace at the appointed time and walked from the outer gate to the throne room. It was as impressive as it had been on previous visits. The palace remained majestic simply by the sheer amount of space it occupied. The enclosures and gardens which led to the actual residence seemed to have taken a plan from nature, resembling the rose and its concentric layers of petals.

As they passed the enclosures, each increasing in refinement to the center, Alric felt an added sense of awe. The last of these, which abutted on the Caliph's private rooms, was planted almost entirely with roses and exemplified the incredible skills of the gardeners. The scent of roses and numerous other blooms intermixed and made Alric feel intoxicated.

On reaching the entrance to the Caliph's private rooms, the visitors were announced by the captain of his personal guard. Harun was waiting for them; he was alone, seated on cushions. He looked calm, his eyes fixed toward Alric and Ahmed. On the floor around him, more cushions were comfortably scattered. Colored flagons of juices and bowls of fruit were on the table. A gathering of servants arrived, ready to do the Caliph's bidding, after which they would withdraw.

Harun arose from the cushions and looked at his visitors with pleasure. As always, his clothes were immaculate. A tunic of rich brocade, faced with bands of silk and inlaid with pearls, made him appear just as spectacular as the first time that Alric had seen him. This time, he was not wearing a turban, and his long black hair was pulled back from his face and hung down his back.

"Sire," Jabir said as he bowed. This gesture of obeisance was followed by Khalil, Ahmed, and Alric.

"Uncle!" Harun responded, smiling, "I always tell you, in a private setting you have no need to kneel before me. Are you not the husband of my dear mother's sister? Rise please," he took Jabir's arm to help him to his feet, "and you also," he said to Khalil, Ahmed, and Alric.

As they lowered themselves onto the cushions, the Caliph indicated that they should refresh themselves. Servants brought in fresh bread, butter, and olives. They all readily partook of the refreshments until everyone was satisfied. The Caliph then signaled the servants to clear away the plates and bring in cool fresh water, then he turned to Jabir to indicate that he should commence.

Jabir introduced the topic for discussion and went into considerable detail. Alric took this as a sign that he should also include the full details of the journey and his findings.

But he had to wait. Jabir suggested that with the Caliph's permission, Ahmed would speak first. Alric noted that once the meal had been completed, the meeting took on a more formal atmosphere. Jabir finished his introduction and at a nod from the Caliph, Ahmed began to relate his story.

"Sire," he began, "Alric and I joined a caravan on the day of . . . " As he talked, Ahmed emphasized certain points. He did not miss any details, even noting the diligence with which Alric followed the cleansing ritual and the five prayer periods each day. Ahmed wished to explain this to the Caliph because he was proud of Alric and he needed the Caliph to recognize that he had made a suitable choice in trusting

307

Alric with the difficult task of the journey to Mosul. One hour later, his story was finished.

"Thank you, Ahmed my friend, an excellent account. I had heard about the possibility of trouble with the tribes. I have men embedded in their midst who are keeping me informed. It seems it is a situation where some tribes are jealous of others because of their closeness to me. I have already taken steps to rectify this situation."

Ahmed smiled and bowed his head in gratitude.

"Now Alric," the Caliph's attention had turned to him. "I will hear you, but please bear with us while we stretch our legs for a few moments and refresh ourselves."

Soon they were all seated again.

Alric, whose use of Arabic was now perfect, even including the tones and intonations of the Baghdad dialect, had no trouble relating the story from his perspective. He did not repeat any of the events covered by Ahmed but described the meetings with the Librarian, his ability to partially read the tablets, and the work he was continuing to do to make his knowledge of the *cunei forma* all encompassing.

Throughout Alric's account, the Caliph showed some surprise at Alric's conversational abilities, as well as his newfound knowledge of the language of the tablet. Harun was pleased to see that Alric had fulfilled the promise he had shown at their first meeting. He looked at his uncle and smiled faintly. Jabir was proud of Alric.

Another two hours passed, and Alric paused, having reached the point where he and Ahmed left the Librarian to return to Baghdad.

"Rest, my young friend," the Caliph suggested, "and take water or juice before you continue."

The Caliph's use of the term *my young friend* did not go unnoticed. Alric had been accepted by Harun into his close circle. "And now, Alric," Harun said as Alric placed the empty glass upon the table, "you have peeled the onion layer by layer for us and we are now at the core.

I assume you have more to tell us?" Alric looked pensive. "You have some concern over your translation?" the Caliph asked.

Alric wondered for a moment how to break the news of his discovery. All eyes were upon him. He needed to deliver his words with the impassionate speech of the alchemist. "I fear that you may have bad news for us, Alric," Harun said, realizing that Alric was formulating his answer carefully.

"On the contrary, Sire," Alric began, and then he bowed his head as he realized that he had contradicted the Caliph. "My deepest apologies, Sire, for appearing to contradict you, but the news is good."

"No apologies needed, Alric," the Caliph responded. "My government is full of men who agree with everything I say, and I find that to be tiresome. It is refreshing to have with me men I can trust and who will speak the truth. Continue," Harun said amiably.

"If it pleases you, Sire, I will read the tablet to you in the form that I have translated. For that, I will need to hold it in my hand."

The Caliph raised his eyebrows. "You have the tablet with you?"

"Yes, Sire. If I may?"

The Caliph nodded.

Alric took the precious item from the inside pocket of his jurbah, unwrapped it, placed the silk wrapping on the table, and then laid the tablet upon it. Harun looked curiously at the tablet. "So," he said, "this is the tablet that was treasured by Ashurbanipal?"

"Yes, Sire." Alric nodded as he responded.

Harun wiped his hands on a cloth and then he picked up the tablet. "Have you, uncle . . . ?" He left the question unfinished as he looked at Jabir.

"We have seen the tablet, Sire, but we thought it best to hear the translation after you." Harun replaced the tablet on the silk wrapping.

"Alric," he said, "we are ready."

Alric took a deep breath, picked up the artifact, looked intently for a moment at the wedge-shaped symbols, and began. "This tablet was written before the time of Abraham, may peace and blessings be upon him, and predicts the future of the country that once existed to the south of present Baghdad. These people called themselves the people of Sumer. However, the writers of the tablet described a man to be born in the future. His home was in a land of continual green and he lived near to the sea . . . ”

“Is that not a description of your home, Alric?” The Caliph asked, his eyebrows raised.

“Yes, Sire, except when the fog arrives from the sea.” For support, Alric looked at Jabir, who gave him an encouraging smile. “This man,” Alric continued, “was born many years after the writing of the tablet. When he was growing up, a sickness overtook him from which he almost died. He recovered and attended a center of learning. His growth in knowledge was miraculous and . . . ” Alric hesitated before going on. “He has the marks of gods upon him, and . . . ”

“Wait,” Harun commanded. “The first time we met, did you not show me your arm that carries the mark of the cross that is the mark of the God of the Christians, as well as the crescent mark that is becoming recognized as the symbol of our faith?”

“I did, Sire,” Alric answered, “and that is what makes this so embarrassing. I feel that I am reading to you a story that I could have written myself.”

“Go on,” Harun said.

“By some means, the tablet is not clear on this point. The man arrives in the Land of Sumer, where he becomes known to the king.” Alric looked at the Caliph. “I am sorry, Sire, for the use of this title. The word for ‘caliph’ is not available in the language of the *cunei forma*.”

“Continue,” Harun urged.

“The tablet then goes on, Sire, to describe this man who, it is written, comes from the western stars and will have stature in the land. Many will try to fight him, but all will fail, as his allegiance will remain true to the king of the land. He will have an iron fist and will shoot fire from his hands in his leader's name. No one will defeat him." Alric paused to sip juice. Silence reigned in the room. "This man will be worth an army to his king. He will remain steadfast and loyal and never turn against the king, even though he was surrounded by enemies. The evil ones shall receive a storm of fire as a punishment. This man will seek them out and there will be no escape for those who will harm the king or his family. At the end of the time of the evil ones, they will be separated from the people in a way similar to that in which corn is separated from chaff. After a trial, the man from the western stars will remain in the land and serve later kings before he will be recalled to the western stars."

"I think," the Caliph looked at Alric, "that we will take another break and have fresh food and drink brought in."

He clapped his hands, and as always, servants appeared from behind curtains and proceeded with their duties. Once more seated on the cushions around the table, the Caliph spoke first as he helped himself to several of the dates. "That is an interesting story, Alric. And now I would like to analyze what you have told us." He popped a date into his mouth. "Uncle, Khalil, Ahmed, you are free to ask questions without fear of interrupting me. But first, I seem to recall," Harun said pensively, "that when my cousin Khalil found you, you were close to death from a sickness?"

"Almost, Sire, but there is another coincidence. Before my capture by the sea raiders, I was taken with a sickness that sapped my strength and energy. My body was weakened by this, but my strength was returning. The summer was good for me. I had been spending more time outside enjoying the fresh air. Hilda, my twin sister, was my guardian. She helped me and I was happy and starting to enjoy life again. On that fateful day, my sister Hilda had the stature and energy that I did not. It was through her goodness and courage that I survived."

"I see from your eyes that good memories of her are still with you, Alric. May she always be close to you," Harun said before he continued. "It seems you may be our man from the western stars."

"Sire!"

Khalil, who had remained silent throughout the meeting, now interjected. Alric's words had triggered a reaction in his mind. "I am interested in the concept that the man, if I may quote the words from the tablet, 'will have an iron fist and will shoot fire from his hands in his leader's name and no one will defeat him.' Being a soldier, I am very curious about this. Alric, is it possible that this is a reference to some new weapon?"

All eyes turned to Alric. The silence was heavy in the room.

* * *

CHAPTER 23

Alric slowly and deliberately placed the glass onto the table, choosing his words carefully. "What I gave you was my translation of the first side of the tablet. There is another side that I will now read to you." He picked up the tablet, carefully protecting it with the silk wrapping.

"The first part of the writing on the tablet describes the use of certain plant extracts for medication. My father is already using some of these recipes to create medicines to heal the sick. The second part describes procedures for extracting the plant medications. But," Alric paused as he looked at the Caliph, "it is the third part that, if I may use your expression, Sire, is the core of the onion."

"As before, Alric," Harun said with deep interest. "Spare us no detail."

Alric held the tablet closer so that he could see the writing more clearly. His face grew serious once again as he started to read. "There are those parts of plants and animals that contain an ingredient that can be extracted for use to generate the fire of which the first side of the tablet speaks. The people of Sumer prepared an extract from cow fat that had been rendered down through boiling and then was mixed with a liquid that we call *spirit of niter* or *aqua fortis*."

Jabir nodded to show he agreed with Alric's use of the name for the very potent nitric acid. "The mixture gives off heat," Alric continued, "and after a period of time," he frowned at the lack of a definition of the time required and added, "the tablet does not specify how long."

Alric looked closely at the writing to make sure he did not miss anything, since some of the symbols could be placed in a different part of the tablet, but all seemed in order. "A pale yellow liquid forms from the two phases. Great heat is given off and it is recommended that the mixture be cooled by immersion of the vessel in a bath of cool water—this helps retain control of the reaction. And," Alric looked closer at the tablet, "there is some indication that the pale yellow liquids float on top of the mixture." Alric frowned. "There are some words here that seem to be out of place. When I first saw them, I wondered if the scribe had made a mistake and not erased it."

Alric looked at Harun. "Sire, the words are: 'My servant Ea-Urki died while doing this.'" Alric paused before continuing. "And now that I read it aloud, I believe the symbols mean much more than when I first translated them." Alric went on. "I had originally assumed that 'Ea-Urki died while doing this' meant that Ea-Urki died while working on the tablet and that he was a servant of the scribe. Now, I believe the man writing the tablet was more than a scribe—possibly a man of science and medicine—and Ea-Urki was his helper in the laboratory!"

"So, Alric," Harun spoke with tones of excitement in his voice, "you believe that this . . . " he looked at Alric.

"Pale yellow liquid, Sire," Alric offered.

"Yes, Alric, this pale yellow liquid has some power and may kill a man working with it?"

"Yes, that is my conclusion, Sire," Alric said firmly and convincingly.

Harun rubbed his brow with his forefinger. He seemed to be at a loss for words. Alric looked at Jabir, who smiled and winked, then interjected: "Sire, I believe the extract Alric describes will be similar to that prepared by the people of Babylon during the time of Ashurbanipal, hence his interest in the tablet."

"Go on, uncle," Harun said.

"Inscriptions from clay cylinders found at the site of ancient Babylon indicate that when animal fats were boiled with wood ash, an extract was obtained and was used for making soap. We prefer scented water and scented pumice, but the ordinary people used what I also believe was called soap."

"That fits, father!" Alric raised his voice.

Jabir held up his hand to indicate that Alric be silent as he looked toward the Caliph, but Harun only smiled. "Ah, I hear the impulsiveness of youth. It is all right, uncle. Please continue, Alric."

"My apologies, Sire," Alric said and then continued. "I am led to believe from the translation that the people of Sumer designed a weapon from this extract that was so great in its explosive power that whole armies could be decimated. It is also my opinion that the secret died with the civilization. No other group of people has been able to decipher this new knowledge."

Alric had reached the final stage of his assessment of the tablet. "It is also written, Sire, that this extract, the explosive I will call it, can be used in small amounts to cure ailments of the heart, especially when breathing is difficult."

"That is most interesting, Alric, and my uncle has told me that certain extracts can be used as poisons or as cures, depending upon the amount. If you are correct, we have an extract that can be used as a violent weapon on the one hand and as a cure for heart ailments on the other?"

"That is correct, Sire," Alric said quietly.

"The soldiers of Ashurbanipal were known for their ability to bring down city walls and thus destroy cities. Is it possible they used this weapon?"

The response from Alric was simple. "It is, Sire."

The Caliph looked at each in turn. "However, I am curious why the secrets of this extract and the resulting weapon were not passed down through time?"

"If I may respond, Sire?" Alric asked. Harun nodded. "There are words written elsewhere on other tablets explaining that the people who made this extract and knew of its power, let us say it was the Sumerians, abhorred war. It was not until the time of Sargon, who unified the various tribal groups, that war became a natural outcome of their activities. My interpretation is that the knowledge of the extract and its power may have been deliberately kept secret, and it was not until the time of Ashurbanipal that the knowledge was sought again."

A silence descended like a dark cloud upon the room. For a moment Alric could not even hear anyone breathing. He looked at Jabir, who indicated that he remain silent. Then the Caliph gathered his jurbah about him and stood up. Everyone was about to stand. "No, no," Harun informed them. "I only need to stretch my legs and think about this issue. Please," he gestured toward the juice and fruit that remained on the table.

Minutes later, after walking around the room, Harun returned to his seat.

"It seems, my friends," he said, "that we are on the verge of a major discovery. Jabir, Alric, what are your plans for the next steps?"

"It is better," Jabir spoke quickly, "that Alric explain this to you. In this current matter, I can offer experience, but Alric has a new line of thinking."

"Thank you, father," Alric responded. He turned to face the Caliph. "Sire, this will be a challenge in which we must not be afraid to try something new, and I am sure we will learn more about our goal as we proceed. The project is complicated, and there is no guarantee we will succeed. However, we will spend time gathering as much information as we can."

"That sounds admirable, Alric. Is there anything else?" Harun asked.

"Yes, Sire. We will send you a detailed notebook of our findings. During our work, there will be failures and we must not become discouraged if we run into problems."

Jabir smiled and said "Alric, you have laid out a series of thoughts that are logical and well explained."

Khalil and Ahmed also approved. Harun beamed. He was more than satisfied with Alric's performance and was impressed at his command of the old *cunei forma* language and his abilities as a budding scientist. "Well done, Alric," Harun exclaimed. "And well said, uncle. You will have my full support, and all the necessary assistance will be at your disposal."

As the Caliph rose to his feet, they all stood and bowed in unison. "As you may have gathered," Harun said, "you are to my liking, Alric. You have the fire of learning in your eyes. I am pleased, uncle," he looked at Jabir. "Your protégé will be a great benefit to this court." The Caliph turned to Khalil. "My dear cousin, yesterday the general of my armies fell from his horse and sustained a back injury that may prevent him from his duties. I need someone to replace him that I can trust. I hereby appoint you in his place as General of the Armies."

Khalil bowed his gratitude. Then the Caliph addressed Ahmed. "Ahmed, loyal friend, I need someone to send spies into the streets to be my eyes and ears. I hereby appoint you to this position to control all such activities." Ahmed bowed and accepted the honor. "I will leave it to you and Khalil to choose suitable men from the army. These men will retain their respective ranks and receive army pay. I will not have such an important job metered out to the vagabonds in the streets."

Harun looked at Khalil and then back to Ahmed. "How long will it take you to prepare the men for their tasks?"

"Perhaps two days, Sire," Ahmed answered. "No more." Khalil agreed.

"These men will need to wear street clothes and be suitably armed for their own protection," Harun suggested.

"I already have men, Sire," Khalil explained, "who are skilled in the art of unarmed combat and in the use of light weapons. Ordinarily I would advise three months for such training, and forgive me for being presumptive, Sire, but after you explained that someone close to you may place you in danger, I took the liberty of starting such training."

"So be it," said the Caliph. "As long as it is you, cousin, I have no problems."

Khalil then added. "I beseech you to be cautious, Sire. Your tendency to walk in the streets at night is known to many, and your disguise may not always secure your safety!"

Ahmed spoke. "May I suggest, Sire, Khalil or I accompany you on such walks? Then you will have the extra protection needed."

An expression of infinite gratitude spread over the features of the Caliph. "Your suggestion is accepted, Ahmed. Now let us not ignore my uncle and Alric. You will keep me abreast of any developments, uncle?" Jabir agreed. "And you, Alric," Harun's face took on a serious look, "must be cautious. This product of the laboratory that you seek seems to have extreme danger associated with it. You will exercise all means of caution but still be close enough to others who can rush to your aid should the need arise. I will expect regular reports every seven days through my uncle and you may also be called to attend me when necessary. Is that understood?"

Alric bowed. "It will be my pleasure, Sire."

"And now," the Caliph said as he clasped his hands and looked at the four men, "the meeting is over."

* * *

Alric and Jabir assembled all of the necessary equipment and resorted to making animal and plant extracts in the laboratory over the next two weeks. On the first day of the third week, Jabir left the house to brief the Caliph on their progress. All was well. Two servants had been assigned to watch Alric and to assist when required.

Amira was taking tea in the company of Abal, Buhjah, and Maha when one of the servants rushed in. "Smoke! Smoke!"

"Alric!" The name burst from Amira's lips. She knew from what Jabir had told her that Alric was working with dangerous substances. Amira looked at the three maidservants. "Come with me, and you," she pointed at the servant who had raised the alarm, "take us to where this is happening. Now!"

The servant led them to the laboratory. Smoke pouring out of the laboratory door almost blinded Amira. There did not seem to be any fire, she was thankful. The smoke curled in an ominous gray-black pillar from the door to the laboratory. Amira's ears were ringing from the sounds of the other servants screaming for Alric.

Suddenly, a form appeared from the smoky atmosphere and Alric strode out of the laboratory looking worse for wear. His jurbah, once white, was now a blue-gray color. In his right hand he held the remnants of a glass flask. His face and hair were blackened and flecks of blood stood out against the remnants of his sleeves.

"Alric," Amira exclaimed, moving forward hastily with her arms ready to embrace him.

"Mother, I have done it!"

"Done what?" Amira asked somewhat angrily at his nonchalant attitude.

"I was thinking about the project for the Caliph, which I designed from reading *Materia Medica*, and suddenly it occurred to me that I was doing it all wrong. I changed my technique, and the product was there in the flask, in my hand."

Amira's patience was wearing a little thin now, having recovered from the initial shock of seeing Alric emerge from the smoke. "But the smoke?" she exclaimed looking for an explanation. The three servant girls who had started chattering from nervousness were silenced by one look from Amira. "Bring hot water, towels, and the medication for cuts and abrasions," she commanded. They stood mesmerized by the sight of Alric before them. "Now!" Amira said in annoyance. "Not tomorrow. Now!"

"Alric, my son," Amira said more calmly as she placed her arm around his broad shoulders. "Sit on this seat and tell me what happened."

Alric sat on the garden bench; he was a sharp contrast to the red flowers that bordered the path. Seemingly oblivious to the worried look on Amira's face, his eyes burned with the fire of discovery.

Amira spoke to the two male servants who had been assigned to watch and help Alric when needed. "Go in there and determine the extent of the damage, but," she added emphatically, "be careful." They looked at each other nervously.

"It is all right," Alric offered by way of comfort, "there was a small bang, and more smoke than anything else. Hold a wet cloth over your noses to filter out any noxious fumes."

The servants did as Alric told them and disappeared, somewhat hesitantly, into the laboratory.

"Now, Alric," Amira said on a serious tone, "what happened in there?"

"I was trying to prepare the extract when I noticed that something was wrong. I changed the method and . . . "

At that point Abal, Buhjah, and Maha returned hurriedly with the hot water, towels, and the liniment that Amira had requested. Wahid appeared moments later, wondering if he could help in any way. The songbirds in the garden, deciding that all was well, were giving voice once more.

Then the three young women knelt before Alric and started to bath the cuts on his hands and lower arms. As they did this, the two servants reappeared from the laboratory. "There seems to be little damage, Lady Amira," one of them reported.

"Now that the smoke is clearing, it appears the only damage might be some discoloration of the walls from the smoke," the second man added. Amira nodded her thanks and indicated to Wahid that he should see to supervising a team of servants to clean the laboratory.

"Please, mother," Alric pleaded, "only under my supervision or father's."

Amira reconsidered and agreed and then looked into Alric's eyes. "Talk, while we attend to your face and arms."

"But, mother!"

"Explain!"

Alric could not refuse his mother's firm command. "I noticed that the product did not seem to be quite right according to the instructions. The extract of animal fat and the *aqua fortis* did not mix. Nothing seemed to be happening. I was thinking the mixture should be discarded when suddenly the two layers became one and the single layer had the light yellow color that was described. I placed the flask onto the laboratory bench when it rolled over. Thinking the liquid would spill, I caught it rapidly, causing the contents of the flask to mix, and flames shot out of the top. Then the flask erupted into thousands of pieces. If the flask had been iron and closed with a stopper, I fear it would have been worse."

Alric paused, a light of recognition in his eyes. The words "He will have an iron fist and will shoot fire from his hands in his leader's name" shot across his brain. The glass, being weaker than iron, had shattered immediately, allowing the potential explosion to dissipate without much damage, only a lot of smoke. But if the flask had been iron and stoppered . . .

"Ouch!" Alric exclaimed as Abal removed a piece of glass from the palm of his hand. She recoiled in fright at Alric's reaction.

"Do not let him bother you, dear," Amira said gently to Abal. "Just continue to cleanse the wounds. Any pain that he suffers was brought upon him by his own actions."

The excitement came back into Alric's eyes and he forgot about the discomfort.

"It was incredible, mother. I saw the fire in the flask and it was as though I was in a dream. The flame seemed to move in slow motion and suddenly there was a flash, like the lightning that appears in the sky during a storm, then the glass vessel disintegrated before my eyes."

Amira frowned and then said tenderly. "You were lucky it was not in your eyes, my son." She was now fully recovered, and her anger had abated.

"And this was such a small amount," he indicated with his thumb and forefinger. "Just imagine what it would be like if I had prepared a large amount of this amazing product!"

Amira preferred not to think about that possibility.

Alric was quiet for a few moments while the three girls inspected him for possible glass fragments. "I apologize to you, mother, for the shock that you must have felt." He kissed Amira's cheek, and then continued. "I knew that something was wrong, mother. Even with the warnings of danger screaming through my mind, I had to proceed. I have never seen anything like this before. When I think about it, it is difficult to realize it is real, and I will never forget it."

* * *

The commotion had been heard elsewhere within the grounds. Gardeners working at the opposite side of the house and other servants had appeared, wondering about the reason for the fuss. Wahid shepherded them back to their work, saying that he would explain it all to them later. Even with the reassurance from Wahid, an air of uncertainty was evident. They were accustomed to Lord Jabir's experiments, but they had never seen anything like this. Smoke still seeped cautiously from the laboratory.

"And now, Alric, you will bathe," Amira announced. "I have decided you will not go near the laboratory again today. You will stay in the safety of the house for the remainder of the day, during which time you can collect your thoughts to make a full report to father when he returns. Girls," Amira addressed her three servants, "enough of the fussing. Go and prepare a bath for Alric. And then," she added firmly, "attend him to make sure that there are no other pieces of glass embedded under the skin."

"Mother!" Alric protested but in vain.

"Such remnants," she continued as if Alric had not spoken, "can cause infection, and must be removed." Then she looked at each of the young women in turn. "If I see so much as a smile on your faces or hear any gossip, it will be worse for you. Return the towels and other items to their correct places and attend to the bath."

Alric's face was suddenly remarkably sober, and the light of discovery that had been there dimmed as he realized that Amira was resolute. They could hear the girls engaged in animated chatter as they walked to the house, their arms laden with towels.

"Those girls will try my patience too much one day!" Amira mused.

"Is there anything I can do, Lady Amira?" Wahid asked.

"Alric?" Amira looked at Alric questioningly.

"No mother, the first report indicates all is well, and the laboratory can be left until father and I check at a later time."

"Please make sure, Wahid," Amira cautioned, "that this does not become part of the household gossip." Wahid left to do Amira's bidding. "And now, my dear son, it is time for your bath, and then you can prepare yourself to report to your father and to my nephew."

Under normal circumstances Alric would have taken a shower, but he looked forward to the bath. Suitably clothed in a large towel, he allowed the girls to check for any remaining pieces of glass or wounds. When they were done, he told them, in no uncertain terms, to leave.

The bath was comforting and relaxing, and it gave him time to think. An iron vessel would send metal shards into an enemy, but the means by which he could control the behavior of the pale yellow liquid was not apparent. Every available cell in his brain was active, working overtime to determine how he might control the process. His mind wandered as he looked at the mosaic surfaces of the floor and the paintings on the walls that depicted gloriously colored birds. The bathwater was relaxing and helped him to control his emotions after the explosion. Then he let out a whoop of joy and jumped out of the bath as the answer came to him.

Abal, Buhjah, and Maha, who had been waiting outside in case they were needed, ran into the room thinking that something terrible had happened. Seeing Alric standing there, they covered their open mouths with their hands and averted their eyes. Amira arrived moments later.

"Mother," Alric, exclaimed, "I have done it!"

"Alric," she said smiling. "May I suggest you wrap the towel around yourself so that my three girls can stop pretending to avert their eyes!"

Alric quickly picked up the towel and covered himself.

"You have," Amira said slowly, "from the expression on your face, found the answer you seek to control any future fires?"

"Yes, mother. It is so simple; I should have recognized it earlier."

"Let me suggest," Amira said calmly, "that you first return to the bath, since I see that you still have considerable dirt and grime on your arms and legs. The girls will bring more hot water and make sure that you are cleaned correctly."

With that, Amira turned on her heel and left.

* * *

CHAPTER 24

Alric was not surprised to be called to an audience with the Caliph. Jabir, Khalil, and Ahmed had listened intently to his story regarding the laboratory incident. Alric had he even produced his notebook to show Jabir that the events leading up to the incident, as well as the aftermath, had been recorded just as they'd happened.

"The Caliph has two issues that he wishes to discuss with you," Jabir said before they left the house that afternoon, one day after the incident. "This morning, when I told him what had happened, he was very concerned for your safety. Do not make light of this when you talk with Harun."

Khalil and Ahmed had other matters that required their attention. They slapped him playfully on the back, Khalil adding, "My brother, be careful. I have grown to like this house. Do not burn it down!"

The weather was dry and hot, now being almost midafternoon when Jabir and Alric made their way to the palace. As always, Alric had his head suitably covered to avoid recognition.

Jabir was known by the palace guards, and soon he and Alric were walking through the now-familiar enclosures to the Caliph's private rooms. After their arrival was announced by the captain of the guard, Harun waved them forward. Alric dropped his face and head covering.

The Caliph breathed a sigh of relief. "Greetings again, uncle. I see that our friend from the western stars appears to be in good health."

"I am well, Sire." Alric took it upon himself to respond, even though the Caliph had not addressed him

"And in good voice, I see," Harun remarked with good humor. "Please sit."

Jabir and Alric took their places on the cushions that were opposite to the Caliph. "After you have received refreshments," he signaled to the two servants who hovered close by, "you can tell me all that transpired yesterday."

When the servants withdrew, Alric spoke. "Sire, as you were kind enough to allow me to continue this task, I have worked steadily to find out the truth about the production of this material. It is now my pleasure to tell you that I have discovered, through experimentation, perhaps through happenstance, the secret of generating the product. I have also learned of its extreme sensitivity to movement!"

The Caliph glanced at Jabir and then admiringly at Alric. Alric's speech was sober and articulate. He continued and told his story without missing a detail. Finally, out of breath after his account of the events of the previous day and with the excitement that accompanied his story, he concluded his speech. "I have my notebook for you to inspect, Sire. I apologize for the stain on the page. Some of the liquid spilled onto it before the fire occurred."

Alric produced the notebook from the waist pouch strapped to his belt hidden under his outer robe. He stood up and looked at the Caliph. "May I approach, Sire?"

"Of course, Alric."

Harun looked at Jabir. "I see Alric observes all of the necessary formalities, even in an informal setting such as this," the Caliph gestured around the room. "Good!"

Harun took the book from Alric and looked at the page Alric indicated.

"This is in Latin!"

"My apologies Sire."

Alric flipped the book open to what would have been the last page in the Latinized world but was the first page in the Arabic world.

"It is in Arabic starting at this page, Sire."

The Caliph was pleased that Alric had taken considerable pains to produce a notebook that would be readable by both Latin and Arabic scholars. "Sit next to me, Alric, and point out the highlights of yesterday."

Jabir was pleased that Alric was building in confidence with Harun. There were many who would feel uncomfortable, even humiliated, in this situation. Harun took his time asking questions and then closed the notebook. "You have done well, Alric," he said, then returned the book to Alric and settled back on to the cushions. "What are your next steps?" he asked.

Alric spoke slowly. "I have discussed this with my father and I now know what happened to cause the violent reaction." Alric went on to describe in detail what he planned in order to make sure the work was a success.

The Caliph nodded in agreement several times and even interjected with a few highly thought out questions during Alric's description of his plans. "I understand, Alric, and so I will allow you to continue this dangerous work. However, I urge caution, and I am wondering, uncle," he looked at Jabir, "if we cannot find some safer means by which Alric can work without relying on two servants who are outside."

"May I suggest, Harun," Jabir said, "that we take a few days to resolve this issue? I will report our plan to you."

Alric had time to study the Caliph intently. No man, he concluded, could be more fitted for the role. He was interested in all subjects and was strong willed, but not so much that Alric's freedom to experiment would be challenged. The Caliph's face was calm but his eyes flashed. Alric detected signs of excitement in his eyes.

"You have satisfied me, Alric," Harun exclaimed. "Continue with your work. When you have performed a successful outcome, my uncle will advise me." He twisted some of the hairs of his beard between his thumb and forefinger before continuing. "If there is another incident, I am sure I will hear from my aunt!"

Jabir laughed out loud. Alric could not help but smile.

"Ah, I see, Alric," Harun said, "that you understand the humor in my words."

"I also understand, Sire, my mother's determination to see that her family is safe and well. I have no wish to be bathed again by three girls who giggled as they picked glass fragments out of my skin!"

Harun al-Rashid, Caliph of Baghdad and the leader of the Islamic world, laughed so heartily and uncontrollably that he had to clutch his stomach lest he roll off the cushions.

* * *

For what remained of the afternoon, Jabir and Alric, having returned to the house, much to Amira's relief, remained closeted together, ceasing their conversation only for the evening meal, constantly discussing the next steps they would take. Amira was at a stage where she did not know what her husband and son would be doing next. However, she did make it clear that although the laboratory was clean again, there would be no work carried out that night.

"Tired brains make mistakes," she announced as she fixed her eyes on Jabir and Alric, "so you will remain in the house." She had decided.

Alric knew that he was close to performing a successful experiment.

* * *

The next morning they arose at sunrise and made their way to the laboratory. They were both trembling with the anticipation of discovery. The first task was to prepare a fresh batch of animal fat renderings. As the flames lit up underneath the copper kettle, the fat started to bubble. Alric indicated that this was what he expected. The odor became stronger as the fat decomposed. Alric adjusted the flame from the fire so that the reaction in the kettle did not get out of control. He watched the liquid thicken. Then he added the wood ash from a supply that had been prepared for other uses but had not been completely exhausted. The mixture seemed to become homogenous. He started to speak out loud so that Jabir could hear what was transpiring as he worked, so that if anything went wrong . . .

"And just what, might I ask, are you doing?" Amira's voice broke into their thoughts. Alric turned to see his mother standing in the doorway. "And the smell!" she added.

"My dear," Jabir responded, "you look absolutely stunning, even at this time of the morning."

"Thank you, my dear husband, but that," she said, "is not the answer to my question." She looked at Alric. "You are making that," Amira paused as she searched for the correct word, "stuff again? Aren't you?" She looked at the copper kettle. "That had better not be one of my water pots!" A guilty silence followed. "Since you are determined to make that stuff," said Amira, as Alric tried to mask his amusement at Amira's terminology, but failed. "And what, my dear son, is so amusing?"

"Just a passing thought related to my thanks for all you have done for me, my dearest mother."

"You are both making me really frustrated!" Then she smiled and said, "Can I assume that you will join me for tea and oatmeal cakes sometime in the near future?

"Yes, my dear."

"Yes, mother."

Alric looked at the mix. "In fact, it might be as well to leave this and allow it to cool." He looked at Jabir. "Yesterday, I may have added the *aqua fortis* when the mixture was still warm, and that may have caused the violent reaction."

Alric turned and lifted the kettle from the fire and placed it on a nearby bench. As they walked from the laboratory, Amira stopped them in their tracks. "The smell of whatever you were doing hangs onto your outer robes. I suggest that you leave them here."

They quickly removed their work robes. Amira moved closer to them, sniffing the air to assure herself that they were presentable.

* * *

After breakfast they returned to the laboratory. The renderings had cooled sufficiently. "Now, Alric," Jabir said, "this is our moment of truth."

"It is, father, but I cannot allow you to endanger yourself. If you stand outside I will talk my way through this and speak out loud so you will know what needs to be done to complete the production of the mixture."

Jabir was about to protest but saw the wisdom of Alric's thinking. He nodded in agreement. "But," Jabir added, "if you need me, I will be with you in moments." Jabir looked into Alric's eyes. He not only saw the confidence of youth but also a steadiness, and the will to succeed was unmistakable. They were about to enter an uncharted area of science.

"All will be well, father," Alric assured him.

* * *

Alric recalled, from the first time he had poured the *aqua fortis* into the fat renderings. He had added the acid to the mixture, and the liberation of heat may have caused the violent reaction. He decided to reverse his procedure and add the fat renderings to the acid to see if any heat liberated would be dissipated. He poured a small amount of the acid into a glass container, which he then placed into a larger vessel containing cool water. The glass vessel now had a cool water jacket surrounding it, and he allowed the acid to cool to the water jacket temperature. Outside, Jabir feverishly took notes as Alric talked.

Alric slowly added small amounts of the fat renderings so that no heat appeared to be liberated from the mixture. He stirred it gently, all the while watching for any signs of a problem. Thoughtfully, knowing that heat was produced by the mixing process, he had placed a large vessel of cool water close by. At any signs of heat being generated, he would immediately dump the solution into the water. After a few more minutes, he noticed a layer forming on top of the *aqua fortis*. The acid layer and the ash that he had added formed a dark gray layer at the bottom of the container. He then carefully stirred into the mixture more wood ash until there appeared to be no more *aqua fortis* remaining in the container. He poured the product very carefully through a cloth to remove the residue of wood ash.

The pale yellow liquid appeared to sparkle in the receiver as it settled to the lower level with the water on the top. He slowly poured off the water and took a few drops on a metal knife edge. The aroma was not that of fat renderings or *aqua fortis*. The product had a sweet odor. He had succeeded.

Remembering the sensitivity of his experiment, Alric carefully placed the stoppered container and its valuable contents behind several large stones that he had collected for other purposes. This would form a protective wall around the product.

The next test was to determine under what conditions the product would explode and flame. He walked out of the laboratory and beamed at Jabir. He was happy.

* * *

Now that the work was complete, the clean up remained, and they would seek a safer storage for the product. If it showed the same sensitivity as the first time, Alric doubted that a pile of stones would serve as protection.

Alric and Jabir cleaned up the laboratory, washed all of the equipment that had been used, and disposed of the excess acid. The extra wood ash proved to be very valuable for this task. As they finished, Jabir suddenly paused. "There is," he said, "a below-ground storage box at the other end of the garden that I have used for products that have an unknown nature. It is small but deep enough and well reinforced that it might be the ideal place to store the product. Moreover, it is in the shade of several trees and should be sufficiently cool enough."

As they walked to the house, Alric paused. "Alric," Jabir said as he turned, "is everything all right?"

"Yes, father. I realize that we have carried out the Caliph's bidding and produced this dangerous product, but we have no way of knowing its true nature. We are still uncertain about its sensitivity, method of storage, and also ways of transporting it!"

"In other words, we know nothing of its character," Jabir added. He paused as if in deep thought. "Yes, Alric, I am aware of that, and I am very concerned. It will be a topic of conversation when I meet with the Caliph tomorrow." Alric nodded. "Now, I suggest that we adjourn to the house, where we can think out this problem—without, of course, telling mother too much about what we do not know."

"I agree, father!"

* * *

The days passed and became months as Alric worked diligently in the laboratory to determine if his first method of preparation was correct. In the interests of safety, Jabir worked with him as often as he could. When Jabir was not able to be there, two servants were posted at the door and instructed how to watch for potential accidents and to act quickly.

Alric estimated that if he maintained this pace of work for another week, he would quadruple his supply of the product. But the more he worked with it, the more uncomfortable he felt. He did not wish to disappoint the Caliph, and even though he was happy in his work and thought about it most of the time, the danger forced him to reconsider the options. Based on the explosion and fire that had occurred, he knew that a larger amount had the potential to demolish the laboratory building, and Khalil's laughing remark—"My brother, be careful. I have grown to like this house. Do not burn it down!"—was a constant thought in his mind.

"If we have a mixture that we cannot control, we may be in danger, as will those around us," Jabir observed when Alric talked the matter over with him.

Alric had learned some important things, such as how to repeat the work that led to the formation of the pale yellow liquid; that when it was kept in the cool storage area, it became solid; and that the solid was even more dangerous that the liquid! One observation in particular came to him.

A drop of the liquid had solidified on the side of the container. As he lifted the vessel out of the storage hole, the solid had started to liquefy and fell to the ground. The resulting explosion shocked him. It was too small to do any damage. Jabir had not been present at the time but had been extremely surprised and worried at the outcome from one small drop. Then, by accident and before Jabir reported their fears to the Caliph, Alric found the answer.

During a further experiment, he sensed Hilda's presence, and she was begging him to be careful. He suddenly caught sight of a jar of clay on the laboratory shelf. He had used the clay to clean up chemicals that spilled onto the laboratory floor and had noticed that the properties of the chemicals seemed to have changed.

He placed a pile of clay on the bench and carefully added the liquid mixture. The clay adsorbed the mixture without any obvious effect, except that Alric could not detect the presence of light yellow liquid on the clay. Emboldened by this act, he experimented with varying amounts of clay per standard weight of the mixture. At the end of the day, he knew exactly which mixtures were benign and offered no danger, which were dangerous, and interestingly, which mixture when molded in the form of a ball presented danger when thrown hard against the ground. Even then the extent of the explosion was muffled.

His eyes sparkled when he explained this to Jabir on his return from visiting patients. Jabir's eyes lit up and then dimmed again. "But, Alric," he said, "we still have the danger associated with the preparation of the mixture."

"But only, father, if we allow the mixture to overheat during preparation!"

That night, they talked about the discovery. Alric continued the work for another week, thinking only of the precautions he needed to follow in order to avoid accidents.

He even discovered that the liquid could be separated from the clay by washing with an aromatic liquid that Jabir had prepared using the bitumen from Hit, the old town of antiquity that lay to the northwest of Baghdad on the Euphrates River.

Hilda's voice continued to warn Alric to be cautious when he worked with the mixture. Her words were often the language of omens, always ready to show him what his eyes had failed to observe.

On the seventh day after his latest discovery, Alric and Jabir were ready to make a report to the Caliph.

"This seems like the beginning of a journey," Harun said to Alric. "I congratulate both of you for having pursued the task to this point, and you have learned much along the way. It is better that this secret be in our hands than in the hands of my enemies, although I suspect that they would not have been as careful as you and may have negated our worries in a cloud of fire. I thank you."

They might have succeeded, Alric thought but decided against speaking his mind on this point. "We had to learn, Sire," was all that Alric could find to say.

"There is only one way to learn," Jabir said, knowing Alric's thoughts, "and that is through careful action. For the moment, everything that we need to know about this secret we have learned through Alric."

"Your hands do truly shoot fire, but I am still very curious about the iron fist!"

* * *

Two months later, Alric was working in the laboratory performing a series of exercises with equipment that Jabir had described and urged him to use to distill more volatile spirits from the tarry semi-solid from Hit, when he heard muffled footfalls. Alric turned to see Jabir approaching.

"I see you are making progress, Alric. But," he said casting his quick eyes over the glass equipment, "why did you make changes to my apparatus? I do not much like change, especially when it involves dangerous liquids that might burst into flame if they were to touch heat."

"I saw or rather I smelled that the liquids escaped from the apparatus and that they seemed to spread along the floor. My feet sensed the coolness as they evaporated and came into contact with my skin. And so . . . "

"You sought to be careful and safe!" Jabir exclaimed. He looked at the apparatus quickly without seeming to blink. "And what did you think it necessary to do?"

Alric bowed his head in deference as he answered. "I reset the connections from the pot where the liquids are heated, the *still pot* you called it, and made sure that the vapors from the still pot passed straight into the water receiver and could not touch any hot surface." Jabir smiled. "There is something else that I need to tell you, father."

Jabir raised an eyebrow, knowing from the tone of Alric's voice that he had a secret to disclose. "I am listening, Alric," Jabir responded solemnly.

Alric licked his lips to remove the dryness and said, "Excuse me, father," as he moistened his throat with fresh cool water, then proceeded to outline to Jabir his latest discovery. "As you are aware, there is a weapon of war known as Greek fire that was employed by the Byzantines to save Constantinople from invasion by Arab fleets almost one hundred years ago. A veil of secrecy has surrounded its composition, and it seems that even the Byzantines have forgotten the means by which it was produced. In fact, from my reading, I conclude that its nature remains as mysterious today as it was in the past when it was first unleashed."

Jabir, sensing he was about to hear another important discovery from Alric, sat quietly at the desk. He motioned that Alric should do the same.

"It seems that this weapon was discharged from tubes mounted on the prows of Byzantine ships. It adhered to whatever it struck and could not be extinguished with water. We do not know its precise nature nor do my readings teach us how it was ignited."

Alric looked at Jabir and saw his father's face deep in thought.

"I believe that Greek fire was a mixture that was very similar to that which I have recently distilled from the Hit tar. It was also thickened with some other agent that would have prevented it from being quickly extinguished or washed away by water. As to its delivery, I have reasoned that the mixture was in vats and projected from a pump similar to the one the gardeners use for spraying water into those areas of the garden that are difficult to reach without stepping on valuable plants.

However, it cannot be discharged as a flaming material because of the danger to the pump operator."

Jabir listened intently to Alric's description. The generation of Greek fire and the means by which it could be discharged to the enemy was of prime importance to the Caliph's soldiers and sailors.

"I realized that chemical compounds can be made from the lime stones in the mountains. I became curious when I read in the Bible about the *burnings of lime*. If I take the lime stones and heat them, I produce lime, which when water is added, generates considerable heat."

A light went on in Jabir's eyes.

"And so, if I mix the lime with the liquid that we use for Greek fire and drop water onto the mixture, the heat liberated from the lime ignites the liquid!" As if to demonstrate his findings, Alric got up, walked to the bench, and splashed water onto a liquid that seemed to contain a suspended milky solid. The mixture inflamed immediately.

"This is infinitely safer than the explosive liquid that I produced last month, but we may still need to protect the men who operate the pumps by use of large iron shields. The need to discharge a flaming liquid is no longer necessary. We must, of course, ensure that the lime meets with the water after the discharge. If it is a naval battle, the ships are surrounded by water and are wet, whereby the liquid will become inflamed immediately. In a land battle, we may use a second pump that will discharge the necessary amount of water for the incendiary effect!"

"Alric, you amaze me!" Jabir responded enthusiastically. "I will see that this is brought to the Caliph's attention." Jabir rubbed his chin. "It is very important," he went on, "that you have used your senses to detect that something was amiss with the equipment. Had anyone else been operating the apparatus, there might have been a fire. Making a mistake in this profession can have serious effects; it matters not whether the operator is rich or poor. It is a precise science that is a joy to behold but can be fraught with danger. And we who follow *al-khimiya* have to live with our mistakes. Or," he said as he looked very seriously at Alric, "die by them. Equally important, you have used your powers of thought to project backward in time to discover the means of the operation of Greek fire. Well done, indeed."

Alric smiled with pleasure.

"There is still much work to do, Alric," Jabir continued, "as we find out about the nature of our world. It pays not to hurry the work we do, and although there will be failures, we have to take advantage when luck is on our side. It is called the principle of favorability. Others may refer to it as beginner's luck. In your case, you observed, you saw what might happen, and you made changes to ensure that the inevitable would not happen. However, there is a theory of mine that no matter how well you plan, the unexpected is inevitable. Bear that in mind, Alric."

Jabir was silent for a few moments before he spoke again. "The Prophet, peace be upon him, gave us the Qur'an and left us just five obligations to satisfy during our lives. The most important is to believe only in the one true God. The others are to pray five times a day, fast during Ramadan, and be charitable to the poor. Keep these in mind, Alric, especially the first, and you put your life in the hands of the Almighty. He will keep you and preserve you!"

Jabir stopped there. His eyes had filled with tears as he spoke of the Prophet. Alric could see that he was a devout man and that even with all of his learning, he wanted to live his life in accordance with Muslim law.

"What is the fifth obligation?" Alric asked.

"The fifth obligation of every Muslim is a pilgrimage. We are obliged, at least once in our lives, to visit the holy city of Mecca. If you follow the teachings of the Prophet, peace be upon him, and accept the protection of Allah, you will one day make the journey of pilgrimage." He saw the questioning look on Alric's face. "Mecca is a great distance from here. Many days' travel. All who make the pilgrimage are happy at having done so. They place the symbols of the pilgrimage on the doors of their houses. And . . . "

Jabir paused and then said, "It is time that we took this to the Caliph. He has requested an update whenever we have a new discovery, and we should attend him now. Shut down the apparatus and wash your hands lest the smell of the chemicals follow you into the Caliph's palace!"

Alric quickly did as he was asked and they left the laboratory. Alric covered his face as was his custom when leaving the house and the surrounding gardens, and they strode toward the palace. "For the moment we must focus on our visit to the palace, but I think the Caliph has other issues on his mind."

I wonder . . . , Alric thought.

"It is not worth trying to read the Caliph's thoughts," Jabir said, "or we can worry ourselves into madness. Let us hasten to the palace, where, I am sure, his thoughts will be revealed."

* * *

CHAPTER 25

Jabir and Alric were shown to a room that was a private antechamber in which the Caliph met privileged guests. As in other parts of the palace, the furnishings were luxurious. The Caliph was sitting at a table reading as Jabir and Alric approached. Alric's eyes took in the décor, the patterned silk curtains, and the numerous cushions which brought lively colors to the room. He kneeled before the Caliph and was requested to rise. Jabir, being a family member and therefore excluded from this form of homage, remained standing, his head bowed in respect.

The Caliph spoke. "You may remove your face covering."

Alric obeyed and allowed himself to relax. If the Caliph asked, he would relate that he had learned some important aspects of his new life, such as the manner in which various chemicals should be handled, and the new language that was all part of *al-khimiya*, the chemical science.

His thoughts were interrupted by the Caliph. "You must always be aware what it is you want, Alric," the Caliph was saying as Alric refocused himself, being helped by a prod in the ribs from Jabir. He realized that it was fate, *kismet* as Jabir had called it, to have arrived in this land, meet with the Caliph, and commence a life anew as an apprentice to a man who was the most eminent physician and scientist in the land.

The Caliph raised his right eyebrow as he looked at Alric questioningly. "Do you hear me, Alric, or do you daydream?" Alric did not respond but bowed his head dutifully to show that he was indeed paying attention. Harun continued. "I have need of your services. I have asked Ali al-Maslawi to join us," the Caliph looked toward the entrance of the room, "and I see that he awaits my signal."

The Caliph nodded to the guard at the door, and Ali al-Maslawi was admitted. He strode into the room with purpose and character. This was a man who was full of confidence.

For the first time since his initial encounter with al-Maslawi, Alric had a chance to examine him. He was a man of more than fifty summers. His weather-beaten, bearded face bore witness to his life in the outdoors. His clothes were modest, in comparison to the rich flashiness of the First Minister, but they were well cut and fitted perfectly. His head was uncovered, his turban having been left at the door with the soldier, lest there be a concealed weapon. Undoubtedly, Alric surmised, the soldier had also checked al-Maslawi's garments for weapons.

Al-Maslawi fell to his knees before the Caliph, who bade him to rise and then turned to smile at Jabir and Alric. "Now," the Caliph said, "there are serious matters to discuss. I always find that such matters are better considered over tea and cake." As an afterthought, he added, "These chairs are uncomfortable. We shall adjourn to sit on the cushions, where we can take our refreshment in comparative ease," as he pointed to several thick luxurious cushions that were placed around a low table.

Before they had time to make themselves comfortable, the tea and cake were delivered by the ever-dutiful servants who flitted into the room like ghosts and exited in the same manner.

After the amenities were observed, in which they took several sips of tea and Alric ate a piece of cake, the Caliph looked thoughtfully at his three guests. "Alric, you are here because you may be able to help us in this political matter. My uncle," he nodded in Jabir's direction, "has kept me abreast of your activities in the laboratory, and I am told that you are making great strides in your work. Personally I have found that you are a man that I can trust and I would like to discuss the work with you sometime. But there is another issue that needs attention first."

Harun paused and sipped his tea. Alric frowned, curious about the other issue that the Caliph wished to discuss with him. "Almost one year ago," Harun looked at Jabir, "on the day of Alric's arrival, I told you that I had reason to believe that one close to me was ready to align himself with the Umayyad administration, not so much for his beliefs but more to satisfy his own ends. It appears that he harbors a grudge against me."

Harun looked from one to the other before continuing.

"Ali," Harun addressed al-Maslawi, "has news that is better heard by you, uncle, and then we can decide what actions need to be taken."

Hearing this, Alric made a move to stand and leave the room, but the Caliph uttered one word. "Stay."

"Oh, and I might add," Harun said, "that any questions should be asked as they arise in your minds. A question that is delayed can lose its impact."

Then he indicated that al-Maslawi should proceed. "Thank you, Caliph," al-Maslawi said. "If you do not mind, I will present some history first to set the stage for my findings to Lord Jabir and Alric." Harun agreed. "Just prior to your arrival," Ali looked at Alric to underscore his words, "the Caliph asked me to undertake this task. I will not define the task, as I think it will become obvious as my story unfolds." Ali had their full attention. "To accomplish the Caliph's request, I recruited some of my colleagues from Mosul to aid me in my investigations. These men," Ali looked at the Caliph, "were not told the reason but were asked to investigate the possible misappropriation of funds or other scurrilous dealings that related to matters of the palace. My colleagues were merchants who had good reason to visit Baghdad and so went about their work unnoticed.

"They are merchants, and when it comes to numbers, they can look at columns of data and, without even putting pen to paper, they find a mistake immediately! They asked questions, got involved in discussion, and observed the actions of many people. My findings, Caliph, may be hurtful, but I feel that you need to know the outcome." Ali bowed his head.

"Please continue," Harun said encouragingly.

"My investigators found that questionable dealings commenced shortly after the coming of Abdul al-Warith to the palace, as the First Minister," Ali announced. "Great excitement reigned throughout the government. Word had spread of Abdul al-Warith's business and financial accomplishments, and there was talk, the source of the talk being a veiled rumor that now seems to have been put out by al-Warith himself, that he with his considerable knowledge of fiscal matters would lead the country into a strong financial position. Trade with other countries would increase, and money management would replace wars for profit. A time of peace, tranquility, and financial stability was anticipated, even expected."

"I do remember that day," the Caliph interjected, "almost as though it were yesterday. At the first meeting of the government in the council chamber of the palace, I had assembled many great men of accomplishment from throughout Mesopotamia, some of whom," he looked at Alric, "you saw on the day of your arrival."

"The Caliph's concern," Ali continued, "was to forgo war and enter upon a time of peace, prosperity, and scholarship. The Caliph decreed that there must be no war unless decided by this auspicious group of individuals, who were recognized as the government of the country. Individuals who decided to take it upon themselves to bring this country into war would be apprehended and punished according to the law. And anyone so apprehended would be required to show good cause for his actions. Even then, innocence may not be presumed, and guilt by association would be the order of the day."

Ali paused. Jabir and Alric remained silent as the Caliph looked from face to face, making eye contact with each one of them. "You may know this, Lord Jabir," said Ali, "that the Caliph has said that the only way a man may convince me and this group to go to war is to bring convincing evidence that an unprovoked attack has occurred, or will occur, at the instigation of the aggressor. It was then that the Caliph conferred upon the First Minister the authority to speak in his place at times when he was unable to attend a council meeting."

Ali sipped his tea before he went on. "From that time, the First Minister has had the right of speaking for the Caliph, in the Caliph's absence, of course. The decision was made in the council chamber before the whole council and recorded by the scribes present at all such meetings. At the conclusion of the meeting, the scribes left the chamber and hastened to their communal room to compare writings and make sure that nothing was missed, and the collective work was finalized as one written record of the proceedings of that meeting."

"May I?" Alric asked.

"Of course, Alric, please go ahead," the Caliph responded.

"Sire, do the records still indicate that the First Minister has the right to speak for you?"

"Yes, Alric, they do," Harun responded. But . . . " he left the word hanging in the air as he signaled to Ali to continue.

"And that," Ali said, "is where matters get very interesting." He took a deep breath as he looked at the Caliph. "The Caliph asked me to start with the records and whatever else I needed to begin this investigation. The proceedings of the meeting in which the First Minister was given the authority to speak for the Caliph are not entirely correct. Words have been changed in some of the sentences. The changes are subtle, but my indications are that there has been a deliberate attempt to usurp the Caliph's position."

"But," said Alric, "is it possible that the scribes took down slightly different words to those actually used in the . . . " he thought for a moment then added, ". . . resolution?"

"That is always a possibility, Alric," Harun responded, "but after the scribes have finished agreeing upon the exact words used, they commit the proceeds to paper and I always check the finished document. It is only after my inspection that the report is entered into the official records. After this, the individual notes are destroyed, as they are considered to be of no further use."

Harun pulled a document from a folder that he produced from under a cushion.

"Uncle," Harun said as he passed the one-page document to Jabir, "when you have read this, please pass it to Alric."

In the silence that followed as Jabir read the document, Ali and Alric took the opportunity to sip the tea. Jabir then passed the document to Alric, who looked carefully at the words written before him.

"Your sharp eyes and scientific curiosity," Harun said, "may help us as you read the words, Alric. Here," Harun proffered an object, "I have a glass that magnifies words that you may wish to use."

The palm-sized round glass, which was encased in a silver rim to which a silver handle had been attached, was handed to Alric. He looked at the document through the glass for a few moments. "Sire," Alric looked up from the document, "may I assume that the scribes are always neat and careful, taking a pride in their work?"

"They are extremely precise, Alric" the Caliph responded. "They take a great pride in all they do, and their work is almost unsurpassed by any other group of craftsman. A line or word out of place will cause them to redo a whole page, even a whole multi-page document, if the placement of a word or a line interferes with the succeeding pages."

"As I see it, this document has three word changes that are not readily visible without the glass. These changes are not in accordance with the work of your scribes and appear to have a different shade, as though the words were inserted at a later date."

Alric thought for a moment and then asked, "From your explanation of the recording process, Sire, I assume that such changes would have caused the scribes to rewrite the whole document?"

"That is true," Harun nodded at Alric.

"Then my conclusion, Sire, is that these changes were inserted at some time after the document was completed by the scribes and acknowledged by you as a true record of that particular meeting!" Alric looked up to see three pairs of eyes looking at him intently. Without waiting for any comment he continued. "This is a document that allows the First Minister to speak at all times for the Caliph. This, Sire," Alric looked at Harun, "is not my understanding of what you have informed us, insofar as the First Minister was only to speak for you in your absence. But," Alric went on, "three words are out of line and appear to have been added over the top of erased letters. The words that have been added are: *even*, *present*, and *or*."

Alric frowned slightly as he interpreted the sentence from the Arabic script. He took a deep breath and said, "The sentence as written here in the altered form reads as follows: 'The First Minister has the authority to speak for the Caliph *even* when the Caliph is *present or* has indicated to the officials of the government that he, the Caliph, intends to be absent.'"

He then continued and added, "From what you have said, Caliph, the correct version of this sentence should be, and I am putting my own words in here: 'The First Minister has the authority to speak for the Caliph *only* when the Caliph is *absent and* has indicated to the officials of the government that he, the Caliph, intends to be absent."

Jabir looked serious. The Caliph and Ali looked at each other as if congratulating themselves on Alric's efforts. "My final conclusion," Alric said, "is that the new version of this document gives supreme authority to the First Minister. The substitution of these three words has made a world of difference to the meaning."

"I see that you have worked diligently, Alric!" the Caliph exclaimed. "Your version of what the sentence should have been is precisely what was written when I examined the document for accuracy shortly after the conclusion of that meeting."

The Caliph nodded to Ali, indicating that he should continue.

"The obvious suspect," Ali emphasized the second word, "is the First Minister. He has access to the records and could have bribed a scribe to make such changes."

"Pardon me, Ali al-Maslawi," Alric interjected, "but should we not look for the scribe?"

"That is precisely what my colleagues have done. Despite our efforts, there is no indication of any such scribe. Now, I do admit that scribes come and go for a variety of reasons. However, we do suspect that any scribe who participated in such a scheme would be paid, not in money, but in the form of a quick death."

Ali picked up his glass and sipped the tea as he formulated the words to conclude his account. "In short," he said, looking at the Caliph, "all we have are rumors and innuendo. There is no real evidence to incriminate the First Minister. This could even be an attempt by others to implicate the First Minister and thereby remove him from power. I feel that we may have exhausted our resources. But there is . . . "

"I agree with Ali's assessment," the Caliph interjected, "but there is one more item that Ali has discovered. Please continue."

"By happenstance," Ali said, "some weeks ago, I talked with an old man at a tea shop that I frequent. The old man did indicate his intent to leave the city, so I do not suspect foul play; in fact I hear that he has left the city. The old man, his name is unknown to me, seemed to be of some high station, from the clothes he was wearing, told me that the First Minister is subject to intense violent rage, and is even given to beating women. What is even more interesting is that the old man seemed to have a close personal knowledge of the activities and behavior of the First Minister. I might even speculate that he was a relative, but I have no proof."

Jabir and Alric were shocked at this news. "But," Ali continued, "the deeper one peels the onion, the more one sees. I have had some of my colleagues talking with the soldiers and guards at the various coffee and rest houses. And there a situation has arisen that may help us."

Jabir and Alric eased forward on their cushions, making sure they would not miss a word. "For the past two days, there has been an occupant of the prison that may be of interest to this case." Jabir and Alric edged even closer. "The prisoner was brought in by two of the palace guards. They saw the captive being escorted by two men who did not seem to have any authority to do this.

"The interesting point is that the palace guards recalled seeing the two men in the company of the First Minister, as though they were members of his own personal guard. When the men were challenged, they ran away, and the palace guards assumed the custody, authority, and responsibility for the prisoner, who since that time has refused to speak to anyone. More important, there have been inquiries about the prisoner from outside sources that are unknown, but the prison guards have refused to comment or allow anyone to have contact with the captive."

Ali contemplated his audience. "There are also rumors that someone of a high station is behind this affair. When the Caliph and I first heard of this, we were uncertain of what was happening, rumors being what they are! As I discussed my findings with the Caliph earlier today, you might say a candle was lit. We saw the light and concluded that this person may be of some interest to the Caliph, so we need to investigate."

"And that," the Caliph said, "is where you come in, Alric. This is the other item that I need to discuss with you!" The Caliph had Alric's full attention. "Alric," he said, smiling, "I need you to find out for me the origins of this person. My captain can sense good people from bad and advises me that there is something strange about the behavior of this prisoner."

Harun looked intensely at Alric, who felt as if the dark brown eyes had darkened further and were reaching into his innermost soul. "Are you up to the task?" Harun asked.

"Yes, Sire," Alric responded in a very confident tone. "Whatever you wish will be done."

Harun smiled at Jabir. "It seems, my uncle, you are teaching him well. I am pleased. Now let us take tea and we will discuss what I need to know about the person in my jail. He clapped his hands and the tea was delivered.

"Before you arrived this afternoon," Harun spoke without even seeming to take a breath, "I was thinking about prisoners, especially those who could offer much in the way of knowledge about their lives and countries. I may have missed the chance for knowledge by not pursuing their backgrounds further. This prisoner of interest has not spoken, and I have not yet offered him the hot irons. My captain noticed that even though the prisoner has unkempt dirty hair, it could possibly be fair, like yours, Alric, and the blue eyes are also like yours. Beneath the dirt and grime it is impossible to make out any other features. My guards are not too happy about being close to someone so dirty. They fear that disease and other malevolent spirits might pass from the prisoner to them."

Harun sipped his tea before continuing. "It was the ever-vigilant Ahmed who suggested that we may be able to use your talents to determine if the prisoner can speak the same language as you or any language that is known to you. My captain also made an estimate of the prisoner's age, and he and Ahmed are of the opinion that it may be close to yours. What better to offer a captive than someone who, hopefully, speaks the same language and may even be a countryman?"

Alric suddenly understood why he had been invited to this meeting, which would otherwise have been privy to Jabir and Ali al-Maslawi. The Caliph continued. "You may be a gift from Allah, Alric. I have plans for you, and my aunt and uncle are helping me to put them into place. After the conversations with my captain and with Ahmed, I understand something I didn't see before. Every blessing ignored becomes a curse. You are becoming a blessing to my house and I am looking at horizons I have never known. I am determined that you should, with careful tutelage, accomplish many things."

Having declared his plan, Harun was in good humor as he contemplated the fresh tea and another platter of sweet cakes that had been laid before them. They talked and ate cakes and drank tea for another hour. The afternoon passed quickly in conversation and the sun began to set.

Shortly after they were dismissed, Jabir and Alric turned to leave and walked to the door, in the company of al-Maslawi, when the Caliph called out as they were about to exit the room. "Uncle," Jabir stopped and turned to face his nephew, "it goes without saying that my cousin Khalil and Ahmed should be acquainted with this conversation."

Jabir's answer was simple.

"It will be done," he said.

"Alric, your work begins tomorrow," the Caliph said in clear and commanding tones. "I am hopeful that you can shed some light on this mystery that has arisen and bring it to a satisfactory conclusion."

* * *

CHAPTER 26

Khalil and Ahmed had returned as expected, and Ahmed was ready the next morning to accompany Jabir and Alric to the prison. Khalil did not go with them, since he had to give a report to the Caliph on his excursions into the eastern part of the country and he needed to make sure his men were given adequate rest.

The prison was located a short distance from the palace. As they approached the building, Alric looked up at the well-guarded fortress before him. It was surrounded by walls built from large stones. Seeing Alric's curious look, Ahmed explained. "This prison was not a place for prisoners serving a sentence, but for those awaiting a trial. The ground floor is usually used as living quarters for the guards, who are often required to spend extended duty time at the prison. The actual cells that house the prisoners are below ground—this makes escape more difficult. The first floor below ground consists of cells where prisoners are held for trial and for those prisoners whose future has not yet been determined. The floor below that is for the persistent violators of the law who await trial. The third consists of death cells where prisoners await execution. Residency in these cells varies from a day to less than one week. In the center of the enclosure, you will see the well house for the water supply."

At the prison gate, Jabir, Ahmed, and Alric were greeted by the captain of the guards, who was expecting them. The captain nodded in recognition of Ahmed, as one soldier to another. He then led them to an anteroom where they were offered refreshing black tea to combat the heat that had already taken the morning temperature to a higher degree than usual. The prison was cool because of the large stones from which it was constructed, but there was still an uncomfortable humidity that pervaded the building.

In spite of the ominous surroundings, the tea was served in beautiful crystal glasses, and the captain offered them a cushion each so that they might drink the tea in relative comfort. The dark liquid had sugar in the bottom of the glass that, when swirled to taste, would help to revive them from the discomfort of the energy-sapping heat.

"So, captain, you have an interesting prisoner who has caught the Caliph's attention," said Jabir. "What can you tell us?

"This is a most interesting problem," the captain looked around as if to ensure that no one else was listening, before adding, "uncle."

Alric's eyes opened in surprise. Jabir smiled. "You did not know?" he said, looking at Alric, and then added rhetorically, "but how could you know?" Alric remained silent as Jabir explained. "The captain, Bashir, is the grandson of my wife's older sister, Durah," Jabir continued, "and you may meet her one day. Her husband died in a skirmish with infidels almost one year ago, so she may not be prepared to meet you at this time. In her place, Bashir welcomes you to our family."

Jabir took a sip of the sweet hot tea and smiled at Bashir. "Will you join us?"

"No, Lord Jabir." Two guards were now within hearing range, and Bashir preferred to be more formal with his uncle.

"There are those," Jabir said to Alric quietly, as if to explain Bashir's return to formality, "who prefer to flaunt their family relationships. We do not do this and so maintain a dignified relationship. You may have noticed that my wife is not inclined to adhere to formality." He paused and added, "If she were here, thanks be to Allah for her, she would be fussing over Bashir to make sure that he was well."

Alric wondered how many more relatives were tucked away in places of importance. Jabir remarked that the tea was always more delicious when it was served in crystal. He added, for Alric's benefit, that it was a tradition to use crystal glasses for tea because the aroma was retained.

* * *

An hour passed, leaving Alric to wonder about the prisoner and if he would ever see him. As if in answer to his thoughts, the quiet voice of Bashir announced, "We are ready whenever you are, Lord Jabir."

Jabir turned to Alric. "I suspect that you are wondering why we waited so long to enter the prison?" Alric waited for the explanation. "If we had gone into the prison immediately," continued Jabir, "the increased temperature of our bodies from the walk here in the hot sun, coupled with the humid conditions in the prison, would have made it extremely uncomfortable for us. We would have succumbed to a condition that I call heat stroke."

"And, I will add," Ahmed concluded, "that Lord Jabir has devised a regimen for our soldiers so that they do not suffer heat stroke when on the march."

Alric wondered how armies could march in this heat but now he understood Jabir's rationale for frequent rest periods and the ingestion of liquid to rejuvenate the body and bring back energy. Alric could already feel the beneficial effect of the hot, sweet tea as he rose from the cushion.

* * *

They entered the prison, accompanied by Bashir. As they descended to the first floor, the stench that pervaded the building was sufficient to cause the visitors to cover their noses. "The prisoner is in this cell,"

355

Bashir said as he led them to the door of a cell that was set back from the remainder of the others on that floor. "Because of the interest shown in this prisoner, we decided to isolate him from the others."

"Lord, Jabir," Alric said, "If I may make a request?"

"Yes, Alric."

"I think it may be better if I enter the cell alone. It may give the prisoner some confidence in me."

Jabir looked at Bashir, who shook his head advising against such an action.   "This prisoner is unknown to us, so we prefer not to take chances," Jabir responded. "I am inclined to agree with the captain, Alric. But I wonder . . . " and an unspoken thought seemed to pass between Jabir and the captain.

The captain nodded as if reading Jabir's mind. "It will be done, my lord," he said. "Restraints will be applied. It will only take a few moments."

The captain spoke quietly with two of the guards, who then entered the cell, returning quickly to signal that all was prepared. Alric noted that there had been no sounds of a struggle, no words spoken by the guards, or sounds of protest from within the cell.

"Now, you may enter, Alric." Jabir gave him a nod of assent. "But," he added, "if we hear one sound out of the ordinary, we shall enter forcefully."

Alric stood at the door momentarily and was overcome by the filthy conditions that emanated from every corner of the cell. He wrapped his face covering even tighter over his nose. It took moments for his eyes to become accustomed to the dim light sparingly provided by the flickering candles placed in the wall sconces by the guards. When he could make out the features of the cell, it appeared to be about eighteen feet by twelve feet. This prisoner was the only occupant of the cell that would have normally accommodated several villains. In the center, a stake had been secured into the floor, and menacing shackles secured the prisoner's hands and feet so that any movement beyond one pace from the stake was impossible.

Alric approached to get a closer look at the prisoner, and even in the dim light, he could not help but notice the blue eyes that appeared to add light to the gloom. As he stared at the luminous eyes, he noted that the prisoner was indeed taller than the usual inhabitant of the city. In fact, as near as Alric could tell, the prisoner was close to his own height of six feet. The filthy garments that were draped on the figure before him had seen better days. At some time in the past, the garments had been well cut, as though they had been made for someone of a high station. The head covering, the clothes, and the thick dirt and grime masked any other features.

As a test, Alric asked several questions in Arabic and Greek, but there was no answer from the prisoner. He repeated the questions in Latin and noticed a flicker of recognition in the prisoner's eyes.

"Ah, you understand Latin, I see."

There was still no response.

"This one must have no tongue," Alric muttered instinctively to himself in the Saxon language.

"You speak the language of the north and of my people?" the prisoner said.

Alric stepped back in amazement, not so much at the words themselves, since he suspected that the prisoner might be from northern Europe, but at the sound of the prisoner's voice. Without thinking, he removed his face and head covering, crossed himself, and moved closer to the prisoner, straining to get a better look.

He could hear the sharp intake of breath that signified surprise at his appearance. There was an attempt to stand erect, but the captive's shackles became entangled in the hem of the tattered garments. Alric's eyes opened wide, not from terror or fear, but from utter astonishment. The entangled robe had emphasized the prisoner's torso and caused Alric to exclaim in his native tongue.

"*Þu is wif.*" "You are a woman!"

She nodded her head.

Alric continued to speak quietly in Saxon and asked her to cease any movement and not to speak. He then released the robe from its entanglements and made sure the clothing covered her body to disguise her gender.

He looked into the blue eyes and, continuing to use the language of the Saxons, said, "Have faith, I believe that I can help you."

The words gave her the courage to speak. "I am Bemia," she said, "from the Kingdom of . . . "

"I know where you are from," Alric smiled as he interjected. He recognized her name as being a customary name from a Saxon kingdom that lay to the south of Northumbria.

"I am Alric of Wearmouth," he said, "a monastery and village in the Kingdom of Northumbria," he added. "In this country I am called Alric al-Biritaanya ibn Jabir, which means . . . "

"Alric of Britain, of the House of Jabir," she exclaimed. "I have sufficient knowledge of the language of this country to know the meaning of your name."

He held up his finger to indicate silence. "I will return immediately." He smiled, and added as an afterthought, "Do not go anywhere."

The icy blue eyes stared at him, at first not recognizing his humor, and then she smiled faintly as she understood the innuendo of his words. "Alric, I need to ask caution of you."

The plea made him stop in his tracks. As he turned to look at Bemia, he could see the fear in her eyes. "I have offended a man of great power and I need to confide in you. I worry that he may want revenge!"

"You shall have no fear of my adopted father and the people of his house. They are honorable men and do not seek revenge on women." Alric saw the look of surprise on Bemia's face. "Yes, I have been adopted by Lord Jabir and Lady Amira as their son. I am proud to be recognized as a son of their house!"

* * *

Alric left for a few minutes and returned with Jabir, Ahmed, and Bashir. They had listened to his words intently and out of earshot of the guards, and even Bashir was surprised when Alric told them that the prisoner was, in fact, a young woman!

Ahmed and Bashir held shimmering candles aloft to bring more light into the confined area. The girl had sat down, but again she stumbled against the post as she tried to stand erect. Alric moved forward and helped her to stand upright. Jabir, Ahmed, and Bashir were surprised.

"*Wes pu hal*," she said. "Good health to you."

Alric translated for them. "It is her way of saying *thank you*."

She looked at them with fear in her eyes. From Jabir's clothes she could see that he was a man of substance. Her look of fear did not go unnoticed by Alric, who spoke to her quietly and soothingly in their language. Then he turned to Jabir.

"She is concerned about secrecy, father. It does seem that she is in fear of the man who held her captive. She believes that he was a man of power."

At Jabir's request, Bashir loosened the shackles. Bemia stumbled forward toward Alric, who made sure that she did not fall, but the stench almost knocked him over.

"Father," Alric said, "if I may so bold, she needs a bath!"

"Yes, Alric," Jabir said smiling, "I do agree that there is need for a hot bath and clean garments. I suggest that we spirit her away to my home, where mother can see to her needs, after I have the Caliph's permission. Then we can talk with her to gain information and find out who is behind this mystery."

* * *

After the Caliph had approved the release of Bemia, she was deposited into the care of Amira, who had been informed of Bemia's removal from the prison by Jabir and Ahmed before they left for the palace.

Amira looked at Alric, who seemed to be hovering in the near vicinity, and told him to find something to do in the laboratory, as he would not be needed for the next hour or so.

"But, mother, I may be needed to translate . . . "

Amira looked at Bemia and then at Alric. "I was under the impression from your father that the young lady understands our language?"

"Yes, mother, she does," agreed Alric.

"Good," Amira responded and then turned to face Bemia. "If I speak too quickly and you lose the meaning of my words, please tell me."

Bemia nodded to show she understood.

"Your clothes will be burned," Amira said, "and we have ointment that will ease the discomfort to your wrists and ankles caused by the shackles. And now . . . " she paused, looking around at Alric. "Alric, you may go to the laboratory!" she commanded.

She had assumed control of Bemia's health and welfare! Alric left the room quickly, not wishing to incur any more displeasure from Amira.

* * *

Amira led Bemia to the room where the bath was being filled with warm water. The odors of the scented oils were heavy in the air, and Bemia smiled at the thought of a luxurious bath.

"These three young women," Amira said to Bemia, "Abal, Buhjah, and Maha, are my maidservants and they will make sure that you are bathed and clothed in clean attire. They will also keep their lips sealed," she added to allay Bemia's fears about being discovered.

360

As Abal, Buhjah, and Maha helped Bemia to remove her clothes, Amira observed the extent of the dirt that covered every part of her body. "I think," Amira said, "that a shower would be better first. This will remove the grime and then you can relax in the clean bathwater."

The maidservants obeyed accordingly. Amira supervised Bemia's shower and was visibly shaken when the dark blue bruises appeared as the dirt was washed away. "You have suffered, my dear. Whoever this man was, he will be brought to justice. Relax in the water; I have a lotion that will ease the pain of those bruises. Then," Amira continued, "you will have the most relaxing bath that you have had for many a year, perhaps even in your life."

Amira stepped back to allow the maidservants to take over. "My son, Alric," she said "tells me that you may have incurred the wrath of someone in a high place. That remains to be determined. For the most part, you are not to worry. Relax and allow my maidservants to help you."

Amira signaled for the servants to begin, and walked from the room. Bemia closed her eyes as the warm water enveloped her body. She had never known such luxury. The gentle hands of the three maidservants helped her to relax. She felt the dirt peeling from her body. Her skin tingled. As she stepped from the shower, warm towels were draped about her. Bemia would have stumbled from the pain in her legs had not Maha held her upright. Abal tested the water temperature, and Buhjah and Maha assisted her to step into the bath and then into a comfortable sitting position. The warm water in the bath helped to relieve the pain that came from the numerous bruises, as well as those that marked her ankles where the shackles had been fastened. The three maidservants looked at each other as they saw the bruises. Abal quietly left the room to inform Amira of the condition of Bemia's body; she returned moments later.

Being unaware of Abal's momentary absence, Bemia felt content as she looked up beyond the ceiling and spoke in her native tongue. "I asked you for survival and you gave me my request. What must I do to thank you?"

The words came into her mind. "You must do what you believe to be correct, irrespective of the pain that you may suffer."

She smiled and said, "I will."

The three girls giggled, not knowing the Saxon language but glad to see the look of contentment on Bemia's face. Maha responded, "Please sit back in the warm water, and we will do the rest. When we have finished, Lady Amira will bring the ointment to ease the pain of your injuries."

Bemia lay back to allow the warm water, the perfumes, and the three maidservants to do their work. Amira soon returned with the ointment and lotion, which she applied to Bemia's body, after Buhjah had dried her with soft towels. Abal and Maha brought in clean clothes and helped her dress. Bemia, who had never worn silk garments, was surprised at the fineness of her new clothes. The silk caressed her skin and molded itself to her body.

Amira stepped back to look at her and was pleased. The light blue sheen of the silk complemented Bemia's blonde hair, which seemed to project its color into the room. "It looked, my dear, as if a camel had chewed your hair," Amira observed, "but it is now clean and presentable. I suggest that you allow it to grow, then we can trim the rough edges so it will grow evenly. In the meantime, tie your hair with this silk ribbon."

Pulled back and tied behind her head, her blonde hair framed her face like a halo, and her blue eyes sparkled like diamonds. Bemia displayed the kind of beauty that would command a respectful silence when she walked into a room. There was no contact between the two women, but Bemia felt several moments of tenderness pass between herself and Amira.

"Abal, while Buhjah and Maha attend to clearing the towels and cleaning the bath, inform Alric that he can now join us in my day room."

"Come, my dear," Amira held out her hand to Bemia and they left the bathroom and walked in the direction of the day room. "If you are able, we have much to talk about."

Bemia smiled and nodded. "Yes, Lady Amira." She felt safe.

* * *

Amira and Bemia seated themselves on the soft cushions in the day room. Bemia at last felt clean and human again. The months of pain and living in squalid conditions seemed to have been swept away in the bathwater. At that moment, Alric charged into the room like a whirlwind.

"Mother, where is . . . ?"

His question was cut short by Bemia, who rose elegantly from the cushions and smiled, lighting up the room. "I am here, Alric," she said, and the sight of her took Alric by surprise.

"Allah be praised," was all that Alric could manage to say.

Bemia did not know how to respond to Alric's open-mouthed expression. She was pleased that she had met one of her own kind. A man from Wearmouth who may be able to understand what she had been through these past months.

She stood in front of him and allowed her hands to feel the new garments. The coolness of the silk made her skin tingle with excitement. The scented water had relaxed her body and the aroma had remained.

"Alric," Amira intruded on the heavy silence that hung in the air between them. "I think it wise that you close your mouth and sit opposite me."

She indicated the cushion on the other side of the tea table. Then she patted the cushion on her left-hand side. "You may sit here, my dear," she said to Bemia.

Once they were seated, Amira clapped her hands, and tea and fruit were produced by Abal and Maha. At that moment Buhjah appeared and whispered to Amira that Lord Jabir and Ahmed had returned.

Maha poured the tea just as Jabir and Ahmed entered the room. Alric stood, moved behind Amira, and indicated to Bemia that she should do the same.

"My dear Amira," Jabir began, "where is that poor girl . . . ?"

The words ceased on his lips as he saw Bemia standing next to Alric. He looked around the room. "Surely . . . " he began and stopped once more.

Bemia was momentarily startled by Lord Jabir's hawklike stare. As if seeking reassurance, she moved closer to Alric and took hold of his hand. Alric moved forward, still holding Bemia's hand. "If I may, mother?"

Amira nodded, barely able to conceal her beaming smile at the sight of the two fair-skinned young people. "Father, this is Bemia of the province of Deira in Britain. Bemia," he turned to her, "I present to you my father, Jabir al-Hajjaj ibn Yusuf abu Asad abu Khalil, physician and surgeon to the Caliph and to the people of Baghdad."

Bemia bowed her head.

"Welcome, my dear, to this house. Such a transformation as I have never seen!" Jabir could not help exclaiming. "My dearest," he said to Amira, "you have done wonders!"

Amira looked pleased. "It is nothing on my part. Bemia already existed. I merely helped her remove the dirt and grime of prison."

"And this gentleman," Alric continued to Bemia, "is Ahmed, my brother, my friend, my *mu'al-alim*, my teacher, and a member of this family." Bemia bowed her head again.

"It is my pleasure to meet you, Bemia, but you need not bow to me," Ahmed responded. "I am not of noble birth."

"If you are of this house, I bow to you in gratitude and my appreciation."

Ahmed smiled.

Khalil's entrance broke the silence. He strode into the room, bowed his head to Jabir, then bent over and kissed Amira on the cheek and nodded to Ahmed. "Alric," he winked, "it seems to me, from her coloring, that this young lady has similar origins to you?"

Alric made the introductions, and Bemia bowed once more to Khalil.

"Now, my dear Bemia, sit next to me and we will talk over tea and a meal," Amira said as she looked at her husband, Khalil, Ahmed, and Alric. "The menfolk can sit wherever they wish. Alric, perhaps you can sit opposite so that if Bemia has trouble with a word, you will be able to draw our attention to it."

Alric said, "With your permission, mother, I would like to speak in the language of my birth to Bemia." Amira agreed. "You must not fear," Alric explained to Bemia. "My mother suggested that if you have any trouble with the words, I will help. She also said that she will take care of you. You must be honest with her, for to be dishonest would cause you to be expelled from this house."

For effect, Alric added words of his own. "Any dishonesty and disrespect to my mother, and I will throw you out myself. Our common country of birth and our common language will not protect you. Do you understand?" Alric smiled to relieve the tension he saw in Bemia's face, and she returned the smile. "All will be well, mother," Alric said. "Bemia understands."

"*Shukran.* Thank you, Lady Amira," Bemia said as if to emphasize Alric's words.

"Now that you have met all of the family, my dear," Amira said to Bemia in gentle tones, "come and let us take tea."

"You will find," Amira said, "that we use the tea break as a means of getting to know each other, to talk business, and also to relax as a family. Take your time, my dear, and tell us about yourself. You must have an interesting past, especially since you existed dressed as a man."

When they had drank the last of the tea, all eyes focused on Bemia. She looked at Amira, awaiting a sign that would herald the next chapter in her young life. There was confidence and trust in her eyes. Amira took Bemia's hand in hers. "Do you feel ready to relate your story to us?" Bemia nodded. "Because of the nature of this crime, we need to hear what happened to you. It may have a bearing on the issues that my husband," she looked at Jabir, "and my sons," she looked proudly in turn at Khalil, Ahmed, and Alric, "are handling now for the Caliph. We are afraid that my nephew . . . "

Amira stopped as she saw the surprised expression on Bemia's face. "You did not know, my dear? Well, the Caliph is the son of my sister, Khayzuran, and Harun, the Caliph, has remained very close to me since Khayzuran's death some years ago."

Bemia took a deep breath. She was the focus of attention. She closed her eyes, and for a moment she seemed oblivious to Alric and the family, gathering herself for the memories that she was about to recall. Then she started to relate her story.

* * *

CHAPTER 27

"My story begins a long time ago," Bemia said after clearing her throat. "I will give as much detail as you wish."

Amira held up her hand to indicate that Bemia wait a moment. "If I may, my dear," she said. She clapped her hands and Wahid appeared. "A pitcher of cool water, Wahid. We do not wish our guest's throat to dry as she talks."

Wahid bowed his head, left the room, and reappeared moments later with the pitcher and glasses.

"Thank you, Wahid," Amira said, "and it is preferable that no one hear this. Of course, you are excluded from this edict. You have the family's trust."

"As you wish, my Lady. It will be done."

Alric could hear the rustling sounds as the maidservants and others, ever in wait for commands from Amira and Jabir, were given permission by Wahid to leave and attend to other duties.

Wahid reappeared to inform Amira that her instructions had been carried out. Wahid," Amira said, "we would all feel comfortable if you will remain at the door to make sure no one approaches us without adequate warning." He nodded. "Now, my dear," Amira looked once more at Bemia, "please continue."

Bemia cleared her throat once more after a sip of the cool water and started to relate her story. "The events that led me to Baghdad started in the year . . . ," she thought for a moment. "I am sorry I do not know the year, but it was around ten or twelve years ago. The weather had been so bad that winter, food was in extremely short supply, and by the end of the year it was cold enough to freeze the river, close to my home village of Hoton near to where the Humbre joins the sea. Because of this, starvation and death followed."

Her gentle tones took Alric by surprise. This was the woman who had spoken harshly to him in the jail. "As a result, a group of militant peasants turned against their overlords. As the daughter of a peasant, I had little hope. The crops had failed, and there was the promise of another harsh winter. A sickness that brought coughs, headaches, and internal pains eventually killed many of the people."

Alric looked at Jabir, who he knew had recognized the sickness as a form of the plague, strong enough to kill. "For my parents," Bemia continued, "there was only one consideration. Across the sea to the east stretched the kingdoms of Europe. Here there was food and shelter. My parents made their decision. I was sent to a land that had been the original home of the Saxons; it is often referred to as Saxony. There I was to live with an aunt and uncle, who would care for me. A passage was secured on board a fishing boat and I landed, with several other children, on the shore of a new country.

"Bemia," it was Khalil's voice that cut into her story. "I believe that we may have visited that area." Khalil then described the coastline he had explored when they had found Alric.

Bemia listened and nodded in agreement. "My uncle met me on this . . . ," she looked at Alric and said two words in Saxon to which he responded, "desolate shore." "Like the other children," Bemia continued, "we were saddened to leave our parents, but we looked forward to a new life, hoping that at some future time we would see our families again. We were taken along a wide, rutted road to a village of huts built of clay and wattle and roofed with river reeds. This led to the marketplace and church. Beyond that, the road continued, and it was only a short distance to the cottage where my aunt, uncle, and cousins lived."

"Fortunately, my uncle and aunt were weavers and were able to supplement their subsistence plot by selling various fabrics and support the family's needs. I was expected to work alone and unsupervised. During this time, I also received lessons from a priest and I learned the basics of reading and writing. The priest was a good man who taught many of the children to read and write, but when this became known, he was made to leave the village. The older villagers especially were annoyed that a priest should teach girls to read and write; we were to be nothing more than workers and bearers of children."

The emotion of her words showed in her voice and Bemia paused to take another sip of water. "Even after the priest left the village," Bemia continued, "I continued my learning in secret, using books he had concealed. I allowed the winds of curiosity to carry me to places far beyond the limits of my imagination. I was able to glean enough Latin from others that allowed me to work my way through the first five chapters of Genesis. It was, however, a project that was fraught with danger, since I, a girl, was strictly forbidden to be educated."

Bemia paused. As she drank more water from the glass that Ahmed had refilled for her, Alric took the opportunity to give a brief explanation of the situation in Britain during times of crop failure, famine, and disease.

"By the time I had reached the age of fifteen," Bemia continued, "word reached me that my parents had died two winters after I had left home. At the same time, my uncle was beginning to take more than a friendly interest in me. His hands touched me in places I thought were forbidden. I confided his unwanted advances to my aunt, who immediately accused me of sorcery. 'You have,' my aunt screamed, 'bewitched an honest man. Leave this house immediately!'

"I feared that I could be burned or my body examined by wanton priests if the holy church heard my aunt's accusation, so I decided to leave. I realized that my life would be more difficult as a girl, so I took some of my male cousin's clothes and decided to travel, as far away from the village as possible."

There were tears in her eyes as she paused to allow Amira to pass her a lace napkin. The tears clouded her vision and as she reached for the napkin she knocked the glass over and spilled the water onto the floor. She closed her eyes for a moment as if to clear her head of the unpleasant memories, and then she appeared unsteady, sliding from the cushion.

"Alric," Amira commanded, "Bemia needs your help."

"No, Lady Amira. I am recovered now. I suddenly felt very tired."

Alric helped Bemia back onto the cushion while Ahmed called for Wahid, who entered the room wondering what had happened. "My maidservants, Wahid," Amira responded, and within minutes Abal, Buhjah, and Maha entered the room.

Jabir examined Bemia, and he could see that all was not well. Her face was ashen.

"Is there anything you can do?" Amira asked.

"Perhaps, my dear, if she can retire to a bed, I think that a good night's rest will cure this fatigue."

Bemia closed her eyes as she felt Buhjah and Maha's arms around her. Abal went ahead to prepare the bed. Once Bemia was on the bed, the merciful darkness of sleep overtook her.

"It has been a long day for her," Amira announced. "We will reconvene here in the morning when I call you. And," she added, "not before!'"

Jabir smiled at his wife's control of the situation.

"We can all wait until the morrow to hear more of Bemia's story."

"It seems to me, mother," Alric observed, "that Bemia has information that may be helpful to the Caliph."

"We shall see, my dear. We shall see."

*   *   *

It was close to the middle of the next day. Jabir had just returned from the palace to report to the Caliph on the events of the last evening and was talking with Alric in the laboratory. They were in a heads-together conversation about a jar of volatile spirits that Alric had recently isolated from the Hit tar when word was brought by Wahid that Bemia had arisen and was in the day room with Lady Amira.

"And so," Alric said, in conclusion, "I believe that this mixture of the volatile spirits may also have uses. It is not as lively or volatile as the other material, and its potential to break into flame is less when heat is applied. And," he said, taking a damp cloth, "it can be a mixed with this fragrant oil and there is no sign of a division of the two liquids."

"You have done well, Alric," Jabir commented. "Fragrant oils are expensive, and if there is some way to extract the oil from the jasmine plant in greater quantities without changing the properties of the oil, that will be a great success. We will need to purchase much less from the merchants who travel here with the caravans along the Silk Road."

Jabir smiled at the thought and then added, "Although we use the oil to treat soreness of the throat and to ease the pain from coughing, I am sure that you have some alternate use in mind. But," he paused, "we must go. Mother has sent for us and to be late when we are called . . . "

Jabir left the rest unsaid as they washed their hands, left the laboratory, and walked to the house.

*   *   *

Amira was seated with Bemia on her left, as they had been the night before, with Khalil and Ahmed. "I wonder what is keeping father and Alric . . . ," Amira was in the midst of asking when they entered. Bemia,

371

resplendent in fresh clothes that were a delicate shade of green, stood up to greet Jabir.

"Sit, my dear," he said, "no need for formalities in this house."

They had just started to eat fruit, drink juice, and converse about the day and of how Bemia had slept when Wahid appeared. Amira looked up. "Yes, Wahid."

"You have a visitor, my Lady. He stated that he is a close relative from a distant place." Wahid's face showed no emotion. He was familiar with the code words that were used among family members. Usually he would have determined the name of the visitor and announced the person by name.

"Show him in please," Amira responded knowingly.

The man entered and was unrecognizable to Alric because of the long robes, and his face and head were completely covered.

"Welcome. Come, sit with us, dear nephew," Amira said, indicating a cushion to her immediate right. Jabir, Khalil, Ahmed, and Alric had placed themselves opposite Amira and Bemia, as before.

Alric jumped up from the cushion, realizing what Amira's greeting meant and then recognizing the Caliph's face as he removed his head and face covering. He fell to his knees, as did Ahmed, and following their actions, so did Bemia.

"Please rise," Harun said quickly. "I am in one of my walkabout moods and thought that I would visit my dear aunt and uncle." The Caliph turned. "You may rise also, Wahid, faithful servant. Some of my guards, out of their usual uniform lest I be recognized, are just inside the gate. They would welcome refreshments."

"It will be done, Caliph," Wahid responded, then turned on his heel and left quickly.

"Harun," Amira said as the Caliph divested himself of his outer garments, "to what do we owe the pleasure of this visit? I suspect there is some reason other than a mere walkabout."

"My dear aunt," the Caliph replied as he kissed her cheek before continuing, "I could never cover up my actions from you! I came to see for myself the young woman who was until recently my prisoner, and perhaps hear some of her story."

"She sits before you Harun." Amira announced, smiling.

The Caliph looked at Bemia. She immediately rose to her feet and bowed her head. "Raise your head, my dear," the Caliph said. He looked at her with much curiosity. "You may sit, my dear," he said. Then he turned to Alric, who had also risen from his seat. "Are all of the women of your land this beautiful?" It was a rhetorical question. "Please sit, Alric."

When everyone was seated again, Harun spoke, looking directly at Bemia. "The reason I am here is that I understand from my uncle that your story could be of great interest to me. If I may, I suggest, aunt, that we finish our midday refreshments before Bemia continues her story. As a result of my uncle's visit this morning, I am acquainted with the details as of last night."

* * *

The remnants of the meal were cleared away by Wahid; the three maidservants were not privy to visits by the Caliph. Wahid returned and placed fresh pitchers of water and orange juice before them. He looked at Amira, who indicated that he should again wait watchfully by the door.

All turned their focus on Bemia. "When I left the house of my aunt, I made my way to the coast," she began. "I remember my aunt telling me that people from all the lands around the Middle Sea came to the coastal ports, and I was determined to seek my new life wherever I could."

She paused and looked at the group, who waited with great interest for her to continue. "I realized that I needed protection from those

373

who would victimize a woman, and that is why I dressed myself in my cousin's clothes. By such subterfuge, I was able to gain work on ships, until one day the ship I was on reached the port that you call Basra. During this time, I deepened my voice so as not to give the sailors any cause to doubt my gender. When I was in Basra, I noticed that men and women, because of their clothes, did not seem to be so different from one another. I decided to leave the ship and stay. The sailors had told me about the magnificent city called Baghdad, and since I had the urge to see the city, I looked for the means to make my way north. I knew the risk, but in my circumstances I considered it justifiable." She thought for a moment. "If I had left the ship in a western or northern European port, it would have been more difficult, perhaps even impossible, to exist as a woman who lives in the streets."

Amira looked quizzically at Bemia. Bemia responded, "I was desperate to survive. I maintained my guise as a man, for I did not feel strong enough to face life here as a woman. I had requested that the captain of the ship allow me to go ashore to make one or two purchases. For this I would need money, and he gave me an allowance on my wages. If I had requested all of my wages, that would have aroused his suspicion. The money was sufficient to buy clothes and food for several days."

Alric recalled his journey on the ship with Khalil and Ahmed. "How did you learn the language of this region?"

Bemia looked at Alric and smiled. "Some of the sailors were from cities that fall under the Caliph's rule," she bowed her head in Harun's direction, "and when I showed an interest in the language, they started to teach me words and phrases. They also told me of Baghdad and how the Caliph encouraged education. They used a name . . . " Bemia put her forefinger to her lips as she tried to recall the word. "Ah, yes. 'House of Light' they called your library and palace because, they said, it shed its light to the world through learning and education."

Bemia bowed her head again in the Caliph's direction. She paused for a moment and sipped the water from the glass, then, hearing no questions, continued. "I was able to secure work on a barge that carried trade goods from Basra to Baghdad. This was an uneventful journey, and on my arrival in this city, I took my wages and sought work here."

"Where did you live?" Amira asked.

"I found a building near the river that had not been used for some time. It seems that the roof had collapsed during a wind storm. I decided to spend the night there, so I swept the floor with some of the tree branches that had been broken by a more recent wind. Those first few nights, I slept on the floor and I used my arm as a pillow. I realized I would need to find a more comfortable arrangement. As the days passed, I was able to construct a shelter using the materials from the collapsed roof."

"You say this building was near to the river?" Harun asked.

"Yes, Caliph," Bemia answered.

"I will make inquires to see who owns such a building and have it repaired and put back into use. Continue, Bemia."

"By presenting myself to the stall owners as the morning market opened, I was able to secure work each day. As the days passed, I was excited at the possibility of a new life, but at the same time, I was cautious.

"Each night I would pick up a handful of small stones from the alley next to the building. I would then drop the stones in the entry to the building and mark their positions. Each morning I would check the position of each of the stones to see if they had been moved by anyone entering the building. All was well until seven days before my capture. I suspected that someone was watching me as I performed my morning and evening cleansing routines. For the following nights, sleep did not come easily. I could not get the thought out of my mind that someone knew my secret. Each day, I checked the stones and I noticed one morning that they had been moved. Someone had entered the building during the night."

Amira reached across and touched Bemia's arm in a gesture of sympathy and understanding.

"It was at that time that I decided I needed to seek other accommodations. However, this was not to be so. That last night, I awoke suddenly, as if my mind had sounded an alarm. The sound of stones rattling under heavy feet advised me of the entry of someone into the building. I arose, and in the dim shadows I saw two men with swords in their hands. I tried to conceal my movements by staying in the shadows of the room. Then I leapt forward in a futile attempt to escape, but some of the men anticipated my intent. They positioned themselves in front of me. One of them called me 'the light-eyed woman' that my master, Malik Lail, desires."

"Did you say Malik Lail?" Alric asked. "Master of the Night," he added.

Bemia nodded. "I rushed at him, and that is the last I remember before regaining consciousness in a strange room."

At this point, Amira suggested that they take a break to stretch their legs while Wahid replenished the orange juice and water and brought in more fresh fruit.

*   *   *

Within a short time, Bemia was ready to continue, and all eyes were focused on her once more. "I awoke in that strange place and heard the voice from behind me. 'I see that you are conscious,' the man said. 'It is a pity my men had to bruise such a beautiful face to capture you.' I moved so that I could see him, but his face was covered by a mask. He said he had first heard about me some days before when his spies had reported that a woman in the guise of a man was living in the old building. From their descriptions of me, he decided we should meet. He also knew from his investigations that I appeared to have no friends.

"He told me that he would give me a choice. I could be his friend—he did not define what form of friend, but I guessed—or on the morrow I would meet the first of many lovers who were not gentle in their treatment of women. It is said that the caravaners can be very brutal when they have a woman for sport. At that point I lurched forward to try to pull down his mask, but he hit me with his clenched fist and knocked me to the ground. I was determined that this man would not dominate me. He looked at me through evil eyes and told me that if I behaved myself, I would be handsomely rewarded."

"It is as well that you were unable to pull down his mask and see his face," Amira interjected, "or you may have suffered severe consequences. Obviously he does not wish to be identified. Please go on, my dear."

"He led me to a high table and told me to lie facedown on it. I did as he commanded. I knew exactly what I had to do. As he leaned over me, I raised my head suddenly and caught him on the nose. It was not sufficient to break the nose but enough to bring tears to his eyes. I turned onto my back and thrust my foot into his groin."

"My dear Bemia," Khalil interjected, "you have used a method we use in the training of the Caliph's soldiers. Where did you learn such tactics?"

"There is more, Khalil," she said. "As he bent over in discomfort, I remembered all of the times I had kicked a ball of rags around with my brothers, and the tactics of the game came to mind. So I kicked his face, grabbed whatever clothes were available, and fled before he could catch his breath and give warning to his household servants."

She touched her forehead as if recalling another memory of that night. "Yes," she said, "there is one other thing. As I ran through the house, I felt that I was guided by a woman's voice, and then I found myself in the garden, but it was all to no avail. My escape ended in darkness brought on by the hilt of a sword. As I came back to consciousness, I realized, from the soreness of my body, that I had been beaten.

"Malik Lail, or the Man-With-No-Face as I preferred to call him, was cursing me and he also cursed a woman servant who, I remember, he called Maria. I was conscious of her being close to me as two men pulled me to my feet. Malik Lail's orders were to dispatch me by whatever means they decided, and my body was to be cast into the river. In my barely conscious state, I heard the woman protest and then I heard the sound of his fist hitting what I believed to be her face. Then the two men threw me to the ground and I passed into a world of darkness again."

The stress was beginning to show on Bemia, and she lapsed into her more comfortable and instinctive Saxon language.

"Bemia," Alric said gently, "if you speak our language, only I can understand you."

She apologized profusely and when asked by Harun if she needed to rest, she politely declined, stating that she would rather finish her story. "I was conscious of being taken, I assume, to the river, where I would be killed and my body thrown into the water."

Harun held up his hand to indicate that she should pause. "For everyone's information, Maria is safe. She was extracted from the house by two of my men, who made it appear that she had been abducted. She made full statements of the happenings in that house, but she never knew the identity of the owner. She is now in a safe place where she cannot be harmed, with money to serve her needs for the remainder of her life."

"Thank you, Sire." Bemia was relieved to hear the Caliph's words. "I feel," she continued, "that Maria was instrumental in saving my life, and I was concerned that some further ill had befallen her.

"After and the two men hauled me to my feet, I heard other voices. I believe that this was the time the two soldiers arrived and interfered with the plans for my death and so took me to the prison. Rather than go from one cruel situation to an unknown fate, and since my captor was a man of some position in the city, I decided to maintain my silence in prison, hoping that someone would be called who might be trustworthy."

She looked at Alric and smiled.

"You said," Amira spoke, "that the man who attempted to . . . well, we will not go into that now, this man remained masked all of the time?"

"Yes, my Lady."

"So there is no way that we would recognize him again?"

"By his voice, my Lady."

Amira raised her eyebrows in question.

"And," Bemia added, "I recall he boasted about holding a high position within the Caliph's government."

"He did not tell you any more?"

"No, my Lady."

"You should know that I," Harun spoke, "strictly forbid such treatment of women. What makes this worse is that we seem to have a man highly placed in my government who believes he can do as he pleases, even acting against the law. Such a man is dangerous."

"I can clearly remember Malik Lail's voice, Caliph. His words are imprinted on my mind, but I can identify him only by this means. It is also my understanding that very few of his other female servants have seen him, as he prefers to remain masked."

"Do not worry my dear," Harun spoke in a comforting voice, "I have learned through my uncle," he nodded at Jabir, "that patience can truly be a virtue. Based on my suspicions, I have a suspect in mind, and by careful observation we will bring him to justice."

"I am reading your mind, Harun," Jabir said. "There does seem to be some connection between this man's treatment of Bemia and the issue that we discussed some time ago. Someone who would ignore the law to this extent is the type of person who may try to control the law, and there is only one way he could do that."

Harun looked at Jabir. "Yes, uncle, he would have to depose me." The Caliph stoked his beard. "We must remain vigilant and be proactive rather than reactive. We need to give this much thought."

Amira touched her chin with her forefinger as she carefully considered her next words.

And then, for the first time in several days, Hilda's voice came to Alric as gentle as always. *I foresee Lady Amira's words and I think you will be pleased. This is a good family. Now listen and rejoice, my brother.*

Alric listened intently when Amira began to speak to Bemia. "You, my dear, need protection, and if my nephew and my husband agree, you will become a part of this family."

Jabir smiled and said enthusiastically, "Yes."

"I have always wanted to have a sister," Khalil added.

"Consider it done," Harun commanded.

Alric was silent. His beaming smile had the brightness and energy of the noonday sun. Ahmed winked at him.

The tears ran down Bemia's cheek. She, like Alric, had found a home. Amira suggested that Alric help Bemia to her feet, and in doing so, he pressed a piece of silk into her hands. "Use this to wipe your tears," he whispered in Saxon. "My mother welcomes you to her home. How well you are accepted depends upon you. I will gladly help you to become a daughter of this family."

No one else could understand his words, nor was anyone curious about them, believing them to be words of sympathy for her ordeal. Suddenly, Bemia was on her knees before Amira, kissing her hand and forgetfully speaking in Saxon. "I thank you for your generous offer and I accept you as my mother." Alric translated Bemia's tear-laden Saxon words. "I will not disappoint you. I will protect you and the family to the death. This I swear before your family as witnesses."

Amira was not certain that she understood the words, but Alric explained. "Mother, Bemia speaks from the custom in the land of the Saxons. She first had to accept your offer and then to swear fealty to you and then to the family. By doing this, Bemia's promise is her bond to you. That bond is unbreakable. She will protect you from harm as I will also, even at the cost of our lives."

Amira smiled and stroked Bemia's hair. The soft strands were so much like those of Alric. Amira smiled wistfully to herself as she thought about the future. "Welcome to my family, Bemia. Your oath to me is precious. I want you to know that we will also protect you."

Alric looked at Amira. He wondered if her thoughts were about the man who might betray the Caliph, her nephew. Perhaps, as Jabir and the Caliph had suggested, there was something deeper to this.

They needed to be able to disclose, with undeniable proof, the identity of this man, and this would be difficult. It all depended on Bemia being in a position to recognize the man's voice. It would require caution and subterfuge, as the man would undoubtedly recognize Bemia.

To Alric, there was a real threat to the Caliph from Abdul al-Warith, his First Minister, who seemed to have an agenda of his own to satisfy. Then there was the experience suffered by Bemia and other women, many of whom had disappeared without trace. In either case, Alric thought, the lives of all his family could be in extreme danger. He felt an increasing uneasiness.

* * *

CHAPTER 28

Two months passed, and Bemia brought new life into the home. Jabir and Amira were overjoyed to have a daughter, and Alric was thrilled to have, in name, a sister, but in reality a friend of similar background to his own. At first, he had felt anxiety at having her around, as she made frequent visits to see him while he worked in the laboratory. Her flowing robes presented a constant danger as she walked around the laboratory peering curiously at the contents of the glass storage containers and the experimental equipment. She was allowing her hair to grow, at Amira's suggestion, but long hair was also a potential danger in the laboratory.

Other than her daily excursions to the laboratory to talk with Alric, she had shown no inclination to leave the house and venture forth into the outside world. After several days, Alric had succeeded in persuading Bemia to leave the laboratory and sit outside in the shade.

Amira, always the observant mother, took a great interest in Bemia's daily and increased visits to Alric. One day, she mentioned it to Jabir as they awaited Alric and Bemia's presence at dinner, but her husband was noncommittal in his response. Khalil and Ahmed smiled but did not comment. After further discussion they collectively agreed that it was time for Bemia to familiarize herself once again with the outside world, specifically the marketplace, where the throng of people would offer some anonymity.

As dinner progressed, Amira suggested an outing, and Bemia was overjoyed. She would go to the marketplace! Her escapades there before her capture were just a distant thought. She was happy now and had put behind her the days when she had inhabited the back streets and alleyways of the city.

Amira cautioned her and indicated it was safe to leave the house only in the presence of Alric and Ahmed using a suitable disguise. Alric, hovering and ever-present as Bemia's protector when he was not in the laboratory, suggested the use of his cream that would give sufficient coloring to her face and eyebrows as means to disguise her northern European countenance.

Since his journey to Mosul, Alric had continued to use the cream on his own face and hair several times and found that it caused no irritation of the skin or damage to his hair as long as he removed it with warm water. And so, when the time came for Bemia to leave the house, she had changed from a blonde Saxon into a tanned, dark-haired young woman who looked no different from the citizens of the country.

Clothes were produced and Amira decided that Bemia would not wear the *hijab*, or traditional head covering and veil, that some women wore, but because of Bemia's height, she opted for the head and face garments that were worn by many men. By the time that Amira had completed her work on Bemia, there was little of her to be recognized, and the clothes made it difficult to tell that she was not a young man.

The language was not a problem, since Bemia used the language daily. She no longer used the pidgin language of a streetwise foreigner but that of the upper-class society. She could, however, lapse into the dialect when it was required.

Bemia felt her outing was an omen and she was ready. Amira had several last words of advice as she cast her approving eyes over Bemia: "Your blue eyes are less suspicious than your other features. There are those who live north of Mosul in mountainous regions who have blue eyes. If questioned, you can admit to being from Mosul." She continued to look at Bemia admiringly. "Do not remove your head or face covering at all, my dear. There is no doubt that your hair and facial features will show you to be a young woman who is not of this country." Amira kissed Bemia on the cheek. "Use caution, my dear."

Bemia smiled. "Yes, mother."

* * *

As Bemia walked to the market, accompanied by Alric and Ahmed, she felt excited. Ahmed, ever watchful, looked for anyone behaving in a suspicious manner. The merchants had set up their stalls, and people of different creeds and cultures were busy making their daily purchases. They were too occupied to notice three more persons in the market. Bemia walked slowly, staying close to Alric and Ahmed and maintaining her poise to give the impression that she was a young man. Alric continued to talk in Arabic, much as friends would do walking in the market. Ahmed encouraged Bemia to speak with different merchants about several items of general interest to test her speech.

As the time passed, Bemia admitted that she wished the day would not end. She recognized that she was feeling something she had never experienced before, and that was the desire to live in comfort in one place forever.

As they walked home, Alric felt that they had accomplished the first step. It had been a good experience. Bemia had enjoyed herself and passed the test. At times like these, he thought, the joys of living overshadow the concerns that there may be someone in the city who wished harm to Bemia and the remainder of the family.

* * *

A week later, Alric awoke to the coolness of the early morning. This time was the most comfortable for him, before the heat of the day took over. The heat of the previous day had been almost unbearable, and the city had been unusually quiet as the inhabitants had preferred to stay indoors. Bemia mentioned at breakfast that a trip to the market that morning would be a welcome change in their activities. Alric looked at Amira; her face remained impassive.

Alric had no experiments that required his immediate attention, so he thought that this was a good idea. "We can," he suggested, "visit the stalls of the merchants who bring the ores from the mines. I have need of fresh supplies."

Ahmed was not available, since his duties required that he accompany Khalil to a meeting with the Caliph later in the morning. Alric saw the doubt in Amira's eyes, but after some moments of thought she agreed, though hesitantly, provided they took the same precautions of covering their identities as they had on Bemia's first outing.

As she watched them apply the cream that changed their complexions from northern European to Mesopotamian, she warned them to stay away from the merchants who used the hookah, that strange pipe used by many visitors to the marketplace. "You will find," she warned, "that, on occasion, pipe users often place other materials into the pipe." She rubbed her chin as if trying to find the next words, at the same time carefully looking over Bemia to make sure her clothes were correct, and then added, "Those substances can alter your mind and cause you to lose control of your actions."

Alric and Bemia understood and assured Amira that they would not go into such places. She took one more look at Alric and Bemia and was satisfied.

* * *

When they arrived at the marketplace, it was busy. This was of no concern to Alric; he knew the crowds would enable them to be less noticeable. The merchants were in good voice as they advertised their wares. Some were even attracting buyers by offering a free portion of food to anyone who purchased their goods.

"What is it that you are looking for?" the old merchant asked as he offered Alric and Bemia a plate of large, juicy dates, thinking that it would help with a sale. The shade of the canopy over the stall offered Alric and Bemia welcome relief, but they declined his offer, not wishing to remove their facial coverings.

"I have already told you," Alric responded. "I am an assistant in a shop that sells medicines to heal the sick. I need to buy ores to make medicines."

The merchant knew of the men who made medicines; some worked and cured sickness, while others did not. But supplying such a shop with different ores on a regular basis could lead to a very steady income and a handsome profit that would make his business much easier.

Bemia stood behind Alric, waiting for his response. There was only silence while the merchant considered the good fortune of having a regular customer. Alric turned to leave and move on to the next stall where ores were also for sale. Seeing them move away, the persistent merchant continued, not wishing to lose his customers. "I have had this shop for thirty years," the merchant said. " I know good ores from bad, and everything else there is to know about the ores you seek. If you care to join me for a cup of fresh tea and juicy dates, we can discuss your needs." Alric and Bemia stopped and turned to face the merchant.

"Already this morning, I have had a visit from a powerful man," the merchant stated proudly, attempting to show that his stall was important. Alric realized the merchant was trying to impress him. "He is a man of high position who is in the habit of walking in the morning air and," the merchant looked around furtively as if to make sure that no one was listening, "and often stops here to relax with the hookah."

The merchant smiled as though he were privy to the man's habits. "He seeks peace and quiet here. Today, he seems to have much on his mind and has tarried here longer than usual. He remains under the shelter of my tent in the back, where he cannot be seen."

The merchant could not hear, nor would he have understood, any of Bemia's whispered words to Alric in the Saxon language. She had been uncomfortable ever since Alric had started to talk with the man. And now his admittance that he had an arrangement with customers to partake in the false pleasures of the hookah as they sat concealed in the back of his stall made her fearful. She felt it was a bad omen!

Alric listened intently to Bemia's whispers and then nodded his head in agreement. He whispered in response, "Keep your face covered, and follow my lead."

Bemia bowed her head and said quietly in Arabic, "Yes, master."

He saw the smile in her eyes and acknowledged the mock gesture of her servitude. Alric inspected the ores in the many boxes and chose malachite, the ore of copper, for use as eye salve, magnesia for ailments of the stomach, and the oxide ores of iron and zinc to dry and soothe the oozing and weeping of skin rashes. He paid the merchant and was about to give instructions for the delivery of the ore but at the last moment remembered about his anonymity and decided against it. He did not wish to give away his association with the House of Jabir.

"Pack each ore in a separate bag, I will take my purchases with me," Alric said.

"Let me offer you tea," the merchant suggested as he continually tried to ingratiate himself with Alric for this sale and, hopefully, he thought, for future sales. "For you," he looked at Alric, "and for your servant?"

Alric nodded in agreement, and as the merchant prepared to make the tea, Bemia nudged Alric gently. "Hah," she whispered in Saxon as she smiled under the face covering, "he thinks that I am your servant. That will be the day, master!"

Alric suppressed a smile. Yes, he thought, she has spirit.

The merchant offered them cushions to sit upon, and as they made themselves comfortable, he proudly informed them, "The tea will, of course, be served in crystal glasses."

It was served, as the merchant had promised, in beautiful clear crystal glasses. Alric was truly impressed by the beauty of the glassware. The merchant remarked that tea was always more delicious when served in crystal, because the aroma was retained. He added that it was a tradition to use the crystal because it had magical powers. As they drank the tea, they became aware of someone moving in the back of the tented enclosure. A man appeared from behind the curtain. He was dressed in garments of white silk. His face was partially covered, and his head cloth was secured with a ring made of camel skin.

He looked at them in silence, regarding them for a few moments, then reached into his pocket and withdrew a coin. "I must leave now," he said.

The merchant said nothing. Alric and Bemia remained motionless with their heads bowed. The man dropped the coin near to where the merchant sat. "I will see you in one week."

The coldness of the man's voice and the words seemed more of a threat than a statement. As he turned to leave, he looked at Bemia, who remained as she was, her head bowed, as if in respect to the man.

"This one is your servant?" he asked Alric. Alric nodded.

"Then, I suggest," the man said, "you teach your servant a lesson with the whip. Servants do not take tea with their masters."

Alric knew at once where he had heard the voice. It took his mind back to the day of his arrival in Baghdad and his visit with the Caliph. He could not forget the voice of Abdul al-Warith, First Minister to the Caliph.

The man turned on his heel and left the shop. The merchant rose from his cushion and went into the back of the shop to clear away items left by his visitor.

Once again, Alric had the strange sensation that Hilda was nearby. Then he heard her words: *You must beware of this man,* she said. *The omens tell me it is time for you to go.* Alric looked at Bemia. She had not raised her head. He put his hand on her shoulder.

"It was him, Alric!" she spoke in Saxon but kept her words to a whisper. "That voice. I recognized the voice. It was him! We need to go from here immediately."

Being with her these last months had taught Alric something even more important. Her language had always been one of enthusiasm and of things accomplished with joy and purpose. Even when he had first met her in prison, she had been independent and unafraid. Now she was filled with fear.

They raised themselves from the cushions as the merchant reappeared. People were continuing to throng the marketplace. Alric picked up the package that had been thoughtfully bundled and slung it over his shoulder. The merchant bowed several times to show his appreciation for the purchase.

As Alric and Bemia left the shop, there seemed to be more activity than usual. From where they stood, there was no sign of the First Minister, but Alric sensed Bemia's concern. "We will not return home immediately," he said. "That might arouse suspicion. I sense that the First Minister will not have forgotten you. You are the one that escaped, and it is quite possible he has his spies watching the main thoroughfares of the city."

Alric paused as he thought about his next words. "It is better," he said, "that you do not speak. I had forgotten, until the First Minister spoke to me, that there are those who are suspicious when a servant is seen to talk, let alone take tea with a master, so you must retain your composure as you would if you were my servant. We are lucky that the First Minister did not chastise us further and demand that we stand when he addressed us. That might have given us away!" He looked directly into Bemia's eyes. She nodded to show she understood. "To maintain our disguise, it is better that you carry this package for a while. It is not too heavy and should be manageable."

Bemia took the package of ores and easily slung it over her shoulder. She moved to follow Alric when he stopped her and looked around to make sure they were not being watched. The merchant, ever busy, had started to rearrange his display of ores for the next customer.

"We will walk for a while around the stalls," he said, without looking directly at Bemia, "and then we will return home casually as we would after a day shopping. We will use a less direct route so that we may determine if anyone follows us." After a moment's pause, he looked at Bemia again. "You are sure, that was him?"

She nodded. Under the robes, her body quivered, but outwardly she appeared calm.

* * *

They walked along the narrow lanes between the market stalls, Alric giving the impression of a master with his servant and unconcerned that his servant was carrying a heavy weight. All around, people were coming and going, shouting and buying, and there was the ever-present aroma of food.

Alric never allowed his attention to wander. He knew the ways of thieves and pickpockets; even the random actions of one of these men could reveal Bemia's identity. In spite of appearing to visibly struggle with the package, she continually reassured him the package was not an imposition and that she could manage the weight quite well.

The sun climbed into the heavens as they slowly made their way to the area of the market that was farthest away from Jabir's house. The midday sun seemed to serve as a reminder that people should be in their houses, and the market would close until the heat abated.

Suddenly, they found themselves on the outskirts. Even here, the sounds of the merchants and the people there, arguing, selling, and buying, did not diminish. They never allowed their vigilance to waiver. "Without drawing attention to us," Alric whispered, "look around occasionally, and make sure we are not being followed."

Bemia smiled under her face covering. This was nothing new to her. Even though she had been adopted into the House of Jabir, her memories of life in the streets remained strong. She realized that those experiences could now be used to their benefit! And, on the pretense that she was periodically checking the package she carried, she glanced over her shoulder. Her eyes swept the crowds of people.

Relaxed and unhurried, Alric chose to continue their journey through the long, narrow streets that would eventually bring them home. By doing so, anyone following them would sooner or later become visible.

They continued at a steady pace as they journeyed home. The houses they passed formed a stark visual contrast to the stalls of the marketplace. Many had high walled enclosures and deeply inset entry gates which formed ideal spots for an ambush. But they passed only the occasional man or woman making his or her way hurriedly to the marketplace.

Alric whispered to Bemia, as they approached the house, that they still needed to maintain their vigilance. Lonely streets were prime spots to stage attacks. They reached the gate to the garden but walked past it as Alric had planned. Bemia made sure that they were not followed, and then they doubled back and walked quickly through the gate. Once the gate was closed, Alric took the package from her. She removed her face covering and smiled.

"Let us find mother and explain what has happened and the discovery that you have made," Alric said. "Please bear with me a moment until I put the package of ores into the laboratory."

Realizing that every blessing ignored becomes a curse, he suddenly felt glad and counted the day as a blessing. Bemia had identified the man who had held her captive and disobeyed the Caliph's laws. Alric doubted that the First Minister had recognized them, but he could not be absolutely sure.

Bemia looked tenderly at Alric. She could not put him in danger. He had saved her from the prison and from a very painful death. If Alric was threatened, the family was also in danger. This could not be. Her emotions were high; she had not felt this way before. She lowered her head as her eyes moistened. She could not afford the tears to flow, leaving streak marks on her cheeks and staining her robe.

"Alric," she spoke quietly, "may we talk?"

"Yes," he said quickly. "Speak in the Saxon tongue."

"This day has had its purpose," Bemia said, "as if to remind me of my captivity. If this man discovers who I am and where I live, we will all be in extreme danger."

"Bemia, this is very difficult for you," he put his arm around her shoulders to comfort her. "Let us find mother and father and explain our discovery."

Bemia shivered at his touch, and Alric felt perturbed with a new sensation. He realized that his fingers traced the line of her shoulders and that she was not objecting. At that moment he had to resist the desire to hold her in his arms.

As the breeze rustled its way through the leaves on the trees, he heard Hilda's gentle laugh: *You are in love, dear brother!*

* * *

CHAPTER 29

It took only a few minutes for Alric and Bemia to make themselves presentable for Amira. Amira was busy giving her maidservants instructions as they arranged fresh flowers in vases placed throughout the room, and she smiled when Alric and Bemia rushed in. They stood before Amira, who sensed that an important issue needed to be discussed and promptly dismissed the three maidservants, telling them to return with tea. She indicated that Alric and Bemia should sit on the cushions. She was concerned that they had run into trouble at the market.

Once they were seated, Amira noticed that Bemia was trembling and Alric was holding her hand to ease her discomfort. Rather than allow them to launch into their story immediately, the tea having been delivered by Maha, Amira talked of generalities while Bemia drank the tea and looked calmer.

As if by design, Jabir came into the room minutes later to bring them up-to-date on his meeting with the Caliph. He bent over, kissed Amira on the cheek, noticed Bemia's flushed face, and chose his words with care: "It seems, my dear, that something has taken place that affects your demeanor? I would say this promises to be an eye-opener, so please let me pour myself some tea and then commence."

At that moment, Abal and Buhjah entered the room, quietly bearing trays of fresh fruit and juice for midafternoon refreshments.

Amira, realizing that Alric and Bemia had probably missed lunch, insisted that they help themselves to the fruit. Not able to contain their news, they both blurted out words in Saxon, then, realizing this, translated the meaning for Amira and Jabir.

"Mother, father, we have found the man!" Bemia said.

After taking a sip of tea, Alric briefly related the events leading up to the point when Bemia had recognized the voice. Amira and Jabir were astounded by the revelation that the voice belonged to the First Minister. At the same time, Alric felt that a weight had been lifted from his shoulders.

Amira suggested that they rest and then have a cleansing bath that would invigorate their minds and bodies. Noticing Bemia having a little difficulty as she attempted to rise from the cushions, Alric helped her to her feet by offering his arm for support. As they walked across the room to the door, Amira turned and smiled at Jabir who merely raised an eyebrow.

It was two hours later, after she had rested, that a bath was prepared for Bemia in her room by the three maidservants, after which Abal remained with Bemia to offer any assistance she needed. Alric, who had not rested at all but had read his laboratory notes, preferred a shower, and Wahid, thoughtfully, delivered fresh, warm towels to the bathroom and then withdrew to leave Alric to his thoughts.

The soap that Wahid had left had an aroma that Alric could not identify but found pleasant. As he allowed himself to luxuriate in the water, he felt his skin tingle while the gentle sprays of water massaged his body. He had not minded being alone with his books and laboratory work, but all of that seemed to be changing. His thoughts were on the discovery of the First Minister as the man who had held Bemia prisoner and almost had her killed.

As the water poured over his body, he suddenly realized that it was Bemia's word against the word of the First Minister, Abdul al-Warith. Even when the testimony of Maria the Spaniard was taken into account, it remained still the word of two women against the leader of the Caliph's government. This could be perceived by other members of the Caliph's cabinet as petty jealousy against the First Minister. Any charges against Abdul al-Warith could easily be dismissed for lack of conclusive evidence. Suddenly, Alric had begun to perceive the barriers that the Caliph had to overcome.

Harun al-Rashid had guaranteed a just society in which every person accused of a crime would receive a hearing before his peers. Evidence would have to be presented that was conclusive and not rumor. His eyes closed as steam filled the room and his mind took a dive into the depths of reality. Then he heard her voice as the unspoken words silently entered his mind: *I see, dear brother, you have a lot on your mind!*

Alric raised his eyebrows in response, as if to ask, How did you guess? He cast his mind back into his past. He did not go far back in time, only over the past year. He replayed his thoughts and actions, and then the thought came to him.

He stepped out of the shower and wrapped the towel around his waist. He turned to see Hilda's form materialize from the shadows that enveloped one corner of the steam-filled room. She looked healthy, and her clothes had an aura that lit up the room. She smiled at Alric and took his hand. He gave her a beaming smile.

Suddenly he spoke. "The tablet," he said as the light of recognition came into his eyes.

Yes, my dear brother, she smiled. *What does it tell you?*

In spite of his earlier doubts, he now felt completely at ease, and his thoughts focused on the words from the tablet. He looked at Hilda as her form seemed to shimmer and suddenly she was gone.

He got up from the couch and was in the midst of drying himself when he heard her soft voice. *I must tell you, dear brother, I like this woman, Bemia. She is good for you.*

*   *   *

As Amira was overseeing the final arrangements for dinner, Khalil and Ahmed returned and greeted her. They excused themselves to get ready for the meal. In the meantime, Alric and Bemia had decided that a walk in the garden before dinner would be pleasant. The heat of the day was dissipating; the cool breeze and the shade from the various trees offered peace and tranquility.

The hardy date palms had been carefully cultured for ornamental purposes and grew to a height of only about seven feet. Olive trees, orange trees, and flowering almond and other blossom trees offered shade from the sun. They had been brought from the north and needed constant attention and irrigation.

Alric and Bemia sat on a seat below one of the olive trees to consider the surprising events of the morning. When Bemia had first arrived at the house after her release from prison, the man had been unknown. And now, suddenly, and without fanfare, he had reappeared. He was none other than the First Minister!

As they talked of the morning's activities, Alric realized that they all had to proceed with care and considerable planning. The potential threat the First Minister offered was worrisome, but Alric was sure they would come through this with honor. Looking up through the branches of the tree, he could see the clear blue sky. Then he touched Bemia's hand and she held on to his as if seeking reassurance. They looked into each other's eyes. He felt as if he were in a dream. Again he heard Hilda's voice: *I sense that you are happy with this woman, my dear Alric. I have told you I like her and I am happy for you. But there are difficult days ahead. Beware, brother!*

He related his misgivings to Bemia about not having conclusive proof of the identity of the man who had held her captive and to what extent her statement would be believed if she had to give testimony before the Caliph's cabinet members.

Bemia looked surprised at first, then, after giving thought to his words, agreed.

"You are correct, Alric," she responded. "It hurts me to say this, but if I am to see justice done, we must seek conclusive proof and not the words of two women who, in some men's eyes, are not of much value or credibility. What you say must be taken into account before we can decide on a course of action."

Alric felt relieved, looked up into the tree, and noticed that the birds had made a shelter there and had stopped singing. "I suspect," he said, turning to Bemia, "that Wahid or one of the maidservants is about to announce dinner." He could hear the sound of footfalls and announced, "It is Wahid."

Moments later, he appeared. "Dinner is prepared and your presence is requested," Wahid announced. Alric followed him, taking Bemia's hand in his.

Amira, Jabir, Khalil, and Ahmed were seated around the table as Alric and Bemia entered the room. Amira, ever vigilant, noticed the color in Bemia's cheeks.

I wonder . . . , she thought to herself.

After a day of eating lightly, Alric licked his lips when he saw the table, laid with fresh bread, butter, and smoked and boiled fish, as well as oatmeal cakes and a variety of lamb dishes, each one prepared differently. There was ample juice and cool, fresh water. When they were all seated and had partaken of some of the food and drink, Amira looked at Bemia.

"If I may, mother and father," Bemia said, "I will relate to all of you," she looked at Khalil and Ahmed, "this time in greater detail than I did when we first returned. Alric has suggested that it is better if the story comes from me, and he will offer any other comments that are needed."

"Excellent suggestion, Alric," Jabir spoke before anyone else. "Go ahead, my dear."

Bemia described her surprise and initial horror at her recognition of the man's voice as he came out of the rear area of the stall and stopped to talk with them. "Well," she added, "it was not so much to talk with us but to sneer and chastise Alric for allowing a servant to drink tea with him!" She stopped and nodded to Alric, who went on to describe his thoughts when he'd realized that the unknown man was the First Minister.

Alric spoke of his latest concerns. It was Bemia's word against the word of the First Minister, and even when the testimony of Maria was taken into consideration, it still remained the word of two women against the leader of the Caliph's government. "I have discussed my thoughts with Bemia and although she would like to see justice done, as would we all, she agrees with me that the evidence which we have, although the truth, may be dismissed.

"So I fear we may come up against a barrier and that to give away any evidence at this point in time would be to no avail. The First Minister will be free and will, I fear, pursue us relentlessly to seek vengeance."

A profound silence reigned after Alric completed his summation. Suddenly, in the midst of it, three light, quick taps struck against one of the door pillars, which caused them to look at the entrance. It was Wahid. He waited and then advanced at a signal from Jabir.

"Yes, Wahid," Jabir responded to Wahid's whispered question. "Tea and honeyed cakes will be in order."

The conversation focused on other matters, as servants, under Wahid's direction, cleared away the dishes of the main course and brought in the tea and cakes. When the table was once again ready, Wahid ushered the servants out of the room and left also, making sure that the doors were closed. As was his usual custom, he remained outside the door and out of earshot to ensure that no one could overhear the matter under discussion.

"What I find interesting," it was Khalil who spoke as he helped himself to a honeyed cake, "is that the First Minister was in the rear of the stall to use the hookah. This is unusual when the hookah is only used to inhale the odors of the additives to the water. There are those," he bit into the cake, "who seek other comfort from the hookah."

"This merchant," Ahmed added, "if I have the correct one from your descriptions of his stall," he looked at Alric and Bemia, who nodded their heads in agreement, "is known to receive the white powder from the east that sends men into the world of dreams, even nightmares. We can surmise from the prisoners in the Caliph's jails that once the white powder is used, it controls the user from that moment. He then needs more and more to satisfy his craving."

"It is the same white powder derived from the poppy," Jabir contributed, "that I use in small amounts to ease the pain of patients with serious injuries or those who have had the painful disease that we have called the *crab* or *cancer*, which destroys the body from the inside and for which there is no cure. It is an example of a medicine that when used in the incorrect amounts, or for the wrong purpose, can kill."

Alric noticed that Jabir was relaxed as he sat on the cushions, perhaps more than he had been in recent weeks. Amira also seemed to have lost some of the anxiety that had shown in her eyes recently.

"Perhaps," Alric suggested, "with the identity of this man now known to us we can start planning on how to handle this situation as regards the Caliph?"

"I never thought it would come to this," Jabir said as he looked at his audience, taking Amira's hand in his to offer comfort.

"It seems that our friend," he used the word sarcastically, "Abdul al-Warith is plotting for his own benefit and to satisfy his other cruel needs. When Harun indicated he had reason to believe someone close to him was ready to take sides with the Umayyad administration to satisfy his own ends, it made me think at length as I considered his statement. There is always someone from among Harun's ministers plotting and planning, but for it to be Abdul al-Warith, Harun's First Minister, is almost beyond comprehension." Jabir reached across the table to refill his glass with the hot tea.

"If I might add, father," Khalil broke into everyone's thoughts, "we have evidence from Bemia and from Alric, who both, for different reasons, recognized the First Minister. We do not have any evidence of al-Warith's role with the Umayyads. That," he scratched his chin, "may be difficult to accumulate." Khalil looked at Ahmed. "If we approach the Caliph with what we have, I agree with Alric that al-Warith may evade justice and slip away to carry on his malevolent work elsewhere. So . . . " he looked at Ahmed and nodded.

Ahmed continued, "We have talked about what course of action we would consider when a suspect arose."

"And . . . " Jabir led, almost impatiently as Amira laid her hand on her husband's arm, seeing that he was no longer relaxed and needed her calming influence.

Ahmed explained, "First, we accept that there is more to the First Minister's actions than kidnapping and, we strongly believe, mistreating, torturing, and even murdering young women. Second, we also have reason to believe that he is a user of the powder from the poppy. Third, there must be more to this, and I believe the First Minister's actions must lead to a much bigger plot than any of us initially thought."

Ahmed looked at his audience and then spoke with conviction. "Therefore, Khalil and I propose that, now we have identified the suspect, we start monitoring his movements, using only trusted men who will not give the game away. By this means, he may incriminate himself."

Jabir nodded his head. "I agree," he said.

"But," Amira broke in, "we cannot allow my nephew to remain in the dark. Indeed, if it is al-Warith who poses a threat to the Caliph,

Harun's life could be in danger any time he meets with the First Minister."

Jabir looked at Amira thoughtfully. "I agree, my dear," he said. "But to break this news to Harun and lay out our suspicions, I think you will agree it should be done here rather than in the palace. I would rather play out this game, dangerous as it might be, until we have the necessary and undeniable proof of al-Warith's activities!"

Jabir was in his element. Alric studied his expressions. He knew that Jabir had unraveled the truths behind important questions in his study of medicines. He had also established a connection between the body and the mind, and the First Minister's apparent use of the white powder from the poppy was one more step in proving that the cravings of the body controlled the mind.

"But, father . . . ?" Alric was about to finish the question when his eyes lit up. "Ah, I see where you are going," Alric said. Jabir smiled.

"The first step," Khalil interjected, "is to determine if, indeed, al-Warith uses the white powder."

"And how, my dear brother, do you propose to do that?" asked Bemia. Before anyone could speak, she answered her own question. "I suggest that I do it for you!"

Alric reached out and gently touched her arm. She looked at him. "I must do this. I do not mean any disrespect to your loyal soldiers, but these men are trained in the ways of war and discipline. They will be recognized immediately. If al-Warith is the man, he will have his own people looking for spies."

"But we cannot allow you to put yourself in danger, my dear," Amira said tenderly to Bemia. "You must have protection. You will need Ahmed, Khalil, and Alric . . . "

"Mother," Bemia moved off her cushion and knelt before Amira, "you have given me a home, a family, and a new life. I will not stand by and allow this family, my family, to be hurt. And," she took Amira's hands in hers, "I am skilled in the way of life in the city streets. Who else in this family," she looked around for emphasis, "has such a skill? As I sit here before you, I am convinced that this is a good plan. I realize that such a course of action could be dangerous, but inside I feel I can contribute to bringing this man to justice."

Khalil was about to protest until the determined look on Bemia's face. Bemia reached over and in turn took Khalil's and Ahmed's hands in hers and squeezed them gently and affectionately. "I know that you and Ahmed will want to protect me," she continued, "and I love you for your thoughts. You must understand that I need to do this for the family. That is the Saxon way. In times of trouble, the women do not stand behind their men; instead they stand alongside them fully armed and ready for battle, whatever the cost might be."

She turned again to look at Amira and Jabir. "I have sworn an oath to protect you, mother and father. If you will allow me, I propose that I go once again into the streets and implement this plan of action."

Amira's eyes opened wide. Jabir, as always, remained calm, knowing that there was more to come.

"But I do have one request," Bemia said and paused before she went on. "I would like Alric to be my companion. He knows the ways of the people and the streets of this city, as I evidenced when we returned from the market."

Alric was proud of her. Amira looked at the others; she felt they would accept Bemia's plan. "We agree to this, Bemia," Jabir said, relieved that she would have a reliable companion. "I hear," Jabir continued, "that Abdul al-Warith has left town on some errand. But that does not mean you can relax. His spies will be everywhere and you must exercise caution."

"And," Amira added, "at the slightest indication of trouble, you must seek the help of Khalil and Ahmed. You will not see them, but I know they will be watching you."

"I understand, mother," Bemia said. "One mistake could mean death, not only for me but for all of us!"

* * *

Alric and Bemia, in appropriate disguises, left the house the next morning to seek out any information they could glean about the habits of the First Minister.

The merchants had already set up their stalls and were too busy to notice their arrival. They walked around, taking their time. As the minutes passed, both found themselves thinking that the day would come when they would not have to live this kind of life, but live in comfort in one place forever.

No one knew their names. Their clothes were the nondescript clothes of travelers seeking work and not those of people of a higher class. Their story, if anyone asked, was that they were two young men who had arrived at a port city on the south coast; Basra was the name the sailors had called it. They had decided to leave the ship and travel upriver on a barge that carried trade goods to Baghdad. In a very short time, they learned the customs and language of the people.

They were limited in the questions they could ask without drawing suspicion upon themselves, so they decided to visit the market stall where Bemia had recognized al-Warith's voice. The stall was closed and other merchants could give them little information about al-Warith's activities, other than that he was a private man who preferred to remain at his home, undisturbed, and in quiet seclusion.

They left the marketplace and, after making sure that they were not followed, entered the street where Ahmed had told them that the First Minister lived. His description of the house was precise, and they located it without any trouble. They decided to observe any comings and goings, and they settled in a tree-shaded spot to munch on fruit and nuts. Alric had been curious to see how Bemia would react after her return to the streets. He wondered about the effect imprisonment had on her. After living with a favored family under the best of all possible circumstances, he hoped she still had her wits about her. As these thoughts crossed his mind, he realized how fortunate he had been. So far, she did not seem to hold any fears about being in the streets again.

Two hours passed, and they found, by quiet observation, that the First Minister's house and surrounding gardens appeared deserted, but, they observed, it would be folly to attempt to enter the premises, even under the cover of darkness. Even if an open gate to the garden presented an opportunity, there would undoubtedly be guards inside the house. Their walk past the wall that surrounded the First Minister's house and garden did not offer any further clues.

As the shadows lengthened, the setting sun reminded them that they should be returning. They were disappointed insofar as they had not heard nor been able to discern any word of the First Minister's actions, in particular his visit to the merchant for the white powder. Throughout the day, they had talked and listened to many men in tea houses and in the marketplace, but it was all to no avail. It was time to rethink their actions and plan future activities.

They made their way back to the house. As they walked in the dim light of the evening, it was a heart-stopping moment as Alric realized that they were not alone. His eyes, having become accustomed to the dim light, were able to make out the outline of a man crouched several feet away. He could feel the man's eyes staring at him intently, and he allowed his hand to clench the hilt of his knife, which was still attached to his belt.

"I see that you are both are well!"

Ahmed's voice came out of the darkness. Hearing the familiar tone, Alric relaxed. "Ahmed, my brother," Alric whispered. "How did you find us?"

"I had the need to be in the guise of a beggar as I watched over you. Father and mother felt that it would be better if you had a guardian angel!" He looked at them both. "I am pleased that you were not tempted to enter the house of the First Minister. I knew you would not be able to resist looking at it. You chose wisely when you deiced not to enter. You would have been discovered!"

"Yes," Bemia responded, "but . . . "

"No more. You are to return home without delay. My orders from father were that when the night started to descend upon us, I was to escort you home."

In the dimness, Alric saw Ahmed hold up his hand to forestall any further conversation. "My instincts," Ahmed went on, "tell me you would have been caught and then it would have been difficult to *help* you! Your lives would have descended into squalor and, eventually, death. In the jails, the lucky ones die quickly, while those who live talk under persuasion from hot irons and give away all they know. There are many such people who have gone missing, but nothing is being done. The Caliph has decreed that such practices are to cease, but his words have no effect on some of the richer, more powerful men in this city. There will, I might add, be a day of reckoning!"

Ahmed looked around furtively. "Let us go home." They could see his smile even in the dim light. "Mother will be pleased to have you home once more!"

*　*　*

CHAPTER 30

They were welcomed by Amira, accompanied by her three maidservants Abal, Buhjah, and Maha. The three young women had been warned that any unnecessary chatter would be frowned upon. They helped Bemia to bathe and remove the applied skin coloring, while Wahid, who had supervised the preparation of the baths, saw to the needs of Alric.

After the relaxing baths had taken effect, Alric and Bemia fell into their individual beds, where they slept soundly. Bemia had a dreamless sleep that lasted well into the afternoon. Both were exhausted from the long days and the tension.

Alric dreamt he was in the garden under the fragrant blossom-laden branches of a hemlock tree, until finally he awoke. As soon as he stirred, Wahid appeared and advised him that a bath would be ready for him. He washed away the tiredness, dressed in fresh clothes, and then decided to walk in the garden. He heard the approach of someone from the house. It was Amira.

"Alric, she said, "you are well?"

It was the first question she had asked since their return. "Yes, mother. I am well."

"You look troubled, my dear. I sensed that when you first returned. Let us sit here," she indicated the wooden seat, "and we can talk. She took his hand in hers. "Now, what troubles you?"

"It is Bemia, mother. I . . . "

Before he could finish the sentence, she placed her forefinger on his lips to silence him. "I know. I have noticed how you look at her."

"Then, what do you think I should do?"

"You must follow your instincts. I will never tell you what to do. Your father and I will advise you, but you must make your own decisions and live with them. Whatever you decide, we will support you. And by the way, Ahmed also suspects something."

Alric's mouth opened, Ahmed had noticed! Alric's confidence returned. He reached over and kissed Amira on the cheek. She patted his in response. Then he smiled. He was about to confront his emotions. Should I disclose my feelings to Bemia? he asked himself. What will her reaction be? Will she accept what I have to say? A pang of fear and worry made him shudder.

"Take it one step at a time, my dear," Amira's words broke into his thoughts. "I assure you, all will be well. Now," she said rising, "I will have Maha bring you some refreshment. You remain here. I know you will do the right thing, Alric."

* * *

Alric had finished the last oatmeal cake. Knowing that Alric and Bemia liked these, especially when they were dipped in honey, Amira had prepared a basketful of the cakes.

Time sometimes passes too slowly, thought Alric as he watched the bees circle the blossoms on the tree. They were too busy to notice him. The garden was such a refreshing change from the marketplace. It was as if the last day were a distant dream. The sellers and buyers had talked incessantly, sometimes laughing but other times shouting, as though they had emerged from a year of silence and were once more able to speak. He decided to concentrate on other matters and leave the bees to their own business.

During the past months, he had concentrated on his work, but now thoughts of Bemia occupied his mind much more. Before her arrival, Jabir's family had been the company he'd needed. Then Bemia had arrived and he felt enslaved by her mere presence. As his feelings became stronger, he had tried not to show them, but Ahmed, may Allah protect him, had been the first to notice his growing affection for Bemia.

To Alric, merely having Bemia in his presence was what he most desired. When she entered a room, her blonde hair, sparkling eyes, and shining countenance became embedded in his thoughts. "This," Alric decided, "is what it means to be in love."

He felt that there would be no other who could take such a hold on his life. He realized that he had a truly unique connection with Bemia. He was certain that she had been sent to him for a reason. The reason, God willing, was the relationship of husband and wife.

He heard the sound of soft footsteps, arose from the seat, and turned. The sight of Bemia took his breath away. She was dressed in a silk robe that accentuated the curved lines of her body. In the background Ahmed, always present to make sure all was well, smiled and motioned the servants away from the area. These two young people needed time to talk.

Bemia's voice was soft and calm above the sound of the bees as she spoke in the Saxon language of her homeland. "I have been looking for you in the house, Alric."

"They tell me that a beautiful young woman with the blonde hair and blue eyes of the north lives here," Alric responded, also in the Saxon language. "I believe I have found her."

At that moment, it seemed to him that time stood still, and his heart surged within his chest. When he looked into her eyes, the hardships of the past days were forgotten. He could see the love returned. It required no explanation.

"I think, my dear," Bemia said cautiously, "we should sit here," she indicated the same seat where she and Amira had sat a short time ago. "Mother thought that you may wish to talk with me." She paused as she arranged the folds of her robe. "Will you take water?" she asked as she filled a glass with the cool, clear water and handed it to him.

"These many days," Bemia admitted, "I have realized that I love you and I feel that I have become a part of you."

Alric listened with joy to the sound of her voice. Then he said, "I want to tell you just one thing, Bemia. I love you and I would like you to be my wife."

Bemia was overjoyed. "Yes, Alric. Oh yes, Alric. I am honored!"

Alric knelt before her and she took his hands in hers. Her voice was sweeter than the sound of the gentle breeze above them as it rustled through the palm trees.

At that moment, Amira approached and, seeing Alric kneeling before Bemia, smiled.

"Mother," Alric's voice changed to a more formal tone. He remained on his knees and took Amira's hand in his. "Lady Amira, as the mother of this house, I wish to inform you that I have asked your daughter, Bemia, to be my wife."

For a moment, silence filled the air. Even the bees seemed to be listening. "My dear," Amira finally broke the silence, "I am so happy for you. You have my blessing."

She looked at Bemia. "The day after you came to our home and was accepted as our daughter," Amira continued, "Father and I had hoped for this. In fact, these two," she motioned in the direction of Khalil and Ahmed, who had suddenly appeared behind her, "were talking about a wager as to when you, Alric, would make the first move."

She pretended to scowl at her son and Ahmed. "And who might I ask, won this noble wager?"

Khalil smiled. "Ahmed won, mother. As soon as Bemia arrived in the house, he predicted the day. He looked up at the sun that shone through the leaves of the date palms. He was even close to predicting the time of day." Khalil looked at Alric. "Congratulations, my brother."

He moved close to Bemia, taking her hands in his. "This is a happy day, Bemia. I am pleased to call you sister as well as the wife of my brother, Alric."

Ahmed patted Alric on the shoulder. "Congratulations, my Saxon brother. May you have the children you deserve and may they always honor their father and mother."

"But," Khalil broke into everyone's thoughts, "are we not forgetting that my adopted brother and sister living in this house under my father's name means we must ask father's official permission and since both of you," he looked at Alric and Bemia, "are wards of the Caliph? We shall . . ."

Amira interrupted her son's thoughts as she looked at Alric and Bemia. "Do not bother your young heads with such thoughts. Wards of the Caliph you might be, but I still have a say in my nephew's decisions, especially when it comes to matters of the heart and of this house." Amira had decided. "And," she added, "I will tell my husband of this joy. He will be pleased. We will meet formally with the Caliph so that he might bless this union. Then I am sure my niece, Harun's wife Scheherazade, will entertain us with her stories. The tales you can relate to her will give her enough stories to last for another thousand and one nights."

Alric took Bemia's hand. "Being with you, I fear nothing, because I feel it is written that you and I were meant to be together."

"And, my dear Alric," Bemia spoke up, "when the Caliph has given us permission to marry, if Allah wills it, we will have children."

Alric took her in his arms. As he did, he could hear the voice of his beloved sister, Hilda: *My dear brother, you have found the woman of your dreams. Treasure her as she will treasure you.* Alric was visibly moved.

Bemia had taken on the role of the Saxon warrior who stood by her husband in battle, her shield linked to his, and ready to swing her axe to protect him. Alric realized his Saxon origins were still strong and no matter how long he lived in this land of Mesopotamia, he felt that his instincts would always be Saxon. "Hilda," the whispered word seemed to explode from his lips, but only Bemia heard him.

Alric? she whispered in return.

Bemia heard the soft tones.

Amira had left, saying she had housework to oversee. Khalil and Ahmed had duties with the Caliph. Alric and Bemia were left alone once more. They sat together as Alric told Bemia of the presence of Hilda during his journey and of how her spirit has guided him.

She looked into his eyes. "My dear, death takes our family and friends from us. We know that. We never get used to it, but we learn to adapt. You have been fortunate to have had your sister with you for these many years. I feel she wishes us to seek our future together."

They both heard the soft voice speaking the language of the Saxons: *It is with pleasure that I speak to you, Bemia of the Saxons, who is now my sister. I entrust my brother to you. May God be with you.*

Then there was silence except for the sound of the wind as it whistled through the leaves of the date palms. Blossoms fell gently to the ground from the hemlock tree. All was peaceful in the garden.

* * *

CHAPTER 31

Alric and Bemia, well disguised and in the company of Jabir, Khalil, and Ahmed, approached the guard at the front of the huge white wall in the center if the city. "We have urgent business with the Caliph," Jabir announced.

Recognizing the visitors, the guard allowed them to enter. Once inside, they were met by the Caliph's secretary, who, as before, was dressed in white and gold garments. At this time, Khalil and Ahmed left to discuss business with their commanders, saying that they would be ready when the meeting with the Caliph was over. Jabir, Alric, and Bemia followed the secretary to the Caliph's private rooms.

The Caliph was, as always, immaculately dressed in loose-fitting white pants, white shirt with gold piping, and a gold turban—a sharp contrast to his dark features. He was engrossed in a document and at first appeared preoccupied. Alric sensed that the Caliph's mind was on matters relating to the First Minister. Then he saw a flicker of recognition followed by a smile as the Caliph rose to greet them.

They kneeled before the Caliph. He bade them rise and at that time Alric and Bemia removed their face coverings. Everyone remained silent. The awkward pause that followed seemed an eternity, and the silence hung like a thick fog. The Caliph rose from his seat and stepped toward Alric and Bemia. "Alric al-Biritaanya ibn Jabir," Harun addressed

Alric, "I offer my congratulations on your forthcoming marriage to the beautiful Bemia, also of the land of the Saxons."

The Caliph's words took Alric and Bemia by surprise. "You are a very fortunate young man. I was told of your proposed marriage by my aunt in a note she sent me by carrier pigeon. She even mentioned I would probably have no objections to such a union." He looked at Jabir. "That is quite a woman you have married, uncle!"

Jabir nodded his appreciation of the Caliph's comment. "Even though my aunt has given me little choice," Harun said in jest, "I willingly grant the request that these two young people be married at the earliest opportunity. I see a union between them that will be everlasting. And who am I to deny my dear aunt?"

Harun's laughter filled the room. He looked at Alric and Bemia. "You do understand that the law requires that you respect the institute of marriage? Since such a union is not to be taken lightly! Marriage requires that you be respecters of each other's persons. Do you understand?"

Alric and Bemia responded, "We do, Caliph."

"I am a realist," Harun continued. "I am aware you will have differences of opinion, but it is my advice that you never end the day in a state of anger with each other."

They bowed their heads and chorused, "We will do as you suggest, Sire."

"I have one last request."

"Yes, Sire," Alric said.

"Since you are my wards, I anticipate an invitation to the wedding."

"Of course, Caliph," Bemia responded before Alric could say anything. "I would be pleased to welcome you and your wife Scheherazade to the wedding."

"May I, Alric?" Harun asked.

"As you wish, Sire," Alric said, wondering what was coming next.

Harun took Bemia's hand and kissed her on the cheek. Then he touched Alric on the shoulder. He took their hands and placed them together. "This holding of hands formalizes my approval of your wedding. Furthermore, as the adopted son and daughter of my aunt, we are cousins. If you ever require anything, you have only to ask. From this day on, the guards will recognize your names and that is sufficient to guarantee your entry into my presence."

"Scribe!" the Caliph turned, and the man standing by the curtains snapped to attention. "Record what I have said regarding the marriage of these young people. It is an agreement between Alric al-Biritaanya ibn Jabir," he paused for a moment, "and Bemia al-Biritaanya binit Jabir that they will marry with my blessing. We will need five documents. There is one copy for the groom, one for the bride, one for my uncle and aunt, one for myself, and one for the records." The scribe bowed deeply and left.

"With your permission, Sire, may I speak?" Bemia asked.

"You may, Bemia," Harun responded. "After all," he added, "you are family."

Harun al-Rashid was the most important man she had ever known. He was the spiritual and secular leader of the people. "It is with great pleasure that I thank you for giving us permission to marry. I request that my father, Lord Jabir, present me to Alric at our marriage ceremony."

"If that is your custom, so be it," Harun responded.

"Sire," Bemia continued, "I also request that my brothers Khalil and Ahmed stand with my father."

Harun smiled. "Your request is granted. Do you have anything else?"

"Yes, Sire. Our church is absent from this land. Alric and I request that you, as the spiritual head of Islam, bless our marriage."

"I will be delighted. It seems, uncle," Harun said thoughtfully to Jabir, "that with my aunt and . . . ," he motioned with his head to Alric and Bemia, "you will have your hands full!" Jabir chuckled at the comment. "Now, let us all sit and take refreshments. We will have tea and oatmeal cakes, for which," he looked at Alric, "I know you have a liking."

As they sat, Bemia moved to serve the tea, but Harun raised his hand. "You are my guests," he said. "I will serve you. It is my pleasure."

The tea was poured from the floral-patterned china pot when Harun said, "Tell me of the events leading up to your wedding. If I am to be present at the ceremony, I need to know the details. But please wait," he suggested. "There is someone more skilled in these matters than I."

At that point Scheherazade appeared from a direction behind the Caliph. Jabir, Alric, and Bemia rose and bowed to her. Scheherazade moved to Harun's side. Her beauty filled the room, and Alric could see the reasons for the rumors that she had bewitched the Caliph. She wore a simple but perfectly draped white silk robe that rustled in the silence of the room. Her black hair was immaculately coiffured and her dark, intense eyes focused on Alric and Bemia.

Harun introduced Scheherazade to them and bade them sit once more.

"Greetings and welcome to my home," she said as she made herself comfortable on the cushions between her husband and Bemia.

"There are those," Scheherazade said to Bemia, "who call me *the story teller*. I have wished to meet you for some time. And," she added, "I am skilled in several languages, one of which is the language of the Romans, should you ever desire to converse in that tongue.

"I am told that both of you have had an arduous journey here. I would like to hear of it sometime. Now I would like to suggest that we take tea. My husband," her dazzling smile lit the room, "does like tea."

As they drank of the tea, Scheherazade said to Bemia, "I will of course talk with Lady Amira to finalize the arrangements for your marriage.

After the arrival of Aunt Amira's pigeon, my husband indicated that it is preferable that the ceremony be private for security reasons."

"Those were my thoughts as you entered the room," Harun interjected. "But do not let me interrupt your conversation, my dear," he said, smiling at his wife.

Bemia bowed. "Thank you, my lady, for your kind offer," she replied. "I know that since my wedding is in your hands and mother's, all will be well. If it is to your liking . . . "

Scheherazade and Bemia fell into an animated discussion in Arabic, much to Alric's delight. On occasion when there was a word she could not pronounce, she spoke in Saxon to Alric, who translated.

* * *

When they had finished with the refreshments, the Caliph decided to change the topic of conversation. He had not participated in the discussion regarding the details of the wedding but left that for Scheherazade and Bemia, who would later consult Amira. His expression had become serious.

"My thoughts were elsewhere when you entered the room. And now, I turn the conversation to this very serious matter." He paused and sipped fresh tea. "Some time ago," Harun began, "I informed you that I had heard rumors of a man who may be plotting to take over my throne. As a result of your efforts," his eyes flashed as he looked at Alric and Bemia, "you have brought to me, through my uncle, the reality of this situation. It is critical you do not tell anyone of this."

Harun paused and addressed Alric. "Your story of the search for the tablet is interesting, Alric. As you know, I have considerable interest in the *cunei forma*. It seems that as you worked through the words on the tablet, there was something we can use. But I advise caution on your part.

"Tomorrow, I am going to talk this over with you, uncle. We will formulate a plan of action." Harun stroked his beard. "I know that Khalil and Ahmed are aware of my thoughts." He turned to Alric and Bemia. "I say from this day on, be wary of your enemies."

With that final comment, the meeting was over. Scheherazade briefly touched Bemia's hand as she said, "You will be hearing from me through your mother."

They were led to the gate by the young man who had given them entry and were surprised to see not only Khalil and Ahmed but also several soldiers waiting for them.

"By order of the Caliph," Khalil announced. "They will escort us home. The Caliph has guaranteed your safety."

They walked in silence, surrounded by the soldiers, until they reached home, where Amira awaited them. Here the men withdrew, leaving the two women alone so that Amira could relish in the details provided by Bemia of the meeting and conversation with the Caliph.

* * *

The next morning, before the sun had reached its high point, Jabir met with his nephew, the Caliph. It was dark before he returned. "I am here," he said announcing himself as he walked into the room where the family members were gathered. He looked at each one in turn.

"Sit down, my dear." Amira said commandingly. "We'll have something to drink while we talk."

She signaled to the unseen figure behind the curtain, and soon a delicious aroma filled the room. "It is a new drink," Amira added, "it is not made from leaves but from beans that are roasted and then boiled in water. I believe it has a name that is pronounced *coffee*. It seems that sailors have found a land where this is grown. The inhabitants there showed them how to make the drink. The ship's captain brought back a bag of the beans; it was just given to me this morning."

The coffee was served in silence. Amira spooned fresh cream into each cup; it made the most delicious drink they had ever tasted. Jabir drank the coffee and he began to relax. "As you know," he began, "Harun is adamant that he must squash the movement to displace him," he said. After making this pronouncement, Jabir said nothing further for a few moments as he sipped the coffee. "There are strong indications," he continued, "that the First Minister is the man behind the plot."

"But to entrap the First Minister is proving difficult," Amira said. The other members of the family, Khalil, Alric, Bemia, and Ahmed remained silent.

"I know. He is a wily fox." Jabir responded. But, he added, "Even the fox is sometimes caught." He looked at Bemia. "You, my dear, have opened a nest of vipers. Had you not been willing to disclose what happened to you, this plot could have gone undiscovered until it was too late and with disastrous consequences. Harun commends you for your courage."

Alric reached over and held Bemia's hand. She smiled at him for the comfort that his touch offered. "I am going to guide our next actions, just as a guide would help you cross the desert." Jabir said. "Imagine we are at an oasis and we have the upper hand because we can tell who is approaching us. The First Minister, Abdul al-Warith, does not know he has been identified.

"Abdul al-Warith may feel that he is being far-sighted and is safe. As yet, we have no definite proof. Because of his high position and powerful friends, the law prevents the Caliph from arresting him to put him on trial. But al-Warith's lack of knowledge of our activities is our strength and the means by which we will draw him out. I believe that the tablet Alric brought back gives us the means to do just that!"

Jabir sipped more of the coffee and indicated he would like his glass refilled. This being done, he continued. "Many men have walked a dangerous track similar to that of the First Minister. He will eventually make a mistake, perhaps because he refused to take advice, perhaps because he was greedy or because he felt that time was running out. Whatever the reason, he will make an error. Then it will be too late.

"And now, here is the plan that Harun and I have hatched. It does involve you, my dear," he said looking at Bemia. "I know you have been courageous to this point. All that Harun and I ask of you is one more final effort."

All eyes turned to Bemia. No one questioned Jabir's logic. This had come to them from the Caliph. Bemia looked at Jabir. This was the man who had taken her into his home and made her his daughter. Next to her beloved Alric, she trusted her adopted father more than any other man in the world.

"My father," she said, "you have asked nothing of me until now. As I have told you, my dear Alric and I come from a culture where the women are expected to take up arms and fight for what we believe to be right. I stand with you as part of this family. Whatever I must do, so be it." She paused and then added the well-known words of the Saxons. "*Ich eom gearu.*"

"I am ready," Alric translated.

It was the creed by which the Saxons lived, and Bemia was committed to that creed.

* * *

Alric spent a sleepless night. Shortly before dawn, he awoke, dressed, and went into the garden. The cool air offered refreshment to his troubled mind. He paced back and forth between the ornate sleeping flowers and the date palms. He was visibly startled as the voice behind him came through the stillness. He had not heard Bemia's soft footfalls as she approached.

"My dear, you are troubled?" Bemia's beauty lit up the gray light.

"I am worried about your participation in this plan," Alric said. "I do understand that it may be the only way to flush the First Minister from his lair and make him commit himself so that his guilt is beyond question. But I worry about the risk to you."

"The risk will always be there, but it will be greater if we do nothing. From what mother has told me, it seems the journey you made to Mosul was an even greater risk. Then for you to work in the laboratory on the recipe for a mixture that has the powers of creating such destruction! Was that not a risk?"

"That is different," was all Alric could find to say.

"Why?" Here blue eyes bored into him.

"But you are . . . "

"I am a woman?" Bemia finished his sentence.

"But that is . . . "

"Different?" She finished his sentence again, much to his dismay. He felt he could not express himself fully because of her determination.

He continued. "I realize that you have been taught to fight, but this is a very dangerous situation. Do not under any circumstances take this lightly. Promise me that."

"You have my solemn promise."

"Thank you."

Bemia looked at him. The tears on her cheeks glistened in the moonlight. A spark seemed to pass between them, and they embraced. It was the first time either had touched the other in this manner.

"Before this, and after the death of my parents," Alric said, "I never had anyone to care about. You have given me love and hope for a future."

They said nothing more as they continued to walk, arm in arm, among the palms in the grayness, and then decided they should return to the house. Alric left Bemia at the entrance to her room. Her eyes were still filled with tears.

"You continue to cry?" It was an obvious question.

"I may be a woman of the Saxons," she said, averting her face, "but above all I am a woman, and I need to give vent to my emotions at this moment." She smiled and went into her room.

*   *   *

When daylight came, Bemia arose, washed, and dressed. Her mind was no longer that of the girl who wandered in the streets of Baghdad. Her life would never again have the same meaning. The house was now her home. This was a family that deserved her protection.

Each day when she did not meet with Alric, she would send her kisses on the wind, hoping they would touch his face and tell him of her love. She also thought of the ceremony that would bind her to Alric for the rest of her life. She would make plans with mother and Scheherazade.

Already, Amira had received contacts from the palace about a possible meeting in which Scheherazade would visit her in the guise of a lady friend, invited to take tea.

Bemia was told of the visit and anxiously awaited the meeting

*   *   *

Later that morning, Ahmed and Alric rode out on horseback to allow Alric time to relax and rest from work in the laboratory. As they crossed the bridge and left the city, the horses whinnied and stomped impatiently and Ahmed suggested they give the horses their heads. Their steeds surged forward, competing as if in a race.

The wind swept across Alric's face, clearing his mind. As they reined the horses to a walk, Ahmed said, "Do not think about what may happen. Do not forget, everything is written by Allah and cannot be changed."

It was difficult not to think about the danger to which Bemia might be exposed. He could still clearly see the palm trees, the flowers, and the face of the woman he loved. As they rode, Alric noticed hawks circling in the distance.

"There is only one way to learn," Ahmed broke the silence. "It is through action. Everything you need to know you have already learned in your journey through life. But you need to learn one thing more."

"What is it I still need to know?" Alric questioned.

Ahmed looked to the horizon, watching a hawk dive and take its prey. Then he said. "I am a soldier. I learned the art of soldiering from my father, who learned from his father, and so on. In those times, a soldier did as he was told. We must obey orders. If there is no discipline, armies lose battles and wars. The flight of those hawks cannot be understood by reason alone. In the laboratory, there is a correct way to study and understand the results of your experiments. But what you feel is an emotion. Emotions are difficult to understand. When I lost my family, I believed that the world would end. It did not and here I am."

"What did you do?" Alric asked.

"I did not try to understand, I contemplated a simple grain of sand, and from that I recognized the marvels of creation and that Allah, the Lord of all, would help me. He did and I immerse myself in all of the activities in which I now show an interest." He reached across from his horse, placed his hand on Alric's shoulder, and gave him a gentle pinch. "Listen to your heart, my brother. Your heart knows all things, because it came to you from Allah, who knows all things and will not leave you in your time of need."

Alric's eyes lightened.

"You have a thought?" Ahmed asked.

"Yes, Ahmed, a very important one. The tablet that I brought back from Mosul holds the secret. If what I am thinking is correct . . . "

He allowed the words to trail away into the air. Then he announced the excitement showing in his voice. "I have work to do, Ahmed. Much work!"

*   *   *

Alric became immersed in his reading of the tablet and was lost to the world. Only Bemia could shake him from this task. He spent another two days thinking about Ahmed's words of advice. He had become much more cautious when he left the house.

Whenever he saw travelers or armed tribesmen in the city, he was even more vigilant wherever his excursions took him. His fear was that he would lose Bemia as he had lost Hilda. But he had protection this time. The sea raiders would not come again, but, he wondered, who would come in their place?

"*Insha'allah.*" "As God wills it," he said to himself.

He felt himself relax, and that night he slept deeply. When he awoke, he no longer saw the world as a threatening place, only the challenges ahead. From that moment on, he understood what Ahmed had been trying to tell him. He swore he would heed that message.

He remembered an old proverb that his mother had taught him before the sea raiders had come: The darkest hour of the night comes just before the dawn.

*   *   *

CHAPTER 32

Later that week at the time of the evening meal, Amira announced that she had heard from Scheherazade and that she would arrive the next day at about midmorning. Alric and Bemia assumed that Amira's pigeons were getting plenty of exercise as notes passed from the house to the palace and back.

As promised, Scheherazade arrived the next day without fanfare. She was in the guise of a high-born lady but not recognizable as the Caliph's wife, lest those watching become suspicious.

She was accompanied by a captain and four soldiers. This was not an uncommon sight for those of a high station. The captain of the guard was, in fact, Bashir, the son of Amira's niece, whom Alric had met at the prison when he had been taken there to interview Bemia.

Within minutes Scheherazade was welcomed by Amira and seated on cushions before the small table that contained all of the accoutrements for tea. Scheherazade shed the outer beige robe to reveal a blue dress trimmed with silken threads of red and gold. She wore a dazzling necklace of sapphires and emeralds. Alric and Bemia marveled at her beauty and loveliness.

After the greetings of the day had been passed, Jabir, Alric, and Bemia joined Amira and Scheherazade at the table. Amira had thoughtfully placed Alric and Bemia opposite Scheherazade.

"Khalil and Ahmed are maintaining a watch to warn if anyone undesirable approaches the house and garden," Jabir explained.

Since Scheherazade was a female guest, Alric noticed that Amira had changed the type of service. A selection of juices and water was offered first. Alric had seen Wahid and Maha making the delicious juice earlier from oranges, lemons, limes, peaches, mangos, and strawberries.

Wahid had been told by Amira to keep everyone away from the room, and only he would be allowed to serve them. He had been advised that the visitor would be Scheherazade and his preparation was immaculate. He placed small dishes of yogurt on the table with fresh-cut sweet melons for each guest.

At a signal from Amira, Wahid commenced the tea service. In addition to the usual pot of black tea, he had prepared a mint tea that had been strained after boiling. In keeping with tradition, the black tea was served from a glass teapot, while the mint tea was placed in a silver one and then poured into glasses. Sugar and honey were provided.

Scheherazade nodded knowingly at Amira as she sipped the tea. As they enjoyed the hot, rich liquid, the talk focused on generalities. There was a variety of things to eat, including sweet bread, biscuits, and cakes. The serving dishes were filled and stacked like a pyramid with the varieties of food. Wahid responded to everyone's needs.

Scheherazade placed her tea glass on the table and looked at Amira. "Of necessity," Scheherazade commenced, "my husband has decreed that this will be a quiet wedding. She took another sip of tea. "You know, this mint tea is delicious, aunt. I must have the method by which you prepare it."

On hearing this, Wahid immediately stepped behind the curtains to write down the recipe. The secret was simple. Pinches of cinnamon were added to the fresh mint before it was boiled.

Scheherazade looked at Alric and Bemia. "Now, let us return to the business of the moment. I need to tell you more of our marriage customs. The wedding ceremony should take place here. For reasons of security and secrecy, my husband thinks it best." Amira and Jabir nodded in agreement.

"We will be flattered," Amira said.

"Good. That is settled. Now," Scheherazade turned her head once more toward Alric and Bemia. "It is our custom to encourage a man who can afford to marry to do so and have a family. Marriage is sacred. The husband should show justice to his wife in every aspect of their life, to provide protection, to love and care for his wife. Taking more than one wife is not an encouragement or an obligation but merely an allowance. When a man takes more than one wife, the first marriage is still valid. In such multiple unions, we expect the husband to deal justly with each of his wives, but because of your customs, I doubt this will happen. Is my assumption correct that the culture of the country of your birth and your church are against this?" She looked questioningly at Bemia.

"Yes, my lady," Bemia responded.

"You may call me Scheherazade. We can afford to be less formal here than at the palace. As my husband said, 'Even at the palace, the walls can have ears!' He and I agreed that this is the most appropriate place for the plans to be made. There will be no formal ceremony, Bemia. Other girls often prefer to be led to the husband's house in a camel litter. Musicians play and men carry her gifts and dowry. However, since this marriage was not arranged by parents," she looked at Amira, her eyes smiling, "there will be no contract."

Bemia sighed. In Britannia, Bemia thought two young people would attend a mass in the church, the priest would give them his blessing, say a few words, and they would be married!

"This," Scheherazade said, as if reading Bemia's mind, "as I am led to believe, is a marriage based on love."

"Since you are both of the same house," she continued, "but not of the same natural mother and father, my husband has decreed that there is no conflict." She stopped suddenly and took papers from the voluminous sleeves of her dress. "Here are the copies of the marriage document."

She gave one copy to Bemia and another one to Amira. "Finally, my husband has also stated that Bemia is free to wear the clothes of her choice, being of foreign birth. Many married women here wear the long-sleeved black *galabia* with a black scarf tied low over their forehead." Scheherazade took a deep breath; her part of the conversation was over. "And now, aunt, having given Bemia and Alric the main points of the wedding, I am done!" She looked at the plates of food. "May I partake of more of your delicious sweet cakes?"

Amira smiled and Wahid immediately took up the challenge, hurried to the table, and passed the plate of cakes to Scheherazade first and then to each one in turn.

* * *

In three days, the wedding would take place in the house of Jabir. Amira lamented that she did not have enough time to make the necessary preparations, but Jabir calmly advised, "You can do it, my dear. If anyone can, you can."

Jabir was the *wali*, or guardian, of the bride. He had made sure that Alric's offer of marriage and Bemia's acceptance were recorded and that the document was explicit in mentioning the word "marriage." Both statements had been made shortly after Scheherazade had presented the written documents stating that the Caliph had given his permission for the marriage to take place.

Khalil and Ahmed were specified to be the two male witnesses. The *sadaq* or *mahr*, or dowry, the required marriage gift that Alric would give to his bride, was in the form of a St. Cuthbert's cross he had fashioned from lead in his laboratory. The cross was to represent the saint who had spent part of his life at Wearmouth and represented

Alric's commitment to take care of all the family expenses, including his wife's personal needs.

* * *

The wedding day dawned. Alric and Bemia were up early but were not allowed to see each other. When the ceremony began, Alric looked at Khalil and Ahmed, who stood to his right. It was late morning and he wondered what had happened to Bemia. The wedding had been prepared and Ahmed informed him that the post-ceremony reception would be a sumptuous lunch. Amira and Scheherazade sat behind Alric. They were patient and waited for Jabir to enter with Bemia. The room in which they waited was Amira's personal day room, where Alric had been many times before.

Wahid was also present as the usher and doorkeeper, maintaining a vigil for the Caliph and making sure the ceremony would remain private. Abal, Buhjah, and Maha stood behind Amira and Scheherazade and were sworn to secrecy and silence. Wahid would watch them carefully.

Alric thought, The Caliph has not arrived and that may be the reason that father and Bemia have delayed their entry. He looked toward the door, which, for the occasion, was hidden by curtains. There was a sudden movement of the drapes and the Caliph entered. Scheherazade rose and walked toward him and they embraced. Harun moved toward Amira, bent over, and kissed her cheek.

"Aunt," he addressed her, "greetings on this joyous day." Harun then acknowledged, in turn, Khalil, Ahmed, and Alric. "Well, Alric, how are you feeling?"

"Excited, Sire," was all Alric could find to say. At that moment, Alric turned and saw Bemia enter, escorted by Jabir.

Bemia was radiant. She wore a blue robe edged with gold and had delicately embroidered white slippers on her feet. She did not wear a veil, as was the custom in weddings. Her face was framed by her blonde

431

hair, which was interlaced with white ribbons. Alric's eyes opened wide in awe at the vision before him. The group focused on Bemia and marveled at her beauty.

It took a nudge from Khalil to get Alric's attention. "Close your mouth, Alric, lest you swallow a flying insect!" Khalil advised.

"It seems all are now present," the Caliph announced.

Jabir led Bemia to Alric. Their smiles were of young people in love. Amira wiped her eyes with her lace handkerchief. Scheherazade followed suit. Bemia released her hold on Jabir, kissed him on the cheek, and placed her hand on Alric's. It was the symbolic way of accepting Alric's protection.

The Caliph declared that all should be seated. "Step forward, please," he motioned to Alric and Bemia.

Alric's mouth felt dry. His arms and legs did not seem to want to move, but he nodded to show he was ready. He looked at Bemia once more. "You look lovely," he whispered. She smiled as a tear rolled down the side of her face. Alric leaned forward and wiped it away. "Do you remember the first time we met?"

The memory hit her so hard that it almost hurt. If she had not had hold of his arm, she might have fallen. She had tried to forget the prison, but the memories were fixed, and the hatred of the First Minister lingered on. She would be happy only when justice was meted out. Alric's strength seemed to pass through his hand and into hers. She snapped out of the nightmarish memory and smiled at the Caliph. He looked directly at them.

"These two young people standing before me are to become united in marriage," the Caliph began. "It is a bond that unites a couple. Promises made by you this day to each other will remain with you always. I know that your mothers and fathers are gone, but in this room this family loves you as if you were their own.

"In the name of Allah the Merciful," he continued, "the Mercy giving, Praise be to Allah, Lord of the worlds, and Prayer and Peace be upon the Prophet Mohammed and his family. I marry you in accordance with the law and the tradition and for the *sadaq* agreed between us."

To which Alric answered, "In the name of Allah, I accept marriage to Bemia in accordance with Islamic law and for the *sadaq* agreed between us."

At that point the Caliph added, "May Allah bless you both."

He then addressed the group before him. "Brothers and sisters, we are uniting in the bond of marriage and in obedience to the guidance of our Creator our brother Alric and sister Bemia, who have decided to live together as husband and wife, sheltered with the blessings of Almighty Allah and His divine Benevolence. May Allah fill their lives with joy and may He grant them peace, health, and prosperity. May they always live together in tranquility and unending love for each other.

"And now," Harun announced, "*Al waleemah*. The reception."

They all adjourned for the reception, which under normal circumstances would have been to make the marriage public, but the secrecy of their ceremony had to be maintained.

* * *

Being the host and hostess, Jabir and Amira led the group into the large reception room where Amira had everything prepared. Ma'ruf and the other servants, all sworn to secrecy and loyal to Jabir and Amira, stood obediently at the tables, ready to assist in every way.

A man standing alone in the corner of the room puzzled Alric until Amira explained. She said, "He is here to observe both of you. He will then use the scenes that will be etched in his mind to create a wedding painting for you."

"Mother," Bemia exclaimed, "how lovely. That will be a precious memory." She kissed Amira on the cheek. "How can we thank you?" Bemia asked.

"By living a long and happy life as my husband and I have done," Amira responded through a mask of tears.

Alric kissed Amira on the cheek and hugged her for several seconds.

"May we," a voice boomed, "interrupt?"

Alric turned to see Harun and Scheherazade standing close by. Bemia curtsied and Alric bowed. Scheherazade spoke. "May we borrow Bemia for a moment?"

Alric nodded. It was the happiest day of his life. He took Amira's hand and walked over to where Jabir, Khalil, and Ahmed were standing. "I assume," Jabir said, smiling, "that tears have been shed by the ladies and all is well now?" He took Amira's hand in his. "Come, my dear," he said. "This is a happy day. Let us rejoice. We have a son and daughter who are man and wife."

At that moment Harun and Scheherazade approached with Bemia. "Alric, look!" Bemia said excitedly as she caressed a large diamond that hung around her neck. The stunning precious stone was the size of a large grape and was mounted in gold and suspended on a gold chain.

"And now, my dear wife, and guests," Jabir announced, "I suggest that we partake of the food that has been prepared."

"My aunt," Harun addressed the servants, "has agreed that when you are finished serving the bride and groom, you may also join as members of the wedding party. My wife and I," he looked lovingly at Scheherazade, "will help ourselves to the food and drinks. But," he fixed his eyes on each of the servants, "I am not here today, and never was here. Am I understood?"

They all murmured "yes" and bowed deeply in respect.

Without further ado, Abal, Buhjah, and Maha approached Alric and Bemia. Their eyes opened wide at the sight of the diamond that now adorned Bemia's neck. Alric withdrew to where Khalil and Ahmed stood with Harun. They were soon joined by Jabir and Wahid, who had also introduced Ma'ruf to the Caliph and was telling Harun how Ma'ruf assisted Alric in the laboratory.

Harun smiled his gratitude to Ma'ruf and then observed, "A wedding is, I think," he looked at the women, "a device invented and propagated by women. In fact," he stroked his beard, "I might hazard a guess that, any time now, handkerchiefs will appear, eyes will become misty, and each will console the other."

Wahid spoke. "May I make a suggestion, Sire?"

"Of course, Wahid," Harun responded, "I have known you since I was a child, and your family has been associated with my father for many years."

Wahid continued. "Perhaps the party would like to commence eating?"

"Alric, will you please lead the way?" Harun asked.

"I will, Sire." Alric answered. "I see that my brothers Khalil and Ahmed are looking longingly at the table."

"Oh," Harun interrupted. "Wahid, the guards outside in the garden . . . " He did not need finish the sentence.

"I will see they are fed, Sire," Wahid responded immediately.

The buffet meal was a delicious array of food and juices. The table was long and had been covered with shimmering yellow covers. White and yellow napkins were interspersed between the dishes. The light blue plates, which matched the color of Bemia's dress, added a delicate contrast. This color theme was taken up by the flowers that adorned the table.

Amira had planned everything well. Alric, who was used to the sumptuous tables that Amira set, still could not believe the amount of food presented! No one, he thought, will leave the room hungry!

To begin, there was orzo salad with sun-dried tomato, olives and fresh basil, chick pea salad, and couscous salad with diced vegetables and tomatoes. The side dishes consisted of hummus, artichoke hearts, roasted red peppers, fresh pita bread, goat cheese, and a cracked pepper cream sauce. The main dishes included roasted bass with saffron and fresh parsley in a tomato fennel broth, sautéed chicken medallions with caramelized onions, mushrooms, and apricots, slow-cooked lamb with orange and pomegranate, as well as a leg of lamb roast that was infused with olive and lemon.

Soon everyone was seated. The festivities continued. Alric talked with Khalil, and Ahmed and the Caliph also joined the conversation. It was light-hearted and full of joy. Then as evening approached, it was time for the cake.

Abal, Buhjah, and Maha left the room and returned carrying the biggest sponge cake Alric had even seen. The cake contained a variety of wild berries. "How," he spoke aloud, "have I missed the preparations for today?"

"Because," Khalil whispered, "you have had eyes for none other than Bemia. The Persians could have ridden through the city and I doubt you would have noticed, dear brother!"

Amira turned to Harun. "Wahid has informed me that your men in the garden have been fed, as you requested, and Abal, Buhjah, and Maha seemed to have enjoyed the attention given them by the soldiers."

Amira looked at the three young women, who responded by looking at the floor to hide their blushes. As Abal served a piece of cake to each guest, Buhjah and Maha followed and spooned fresh fruit onto each plate according to their taste.

* * *

Hours later, it was difficult to tell that a feast had actually taken place. The table was quickly cleared of any remains. "This," Wahid had decided, "will not resemble a battlefield!"

There were no remnants of food, and he had kept the servants moving to and from the kitchen. As each dish was exhausted, crumbs and errant morsels of food were quickly removed, along with used fingerbowls. The conversation continued light and harmonious until the eating and talking slowed down. The skies had started to darken.

"It seems, my dear," Harun said to Scheherazade, "that we should make our way home. We will leave together." He looked at Alric and then at Bemia. "The reasons that brought you to this land remain unknown, yet my wife," he looked at Scheherazade, "believes it is because you can make a difference in our world. You now have family and friends. I have been fortunate over the course of my life to be surrounded by those who have cared for and protected me."

Harun was engaging, passionate, energetic, and challenging as he spoke. His words were sincere. "The wedding is over, my young friends, but your lives have just begun!" He took Bemia's hand, raised her to her feet, and kissed her once on each check. Harun then grasped Alric's shoulders. "Treat your wife well, Alric. Enjoy each other and you will enjoy life."

*   *   *

After Harun and Scheherazade left, Alric and Bemia, in the company of Jabir, Amira, Khalil, Ahmed, and Wahid, were shown to the door of a new residence on the side of the colonnade that was opposite to where the kitchen was located. "These accommodations," Jabir announced," are a wedding gift from mother and I." On hearing this news, Alric and Bemia were delighted and marveled at how the secret had been kept. "The rooms are furnished and will offer you privacy. Your brothers Khalil and Ahmed thought fit to present you with the gift of a comfortable bed."

Jabir raised an eyebrow as he looked at Khalil and then at Ahmed. "Their story," he added, "is that the bed was made by the finest Persian craftsmen."

437

Amira interjected, smiling, "My dear," she looked at Bemia, "do you remember the stables that we were building for the horses?"

"Yes," Bemia said cautiously.

"Well, they were never intended to be stables!"

"You mean . . . ?" Bemia finally found words.

"But, mother," Alric exclaimed, "that means the building was started long before we announced our betrothal?"

"Alric, my boy, if there is one thing you must learn," Jabir put his arm around Alric's shoulder, "it is that mothers have a sixth sense that allows them to determine the future of their children. So when my dear Amira told me her plans for you, I decided there was but one thing to do: It was not to interfere. From that moment on, mother handled everything!"

Jabir laughed. Alric and Bemia hugged Amira and kissed her cheeks. "And now," Jabir announced, "we will show you our well-kept secret. Wahid, please lead the way."

Alric and Bemia entered the spacious rooms and saw the magnificent furnishings for the first time. "Mother," was all Bemia could say as Alric held her close. Her body shuddered with emotion.

"Why should we not do this for our daughter?"

Alric smiled.

"Our wedding gift to a wonderful son and daughter," Amira whispered.

* * *

CHAPTER 33

Two weeks passed, during which Alric and Bemia's happiness was obvious to all. They frequently walked in the garden, a favorite spot, holding hands, much to Amira's delight. During this time, they were able to put the First Minister and his sinister activities out of their minds.

As allowed, Alric continued to introduce Bemia to the work in the laboratory. She had shown a remarkable curiosity for medicines, mixtures, and extracts. She was neat and tidy—an important quality, since caution was essential for laboratory work, and that pleased both Alric and Jabir.

Bemia's explanation was simple. "Women spend all of their lives cleaning up after men, so why should I not be neat and tidy?"

"Ah, my dear," Jabir said smiling, "you are priceless."

There had been idyllic days since the wedding, but Alric sensed that would soon end. On the evening of the fourteenth day of their marriage, he confessed to Bemia that he could not shake off the feeling that something was about to happen. She responded by stroking his hair and kissed his cheek.

"Mother and I have sensed your unease, Alric. All we can suggest is that you allow us to help you."

"I promise, when my thoughts clarify, we will talk over my concerns."

* * *

The following morning Alric awoke early. Bemia breathed gently at his side. She was asleep and had a look of supreme contentment on her face. Alric felt that lying in bed would not resolve his problems, especially with his beautiful Bemia lying next to him!

He had always been an early riser, and he treasured the hour before sunrise. He bent over and kissed her lightly on the forehead. He looked around in the dim light of the bedroom, then got up, put on a robe, and, as an afterthought lest his continual pacing awaken Bemia, made his way to the kitchen.

There was calmness in the air as he made his way along the colonnade. He was not surprised to find Wahid sitting at the table, a glass of apple juice in front of him. Seeing Alric, he immediately stood up.

"No, Wahid. This is a precious time of day when a man should enjoy his morning thoughts. I can help myself."

Wahid started to protest, then realized the futility of such action and sat back on to the stool. Alric poured himself a glass of orange juice. "May I?" Alric asked and gestured at the stool on the other side of the table.

"Of course," Wahid replied smiling. "If I may ask, Alric, what brings you to the kitchen so early in the morning?"

"Oh," Alric stumbled for the words, "I needed to think about, let me say, a hypothetical situation, Wahid."

"If it is the hypothetical situation that I can imagine," Wahid looked around as if expecting spies to materialize from the wall, "I can sympathize with your thoughts and feelings."

Knowing that Jabir and Amira had taken the trustworthy Wahid into their confidence about the plot against the Caliph, Alric sipped his orange juice and then spoke. "The next steps are always difficult to plan when one does not know the true nature of the enemy."

"My father, who was captain of the guard, was close to the Caliph's father," Wahid offered, "and he faced a similar situation."

Surprised at Wahid's mention of his father, Alric asked with raised eyebrows, "And how was this handled?"

Wahid sipped the apple juice and carefully replaced the glass on the table. "In the situation that had arisen," he said, "my father sent people into the streets to hunt the Caliph's enemies and determine the course of action they planned to take." Alric was about to ask how when Wahid continued. "He did not send soldiers. The Caliph had trusted friends who sought out the plotters for him without anyone identifying themselves."

Wahid walked to the stove, made sure the fire was hot, and indicated that Alric should join him for tea. "I find that a hot cup of sweet tea is so much better for a serious discussion such as ours." Wahid seemed to go into a trance. "Where was I?" he asked rhetorically. "Ah, yes," he answered as the flames lit up under the copper kettle. "It seems to me the issues might need to be forced."

Wahid's eyes kept returning to the flame under the kettle. "Alric, you may find it difficult to draw the leader into the open. If he does commit, he will always have some excuse for his actions, and, of course, this excuse will bear no relationship to the real reasons for his motives.

"Can you remember when you first arrived at this house and you were introduced to the game of chess?" Alric nodded. "It is a game that must be played by thinking four or five moves ahead of your opponent. I notice that you had a penchant for the game. Put your chess mind back into action and use these abilities to think."

Wahid paused and looked at the kettle once more. "It seems that the water is ready for our tea!"

* * *

Alric thought about Wahid's comments during the day. He did not tell Bemia about their early morning conversation. He felt that they were moving further and further into danger. The longer the actions of the First Minister remained unchecked, the more dangerous they would become. Alric made up his mind. He would seek out his father before dinner and talk matters over with him. Something had to be done soon.

Later that morning, an occasion arose for Alric to speak with Jabir, who, sensing that Alric had something important on his mind, ceased his work in the laboratory and prepared to listen. Bemia had been asked to go to the house on a pretext.

"This is uncharted territory for you Alric," Jabir said after hearing Alric's suggestions.

"With respect, father, I think that risks must be taken. Perhaps these risks can be lessened so that there is little chance of being caught?"

Jabir rubbed his cheek as though his beard were causing some discomfort, and then he smiled. "Let me use the analogy of the forest," he said. "At times the forest is so overgrown, it causes damage to the trees. If this keeps up, the forest is in danger of diminishing in size. The forest, by growing so large, becomes, you might say, overconfident almost to the point that it destroys itself. So . . . "

Alric had understood Jabir's logic. "It seems, father, that you are suggesting that the First Minister may be overconfident because he has gone unchecked. We must assume that his actions against Bemia were not the first time he has broken the law."

"And so what is next, Alric?" Jabir questioned.

"The First Minister will definitely not do his own dirty work," Alric said quietly. And so . . . "

"He will hire others," Jabir completed Alric's thought. "And once we have determined his plan of action . . . That is it!" Jabir suddenly exclaimed. He looked at Alric. "Who stands in his way most of all?

Alric thought for a moment. "You, father," he said.

"Who else?" Jabir asked.

Alric thought for a moment, almost at a loss to come up with a name, and then he smiled grimly. "Minister Ali al-Maslawi!"

"Correct, Alric."

"I ask your permission to meet with him, father."

"Then, Alric, if the First Minister has plans for Ali al-Maslawi, he will also have plans for whoever he considers to have the greatest influence with the Caliph."

"And that would be . . . No, we cannot allow it." Alric's eyes opened wide in the realization of what he had concluded. "Mother must be protected at all costs. In our absence, father, I know just the person to do that."

Jabir looked at Alric, then exclaimed, "Of course! Bemia!"

"And what will Bemia do?"

The voice came from behind them. Surprised, Alric and Jabir turned suddenly to face the door of the laboratory.

"My dear, what will I do?" Bemia asked. "And please do not hide anything from me." Alric gave Bemia a summary of their line of thinking. "You are wondering what I think," she said. "Well, I have sworn to protect my mother, and you, father, and this oath means to the death. My dear Alric understands." Alric and Jabir nodded. "Then, it is done," Bemia concluded. "Now I do need to have my brothers provide me with suitable weaponry so that I might practice their use. Must mother know of this?"

Memories of seeing his father and mother and the villagers lying dead at the shield wall and of other women who had chosen to fight alongside their men flashed into Alric's mind. If anything happened to Bemia . . .

"Alric, are you in agreement that we do not tell mother?" Bemia's voice broke into his thoughts.

"Yes, I agree. But . . . "

"I will be careful, my love. Now, if you can find my two brothers for me, I will choose weapons suitable to the task."

Jabir interjected, "I suggest that we go about our business. If Amira hears anything of this conversation, she will immediately suspect that we are up to something!" He grinned devilishly. "Let us take tea in the house and remove ourselves from the laboratory. Amira will already be wondering why the three of us have been closeted away in this place for so long."

* * *

Ali al-Maslawi walked though the fresh morning air toward his favorite outdoor cafeteria for tea and a slice of honeyed bread, his usual morning breakfast. At Jabir's request, he was meeting Alric.

Ali continued his walk. He had long ago lost respect for the First Minister. There was something about the man that did not quite ring true, and the rumors and stories of his background had left too many questions unanswered.

At that moment, two men approached him. Their identities were hidden by face coverings, and they appeared strong and healthy. Ali fingered the small dagger that he carried in his belt.

"Ali al-Maslawi, it is a good morning to be alive."

These were the keywords that Jabir had told him would be used when contact was made. The man continued, "We bring you greetings from Jabir al-Hajjaj ibn Yusuf abu Asad abu Khalil."

He looked at the man who had spoken and relaxed. Even with the head and face covering, the eyes and the voice of Ahmed were recognizable. But who was the other one?

"I believe that you know Alric al-Biritaanya ibn Jabir."

Alric lowered the covering to allow al-Maslawi to see his face. "Greetings, Ali al-Maslawi. I also bring you greetings from the Librarian in Mosul."

Ali stared at Alric. "Of course!" Ali said, relieved. "I remember you. But you look . . . ," he searched for the word, "different!"

Alric and Ahmed smiled. "That is," Alric said, "because I have developed a mixture that colors the face and hair. It serves me well at times like this."

Al-Maslawi smiled and nodded. "Will you both join me for breakfast with my friends or shall we talk alone?"

"We will join you for breakfast," Alric said. "We are curious to meet your friends—one in particular. From what you have told my father, he may be a person of great interest to us."

Ali nodded. "Then let us walk in this direction," he gestured.

* * *

Some of the merchants were already busy assembling stalls, while others loaded packages onto carts to convey the goods to the marshalling point for a caravan. A group of women washed the walls of the gardens to remove some of the dust that had accumulated over the past days and return the walls to their sparkling whiteness.

Baghdad was always busy at this time.

"A veritable beehive," Ali observed.

A few minutes later, just inside the city wall, they turned a corner and the tea shop came into sight. Business looked brisk. Ali's three companions, whom he met every day for breakfast, were already seated. The owner made sure that a table was always available for them. Ali commented that he could not remember the last time they had eaten breakfast at a different place.

The owner of the shop greeted him, looked at Alric and Ahmed, and provided three more chairs. Ali greeted his companions and introduced Alric and Ahmed as Ali and Asad, the sons of his cousin from Mosul. Neither Alric nor Ahmed made any effort to remove their face covering as they sat down at the table.

Al-Maslawi looked at his three companions, although he considered only two of them to be close friends. The third was an acquaintance who had nowhere else to go but, by association, considered himself to be a member of the group. He greeted the two friends warmly and acknowledged the presence of the other man by casting a casual glance in his direction and nodding his head.

Al-Maslawi introduced Jawad and Ma'mun to Alric and Ahmed; the third man was introduced as Mash'al. "I see that we dress alike, Mash'al," al-Maslawi said. "This is a coincidence, and I must compliment you on your choice of clothing."

There was something about Mash'al that Alric did not like. His attitude seemed to be a veil to cover his true intent. Alric wondered how Mash'al had managed to become a member of the group. As the matter faded from his thoughts, he turned his attention to the shop owner. Hot, strong, sweet tea and honeyed bread were laid on the table. Ali smiled at his companions, and breakfast was under way. He looked at Alric and Ahmed.

"You are not eating?" he asked.

They shook their heads.

"Well, perhaps you would like to take tea?"

They nodded and lowered their face coverings and the café owner poured the sugared tea into the glasses. Mash'al stared at Alric. He continued to eat his bread and sip the tea as he looked curiously at the visitors.

Al-Maslawi took the conversation into a direction that Mash'al could not ignore. He brought up the issue of a family concern, and Mash'al readily monopolized the conversation with his own personal issues that were his favorite topics.

Below the surface of his calm exterior, Alric was becoming more and more uncomfortable with Mash'al, and as a result of their ensuing conversation, it occurred to Alric that Mash'al was not just a breakfast associate but perhaps a conduit to the First Minister. The words "Do not be paranoid" sprang into Alric's mind. He was well aware of the First Minister's dislike for al-Maslawi, and what better way to upstage him and discover his plans and thoughts than to have a man placed within al-Maslawi's close circle of friends! He also sensed Ahmed's discomfort with Mash'al.

As the thoughts coursed through Alric's mind, he became even more convinced now that Mash'al was an agent of the First Minister. He had even brought the First Minister's name into the conversation and attempted to goad Ali and his friends into saying something derogatory, but without success.

Alric and Ahmed were surprised when Mash'al gulped down the last of the bread and decided he had to leave. The group, planning to stay longer, promised to meet again the next morning. With a wave of farewell, he left the table, disappeared around the corner, and walked quickly to the back lane between the houses of the next two streets.

Ali nodded casually to the shopkeeper and accepted more tea for himself, Jawad, and Ma'mun. Alric and Ahmed declined, stating that they needed to leave to attend to other business. Al-Maslawi nodded knowingly.

* * *

Alric and Ahmed walked leisurely until they were out of sight of the group. Once around the corner, they quickened their steps in the direction of where they believed Mash'al had gone. They reached the entry to the back lane and saw Mash'al halfway along the path.

The houses that lined the lane had high-walled enclosures in various stages of disrepair. As Mash'al approached a house at the end of the lane, his speed diminished. He stood silent, as if listening. And then, suddenly, two arms reached out, grabbed Mash'al, and pulled him out of sight.

Alric and Ahmed gathered up their robes and ran to the point where Mash'al had disappeared. The gate to the enclosure was open, but there was no sign of Mash'al.

As they moved quietly toward the dilapidated house, faint sounds came from within.

"Listen," Ahmed whispered.

They could hear a voice coming from inside the house. The high-pitched tone made it sound pleading and desperate. "Swords," Ahmed said quietly.

Alric drew his sword and held it at the ready. They crept toward the house. The windows had blinds that were drawn, but the door had been left ajar with barely a hand's breadth between the edge of the door and the frame.

Alric knelt on the ground so that Ahmed could stand above him to see what was happening inside. Two men stood next to the wall, and Mash'al was on his knees between them. There was a third man, in black attire. Alric and Ahmed could see the man in black, but neither could identify him; his face was well covered.

"But it is not my fault!" Mash'al exclaimed in his high-pitched tone as he looked up at the man. "How was I to know that two others would be there?" He looked up pleadingly. "It was not supposed to be that way!" he added.

The sun did not cast much light in the house, but Alric could see the fear on Mash'al's face. The man in black spoke in guttural tones that were difficult to distinguish as he gestured to the other men standing against the wall: "My two colleagues were paid to kill someone today. You did not present them with the correct target, and they will not get paid until they have successfully carried out their task. They are displeased."

As the figure in black looked around, he tensed, then addressed the two men:

"You wanted to kill someone, and so you shall! There is a bonus for ridding me of this idiot!" He gestured to Mash'al. "The bonus is half the fee you will receive for killing the real target, Ali al-Maslawi. Do you agree to these terms?"

They nodded readily.

"He is yours! Do with him as you wish," the man said.

Alric was alarmed. Before he could move, the two men had drawn their swords and killed Mash'al with a savage cut to each side of his neck.

The man in black looked at the grisly scene before him, turned on his heel, and headed toward the door. Then, as an afterthought, he spoke to the killers. "See that the others who sat at the table with this," he pointed with disdain at Mash'al's body, "are dispatched also. Above all, make sure you remove al-Maslawi permanently from this life. After that, meet me at the usual place tomorrow night, convince me that you have done the job, and I will pay you in full." Then he left with a swirl of his black cloak.

The killers looked at each other. "When we are paid," one said, "perhaps we will discover who is rewarding us for this work!"

The second man laughed coarsely, and the meaning was clear. They planned to kill the man in black and be on their way to another murder in another city. Alric rose to his feet and looked at Ahmed.

"These men do not know the identity of their leader. They are of little use to us, but they must not get away with this murder!" Ahmed whispered.

At Ahmed's signal, Alric threw the door open and they rushed into the room. The killers quickly recovered from their surprise and turned, ready to fight. Their eyes glinted viciously and with steely determination in the dim light.

"As we stand!" Ahmed said quickly, meaning take the man on your side, Alric, and I will take the one on mine. The two men attempted to move toward the door, keeping their backs to the wall. They moved apart so as not to interfere with each other's movements, but they were no match for Ahmed and Alric.

As the first one attempted to confuse Ahmed by his feinting movements, Ahmed spun around just as the killer lunged toward him and was able to thrust his sword into the man's torso. His attacker dropped to his knees and crumpled to the floor, dead.

Alric's opponent, bewildered at the suddenness of Ahmed's action and not wishing to join his colleague in a quick death, rushed at Alric. He attempted to block Alric's sword thrust, but Alric, using a swivel movement, locked the man's sword with his own hilt, rendering his opponent's weapon ineffective. The man's confident smile changed to fear as he realized that his sword was no longer useful. The dismay on his face was apparent as Alric's dagger entered his throat.

* * *

When Alric and Ahmed left the house, the lane was quiet. No signs of life were visible in the alley; it was silent and empty. "We will not find him now. Let us . . ."

Ahmed gestured toward the house. They returned and cleaned their weapons on the clothes of the dead men. Then they left the house and the bodies as they had fallen. No doubt they would be discovered and disposed of, most likely in the river. Quickly Alric and Ahmed walked away and into the sunlight at the entry to the lane.

* * *

Leaning over the side of one of the fish ponds, Alric and Ahmed related the events to Jabir and Khalil. "Well done, both of you," Jabir said, and Khalil smiled. "I will see that the Caliph is made aware of this and that my friend Ali al-Maslawi removes himself from the public eye for a while. It is unfortunate that you did not recognize the man in black. I know you have your theory, but the Caliph will also be pleased that you are unharmed."

Jabir paused and then said, "Khalil, will you advise cousin Bashir of this and warn him to be on his guard?"

"Yes, father."

Jabir left them to return to the house. "In these troubled times, mother worries when she sees us huddled in conversation!" he said as he walked away.

Khalil was smiling at Alric. "Ahmed tells me, little brother," Khalil said, "that you dispatched your opponent quite quickly with that dagger of yours."

Alric smiled in return.

Wahid's words about thinking ahead as in a game of chess came back to Alric. In a flash, he had thought of pawns chasing the king, somewhat ineffectively and usually unsuccessfully. What did it take to capture a king? Alric wondered, and then suddenly he had the answer: a knight or a bishop, especially a well-positioned knight or bishop who had the support of others. But in this case, he smiled inwardly, a knight or bishop with support of others could be detected. It had to be a single person who is secretive and clever at his trade!

"Let us say," Alric broke the silence, "that whoever the man in black is, he believed that he was successful today and that al-Maslawi is now dead." Alric looked serious and paused before continuing. "If this is the case, the Caliph will most likely be the next target. We should look for

451

an assassin who thinks he has the freedom of Baghdad! We will find him and confine him. Just like the fish in this pond!"

Khalil looked at Ahmed and then at Alric. "Yes" Alric, you make a very good point."

"And," Alric added, "let us assume that the First Minister will hire an assassin. This man will be twice as observant and many more times as proficient as the two killers that we dispatched today. It is also in my thoughts that this hired assassin will know the identity of the man in black."

"If that is so," Khalil said, "Alric, we must find and apprehend him before he strikes. We can only hope he also has the temerity to believe he is infallible."

* * *

CHAPTER 34

Alric suggested to Bemia that she venture out only if absolutely necessary and pointed out that at home she could protect Amira. Bemia agreed with a smile and immediately asked Ahmed, who had remained silent throughout the conversation, to provide her with weapons.

She chose two short swords, ideal to use at close quarters. The swords reminded her of the Saxon *seax* she had learned to handle as a young girl and so felt comfortable with them. The twenty-four-inch blade of each weapon was almost a half inch thick at the base and offered strength. The blade of one was inlaid with a brass decoration, and the hilt was a combination of steel and engraved brass in a stylized wolf's head. In contrast, the other weapon was plain and unadorned. The scabbards were leather with markings that reminded Bemia of a Celtic motif. She swirled them around, testing each sword for weight, and balance.

Ahmed nodded in agreement. "My sister has knowledge of weapons," he said to Alric who looked on proudly.

Bemia smiled. "We were taught the use of weapons from a young age." She said as she looked at the swords and replaced each one into its scabbard. "I will strap each scabbard to my body so that the sword is reachable through the opening in the side of my dress."

Alric kissed her on the cheek. "Be careful, my love."

She smiled and kissed him in return. "You be careful, also. Do not get into any trouble!"

*   *   *

The following week, the next sign of danger came during an excursion made by Alric and Ahmed to the marketplace. Alric was disguised as he had been during previous outings.

In the meantime, and believing that he was alone, three armed men approached Alric as he turned into a lonely lane. One of the men, the apparent leader, asked what business he had in the marketplace.

Alric did not respond. Then the man questioned him again. "That is my business," Alric answered.

"We are going to have to search you to see if you are armed," the leader said.

Alric stepped backward cautiously so that his back was protected by the wall of a garden enclosure.

"Perhaps you have money?" another one ventured a brave statement.

Alric remained silent.

The men moved closer. They saw Alric as an easy victim. They drew their swords and were ready for action.

Alric remained calm. "I will now show you one of life's simple lessons," he exclaimed as he produced the sword that had been concealed under his robe. The blade glinted in the morning sun. "Now, do you have a request of me?" he asked.

"You are one against three," the leader said. "What hope can you have against us? Just give us your money and we will be on our way."

"No," Ahmed's voice came clearly to Alric from behind the men. Having seen the men approach Alric and knowing that their business was suspect, Ahmed had quickly circled around the garden wall and come up behind them.

"Well, it seems, my friend, that we are now two!" Alric exclaimed as he made a quick movement with his sword and laid open the cheek to the bone of the man who was closest. Alric's skill with the sword took them by surprise. The one that was cut bled profusely and screamed for help from his comrades as he moved closer to Alric, wanting revenge.

"You handled yourself very well, my brother. Do you need help?"

"No, Ahmed," he responded as he moved away from the wall and his attacker, seeing this as his opportunity, lunged at Alric. A swift movement of Alric's sword and the man fell as the life blood poured from the cut in his throat. The two remaining would-be assassins could not move. With Alric in front and Ahmed behind, they had no choice but to fight. The leader weighed the opportunity very quickly. At a sign to his colleague, they rushed at Alric, thinking to overcome him and escape. Instead, Alric's deadly singing blade whistled through the air, and both men died in the same manner as their colleague.

"Thank you," Alric said to Ahmed.

"For what?" Ahmed asked.

"You have been my teacher!" he exclaimed.

Ahmed smiled and said, "A teacher is only as good as his weakest pupil. And you were the best!"

The attack had provided a stimulus and given Alric strength. He realized that it had brought out his courage and strongest qualities. It reminded him of the day that Hilda had died. She had attacked the two sea raiders at her own peril. She had made them change their plan; otherwise, they both may have been killed.

* * *

Alric and Ahmed returned to the house and related the incident to the family. "I fear that the time is close," Khalil observed. "This was an attempt to remove you, Alric, since the First Minister must also consider you a threat. If the plan is to draw him out so that his guilt is beyond doubt, this is only the beginning. There may be other incidents of this kind. We need to discover the assassin."

"And once we have him," Ahmed interjected, "we will be in a much stronger position."

"With every day that passes," said Jabir, "we must be more and more vigilant. Abdul al-Warith, First Minister to the Caliph, is no fool. He will plan accordingly. I deem it no longer safe for anyone to leave the house alone." He looked at Khalil, Alric, and Ahmed. "You will leave only in twos or threes. And my dear wife is not to venture forth at all. Bemia, my dear . . . " The last words were left unsaid as he looked at Bemia.

"I understand, father. Mother will be safe with me. And you, father?" Bemia added.

"I have left word with Harun that I also will remain with you in the house." He put his arms around Amira. "All will be well, my dear. We have three determined sons." He looked at Bemia and smiled, "And a daughter who stands with them."

* * *

The next morning, as was Alric's custom, he awakened early, bathed quickly, and made straight for the laboratory, having decided he would eat breakfast later when the household servants were fully awake. He felt the same anxiety that he had felt every morning recently.

He spent the next two hours taking stock of the equipment, supplies, and all other items in the laboratory. His practiced eyes scanned every detail of the shelves and closets and saw that everything was in place. He had performed this same task since his second morning in the laboratory, and he knew the waking schedule of everyone in the household. When his task was completed, he left for his private quarters.

He found Bemia at ease, sitting on the cushions and reading the notes he had given her. She also had a book dealing with *al-khimiyam* that had caught her eye. She alternated between reading it and the Latin notes, but the Arabic writing was difficult and took her longer to read. She was fascinated by the language, the symbols, and the theories of nature. Her eyes took in every detail of the book, and she found herself reading with a different perspective.

"You are busy this morning!" Alric exclaimed as he entered the room.

Bemia gave a slight start. She had been so engrossed in Alric's notes that she had not heard him come into the room. She smiled, arose, and walked over to him, kissing his cheek. Alric breathed in the scented oils she had used in bathing. The aroma was pleasant and captivating.

"I have been reading for so long," Bemia said, "that I lost track of time. Have you had breakfast, my love?"

Alric shook his head. "No. I have been taking stock of the supplies and equipment in the laboratory." He sniffed each hand in turn. "It might be better if I wash my hands again. There are some chemical odors that are difficult to remove. I will be back shortly and then we can discuss your reading."

He soon returned after washing his hands using the same scented oil that Bemia had used. "You know," he said looking at each hand, "these oils seem to adhere to the skin. They mix with water very well and . . . ," he paused, thinking out loud. "I wonder if . . . ? I will try that later. Shall we have breakfast?"

They walked along the colonnade to the breakfast room, where Wahid, aware of their coming, was laying fresh bread on the table. The aroma was enticing, even addictive. Once seated, they broke the bread into small pieces, dipped each piece in honey, and popped the fresh morsel into their mouths.

Bemia sipped the orange juice. She had learned a lot of new facts and had become accustomed to the work in the laboratory. It was a new world to her and she had begun to learn and understand the language of symbols and signs. With that knowledge, she felt her world had opened a door to greater learning.

"My dear, I would like to go back to the beginning of your notes and learn everything there is from your work," she said thoughtfully. "This may take me a considerable time, but I feel I need to understand more clearly what you have done. I want to know everything I can about mixtures and the ingredients. I realize the ingredients must be mixed in the correct proportions."

"I think that is an excellent idea," Jabir said as he entered the room.

Alric and Bemia looked up to see him. They welcomed his company, but he expressed the hope that he was not intruding on their private moment. Bemia assured Jabir that he was not, and he settled himself upon the cushions. Hearing the voices, Amira came to investigate, and she too joined them for the meal.

"Do you realize," Amira observed, "that it has been many months since the four of us actually sat down together for a meal?"

"Then I suggest, my dear," Jabir said, "that we make the most of it." He contemplated a piece of bread. "This bread is delicious!"

"It was made for us by Wahid," Bemia offered the explanation. "It is based on a recipe that my . . . " Bemia fumbled for a word.

"Your birth mother," Amira added.

"Yes, mother, and thank you." She continued. "My birth mother used this recipe before I left England. Wahid asked one day if there was anything that I would like, and this bread recipe came to mind. Alric," she smiled, "also likes it."

"So do I!" Jabir was determined not to be left out of this part of the conversation. "I suggest, my dear . . . "

Amira held up her hand. "Yes, my dear husband, I will see to it that Wahid includes this type of bread as part of his daily baking." The bread was thicker and richer than the round, flat type of Arabic bread, and the oatmeal ingredient and the browned crust enhanced the taste.

* * *

Through the high open window of the breakfast room and beyond the garden wall, Alric could hear the sounds of the merchants making their way to their stalls in the marketplace. He was reminded that he needed to be vigilant. Bemia might have to curtail her laboratory work. He knew she could do anything she set her mind to.

Alric glanced through the pages of the book that Bemia had been reading when a picture caught his eye. "This drawing has given me an idea."

Jabir raised his eyebrows in question.

" 'He will have an iron fist and will shoot fire from his hands,' " Alric said as he quoted from the tablet. "Remember, father, the words of the tablet?" As he spoke, Alric showed Jabir the drawing of a man with fire seemingly coming out of his hand.

"I think this is leading me to an answer, father," Alric said excitedly as he excused himself and went in haste to the laboratory.

"That young man never seems to rest," Amira observed.

"That is true, mother, very true," Bemia added, but her mind was elsewhere.

Jabir looked at his wife and winked.

* * *

Bemia joined Alric several minutes after his departure, excusing herself to Jabir and Amira. "I am starting to recognize the intimate aspects of your work, Alric," Bemia said. "So, it's not surprising that I now fully support your intentions. Each day that I work with you seems to be more fascinating that the last."

She went on, fearing that Alric might not understand the intent of what she was saying. "It is in the tablet, is it not? In that very same tablet that you brought back from Mosul? There is something in there that gives you the power to overcome enemies."

"I feel that I am being guided by some mysterious force. But you are right, my love," he said. "I have found the secret written on the tablet. For many years, the cuneiform writing was the language of government and science, but now it is largely forgotten. I am fortunate to have learned the language from the Librarian in Mosul. But to the current issue, the man who made the writing on the tablet must have been a follower of *al-khimiya*."

Bemia put her hand over her mouth to yawn, and then she raised her arms to stretch.

"Don't do that, my dear," Alric said.

"Do what?" Bemia asked innocently.

"Raise your arms like that."

"Why?" Bemia was curious.

"Two obvious reasons!" Alric responded with a mischievous smile on his face.

Bemia playfully slapped his arm. "Is that all you can think of?"

"Yes, my love," he said, taking her in his arms.

At that moment, Amira entered the laboratory. "I am not interrupting anything, am I?"

"No, mother, just my dear husband here seems to have eight arms like . . . what do you call it?"

"An octopus."

Bemia and Amira smiled at Alric's discomfort, and then Amira spoke of her reason to visit the laboratory. "You are fortunate, Alric," Amira said. "A caravan has arrived from Basra, and now I can replace the missing pots. Without realizing what he was saying in the excitement of his new work with you, Ma'ruf—or Rufus, as you seem to want to call him—has told me the whereabouts of my pots.

"Now, let us have lunch together, and tell me of your latest thoughts on this issue of the First Minister and the Caliph." Amira saw the surprised expression on their faces. "It does not take a wizard," she said, "to see that you are both up to something. Young minds are always fertile. And older minds are always curious!"

They talked as they ate fruit and pastries and drank tea. Amira listened intently until they were finished relating the events. "You have translated a *cunei forma* tablet and written the translation on a scroll that is somewhere in this house?" Amira began questioning. "And your plan is to use the information to draw out the First Minister into a form of confession? You do intend to make an attempt, successful or otherwise on his life?"

They nodded in agreement at her quick assessment. "Good," she pronounced. "But to kill a minister of the Caliph is not your prerogative. It is the prerogative of only the Caliph to displace or execute one of his ministers. Your plan may conflict with that formulated by the Caliph and your father." Amira sipped her tea and dabbed her lips with a napkin. "You must tell father, and I will talk with my nephew. He owes me another visit. He is a good man, but his temper is not so wonderful to behold. When the Caliph is angry, even I stay away!"

Bemia got up from her cushion, moved to Amira, leaned over, kissed her on the cheek, and said, "Thank you, mother."

Wiping a tear from her eye, Amira said, "I still have trouble after all of these years knowing what *al-khimiya* really is, but I do realize its hidden power, such as that which caused the near destruction of the laboratory and of you, Alric. But, please listen to your mother."

They had reseated themselves on the cushions and leaned forward in anticipation of her words. "I will make sure this is noised abroad," Amira said. "Khalil and Ahmed have their trustworthy men who will spread the word. Their message is that the one who escaped from death at the hands of the First Minister now lives at the house of al-Jabir and is betrothed, perhaps even married, to the blond northerner. If this does not draw out the First Minister, I will be surprised. I am sure it will force him into action of some kind, and we shall prevail. Be careful, my dears. This is a very dangerous game!"

* * *

Amira and Jabir were granted an audience with the Caliph. He had endorsed their plan with the same caveats and cautions of which Amira had spoken. There must be no attempt to kill a minister of the Caliph.

Khalil and Ahmed, in the presence of Jabir and Amira, were made aware of the plan and gave it a skeptical blessing. Being soldiers, Khalil and Ahmed would not remain hidden like mice but would go about life as if all were normal and take on danger as it arose. When they realized part of the plan was to have Bemia become more visible, they were very cautious. It was obvious that hiding Bemia away would serve no purpose.

"I have heard," Khalil said after the plan had been explained to him, "that there is a new man in the city, and I believe he is the assassin who has been hired by the First Minister."

Ahmed nodded in agreement. "Similar words have reached my ears. And when a stranger arrives in the city and does not appear to have any contacts, there is usually a nefarious reason."

"My suggestion," Ahmed turned to Jabir, "is that we go ahead as planned. Bemia needs to be reintroduced into the streets."

Alric and Bemia, accompanied by Ahmed, left the house for the market the next morning. Even though it had been decided that Bemia would protect Amira, the new plan had brought some changes to that idea. Khalil remained with his mother.

"Even if you do not see me," Ahmed advised as they walked through the streets, "I am always nearby and will come when needed."

Their exit from the house did not go unnoticed. The beggar who sat fifty paces away watched them carefully. He smiled inwardly. His prey was on the move. He would watch them, observe their behavior, and bide his time, and then he would strike. His breath hissed through his thin mouth like a snake.

* * *

"I see that we have an observer outside," Ahmed remarked casually to Alric and Bemia as they entered the garden after their trip to the market.

"Where?" Alric enquired.

"Under the shade of an awning from a nearby stall," Ahmed whispered as if the man were in hearing distance. "He followed us to the market and has managed to return here before us."

"So, what do we do?" Alric asked.

"I have no doubt that he will wait there until darkness, then creep off to his lair. I will talk with Khalil and suggest that we find a vantage point from which we can watch him, and then follow him to see where he leads us."

Alric nodded as Bemia added, "But you need to be very careful. The stall owner may be an accomplice."

Several hours later, when the grayness of the evening had changed into the darkness of night, Alric, with Khalil and Ahmed, left the house and garden as planned. They were armed and dressed in dark robes that would not reflect any light. Jabir, Amira and Bemia had been advised of their plan. Entry into the house would be difficult, as all doors would be locked. Wahid and Ma'ruf would lend whatever support they could, if needed.

Once outside the garden, Alric, Khalil, and Ahmed made their way stealthily into a position where they could observe the beggar. To their relief, the man had not moved.

When dealing with a high-placed enemy such as the First Minister, we must expect anything, Alric thought.

Suddenly, the beggar arose, stretched, and headed in a direction toward the outer city. Alric feared that they might lose him in the narrow streets that lay outside of the inner city.

The three figures glided through the stygian darkness, never losing sight of the man as he twisted and turned his way through the narrow streets. Finally, he stopped at a doorway, looked around furtively to see if there was anyone about, failed to see his three followers, and proceeded through the door.

Alric, Khalil, and Ahmed were relieved that they had not lost him in the darkness. They had been fortunate. Whenever he'd seemed to disappear, a dim light from a window or from a torch carried by soldiers on patrol had given him away.

Then the man reappeared at the door, looked in both directions, and walked quickly in the opposite direction from where his three observers were concealed. Alric's mood was not ameliorated by this nighttime excursion into this area of the city. The wind was starting to pick up strength and seemed to whistle its way through the narrow streets. The houses were crowded together as though they had been built without a plan, unlike most of the streets, which formed a regular grid system.

The man disappeared again around a corner. Alric quickened his pace, but Ahmed put a restraining hand on him. "Careful, Alric," he whispered. "You never know what you might meet at the corner!" Alric took the caution seriously—follow, but do not be observed! This was not a game.

They shadowed the man through several streets, which included a stop at yet another house. The tempo of the man's walk varied; at times he would quicken and almost disappear, and then he would slow his pace as if looking for someone.

As they stood in the shadows, leaning against a wall, the thought suddenly hit Alric. Perhaps the same thought hit Khalil and Ahmed at that moment. "We have followed this man for a considerable time," Alric whispered. "It is now well into the night and he still seems to have no purpose in his walk, unless . . ."

Ahmed stood upright. "It is as if this man *wants* us to follow him!" he growled. "And we have walked a considerable distance from the house!"

"Bemia and mother!" Alric exclaimed.

They turned, forgetting about the man, walked quickly, and then ran in the direction of Jabir's house.

* * *

As they disappeared down the street, the shadowy figure peered out of the last doorway that he had entered and smiled. "The cards that I am given to play are not always worthy of the game," he exclaimed. "But these three may be worthy opponents."

As he watched his three would-be observers disappear into the shadows at the end of the street, the beggar was in a good humor. Everything seemed to be going according to plan. He looked at the man in black, knowing well it was the First Minister whom he addressed.

"I had hoped to distract them for at least another hour," he admitted to the First Minister. "But," he added, "my men should be done with their work by now." He smiled again, his thin lips quivering. He would be well paid for his part in the plot. His final reward would come when the Caliph was removed and his sponsor installed in his place.

"I see," said the First Minister, "that your ruse may have worked. Let us hope all turns out well for us and not so well for Jabir and his family." The First Minister was more sober in his speech and less certain of the outcome of the night's work. "We shall see how many funerals shall be arranged on the morrow. That," he said emphatically, "is how your business will be decided.

"Over the years, my friend," Abdul al-Warith continued, "what appears to have happened is not always so. If we are too confident, danger and death will be lavished on us. The wrath of the Caliph is unknown to many, but I have seen it. And it is not a pleasant experience, let me assure you, my friend. If you are caught, the Caliph will see to it that you die unpleasantly and in such pain that you plead for the peace of death."

The beggar frowned and stood silent, rooted to the spot. It was the worried expression of a man staring at his executioner as he awaited the verdict of death. "At this time," he said convincingly, "or before the night grows much older, all of those present in the House of Jabir will be dead, and the three men running back to the house will join the remainder of the family!"

The First Minister reserved judgment until the deed was done and the body count was official.

* * *

CHAPTER 35

After Alric had left with Ahmed and Khalil, Bemia inspected the house to ensure that all was in order—doors locked and windows bordered up. Khalil had made sure that Wahid and Ma'ruf saw to the security of the house. However, Bemia was still concerned. The trees and bushes that grew close together in the wonderful gardens surrounding the house were ideal hiding places for intruders. The wall that surrounded the garden offered some protection, but a professional assassin would see the wall as only a minor obstacle. The walkways through the garden were well lit, but if the lights were extinguished by intruders, they could remain unseen in the darkness.

There were no guards outside, and Bemia was feeling irritated and restless as she paced the floor of the lobby near the front entrance. In a fleeting moment, she almost yielded to the temptation to make the rounds of the garden, but something seemed to be holding her back. Back and forth she paced; from the lobby into the breakfast room, into the lounge, then through the dining area and the kitchen, with her swords strapped to her body and ready for action.

"Bemia," Amira gently called.

"I am sorry, mother. I feel on edge knowing that something could happen."

Amira took Bemia into her arms. "Whatever happens, my dear, will happen. Now, how about a nice cup of tea?"

Bemia smiled. "Mother, you are priceless. A cup of tea does not cure everything, but that would be nice."

Wahid, who was nearby, immediately retired to the kitchen to make the tea.

Bemia could hear the wind as it began to pick up. It could bring dust from the desert to the north or heat from the south, and there were other sounds coming from the garden which caused her to be suspicious. She signaled to Amira to extinguish the candles.

"Maha," Amira called gently, and the young woman appeared from behind the curtains. "Make sure all of the candles in the house are extinguished. Also, see that the other servants are watchful, and then advise Wahid and Ma'ruf to attend me with Abal and Buhjah."

Maha nodded, and within minutes the only light visible was the moonlight that reflected from the interior walls. A resounding clatter alerted Bemia that intruders had indeed entered the garden and would soon be at the house. She blinked as her eyes became accustomed to the dim light.

"Mother," Bemia whispered, "is all well with you?"

"Yes, my dear." Amira was alert.

Ever since she had agreed to defend Amira and the home, Bemia knew that it would come to this. There had to be a reckoning and now was the time. She did not know how this would end, but she would give an account of herself that the intruders would not forget. She wished Alric were near, but it was not to be.

"Mother, stay here where I know I can find you," Bemia commanded. She did not wish Amira to become embroiled in any ensuing fight and be taken hostage.

"Yes dear." Bemia heard her mother's soft response.

There was a strong kick on the door, and Bemia braced herself for what was to follow. She exhaled to release her pent-up breath. In the shadows she could see Amira crouching in an alcove near one of the pillars that supported the ceiling of the lobby. A man was next to her. Bemia recognized Wahid. He had a knife in his hand and a long-handled large iron pot used for cooking meat!

Bemia looked at the pot; it was strong enough to lay a man low. She saw another man: Ma'ruf. He had a short sword in his hand. Also, she noticed Abal, Buhjah, and Maha in the dimness crouching so that they protected Amira. They also had long-handled iron pots in their hands. She had an army of pot carriers! Dear God," Bemia thought, do none of these girls know how to use a knife?

"Wahid, Ma'ruf," Bemia whispered. "Protect mother at all costs."

She heard the two men chorus, "To the death, my lady," as a loud noise told her that the door had finally given way to the incessant battering it had been taking over the past few minutes and collapsed into the lobby.

With a shout of triumph, the first man came through the door, and others followed, bursting into the entrance. Bemia tried to count the figures and noted, "There must be six men . . . no, eight," she added as two more entered.

The first intruder stopped. Bemia stood before him, and in the dim light, the pale blue color of her dress made her seem like an apparition. She had slit her dress from thigh to hem for ease of movement. Her long legs showed through the slit tantalizingly as she moved toward the intruders; their eyes focused on her.

The first man, who appeared to be the leader; licked his lips. "Ah, my lady," he said self-assuredly, "it seems that I will have to teach you a lesson. You will make a fine plaything for me and my men before we are through with you." His eyes opened wide in disbelief as one of Bemia's swords, appearing magically from the folds of her dress, entered his chest and sliced through his heart. He did not even have time to react and fell to the floor, his life ended.

His companions were taken aback. Their man had fallen because he had been careless with the woman. Bemia moved and placed herself between two entry pillars. These were the fronts of several pairs of pillars that supported the roof and formed the interior decorative colonnade. She remembered a story Alric had told her about *Horatio and the Bridge* that described how an ancient Roman had held an enemy army at bay by taking a position at the entry to a narrow bridge where his enemies could not attack from the side or the rear or use their superior numbers. To enter Rome, they had to fight Horatio one at a time until he was killed.

She waved her sword in a mock salute. "Well, vermin," she said, "it seems we have an impasse." Another man moved forward, half-turned, and smiled at his companions. He would take revenge for the death of his companion. Bemia drew her second sword and attacked. The man suffered the same death-dealing wound as the first.

"Now you are six," she said tauntingly, hoping to anger the men so much that they would do something foolish. They did not realize there were others hiding in the alcoves behind Bemia, and they would have to get past her to reach Amira, Wahid, Ma'ruf, and the three girls.

At that moment, the moon came out of hiding from behind a cloud and shone its beams through a high window. The rays of light illuminated her body, causing it to shimmer beneath the delicate fabric of her dress. The next attacker stood open-mouthed as he gazed at the incredible sight before him. His moment of hesitation was a fatal mistake. Bemia lunged, and before he could react, he died as had his two henchmen. Bemia answered softly, "Now you are five."

"This woman is a menace," one of the men growled. "Deal with her."

The next man stared at Bemia through menacing and lustful eyes. "A cut here and there to disable her," he said, "and then we shall have sport before she finally dies."

Bemia stared back, not moving one iota from her defensive position. The man looked dirty and unkempt, a result of a harsh life spent in the streets of Baghdad. The three men she had cut down were pitiful swordsmen, but this one was different, and she suspected that his comrades might also be the same. Perhaps the three dead men were merely sword fodder to lull an opponent into a sense of false confidence. She decided to wait and not make the first move. She had the defensive position.

"What am I to do with you?" the man snarled. He was aware that his colleagues were moving into an attacking position, to overcome her by sheer weight of numbers.

In the narrow confines between the pillars, Bemia knew that they could still only fight one on one—they could do no other in the narrow space. She would continue to fight each man in turn, and protect her family.

The man attempted to lunge at her and close the gap, but a slashing cut to his arm made him withdraw. The next opponent had seen three of his companions fall to Bemia's sword, and another now was wounded.

Bemia's short swords were in continual motion as she parried the man's thrusts. His longer sword was a disadvantage for swinging in the narrow space, but it had the advantage as a thrusting weapon. Bemia attempted to make an opening that would allow her to gain contact with the man's body, but he was more cautious.

The others watched with intent from their vantage point. Then, quickly, the attacker backed away and a colleague took his place. Bemia now had fresh arms to deal with, and her own arms were now feeling the weight of her weapons.

She noticed when she parried his blade to his right that he stepped back and then quickly forward, seeking to gain an advantage from his move. As he stepped forward, she had been stationary, giving him a moment to recover. She diverted the sword to the left and he moved forward again. She then blocked the blade to the right, and as he stepped back, she moved forward, closing the gap between them. Without realizing what she had done, the man lunged. He gasped his last breath as he realized his error. Bemia grimaced as she quickly thrust her sword into his throat. His blood splashed across her robes.

The floor was now littered with four bodies, which were sprawled in various attitudes of death. Bemia retreated to the next pair of pillars, not wishing to trip over a body or slip in the pool of blood that was spreading across the floor. If she retreated any further, she would be too close to the place where Amira, the girls, Wahid, and Ma'ruf were concealed. She had to protect them. That had been her oath to Jabir. Now that four of the men were dispatched, she felt better, but she was starting to tire from the constant attacking. She sensed that the remaining attackers would realize this.

The next man stepped forward, almost slipping on the blood but managed to right himself at the last moment. "Now, blonde one," he said. "Prepare yourself for a lesson in the mastery of the sword."

He suddenly thrust his blade at Bemia. She was not quick enough to move, her legs weakened from the effort of constant fighting. His blade pierced her dress and the sword blade ran across her body at the point where the rib cage ends. It passed across her flesh like a red-hot iron, causing a deep surface wound from which blood flowed freely.

"Now, he smiled, "I have really spoiled your dress."

Bemia staggered backward, blinded by the pain. The man smiled, but as Bemia moved back, he realized his blade was entangled in the folds of her dress. She turned her body so that the blade could not be extracted from the fabric without a supreme effort by her opponent. As she moved, the man's hand slipped from the sword hilt; he was disarmed.

"Well," he said with glee, "there are other ways to kill a cat," and he reached for his dagger.

Bemia mustered all her strength to wield her weapons.

A flash of red hair shot before her eyes as Ma'ruf took the sword from her hands. Seeing Bemia's plight, he had emerged from his place of concealment.

"So you like to fight women!" he said. "Now, sons of camels, see how you like to fight me!"

Bemia's opponent had not moved but stood in shock and surprise as Ma'ruf calmly stepped up and cut his throat.

"And now, since the lady needs to catch her breath, you can amuse yourselves with me. Who is next?" Ma'ruf exclaimed. "My lady?"

Ma'ruf signaled to Amira that she should look to Bemia. But Amira had already left her place of concealment and was tending to Bemia's wound. "She will be well, Ma'ruf."

Ma'ruf, being of Celtic birth, knew from childhood how to handle weapons. The short swords continued to flash in the dim light, and the man with the wounded arm joined his companions on the floor.

Ma'ruf felt a motion at his side. "I stand with you, Ma'ruf." It was Wahid. He had retrieved the sword from the folds of Bemia's dress and was now willing to use it.

"There are two, Wahid," Ma'ruf spoke the obvious. "I suggest we go one on one!"

The two remaining assassins looked at Rufus and then at Wahid. The first one stepped forward, only to be stopped by Wahid's premature thrust of the long sword. It was a dangerous maneuver, but it did its job, as the intruder stepped back, allowing an opening for Ma'ruf to attack.

As the man's feet touched the slippery floor, he stumbled but managed to keep his balance. He snarled at Ma'ruf and, with a vicious thrust of his sword, knocked one of his swords to the floor. His blood boiling from exertion, he battled on. He would quickly dispatch the red-haired one and then the old one. He looked at his only able companion.

He had seen the others fall one by one. The cries of his men as death had taken them into his arms were ringing in his ears.

Then Bemia's voice rang out in the tortured air. "Ma'ruf! Wahid! They are mine. I will finish them. Please see to mother and the girls." Ma'ruf and Wahid started to protest but were cut short by Bemia.

The assassin's eyes narrowed as he saw a shock of blonde hair and the flash of blue as Bemia stepped forward once more. "And now," she said, her hands holding her two swords once more, "there is business to be settled between us."

Bemia attacked the man with a fury she did not realize was pent up within her body. The pain of her wound and the sworn oath to protect her mother and family had unleashed a frenzied outpouring of anger and violence that could only be dealt with through sheer physical exertion. She was focused on parrying, cutting, and thrusting in rapid succession. She did not even sense the effort she was making.

She had steeled herself lest her pain interfere with her fighting abilities. She fought with a ferocity she had never imagined and showed little emotion. She was automatic, cold, and calculating. She took care not to slip on the blood, at times standing still, her face devoid of expression, staring at her opponents. She could sense the rapid beating of her heart.

She pivoted slowly on the balls of her feet, positioning herself to her best advantage. She faced the next man and knew by the look in his eyes that she had made an impression. She realized that the two remaining killers would not fall for any of her tricks. She had to overcome these enemies by sheer fighting skill.

The blows and thrusts from the man's sword came fast and furious, and even though Bemia was ready and knew the restricted space hampered his movements, she realized that if she relaxed for a second, he would kill her. He ducked and dodged and blocked, avoiding her blows. They fought without exchanging words for what seemed like an eternity, until, panting, they broke apart. Bemia stared at him, trying to catch her breath.

The man held his hands out, wide apart, trying to appear nonchalant. Then he suddenly took up the fight again, knocking one of the swords from her hand. He took a risk and lunged at her heart, but the sword tip was not close enough to draw blood. He had underestimated the distance between himself and Bemia. And now he was extended beyond his own self-control. Using a two-handed hold on her remaining sword, she parried his sword violently so that it fell from his hand onto the floor with a clatter.

He saw her fingers tighten around her own sword. He closed his eyes and stiffened, waiting for it to plunge into his heart. He was willing to make the final sacrifice. He then made one last effort and attempted to escape but slipped on the blood-covered floor. As he fell, he saw Bemia, as if in slow motion, raise her sword. His primal scream filled the room as the sword entered his body. He could no longer breathe and darkness overtook him.

The remaining intruder was struck by Bemia's abilities, but now she had only one sword, a short weapon. The man wiped his mouth with his sleeve. He had made a decision. He bowed and gripped his sword.

"I see that you have made your choice," she said. "So be it."

The man brushed his forehead and glared at the woman who had dared to stand against them. He was filled with rage. Bemia decided that she needed this man alive. He may have had knowledge of the one who'd sent them on this mission of murder.

The next moments were longer and fiercer than at any other time. Bemia was ruthless and without compassion. Amira thought she had seen Bemia at her worst, or most savage, when she had dispatched the other intruders, but that did not compare with what she witnessed next, as Bemia fought the last man.

Every muscle and fiber in her body was tensed and ready. Her eyes were wide with anticipation, the blood lust flowing through her veins. The renewed energy was running through her body. She was wounded but still had passion and power. Any opponent could not help but admire her.

She thought about the events of the past hour and breathed a silent prayer. "In that hour, I thank the Saxon gods that I did not fail and fall to these men. You too, Lord Allah, whatever your name is, I ask you one thing. Please protect my husband so that he shall not befall the same fate as I."

If she was to fall, as long as she could breathe, she had made up her mind that her concealed dagger would take care of any lustful ideas that may befall her. Her side, where she took the thrust from a sword, seemed to have stopped bleeding, but through the warm stickiness she could not tell. She knew she had lost a lot of blood. If she survived, she would have to deal with the discomfort that would come with the stitching of a wound. Her beloved Alric would tend to her.

The last man came at her in a sudden rush. Bemia quickly knocked his thrusting sword aside with a strength that surprised the man. She fought with renewed vigor and opened several deep cuts on his arms and torso, but none were sufficient to take his life. If she could sustain herself, his wounds would weaken him, and then she would have him! Blood spattered everywhere. Bemia could not tell who it came from most of the time. He closed the space between them trying to gain advantage from his size and weight, but he had underestimated her height. She raised herself from her crouching stance to her full height. The man's eyes opened wide just before she struck him in the face with the hilt of her sword. She heard the sounds of bones breaking as his nose flattened against his face.

The man stepped back, but she showed no mercy. The words she uttered were Saxon. In her passion, she spoke her natural tongue. She no longer had to watch her back. The man was weakening. Blood covered his sleeves and chest. He had not been able to touch Bemia. She had protected herself well, but her wound had opened and her blood was flowing again.

Then, as if in answer to her pain, she felt a numbness spread over her body that took away the pain. Her eyes went out of focus and she fell to her knees. The man could not believe his good fortune. His opponent, the tall blonde savage who spoke in a strange tongue, was on her knees with her neck bared and ready for his sword.

He stumbled forward, still feeling his own weakness from the wounds he had sustained. "This," he said, "will more than make up for my wounds and pain."

Bemia leaned on her sword for support, point to the ground, the hilt clenched between her two hands. She was not about to yield. She looked at him as she struggled to her feet. The man looked surprised. "And so, son of a camel," she spoke in Arabic, "you thought that you had me!"

The man, sensing victory was within his grasp, was about to make one last supreme effort. By this time, Ma'ruf, who had continued to follow the fight blow by blow and knowing that Bemia was weakening rapidly, made his way around the room and, suddenly rising from the shadows behind the man, wrapped his strong arm around the man's neck and plunged his knife upward into the man's back and into his heart.

The pain that had engulfed Bemia's body was gone and numbness overtook her, engulfing her body, threatening to take her into the arms of death.

This was her last thought as her limbs, tired from the fight and weak from loss of blood, would no longer support her. She looked at Ma'ruf and she could see the horror in his eyes. By instinct she spoke in Saxon, a language that Ma'ruf understood. "*Ic wes mid hire fan biset al abuten . . .* " "I was besieged by foes on all sides. Please tell my dear Alric I fought well," she mumbled as she sank to the floor.

Ma'ruf whispered "I will, my lady."

He cradled her head in his arms, the tears running down his cheeks, begging her not to die as he yelled for Amira and Wahid.

* * *

CHAPTER 36

Alric, Ahmed, and Khalil rushed into the house to see Bemia lying on the floor, her head cradled in Ma'ruf's arms as Amira and Wahid moved to help her. Their eyes quickly took in the carnage.

Alric surveyed the body-strewn floor. Weapons and blood were everywhere. The tiled floor, shining and vibrant earlier in the day, was now littered with bodies that lay in the various twisted agonies of death by the sword. He had not seen so much death and destruction since he had searched the bodies left by the sea raiders. It brought back tragic memories he had tried to erase from his mind.

Ma'ruf kneeled on the floor between the two pillars, supporting Bemia. She was still, her two swords lying on the floor close by. Ma'ruf moved aside to allow Amira access to Bemia. Alric looked closer, wondering if it really was Bemia covered in blood, but there was no mistaking her blonde hair.

"She fought well, Alric," Ma'ruf said quietly. "Her last words to me were . . . " and he repeated Bemia's words in Saxon to Alric. "She thought of you up to the last."

"But," Amira interjected, "Ma'ruf is not telling you the whole story; he stepped in at the last moment and prevented Bemia from being killed by the last assassin!"

Alric nodded thankfully to Ma'ruf as Khalil approached and put his arm on Alric's shoulder. Alric then moved close to where Amira sat with Bemia.

"All is not lost, Alric," Amira said with purpose. "Your dear wife, my beloved daughter, has life. She breathes, very slowly and shallow, but she breathes."

Alric closed his eyes, looked at the ceiling, and gave thanks to God. "Ma'ruf," Khalil commanded, "find father. He will be at the palace. And be careful. There may be others . . . "

Ma'ruf left at a run. Within a half hour, he returned with an eight-man troop of soldiers commanded by Bashir. They were followed by a further twenty soldiers, even more heavily armed than the first group. They immediately took up defensive positions around the house and garden.

* * *

After surveying the scene, Alric heard a rasping sound. Ahmed heard it too and began to move among the bodies of the assassins, nudging each one with his boot. "This one still breathes," Ahmed said as he stirred one of the bodies with the tip of his sword.

Alric moved quickly to inspect the wounded man. Without further thought, he raised his sword to strike the fatal blow against Bemia's still-living opponent, but Khalil prevented this action.

"Stand firm and stay your hand, brother! "Khalil commanded. "While he lives, we have use of him. Tend to your wife while Ahmed and I see to this one."

Alric lowered his sword, laid it against a pillar, and removed the belt and scabbard from under his robe. He knelt next to Amira listening to Bemia's breathing, praying that there would be no further deterioration in her already critical condition.

"Mother," he sobbed "do you . . . ?" He was unable to finish the question, being consumed with emotion.

Amira placed her free hand on his arm. "We cannot know until father returns and gives us an opinion of her condition. She seems to have one very serious wound and has lost much blood. Only Allah knows the answer to your question, my son."

Amira looked around to see Abal, Buhjah, and Maha hovering close by, awaiting her instructions. "Girls," Amira said, and they stepped forward, taking in the devastation before them, "food and drink for the soldiers."

As they left to carry out Amira's bidding, Khalil and Ahmed began the task of moving the bodies outside while Wahid began to clean the floor. He had made some headway with this gruesome task when Jabir burst through the door. He had been brought in a litter surrounded by heavily armed soldiers. Once Jabir was inside the house, the remaining soldiers joined the others in the garden.

Jabir commanded Ma'ruf to bring his instruments and medications. He looked at Khalil and Ahmed, who, having removed the last of the bodies, checked the windows to make sure all was well.

"My sons, are you all right?"

"Yes, father," they answered individually.

Then Jabir asked, "Where is my daughter?"

Hearing his voice, Amira called out from near one of the pillars. "Here, my dear."

Jabir rushed to the spot quickly as Ma'ruf returned with Jabir's medical bag. "Let me get to work. Alric, my son, I need space to work." He looked at Ma'ruf. "Ma'ruf, I hear that you saved my daughter's life. For that I thank you. Now assist Ahmed to bar the windows and cover them with heavy curtains. Amira, have the girls stop whatever they are doing and bring me water and cloth for bandages."

Jabir felt the urgency to tend to Bemia, and time was of the essence if he was to save her life. He looked around and spoke to Alric. "My son, I realize that this will be difficult for you, but go with Wahid and see what can be done in the kitchen to provide for the guards. We will need plenty of water. I need your mother and the girls here.

"Khalil," he looked at his son, "a little privacy please, for Bemia." As an afterthought he added as he saw Alric, who still hovered close by, "Please take Alric with you to the kitchen, even if you have to carry him!"

Now that he was alone with Amira, he looked closely at Bemia. She was pale, barely breathing, and her thin dress was covered with the blood that had drained from the wound. "I cannot hold out much hope," Jabir whispered to Amira. "But I will do everything I can. After that, her life is in Allah's hands."

Amira put her hand on Jabir's shoulder as he knelt over and looked at Bemia. "Do what you can, my love."

"Amira, a surgical knife, please."

She handed him the sharp instrument from his medical bag. Jabir then gently tore the dress to expose the wound. "Abal, a cloth."

He wiped away the congealed blood with the soft cloth. "Ah," he said, as though satisfied, "I see it." He carefully examined the place where the sword had cut into Bemia and done its work. "I sense my dear," he looked at Amira as he spoke, "that it may not be as bad as I thought. This looks to me," he said as he bent over and inspected the wound more carefully, "that the sword cut a large gash in the surface rather than damaging the subsurface of her body. However, the weapon has done a lot of damage to the tissue and she has lost much blood, and that is the matter at hand. I will clean the wound and then she must rest so that she can regenerate."

He allowed his fingers to explore the wound. "It is deep," Jabir observed. "Abal, bring several pieces of cloth and warm water in a dish. Buhjah and Maha, bring a mattress." He wiped away the blood that surrounded the wound and cleaned the edges where the skin had curled back. "It seems the bleeding has stopped."

He looked at Buhjah and Maha. "As I lift her gently, ease the dress from under her body. Abal, apply gentle pressure on the wound using a piece of clean linen. Then, Buhjah and Maha, you will ease the soft mattress under her so that she is not lying on a hard surface."

Bemia lay naked on the mattress, the ghastly wound now exposed. "Maha, fetch two bedsheets that we can use as covers. My dear," he looked at Amira, "help me further clean the wound and also check her body for any other wounds she may have, although I am sure this one is the only serious one."

Jabir peered at the gash in Bemia's skin. "We will also make sure," he said, "that a broken sword tip does not lurk inside the wound." Jabir bent over and placed his ear next to Bemia's mouth. His face changed from concern to mild relief. "She breathes," he said. "Slowly and gently."

"Now my dear," he looked at Amira, "you and I will go about the business of saving our daughter."

An hour later, they were satisfied at having done all they could to tend Bemia's wound. They had found no evidence of any others. They made sure that Buhjah and Maha cleansed Bemia to remove all evidence of the blood—her own and that of her opponents. As they did this, Amira related to Jabir the details of the events which had led to this situation.

"I believe," Jabir looked carefully at Bemia, "that if we keep the wound clean and watch her carefully, our warrior princess will have a chance of recovering."

Amira turned to the three girls. "Cover her with the bed linen and leave us for a few moments." Then she added, "And see to it that our sons are fed. Assist Ma'ruf and Wahid wherever they need you."

Once they were out of the room, Amira laid her head on Jabir's shoulder and wept. Minutes later, the terror of the evening was swept away in Amira's tears. She stroked her husband's gray hair. "Thank you," she said.

Jabir smiled. "You are very welcome, my dear. Now dry your tears, as I believe that we have three sons who, I suspect, are bursting to know what we have done. Also," he looked at Bemia, "we cannot leave her here." He paused. "I have it. Remain here." Moments later, Jabir returned with Alric, Khalil, and Ahmed in tow. Ahmed carried a large wooden board. Amira sensed that something else had transpired.

"Mother," Khalil said, recognizing the look on Amira's face. "We have had a chat with our surviving friend. Unfortunately he has decided to leave this life, but not before he gave us the information we required. I will add that our brother Alric has a masterful touch when it comes to asking questions. Some of those medicinal extracts he has made in the laboratory certainly can loosen the tongue!"

Amira grimaced and then smiled. "*Insha'allah*. As God wills it."

"If we can return to the situation at hand," Jabir interjected. "Lay the board next to her, as close as you can. That's it," he said as he watched. "Now we need to ease her onto the board very carefully, since we must not start the bleeding again." He looked at Alric. "Alric you take her shoulders. Khalil, ease your arms under her waist. Ahmed, support her behind the knees. Now on my command gently move her with as little movement of her body as possible onto the board. Amira, my dear," Jabir looked at his wife with tenderness, "stop fussing for a moment. We will have her in the bedroom soon enough." Once she was laid gently onto the bed, Jabir and the family withdrew to give Alric a moment of privacy with Bemia.

He stared down at her. She continued to breathe softly as Alric's fingers gently moved through her hair. He allowed his hand to wander to her cheek. She didn't stir but continued to sleep, her chest rising and falling, her lips partly opened, allowing an occasional sigh.

"My love," he said, "I will have my vengeance on whoever did this to you." He sliced his dagger across his palm, allowing the blood to seep from the cut. "I swear that to you on my blood."

* * *

Alric continued his vigil, refusing to leave Bemia's bedside. He sat through the dark nights, holding her hand, giving her comfort from his touch, and talking in soothing tones so that she would know he was there. Each morning, the rosy cheeks of dawn graced the sky before Alric would allow his eyes to close. He slept at the bedside for a few hours during the day, and apart from the necessary bathing and eating, he would not leave Bemia.

On several occasions, Khalil offered to take Alric's place, but he knew what the answer would be. "Khalil, my brother," Alric responded to the offer, "you can understand that I cannot leave my wife. I would prefer that you find the man who planned this, and when Bemia is awake and well, we can seek our vengeance. I have sworn to her that I will have my vengeance. I will find the man who is responsible for the attack on this house and on my dear wife. He will pay. And then I will deal with the First Minister, who we know is behind all of this. But, for the moment, Khalil, one step at a time."

Khalil squeezed Alric's shoulder affectionately. Ahmed, standing in the background, nodded in agreement. Amira made sure that Alric had an ample supply of food and drink for the night; bread, fruit, and sweetmeats. Wahid and Ma'ruf periodically checked to make sure that all was well.

Five days had passed since Bemia was wounded, but night and day had no meaning for Alric, since he had refused to leave her side. She moved in and out of her dream state, sometimes speaking in the Saxon tongue, and other times just moaning. Alric watched her body rise and fall as she breathed. His heart pounded with each breath she took.

He kissed her forehead gently. His memory strayed to the time when they had talked about the future, the possibility of a family. He frowned. Jabir had told him that Bemia had lost a lot of blood, she was weak, and the danger of infection to the wound was ever-present.

"Bemia's recovery, my son," Jabir had said, "is in the hands of Allah. It will take time, but she will recover." He was proud of her. She was a wife any man would hold dear.

She stirred, then continued to breathe slowly and evenly, as if nothing had disturbed her. Carefully he took her hand and held it. She looked so peaceful and serene.

* * *

The next morning, when Alric was bathed and dressed, Khalil quietly announced that Ahmed had a man under observation. "Ahmed thinks this man is a likely candidate behind the plot and may even be the beggar that led us away from the house at that crucial time."

Alric raised his eyebrows and Khalil continued. "Early this morning, Ahmed spotted him in a quiet corner of the marketplace. He is currently watching him while I find two of our best men to help observe. We will find out who he is and the places he frequents."

For the first time since he had seen Bemia lying wounded on the floor, Alric allowed himself a brief smile. The past night had been uneventful, as she continued her sleep. On occasion, Alric could hear the muffled sounds of the soldiers guarding the house. They had sealed the house well. No one could enter or leave without Bashir or one of his men knowing about it.

Abal, Buhjah, and Maha enjoyed taking meals to the soldiers. The attention that the young women received was welcomed. There was only one occasion when Amira had to give them a minor reprimand because of the noise of their laughter.

* * *

One night when Alric could not keep his eyes open any longer but had slept deeply before the dawn, he awoke to see the rosy hue in Bemia's cheeks. He continued his vigil as the sun slowly made its way into the sky. He sat contentedly looking at her. He refused to eat lunch, sensing that something was about to happen. As he reached out and touched her hair, she opened her eyes, looked at him, and smiled. The smile took his breath away.

"If this is heaven, my love," she said, "I am happy to be with you but sorry that you died too."

"You are not dead, my dearest. Father and mother saved your life. They cleaned and stitched the wound and you have slept since then."

"Is it morning? What time . . . ?" She left the question unfinished.

"Afternoon," he smiled. "It is early afternoon of the sixth day since you held those men at bay." He grinned at her, his blue eyes focusing on her own. Bemia yawned and smiled. "Your opponents are all dead. One survived for a short time after our return and then died, but not before Khalil, Ahmed, and I talked with him."

She made the effort to sit up. "No," Alric continued, "do not get up. You are still weak. And bedsides, you are naked! Moreover, Khalil and Ahmed are waiting to see you."

She peered below her bed covers.

"Then who . . . ?"

"Mother and father took command of you as soon as they could. Khalil, Ahmed, and I took care of your opponent." Alric paused thoughtfully. "He had an amazing voice when encouraged to talk." Alric lifted the bed cover and looked underneath. "Yes, indeed," he smiled. "You have no clothes on!"

If she could have stood the pain, Bemia would have laughed out loud. "Alric, I will see to you when I am feeling well."

"Promises, my love. Promises!" He smiled and helped her to position herself comfortably on the pillow.

"Well, if my brothers wish to see me, I am ready."

* * *

At Alric's invitation, Khalil and Ahmed entered the room, full of energy and with a vibrancy Alric had not seen since they had rescued him from the sea raiders. Without hesitation, they walked to the bed where Bemia lay, ignoring Alric as if he were not present.

"Well, sister," Khalil beamed, as did Ahmed, "you are looking much better than when we last saw you. How do you feel?"

"I ache and feel weak, but seeing the two of you," Bemia smiled at them, "I now feel much better."

They both turned, finally giving Alric attention, and sat on the cushions close by the bed. "When we returned from our fruitless chase, your husband was as angry as I have ever seen him. He does you credit, Bemia. Your living opponent was about to be dispatched by Alric's sword when we stayed his hand. We now have no doubt the First Minister is behind this, and we also have information from our late lamented friend."

"What is more, we now know where to find the assassin!" Ahmed exclaimed.

"And so," Bemia deduced, "your next plan is to waylay this assassin and find out more information from him. He will, most likely, have been hired directly by the First Minister. Once you hear him admit to this, the chain will be complete, all of the links in place."

Khalil, Ahmed, and Alric nodded enthusiastically. "But, my dear," Alric said as he read the look in her eyes, "you will not be part of this. Father and mother are adamant. Also, father is concerned that if your wound opens again, he may not be able to protect you from infection." Bemia's look of disappointment was obvious.

Khalil rose up from his cushion and took Bemia's hand in his. "Ma'ruf," he said gently, "told us that you fought well and saved mother and the others. For that," he looked at Ahmed and Alric, "we are eternally grateful. Now I suggest that the three of us adjourn from here and leave you in the capable hands of our mother. Resting is most important to your healing, and we," he looked once more at Ahmed and Alric, "have much to discuss." Khalil leaned over and kissed her cheek, followed by Ahmed.

Bemia felt that she would like to face the man who was responsible for the attack but realized the wisdom of Khalil's words. She felt anxious not knowing the status of their efforts against the assassin and the First Minister. Alric looked at Bemia and seemed to be reading her mind. "We will, of course, keep you informed about what we do."

She smiled at her husband. "I should not have expected to be with you. I will concentrate on recovering my strength so that I can be of use here in the house. I am not sure if I could lift a sword, let alone use it for fighting." She smiled at the three men. "Please tell mother that I will sleep now."

She closed her eyes and was soon asleep. Alric kissed her on the forehead and left the room following Khalil and Ahmed. "We do indeed," he thought, "have much to discuss."

* * *

Alric looked with satisfaction at the neat row of jars lining the wooden shelf on the wall of the laboratory. His worst pain was gone now. Bemia's wound was healing, showing that her body was not succumbing to infection. He needed to be busy to take his mind off that vicious night and focus on finding the assassin.

Khalil and Ahmed had taken to the streets and were seeking the man. The attack, everyone realized, had been a planned and coordinated effort. The failure had been the reliability and fighting skills of the eight men sent to do the deed. Under the usual circumstances, they would have succeeded, but when Bemia had blocked the way for entry into the main area of the house, their plan had failed. Obviously, the mastermind behind the attack would know by now that something was amiss. His hirelings had not returned.

Khalil had reasoned that the plotter would be curious but displeased that his plan may have gone astray. He warned Alric and Ahmed that the man may decide to take risks. His pay would depend upon success, and if it failed, he would need to seek other ways of recouping his money. He may even venture out onto the streets himself.

*   *   *

Alric continued to examine the shelves of the laboratory. He would find solace and comfort with his extracts and mixtures.

As the days passed, Bemia's strength returned, and the healing of the wound showed remarkable progress. The ointments and salves provided by Jabir and applied by Amira were working. Alric spent his days between visits to Bemia and conferences with Jabir, Khalil, and Ahmed.

He had a plan for dealing with future attacks but, he explained to his father and two brothers, "we should now take the attack to them where they live!"

Alric noted that he was almost out of clay, as he surveyed the jars on the shelves. "But there is enough for another mixture." He paused to check the other containers on the shelves and to make sure that all of the extracts and chemicals were in good supply. On occasion, he stopped to make a note in his book, which was turning out to be quite a work in progress. He was well into his second thick volume, and he knew that soon he would require a third one.

Suddenly he had an idea. He took two jars from the shelf, mixed two of the extracts, and watched as the liquids merged into one. The light yellow color, which he had seen when he had first mixed these same extracts that caused the explosion and fire, was still evident. The odor gave it away. He carefully placed the jar on the bench and added the remaining clay to diminish the potential of an explosion. He stoppered the jar and placed it on a lower shelf that benefited from the coolness of the floor.

He felt that the laboratory held the answer to his search for the planner of the attack. He took a closer look at the jar containing his recently prepared mixture. The clay would prevent any mishaps, and he knew what he needed to do to cause fire and an explosion. He stepped out of the laboratory and looked at the sky. The sun was beginning to sink behind the wall that surrounded the garden. He could not see the soldiers, for they were placed inconspicuously behind the luxurious foliage of the grounds. His heart pounded, and he felt a sudden flush. This whole matter, one way or the other, would be brought to a head soon.

As he stood in the garden, the sun finally sank behind the wall. In an hour or so the moon would rise, bringing its pale light to the streets and back alleys of the city. He had watched this scene many times as Bemia fought to recover. Thank God she was well on the way to good health. But now, it was his time for action.

He bit his lip. The memory of seeing Bemia that night still pained him. He tried to push the scene into the back of his mind, but it was difficult to erase. At first, he had felt a mad urge to seek vengeance, but the cooler heads of Khalil and Ahmed had prevailed, and he had heeded their wise counsel.

* * *

Later, unable to sleep, Jabir, Khalil, Ahmed, and Alric sat quietly drinking tea as they discussed once more the attack on the house and the role of the First Minister in this plot.

"It seems to me, and I am sure that you are aware of this, father," Khalil finally said, "that we need something more definitive to take to my cousin," referring to the Caliph, Harun al Rashid. "Unless we do that, this becomes a he-said-he-said situation, and I am sure the First

Minister can assemble enough support to deny any such claims that we are inclined to make."

"That is the situation as I also see it," Jabir replied to his son's comment. "I am not going to request that the First Minister be charged as a result of tonight's deeds, but as soon as it becomes evident that charges have been made against him, the First Minister will be on his guard and it will be more difficult, perhaps impossible, to gather the necessary evidence."

Jabir stroked his chin with his thumb and forefinger, then looked at Ahmed. "By the way, Ahmed, how are your observations proceeding?"

"Quite well, father," Ahmed replied. "With the help of some of my men, who work very well under cover, I have good reason to believe that I have identified the potential assassin. I need a little more time, a day or so, and then we can make plans."

"Excellent!" Jabir exclaimed. "No doubt you will succeed, and then we will act without delay," Jabir concluded.

Ahmed bowed his head in acknowledgment as Jabir added an afterthought. "I have a plan to bring the information before Harun.

"It is a pity we could not bring this to fruition before tonight. But we must remember that Harun needs conclusive proof that the First Minister is the man behind this scheme. We do not have barbarians at the gates, as happened at Rome almost four hundred years ago. We have them within the city gates!"

He paused to sip his tea and munch on a cake. No one spoke, waiting for Jabir to continue. "I suggest that we wait patiently and give ourselves the time to think before following any instincts or plans we formulate."

They all murmured in approval. "Abdul al-Warith is too wily a fox to be trapped easily," Jabir said. "As we seek the assassin, we must occupy the First Minister with other events." Jabir continued, "We know of his greed, his vanity, and his designs on the throne. His pride and caprice could be the cause of his downfall."

"Being a man who is paid for his work," Khalil spoke, "I am sure that the assassin will talk, with the right kind of persuasion!"

"If that should happen," Jabir concluded, "then we will have conclusive information for the Caliph."

Ahmed looked at Alric, who was suddenly alert. "Father," Alric said as a thoughtful smile creased his face, "I may have the answer to both issues."

* * *

CHAPTER 38

"It is well known," Alric began, "that the First Minister, Abdul al-Warith, has wealth. In fact, he has great wealth and commands obedience from many people in this city. With such wealth and power there comes greed!"

Jabir, Khalil, and Ahmed focused on Alric's words as he continued. "It is not unusual for a man such as the First Minister to think himself above everyone. He is well guarded like a caliph and he holds the property of others equally at his disposal. It is therefore my suggestion, before I lay out the details of my idea, that we become proactive and have the First Minister watched day and night, his every movement followed, but not so obviously that we provoke him to further action. I think that he will need a period to recoup his plans, and it is during that time that we can play to his weakness—the greed for more wealth. If we plan meticulously, we can occupy the First Minister's mind and take him away, momentarily from his goal. That will give us the time to recoup."

"What is your idea, Alric?" Jabir asked, wishing to get to the heart of the matter.

"My idea, father," Alric announced, "is that one action would involve a demonstration of *al-khimiya* that would appeal to the First Minister."

Jabir, Khalil, and Ahmed listened intently, their eyes fixed on Alric, waiting for his next words. Alric continued. "I have an idea that should appeal to the First Minister's greed. We can assume that he will, in spite of his wealth, require even more money to carry out the final steps of his campaign to depose the Caliph. I doubt he will risk much of his own capital and, given the chance, would prefer to secure other funds for his nefarious plan. I will hold a genuine demonstration, during which it will appear that gold can be produced from a metal such as lead!"

Alric noticed Jabir looking askance at him, one eyebrow raised, wondering what was coming next.

"No, my dear father, I am not lapsing into charlatanism."

Ahmed started to smile, having a good idea what was coming.

"The First Minister knows who we are," Alric stated as he looked around the room. "But there is one he may not recognize."

The heavy silence was broken by Jabir as he voiced, "Ma'ruf?"

"Yes, father. Ma'ruf!" Alric smiled at Jabir's intuition. "A week ago," Alric continued, "I demonstrated the means by which the metallic color of lead could be changed to resemble gold. Bemia and Ma'ruf were present at the demonstration. Ahmed came to me toward the end of the demonstration, so he has an idea of what this involves."

Alric described in detail the entire process of changing the color of lead to that of gold. He explained how the entire process depended on a number of factors and how sometimes just relying on one product— for instance, a color change—was still fraught with difficulties. He was convinced that Ma'ruf could handle the task but insisted that it was vital for Ma'ruf to be told of the danger involved, since they would be dealing with men who would not hesitate to kill them. Alric stressed that even when there were reports of the apparent lack of activity on the part of the First Minister, this did not mean that he was idle in thought and word.

"You are convinced that Ma'ruf can make the demonstration? Is it so easy to do?" Jabir asked.

"Yes, father, it is. But I need to know that we can be sure the First Minister has not seen Ma'ruf."

Jabir answered, "Yes, I am sure, Alric. Ma'ruf has remained in the house and has never had cause to venture outside. The First Minister has not visited this house, although he does know where we live. However, he has not chosen to grace us with his presence."

Excitement was in the air, and they all wanted to talk at the same time, but as head of the household, it was Jabir who prevailed. "We should not bombard Alric with questions," he said. "Let us start with you, Khalil and Ahmed. What do you both think?"

Khalil nodded at Ahmed to show that he should proceed. "There is risk, as in all ventures," Ahmed said, "but the potential benefits outweigh the risk. I also see cunning in this plan." He looked at Alric. "Well done, my brother.

"Imagine the First Minister thinking he has a lump of gold and then attempting to bribe others or use it to pay soldiers! That, I believe, is treachery and fraud in the eyes of our Caliph."

"And," Khalil, interjected, "that would send waves of anger through my cousin! Harun will have his reason to depose and even imprison the First Minister!"

"Hmm," mused Jabir as he considered the plan from all angles. "It is important that Harun see for himself what the First Minister is doing. This is an important tactic, and we must put our trust in Ma'ruf. He saved Bemia from death, and it was only upon her wishes that he did not take an earlier role in the fight."

"I agree, father," Alric was quick to answer. "When he worked with Bemia and me, he was talkative. He even told us he would like to return home one day. Because of his bravery, he saved Bemia's life. Perhaps we can tell him that after a further period of service, full passage to his home and freedom for the remainder of his life would be the reward?

Even," Alric looked tentatively at Jabir, "with a small pension so that he may live comfortably?"

"Done," Jabir responded without hesitation. No one was shocked at Jabir's immediate agreement to Alric's suggestions.

"Now," Jabir continued, "let us assume that the First Minister takes the bait and will be present to see the remarkable transformation of lead into gold. Have you considered how you will tempt him, Alric?"

"Yes, father," Alric answered quickly. "There is so much at stake and I am counting on al-Warith's greed to be his driving force. I am expecting him to send others, but I am sure that a man such as the First Minister will prefer to be close at hand. He will, after all, want to see the results for himself rather than believe in the word of others!"

Jabir looked thoughtful, then said, "A good point, Alric."

"And then," Alric concluded, "we can keep the First Minister busy for a time as he thinks of the gold while we attempt to discover more details of his future actions." Khalil and Ahmed nodded in agreement.

There, in the quietness of a private family room, the plot was hatched. If it worked, their names would be long remembered. It was most important that they succeed—the consequences did not bear consideration.

After a pause, Jabir asked, "What follows next, Alric?"

"Over the past weeks I have come across an extract of a plant that grows in the garden," he waved his hand in that general direction. "This extract, when administered, has the ability to cause a man to tell the truth without duress or prejudice."

The room was silent.

"But have you experimented with the extract?" Jabir asked.

At that point, Khalil broke into the conversation to answer his father's question.

"Indeed he has, father! I watched Alric administer the extract to the one intruder who remained alive. I believe that although severely wounded, the man was cognizant of his responses and responded without prejudice. He did not seem to have the ability to lie."

"How . . . " Jabir started to ask.

"Excuse me, father," Ahmed interrupted, then looked at Alric. "May I?" Alric nodded and Ahmed continued. "On our first journey across the desert, Alric observed the actions of a scorpion and became interested in the operation of the stinger. So between us, we have prepared a modified scorpion's stinger from a hollow needle so that it can be used conveniently. And through the use of a small reservoir, constructed from sheep's bladder, which is connected to the needle, we can inject the liquid into whatever the needle pierces."

Jabir laughed. "I must tell mother that I am no longer the crafty old man of the house. I am being displaced by my three sons!" Jabir wiped tears of laughter from his eyes and then added, "Please Alric, go on with your discovery."

"So this," Alric said, "is what I plan to do . . . "

* * *

"I need some wool, fairly coarse so that it does not break easily and is also able to soak up liquids," Alric said to Ma'ruf, who immediately left the laboratory. Moments later, he came back proudly proffering the wool, recently purchased from a local shepherd. Alric looked at the ball of wool carefully. "Good," he said, "exactly what I need."

He made sure the wool was rolled tightly and tied so as not to unravel. It could easily be concealed in a pocket and be only just visible when held in a closed hand. He placed the wool into an open flask containing the premixed ingredients, using a stick to stir the contents, not wishing to get the mixture on his hands.

"This," Alric said to Ma'ruf, "will give you an extra piece of insurance. The liquid that I have used is far more explosive than anything I have made before. It is relatively safe to carry, but to detonate the mixture you need to throw the wool violently at the feet of any would-be oppressors. It is guaranteed to cause much harm to the body. I am also placing a clay shell around it to form a vessel with a hole in the top. When the clay dries, it will break when thrown to the ground. Even if the shell survives being cast upon the ground, the mixture will not withstand the shock. It will explode and the main force will initially drive through the hole before the shell itself is destroyed. Do you understand how to throw it for maximum effect against any persons facing you?"

Ma'ruf nodded. Alric continued. "If you do this as soon as the vessel leaves your hand, drop to the ground for your own safety!" Alric was silent as he finished soaking the wool and placed it on the counter to dry. "There is a risk. You understand?"

Ma'ruf nodded again, then added, "To do something good for the people who have given me shelter and treated me well, it is worth it. I am eternally grateful to Lord Jabir and to Lady Amira."

"What is this risk that I hear being talked about so boldly?" Jabir asked as he entered the laboratory and saw the ball of wool.

"Is this another item from the scroll? Or should I say the tablet?" he asked.

"No, father," Alric responded. "I discovered it by accident. I was attempting to bleach wool," he went on, "by another method. It did not work. I had soaked wool in the mixture, and never thinking, I allowed the wool to dry before I threw it onto the rubbish heap near the back gate."

Jabir's eyes opened wide. "So that was the noise and disturbance I heard early the other morning . . . " His words trailed off. Then he added, smiling, "I should have known."

"I usually learn more from my experiments than from books," Alric answered and then bowed his head toward Jabir. "That is, with the exception of your books, father, from which I learn much!"

Jabir smiled, enjoying the recognition from his son.

* * *

During the next two hours, Alric showed Jabir and Ma'ruf how to make more of the explosive devices.

"How did you learn to read?" Jabir asked Ma'ruf when he noticed him looking at the recipe that Alric had written on a piece of vellum.

"In school," he responded.

"Here?" Jabir asked.

"No, when I was a child. Every child in Brittany had the chance to learn. The schools are not all church schools, as you may think. Parents serve time as teachers so that all have the chance to teach their own children as well as others."

"What a wonderful idea," Jabir exclaimed.

Ma'ruf did not answer, feeling too embarrassed at being the sudden focus of their attention. He had been sure that the people of other cultures would never understand, so he had never talked about it.

"And if you can return to Brittany, Ma'ruf?" Jabir asked.

"I will teach the children, whether or not I ever have any of my own."

Jabir caught Alric's eye and nodded. It was time. "Ma'ruf," Jabir began, "this venture that you are undertaking is dangerous. However, this is a time for us to move forward and engage this enemy head-on. Loyalty and the willingness to accept danger will be rewarded." Jabir paused then continued. "When this is done, I grant you the freedom to return to your homeland."

Ma'ruf took deep breath and then mumbled, "Thank you, Lord Jabir."

Jabir smiled. "I am not finished, Ma'ruf. I have also decided to give you a pension so that you may live comfortably, and I will pay for the construction of a schoolhouse that will carry your name, where you can live and teach the children."

Alric was surprised at Jabir's last words. His father was often full of surprises.

"How . . . ?"

Ma'ruf was about to ask, but Jabir cut further into his thoughts. "The Caliph has exchanged delegations with Charlemagne, King of the Franks. My promises to you will be accomplished through our ambassadors."

"Now," Jabir announced, "I will leave you to your devices. May Allah protect both of you."

* * *

The day was dawning, but Alric had been awake for some hours. The excitement in him was growing, and yet at the same time he felt uneasy. Nothing could go wrong. He was consumed by what they had to do. The planning had taken seemingly endless hours between sunrise and dusk during the past week.

He knew that their future depended on this day. He longed for the time when he could return to the laboratory and the joys of *al-khimiya.*

Alric had experienced the same dream for a second time, and it was causing him to feel hesitant about the role that Ma'ruf had to play. He drank from the water container he always kept by his bed at night. He realized that a few hours from now, with the sun at its zenith, it would be decision time.

This was the time of day when the silence was so profound. The city was asleep. There were no sounds from the bazaars, no arguments among the merchants, no men chanting the call to prayer. Alric lay in quiet meditation on his bed.

He decided to get up, went through his morning cleansing ritual, and dressed in the clothing of a merchant that had been set aside for him. He carried his head covering to the kitchen, prepared himself a meal of fruit and milk, and poured hot tea into a crystal glass. He sat in silence. listening to the sound of the wind that brought the scent of the desert. He waited patiently for Ma'ruf. Then he would have more tea, and perhaps an oatmeal cake.

"I have all of the materials," Alric announced as Ma'ruf entered the kitchen.

"I hope that Allah gives us his blessing," Ma'ruf said. "May he help us in what we have to do."

Alric continued to prepare his tea, saying nothing. Then he turned to Ma'ruf. "I am proud of you," he said. "We must succeed, so let us quickly talk through our plan once more."

* * *

"Follow my lead, Ma'ruf," Alric said, "until we perform the magic, and then take care. I suspect that is when the skullduggery will commence. This man," he said referring to the First Minister, "holds the power of life and death over every person he sees, with the exception of the Caliph. The royal court is a capricious place and has been known to take men's lives! I have no wish, as I am sure you do not also, to join that illustrious but headless group!

"Late last night, after father had returned from the palace, he sought my attention and told me that he had seen the First Minister in hushed conversation with his assistant minister. Father and I are of the opinion that he may have others within his sphere of influence at the palace involved in his evil plans."

* * *

Before leaving the house, Alric and Ma'ruf made sure their head coverings were secure, and Alric had taken the usual precaution of using his skin dye to disguise his face and hair coloring. Posing as Ma'ruf's assistant, he carried a bag containing the necessary equipment that they would need for the demonstration.

They walked in silence from the house. This quiet time was soon replaced by the sounds of the market; vendors shouted their wares, children cried, and animals whinnied, all this mixed with the nervous voices of mothers making sure that their children were safe in the crowd. There were at least four hundred people gathered throughout the marketplace, along with numerous animals, camels, horses, mules, and fowl. The cacophony of sounds camouflaged any words that passed between Alric and Ma'ruf.

"Ah, here we are," Alric said. He looked around cautiously as he attempted to determine if they were being watched. Ahmed had already leaked the word to various trustworthy sources that there were two newcomers in the city who could turn lead into gold. He had made sure that full descriptions of the clothing that Alric and Ma'ruf wore were also given.

Unknown to them, they were watched as they approached the marketplace, and within moments of entering it, they were accosted by two men. "We are here to take you to a man who has an interest in your talents," one of the men said. Alric and Ma'ruf nodded.

"Then follow us," the second man commanded.

The two men remained silent as they escorted them toward a building at the corner of the marketplace. At one point, Alric thought he caught a glimpse of Ahmed, but then the shadow was gone. He did, however, observe the First Minister's bodyguards, who always stood in strategic positions close to their leader. He knew that the First Minister, Abdul al-Warith, would be close by.

Alric concentrated on the thought of what was to come. He had expected the presence of the First Minister's bodyguards. Khalil also had his men close by. They were the very same men who had accompanied Alric on the journey after his rescue from the sea raiders. *Maktub,* he said to himself: It is written.

The crowds of people and animals made their progress slow. "Now," Alric whispered in Ma'ruf's ear using the Celtic language, "be on the watch. I sense we are close to our goal." They both said a silent prayer that they would be protected.

The crowd seemed to thin at that point. Alric had spotted Ahmed as he moved across the market square, unobserved by the men escorting them across the marketplace. They entered a building to find another six men waiting.

* * *

From the outside, the building looked old and dirty, and the men who were present were equally unkempt and disheveled. Alric and Ma'ruf were led into a large room that was dark and dingy and had not been used for some time. Alric continued to feel danger in the air, wishing that he and Ma'ruf could leave. But they had not come this far into danger to turn and run!

Quickly, Ma'ruf, as the leader, with Alric's assistance, got to the heart of the matter. He communicated effectively, in short sentences—sometimes two words, sometimes only one. His presentation was concise and to the point and refreshing. Ma'ruf had removed his face covering so that his words might carry better to the surrounding spectators and to emphasize that he was not of the Caliph's kingdom, and he allowed his Celtic accent to be noticed by the listeners, certain that his origins were known only to Jabir and the family.

As Ma'ruf talked, Alric, who remained masked, set up the apparatus. This consisted of a three-legged stand on which he suspended an iron pot above a heater that produced the necessary heat through the combustion of a thick fuel oil that Alric had prepared in the laboratory from bitumen from the seepages at Hit. The heat from the burner quickly melted the lead, and the liquid had the bright silvery sheen characteristic of melted lead.

The six men who surrounded Alric and Ma'ruf were fascinated when the yellow slivers were added to the melted lead and the lead appeared to turn into gold. Alric poured the molten metal into another container that was surrounded by cool water, and the goldlike liquid quickly solidified.

One of the men hung back, not getting too close to Alric and Ma'ruf, but Alric had already identified him, from his demeanor, as the First Minister. Alric doubted the First Minister had identified him, since his eyes were focused on the gold. As the metals shimmered in the dim light, Alric glanced up and saw the fascination in the First Minister's eyes. His preparation had been immaculate, and Ma'ruf carried out his part without fault, using Alric as his servant. The observers could see that the change was not merely a surface effect; the solidified liquid metal even had the appearance and behavior of pure gold.

"That is the principle that governs *al-khimiya*," Ma'ruf said, lapsing back into his Celtic accent. "In alchemy," he continued, "when you desire something and have the correct ingredients, it is the time when you are closest to the truth, and the ability to change metals is a positive force."

Alric looked around the building. Then he saw the sign, scratch marks on the door that were characteristic of the birthmarks on his arm, and he knew that Ahmed was nearby. He wished he could tell Ma'ruf, to give him a modicum of security, but then again, Ma'ruf was becoming comfortable in his role of alchemist.

As his assistant, Alric had occupied himself setting up the equipment and had been surprised when Ma'ruf had immediately assumed the role of master. He had expected some fumbling, but it was not so. Ma'ruf had done well.

Ma'ruf requested that one of the men inspect the equipment to be certain of no trickery. After a few moments, the First Minister stepped forward and pronounced that it was without flaw. At a signal from the First Minister, one of the men produced an ingot of lead for them to test, so that there would be no suspicions that the metal had been pretreated. The test was completed in a matter of minutes; to delay any longer would have been hazardous to the health of Alric and Ma'ruf!

To the observers and most especially to the First Minister, the test had been nothing short of amazing. In the time it took the melted metal to solidify, it had become gold. "Everything on earth is being continuously transformed, because the earth is alive and we do not always recognize that it is working for us," Ma'ruf proclaimed. "I have discovered the means to produce gold."

Alric saw the First Minister's eyes narrow as he realized the potential of this demonstration. He looked at Ma'ruf and the gold. "I have need of such money," the First Minister whispered to himself, "and it is limitless. Gold speaks the universal language of power. I must have it!"

* * *

CHAPTER 38

Alric roused himself as the sun started to lighten the sky and cast its yellow rays on the Tigris River. He looked at the second bed in the room, where Bemia had slept since her injuries, and saw her sleeping peacefully. Silhouetted by the morning light, he moved quietly to her and kissed her forehead. Then he made his way to the bathing room and allowed the water to wash the sleep from his mind.

He returned to the bedroom and saw Bemia beginning to stir. She awoke as the sun sent glowing images through the curtained window. Alric watched her as she opened her eyes and smiled. He handed her the glass of cool water he had brought from the kitchen. After she had taken a sip, she eased herself into a sitting position and smiled as the energy flowed back into her body. "See," she said lifting her sleeping robe and showing Alric the scar. "Father says that I am healing quite well."

Alric looked down at the scar. The dead tissue was gradually disappearing, and the wound showed as a faint pink scar against her white skin. Hope thundered through Alric's chest. The possibility of infection had diminished as the days passed, and Jabir's healing ointment seemed to be working.

Bemia looked at Alric and reached out to stroke his cheek. "Now, my dear husband, will you help me from this bed and into the bathroom?

I am going to have a relaxing bath and," she smiled, "I will need your support, since mother has recommended I do not allow the warm water to soak the wound, and I am not sure if I can stand on my own."

"But . . . " Alric attempted to protest.

"I discussed this with mother yesterday evening while you were skulking in the garden with Bashir and the soldiers. She has agreed to my suggestion if you help me." Bemia's eyes twinkled, "Mother also advised that any other activity is strictly forbidden."

"Really!" Alric exclaimed as his face broadened into an uncontrollable smile.

"Well, at least for the moment," Bemia added. "And while I cleanse myself, you can tell me of the latest developments."

* * *

For the remainder of the morning, Alric helped Bemia regain her balance as they walked together a few steps at a time. Every time she felt a little weak, he stopped and helped her to the chair that had been provided by Amira.

Finally, tired from the exertion, Bemia lay back in the bed of cushions on the chair. Unmindful of her own condition, she asked question after question about the fallen intruders and if anyone else had been hurt. Satisfied that all was well with the other members of the household, she announced that she felt hungry.

Alric's whoop of joy brought Jabir and Amira quickly into the room. When they were told the reason for his joyous sound, Jabir looked carefully at the wound and declared it was healing so well that Bemia would be allowed to take gentle exercise every day.

She was now well on her way to recovery. Amira immediately started to plan the meals that Bemia would eat. Amira would take charge, and although all was well within the house, it was the world outside that worried Alric.

* * *

Several days later, having the strength to walk without assistance, Jabir announced that it was time that Bemia had an outing in the garden. After much discussion with Amira about what to wear, Bemia chose a dress and robe of her favorite color, blue.

Alric accompanied her into the garden to find Wahid, and Ma'ruf had already set up a comfortable chair, a resting place from which Bemia could make the most of the scents and sounds of summer. She found herself with a host of visitors; Bashir and several of the soldiers who stood nearby stopped to pay their respects and marvel at the woman who had held eight assassins at bay for almost two hours.

As he was about to leave, Bemia said, "Bashir, dear cousin, I appreciate your efforts to protect me and my family. As the remainder of your soldiers take a break from their duties, I will willingly meet each man and give him my thanks."

Bashir felt happily honored when Bemia called him by the familiar name *cousin,* and he even tarried a few minutes to chat with her and Alric. He passed on the message to the soldiers at their posts throughout the garden and they all, in turn, visited Bemia, accepting her gratitude.

The air was tainted with the intoxicating aroma of the blue flowers. It seemed as if the gardens were welcoming Bemia's return to health.

* * *

Throughout most of the day, Amira made sure that Bemia had everything she needed. Maha was given this duty. Morning gave way to afternoon, and the shade provided by the trees allowed Bemia to get much needed fresh air without the cruel heat from the direct sun.

"Our dear daughter," Jabir observed to Amira, "seems to be more of a politician than many of the men who frequent the palace. She now has all of these soldiers sworn to protect her and the family!"

Bemia slept for a short while in the coolness and quiet surroundings of the shaded garden as Alric watched. She slept with a smile on her face, and seemingly happy with the world. She awoke as the sun filtered through the foliage and fell upon the coverlet that Alric had placed over her. She tried to sit up, but winced. She looked up and saw Alric and Maha standing close by.

"What happened?" Alric asked.

"I have a minor discomfort in my side. Perhaps it is a muscle advising me to be cautious next time."

Alric fussed as Maha went to the house to fetch a cool drink. Amira and Jabir appeared to be assured that all was well. "You are awake!" Jabir pronounced. "Good."

Amira bustled around, attempting to fluff the cushions to support Bemia as she sat up. "Before you get too comfortable," Jabir said quietly, "I would like to take a look at the wound again."

Amira and Maha held a privacy sheet in front of Bemia while Jabir examined the wound. Seeing that the bandage had remained fresh and the wound showed no sign of deterioration, Jabir pronounced himself satisfied. He then retired to the laboratory while Amira made arrangements for a late afternoon meal.

As Alric sat with Bemia, the shuffle of soft shoes on the stones of the garden path announced the arrival of Ahmed. "Ah, dear sister," Ahmed exclaimed, "you look well!" He looked at Alric. "May I?" Ahmed leaned over and kissed Bemia on the cheek.

"I assume you both have something to discuss," she said. Seconds later Khalil arrived.

"We have found the wolf," Ahmed said. "We do not have his lair, but my men reported that we have him. His habits have not varied over the past few days. He may be ripe for the picking! And your ruse has worked. There are many questions being asked about the two men who can turn lead into gold. It seems, from what my men and I hear, that the First Minister is consumed by the idea of turning lead into gold.

He has not discovered that the lead ingot that he gave you as a test has not been turned into gold."

"Nor will he discover it," Alric said. "If the First Minister had bothered to notice the contents of the dealer's shelves where he took his hookah, he would have noticed that certain ores are yellow in color. All I did was isolate and convert the lead back to its original ore, which, through the agency of heat and the materials that I added, melted and then, when cooled, the mixture took to the shape of the vessel that contained it. The First Minister's greed—and I counted on this—prevented him from determining what I had done. Gold seems to make men blind to the facts!"

Khalil and Ahmed looked at Alric open-mouthed and then smiled. "Does father know of this?" Khalil asked.

"Yes," Alric responded. "He knew what I was going to do as soon as I described the general procedure to him. In fact, he recognized it from some of his earlier work with metals and alloys.

"So, now we have time, since the First Minister is involved in a hopeless search for Ma'ruf and me. What are the next steps?"

"As you say, we have valuable time, and I propose that we do not rush into the next steps." Ahmed responded. "I doubt that the Caliph will be in much danger until Abdul al-Warith comes to his senses and starts to refocus on his matter at hand. There is too much at stake for us to be hasty, and we must not arouse suspicions and allow the assassin to escape. He is our key. Even now, my men are watching him. Their duties are varied, so the chance of recognition is very slight. I believe he does not suspect he is being watched."

Ahmed took a deep breath and exhaled. Just then, Jabir and Amira approached.

"We hope," Amira said, "that you are not disturbing Bemia. Oh, and greetings to my three sons!" she added.

Bemia smiled. "No, mother, they do not disturb me. In fact, it is reassuring to know what is going on."

She coughed lightly and eased herself higher in the chair. "Now," Bemia continued the conversation, "what are the plans for us to capture this assassin and perhaps discover the truth behind his actions with possibly dire consequences for the First Minister?"

Jabir looked at his wife. Amira's face was flushed as if to echo her thoughts. He then addressed Bemia. "There is no 'us,' my dear. I cannot risk you getting into a fight at this stage of your recuperation. It could cause complications from which you may not recover."

"But . . . " Bemia started to protest.

"It is for the best, my love," Alric spoke reassuringly. "Besides, if we," he looked at Khalil and Ahmed," are seeking the assassin, mother will tend to you here and make sure your wound continues to improve."

Bemia nodded and said, "You are right. I was fooling myself to think that I could be of help. It was revenge, pure and simple, that filled my mind."

Bemia shook her head to clear her thoughts. She wiped away a tear. "But once my wound is healed, I would like to be involved."

Khalil and Ahmed looked at Alric. Alric took her hand. "And so you shall, my love, when you are fully recovered."

He winced at the thought of Bemia being hurt again. He looked at the faces of the family and knew that they had the same thoughts. Bemia had come very close to losing her life, but she had fought that battle and won. He could not tolerate another shock of seeing her lying on the floor in a pool of blood. The strength necessary for wielding a sword would take some time to return.

Khalil and Ahmed sat, looking pensive. Finally, to end the silence, Khalil spoke. "I do not know what this man's strategy might be, but we understand that he is a particularly vicious assassin. He has a long history of murder and creating mayhem to cover his murderous actions. However, we see a flaw in his cloak of secrecy. We know his actions and the places he frequents most. It will take some effort, but I believe that we can run him to earth and seek answers to our questions."

"And so we begin the final phase . . . ," Alric said allowing his words to trail into the air.

* * *

The next morning, Alric, in the company of Khalil and Ahmed, all suitably disguised, quietly left the house. They passed a group of men seated, smoking their hookahs, and trading stories from their recent travels. No one paid any attention to the three men in nondescript robes.

"There is no danger," Alric whispered as they approached the group.

"Trust in your instinct," Ahmed said, "but never forget that when men are at war with one another, both can suffer the consequences."

* * *

The sun had started on its descent toward the horizon, and as the shadows lengthened, the marketplace became deserted. Ahmed and Khalil halted. They turned to see a group of men approaching. They were dressed in dark brown, well-worn robes. Black rings encircled their turbans, their faces hidden behind veils with only their piercing eyes showing.

"Quickly," Ahmed said, looking around for a defensive position, "the alley."

They feared the worst and instinctively backed themselves against a wall to prevent a rear attack. Khalil and Ahmed had their hands on their swords, ready for action. No words were spoken as the dark-robed men halted and faced them several paces away. One of the men, speaking in a northern dialect, attempted to approach menacingly. His dark brown eyes were black with anger and hate.

"It would appear that you need to speak with us," Ahmed said.

"Who is your friend?" The man nodded in Alric's direction.

"A man who works with plants to make the mixtures that cure ailments," said Ahmed. "He understands the forces of nature."

The leader listened quietly but without any sign of understanding.

"What is a foreigner doing here?" asked another of the men, also speaking in the same dialect.

"He has brought his knowledge that he may help us."

The leader did not accept Ahmed's explanation. "How can a blue-eyed one help us?"

At first, Alric and Ahmed were surprised at the willingness of the leader to engage them in conversation. But as they watched, the men appeared to be trying to form a strong semi-circle around them to cut off any means of escape.

"How does he work with plants?" The leader continued the ruse of trying to surround them without drawing attention to the tactic.

"He understands nature and the world. If he wanted to, he could destroy all of you with a power you would never understand."

The assailants laughed. They were used to the ravages of battle and knew that no one had such power. These were men of the northern desert and did not understand sorcery.

"What can he show us?" the leader asked.

"Just give him a moment," Ahmed replied as he turned to look at Alric, "and he will demonstrate his powers. If he cannot do so, we humbly offer you money, for your honor."

"You cannot offer me something that is already mine," the leader said arrogantly. "Look about you," he smiled, showing blackened, crooked teeth. "I already have your lives in my hands."

There was the ring of triumph in the leader's voice. But he felt the need to indulge them to demonstrate his command of the situation.

Alric was calm and collected. Fortunately, he had seen an alcove in the wall where they could take refuge. In addition, Ahmed's advice several days ago had helped him master his emotions. He looked at

Khalil and Ahmed as he spoke in the northern dialect, hoping that the assailants would understand his words.

"These are brave men, my brothers," he said and then addressed the leader. "You threaten us. You realize this could be your last day on earth."

Alric's voice was steady, and the group of men quietly observed the coldness in Alric's eyes. The leader did not speak. His dark eyes showed signs of curiosity and then nervousness, which had replaced the confidence that had been there moments ago. To hear this blue-eyed one speak in the dialect of the north made him suspicious. He signaled his men to move forward slowly to form an impenetrable wall.

"I suggest that you walk away," Ahmed said nonchalantly, but the leader only snarled a series of unintelligible words. "So be it," Ahmed commented and then turned to look at Alric and Khalil and gave them a signal before looking back at the assassins. "Now you shall reap your rewards," he said quietly.

Alric had prepared for such an attack, but he had diverged from his original plan. He had packed one of Amira's fist-sized iron vessels with wool before adding nitroglycerine in the correct amount to soak it. Then he had covered the pot with clay to minimize any motion shocks as he walked with it in the pocket of his robe. His tests had shown him that the mixture would still explode, causing the pot to fragment and spreading deadly shards of iron into the air.

He took the ball of clay from the pocket of his robe. The clay ball appeared to offer no threat. The men hesitated when they saw the object in Alric's hand. It was so small and looked like a ball of dirt.

"That is no threat," one of them mumbled. A wave of relief showed on the faces of the aggressors. They were going to enjoy this. A lot of pay for very little effort!

"Do not give in to your fears," Alric said in a strangely gentle voice. "If you do, Allah will never forgive you."

"We are not afraid of death," the leader said. "What can you do without weapons? We are many against three."

"You will die in the midst of your men. *Maktub*. It is written."

Alric threw the ball of clay toward the feet of the leader. The clay hit the ground in front of the man and ricocheted two feet into the air. The assailants laughed at this action, wondering what effect a ball of earth could have on them. But as the ball left his hand, Alric yelled to Khalil and Ahmed to get into the alcove. They did and fell prone to the ground, causing the assailants to laugh even more.

When the clay ball rose into the air, Alric joined Khalil and Ahmed so that they were sheltered from any outcome of his actions. At that moment, pieces of the dry clay were shed from the ball in front of the assailants. Suddenly, as the last of the clay fell away, the dull glint of iron was evident to the assailants. As the pot rose to waist height, its open end toward the men, a sheet of flame erupted from the narrow neck, followed by an explosion and fire that smothered them.

In the moments before they died, first surprise and then fear appeared on their faces, with the last vestiges of their laughter ringing through the evening air. The men who were not killed outright were consumed by the flames that accompanied the explosion.

The final sounds of the deadly explosion were carried away by the wind, and silence filled the air. Alric had felt its force as it passed over his body and then the heat from the flame. Pieces of the iron pot rattled against the wall, and he knew that their low profile and protection by the alcove had saved them from injury. Other than dirt on their robes, they remained untouched.

Khalil and Ahmed raised themselves from the ground and looked at the death and devastation. "My brother," Khalil exclaimed as he surveyed the blackened and charred bodies of the would-be assassins, "you certainly have a way of producing devastating mixtures! I am surprised we are untouched, but you did tell me it would be so. These men had no idea of how they were going to die."

"And would you believe it Ahmed," Khalil exclaimed, "Alric has told me that the mixture that caused that explosion also has the power to cure a disease of the heart, if administered in the correct amount!"

"Yes, Khalil," Ahmed responded. "Alric has also told me of other mixtures and extracts that can destroy but can also cure when used in the correct amounts."

"We must leave this place now," Khalil ordered.

Alric looked once more at the scene before him. It had worked. Father would be pleased!

* * *

That night as they prepared for supper in Amira's day room in celebration of Bemia's recovery, Jabir commented that he had just heard a rumor of a man who could turn earth into fire and death.

"I have heard," Jabir said, "that there was an incident near the marketplace in which eight men, as near as can be told from the remaining parts, died violently. Other than the remains of the men, the only other evidence seems to have been pieces of iron that had hit the nearby wall." He raised an eyebrow and looked at Alric, Khalil, and Ahmed. "You would not, by chance know anything of this, would you?"

"Now I know the fate of my old iron pots!" Amira said, placing her hand gently on Bemia's arm as she looked into her blue eyes. "I did not think that your husband had taken up cooking."

"My dear," Jabir looked at his wife, "you are priceless. However, the Caliph is wondering what type of weapon has been turned loose!" He looked across the table at Alric, Khalil, and Ahmed. "Do you have an explanation for the Caliph that is just believable enough to sound true so that he will not have my head on a platter?"

"Sire," Alric spoke up, "if I may so bold?"

"Yes, Alric."

"At this time of the year, Sire, the dryness of the weather can cause the forked light to strike from the sky."

Jabir almost fell off his cushion. Amira smiled in amusement, and Bemia looked at the ground as if attempting to admire her feet. "I pray Allah will protect us from my northern son," Jabir said. "However, I would prefer to hear the true story."

"I should imagine," Bemia said quietly, "that my husband and my two brothers were the source of this event. And," she looked at Alric, "if my father tells such a tale to the Caliph, all will not be well. So, my dear husband, you can relate the whole story or," she smiled sweetly, "when I am fully recovered I may have to beat you!" Everyone dissolved in laughter. Bemia held her side so as not to irritate the wound.

"Well, it seems," Alric said with barely a straight face, "I had better relate the whole incident from start to finish. My brothers will of course help me and protect me from my dear wife!"

Alric, with the occasional words from Khalil and Ahmed, related the incident to his father, mother, and wife. When he had finished, Jabir nodded. "It seems, my son," he said, "that you have brought forth a weapon of great power. It may even pose danger for those who prepare it." Alric agreed. Jabir continued, "At a later time, Alric, I need you to show me how to make this mixture."

* * *

"I do not understand what you are talking about, Alric," Bemia said the next morning. They were sitting in the shade of the garden, on the seat that Bemia preferred. The sunlight provided gentle shadows as it made its way through the branches of the trees. Wahid and Rufus had, under Amira's supervision, provided supportive and comfortable cushions for Bemia so that she would be at ease.

She was able to walk confidently without requiring assistance from Alric, although her preference was to lean on his arm. Her progress was, in Jabir's words, nothing short of remarkable, but as always, he advised caution.

The branches of the trees swayed gently in the breeze that meandered through the garden, and Alric became lost in thought.

"Are you listening, Alric?"

"Of course, my dear, I would not do anything else!"

"You need help," Bemia announced.

"Yes, my dear," Alric smiled.

"Khalil and Ahmed may be of some assistance, but they are not skilled in the work that you do. I know you have your alchemists' secrets, and I have heard you and father talking about your experiments, so I do have some understanding of your work. If I am to be confined to the house, there are many ways in which I can assist you."

His eyes lit up. He could always use another pair of hands! He felt that his ideas and work had no limits, and here was Bemia saying she would like to help! She would not have to work with dangerous extracts and explosives. She could experiment with medicines and help him formulate curative mixtures!

"This is what we will do, my love," Alric said, seeing the determination on her face. "And you look so beautiful today."

"Alric, please do not try to soften me up or change my mind with your words."

"First," he said "you do not understand the mixtures and their ingredients." Bemia nodded her head. "Second, the laboratory is my domain."

"But . . . "

Alric raised an eyebrow. Bemia forced herself not to interrupt. "Third, mixtures and extracts can heal or they can kill. And fourth, when you are in my laboratory, you will gain some understanding of what is happening, but proceeding on your own is strictly forbidden!"

Bemia was becoming irritated with this conversation, even though Alric was undeniably correct. She was annoyed at having to acknowledge her own limitations.

Alric waited for an answer. She nodded in agreement.

"Finally, you will follow my instructions to the letter. There will be no deviation whatsoever!"

"Alric, my dear, I agree to all of your conditions. You are wise, because you observe everything and record the details. I will transform myself in the laboratory to be your assistant."

"But understand that you are not yet fit to help in the laboratory," Alric said as he tried to explain his decision to Bemia.

She did not answer him for a few moments. Then she said, as if resigned to Alric's decisions, "As my health improves, I will give you assistance whenever there is a need." The sun seemed to shine even brighter at that moment.

Alric and Bemia heard the sound of footfalls on the garden path and looked up to see Ma'ruf. He carried a tray of juice and fruits. They thanked him as he left the tray and returned to the house.

They sat in the garden for the remainder of the day. Bemia did not feel the need to rest and so they talked continuously. On occasion, Amira checked to make sure that all was well. Jabir was briefing the Caliph on the nature of the explosion and fire while Khalil and Ahmed were debriefing their men regarding strange happenings in the city.

Bemia and Alric talked about their lives as children and of people they knew in the distant lands and those they had met throughout their journeys. They even suggested that they might return to Britannia one day.

By the time they had finished reminiscing, the sun had set and a full moon had started its journey into a starry sky. The moonlight cast shadows through the palm trees and the servants started to light the bitumen-soaked torches in the garden. The trees, illuminated by the light of the moon and the torch flames, stood solemn and majestic.

Alric and Bemia sat in silence, each confined to their own personal thoughts. Their simple life had passed by.

"One day," Alric said, "I would like to go back to Wearmouth." He had a recurring thought from their earlier conversation. "I would like to see the monastery, the people, and what changes have occurred."

"I was having the same thought, my dear," Bemia added. "Exactly the same. Perhaps one of these days we shall do so."

"If we continue to live here in this glorious city and in the Caliph's House of Light," Alric said, "and even though we understand the language and the customs, we are still a man and woman of northern Britannia. So let us make this pledge to each other."

He looked down and, in the light cast by the torches, saw a beetle scurrying for its hole. Even this insect was going home! "I hereby pledge to you, Bemia my love, that when the opportunity arises I will take you home to Britannia. But whatever happens, we shall remain together for all eternity."

"Alric, my love, I pledge the same to you."

*   *   *

CHAPTER 39

The next morning as Alric walked through the garden before breakfast, the gentle rays of the morning sun brightened his mood. Bemia's mental and physical wounds were healing and all looked well. There was, however, still the matter of the First Minister. The man was dangerous and he had shrouded himself in mystery.

"He is a dark shadow," Alric thought. "But," he smiled faintly, "even shadows are caught!"

As he continued his stroll around the garden, he saw Bashir making his rounds checking the guards and reminding them to be watchful for anything out of the ordinary.

"Bashir," Alric whispered to the captain. "Where are Khalil and Ahmed?"

"Khalil has just returned, and the whereabouts of Ahmed are unknown . . ."

Suddenly Alric's senses became alert when he heard the soft scraping sound, then another. Several of the soldiers were at attention, alert, with long, curved swords drawn and ready for action.

Alric's heart skipped a beat. He cocked his head to one side to determine the source of the sound. It came from the other side of a well-protected gate that could not be opened from the outside.

Bashir and Alric hastened to the gate and Bashir signaled the soldiers to follow him. He commanded his men to form a semi-circle at the gate with their weapons drawn. He sent one of the men to inform the soldiers in other parts of the garden to be wary and to guard the house but not as yet to enter. That would cause unnecessary alarm. Bashir took Alric by the arm and led him behind the soldiers for protection.

"You are not armed, Alric," Bashir said by way of explanation. And then he smiled as Alric produced his Saxon dagger. Bashir shook his head, indicating that the dagger would not be much help if a fight ensued.

The scratching sound continued. Alric and Bashir looked at each other for a moment, and then Bashir signaled for the gate to be opened. One of the soldiers partially opened the gate as four others put their shoulders behind it so that anyone attempting to rush the entrance to the garden would find it difficult.

There was no one. Bashir and Alric did not notice the stooped shadowy figure until he was standing close to them. Swords were held within inches of the man's body as the gate was closed and made secure once more.

"Stay your swords!"

The man's strong voice was not in keeping with his stooped, beggar-like appearance. Alric and Bashir recognized the voice immediately. Ahmed, a master of disguise, raised himself to his full height. His eyes glinted as he removed the coverings from his face.

"So, my brother," Alric exclaimed with relief as he recognized Ahmed, "the fox returns!"

The soldiers sheathed their weapons and resumed their watch. One was dispatched to the house to inform Jabir and Amira that Ahmed had returned.

"Alric, Bashir, walk with me to the house," Ahmed said quietly, taking their arms in his strong, firm grip. Once out of earshot of the soldiers, he spoke excitedly.

"I have him!" Ahmed exclaimed.

"You mean . . . ," Alric was about to ask, but his question was cut short as Ahmed continued.

"I first suspected this particular man about one week ago after he was pointed out to me by my men and after I observed his daily actions in the market place. The man was a little too curious to be a casual loafer there. His conversations with others I overheard were anything but casual. As you know, gossip is rife in the marketplace, but he made the mistake of asking questions of several of my men, who, naturally, were unknown to him. Since then, I have followed the man as best as I could, seemingly without suspicion."

Alric knew that Ahmed was a master in the secretive work he had undertaken. "He varies his habits," Ahmed continued, "but eventually he returns to retrace his steps, and his actions reoccur every three days." Ahmed looked at Alric. "We have him, Alric."

"Is there anything that you would have me do?" Bashir asked.

Ahmed shook his head. "Remain vigilant at your post here, cousin."

They started to walk toward the house when Ahmed became conscious of an odor that pervaded the fresh morning air. He sighed as he looked down at his street clothes. They were covered with dirt and stank from the odors of the streets. Alric knew the reality of living the life of a beggar.

"I think, my brother," Alric commented, "a bath and the burning of your clothes is very appropriate at this moment." Several of the soldiers within hearing smiled in amusement. "And I am sure," Alric added, "that mother will see to the disposal of your clothes!"

"She will indeed," Ahmed agreed.

"And," Alric added, "while you are luxuriating in your bath, I will find Khalil and explain your findings to him. We can then spend some time planning our next line of attack!"

* * *

Just like the foxes leaving their lair to quietly track game, Alric, Khalil, and Ahmed left through the back gate of the garden in the grayness of the early morning light. They had spent the remainder of the previous day talking to Ahmed. As the afternoon had become evening, they developed a plan that met with Jabir's approval.

They discussed the means by which they would force the assassin to talk, if they should capture him alive. "I will take the medication with me, father," Alric said.

Khalil and Ahmed had no understanding of what Alric meant, but they did suspect that it would be less violent than the usual methods of making men talk.

As they walked quietly though the streets toward the marketplace, they could hear the sound of the city coming to life. They were barely visible in the dim light, as the gray robes and face coverings they wore blended into the shadows.

They strode swiftly through the narrow, winding streets. Occasionally, a dog barked. They passed several farmers leading their donkeys loaded with goods. Even though the light was dim, buyers and sellers from outlying villages had begun to trade in the market that bordered the northeast gate to the city and spread over the bridge to the eastern side of the Tigris River.

A bend in the street brought them to the buildings that the Caliph had designated as his first university. This was built for the study of the sciences and the philosophical arts. The Caliph had even hinted that he would allow women students to attend.

They stood at the side of the street, facing the wide, well-tended road that could take the Caliph's army to the north or any part of the eastern side of the country. The road, which continued along the eastern bank of the river, was the very same one that Alric and Ahmed had used when the caravan to Mosul had first started out. They walked in the shadow of the city walls and made their way quickly past magnificent dwellings that were surrounded by luxurious gardens full of exotic plants.

When they reached the marketplace, the morning grayness had changed to gold as the sun's rays reflected from the white buildings. The tops of the palm trees glowed with the rising sun.

The wide gate to the outside of the city wall stood open. The marketplace was jammed with many traders from other countries. The men wore a variety of clothes. Some were outlandish in style and color, while others, hired to haul goods or pressed into slavery, were only partly clothed, their upper bodies bare. The women were dressed in traditional attire, many with their faces covered. The traders' voices were loud, and their languages were as varied as their clothing and skin color.

Next to the gate, a tank hewn out of stone had been built into the wall and was full of water for the benefit of all who passed. "This," Ahmed whispered to Alric and Khalil, "is where we will find him. He will be watching this place, knowing that his prey needs water."

"In that case, Ahmed," Khalil smiled under his face covering, "let us hunt the hunter!"

"But first . . . " Ahmed whispered and motioned to the water tank.

They pushed aside the heavy marble cover, filled the copper ladle which was fastened firmly to the lid with a chain, and drank the cold water until they were both satisfied. As one drank, the other two continuously scanned the crowd for any signs of the assassin.

Several men were squatting on benches of baked bricks on both sides of the gate. The sounds of donkeys braying, dogs barking, and camels grunting as they aired their displeasure of the whole situation joined the noise of the traders plying their wares.

The beaten dirt of the ground was covered with bales of merchandise, stuffed saddlebags, packages wrapped in leather, and countless other bundles in the process of being opened. In another half an hour, the market would be in full motion as the traders' efforts to sell their goods intensified.

They looked for a place to rest where they could watch the area without being obvious. Before long they selected a spot that would give them an unhindered view of the water tank and its immediate surroundings.

"This," Ahmed announced, "is where we will remain. I suspect that our man will find a place in the shade yonder. I suggest that we make ourselves comfortable."

At that point the road curved, giving them a panoramic view of the market. They squatted on their haunches, ready for a long wait.

"My men are in place," Ahmed announced, to Khalil and Alric's surprise. They looked around. Stalls that catered to early morning appetites by selling fresh bread and hot tea were already doing a brisk business.

"We have plenty of time," Ahmed announced, "so I suggest that we purchase bread and tea from this stall, and sit here and wait. If the man is true to form, he will follow the same path and appear soon." Ahmed nodded in the direction of the opposite side of the square. "The lane between the stalls allowed me to maintain my vigil of the other side of the square and the bridge across the river without losing sight of the man," he added.

Just as they finished the bread and tea, Ahmed was alerted. "Be aware," he whispered. "The man approaches."

At the far end of the central square, the arches of the bridge across the Tigris were lit by the sun's reflection on the river. Ahmed had seen the man crossing the bridge keeping to the crowded areas so as not to be easily noticed.

As he came into sight, Alric noticed that the man wore a nondescript dark robe that helped him blend into the shadowy areas without drawing attention to himself, but he had not counted on being observed by Ahmed!

"A good disguise for a person with nefarious deeds in mind," Alric thought. "So, this is the man who plotted the attack on my father's house!"

The man picked his way with ease through the shadowy arches of the building that ringed the market square and stayed close to a high wall that offered shadow.

"Now, observe," Ahmed whispered.

The man stopped at a building opposite to where Alric, Khalil, and Ahmed sat. He used the hilt of his sword to strike the nail-studded door in what seemed to be a predetermined pattern.

"That seems to be a signal he uses to indicate all is well. You will see a small window open and the man will then step through the door."

Just as Ahmed had predicted, the door opened and the man disappeared inside.

"The house is grander inside than it looks from the outside," Ahmed offered. "The furnishings are sumptuous and the gardens are immaculate, with exotic plants and several ornamental pools. There is a large patio that has rooms on three of the four sides. The owner of the house is not generally known, but I have it on good authority that it is owned by the First Minister!"

Ahmed looked at the two pairs of eyes staring at him in amazement. He had amassed more information than they realized. "Before all of these recent events took shape, I believe I told you I happened to meet an old man one morning. He and I took tea together. He said he was leaving the city and he had an intimate knowledge of the house. I had the distinct impression he had lived there. I also suspected he had some relationship to the First Minister."

"If that is the case," Khalil said, "it is my opinion that the First Minister is in the house at this moment. He may still be in doubt about the success of the attack in which Bemia was wounded. No doubt he has received word of the death of the eight men. He will be wondering about the success of his plan."

"Father told me," Alric interjected, "that the Caliph has found large sums of money to be misappropriated from the treasury. He is sure that this is the work of the First Minister."

* * *

It was one hour later when the man reappeared and moved to the spot that Ahmed had indicated. He then sat on his haunches, his back pressed close to the wall of a building, blending into the environment. Even at the distance across the market square, Alric, Ahmed, and Khalil could see that he was constantly watchful.

"The building behind the man," Ahmed whispered, "used to be an animal barn, and then it was a warehouse. The man's name is Rasil." Ahmed continued. "It may not be his original name; that seems to have been lost in the annals of time. Some say that he is also called the Messenger of Death.

"He has been given this task," Ahmed whispered, "because of his ability to disguise himself effectively. On occasion, his knife, which he is now using to sharpen a stick, is his weapon of choice. He will use all means at his disposal, which I hear are multitudinous, to accomplish his goal."

"It is said," Ahmed continued in a whispered voice, "that he was high born, but drinking and gambling took him from riches to poverty. He has a quick brain and an agile mind, so he learned the art of the assassin quite easily. His activities brought him to the attention of important persons who have often sought his services."

Alric continued to be amazed at the depth of information that Ahmed had learned about the assassin. Khalil was expressionless. He knew well of Ahmed's capabilities.

Ahmed shrugged. "My men are thorough," he said. "It is rumored that one of Rasil's early clients declared that he would not honor the contract for murder that he had arranged with Rasil. The man was found tied and hanging by his feet from a tree. He had been garroted, and several of his body parts had been removed. Rasil's future services were then in greater demand!"

Ahmed looked around to make sure that all was well before he continued.

"Rasil came to Baghdad about one year ago and spent much of his time in the library. His gambling and drinking habits are in the past. He is a very dangerous man." Ahmed coughed lightly. "I think, my brothers, that it is time for us to make our move. Remember, this man is vigilant, and by the way, he is left-handed."

*   *   *

Alric was the first to approach Rasil. Alric had taken on the appearance of a young Arab, loaded down with baggage that had been provided by some of Ahmed's men who were stationed in other parts of the market square.

Alric slowly moved through the crowds at first, out of sight of Rasil, and when he was within speaking distance, he unloaded the baggage from his shoulders, moved close, and sat down to the right of him. Alric's reasoning was simple. Having been informed that Rasil was left-handed, he deduced that Rasil would have a knife sheathed and attached to his belt on his right side beneath his outer robe, and so he would need to reach across his body to withdraw the knife. Alric's position gave him an advantage should Rasil attack.

"*Salaam aleikum*," Alric greeted Rasil. "Peace be with you."

"*Aleikum salaam*," Rasil growled in response. "And with you."

Alric's face was almost completely covered, to give him the appearance of being a Bedouin. Rasil was so intent on watching the activities in the square that he did not even bother to pay much attention to Alric, except to shift uncomfortably on his haunches.

"Where are you bound?" Alric inquired matter-of-factly, as would be expected from one traveler to another.

"Nowhere," Rasil replied curtly and then added, "Just resting before the day's work starts."

"I am going into the desert," Alric added, "my brothers, the Bedouin, offered to help me get back to my home."

"You do not have a home?" the man asked with a note of suspicion in his voice, looking at Alric's clothing. "You are a nomad!"

"The desert is my home," Alric said.

Rasil shrugged at the response.

Alric knew that Rasil did not want any further conversation, so he said nothing more as the morning sun rose higher in the sky and its heat shimmered in the air. If Rasil decided to move, he would have to act, but Ahmed had assured him that once he had settled, he rarely moved for hours.

Alric spotted Ahmed and Khalil surreptitiously making their way through the crowds. Ahmed nodded his head; that was the signal for Alric to act.

Alric took out a small scroll from the deep pocket of his robe and began to read. Rasil's eyes opened wide as he focused on the script. The writing on the scroll was in Latin. Alric guessed that Rasil, by virtue of his education and visits to the library, would recognize the script.

It was time to act. Rasil's attention on the script distracted him from the activities around him. He was blind to the movements of Ahmed and Khalil. Suddenly he became suspicious and started to reach for his knife. Alric's supposition had been correct. Rasil reached across his body with his left hand, feeling for the knife. As his fingers closed around the handle, Alric took a firm hold of Rasil's wrist and held it in place. Alric's grip was viselike, causing the assassin to look at him with a mixture of curiosity and anger.

"Take your hand off me, you miserable Bedouin!" Rasil exclaimed. "Or your body will feel my blade."

It was at that moment that Alric pricked the needle into Rasil's free hand. The needle was hollow and had been fashioned in the likeness of the scorpion's stinger. As the point entered Rasil's skin, Alric squeezed the small balloon that had been carefully crafted from a sheep's bladder and which was attached to the other end of the needle.

"What . . . ?" Rasil never finished the question.

Khalil and Ahmed, seeing Alric's actions, moved in quickly. Alric prevented Rasil from falling over, while Ahmed and Khalil positioned themselves around the assassin. Rasil's eyes glazed over, his eyelids closed, and his head slowly came to rest on Ahmed's shoulder.

"Well done, brother," Khalil whispered. "Now, let us take him where he can be of use to us."

"In the meantime, I will dispatch two men to give father the news," Ahmed said, turning to signal his men standing close by, who immediately departed for Jabir's house.

*   *   *

The air in the building still carried the odor of animals, sweat, and dust. It had been a simple task to move Rasil's unconscious body into the structure through the nearby door.

Once inside, Khalil and Ahmed tied Rasil between two posts so that his legs and arms were at their maximum extensions—a spread-eagle position.

"I see you are joining us. Welcome back!" Alric announced. "Please do not feign unconsciousness, as I am well aware that the medication wears off as quickly as it takes effect. By my count, you are now coherent and quite able to understand my words."

Khalil and Ahmed watched as Rasil tried to move but to no avail— he was held fast. "My brother, Ahmed," Alric smiled, "ties knots very well. You will not escape, Rasil, so accept your situation."

Alric noted the man's surprise when his name was spoken. Alric, Khalil, and Ahmed had lowered their face coverings. They could see Rasil's further surprise as he stared at Alric blue eyes. "Who are you?" Rasil asked.

"That is of little consequence" Alric answered. "But, for your information, I am from the northern climate, so my blond hair and blue eyes set me apart from my brothers." He looked at Khalil and Ahmed and smiled. "But we are as close as any brothers can be; we are the sons of Lord Jabir! He is the man you were stalking in an attempt to get close to the Caliph, and it was my wife that your men attacked in their raid on my father's house." Rasil's eyes opened wide in fear as he realized the identity of his captors.

"However, she lives, and no matter what you have heard, my wife killed seven of your men, and the survivor told us, under the effects of the medicine I will administer to you, what we needed to know before he died!"

All Rasil could do was snort in disbelief that anything or anyone could make him talk.

"Khalil, Ahmed, what do you think?" Alric asked.

They looked closely at Rasil and both nodded. "He is ready," Ahmed concluded. "It appears that he comprehends the situation well enough."

A noise at the other end of the building announced the entry of Jabir, Bashir, and four of the soldiers.

"My sons," Jabir exclaimed as he surveyed Rasil, "you have done well. When I heard of your success, I could not prevent my daughter from accompanying us."

Bemia, dressed in the robe of a soldier, smiled at her husband. She turned to Bashir and the three soldiers. "Thank you for helping me to get here. I feel well, thanks to you."

The men bowed their heads in acknowledgement. Then, with Bashir, they moved away to guard the door and prevent any intrusion. "Now," Bemia said, turning to look at the quivering Rasil. "What do we have here?"

As she spoke, she removed her head and face coverings and saw Rasil's eyes open in astonishment. "You, the blue-eyed one . . . ?" Rasil was not allowed to complete the question.

"Yes, as you can see, I am." Bemia answered.

"Ah, yes," Alric said. "Allow me to introduce my wife, Bemia. She was the intended victim of your men. Is it not interesting how the hunter can become the prey?"

Rasil was silent. He was not in a position to do anything about his current situation. Nevertheless, he had escaped before. He licked his parched, cracked lips, but his tongue felt dry. "What are your plans for me?" he asked, thinking that there might be a point for negotiation.

"Do not concern yourself with your future," Jabir said. "You will tell us what we need to know before we are done with you. "You have information that we require," Jabir continued, looking at Rasil through dark eyes that showed little emotion.

"I will tell you nothing," Rasil responded defiantly.

Jabir fixed his eyes on Rasil. "I want to tell you a story about dreams," Jabir said. "You are, I hear, a learned man who visits the library on regular occasions." Jabir paused and watched Rasil's reaction before he continued. "Through my son Ahmed, we have learned a lot about you. It is amazing what can be learned from the street beggars and what they will tell for a few coins. You have been under surveillance for some time now."

Jabir paused again as Khalil and Alric brought wood and stone supports to construct a makeshift seat for Bemia. Jabir continued. "As you may know, I have studied the arts of *al-khimiya* for several decades. My son Alric is my assistant, and he has studied the ingredients of mixtures that will heal the sick. Some of these ingredients, used in higher doses, can kill. The prick that you felt before you went into a deep sleep was the introduction of one such ingredient."

"I will tell you nothing. I will piss on you first!" Rasil exclaimed, realizing that his situation was becoming more and more hopeless by the minute. Alric drew his knife but was restrained by Khalil.

Jabir interjected, "If I turn all three of my sons loose on you, they will surely get the information we need. I suggest that you listen."

A heavily robed figure entered through the door. Alric noticed another surprised look from Rasil at the deference shown by them to the new arrival. "By the way," Jabir smiled, "this gentleman is my nephew. Better known to all as Harun al-Rashid, Caliph. He is here to listen to what you have to tell us."

Rasil glared in anger.

"Thank you, uncle," Harun said. "Please proceed, but before you do . . . ," Harun hesitated and turned to Bemia. "I hope you are recovering well?"

"I am, Sire," Bemia said, having arisen when Harun entered.

"Sit, Bemia," the Caliph commanded. "Rest yourself." He turned and nodded to Jabir to continue.

"Now, as I was saying," Jabir looked at Rasil, "you will tell us everything. The extract that put you to sleep will, when administered in a smaller dose, send you into a physical state so that your resistance will be impaired and you will have no willpower. Under such influence, you would even sell your mother into prostitution. I assume that you did have a mother?"

Rasil thought for a moment, then seemed to recover his confidence. "What do you want of me?"

"We need to hear from you the name of the man or men who hired you and for what reason."

Even though there seemed no hope of escape at this point and every movement caused the cord to bite into his wrists and ankles, Rasil's eyes gleamed craftily. "What is in it for me?" he asked.

"Well, it seems," Alric answered, "that we are not be able to trust you. So whatever you tell us consciously will have to be checked by administering the sleeping ingredient. If you may be thinking of a negotiating ploy, that is not an option. Do you wish to talk?"

"What will you do to me afterwards?"

Alric answered, "Your life is in the hands of the Caliph."

Seeing the desperation of his situation and realizing that his secrets would soon be known, Rasil's attitude hardened. "Damn all of you! I will not talk." The words exploded from Rasil as he struggled in an attempt to show defiance. It was futile, since the cords that bound him were secure. Pain shot through his arms and legs.

"No matter, you will talk under the influence of this extract," Jabir concluded and nodded to Alric to proceed.

Rasil felt the prick in his arm. He muttered an expletive and soon his eyes took on a glazed appearance. He was conscious, but after several minutes he seemed to lose all resistance. The cords that bound his wrists and ankles lost their sting. Alric knew he could see all of them through a semiconscious mist.

"Now we will start with your name," Alric's voice came clearly through the haze.

* * *

An hour later they had all acquired the information they needed. Rasil had not been able to resist the questions. The answers had flowed from his mouth without hesitation.

As the haze cleared, Rasil saw the Caliph approach.

"What do you intend to do with me?" he asked, his words slurred.

"Do?" the Caliph said. "Now that I have conclusive proof that the First Minister is behind this, I have no further use for you."

Rasil felt the urge to smile in relief as the thought passed through his mind that he would be allowed to go free. But this premature emotion disappeared as the Caliph continued. "My friend Alric will administer a stronger dose of this extract that will finish the job for us. You will not ply your trade anymore. You will die just as many of your victims have died. If you have a belief in Allah, make your peace now."

Rasil tried to speak, but his ability for conscious action diminished. His lips parted, but only a low groan escaped as the sharp prick in his upper arm indicated that the extract was being introduced once more into his body.

Alric was well aware of Rasil's next sensations. When the liquid entered his bloodstream, the effect was immediate. Rasil's limbs became numb, incapable of movement, and his breathing was difficult. His chest muscles tightened in response to the chemical that was coursing through his body. Realization finally came to Rasil that he was dying. He would not feel any pain, as might be expected from the thrust of a sword or dagger, only numbness.

Rasil's heart started to beat rapidly and his pulse quickened. The blood flooding through his arteries and veins would be as if a dam had burst inside him. The strain was too much on his body. His heart stopped.

Harun spoke without emotion as he looked at the prisoner's body. "I will have my men dispose of him." He looked at Jabir. "Uncle, I will have a litter made available to carry Bemia home. Alric, Bemia, you have done well. It seems that your medicine has incredible properties, and your method of introducing it into the body using a hollow needle is indeed amazing. I anticipate that you will be making written notes of these . . . ," Harun thought for a moment, "proceedings?"

"I will, Sire," Alric answered, after which he and Bemia chorused, "Thank you, Sire," with a bow of their heads.

"Ahmed, I thank you for your devotion to duty. As always, your actions are commendable." Ahmed bowed his head in gratitude. The Caliph then turned to look at Khalil. "Khalil my cousin, I can always count on you, and you always have my trust. Thank you." Finally, Harun spoke to all before him. "I have made preliminary arrangements in preparation for the time when this event would come about. Uncle," he looked at Jabir, "a hug for my aunt, if you please."

In a flurry of his robe, Harun turned on his heel and left. No one paid any further attention to Rasil's body, suspended between the two posts. They had accomplished what was necessary.

*   *   *

CHAPTER 40

Alric walked close by the litter that carried Bemia, wondering about her ability to withstand the ordeal of her first excursion out of the house since she had been wounded. His face betrayed his concern, but Bemia reached out and held his hand. "My dear husband," she smiled to comfort him, "I am well."

It had taken most of the day to capture and extract the information from Rasil. Now it was evening, and the air was pleasantly cool.

Alric looked at his wife. She did appear well and her color and attitude were excellent. The freshness of the rose water she used to cleanse her skin intoxicated him. Then his thoughts focused on the latest events. He knew the saga was about to come to an end, but the treachery of the First Minister still gnawed at his innards. Now the Caliph would handle the remaining business from this point.

With every step he took, Alric felt delivered from the hand of evil.

* * *

When they returned to the house, Amira, who had been concerned by their prolonged absence, greeted Jabir somewhat less formally than usual. She had taken his hands in hers and looked into his eyes. Not a word was spoken; the relief was evident on her face.

An hour later, they were seated in the lounge making the most of a pleasant meal of delicately cooked lamb, rice, a variety of vegetables, and fruit. The lamb and rice lay on a platter supported on a metal stand above several open containers that burned an oil to provide the heat.

Seeing this arrangement, Jabir looked at the food and then at Khalil, Alric, and Ahmed. He rolled his eyes, knowing that they would not eat until Amira had heard of the day's events.

"Now," Amira said, on cue with Jabir's thoughts, "I will hear of the events before we eat. Alric, please tell me what happened up to the point where Bemia arrived, and then perhaps she can finish."

Alric nodded, "Yes, mother."

When he had related his part of the story, Amira turned her attention to Bemia. Omitting some of the more lurid details, Bemia described what had happened to the assassin at the warehouse. She concluded by stating, "And that is when the Caliph left."

She looked around to see if there were any comments. No one spoke.

"Harun did request," Jabir added, "that I give you a hug." He reached out and held Amira's hand.

"He is such a dear boy," Amira said and then added, "This is a most interesting series of events."

She looked lovingly at Jabir and then proceeded to serve tea. At this signal, Wahid and Ma'ruf entered bringing chilled fruit drinks.

* * *

The evening meal was a joyous affair. Amira fussed over Bemia, and Bemia fussed over Alric, much to his discomfort. After the meal, Alric and Bemia retired to their bedroom, where Alric spread himself upon the snug cushions and stretched out his body on their softness with a satisfied groan, relaxing deeply into the thick fabric until he was satisfied that he was comfortable. The coolness of the house was most welcome after the heat of the day. Amira and Jabir had retired to their own private room while Khalil and Ahmed left to check the security of the house.

Alric, with Bemia's help, then spent two hours writing a description of Rasil's capture and interrogation. He included every detail that came to mind, and even more details when prodded by Bemia's gentle questioning. Finally, he was done. Bemia was perched on a seat as she brushed her waist-length, corn-colored hair.

The quietness of the night after an exhausting day overtook Alric. He closed his eyes and surrendered to the sleep that had eluded him for the past nights. Seeing that Alric had fallen asleep, Bemia put down the brush, walked over to where he lay on the cushions, and sat next to him. She leaned over and kissed him gently on the forehead, then reached over to him and cradled his head on her lap. In his dream, Alric could smell rose water.

*   *   *

Alric slept as if in a coma and awakened only when the sun was at its midpoint journey through the cloudless blue sky. He did not know where he was, and his first instinct was to reach for his dagger. Then he felt the gentle touch of Bemia's hand as she stroked his hair.

"My dear," she said, "you have had the sleep that you desperately needed. And," she added in response to the question that was forming on his lips, "I am feeling well. The outing yesterday was a little strenuous, but the exercise was good for my muscles and will help my recovery." She smiled mischievously. "It is time for your morning bath, Alric, and I will supervise. Father says that I must make sure the water does not soften the flesh of my wound and open it up again, but I can remain dry while you will be bathed thoroughly!"

Alric was soon relaxing in the glittering white porcelain bath, and the sunlight that flooded into the room from the high window made him feel alive. At the same time, Bemia stood under the shower, and the luxurious feel of the water rejuvenated her.

A gentle tap on the door heralded the arrival of Amira, who was bidden to enter. Alric scowled and lowered himself further into the bath water. "Good morning, mother."

"Well, my son, from what I can see of you, it is obvious that the rest has done you well." She looked at Bemia, who was wrapped in a large towel. "Your dear husband," Amira nodded toward Alric, "seems to be in good spirits this morning. The worry has gone from his face and he is looking quite normal once more."

"I am fine, mother," Alric said with slight irritation. "Now I would like to get dressed!"

"Take your time, both of you," Amira suggested. "I will have Abal and Maha bring refreshments."

Alric smiled. "Thank you, mother." Yes, he thought, food and refreshments would be very welcome! "Mother," he said as an afterthought, "is father around?"

"No," Amira replied, "he was called to the palace early this morning. Harun summoned him on a matter of some urgency. I am not sure when he will return."

After Amira's departure, Abal and Maha arrived with the food and drink. When they left, Alric arose from the bath and wrapped himself in the towel that Bemia held ready for him.

After they had eaten the fruit, oatmeal cakes, and tea, a tap on the door and Wahid's voice advised them that the family was to assemble in the lounge.

*   *   *

When they had all gathered together, Khalil and Ahmed being the last to arrive, Jabir was ready to begin. All eyes turned to him. He had just arrived from the palace.

"You will be pleased to know that your efforts have not been in vain. The Caliph called a meeting of the council this morning. Every council member was required to attend and no excuses were allowed. At the meeting, the First Minister was arrested publicly before all members of the council. He was officially charged with treason. At the same time, several of his accomplices, one of whom was his assistant minister, were also arrested at their homes or places of work. The Caliph was thorough, and no one who had showed even a modicum of support for the First Minister was allowed to remain free. Fortunately, there were not many such men."

Jabir tapped his finger on the wooden arm of the chair. "This being the case," he said," I now suggest that we all take the time to relax, take tea, and talk among ourselves, during which time I will give you the remainder of the details."

Tea was duly served, and the excited chatter reflected the family's mood. After the recent weeks of stress, Bemia's near-death incident, and other risks, the tone in each person's voice was much more even and echoed happiness. Finally, Alric could wait no longer. "Father," he said, "I am sure the Caliph will have taken the necessary precautions, but the First Minister is a crafty and resourceful man. After all, my wife.. . . . "

Before he could finish, Bemia put her hand on Alric's arm to restrain him. Jabir smiled as he answered. "I share your concern, Alric, and I did indeed broach this subject with the Caliph." He sipped tea from his cup. "The First Minister is not under house arrest," Jabir was emphatic in his words, "and he is not in, what we might call, an ordinary prison, or even a temporary one used by the Caliph's patrols. He is locked in a secure cell that is separated from all other cells. The Caliph feels that this is imperative. In addition, the members of the Caliph's council are sworn to secrecy under pain of death. All council members clearly understood the meaning behind the Caliph's words of caution."

Jabir looked at Alric and Bemia. "You have no need to worry. The cell he is in was formerly used for prisoners awaiting execution. It is situated on the lower floor of the prison and is watched over constantly by six trustworthy men. All are soldiers commanded by Bashir, I might add. The guards are not allowed to converse with a prisoner in that cell. The First Minister will be too preoccupied by thoughts of his fate to take much interest in his surroundings. In other words, bribing the guards is not an option for Abdul al-Warith! I hear it from a reliable source that he yelled and screamed for an hour after he was first incarcerated, but no one paid any attention. And now . . . "

"My dear husband," Amira interjected, "I am hoping you get to the point soon. You do have something else to say."

"How could I ever fool you, my dear wife?" Jabir responded. Then he turned to look at Alric. "The Caliph has asked that you appear before him. His request is that you use your extract to make the First Minister speak the truth before the members of the council. Harun, the Caliph, feels that the council members must hear the truth behind the arrest from the First Minister himself. This would remove any lingering doubts in their minds about Abdul al-Warith."

Jabir turned to look at Khalil and Ahmed. "You are also requested to be present for commendations from the council. And you, my dear," Jabir looked at Bemia, "are to receive the Caliph's recognition for your bravery."

Bemia bowed her head in deference. Jabir continued. "And, mother, I think you should be there . . . "

"I will indeed be present to tend to the well-being of my daughter! And, of course, to see my nephew."

"Mother, we need to decide what I should wear!" Bemia exclaimed. The laughter from the men was thunderous.

Jabir tapped on the arm of the chair using a cane he had miraculously retrieved from the pocket of his robe. "Before we leave," he said, "there is a promise that I made to Alric on behalf of Ma'ruf. I must fulfill that promise here and now before all of you as witnesses. The Caliph has given me the authority to do this. Wahid!" Jabir called out and the man appeared. "Summon Ma'ruf, please."

* * *

They awaited Ma'ruf's arrival with a calmness that came from knowing what was about to take place. "You sent for me Lord Jabir?"

"Before you undertook to accompany Alric to entrap the First Minister, Ma'ruf," Jabir began, "I made a promise that your loyalty and your willingness to accept danger should be rewarded. This reward was that you would be allowed to return to your home as a free man for the remainder of your life. I also said that I would provide you with a pension so that you may live comfortably. And I also made a commitment to pay for the construction of a schoolhouse that would carry your name where you can live and teach the children.

"This morning, my nephew, the Caliph declared that my promise to you will be fulfilled and that you would travel as a free man with the next delegation of ambassadors that he, the Caliph, sends to Charlemagne, the King of the Franks. They will explain the reason for my gift to you." Jabir reached into a pouch that lay beside him. "This document," Jabir went on, "explains your situation. It is written in Arabic and Latin to cover all eventualities."

Lines of emotion suddenly appeared on Ma'ruf's face. His body shook as Alric walked up to him and put his arm around his shoulder. "Well, done, my friend. The family is truly indebted to you for taking on such a dangerous role and helping us through this troublesome time. I particularly thank you for the defense of my wife as she became exhausted during the fighting that took place here."

Alric was joined by Khalil and Ahmed, who in turn embraced Ma'ruf. Ma'ruf turned to Bemia and bowed his head to acknowledge her presence. Bemia smiled at him before he turned his attention to

Jabir and Amira. "Lord Jabir and Lady Amira, I will always be grateful for your kindness. You have treated me with respect, and for that I owe you much. If it were not for the thoughts of teaching children at school, I would stay here, but my destiny is to return to my homeland."

"As the time for your journey approaches," Jabir said, "Wahid will help you make the arrangements. You may not know it, but when presented with a similar opportunity some years ago, Wahid decided to stay with us."

Ma'ruf addressed them. "I look forward to making this journey and to start a new life. I have often silently expressed a desire to see the land where I was born, and you have given me that opportunity."

"You can do so much for the children of your homeland," Amira replied. "That is all we ask."

"Before you leave this house," Jabir's tone became serious, "you will be given a package in your name. It will contain this discharge," Jabir indicated the document that he had taken from the pouch, "and yet another document states that you fall under the guardianship of the Caliph and that you are not to be detained in any way. You will also be given letters of credit for a sum of money that is sufficient to allow you to complete the schoolhouse. The ambassadors will use this letter of credit to help you recruit the labor for the building of the school and pay for all of the materials needed. A second letter of credit will contain sufficient money for a pension for five years. As the fourth year comes to its halfway point, more money will be deposited with the King of the Franks with a request that he also see to your well-being. That is your money to do with as you wish. We hope that you live for many years and that you marry. If so, at the time of your death, your wife will be paid a pension until the time she follows you in death. Any children of such union will not receive a pension. They can learn from their father the meaning of hard work and its rewards."

Ma'ruf beamed, bowed his head, and left the room radiant. They watched him as he walked with a new spring in his step. His cheeks were flushed with pride, and his red hair seemed to shine even more than usual.

Within moments of Ma'ruf's leaving the room, they heard a loud whoop fill the air. Khalil and Ahmed rose from their seats, drawing swords as they did so.

"Stay your hands, my brothers," Alric exclaimed. "That was Ma'ruf. It would seem, father, that he is pleased with your announcement, and he has just expressed his happiness!"

All laughed at Alric's understatement.

* * *

Two hours later, Jabir and his family were led into the council chamber and formally introduced to the members of the council by the Caliph. "I am sure," Harun said to his council, "that you all know my uncle, Jabir al-Hajjaj ibn Yusuf abu Asad abu Khalil."

Nods of affirmation and smiles greeted Jabir.

"Now, Harun continued, "let me introduce his family."

Starting with Amira, whom Harun introduced as his dear aunt, the other family members were introduced one at a time. This was followed by the introduction of Alric as Alric al-Biritaanya ibn Jabir and as Bemia al-Biritaanya binit Jabir. During this time, Bemia had retained her head covering, but at a signal from the Caliph, Alric helped her remove it. A murmur of surprise came from the council members as they noticed the color and length of her hair.

"This young lady, who is also under my protection, stood alone and faced eight assassins. Even though severely wounded, she dispatched each one in turn with her sword and made sure no harm came to my aunt, Amira, and other persons in the house." Words of approval rang though the chamber.

"She is the wife of Alric," Harun turned to nod and smile at Alric. "I now request that Bemia al-Biritaanya binit Jabir, Bemia from

Britain, daughter of Jabir, stand before you to receive the thanks of this council."

The council members stood, and the thunderous applause brought a blush to Bemia's cheeks and a tear to Amira's eye as she remembered Bemia's efforts that night. Ali al-Maslawi, who was sitting in the front row, winked at Alric.

As the applause died down, Harun ushered the family to their seats, smiling all the while. Then his face took on a serious look. "The reason I have called this special meeting of the council," he looked at the members, "is to bring to your attention a very serious matter. The issue at hand is treason by one who was close to me. I speak of none other than Abdul al-Warith, formerly the First Minister in my government."

The Caliph remained in the center of the chamber awaiting any response.

Alric was somewhat nervous about the nature of the proceedings, not knowing what to expect. But the council members remained silent, their eyes focused on the Caliph, awaiting his next words.

"This is a story of treachery of the highest order. Several years ago, I elevated this man to the post of First Minister. This is a man whom I trusted with my kingdom and therefore with my life. I thought that I knew him, and even now I do not understand nor will I probably ever understand why he acted in this way."

Harun paused and looked around the chamber. "When I first heard of his treachery," he continued, "I found it difficult to believe he was capable of such acts. When I received word of his actions, I would have been satisfied with his banishment from the kingdom for life. But the attack that he ordered on the house of my aunt and uncle was too much. Had it not been for the valiant efforts of Bemia al-Biritaanya binit Jabir, the attack would have been successful. The assassins would have lain in wait for Khalil, Ahmed, and Alric, as well as my uncle, and there would have been more bloodshed. Such were the plans of Abdul al-Warith."

All eyes were fixed on the Caliph as he walked back and forth in front of the seats where they sat. He carefully formulated his next words, and then he looked at the council members. "As for the consequences of the First Minister's actions," he said, "I ask you to decide. A simple majority will mean death. Any other vote will mean banishment from the kingdom for life. Should the latter be your decision, any return to the kingdom after banishment will result in his execution."

Ali al-Maslawi shifted in his seat, as if feeling some discomfort.

"Ali, you have a comment?" the Caliph asked.

"Sire, with respect, some members may feel that the council is lacking the proof for us to make such a decision."

"Well said, Ali," Harun replied. "As always, your words are very eloquent and to the point." The Caliph cleared his throat and looked to where Alric and the family sat at one side of the council chamber. "Alric, on his own and without the tutelage of my uncle in this matter, has developed a new extract from plants which makes men tell the truth under questioning even when they are the most steadfast liars. The extract is administered quite conveniently but carefully, and I am allowing a demonstration now. The subject is, of course, Abdul al Warith. Each of you can formulate your own questions and then address them to al-Warith. I suggest that to convince yourselves of the truthfulness of his answers, you ask him personal questions, whispered if you wish, for which only you know the answers. After the session, you will be provided with refreshments."

Harun turned to Alric. "Are you ready?"

Alric bowed his head and responded, "Yes, Sire."

The Caliph retired to his seat on the dais at the head of the council chamber and addressed Alric. "Before you commence your work, Alric, I suggest you give the members a brief description of what you will do and how the drug affects a person. I have seen this for myself on another subject who had to be questioned. You will see that there is no need for the use of hot irons to turn a man's tongue, since he will say anything to relieve the pain." Harun indicated that Alric should proceed.

"Sire, members of the council, I stand here before you today to explain how the extract works and to make sure that you do not see a miscarriage of justice. What you see and hear is open for the closest of inspections. I would even suggest that once I begin, you come closer to the prisoner. You will see that there is no obvious interference on my part."

Alric then gave a description of the means by which the extract was introduced into a person and the subsequent effects. The council members listened intently as Alric continued his speech. Other than the sound of Alric's words ringing through the chamber, not a word was spoken. A cough here and a shuffle there were the only sounds that competed with Alric's clear tones.

When he finished, he announced, "If you have any questions, I will be happy to answer them for you." There were none. Alric turned to the Caliph, bowed his head, and said, "Thank you, Sire." Then he returned to his seat to await the arrival of the First Minister.

* * *

CHAPTER 41

The venue had changed to another room in the palace. Chairs for the council members were placed in a semicircle, with a single chair at the focal point. Other seats were set aside near to a wall; these were for the Caliph, Alric, and the remainder of the family. Scheherazade sat next to Bemia.

Once the council members were seated, Abdul al-Warith, formerly First Minister to the Caliph Harun al-Rashid, was led into the room by two soldiers. His hands were bound in front and his clothes were disheveled, but for a man who had spent a night in prison, his condition could only be described as good.

The First Minister appeared angry. Without taking in his surroundings, he looked at the council members with scorn. "By what authority is this being done?" al-Warith demanded.

"By my authority," Harun al-Rashid responded as he rose from his seat. "By the express authority granted to me by the law. I act by the laws of this land and not by any implied authority."

For the first time, al-Warith saw the Caliph as he turned to the source of the voice. It was then that he recognized Alric and Bemia, as well as the other members of Jabir's family.

"Then, tell me why I am here?"

"You will change the tone of your voice," Harun commanded, "or I will have you gagged. This council has been convened to discuss your unlawful actions within this institution of government."

The Caliph looked at the council members. Their faces showed no emotion.

Ali al-Warith smiled confidently. "On the contrary, I have done nothing wrong. An internal investigation will establish that fact."

"Such an investigation is now under way, and there is evidence that your colleagues, who also participated in your scheme and who, at this time, are under arrest, misappropriated funds from the treasury, mistreated women, and either murdered or attempted to murder innocent people. You have become a major liability. Thus, it is my determination that the council members will sit in judgment of you. They have not been informed of all of your activities, but they will hear about them as the day lengthens."

From the look on his face, everyone could see that al-Warith was stunned. He stuttered breathlessly for a moment but finally managed to speak. "This is outrageous! I have never seen such hypocrisy in my life! You," he looked at the council members, "have no idea what you are doing, and I can assure you, you haven't heard the last of this. When you hear the truth, you will wish . . . "

"And that is precisely what we propose to do," Harun said.

The Caliph nodded, and instantly two of his soldiers took a secure hold on each of al-Warith's arms and legs and bound them to a chair. Now that he was restrained, he was finally at a loss for words, and remained silent as he realized the seriousness of the proceedings.

The Caliph continued. "You will not be subjected to hot irons or any other form of physical discomfort. It would be easy for anyone to deduce that you talked under duress in such a situation. Your treatment will be quite different." The Caliph looked around. "Alric," he said quietly, "please explain to Abdul al-Warith the nature of your method of persuasion."

Alric stood where al-Warith and the council members could see him. He spoke quietly and with confidence as he related the story he had told the council members earlier. Abdul al-Warith closed his eyes and put on a slight, and seemingly genuine, smile. When Alric had finished, al-Warith opened his eyes, looked at Alric, and sneered. His words were not gracious, and he turned his attention to the council members, saying, "I find it hard to believe that such a scheme will work."

"Oh, it does work," the Caliph said. "I saw the effect the extract had on your man Rasil, who, I am told, is also known as the Messenger of Death. He told us everything before he died. You will tell us everything and then we will decide on an appropriate punishment."

Al-Warith drew a deep breath and was about to respond but he was again stopped by the Caliph. "Alric, it is time."

On that cue, the soldiers took a firm grip of al-Warith's arms and held the chair firmly in place. Alric approached him from the rear and gently inserted the needle into the First Minister's arm. He felt the sharp prick of the needle. Alric continued to exert gentle pressure on the bulb containing the extract. The expression of hatred on al-Warith's face changed to that of benevolent tolerance as the chemical took its effect.

Alric could see from his eyes that he did not realize what was happening. Then Alric turned to the council members.

"Gentlemen," he said, "I have used my hollow needle to introduce the extract into Abdul al-Warith's arm. As you can see, he is now silent. However, I have introduced only as much of the chemical as is necessary for him to tell us the truth. It is safe to approach, Sire," Alric said looking at the Caliph, who sat next to Jabir and Amira. Bemia, Khalil, and Ahmed, having seen this effect once before, remained attentive and on the edge of their respective seats waiting for the proceedings to commence.

"Gentlemen," Alric gestured with his arm in the direction of al-Warith, "I offer you the opportunity to approach the prisoner."

As the council members cautiously left their seats to observe the effects of the extract, al-Warith continued to remain calm.

The Caliph's voice rang throughout the room. "As I suggested earlier, you may now question him regarding personal events."

* * *

When the last of the council members had talked with the First Minister, they all stepped back; the initial examination was done. No one who asked questions excluded their colleagues. All was done openly.

"Are you satisfied that al-Warith speaks the truth?" Harun asked. Heads nodded affirmatively. "Then we shall begin the serious questioning," the Caliph added. "I have provided scribes to make a record of these proceedings. I suggest we begin with Ali al-Maslawi. And," Harun passed, "I will appoint Ali as the chair of the council for this session." A murmur of approval ran through the room.

When al-Maslawi was finished, the others of the council asked questions one at a time. One by one, each of the members was satisfied and outraged by the responses they heard. Alric could see the First Minister's eyelids fluttering as he fought to regain control.

* * *

As the effects of the chemical began to wear off, al-Warith regained his senses. He had no idea what had transpired. "I am rather tired of this game," he said. "That prick in my arm did nothing but irritate me. You," he focused his eyes on al-Maslawi, "are attempting to destroy me, but you shall not succeed. This has, indeed, been an ineffective and useless exercise!"

"You may think that at this moment," al-Maslawi replied, "but you are very much mistaken. While the sun climbed into the heavens, we have learned much from you about your actions." Ali looked at the Caliph. "Sire, my fellow council members have indicated to me that they are ready to convey their decision to you."

The First Minister looked around in amazement. "Tell me your decision," he begged.

"I cannot do that," al-Maslawi answered. "After we convene to discuss our finding, the decision will be conveyed to the Caliph first, and he will pronounce judgment that is in accordance with the recommendation of this council."

Abdul al-Warith became very pale. He attempted to stand, but his leg and arm bindings restrained him. The soldiers approached from where they had been standing and laid their hands firmly on his shoulders so that his movements were even more limited. A look of terror spread across his face. He struggled against the bindings and the hands of the soldiers. It was several hours since he had been brought into the room.

Alric and Jabir watched al-Warith's reactions with the curiosity of men of science, but they had little remorse. Bemia and Scheherazade watched with curiosity. The faces of Amira, Khalil, and Ahmed were devoid of emotion.

A tap on the door broke the silence. "Come," the Caliph's voice rang out.

The door opened and a cold-faced young officer stepped into the room. He walked to the Caliph, words were quietly exchanged, and with a brief movement of his hand, the officer indicated to the soldiers that the First Minister should be freed from the chair and taken back to his imprisonment.

Visibly shaken and stunned, Abdul al-Warith was led out of the room and marched between the two soldiers, his face vaguely perturbed, but still not fully comprehending what had occurred. Before he reached the door, he seemed to recover, straightened up and, mindful of the danger that he was in, turned and looked back at the Caliph. Harun remained stone faced and impassionate as Abdul al-Warith was led away.

* * *

After al-Warith's departure, the Caliph rose from his chair and approached the council members. "I presume," Harun said, "that you need time to deliberate?" Ali al-Maslawi bowed his head in agreement. "You may remain here," the Caliph said to the council, "to consider the evidence that has been put before you today. The issues to be decided are whether or not Abdul al-Warith shall be sentenced to death or be banished from the kingdom."

Harun looked thoughtful. "I know you will give much consideration to your decision, and I will abide by it. I will have refreshments brought to you, and as soon as you have made your decision, please send word to me and we will reconvene here."

With that, the Caliph, Scheherazade, and the Jabir family withdrew, leaving the council members to their deliberations.

The discussions were thoughtful and intense. The council recalled Alric and Jabir on two occasions to ask questions about the nature of the chemical. They also had questions regarding the interrogation of Rasil and of his background. Alric did not have his notes, in which he had recorded the details of Rasil's capture and interrogation. Two of the soldiers were dispatched to Jabir's house and returned with Ma'ruf and the notebook. Ma'ruf had informed the soldiers that the notebook would not leave his possession until it was delivered into the hands of Jabir or Alric.

The council listened intently to Alric's description of Rasil's interrogation and recognized the serious consequences that would have ensued had Rasil been successful.

When Alric and Jabir withdrew from the council room, the deliberations continued. After almost an hour of further discussion, al-Maslawi called for a vote.

* * *

Scheherazade, Jabir, and the family were once more seated in the council room as the Caliph faced the members of his council. "I presume," Harun said quietly to Ali al-Maslawi, "that you have reached a decision?"

Ali looked at his colleagues. "We have, Sire."

"And that decision is?" the Caliph asked.

"We find Abdul al-Warith, formerly First Minister to you, Sire, guilty of treason by his own words. We also add that he has willfully broken several laws of this land. Each breach of the law is an offense against you and the people of this land."

"And your recommendation is?" Harun asked, raising an eyebrow.

"The decision of the council, Sire, is that Abdul al-Warith be taken to a public place and executed for his crime of treason. Each law that he broke is punishable either by banishment, life in prison, or death."

The Caliph looked at all of the members. "Is your decision unanimous?"

"It is, Sire. Each member has indicated his willingness to stand before you and be heard so that every vote can be recorded." Al-Maslawi indicated that there had been no dissent, and so that the scribes could record the individual votes, each man's name was called and he declared his vote on the various counts.

When all was done, al-Maslawi spoke again. "With your permission, Sire?" The Caliph nodded. "The council would also like to record a debt of gratitude to the family of Jabir al-Hajjaj ibn Yusuf abu Asad abu Khalil, who valiantly stood against this man. We particularly thank Bemia al-Biritaanya binit Jabir for her valiant efforts at staying the hands of the assassins, almost at the cost of her life. The council members are also appreciative of the efforts of Alric al-Biritaanya ibn Jabir, who has followed in the footsteps of his father, Jabir al-Hajjaj ibn Yusuf abu Asad abu Khalil, and shown us that *al-khimiya* can be used beneficially. We also thank Khalil and Ahmed, the sons of Jabir and Amira, for their role in bringing this case to a conclusion. And finally, the council members offer a vote of thanks to the two men known as Ma'ruf and Wahid. The council recognizes that their roles were most important on the night that Bemia stood valiantly against the eight assassins."

Harun turned to the scribes. "Let it also be recorded that I accept the decision of the council, and the execution will be carried out at the first opportune time. Finally, my gratitude goes to Ali al-Maslawi, chairman."

As the scribes carefully recorded Harun's words, he turned to the council. "Members of the Council, I offer my thanks to you for undertaking this difficult task."

The silence hung heavily in the room. "It is done. You are adjourned," Harun said in conclusion.

* * *

CHAPTER 42

The day dawned bright and sunny, and the trials and tribulations of the previous day were now events of the past.

City criers, men who were paid to go from street to street, to bang on a drum, and to shout their message to the people, had spread the word that an execution was to occur in the marketplace. The man to be executed was none other than Abdul al-Warith, formerly First Minister to the Caliph, Harun al-Rashid.

By midmorning, hundreds of people had lined the broad thoroughfare of the marketplace. The vendors were prevented from setting up their stalls but were permitted to relocate in the streets radiating from the market square. There was to be no price gouging, upon pain of imprisonment, and the Caliph had announced that the palace would cover the cost of all refreshments sold by the merchants. Soldiers patrolled the streets and rooftops of the buildings, peering down on the people as they made their way to the square.

The fresh breeze from the south continued to cool the crowd as Jabir and the family entered the square. They were led to a row of seats in front of the dais. There were whispers of wonderment too, as many, for the first time, saw the blonde northerners who accompanied the family. Word spread quickly that the tall blonde female was the one who, it was rumored, had stood against eight assassins and had

563

triumphed, almost at the cost of her life. Because of the presence of Jabir and his family, the crowd was aware that someone of importance was to be executed. The noise of the multitude reached a crescendo—execution day belonged to the people.

Shortly after Jabir was seated, the loud clip-clop of horses' hooves was heard. Transportation to the place of execution by open carriage was reserved for those of a high station in life.

*   *   *

Al-Warith did not even look at the crowd. A cordon of thirty-two soldiers, commanded by Bashir, Jabir's nephew, formed a wall of steel around the carriage to prevent anyone from getting too close. The carriage stopped at the rear of the dais and was visible to everyone in the square. Bashir ordered his men to surround the dais.

The market square was filled to capacity. The Caliph had decided to make everything as secure as possible, since he was uncertain about the degree of sympathy for al-Warith. It was the first time within living memory that a minister of a Caliph's government would be executed. There were those in the crowd who were curious, others who were determined not to miss it, and those who wanted to see if a minister would die with dignity or, like many other criminals, whimpering as he begged for mercy.

Alric sensed a change in the mood of the crowd. There were shouts of derision and hatred at the sight of al-Warith. Alric leaned over and spoke to Bemia. "If Abdul al-Warith is expecting someone to come to his aid, I sense he will be sorely disappointed."

Ahmed overheard Alric's words. "You are correct, brother. I see the mood of the crowd growing darker, and Bashir needs to be on his guard in case anyone decides to take the law into his own hands! If trouble starts, protect father and mother."

"I will," Bemia responded instinctively.

Alric, Bemia, Jabir, Amira, Khalil, and Ahmed watched from their front-row seats as al-Warith, trussed and fully clothed, was made to kneel on the dais. The crowd suddenly fell silent, and the executioner appeared from the rear. As he laid his hand on the al-Warith's shoulder, the noise of the crowd soared to a crescendo of approval.

The executioner carried a powerful, curved, long sword, still sheathed. His face was covered, only his eyes showing. He moved to a position at the rear edge of the dais, where he stood at attention. Both hands rested on the leather-bound hilt of his sheathed sword. Alric knew from the descriptions of executions that the sword was sharpened to a fine edge.

The crowd had settled, and Alric felt that the fear of a riot was unfounded.

*   *   *

He cast his mind back to the early morning. Amira had at first decided that she did not wish to see the final phase of al-Warith's life. "All I feel for the man is disdain," she told Alric and Bemia that morning, "because of the way he misused his office and trust. It is better that I ignore him. Later, father will give me any details that I require."

However, when she saw Bemia preparing to leave, and remembering her near death struggle for life, Amira changed her mind.

Alric turned his attention to al-Warith. He could see the man's lips moving but was unable to hear the words. He assumed that al-Warith would be praying for his life.

However, he remained silent as the executioner's assistants, kneeling next to him, asked for his forgiveness and then raised him to his feet.

The words of al-Warith's response carried across the short distance from the dais to where Alric was seated. "I certainly will not forgive you," al-Warith growled. "May you all be cursed." His words had no effect.

A roar came from the crowd. Al-Warith turned and looked at the people with a venomous expression on his face. At that moment he saw Jabir and his family sitting at the front. He recognized Ali al-Maslawi and the members of the council, expressions of satisfaction on their faces.

Al-Warith had hoped that a last-minute effort would save him. His appeals and demands, continuous throughout the night, for an audience with the Caliph had not been answered. He then wished to appeal to the crowd, and the mob would save him. There was no mob; this was a noisy but an orderly group that expected only one thing, for him to die.

The assistants began to disrobe him, laying his clothes aside. During the time this took, the look on al-Warith's face never changed. It was a mask of evil, a reminder of his treachery to those who saw him for this last time. Finally, being stripped of all his clothes except the undershift, the two assistants forced him to kneel once more. One of them produced a cloth to cover al-Warith's head, but he shook his head to show that he refused the cover. The executioner nodded and the man withdrew. The assistants' work was done and the executioner took center stage.

In the meantime, Ali al-Maslawi had ascended the dais, where he commenced to read the charges, the verdict on each charge, and the resulting writ of execution that had been signed by the Caliph and all of the members of the council. The list of the First Minister's crimes was impressive by any standards. Knowing that the moment was near, the people began to shout angrily at al-Warith.

"Where is the Caliph?" al-Warith asked.

"I am here, Abdul," the voice came from behind.

Al-Warith looked around. There was no one, save the executioner. Then the truth dawned. The Caliph was the executioner. "You have committed crimes against me, against my land, and against the people," Harun said. "For that, I will execute you myself."

Al-Warith attempted to reply, but gasping from thirst, he asked for water.

"Give him water," said the Caliph. He looked down as Abdul gulped the water. "And now, Abdul," the Caliph said, "it is time." Harun paused. "You have heard the charges and the verdict. Prepare yourself."

As the Caliph raised the sword, al-Warith tensed, lowered his head, and waited for the fatal stroke. Bemia took hold of Alric's hand and squeezed it, knowing at last that justice was about to be done. Harun's sword descended swiftly in an arc, severing the head of the former First Minister.

The loud roar from the crowd startled the pigeons around the square, and the flapping of their wings added to the resounding noise. The Caliph looked across the dais at Alric and other members of the family. "My friends, I thank you for your efforts," he said quietly. "I know that I owe you my life."

Assistants approached the Caliph with towels and water to wash his hands. Then one of them exclaimed in a loud voice, "So perish all enemies of the Caliph!"

Bright sunshine flooded the dais. Alric suddenly felt the anticlimax. The execution was over. He held Bemia's hand and looked at Ahmed and Khalil. They remained motionless in their seats. Jabir turned to Alric and said simply, "So be it."

The crowd started to disperse, most of them making their way to the vendors' stalls. Shouting and voicing approval of the execution was thirsty work. Some took a longer route to the thirst-quenching stalls to catch a glimpse of Bemia and Alric.

The square, which had been packed to capacity a short time ago, was soon deserted. There would be stories to tell, opinions to voice, and rumors to accept or deny as the conversation about the reasons for the First Minister's execution were discussed over and over again.

Alric felt now that now was the time he could return to the laboratory and the joys of *al-khimiya*. Many of the people had never read a book in their lives and concerned themselves only with surviving the trials and tribulations of everyday life. He wanted more. He not only wished to help people survive, but he wanted to help educate them.

The clusters of palm trees threw the shadows from their leafy heads far over the roofs of the buildings lining the square. As he and Bemia walked back to the house, Alric thought of the events that had led him to this moment. He suddenly felt relaxed, and a sense of calmness came over him. In the silence of his mind, he knew that he and Bemia had closure. He looked into her eyes and smiled.

* * *

The remainder of the year was surprisingly peaceful, after the turmoil of events leading up to the execution of Abdul al-Warith.

Alric continued his work with extracts and medicines and assisted Jabir on his visits to home-bound patients. There was not a person who lived in Baghdad who did not recognize the blond northerner who had the ability to heal the sick. Every day, Alric expressed his love for Bemia and for their life together. He continued to write the events of each day in his journal.

It seems almost an anticlimax to write about Ma'ruf's departure for his homeland. Alric and Bemia missed him, but they stayed in contact through frequent letters carried by the ambassadors from the court of Charlemagne to Baghdad. Ma'ruf was thrilled to be back in his homeland and he did marry. Bemia had been forecasting Ma'ruf's marriage for some time, and when she received word of the marriage by letter, she gave Alric an I-told-you-so look.

Bemia continued to work in the laboratory with Alric, although she also spent a lot of time with Amira, who was happy to relax in the company of her northern daughter. They even made regular trips to the market but, at Harun's command, always under eyes of four of his guards.

Alric took over Jabir's duties as the passing years slowed down his aging father. Jabir even started to write a journal and in addition to recipes for the preparation of medicines, recorded the correct methods of administration for them. As a result, Alric and Jabir were able to gain experience from this exercise and often revise their methods of treatment.

Khalil and Ahmed continued in service to the Caliph and rose to the top of their professions. Their methods of military training and discipline were adopted as those methods of choice for the Caliph's armies. Individually, they were often deployed to various parts of the kingdom only to return to Baghdad when they were satisfied that the soldiers were trained to their maximum capabilities. Their return was always a joy to Jabir and Amira, and Bemia would take on the duties of organizing a welcome-home reception for both her brothers.

For many years, Alric, Bemia, and the family continued their work together, and the pain of their past experience gradually faded into dim memory.

* * *

PART IV: THE RETURN

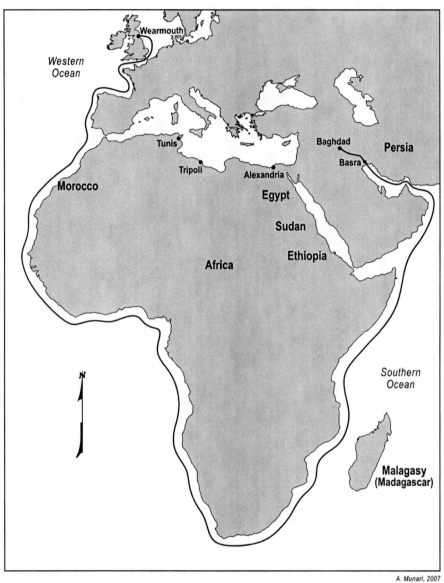

Map 4: The journey around Africa.

CHAPTER 43

I, Alric of Wearmouth also known in this land as Alric al-Biritaanya ibn Jabir, declare that the story of the first part of my life is now complete. I have related the events that caused me to be adopted into the house of Jabir and Amira as their son and to be introduced to my dearest Bemia.

Surprisingly, as a stranger in a strange land, I found that I had much in common with many of the people of the land. There were those who helped shape my life, and my gratitude is with them forever, wherever they may be at this time. Now as I look back on my life, I see the many stories that remain to be told and the changes that have occurred since the day of the execution of Abdul al-Warith.

As for the stories, perhaps one day I will write them down for posterity and for the amusement of younger people. But the changes that have occurred during my lifetime are worthy of consideration now.

My friend the Caliph Harun al-Rashid and his wife, Scheherazade, have been dead these many years. Nay, they have been dead these many decades—it is almost sixty years since the day of Harun's death and thirty years since the death of Scheherazade. Harun has been succeeded through several generations by Caliph al-Mutawakkil.

There have been numerous rumors about Harun's death in the year 809 of the Christian era, but I know from my experience that he died of an illness which had long given him trouble. As he was getting ready to march once more into the Roman provinces, a revolt broke out in one of the eastern regions of the kingdom, and while on his way to suppress it, he died. His remains lie in the eastern city of Tus, Persia. I know for a fact that the sickness for which he received my treatment was incurable and was gnawing at his inside. I have heard such sickness called the *crab*, or *cancer*, as is the name given to the disease in Roman literature.

Under several Caliphs since Harun, the scholars in the library, or House of Wisdom, as it is now called, have continued their work translating many Greek texts, and these translations have been copied and read widely throughout Mesopotamia, Egypt, and the provinces that border the western edge of the Middle Sea. There have been many internal arguments and rivalries between the librarian scholars, and it is this strife that has made me think and decide on a course of action.

Of late there has been trouble in Constantinople. The city has been attacked by the sea raiders, and my experience with them tells me that they will return. All of these activities have caused me to think about my future and my promise to my beloved Bemia. So it is with joy that I have made the decision, but with heavy heart that I leave the city that became my home for almost seven decades. However, this is dependent upon my audience with the Caliph.

My father Jabir and my mother Amira died several decades ago of a good age. Father died first. He was taken suddenly in his sleep. He had been active until dinnertime one day, when he declared that he felt tired and had to retire for the night. He never arose from his bed. One week later, mother died after declaring that she could not live without father in the house and his experiments in the laboratory. They had been married for more than fifty years, perhaps even sixty, but no one knows for sure. At the suggestion of Khalil, my parents willed the house and gardens to Bemia and myself. In return, we decided to leave the house to the oldest living son or grandson of Khalil when the time came for us to pass on into the world hereafter.

My brothers Khalil and Ahmed still live, even though they have several years on me. Had it not been for them, I am probably the oldest man that I know!

A year after Abdul al-Warith was executed, they had both announced their intention to marry—Khalil for the first time and Ahmed for the second time. It had been many years since Ahmed's wife and son had died, and he had found a pretty and pleasant young woman to take to wife. The first sons of both Khalil's and Ahmed's marriages, who are now men, became highly placed in the service of the Caliph, and currently both are ambassadors. Khalil's son is ambassador to the court of the king of Egypt, and Ahmed's son is ambassador to the court of the Chinese emperor. It was through both of these young men, who see fit to address me affectionately as Uncle Alric, that I was able to garner copies of documents of interest over these recent years. I was pleased that Ahmed married again after his sad misfortunes early in life. In fact, his children and grandchildren have been active in the service of many Caliphs.

Unfortunately, the brother that I hardly met, Asad, died in Constantinople during one of the many uprisings that seem to plague that city. But let me return to Khalil and Ahmed.

It is a thrill to see the offspring of my two brothers, whom I am privileged to acknowledge as my nephews and nieces. Some are even wont to call me grandfather, never having met their true grandparents.

The love of my life and my only love, Bemia, died two years ago. As near as I could tell, she was two years older than me, although I never referred to her as being older, yet she always reminded me that I was the youngster, no matter what our age, and that I should do as she bade. She always smiled when she had such a conversation with me, and we would laugh together.

Regrettably, we never had children. It seems that the beating and harsh treatment that Bemia had received from Abdul al-Warith during the time she was held captive by him interfered with her ability to conceive. However, because of the frequent visits from the offspring of Khalil and Ahmed, we were never short of the laughter and company of children.

My Bemia died peacefully. We sat, as we often did, in the lounge reading the stories written by Scheherazade. One day, we were reading the story in which Bemia's valiant fight against the eight assassins had been described and included in one of Scheherazade's tales. Bemia and I were reminiscing about that night when I turned to seek one of the servants and request tea. I turned again to look once more at my Bemia to find that her countenance had changed. She looked pale and was sitting motionless. She smiled at me as I took her hand in mine.

"I have loved you as no other woman loves her husband. My dear, I must leave you now, but I will return for you." With those words, she breathed her last.

I received many letters and words of consolation from all who knew us. The Caliph was kind enough to allow me to send Bemia to the next world in the Saxon manner. She was cremated in a private ceremony, and I have kept the ashes of her funeral pyre in a special vessel that I keep in a quiet corner of the lounge that she loved so much.

I have heard that Ma'ruf made a successful life in his home country and may even still be alive. The school that bore his name became the first of several such schools, and children are being educated due to his efforts.

Wahid, faithful to the last, died shortly after mother and father. As a tribute to his years of service, Khalil had him incorporated into the family as an official uncle a year before his death. He lived with Bemia and I for the remainder of his life, and even in the days just prior to his death, he still took it upon himself to organize the servants and make sure that all was well with the household.

Each of the three girls Abal, Buhjah, and Maha left the house shortly after the death of mother and father to start their own families. Bemia maintained contact with them. The three have since died, but their families live on and visit me on occasion.

So, the times pass, and so do the caravans of the desert and now I, Alric al-Biritaanya ibn Jabir, am being escorted to an audience with the Caliph, who has made the journey from Samarra to meet with me.

*   *   *

The escort that the Caliph sent to accompany me to the palace was a small unit of men from his own elite guards. It is said that he reserves such escorts only for people of importance. I have never considered myself to be one of those persons, but apparently the Caliph looks upon me that way.

The captain, a young man unknown to me, greeted me with courtesy and decorum. His message from the Caliph came with good wishes and a request that I attend the palace. I accepted the Caliph's kind invitation, and the captain immediately dispatched a runner to herald my impending arrival.

I declined the use of the litter that was brought by carriers and told the captain I was a firm believer, like my father, in the beneficial effects of a daily walk. He smiled and nodded his agreement and indicated that he and his guards would accompany me. As we set off for the palace, I suddenly considered the invitation. It was not a command, the captain was courteous, and I had an honor guard! I hoped the Caliph was not displeased with me—an old man's imagination can run riot, I mused.

The soldiers marched slowly to accommodate my steps. I must have been a curiosity to many people. Like my Bemia, whose hair was never tinged with the gray hairs of old age and remained golden until the day of her death, my hair had also retained its hue that belied my Saxon birth.

The soldiers marched in silence while the captain engaged me in quiet conversation. After a while, he said, "My name is Sakhr and I am the grandson of Ali al-Maslawi. My grandfather spoke highly of you, even until the day of his death."

I slowed my pace and stopped. The soldiers followed my lead. I looked at Sakhr curiously. "You do have a look of your grandfather about the eyes. I was privileged and honored to meet him. He stood for what he believed in, even though it almost cost him his life. I am honored and privileged to meet you."

"It is I, Lord Alric, who is privileged," Sakhr smiled. "I swore to my grandfather that I would attempt to meet with you. He even predicted the words that you would use when I introduced myself to you! My grandfather often recounted the dark days of the time of the First Minister, Abdul al-Warith." Sakhr's voice took on a very serious tone. "Indeed, those must have been very worrisome times!"

* * *

We passed through the marketplace, which had remained the same since I had first seen it. A caravan had just arrived, having spent the night outside the city and was now making the most of the morning crowds. Many towns and villages looked forward to the arrival of these caravans, having little communication with the outside world. Baghdad, being the capital city of the region, had remained the center of the caravan routes in this part of the world.

People were shouting at the new arrivals, and the children were bursting with excitement at the arrival of the strangers. A faint haze obscured the desert sun. I have seen many people come and go, but the desert remains the same. Only the dunes were changed by the constant wind, but these were the same sands that I had known since I arrived many decades ago. I have always enjoyed seeing the joy of the travelers when they arrive after weeks of yellow sand and dazzling blue sky.

The soldiers gradually made their way through the crowd and moved around the edge of the market square, where there was less congestion. Several individuals looked at me with interest and respect; some seemed to recognize me, although I did not recognize them. There were those who, by the way they bowed their heads, seemed to think I was a man of substance. Perhaps my walk and the style of my clothes gave them cause to think that way.

Finally, after what seemed an age in the heat of the late morning, we entered the palace and arrived at the door to the Caliph's private lounge. I felt that this was a good sign. Perhaps I had done nothing out of order at all.

The Caliph arose and welcomed me by taking my hand in his. "Glad to see you up and about again, Alric," he said, referring to my recent bout with a chill.

I was confined to my bed for three weeks. I had started to feel weak and hot, and I slept feverishly for the first three days. I was conscious of people around my bed, but I was not able to respond and acknowledge them in any way.

Time and rest did its job, and although I was still confined to bed for another week, I began to reread several of my experimental notebooks. By any measure, these books were voluminous, and I was surprised at the amount of detail I had included, even in my early days. I was determined not to forget their contents, as I found they stimulated other ideas.

"Alric!"

The Caliph's voice intruded into my thoughts and brought me back to the present. "Yes, Sire."

"You seemed to have your mind elsewhere, Alric. Are you well enough for us to talk?"

"Yes, thank you, Sire. I am well. And I look forward to this audience with you."

"As always, Alric, you have a smooth tongue. If my tongue were as smooth as yours, I would have no trouble dealing with ambassadors!"

I had noticed previously that the Caliph's style of dress was less gaudy than that of his predecessors. His white, flowing robes and pale yellow headgear were a stark contrast to the colors in the room, which was decorated with flowing curtains displaying vivid colors. The floor was spread with huge blue, gold, and purple cushions. The Caliph smiled, showing his even white teeth.

"How can I be of service, Sire?" I asked.

"Please sit. Take tea with me, and we will talk," the Caliph responded without answering my question. He looked to be in good humor. "Come," he gestured toward a comfortable chair, "sit, my old friend, and let us talk."

Having a chair pleased me, as the days of scrambling up and down onto cushions have long since passed from me. The stiffness in my knee joints does not bode well for such activity. As I made myself comfortable, servants brought tea and sweet cakes, after which they retreated from sight. The Caliph poured tea and offered me a cake. I took the tea readily but declined the food.

"It is said," the Caliph spoke, "that too many sweet cakes make one's waist line expand."

I said that, I thought to myself.

"In fact," the Caliph continued, "I recall reading from one of the books that belonged to my predecessor, Harun al-Rashid, and you pointed that fact out to him."

"I did, Sire."

"And you must have followed your own advice, since you have retained a body that looks fit."

I smiled.

The Caliph laughed and was silent for a few moments as he considered what he was about to say. "Several decades ago, in the time of the illustrious Harun al-Rashid, you came to this country as a young man, not knowing anything of our culture. You had your dreams, assimilated our culture, and have proved yourself over and over." The Caliph paused, his eyes friendly. "Before your time, strangers were allowed into the country, but only under strict supervision."

I nodded as I placed my teacup back onto the table. I was still confused about the Caliph's reasons for inviting me to take tea with him. His words were not strange to me. I had known from the beginning that my residence in the country was subject to good behavior. That father had vouched for me and offered to take me under his wing had made the difference.

"You have never broken the law," the Caliph continued, "and your conduct has been beyond reproach these many years."

"It was my duty, Sire, and it was the correct thing to do," was the only response that came to mind.

The Caliph waved away my words with a flick of his hand as though it were all known to him. "Indeed. Now that you are back in health after my healers tended to you, I felt that it was time for us to talk personally rather than formally as we usually do."

I remember finding it difficult to talk personally with Harun, even though I knew him well as a result of the demise of Abdul al-Warith. I still could not fathom the reason for the Caliph wishing to see me. What was the point if we were merely going to talk personally over tea and cakes? Surely he knew all about me?

The Caliph continued. "While my healers treated you, you talked in your sleep and told them many things. They followed the rules you laid down many years ago. One of those rules was that healers should always listen to the patient."

"You spoke of your beloved Bemia. She was the one who stood against eight and triumphed. Her name is legendary because of the writings of Scheherazade! You also spoke of your homeland."

"I did?"

"Yes. You spoke of monks and a sickness that seemed to put you in the hands of God. You spoke of your birth father and mother, and in fact my healers heard you speak of a muscle weakness that still seems to trouble you."

The Caliph looked into my eyes. I could not respond as the memories flooded back to me. I bit my lip to stop the emotion from overwhelming me. "You talked of an abbot who made you and your sister learn verses from the Christian Bible every day, so that you came to know much of the five books of Moses. But it seems the time you spent with your sister, Hilda . . . ?" I nodded. "You enjoyed her company and sometimes escaped from the monastery so that you could walk along the seashore. In fact, I am told that Hilda was your twin."

He continued. "You described the skies as being the domain of many species of birds. Songbirds, crows, ravens, and various hawks, the more common denizens of the air. From time to time, large birds of prey, golden eagles swept through the skies always on the lookout for anything edible." He looked at me closely. "And then your life changed."

"It did, Sire."

"Because of the coming of the sea raiders."

"That is correct, Sire." I still did not know where the Caliph was going with my story.

Suddenly, all of it came back as clear as the days when the events had occurred. The memories flooded my brain. Memories that had lain dormant all of these years were alive again. I could see Hilda's face. The sorrow, the hurt, the pain, and the anger at the sea raiders. Tears filled my eyes. The Caliph remained silent. I wanted to yell, just as Hilda had yelled at the sea raiders. I wanted to attack them, to get revenge, and kill them. All of these years, I had not been able to do anything. I was in the presence of the Caliph; I needed to regain my composure. Today he had helped me remember my past. I rose from the chair, paced a little, and sat down again. I could see the concern in the Caliph's face.

"Are you alright, Alric?" he asked.

"Yes, Sire. The memories have all come back to me. The good ones and the bad ones."

"Perhaps I should not have reminded you of those painful times, Alric?"

He looked at me closely.

"I seem to recall," I said as he refilled the tea and gave me a handkerchief for my eyes, "that I wrote a book of my early experiences. I believe that I loaned it to Harun . . . apologies, Sire, I mean the great Caliph, Harun al-Rashid."

"No need to apologize, Alric. A moment, if you please." The Caliph clapped his hands. The steward moved out of the shadows and bowed his head. "Send a runner to the Great Library. Have the librarian find this document and bring it here with haste." The Caliph turned back to me and smiled.

For me, life seemed to have started again. Prior to this moment, I was an old man and my existence did not seem to matter, but the Caliph had brought back to me a life that I had forgotten for many years. He conveyed to me in the best possible manner that before I became Alric al-Biritaanya ibn Jabir I was, and still am, Alric al-Biritaanya. This means no disrespect to my father, Jabir al-Hajjaj ibn Yusuf abu Asad abu Khalil or to my mother, Amira. They had always asked me to remember my birth family and the place of my birth. Now through the good graces of the Caliph, this has come to pass.

The Caliph clapped his hands again, and a servant entered. "Bring fresh tea and some of the oatmeal cakes that Lord Alric loves, and honey for dipping," he added.

The servant soon returned with the refreshments.

As the Caliph poured tea, he said, "Is it true that oatmeal cakes are a common food in your homeland?"

"They are, Sire."

He passed the plate of oatmeal cakes and, waistline or not, I could not resist taking one and, after a while, a second one. I poured the warm honey into the shallow side dish and dipped the cake into it before taking a mouthful.

"Now to the point of your visit," the Caliph announced. *Finally!* I thought. "Alric, I can see from the look in your eyes you are relieved."

"I am, Sire."

"We always," he started solemnly, "observe the tradition to grant a loyal servant a last wish that will be fulfilled. You, Alric al-Biritaanya al Jabir, have been such a loyal person to this house. During your sickness, you spoke many times of returning to the country of your birth."

"You did not use those actual words, but you talked so much about the place called Wearmouth," his pronunciation of the name was somewhat difficult and it sounded like "Weeramut." "In accordance with that wish," he continued, "and if it be true, I hereby grant you the privilege to return to the country of your birth."

I was overcome by emotion, and it took me several minutes to compose myself. The Caliph came to me and placed his arm around my quivering shoulders. I did not hold back. The emotion of the decades poured out of me. When I recovered, I said,

"A cup of tea cures everything."

When more tea was provided, all I could utter was, "Thank you, Sire."

"I realize that you will need to make arrangements. I will send a team of men and women to your house in the morning. They will sit with you while you tell them what needs to be done. It will take several months to make all of the arrangements. Also, a young man has come to me to ask that he serve as your apprentice. It seems that he has experience elsewhere. I will send him to you. His name is . . . " The Caliph paused. "Oh, I forget it for the moment, but I suggest that you use him for whatever you need, and he may be useful as the guardian of your medicines and extracts."

"I will, Sire."

"Now, let us rest until the librarian appears with your book." He poured more tea. "I know you have been very prolific in your medical and other writings. I have had your works copied for safety, but I make you the gift of the originals from the Great Library. They are yours to keep. We have the scribes' copies from which to work and use to advance our science and medicine."

The Caliph sipped his tea and nibbled an oatmeal cake. "I have also heard," he said, wiping a crumb from the corner of his mouth, "that the book you brought with you, which is on its way to us as we speak, is very informative. You may wish to continue with your life story."

We sipped tea and engaged in idle chatter for the next hour. A light cough caught our attention. As the curtain moved, we saw it was the librarian. He was carrying a large leather pouch and, at the Caliph's signal, approached and placed it carefully onto the table in front of us.

"Ah, here it is," the Caliph said as he took the pouch from the librarian, who bowed his head in turn to each of us and departed as quickly as he had arrived. The Caliph handed me the pouch. "A ship will be prepared, and as soon as it is finished and you are ready, with all of your affairs in order, you may leave us, my friend."

"A ship?" I asked.

"Yes, Alric, a ship," the Caliph responded. "Instead of the tedious land journey over desert regions, which are oppressively hot, to Constantinople and where also there are troubles with various tribes and the inhabitants of that city, you will sail from Baghdad to Basra and then enter the waterway that leads to the Southern Ocean. At that point, the ship will follow the coastline of the land of Africa until you come once more to a narrow passage that is referred to as the Pillars of Hercules and thence along the coast of Spain. From there the vessel will retrace the first part of the journey that brought you here, until you eventually reach Britannia."

He paused for a moment. "The sea journey will give you the opportunity for much fresh air."

And for writing, I thought without saying it.

"May Allah always be with you, Alric of Wearmouth."

* * *

When I left the palace, I was again escorted by the guardsmen to my home. I still felt alarmed by what had happened, and it had happened so quickly. The Caliph had granted me my wish. This was a wish I had harbored since Ma'ruf left for his homeland.

Now looking back, I have no regrets. If I die tomorrow, it would be because God was not willing to change the future. I have lived every one of my days intensely since I was taken from my home so long ago. I have seen more than many men could hope to see in five lifetimes, and I am proud of that. I have also known the love of my Bemia.

After this long life in a new land, if I have words for anyone, they are very simple and to the point.

Do not think about the life you have left behind. It matters little to your future. Men dream more about coming home than about leaving. If what you find on your travels is only a moment of light from which you carry the memories of life, then you have traveled and lived well.

Now that I am old, it is difficult not to reminisce about what I have left behind. I can see the palm trees and the face of the woman I loved. I can also see the greenness that is the land of my birth. Now, as I remember the promise I made to my Bemia all of those years ago, that promise will preserve me.

The words flow back into my mind. "I hereby pledge to you, Bemia my love, that when the opportunity arises, I will take you home to Britannia where you may find the place of your birth. But whatever happens, we shall remain together for all eternity."

Now I will take her ashes back to the land of her birth and bury her there.

*   *   *

CHAPTER 44

I had no idea the ship was to be specially constructed for my voyage. It was designed to sail in the cold gray waters of the Northern Sea off the eastern coast of Britannia. I had no reason to think I needed to visit the shipyard, since the Caliph had indicated that it would take several months to make all of the arrangements.

The occasion of my first visit to the shipbuilding yard was unexpected. Nevertheless, it came about in the midmorning of the seventh day after meeting with the Caliph. That particular day, Sakhr was shown into my study by one of the servants. I was surprised at his presence and even more so when he told me that his men awaited in the garden. He seemed uncomfortable at being in a room full of books, since he was dressed in his uniform and fully armed. I clapped my hands and a servant appeared. I cannot remember her name. In fact, my servants are so numerous these days that I can remember their names only with difficulty. This is one of the penalties of old age, but they forgive me and are such helpful and dear people.

A young lady appeared. I remembered her name, it was Hana. "Bring us refreshments, Hana, and," I turned to the captain, "with your permission, I would like to serve your men refreshments."

"You are kind, Lord Alric. My men will appreciate this kindness. The heat of the day is already upon us." Hana smiled and bowed her head.

"And, Hana," I said as the thought occurred to me, "please direct the soldiers to the more shaded parts of the garden."

"Now, Sakhr, I expect the same degree of honesty from you that I received from your grandfather, Ali al-Maslawi, may his name live forever. Why are you here? Do sit down across the table from me while we take our refreshments, and please help yourself to bread and butter. Honey goes very well on bread that is covered with fresh butter!"

"But, Sire!"

"Sit!" My command was so firm, I surprised myself. Sakhr unbuckled his sword belt and set it next to the chair. I repeated my inquiry. "Why are you here?"

"The Caliph ordered me," Sakhr responded as he picked up a piece of bread, "to guard you with honor, Sire. He also said that your service to this country and to the people is beyond reproach, and he values you highly. He also suggested you use a litter, as a security measure, whenever you have to leave the house."

"I do not need a litter!" I retorted.

"The Caliph said that would be your response."

"Humph," was the only sound I could utter.

"A litter is to be provided for you at all times, Sire. Whether or not you use it is another matter. It is collapsible and can be carried easily by two of my men." He saw the puzzled look on my face. "One man carries the folded chair while the other man carries the sun shade.

"The Caliph also asked that you allow my men, there are twelve, to be billeted here. He will pay all expenses and they will be at your disposal, night and day. They can, Sire," he said, as if dreading my response, "perform tasks that are beyond the capability of your servants."

"That is acceptable, Sakhr." He looked surprised. "I suppose the Caliph told you that this crusty old fellow would never agree to that?"

"With respect, I decline to answer your question, Sire."

"You just did! I will have Hana and the other servants prepare rooms for your men at the rear of the house. That part is little used these days. I seem to rattle around in this big house. Now let us partake of the tea and bread!"

* * *

Later in the day, I was escorted to the shipyard by Sakhr and his men. As we left the garden, the sun was already blazing down, yet its heat was tempered by a soft, cool breeze that just stirred the leaves above my head. It did not take us long to reach the river.

The flowing water whispered to the ships moored alongside the docks, which teemed with activity. There were vessels of all sizes docked; the smaller boats had a separate mooring area. I could see men passing by on the far side of the river. Windlasses creaked as ships were loaded and unloaded and I heard the sound of men shouting orders.

Sakhr led me straight to the area where the ship was being built, and I was surprised to see that even after such a short time, work was well under way. The size of the hull indicated that the ship was going to be larger and sturdier than most. As best as I could estimate, this one would be grander than the one which had brought me to Constantinople.

* * *

As the weeks passed, the ship grew in size. From the length of the keel, I knew it would be a little more than a hundred feet long and about thirty feet wide. A large enclosure, called a cabin, was built on the stern, from which there was access to sleeping and dining quarters. The area below deck was divided into smaller quarters for soldiers and sailors to share when they were off duty—although I doubt that anyone on such a ship at sea would ever be off duty! Below deck I noted the spaces in the hull where the oars would be placed.

It took many more weeks, but finally the ship was ready and I made my journey to the river docks to be taken to Britannia.

The vessel was spectacular! The timbers creaked softly as it rocked in the gentle swells at anchor. After its launch from the shipyard, finishing carpenters had completed their tasks, and I was told that sailing trials up and down the river proved that the vessel was in excellent condition. After the last trial, the ship had been brought about so that her prow faced to the south leading to the lower river and, eventually, to the sea.

Sakhr invited me to go on board. The ship's captain was not present at this time. Soldiers from Sakhr's brigade stood guard.

The vessel appeared to shine in the sunlight, giving the impression that the wooden hull and deck had been polished to a high sheen. She had not been built for battle. It was too large for that task, but the shipwrights had retained the swift lines. She was built for speed so that it would be able to outrun and outmaneuver any other vessel on the ocean.

The banks of oars on each side would propel her through the water at a commendable rate. The mast bore a single goose-winged black lateen sail that would drive her forward, directly into the wind if necessary.

As I had suspected at the outset of her construction, she would have a shallow draught so she could be moored in rivers and lagoons from which the men could seek additional provisions and we could disembark in relative safety.

All necessary items were loaded. Four latrines were built as out-juts from the deck rail so that personal hygiene was assured, minimizing the chances of disease. Casks were available for fresh water storage; they would be filled to capacity and sealed before the ship left port. Extract of lemons was added to the water to give it a refreshing taste and to reduce the occurrence of seaboard sicknesses. These would be refilled at convenient places during our journey.

I asked Sakhr which cabin was mine. "That one," he responded, nodding his head in its direction. He led me to the room where I would live for at least the next year. I looked around the spacious room and was impressed by the furnishings. There was a comfortable bed, a dining table, and three chairs. The walls were lined with bookshelves that would eventually be filled with my books or at least copies of them—in spite of the Caliph's generosity, I had requested that the originals should remain in the Great Library and I would take copies with me, and the Caliph had agreed to my request. There was also a desk and chair where I could sit and write. An oil lamp sat prominently in the middle of the desk.

I was excited. This was indeed a place where I could spend time and sit with my books. Sakhr watched me as I ran my fingers over the wood of the desk. He told me that the desk had been installed courtesy of the Caliph so that I might continue to write my life story!

* * *

The day arrived when I received notice that we were to depart the following morning. That evening I took a brief walk in the gardens, realizing that I would never see them again. Knowing this day would come, I had already made arrangements through Khalil for his oldest son to inherit this haven of tranquility. The soldiers, whom I had come to know well, showed their respect by standing to attention as I passed each one. When I returned from my walk, the scent of the tree blossoms and flowers was heavy in the air. With this fragrance lingering in my nose, I made ready for bed and slept the sleep of contentment.

When I awoke, I heard someone speaking loudly in the next room. I rose hastily and found Khalil and Ahmed waiting for me.

"Allow me to bathe and then I will join you for breakfast," I said.

They nodded and soon we three crusty old men were enjoying our bread, butter, honey, and tea. This meal was a longtime favorite of mine, and it is rumored that I overdo it, but what other pleasure can an old man have other than indulging himself now and again?

It was a time of great joy for us, although we knew that we would never see each other again. We had enjoyed our lives together and we knew that we would meet again in the afterlife; of that I was sure.

At the teahouses in the narrow streets of the city, old men sip tea and talk of times past or of times to come, some in fear and trepidation, or regret that the good times are gone. We had no regrets. Every day brought joy. For us, life had unfolded like a great work.

* * *

It was time to go to the dock and board the ship. All of my belongings had been taken on board the day before. A trunk full of clothes was the last to be moved, and this had been taken care of while we had breakfast. One item remained. That was the urn that contained the ashes of my beloved Bemia. The urn was packed into its own wooden container and padded with layers of silk to protect it.

We went through the garden and out of the front gate, where we were joined by Sakhr and his men. In a way I was surprised to see Sakhr, but at the same time, it was an unexpected pleasure, which would allow me to express my gratitude to him and to his men for their care and attention, although privately I did not think I needed all of this attention.

Sunshine fell on the leaves of the trees and dressed them in golden hues, giving my departure a colorful send-off. Khalil and Ahmed insisted on accompanying me in the midst of the soldiers, with Sakhr leading.

A crowd of people awaited me at the dock. And there, standing at the head of the walkway to the ship, was the Caliph. He smiled and held his arms out to me as I ascended the ramp. When I stepped onto the ship, he allowed me the time to put down the box I was carrying containing the urn, then he embraced me and smiled at Khalil and Ahmed, who had followed me onto the deck. Behind them came their respective sons with their wives and their grandsons and granddaughters with their spouses. Each member of the family was determined to say his or her farewell to "uncle" or to "grandfather," as some of them chose to call me.

When the family salutations were completed, I heard the Caliph's voice. "Were you really thinking I would let you depart without saying farewell?" he said as he took my hand. "We are truly sorry you are leaving," he said. "I know how much this journey means to you and to your beloved wife."

I was filled with emotion and unable to speak, though I desperately wanted to shout "thank you" and reveal my thoughts to the world and to all gathered there. I recognized faces from years ago who had helped me in my work. There were those I recognized that I had saved from death by administering my healing extracts, and many faces I just did not recognize at all.

I was still trying to recover from the emotion of the moment when the captain approached. He bowed to the Caliph and said, "All is well, Sire," after which he turned to Khalil, and said, "Grandfather."

It was only then that I recognized Khalil's oldest grandson, Faisal. He was a man of thirty summers. I have since learned that Faisal, as master of the vessel, had overseen all of the preparation for the journey and had made sure the ship was in perfect condition. He had held previous sea and land commands, and although he was not prone to talking about his own achievements, it was said that he had never lost a ship or a soldier in conflict. A proud record, indeed! I felt truly safe to be under his care.

Faisal had also taken other precautions. He had made sure that all on board, both soldiers and sailors, had the necessary skills in case repairs were needed to the ship. Pails of thick bitumen, from the seepages along the Euphrates River, were stored. This would be troweled into seams when needed—if we were subject to extremely stormy seas. Pails of grease were available for additional coating on the hull to maintain as little drag as possible.

Faisal had chosen the black sail. When he decided the ship should be berthed at a suitable dock for the night, the black sail and dark hull would not reflect any moonlight; it would be virtually undetectable.

The Caliph then indicated to Faisal that it was time to leave. Faisal gave instructions for a trumpet to sound to signal to all nontravelers to leave the deck.

I embraced my brothers in turn and kissed them on each cheek, as is the custom. Khalil and Ahmed did likewise and then slowly left the ship. I looked at them. To me, we were still young and we would never grow old. To the world, the picture was different. But such is life.

The Caliph said his goodbye in the same manner and disembarked. I was conscious of a presence behind me and then I heard the gentle word "grandfather." I turned to see Marzuq, Ahmed's grandson. As I recall, Marzuq was one year younger than Faisal.

I was delighted. Marzuq told me that his oldest brother was on duty in the north, and he had been given the promotion and honor of being commander for this journey. What better way of having trust and protection than to use a member of one's family?

The final minutes passed quickly. With the "farewells" over and the wooden walkway taken on board, the reality of my departure hit me. I stood at the deck rail and waved to those who were my family and to the place that had been my home for these many years. As the ship moved away from the dock and was guided south by a strong breeze, I waved my last farewell and watched the retreating shoreline, and soon the city disappeared from view.

Faisal and Marzuq showed me to my cabin below deck. Even though they were on duty, they were both happy and content to continue to refer to me as "grandfather." They and their brothers were fine boys and had always given Bemia and me considerable joy when they'd visited us. And now one was captain of the ship and another commander of the guards, sent to guarantee my safety!

I have stated "below deck" in reference to the position of my cabin, but in actual fact, part of the cabin was above deck, so that I could use the sunlight to maximum advantage for my writing. In addition, the light from candles would supplement the moonlight if I chose to work during the night.

The remainder of my first day was pleasant and uneventful. The ship eased its way south on the river and was greeted by many from the shore who had never seen a ship of such size and beauty.

* * *

After I bathed and changed my clothes, I was shown by a servant, Thawab, who had been appointed as my valet, to the dining room, where Faisal, Marzuq, and their officers were seated. After the introductions, I realized that most were relatives of Khalil and Ahmed, either through birth or through the families of their wives and daughters-in-law. Thus, dinner was very much a family affair, and an enjoyable one at that.

As an afterthought, I asked, "Is there any one of you who is not related to Grandfathers Khalil and Ahmed?"

Faisal smiled and answered for them. "We are all cousins, grandfather," at which smiles lit up the room.

As the meal came to an end, Marzuq leaned over and whispered secretively, "I have a request from our cousins, grandfather."

"Go ahead and ask," I whispered.

"It is personal."

Faisal looked at Marzuq, and I knew that they had cooked something up between them. "Ask!" I retorted.

I suspected that he was going to ask me about my dear Bemia. "Those of us who knew Grandmother Bemia loved her." He looked into my eyes to determine my reaction. "But there are those of my cousins in this dining cabin who know Grandmother Bemia only from what they have heard from us or from the stories of Scheherazade."

"And you were wondering?" I did not complete the question.

"Yes, grandfather, we were wondering if—"

I interjected. "I suppose you want to know how my Bemia stood against the eight."

"Yes, grandfather, and, since this is a long voyage, we would also like to know about the land of your birth."

"I will be honored to relate these stories."

Marzuq rapped on the table with the handle of his knife. Suddenly I was the focus of everyone's attention. Marzuq looked at Faisal and then at their relatives. "Grandfather has kindly agreed," he announced, "to tell of Grandmother Bemia and the land of his birth, a land we will see after our long voyage." He looked at me and added, "Grandfather, the table is yours."

It took a few moments to collect my thoughts and to make sure I did not dissolve into a pool of emotion. "I am flattered you wish to know the details of the life of Grandmother Bemia. As the weeks pass, I will tell you all about her, and by the time we reach Britannia, you will feel that you know her. I will tell you from my own experience of loving her with all my heart and soul. Except I cannot relate to you firsthand the details of the time she stood against the eight assassins." I paused as I saw a frown or two. "To this day, I regret that I was not with her." I paused again. "But I can speak to you in the words of Ma'ruf."

Smiles of gratitude returned to the frowning faces. "That night," I began, "as Grandmother Bemia lay wounded in the care of Grandfather Jabir and Grandmother Amira, Ma'ruf told me of the events that had taken place. He had been an eyewitness and, at the right moment, he had stepped in to save Grandmother Bemia. Without his help, I fear that she would have been killed! It was a sensation I will never forget as Grandfathers Khalil and Ahmed and I walked the streets of the city looking for an assassin . . . "

For two hours I related the story, not missing any of the details and taking them to the point where the fifth man fell. Young faces were full of emotion as I described how Bemia placed herself in a protected position. At this point, I interjected the story of *Horatio and the Bridge* and how Horatio had saved Rome.

I related how Bemia had fought and laid the killers low one by one as she defended Amira and the household. I told how metal clanged against metal as Bemia's swords parried their blows and returned their attempts on her life with vengeance. Men died as she thrust, stabbed, and cut. They succumbed to her as though they had merely come to die rather than to kill. They had not expected someone who could use weapons as well as she used her swords.

And then I stopped. I could feel the emotion welling up inside and I felt the urge to be alone. "If you do not mind, young ones, I need to rest and I will continue this story tomorrow night."

They looked disappointed, but Faisal and Marzuq agreed with me and stood up to escort me to my cabin. Then they bade me, "Goodnight and a pleasant sleep."

I could see the expressions on their young faces. They could not wait for the next night when I would finish the story. I smiled to myself at their anticipation. If there is one thing that I learned from Scheherazade, it was the way in which a story should be told so that the audience grasped every word!

"God bless you, Scheherazade, wife of Harun al-Rashid."

* * *

All good storytellers, no matter how many times they relate their story, know how it can stimulate the mind. I was wholly dependent on my memory—the memory of an old man. But the more I talked, the more the facts came back to me. When Faisal and Marzuq left me, they assumed that I wished to go to bed immediately. I did indeed wash, and after Thawab left me, I felt awakened. I had the urge to work, so I turned to my writing materials and started to collect my memories so that I could work on the continuation of my life story, as requested by the Caliph.

The weariness had gone, the returning memories spurred me on, and I eagerly looked forward to this pleasure. I felt emotion from that first night when the memories brought back to me the laughter and relaxation while in the company of my wife. At times, I felt that I could write all night, but there were times that I became too tired and needed to sleep and get up with the sun. I would often continue during the next day and into the night.

I also started to work on my personal journal, which I wrote in parallel to my life story. Without fail, I made entries into it each day, and this is the result that you now see before you.

This plan worked as expected, and as the days passed, my life story and my personal journal grew in size. But again I get ahead of myself. As I slept that night, I had no fear, I was well protected.

The river carried the ship toward the coast where the tidal effect would be sufficient to carry us out to sea. In the early dawn of the next day, we were under full sail. The light breeze of the early morning strengthened and spurred us on.

* * *

Looking back some weeks later, that first night set the tone of many nights to come. The stories continued for the whole voyage, and during that period I must have often repeated the story of the *Northern Woman and the Eight,* as it became known from the words Scheherazade had developed.

Scheherazade placed Bemia's story prominently in her collected works of adventure and mystery that she drew from the lives of others. They will be lodged in the Great Library of Baghdad, but whether any of these works will survive the ravages of time is itself a mystery.

But, to continue . . . The depiction of Bemia's fight, and reliving those times according to what I had heard from Ma'ruf, gave me a lot of satisfaction. I felt as if my Bemia were still with me. As the nights passed and I repeated the story, I realized I was finally coming to terms with her death, and I began to dwell more on the times we had spent together during her life.

But this story would not last forever on such a long voyage. So I chose many tales from Scheherazade's collection, primarily those that focused on adventure and real-life situations. The fact I had personally known Harun al-Rashid, and his wife Scheherazade gave me additional standing in the minds of my young audience. Even when they chose to hear a tale once again, they listened to my words as intently as if they had heard it for the first time. All young men need heroes, and these were no exception. My words provided an escape from the rigors of the voyage.

Now I must rest before another day dawns. I am at an age where waking up means that the day has started well.

* * *

CHAPTER 45

The ship moved easily down the Tigris River, and I spent much of the first few days on deck inhaling the fresh air. After all the years of being a city dweller, it seemed to give my body a resurgence of vigor. Resting my arms on the deck rail, I listened to the sound of the waves lapping against the bow as the ship glided through the water. "Britannia," the water seemed to say.

I kept my thoughts to myself. Now that the journey had started, my memory was drawn to a time so long ago when the first attack by the sea raiders had taken the lives of my family and changed my life.

The journey from Baghdad to Basra was no great distance for the ship. For the plodding camels, which are often called ships of the desert, it was a fifteen-day trek, depending on the sandstorms that blew in from the east. Not wishing to risk damage to the hull, Faisal took a cautious route in the middle of the river and kept to the deepest part of the channel. This gave smaller crafts the opportunity to move away and avoid collisions that would surely cause serious damage to their boats, and possibly to our ship.

* * *

And so, one week after we left Baghdad, Faisal announced that we were approaching Basra. As we neared the coastal city, I could feel a coolness in the air. A mist had formed at the point where the river runs into the sea, and with night approaching, Faisal decided we should dock for the night. This gave us the opportunity to replenish our water supplies. For several hours, the mist hung around the dim lantern light of the ship. The cool air and the smell of the sea were invigorating. The tidal water increased the swell, and the lapping of the water against the ship's hull beat a hypnotic cadence.

It was during our brief stay in Basra that I discovered another reason for the voyage. That night at dinner, I noticed an excitement in the voices of the young officers that I had not heard before. I wondered what was causing this when Faisal held up his hand to quell the conversation. "This is the time to tell you, grandfather," Faisal said. "We were under strict orders from the Caliph not to say anything until the ship was on the open sea. This is a voyage of discovery," he continued with conviction. "It is known from traders that there is a large land to the west where the edge of the world of Islam meets the sea." I nodded. "There are stories from the time of the Egyptians," he explained, "almost one thousand four hundred years ago stating that a ship can sail south of this land, which we call Africa, and then sail north along the coast to the entry that leads to the Middle Sea."

I coughed behind my hand as if my throat were dry. This was known to me, but I did not wish to interrupt Faisal.

"Yes, grandfather," Faisal said and added, "many of our sailors have made the same journey, but the voyages were not sponsored by the Caliph!"

"And," I interrupted, "the Caliph needs to know the exact positions of the land and the number of days it will take. He expects me to take the readings of the stars as we continue the journey!"

"Yes, grandfather, you are correct," Faisal nodded his head as he spoke.

"Why did the Caliph not ask me outright?"

"Because you intimidate him, grandfather! But he knew you would be open to our requests, since we respect and love you."

I smiled. "And what if I said no?"

"You are a man of learning, grandfather. You would not disagree with such an opportunity."

I laughed and the young officers joined with me. The attitude of the Caliph and my sense that something was amiss when I was first summoned to the palace was suddenly explainable. I had been chosen for a task that any man of learning would grab with both hands. "Then I suggest we start tomorrow."

Faisal smiled as he looked at me and said, "I have all the necessary instruments you will need."

I looked at the officers. "Well gentlemen, some of you are about to have lessons in the reading of the stars. Now," I looked sternly at each young face, which had become serious, "you will have to pay for the stories that I tell you each night. I will show you how to use the instruments and you will take the measurement at times set by me."

A sense of anticipation filled the cabin. "Now, captain," I addressed Faisal, "I suggest we eat! Have the crew been informed?"

Faisal laughed. "They have, grandfather."

I put my arm around Faisal and Marzuq as I said, "I see you have picked trustworthy companions. Well done!"

* * *

Late the next morning, after the water and stores had been replenished, Faisal guided the ship away from the dock, and we entered the open sea with the sail greeting the wind.

I immediately started to introduce the instruments to the officers. These instruments were the newest versions available and had, in fact, been made especially for this voyage. It did not take long for the eager minds to understand what was needed, and I retired to my cabin, where I created nightly schedules while the young officers continued to practice.

There were no storms to hamper our progress and I became so engrossed in the mapping work and my writing activities that I did not realize that the ship had entered the Southern Ocean. The discovery came to me when the vessel came upon heavy swells.

The ship slowly moved through these swells all day and night, until later the next day we found that we were in calm water again. Faisal set a course to the southwest to follow the distant outline of the land. After several days, we lost sight of the land. Faisal explained we were passing the entry to the large inland waterway that led to Egypt, the land of the Pharaohs. The land-birds were no longer visible to us, but the gulls dived and hovered around the ship hoping to find something edible. After a while we were able to see land again to the northwest of the ship as we continued our southwesterly journey.

Our first stop on the east coast of Africa came within a few days. It seems that ships of the Caliph had been there before, since we were given a welcome as we came ashore. The first to leave the ship was Marzuq, escorted by ten of his soldiers.

The spokesman for the tribe who lived in the nearby village was courteous and marveled at the sight of the ship sitting elegantly in the shallow water offshore. He was even more amazed at the small boats that were used to ferry soldiers and sailors from the ship to the shore. He indicated that he would be interested in meeting the honored guest who, Marzuq had told him, was on board the ship, and invited us to have a meal with him. Since it would take time to replenish the water casks, Faisal suggested we accept dinner from the tribal leader.

The meal was held outside with all of the villagers present and I was offered the place of honor next to their leader. The menu, I was relieved to find, consisted of no offensive dishes, and food was even provided for the men who remained on board. We did, however, decide to sleep on board the ship that night.

Within twelve hours of our return to the ship we were on the high seas once more. We occasionally saw other, smaller vessels, but they offered no threat. Even though the work continued, I felt relaxed.

Being on board for a prolonged period, which was only interrupted by stops to replenish our stores of fresh water and to take on fresh fruits and vegetables whenever necessary, was strange to me. It had been many decades since I'd made my first voyage in the company of Khalil and Ahmed.

I spent much time on deck, since the weather was pleasant. With Faisal's permission, since he was captain of the ship, I made arrangements for some of Marzuq's young men to carry my writing desk from the cabin into the fresh air. At night, or when the weather changed, the desk was returned to my cabin.

* * *

The ship continued to make good time, and the days flew by. In one week we had left our water stop far behind. During the day, the sea appeared to boil in the wake of the vessel.

I found that I had acquired a taste for life at sea, just as I had for olives when in Baghdad. The confinement to the deck, the motion of the vessel, and the noise of the men became a part of my daily life. Some mornings, I awoke and the floor seemed to be at such an angle that I thought I would fall from my bed. But I became used to this minor annoyance, realizing that the sea had strength and the ship accommodated that strength rather than fighting the greater force.

As we moved south, the sky became grayer and the sea was rough at times, but we had confidence in the builders of the vessel and were unafraid. In the distance the land varied, being more visible at times and other times disappearing below the horizon. The time provided me with ample opportunity for study and to concentrate on writing. My hand was not as steady as it had been decades ago, and my mind was a little slow when deciding the words to use. I remembered that some of the happiest and most valuable hours that my Bemia and I had spent were with our books. The greatest inconvenience I have found at sea is the need to have more light in my cabin.

Fortunately, I had brought several books with me, which afforded me the chance to reread my own works, as well as the works of others. Through these writings, I have learned something new. Hopefully, readers are learning from my books that remain in the Great Library in Baghdad. Faisal told me that under the best conditions, a voyage can be a severe test for a nonsailor, but he was pleased with the way in which we were all keeping occupied. As a testament to our occupation, the chart of our measurements and shape of the land grew in size, possibly to the envy of our contemporary chart makers, who would see it at some future time.

As we neared the land, I marveled at the genius of the shipbuilders who had constructed this large but shallow-draft vessel. Not once did the ship touch ground, a tribute also to the skills of Faisal and his sailors.

We saw coastal villages that seemed to be deserted. We met with people from different tribes and attempted to learn smatterings of their languages. When the tribesmen discerned that we were merely stopping for water and were not on a mission of war and conquest, they were more generous with the provisions we needed. The ship moved farther and farther south, and the hours continued to pass pleasantly. I noticed that both soldiers and sailors seemed to take on a greater respect for each other. The work on board was steady.

Throughout all of this time, Faisal continued to maintain contact with the Caliph by carrier pigeon, which mother had used so well and which a succession of Caliphs had adopted, not only as a tribute to her but because of its usefulness. The birds were housed at relay points throughout the land, and it was even rumored that a post in the northern part of the Land of the Franks was also operative.

* * *

The patches of gray that had appeared in the sky on occasion became more frequent, and the weather took on a cooler aspect. My fear was that it would become too cold, since there was little warmth on board ship, even in the best cabins. As we moved between Africa and a large island land mass that we saw in the distance to the east of the ship, a fog soon enshrouded us, bringing with it a cold dampness.

Faisal told me that the land mass was the home of the Malagasy and was called Madagascar. Two hundred years ago, sailors from Mesopotamia had established trading posts along the northwest coast of the island. Because of the fog, he decided not to stop there. Faisal ordered the cooks to make hot soup so the men would have warmth inside their bodies.

* * *

It was as though my prayers had been heard, for the farther south we traveled, the weather improved, the coolness disappeared after a day, and we were not forced to retreat into our cabins to retain the heat of our bodies.

"I had heard there were bands of cold weather that can change into warmth again very quickly," Faisal said at dinner that night.

"I would not complain if the good weather followed us into the northern climes," Marzuq added.

The next morning, the sun rose above the level of the horizon, bathing the ship with a golden light and causing the deck to glisten as the sunlight reflected off the polished wood surface. Everyone was aware that during the night the ship had turned in a westerly direction.

We were at the tip of the land mass that we called Africa and we would soon be sailing north toward the western end of the Middle Sea.

A day later, as we turned north, it was interesting to see the sun to the north of us rather than to the south. Over the years, the Caliph's scientists had wondered about this and about the earth being a globe rather than flat, as was believed by many, but that is another story. I have recorded my thoughts on this and on the possibility of finding seaways that would allow a ship to make a complete journey around the world, even to parts as yet unknown.

* * *

With the second half of the voyage before me, as near as could be determined, my mood brightened even more. The anticipation of returning to the homeland I had not seen since I was taken forcibly all of those years ago was becoming a reality. The days seemed to get shorter. I spent even more time on deck, looking out to sea. Large fish frolicked near the ship, as though they were leading us farther north. They were everywhere. I had suspected the presence of creatures for several days, as I had heard their sounds nearly every day since we'd turned north. Now they were crossing and re-crossing the path of the ship gleefully, and I wondered if this was the first of many such meetings to come.

The farther north we traveled, the more numerous the friendly fish became, and I even had several occasions to view them closely and was amazed by the ability of these creatures. As near as I could determine, the animal breathed through a hole on the top of its head, much as the whale that swallowed the Prophet Jonah, whose burial place, you may remember, is in the walls of the ruins of the ancient city of Nineveh, but this animal was more the size of a man than a whale. It had a tail, like that of other sea animals, and propelled itself in an up-and-down motion, with the double flukes, that drove the animal forward. The most peculiar aspect was its strange bottle-shaped nose that resembled the bottles I had kept for storage of the liquids in my laboratory. The creatures emitted, almost continuously, clicking sounds or whistles. These were truly remarkable. Perhaps they had even been watching us to determine our intent!

I have written a full description of this so that it would be returned with my notes on the measurement of the land mass to the Caliph for deposition in the Great Library. His sages could ponder over my thoughts at some later time.

These same sea creatures made no effort to leave the ship and were quite happy to accompany us over long distances. At one time, they disappeared for two days after a much larger fish, with very prominent black and white markings, suddenly rose from the sea with one of the animals in its mouth. I also made notes of this phenomenon. It was only when the monster was obvious by its absence that the animals returned to frolic with the ship again.

I had read that the large black and white fish was called Orca by the Romans, while the Phoenicians called it the hell fish or devil fish. Seeing it attack the smaller creatures, I could understand how it came to have such a name!

* * *

We continued our journey north, the ship cutting through the waves as we listened to the clicking and whistling sounds of the fish. At night, after the stories, I settled in my cabin to write and then retired to bed and fell asleep to the music of the waves against the side of the ship.

Faisal and Marzuq kept a watch on me to make sure that all was well. After all, I was the oldest man they knew. In fact, other than their grandfathers Khalil and Ahmed, who are older them me, I am the oldest man that I know!

One morning, Marzuq asked, "Did you dream, grandfather?"

I looked at him and smiled. "I very rarely dream these days. My last dreams were during the night before I met with the Caliph and learned of this journey. You can tell Faisal," I patted his arm to show that I appreciated their concern, "that I am well. I feel settled now. I can keep my promise to your grandmother Bemia."

Marzuq nodded. A question came to him. "What does it feel like to be going home, grandfather?" he asked.

"That is an interesting question, Marzuq. I feel torn. I have left the land that was my home for many decades. My family is there. Grandfather Khalil and Grandfather Ahmed and I formed a close bond that has remained from the early days. But it is the custom of the people of the north that they be buried in the land of their birth. The sea raiders take their dead with them for that very purpose. My ancestors continued this tradition from their early days in Britannia, and I must do this for your grandmother. I swore a solemn oath to her many years ago. In fact, it was shortly after she recovered from her wound fighting the eight assassins. I honor her request. "

"*Maktub*, grandfather." It is written.

One of the soldiers approached us bringing tea and oatmeal cakes. I looked at the young man and smiled my thanks. Something seemed familiar about him.

"My cousin," Marzuq said.

"Is there anyone on this ship who is not related to you and Faisal?" I asked.

"I have not really done a count of the sailors, but I doubt it, grandfather. The Caliph was determined that you would travel with only those that Faisal and I could trust!" We laughed and sat down on the two seats provided for us, sipped the tea, nibbled on oatmeal cakes and looked out at the sea.

As we passed within sight of land, I scanned the landscape, noting the barren hills that stretched before us to the north and south. At other times, there was the lush greenness of the trees and plants that grew close to the shore line. When the shoreline was clear, I could see natives watching us from the beach.

Faisal chose this opportune time to stop for water and to replenish our food supplies. He was a firm believer that fresh fruit kept away seagoing sicknesses that incapacitated many sailors. We were at times lucky enough to kill an antelope or several small animals for fresh meat; this was a treat for us.

All the while, the clicking and whistling fish accompanied our ship. We were thinking they would never go, when one day, at the point where the Middle Sea joins the Western Ocean, they disappeared. We saw no signs of them again.

"I am not sure if you realize it, grandfather," Faisal said the next morning, "but we are now returning on the course that you took with Kahlil. We will need to be careful from this point on as we enter the domain of the sea raiders!"

* * *

Three nights later, I noticed a chill in the air. In fact, it woke me from a deep sleep. As I covered myself with an extra blanket, I knew that we were about to enter the cold Northern Sea that lay to the east of Britannia. And, truly, the next morning, I saw the white cliffs to the north of the ship only a short distance away.

Faisal chose a spot to make landfall that night, and I am certain that it was the same place where Khalil, Ahmed, and I had stopped after they had rescued me from the sea raiders and where the men had berthed their ship. The potential dangers that lay awaiting us on the Northern Sea were unknown. Faisal and Marzuq felt that the men needed a rest from the rigors of the sea and that a night on land would help them recoup lost energy.

Faisal chose a sheltered spot between the white cliffs of southern Britannia, which offered protection from the northern winds. The northern lip of the cleft effectively shielded the ship from prying eyes. The men built fires and killed game, and a feast was prepared that we had not seen the likes of for many a night.

"We will rest until morning," Marzuq announced. Now that we were on land, he was in control. "Faisal will seek the correct time to depart." I nodded before drifting into sleep.

* * *

The sun was well risen when I awoke. The fires had long since burned out, and the wind had picked up again. I sat up quickly and then lay down again as a wave of dizziness washed over me. Closing my eyes for a moment, I oriented myself and then sat up slowly. My clothes were wrapped warmly against my body. Faisal and Marzuq appeared at my side.

"Grandfather," Faisal exclaimed, "you had a dizzy turn!" Their eyes spoke of their concern. Above, I heard the unmistakable sounds of gulls in flight and then they fell silent, as if trying to forewarn us.

"My men," Marzuq explained, "have spotted a group on the march in the distance. They may not be friendly and we must leave. You slept well, grandfather, and while we make ready to depart, drink this hot tea that has been well sweetened with honey to help you regain your strength and energy."

The ship was made ready and not a moment too soon. No sooner had we put to sea than men appeared on the cliffs above the cleft and waved their swords and spears at us. Fortunately, the wind helped us to quickly put distance between ourselves and the shore. While Faisal saw to the operation of the ship, Marzuq commanded two of his soldiers to carry me to my cabin.

"I can walk," I said irritably.

"No, grandfather, you cannot," Marzuq was firm. "You had a dizzy spell when you awoke and you are unsteady on your feet."

I allowed myself to be carried to my cabin. I had no other choice. Young arms held me firmly. I did refuse to go to my bed and commanded that I be put in my chair. The soldiers looked at Marzuq. He nodded, and so I was lowered gently. I think they were surprised at how light I felt.

"Grandfather," Marzuq announced, "you will stay here and your food will be brought to you in this cabin. You need rest and you shall have rest!"

I looked at him. "For how long?" I asked.

"Until Faisal and I see that you are strong enough!"

"Then I will rest," I sighed. Even though I had slept through the night and well into the morning, I still felt tired. Whether it was the effect of the journey, the anticlimax of approaching landmarks that I started to recognize, old age, or all of these things, I did not know. But suddenly, I was tired. I did not awaken until the sun had long passed the midpoint of its daily journey. I arose, washed, walked to the door, and signaled to the soldiers, placed there to watch me rather than guard me, and announced that I was awake. Within moments Faisal and Marzuq appeared.

"How are you, grandfather?" Faisal asked.

"Feeling better, but for some reason, still a little weak. My left arm seems to ache. Other than that, I am well."

They looked at me for a moment, considering this information. Marzuq smiled at Faisal. "I think, grandfather, you will rest from this point on. I recall that your scientific measurements are almost complete. My men can finish the work that remains to be done. You have taught them well. And your writing has progressed?"

"It is done, as the Caliph requested," I responded.

It was Faisal's turn to speak. "You will rest and we will look after you."

"But . . . " I started to protest.

"Grandfather," Faisal's tone was serious, "as master of this ship, that is my order. And my cousin," he looked at Marzuq, "will see that it is carried out."

Marzuq bowed his head in agreement. I decided I had no choice and complied. "You know," I said, "if there is anything worse that one grandson telling a grandfather what to do, it is . . . "

"Two grandsons," they chorused and laughed.

"I suddenly feel the need to eat and take tea. May I?"

"Of course, grandfather, one of the soldiers will inform the cook."

Another urge came upon me. I felt that I had to read the material that I had written and make additions or corrections. The Caliph had provided me with a great deal of writing materials, which allowed me to leave considerable distance between the lines. There was more than enough room for insertion of any omissions or afterthoughts. Being confined to my cabin turned out to be a blessing!

My stories had long since ended, and each night the young officers stopped at my cabin to wish me good health. They did not tarry but merely wanted to see that all was well. Each night, I fell asleep and did not wake until the morning sun cast its golden rays through the window of my cabin.

I was offered fruit every morning but refused it. I knew that such food would be in short supply, and I told Faisal and Marzuq that it should be given to the young men who were working.

It seemed that the enforced rest in my cabin cost me the use of my sea legs. Later, I stood on deck between Faisal and Marzuq and looked at the shoreline. "That building on the headland, if memory serves me correctly," I squinted at the cliffs, "is the nunnery of St. Hilda, and the settlement close by is named Whitby. The monastery of Wearmouth is," I paused and looked at the sea as it caressed the hull to estimate the speed of the ship, "but a day's journey from here."

Faisal and Marzuq looked at me. "Then, grandfather, it will be well for us to take extra precautions, since we will have to move to shore on the morrow."

"I will inform the men and have them make preparations," Marzuq offered and left to see to that duty. I returned to my cabin. I was tired again and needed to rest and sleep.

* * *

When I next awoke, it was dark and the ship was moving slowly. I sat upright, looking about me in the dark cabin. As my eyes became accustomed to the dim light of the moon, I knew that I was back at Wearmouth. Someone was in the cabin with me.

Before I could speak, I perceived darker shapes illuminated by the moonlight that shone through the cabin window. Then I saw them; the dark shapes coalesced out of the darkness and became two women.

Hilda and Bemia stood before me. Hilda was unchanged, but Bemia had the form I remember when we were first married.

You look well, my brother, Hilda was the first to speak.

My husband, Bemia looked at me and I could see the love in her eyes. *We have watched over you for these past two years, but now you are here and we are content.*

Hilda said, *We have much to discuss.*

We talked all night, until the sun appeared on the eastern horizon. Before leaving me, Bemia and Hilda both kissed me on each cheek. Then Bemia wrapped her arms around me. *My love,* she said without tears, *I have missed you*

Just as they had appeared from the shadows, they left.

* * *

CHAPTER 46

I felt excited, but at the same time I had reservations about my return. After all of these years, I was home or, more correctly, in the land of my birth. Mesopotamia had been my home for the past six decades. Wearmouth would be different. I was changed, and the people would seem different, but I had made a promise to my beloved Bemia and I would keep that promise.

Every day for the past week as I stood on the deck and looked out at the horizon, I thought about my Saxon heritage and the language. After the death of Bemia, I had little chance to practice, until, for reasons unknown to me at the time, Faisal and Marzuq had requested that I teach them and the junior officers the Saxon and Latin languages. I had not thought of it at first, but lately it had become clear why they wished to learn these tongues.

I looked at the land. There were hills in the distance and rocks. Plants seemed to insist on living where survival seemed impossible. And as always, the sea looked gray and cold. "How are you today, grandfather?" I heard the soft whisper over my shoulder.

"Starting to feel a little better," I responded to Faisal.

"It seems that you have been able make your way to the deck on your own?"

"I had help," I responded, remembering the two young soldiers. They had brought my chair so that I might rest as I looked at the land and breathe the air once again. I wore extra robes. My body still ached, at times angrily, and the sun no longer warmed my body as it had done. One of the penalties of old age seems to be a perpetual chilling effect.

"How do you feel about your return, now that we are so close?

"The land that we are going to," I said to Faisal, "carries part of me, just as the desert carries a part of you."

And then I saw it. The river mouth. The monastery still sat high and proud on the promontory. There was the greenness of the country that I realized I had missed all of these years. After traveling many miles and spending the best part of a year at sea, we had arrived. It was close to midday and it had started to rain.

During the early morning, as we moved slowly toward the dock, which seemed bigger than I remembered, the soldiers and sailors made preparations to disembark. Activity from the land showed me we had been spotted. Men appeared with weapons. The monks chanted holy songs and prayers. They realized that we were not the sea raiders. I could hear voices clearly and with understanding as they asked each other who we might be.

Faisal hailed the people using the Saxon tongue. The response was a sudden silence, surprised that a person on such a ship, and dressed in the manner that he was, could speak their language. I realized that Faisal's robes, the breeches, and his helmet were a stark contrast to the Saxon style of clothes. His well-trimmed beard and coloring looked strange to those watching from the shore.

A man, who we assumed was the headman of the village, approached us and after much discussion stated that he was a representative of the abbot. Faisal requested that we be allowed to disembark. The abbot, who had appeared by this time, suggested to Faisal that we leave our weapons on board. Faisal responded firmly.

"No. We must carry our weapons. We may need to protect ourselves. You do not have our trust at this time."

To which the abbot responded, "I am a man of the church and you have my word that you can trust all who are here."

Faisal looked at me and smiled, then added. "I have with me my grandfather, Alric al-Biritaanya ibn Jabir, who stands by my side." Faisal saw from the looks on their faces that the name and his pronunciation did not mean anything to the abbot or to the village headman. "He came to our land many decades ago as Alric of Wearmouth. He requests that he be allowed to visit the monastery where he received his early schooling and the village where he was born."

At this point, I removed my head covering so that my gray-blond hair and Saxon features showed clearly. The abbot and the headman opened their mouths in surprise. This was followed by a collective hum of conversation from the villagers and the monks, who stood farther back from the ship.

"I suggest," Faisal continued, "that you check the records of the church and for written memories of this man who was taken from these shores by sea raiders. We will await your invitation to disembark. In the meantime, any attempt to board this ship will be dealt with severely."

Faisal's message was clear. The abbot acknowledged this request by dispatching two monks to the monastery. On board ship, Marzuq posted the guards so that no one could approach without detection. Faisal made sure that I was wrapped in warm clothing as I sat on the deck watching the activities on the shore. The headman placed five armed men on the dock to make sure we did not do anything to arouse suspicion. For the most part, the monks returned to the monastery, but there were several who remained near the dock with the villagers, who did not seem to want to do anything but watch us. Their clothes were much the same as the style of garments that I had worn before my departure from Wearmouth. Colorful but coarse clothing—I had become used to silk fabrics and fine linens. Memories came flooding back of my youth.

I sat and took tea with Faisal and Marzuq and we chatted about the land and the people. I must have dozed for a while, for it was suddenly midafternoon. Faisal and Marzuq were wondering if the delay was not some form of ruse until reinforcements arrived. Suddenly, the two monks reappeared with the abbot and the headman. They immediately started a huddled conversation with the other men, who seemed to have status among the villagers. During the conversation, they looked in the direction of the ship several times. The murmur of their conversation grew louder. Finally, they approached us, and the guards moved aside.

"In the name of God," the abbot declared, "I welcome you to Wearmouth. I also welcome you, Alric, back to the land of your birth."

* * *

Marzuq and his soldiers decided to disembark first and formed a protective line as they faced the abbot. Faisal and I followed, and he helped me to walk slowly toward the abbot. As he did so, he continued to talk to me in Saxon.

"Your secret is out, Faisal. I now understand the reason that you, Marzuq, and your officers wished to learn my language." Faisal smiled.

Once more I stood on the land of my birth. The monks now carried crosses as if to frighten away any demons that we might have brought with us! I realized that even my skin, pale by comparison to Faisal and Marzuq, was tanned when compared with that of the villagers and monks.

Faisal took out his sword, to the consternation of the villagers, but handed it to Marzuq, and then he and I approached the abbot.

"Learned sir," he said by way of respect with a slight bow of his head, "I have the honor of presenting to you my grandfather, Lord Alric, known in my country as Alric al-Biritaanya ibn Jabir, Alric of Britannia and of the House of Jabir."

"You need not fear me," I said by way of introducing myself to the abbot and the people, many of whom were wide-eyed at my appearance. "I am Alric and I was born in this village. I received my first education in the monastery. I was taken by sea raiders and subsequently rescued by the grandfather of this man. I have come back to see the land of my birth once again and to fulfill a promise that I made to my dear late wife."

They looked at me in surprise as someone from another land, dressed as I was, who spoke their dialect perfectly. "My promise to my late wife, made many years ago at the time of our marriage, was that I would bury her in this land of her birth and close to the place where my sister and parents were laid to rest."

"And so you shall," the abbot seemed to relax. "I do not know you, but I hear from my brothers," he nodded to the two monks whom he had dispatched earlier to search the records of the monastery, "that there are indeed writings about you in some of the texts housed in our library. I welcome you and your grandson." Marzuq coughed lightly.

"I have two grandsons with me, abbot. The commander of the soldiers is also my grandson." The abbot looked at Faisal and Marzuq, then exclaimed, "I welcome the grandsons of Alric of Wearmouth and all of their companions." He looked at me. "Come you must rest."

"Not yet, abbot. First I must bury the remains of my wife." I turned, and one of the sailors brought the box containing the urn and placed in into my hands. I opened the box and indicated to the abbot that the urn contained the ashes. I felt that I could not go ashore without my Bemia. "Then will I rest." I saw the look of curiosity of the abbot's face. "I know the spot where my parents and sister are buried. I will point it

623

out to you, and if you would be so kind as to arrange for the burial, I will be in your debt."

The abbot agreed. "In the meantime," he said, "my monks will prepare quarters for you within the monastery instead of one of the individual accommodations used by the monks. I believe," the abbot said, "you will be familiar with these huts and the coldness that comes at night?"

The monks departed toward the monastery and I smiled. I was fully aware of how cold the huts could be during the night when the fire was not maintained with a regular supply of wood. My old bones would barely tolerate such temperatures. "I appreciate your concern, abbot, and I welcome your efforts to give me accommodation within the monastery."

By this time, the fear of a battle had abated, and the villagers approached en masse. Their curiosity was aroused and they edged closer, wanting to know about the old man with the fair skin and his companions from another land.

And so, preparations were made, and within a short time, in a simple service, which was blessed by the abbot and by Faisal as a representative of the Caliph, I buried the urn containing Bemia's ashes close by the remains of my parents and my sister that I had recognized as their final resting place.

When the service was complete, I fell to my knees in a final prayer to my loved ones. I could barely see the ground for the tears in my eyes. A torrent of love rushed from my heart as I began to pray. It was a prayer that I had not said for a long time. In the silence, I gave thanks for all of my blessings. My promise was fulfilled.

* * *

We walked to the monastery in silence. The abbot led the way; Faisal and Marzuq flanked me, and the monks followed. A number of the villagers had also attended the simple service. My return was an honor for them, and they wished to pay their respects to those who had died for the village.

The abbot invited everyone to the monastery gardens to participate in a simple meal of thanks that would commence in the early evening before darkness fell. The food would be provided by the villagers, and the monastery offered what could be spared from their supplies. I recalled the shortage of food and I knew that the fare would be meager, since the villagers could barely spare the food to feed a group of visitors such as ours. I nodded to Marzuq, who, with six of his well-armed men, disappeared into the forest.

They returned an hour later with directions to the whereabouts of six freshly killed deer. The villagers whooped with joy as men and women ran into the forest to prepare the dead animals. Sometime later, they reappeared, carrying pieces of meat. Cooking fires had been started in anticipation of this feast, and the venison was promptly suspended above the flames.

In the meantime, Faisal had overseen the secure placement of the ship in the inlet so that anyone approaching from the north or south would be unable to see it. The shallow draught of the vessel made it ideal for such a berth. The sail was lowered and the mast detached and laid on the deck so that its profile was no longer noticeable among the other small craft berthed close by.

In the meantime, Faisal had requested that his cooks help the villagers prepare the food and to make sure that all was done according to the liking of all. Faisal provided fruit that we had stored on board and that had retained its freshness, being stacked in straw in the coolness of the lower hold below deck.

The meal was a delight from start to finish. Once seated, we were presented with bowls of vegetables, freshly baked bread, and a healthy portion of venison that was cooked to perfection. Much to my delight, we were served small oatmeal cakes and honey. In deference to their guests, the villagers did not partake of the usual mugs of ale. A juice made from rose hips was presented to each person. The twelve men guarding the ship were not forgotten and were relieved from duty early by their comrades, who had already feasted, so that they too could participate in the feast.

* * *

The next day, feeling the effects of the long journey from Mesopotamia and the rigors of such travel, the soldiers and sailors welcomed the rest. Marzuq had continued the original schedule, and on any given day or night at least a dozen men patrolled the beach and guarded the ship. Those who were not on duty were allowed to rest and generally passed the time cleaning their weapons, talking of home and the multitude of other subjects that soldiers can find to discuss. Fraternization with the villagers was strictly forbidden.

Occasionally, I related the same stories to the men I had told to the young officers at the beginning of the journey. The abbot joined us one evening but sat silent; his face remained set and unreadable. A young monk approached me a day later and asked if he might record some of the stories. I suggested that instead of waiting for me to talk in the evening, he should talk with the young officers, several of whom spoke Saxon and Latin, and get the stories from them. He beamed and went straight to the abbot with the news.

* * *

Then the inevitable happened! Word was brought to me that ships of the sea raiders had appeared on the horizon, and it looked as though they were heading to this shore. Remembering their habits of the past, I informed Faisal and Marzuq that the sea raiders would remain out of sight for the remainder of the day and, during the night, would draw closer to the village and monastery and attack early in the morning.

The sea raiders knew how to disappear, but they did not count upon the village being defended by trained soldiers.

Once the men were assembled, Faisal addressed them. "As you know," he said, "this is now a land campaign. As senior officer of this expedition, I relinquish command to my cousin Marzuq, who commands the land forces. You will obey him as you would obey me."

Even before Marzuq spoke, the news of the sea raiders had spread. For many months now, the soldiers had seen little activity other than the minor excitement when they'd first arrived at Wearmouth.

Marzuq looked at his men and spoke in quiet tones. "The men who approach these shores are a formidable enemy. You have heard from the stories of Grandfather Alric of the death and destruction that result from their attacks. These sea raiders are the enemy of this village and this monastery. We have been welcomed here by the monks and the villagers; they are our friends. But, above all these raiders are enemies of my grandfather, Alric al-Biritaanya ibn Jabir, and so they are enemies of mine. I hope you feel the same."

The resounding cheer and the sound of sword blades tapping on shields gave Marzuq the answer he needed. "And now, men, prepare for battle. Grandfather Alric estimates that the raiders will attack at first light tomorrow. But we will double the guards around the perimeter of the village and the monastery in case of a surprise attack. The raiders do not know that we are here, so the ship should be safe, but guards there will also need to be doubled. In the meantime, tend to your weapons. Make sure that your bows are strung and that your arrows will fly true."

He looked once more at the men assembled before him. "I sincerely believe there is a reason we are here at this time. This enemy is a scourge to the people who live here. I invite you in their name to drive out the sea raiders and make them realize that to invade these shores again is at their own peril. These men are not true believers as we are. They worship different gods and believe that they go to a warrior heaven

627

when killed in battle; my grandfather tells me that this warrior heaven is called Valhalla. Let us arrange an early entry into Valhalla for each one of them!"

Once again, the steady drumming of swords on shields broke the silence. The men were ready, and for them to meet a formidable enemy brought a new of sense of excitement into their eyes. When Marzuq had finished speaking, the men formed themselves into companies and made a final check of equipment and weapons.

I had no choice. Marzuq looked knowingly at Faisal. "I will take grandfather to a safe place where he will come to no harm," Faisal said confidently.

"My dear boys," I said quietly out of earshot of anyone else. They looked at me and smiled.

"Grandfather," Marzuq said, "you were placed under our protection. And you will remain under that protection."

"I know a place where you, my dear Faisal, and your sailors can watch as the events unfold." They looked quizzically at me. "The wall of the monastery has a walking ledge on the inside that allows the monks to watch for anyone approaching. We can also use it strategically."

"And," Marzuq looked at Faisal, "we assume you will also wish to be there to watch the battle?"

"Well," I smiled, "if dear Faisal," I put my hand on his shoulder, "has me in his care, I should be with him!"

In spite of the tension, they both laughed. "Grandfather," Faisal began, "I remember some years ago, I was told by Grandfathers Khalil and Ahmed that you were the only person who could talk back to the Caliph. The expression was that you 'had a smooth tongue in your head,' and I see now how you were given that dubious honor." He looked at Marzuq. "He will be safe with me, cousin."

Marzuq nodded and signaled to his men that the villagers should be taken into the confines of the monastery for safety. Some of the men wished to stand and fight, but Marzuq knew that they would be no match for the sea raiders and might prove a weakness in his lines. And then . . .

To one of the monks, Marzuq asked a question in Latin. "Are the men skilled with the bow and arrow?"

"Yes," the monk responded. "They use a bow that is much longer than yours and can hit a deer on the run at over one hundred paces."

"Collect them together and they will form a group under your young captain Bron. But . . . "

The monk replied, "I am not allowed to fight because of the religious oath that I took to enter the monastery, but I will not desert you. I will remain as interpreter to make sure that the commands from your officer to the archers are clear."

"Excellent!" Marzuq was pleased. He then placed his soldiers in strategic positions around the village. Fires were forbidden, but several of the women emerged from the monastery at dusk and brought oatmeal cakes and hot tea.

A whispered *shukran* and a smile told each one how much this was appreciated. It would be a night of waiting. Each man would prepare his weapons and his thoughts in his own way. They would sleep in four-hour shifts so that two thirds of the men were awake at any one time. Extra blankets and robes were brought from the ship to ensure the warmth of the soldiers.

Just before dawn, Marzuq and his officers made sure all was well. Faisal and fifteen of his men were stationed in the monastery with me. Even though I had badgered Faisal to let me talk with the soldiers, I had been brought back to the monastery, after my early morning walk, as dawn stretched her rose-colored fingers into the sky.

"Battle this day for honor and be true to your comrades," Marzuq whispered to each group of soldiers, and then he looked at me. "Grandfather, it is time!"

Against my protests, I was taken into the safety of the monastery. But I was determined to get a full view of the battle. The walkway at the top of the wall had been reinforced and was functional. That would be my lookout point. I sat there with Faisal and his men as we drank hot tea and kept a sharp eye out for any movement.

"We do not know for sure if the enemy is still in the area," Faisal pointed out. "And we do not know where they beached their ships."

"They are here," I said.

Faisal looked out from the wall. "Are you being pessimistic, grandfather?"

I smiled in the dim light. "No I am a realist."

After all of these years I had surprised myself, but that sensation never left me. I told Faisal how I knew. "I can smell them," I replied. "I recall the time I spent in the stinking ship before Grandfathers Khalil and Ahmed rescued me." I paused. "That is how I know!

"They will be here within the hour," I added, "and will be planning their attack. It is always their plan to kill most of the people, and then they decide how to make the most sport of the survivors. They will not use the forest, as it does not suit their open style of fighting. They are most likely to be beached just beyond the inlet to the north. And since the wind always blows from the north, their smell carries from that direction."

Faisal spoke to one of his men. "Go and inform Commander Marzuq. Grandfather Alric is certain they are close."

The raiders had not seen the ship, for it was berthed at the river dock to the south of the monastery and the village. Faisal crouched by my side and signaled his men to keep their heads down. If the time was right, he could launch a flanking attack from the monastery. "This is different from captaining a ship," I said as a matter of fact.

He smiled in relief, knowing the battle was about to begin; the waiting was almost over. "By the way, this is yours, grandfather." Faisal presented my old knife to me as he spoke. It brought back so many memories. "One of the men noticed it in your cabin as they checked the ship last night." I took the weapon and fingered the blade.

"Now grandfather, please do not get that look in your eyes." His tone was serious. "The only way you will use that knife is if I and Marzuq and all of the men are killed by the raiders! Please put your thoughts to rest." He reached over and tapped me on the shoulder. "You are listening, grandfather?"

I nodded. Then I cocked my head to one side and held up my hand to indicate silence. "The smell is stronger. They are approaching."

They heard the cry of a hawk from the direction of the forest that lay to the west of the village. "That is Marzuq's signal," Faisal observed. "I suspect he has seen them. As you suggested, he has his men stationed in a perimeter around the village in case of an attack from the west."

I could hear the sounds of men talking as gray figures appeared on the beach from the north. Remarkably, my eyes adjusted to them instantaneously. As I watched I felt my body was immediately taken back in time to that moment when they had attacked the village and killed my parents and Hilda. I started to shake in excitement, wondering if this was the day when the village would wreak vengeance. I felt as though my body would explode, and my heart thumped wildly in my chest. I experienced some pain, probably because of the excitement, but it did not deter me from watching the men stride up the beach toward the village.

Two dark gray figures walked in front of a small army. As near as I could tell, there were about two hundred men. I remembered the two brothers who had led the first raiding party. As the raiders strode with purpose toward the village, the sun was starting to rise behind them, their outlines becoming obvious to us and to Marzuq and his men.

Faisal reminded his men to keep themselves concealed, and he and I would inform them as the events unfolded.

The raiders continued to advance toward the village and were not surprised at the lack of opposition. They did not expect any! As they moved closer, they formed a V shape, the two leaders in front. On command, the V-shaped line straightened, expecting a shield wall.

They obviously meant to move through the village in that way, killing as they went and trapping all who tried to escape.

They made no pretense of silence as they broke into a run, still maintaining their line and looking for the shield wall. Their shouts broke through the morning stillness. As the raiders approached the village, they slowed their pace. The attack was under way.

* * *

CHAPTER 47

After all of these years I still recall the events of that terrible morning. With each level of awareness I have achieved, the concept that men can do such things is alien to me, but as the thoughts are released into my conscious mind, that is why I return to the events of that day so long ago.

As I sat with Faisal, I did not know what had taken place, but from my high vantage point, I was able to glimpse a movement of men within the village. There was no noise or obvious disturbance, so I assumed that it was not a result of raiders surprising Marzuq and his men but most likely it was due to Bron and his archers returning from the west side of the village.

I unsheathed my dagger and stared at the blade, quickly lowering it so that the early sunlight would not reflect from it and give away our position. Gripping the handle tightly in my hand, I felt the presence of Hilda. She was with me once more! I held my breath and struggled to gain control of my emotions. I heard a cry above me. It was a hawk looking for morning breakfast, perhaps an errant fish on the shore or a mouse in the fields adjoining the monastery.

I turned my attention once more to the beach. Faisal and I watched the sea raiders approach the village. I could see that they were cautious. The expected resistance had not materialized and I could hear the mumbled sounds as the raiders started to question the lack of activity in the village. Then two words shouted in Arabic and in Saxon rang through the morning air. They were simple words but meant so much. Over the short distance from the monastery to the village, I heard the words, "Archers, now" first in Arabic, then in Saxon.

The gulls had been silent as the raiders approached the village, but now their eerie cries once more gave sound to the tableau before me.

* * *

At the signal, Bron and his village archers, fifteen men in all, armed with their long hunting bows and wearing green and brown attire, well matched to blend with the colors of the forest, stepped from their hiding places and loosed a flight of arrows toward the sea raiders. The arrows cut graceful arcs through the air, and each one found its target, bringing death or a serious wound to the enemy.

One of the raiders, perhaps their leader, positioned in the middle of the front line shouting commands, fell first as an arrow passed through his neck, his sword and shield falling to the wet sand. Two others close by also fell, pierced through the upper body. The irony was that one man was killed by an arrow that glanced off the shield of his companion, who, on turning to look at his falling comrade, was struck himself and mortally wounded. All I could hear from the enemy line were shouts of anguish as men were wounded, and the screams of others who died in pain. From the direction of the village I saw flight after flight of arrows as they were released by the bowmen.

There was no respite for the raiders, and death continued to rain down upon them. No sooner had the first flight reached them than the second was on its way. Following this, Marzuq's bowmen appeared, standing beside their Saxon comrades, and aimed straight and true at chest height.

The sea raiders appeared confused, not being prepared for such an onslaught. Arrows came at them from the sky, but when they tried to protect themselves by holding their shields high, their unprotected chests were pierced by iron-tipped feathered shafts. Many died immediately, not knowing what had happened.

I could hear the cries of the dying and wounded raiders as they realized that this was a battle that could not be won. Their shouts were pitiful as the arrows continued to fall into their ranks. One man fell to his knees, an arrow in his chest, and as he struggled for life, another arrow pierced his leather helmet and lodged itself in his head. Another man had both legs pierced and appealed to his comrade for help. One comrade took the man's arm in an attempt to assist him, but both fell under the onslaught of the feathered shafts.

"I think," I said to Marzuq with a smile, "that our brave opponents have met their match. This is not a group of farmers with their women and children being led to their deaths. It is a fighting force the likes of which they have not seen before!"

Men continued to fall upon the wet sand, and as if by a signal, the raiders halted in their movement and made a hurried retreat to the sea, leaving the sand littered with bodies. Even then, men continued to fall. Goose-quilled arrows mysteriously appeared from the sky and pierced their bodies.

As I peered over the monastery wall, a raider looking in my direction, as if seeking shelter from the iron-tipped death, must have seen the movement and raised his sword as if to draw attention to me, only to be killed by two arrows before he could utter a word.

As the raiders reached the edge of the sea, they turned in defiance. In spite of their losses, the raiders were not beaten, and they stood defiantly at the sea's edge as if to make a last stand. At that point, I heard Marzuq shout the command to advance; this was echoed in Saxon by his interpreter monk.

As they advanced, the village archers and Marzuq's bowmen made no sounds. They continued to rain death onto the raiders. For each step that the intruders retreated to the sea, the archers and bowmen advanced, alternating their attacks. With their backs to the morning sun, the raiders formed dark outlines against the sky. This made them easy targets for the archers, and the raiders were unable to protect themselves.

Several soldiers from the main body of Marzuq's group, on command, joined their colleagues and walked among the wounded giving no mercy. The archers and bowmen continued their steady approach to the sea, driving more of the fatal arrows into the enemy. The sea raiders, unable to get close to use their swords, had no means of fighting back.

This strategy continued until the remaining raiders, their backs to the sea, decided that they had suffered enough. With the attackers vanquished, at least for the moment, Faisal and I made our way to the beach. I would have smiled except I knew that the present situation could be reversed in an instant. We were not yet secure.

Then I heard someone shouting jubilantly in the northern tongue, "It is over. It is over." By this time, Faisal and I, the sailors, and the remainder of Marzuq's men had all left our respective positions to stand behind the archers and bowmen. The raiders that remained had dropped their weapons and shields and stood facing the line of archers and bowmen. Each of our men was ready to attack at the first sign of treachery.

Marzuq and Faisal stepped forward, turned, and invited Bron to join them, with the monk as interpreter, if needed. "Grandfather," Marzuq looked at me, "this is your time."

I took a step forward from the formation that the soldiers and archers had formed at the water's edge. I turned to Faisal and Marzuq and spoke in Arabic. "I am going to ask them about the number of ships. If you see the fingers of my right hand move, it means that whoever speaks is lying."

Marzuq nodded in agreement. Then I looked at Bron and switched to the Saxon tongue. "On the signal from Marzuq, please send two arrows into whoever is talking to me." Bron smiled and turned to his men; I heard him give this assignment to them. It was gleefully accepted.

One of the raiders took a step forward, as best he could, in the knee-deep water. He smirked as he spoke to me in rough Saxon. "It seems," he said with much bravado, as if trying to restore courage to his bedraggled and defeated colleagues, "that we have an impasse, old man. Your men in their fancy clothes perhaps do not wish to get wet!"

I wiggled my fingers behind my back to signal Marzuq. Two arrows suddenly protruded from the man's chest and he fell noisily into the water. "There is no impasse. I will question you one at a time and kill you if needed. Now, does anyone else have anything to add?" I asked in the language of the raiders. No one answered. "Is there anyone who will speak for you?" I asked.

A man stepped forward, the look of vengeance in his eyes.

"How many ships do you have? And where are they beached?" I inquired.

"We have two ships, and they are to the south."

He was lying. I knew from the remaining men and the bodies on the beach that there were, or had been, sufficient men to propel four ships. He had lied to me twice.

I signaled again to Marzuq, and the raider fell into the sea to join the first man, whose body rose and fell gently with the swell.

"Now," I looked at the other men, "I will have the truth from you or you will all die here, without a sword in your hand and no means of reaching your Valhalla."

"Who will speak the truth?" I asked. Another stepped forward, and when I looked at him closely, I perceived he was no more than fifteen years old. "You will speak the truth?"

"I will. I have no wish to join my father," he pointed to the body of the first man who had died.

"How many ships and where are they?" I repeated the question.

"Four, and they lie to the north, in the shelter of the cliff."

The truth at last! I translated for Marzuq and Faisal, who immediately sent men to burn three of their vessels. The remaining ship would be used to transport the survivors across the sea to their home. There is no greater deterrent to further attack, at least for some time, than the stories told by survivors who have been shamefully defeated. This would not stop the sea raiders from attacking in the future, but it would give the villagers a period of respite from such attacks. The skills of Bron and his fellow archers would cause any would-be attackers to think twice.

Faisal and Marzuq stepped forward and looked at the remaining raiders. Of the almost two hundred who had landed that morning, only thirty-one remained standing in the sea. "Grandfather," Faisal said, "please ask the boy the minimum number of men required to take one ship back to their homeland."

"Sixteen," he responded to my question, and I translated for Faisal and Marzuq. Marzuq turned to Bron and said, "We need to reduce the number of raiders to sixteen."

"We will gladly do this, sir," Bron responded in his native tongue. Marzuq did not need a translation. He saw the answer in Bron's eyes.

"But first," I interjected, and the men paused. You," I said to the boy who had spoken the truth, "step aside from your colleagues. You spoke the truth and this has saved your life!"

He did and I signaled to Bron to proceed with the work of culling the raiders to the required number. As the arrows flew from the bows of Bron and his men, fifteen more raiders fell into the sea.

The abbot, who had appeared when the fighting ceased and stood behind Faisal, was shocked. Hearing his sharp intake of breath, Faisal turned quickly and looked at him with intense eyes. "Master Abbot," Faisal, in his excitement spoke Arabic, which I translated, "these men would have returned at some time soon to harass and kill anyone alive in the village. It will be many years before they decide to come back here, knowing that the risk to them is high. My grandfather tells me that if a sea raider dies without a sword in his hands, the gates of Valhalla are closed to him. My grandfather has also informed the survivors that this same fate awaits those who attack the village and the monastery. Also, they do not know that we will not reside here. And, as you can see, they are much less arrogant now!"

"And, grandfather," Faisal did not take his eyes away from the shivering raiders. "Please inform them that I hope they have someone in their number capable of commanding the ship. I wish him to return to his home with this story."

I translated Faisal's words. The sullen eyes of defeated men looked at me, the light gone from them. I was confident that they would cause no further trouble. I spoke my thoughts to Faisal and to Marzuq.

"Now," Faisal said as he turned to Marzuq. "I will lead forty of my men and escort these pieces of garbage," he looked at the unkempt and disheveled raiders, "to make sure they set sail." He turned to the abbot. "Master Abbot, I agree with my cousin Faisal, and it is no guarantee, but I am sure that this shore will remain unmolested and safe for some years to come. We do this for our grandfather."

Faisal surveyed his men and the villagers who had collected behind us. Then he addressed Marzuq. "There is the matter of the bodies that needs attention."

The surviving raiders were then set the task of digging a mass grave, beyond the reach of tidal water and offset from the direct path from the sea to the village, in which to place the bodies of their dead comrades. Once this was done, tar and wood were added to help consume the remains by fire. When the last embers of the fire were smoldering, the grave was filled with sand.

The villagers collected the weapons of the sea raiders; they could be used for future protection. It was a miracle that none of the soldiers had been killed or injured.

Faisal looked around with satisfaction.

"And now," I said to the raiders, who were panting from their exertions, "you will be escorted to your ship and you will leave these shores."

* * *

At the end of the day, I decided to meet with Bron and his fourteen companions, the village archers. I learned from him that the ambush had been set up on the village side of the trail that ran north-south, a means of reaching other villages as well as the old Roman road that lay farther inland. The trees had given them adequate cover as they'd watched for movement from the forest.

The archers did not carry swords, and their only weapons, other than the bow and arrow, were sharp daggers, somewhat similar to mine, which I had kept close by me and treasured all of these years.

Bron had uttered a similar cry to that of the gulls, causing his men to lapse into a deathly silence, as though their breathing had stopped. His sharp eyes had seen movement on the edge of the forest.

Sea raiders had appeared in the dim light and moved together, as a group. They made no efforts to spread out, leaving the archers an easy target. Bron had told his men to aim for the hearts or the throats of the enemy. The killing had to be soundless so as not to give any warning to their colleagues, who would, no doubt, be walking from the sea to the village.

Bron sent the word along the line, "On my signal."

The sea raiders were positioned just where he wanted them, and arrows were sent flying into them. Bron had related to me that he and his men had spent years farming and hunting. These occupations had given them enormous patience, the ability to simply sit, lie down, or, in this case, stand immobile for hours and remain alert. I was amazed by this group of farmers turned archers.

He had estimated that the sea raiders were well within killing distance, and a second cry sent his men out of the cover of the trees and into the open. I asked Bron why he'd done this; it seemed to me that this action would put them in danger. He smiled at me and explained.

"Part of the reason," he said, "was that the sea raiders had not at first noticed the archers due to the dimness of the morning light, and the fact that they wore a variety of green and brown clothing had, as I had also witnessed, allowed them to blend in well with the backdrop of the trees."

As Bron had hoped, since he knew his archers would be no match in hand-to-hand combat against the sea raiders, the ambush was perfect. He did relate that his men unleashed five arrows each, one after the other, into the enemy that took down all twenty-four. As near as I could tell, two of the raiders survived the arrows but were severely wounded and tried to escape through the knee-high grass. They were found and quickly dispatched. Only one archer was injured—his bow string snapped after releasing his last arrow and he received a minor cut on the arm. I checked the wound and Bron was right. It was not serious. I told the archer to wash it and gave him an ointment to use.

"And then what did you do?" I asked Bron.

"We retrieved our arrows," he said, showing surprise at my question.

Of course. A goose-quilled arrow is too valuable to leave in an enemy! "And then?" I prompted.

"We walked silently to the village and joined your soldiers to wait for the other sea raiders."

"Oh, Bron," I suddenly remembered. "The bodies?"

His response was simple and to the point. "The creatures of the forest will clean up for us!"

I thanked him for his efforts and added that I needed to know this information to send it back to my supreme commander, the Caliph. Thanks to Bron and his men, Marzuq and his soldiers did not have the sea raiders at their backs.

* * *

Suddenly I was tired. And the discomfort that I had been feeling in my chest and arm was returning more frequently now. I needed to rest. It was night, after all. It had been several days since the aches and pains had started to bother me. The journey and the events of the day had made me weary. I drank water, with a little vinegar to make sure that the liquid would not give me the stomach sickness. A monk brought me a different type of oatmeal cake, which had vegetables mixed inside; it had a delicious savory flavor. I asked him to make sure that Faisal and Marzuq were taken care of and that they would have access to me whenever they needed to see me. He assured me that they were extremely well provided for and that they were also giving out food to the villagers.

Late in the afternoon, Faisal had offered to bring the ship closer so that I could use my room on board, but I declined his kind offer. The ship was safe where it sat, but I did request that he send men to bring my books and writing materials. I knew that once I was surrounded by them, I would feel most comfortable.

* * *

The monastery was quiet. I could see the stars through the high windows. I remembered the time I had lived here as a boy. I had then been given one of the separate huts that were assigned to the monks, but this time, being a special visitor, I was given quarters within the building that were equivalent to those of the abbot.

I sat looking at the stars for a long time. I thought of the many roads I had traveled, and of the strange way that God had chosen to show me how to use my abilities. I remembered the nights in Baghdad and in the desert. These were happy memories.

I fell asleep, and when I awoke, the room was bright with light, as though the sun were already high in the sky. But, instinctively I knew that this was not a natural light. The scent of roses was in the air. I turned over on my bed and I saw them.

Hilda and Bemia were standing next to each other, near my writing table, and just as I had seen them a few days ago, they were both young. Hilda had died young, but Bemia had taken that same appearance she'd had on our wedding day. Their pale robes radiated light, and their faces shone. Hilda's close-cropped hair contrasted with Bemia's long tresses.

We have been waiting for you, my love, Bemia smiled radiantly as she spoke. *How are you, Alric?* she asked and then answered her own question, *You look tired.*

"Yes," I said. "And I have been longing to see both of you again."

Do not worry, Hilda said. *It is not your time just yet, but it will be soon, and then we can be together for eternity. But come, let us talk and remember times past.*

I felt Bemia take my hand in hers and I could feel the warmth spreading through my whole body. The aches and pains seemed to leave me and I felt young again. There was so much I had to tell them, and even though I'd had a long life, I felt I still needed more time to complete my work.

* * *

Two nights later I was sitting comfortably conversing with Bemia and Hilda, as I had before. I felt a sense of elation that I had not experienced

643

for many years. As I stretched my neck to stop the onset of cramps that happen when I sit too long in any one position, I felt that the three of us were being watched. At first, I did not concern myself about the sensation.

I felt comfortable with Bemia and Hilda and I was pleased that they were nearby. I cherished these moments we were together. In fact, I began to take our private moments for granted. Bemia had always been a good judge of my disposition, and I found her looking at me with a look of concern. *My love,* she said, *I have something to tell you.*

I nodded. Since our marriage, we had become accustomed to detecting each other's feelings, to the point where we could read each other's thoughts even before they were spoken. At that moment, she squeezed my hand and indicated that I should look toward the back of the room.

There was nothing to see and then as the shadows darkened, two forms started to materialize. In the dim glow of the candle light, the flickering shadows suddenly took on golden hues, and there were patches of brilliant red, orange, and blue. As I peered into the changing light, I smiled as I knew what was happening.

Dressed as they had been on the day I'd first met them and looking every bit as young, Khalil and Ahmed walked slowly out of the shadows and into the light of the candle. Dressed in their military clothes, they were young once more. The lines of age had disappeared from their smiling faces. "My brothers," I said arising slowly from my seat. "How good it is to see you again, even though . . . "

I kissed both of them on each cheek and they returned the greeting.

We joined Bemia and your delightful sister Hilda several days ago but we were not ready for you, Khalil explained. *Now, we have had much to talk about,* Ahmed added.

We talked for the reminder of the night. As we were about to part, the thought occurred to me. "What about . . . ?" I ventured.

The Caliphs pigeons are on the way to the ship and may arrive within the next day or so. If you feel that you should give our grandsons forewarning of the message that the pigeons carry, you have our blessing.

I attempted to smile, but the strain must have shown on my face. *We know, dear brother, you will do the right thing and find the moment,* Ahmed said consolingly.

I turned away to hide the tears that began to cloud my vision. When I turned to look at them again, all four had returned to the shadows. All that remained was Bemia's soft tones. *We will return tonight, my love.*

* * *

I must have fallen into a deep sleep but was awakened by a light tap on the door. I called out, "Enter."

It was Faisal and Marzuq. "How are you grandfather?" Faisal asked.

"I feel well," I responded immediately. "Perhaps better than I have felt for some time."

Marzuq looked closely at me. "You seem to have a light in your eyes that I normally see in young men, grandfather."

I smiled at his comment. "I do feel better, and maybe that is the reason for the light in my eyes," I said. I could not tell them about the visitation. Who would believe the rambling words and illogical mind of an old man?

"We thought," Faisal looked at Marzuq, "that we should discuss with you the matter of our return to Baghdad?"

"Yes, we should. But allow me to get washed and dressed and we can talk over breakfast."

"That will be in order," Marzuq responded, ever the soldier. "But, grandfather, we are a little late for breakfast. It is early afternoon, and so a light midday meal might be better?"

His words surprised me. I must have slept well. They realized that my plans were firm and that I intended to remain at Wearmouth. I felt that their men had been away from their families long enough and they needed to go home to Mesopotamia. I looked at both men who still called me "grandfather" and smiled. "As you have probably guessed, I cannot leave my Bemia. Her ashes are buried here, and I would not desert her. I will remain in this place of my birth."

I could see the emotion on their faces as they fought not to make a comment. I continued rather than allow the moment to prolong itself. "You have both given me loyalty. I appreciate that and I thank you. I cannot give you a day when you should leave, but I am sure that God will give you a sign. If you will have patience, he will guide you, and when you do leave, I pray that he will watch over you and bring you and your men safely home."

Faisal was able to speak first. "We have always known that we were bringing you here to remain. To have loved as you have loved Grandmother Bemia is to have loved well. We accede to your thoughts and wishes."

I bowed my head in acknowledgment. "Now," I said, "there is something I must tell both of you. I cannot relate the details of how I came by this knowledge, so you must trust me as you always have." They looked at me curiously. "Grandfather Khalil and Grandfather Ahmed have passed on to the afterlife. I am sorry to be the bearer of such bad news, but I needed you to know. The Caliph has sent his message to you both by pigeon, which should arrive within a few days."

They were stunned—not so much because of the death of two men who were older than me, but by the fact that I was sincere and my voice steady as I spoke. And they knew that I would not speak of such matters unless I was sure.

"We thank you, grandfather," Khalil said.

"We had suspected as much, that we would not see them after this voyage due to their great age," Marzuq added.

"This must have been difficult for you, grandfather?" Faisal observed.

"It was, and I thank you both for your understanding. It was told to me that Khalil and Ahmed knew the end was near and were together with both families present at the time."

"We will mourn their loss privately," Faisal said. "For the moment, we must return to our men."

"We will say nothing of this disclosure." He looked at Marzuq. "But we will tell our men to start the preparations for our return home."

I knew the ship needed attention to prepare it for the long voyage back to Baghdad. They would follow the route that had brought us here. Marzuq would allow his men to hunt and stock the larders of the villagers so that food would be plentiful for the winter as well as replenish his own supplies. At this late stage of summer, the promise of a cold winter was in the air.

* * *

CHAPTER 48

A week later, after the evening meal, as I took a little exercise in the monastery garden, I sensed I was almost at the end of my journey. I have pursued my dream and lived by the laws of God and Allah. I have taught others many of the things that I have learned. My books are in safe hands—those I left in Baghdad are in the Great Library and those copies I brought with me will remain in the monastery library as my gift to the monks.

Yesterday, Faisal told me that the Caliph's pigeon had arrived with the news of the death of Khalil and Ahmed. Faisal looked at me gently as he spoke and I knew his mind was filled with questions, but he did not ask and he left me to my thoughts.

I felt that the attacks from the sea raiders were over for quite some time. From whatever village they came, the cream of their fighting men had been eliminated and they had been taught a lesson they would not forget. They would, at some future time, seek revenge, but they would never know whether they would be met by Marzuq and his soldiers again or the archers. In the meantime, I noticed that Bron had taken up the challenge of training more men as archers, and Marzuq's officers were showing the villagers the rudiments of sword fighting. All of this was carried out to the sounds of Arabic, Latin, and Saxon words.

I followed the activities with interest and, choosing my ground for the best vantage point, I often watched the men. Children and young boys watched and imitated the adults, fashioning themselves crude swords and bows and arrows using the tree branches.

At other times, when the air was still and I could not hear the voices of men and women or the sound of laughter, I continued my writing. There were two main volumes that consumed my time. The first, as requested by the Caliph, was my life story, with all of the elements of my work included therein. The other work was more private and was, in fact, this personal journal in which I write my thoughts. At the right time, I would give this to Faisal and Marzuq that they might read of our adventures and my thoughts during this journey.

I was given full access to the monastery library, but, in truth, even though this was a distinct pleasure, it did little to tear me away from my own books. Meager as my collection was, when compared with the several libraries of Baghdad, in particular the Great Library with its hundreds of thousand of volumes, the monastery library did little to excite me.

The abbot, God bless him, was proud of his collection of fifty or so books, but I did notice a distinct rising of his eyebrows and a gulp after I had requested more shelves. He was impressed when he entered my room and saw that the books in my collection numbered almost two hundred. However, he was grateful when I advised him that the books would be donated to the monastery when I had no further use for them. I could see the concern in his face. He smiled when I told him they were all written in Latin, with my handwritten notes added in Saxon in the margins of some of the pages.

Within the hour of my offer, the abbot had made it known to all of the monks that I had offered my generous collection to the monastery. I could tell from the increased number of casual visits I received from the monks that they could not wait to get their hands on my books. The fire of learning was in their eyes!

As my writing progressed, I found that I could not hold out on such a toilsome course, and I often fell asleep during the day. At night when all was still, I was visited by Bemia and Hilda with Khalil and Ahmed. We talked for hours, and so there is little wonder that I often felt tired during the day and was wont to fall asleep. Talking with them brought back the very life and breath of my younger days with these dear souls.

Faisal and Marzuq visited frequently and encouraged me to walk along the beach with them. They were never too busy to visit Grandfather Alric!

I was unknown to many of the villagers, and they had been inclined to stay away from me because of my so-called importance; they also feared my magical powers. Yes, magical powers! To see the sea raiders defeated in such a manner caused them to think of me in this way. But now, as they saw me walking on the beach with Faisal and Marzuq, some took the courage to approach me. Perhaps my Saxon features and conversing with them in the Saxon tongue helped to remove some of the mystique. Both Faisal and Marzuq had improved in their knowledge of the Saxon language.

Through the mists of time, I remembered the village before the first attack by the sea raiders. The stories of Beowulf, the hero who had fought against all adversity and triumphed, came back into my mind. Faisal and Marzuq, seeing the change in me, since I felt happy and content, thought my strength was improving.

I was surprised. The efforts at walking were no longer as strenuous as they had been.

As we walked along the shore, I instinctively watched for ships on the horizon; I saw only the small boats of the fishermen. The villagers told me that they were in the midst of good years. It was just a matter of throwing the nets into the sea and then retrieving them full of fish!

* * *

I felt a great sadness whenever I thought of my Bemia, but this was dismissed from my mind when she came to me at night. The visits of all four became a part of my life, which I did not mention to anyone else. Faisal and Marzuq would have considered it an old man's dreaming of the past, and I did not wish them to feel pity for me, but I knew that the visits by Bemia and Hilda were real.

Each time I took Bemia's hand in mine and looked into her eyes, the years were swept away. Each time I stared at the sea, I could feel her thoughts, which made my eyes brighter than they had been of late, even more than when I was reading my books. Fortunately, I was able to contain my emotions as I took my walks with Faisal and Marzuq.

One day, as we sat and rested on a rock that had been warmed by the sun, I looked up and saw a pair of gulls flying high in the sky. I watched them as they drifted on the wind. Suddenly, I felt sleepy. In my heart, I wanted to remain awake, but at the same time, I wanted to sleep.

* * *

I must have slept for the reminder of the day. I recalled Faisal and Marzuq helping me back to my room, but that is where my memory ended. After that, I recall nothing.

From my bed, through the high window, I watched the moon come out from behind a cloud. It was then that I detected the familiar scent of rose water in my nostrils. Shifting my eyes to the interior of the room, I saw Bemia and Hilda. They had not arrived accompanied by light, as had happened over the past week, and Khalil and Ahmed had not come with them this time. The room was illuminated only by the moonlight.

Let us walk, my love, Bemia said.

I was about to protest but found that the tiredness had gone from my body. In minutes, we were on the beach, Bemia and Hilda flanking me, their arms linked through mine. The moon was bright in the sky, a mist was on the sea, and the wind was low, which seemed to make the mist roll slowly toward me. I sensed that something was amiss, but unexpectedly the mist lifted like a gray veil. I saw myself as a young man, as I'd arrived in Baghdad for the first time.

As the air cleared, I looked at Bemia. Suddenly I was seized with a great joy and longing. *It will be soon, will it not?* I said.

She squeezed my arm in response. *Yes,* she said, as a feeling of euphoria swept though my whole body. *You have but a short time.* The heavy weight that had been on my shoulders for the past months had been lifted.

Suddenly I was back in my room. Bemia and Hilda were gone. The wind came up with the darkness, and then the gentle sun of that late summer morning signaled the arrival of the day. As I sat in the early morning light, I took the time to consider my next actions. I knew what I had to do.

All that day I stayed in my room, telling Faisal and Marzuq that I was not up to my daily walk along the beach. The sun shone, the sky was blue, and my heart was filled with joy. When night fell, I found comfort, for then I knew that this was the path chosen for me.

I looked at my writings that were stacked neatly on the desk. I will lie down soon with peace of a mind. I thought of my birth family, especially my sister Hilda, who lives on in my memory. I thought of my wife Bemia, my father Jabir, and my mother Amira, my brothers Khalil and Ahmed, the great Caliph, Harun al-Rashid, his wife Scheherazade, who memorialized Bemia in her stories, and all those who have helped me over the years and whose lives have touched mine.

Bemia and Hilda have appeared to me each night since the battle with the sea raiders, and we have shared many memories. Each day, I have slept until the midday sun shone its light into my room. This was a wonderful time for reflection.

I remembered the tablet that I received from the Librarian in Mosul all of those years ago. It was written many centuries ago by a wise man who understood this natural world. I have never told anyone what was written on the tablet. Most assumed that it was a recipe for weapons. I did not wish to disillusion them. The tablet held a secret that gave me an understanding of the world and allowed me to see into the future and to know the course of my life.

And now I know what must happen. *Maktub.* It is written.

* * *

PART V:
EPILOG

CHAPTER 49

Faisal was on board the ship that next morning when he received a message delivered by one of the monks requesting that he and Marzuq attend the abbot. Faisal quickly informed Marzuq and they hastened to the monastery. On their way, they received cautious looks from the villagers, who had started their morning work.

They were met at the monastery gate by the abbot, who, from his expression, told them everything without having to say a word. A monk, who was assigned to deliver Alric's breakfast, had informed the abbot that their distinguished guest had passed away during the night.

Faisal and Marzuq were taken to Alric's room where his body lay prone on the bed. For Alric, the sun had set for the last time. He had departed happily and was now with Bemia and Hilda.

The two grandsons requested a few moments alone in the room to offer prayers for their departed grandfather. As they left the room, with one last look at Alric's body, they found the abbot awaiting them. "If you would be so kind as to accompany me to my room, there are several items that we need to discuss." Without speaking, Faisal and Marzuq followed the abbot. "Please sit," the abbot offered chairs as they entered the room. "We need to decide on the disposition of the body of Lord Alric."

Faisal and Marzuq mumbled their thanks. "I am aware of Lord Alric's wishes," Faisal said quietly as he sipped the hot beverage provided by one of the monks. It had the pleasant taste of rose hips. "Our grandfather," he continued, "wished to receive the Saxon cremation and have his ashes buried alongside those of his wife."

"I see," the abbot responded. "That being the case," he added, "I suggest we perform the ceremony within the day."

"It shall be done," Faisal responded.

"I will arrange," Marzuq added, "for my soldiers to form a guard of honor at the funeral pyre. I suggest that your archers who stood with my men also be included in this guard of honor." The abbot agreed. "Perhaps, abbot," Marzuq asked, "you could make the arrangements for the villagers to provide the wood?"

The abbot nodded and looked at the desk, upon which were collected Alric's papers. "As you can see, captain, I have not disturbed Lord Alric's papers. He has marked each of the two piles clearly. One for your Caliph and one you," he said as he looked at Faisal and Marzuq.

"And we understand, abbot, that Lord Alric donated his collection of books to the monastery library." Faisal waved his hand toward the full shelves. The abbot nodded, his expression showing his gratitude.

Faisal and Marzuq rose from the chairs. "We must inform our men of Lord Alric's death. We will then leave tomorrow on the first suitable tide."

Faisal rubbed his chin. "If it is not an imposition to you, abbot, we will send two men to help prepare Lord Alric's body."

The abbot agreed and as an afterthought said, "One last thing . . ." At the door, Faisal and Marzuq turned toward him. "Among Lord Alric's possessions there was an old dagger, a gold coin, and two ancient tablets, one of which appears to have been broken at some time. There is also another tablet of baked clay. What do you wish to have done with them?"

Faisal and Marzuq looked at each other. "It is Lord Alric's wish that they accompany him to the grave," Faisal said. "The dagger is well known to us, and it is a personal possession that he has treasured since leaving this shore. The gold coin was given by my grandfather Khalil to grandfather Alric when he first arrived in Mesopotamia and visited the ruins of the old city of Troy. The broken tablet was found among the ruins of the city of Nineveh and was given to him by Grandfather Ahmed. The other tablet is a mystery, but we know that our grandfather would prefer that it accompany him to the grave. "

Both Faisal and Marzuq had no more words to add; they both felt the emotion of Alric's passing.

* * *

Both soldiers and sailors mourned Alric's death but celebrated his life. To have known such a man was an honor beyond their wildest dreams. As one who practiced the art of *al-khimiya*, he had taken the fledgling science to new heights of achievement. The apparatus used in alchemy had been part of his daily life. The books, neatly stacked on his shelves, had been his passion.

He had been a patriarch among his people. He'd been already advanced in years when his wife had died. At Bemia's grave he had tried to speak, but his voice had faltered and broken. Though he'd lived two years longer, he had continued his work, always seeking new knowledge. Although he'd sensed his impending death, during these past weeks he had retained his energy, but gradually this too had waned, as was to be expected in a man of his great age. As near as the sailors and soldiers could tell, Alric had passed his eightieth year some time ago. They felt that the world had lost a light with his passing.

As time went by, the pain of his death would diminish, but he would always be remembered. He had never spoken of it, but Scheherazade had immortalized Alric in some of her stories whenever she had written of an alchemist. These would never die. She had provided an inheritance for Alric, just as she had for Bemia.

* * *

The funeral pyre and the burial took place in the late afternoon. The entire village attended Alric's funeral, and twelve sets of bearers in turn carried his shrouded body to the pyre.

The day was bright and cheerful, characteristic of late summer. The birds and the ubiquitous shrieking gulls maintained their silence while Faisal and the abbot spoke the last words over the body. The gray sea even looked blue that day, as if to honor Alric.

When the pyre had burned its last flame, six of the men dampened the hot ashes with water, recovered them, and placed them in an urn which Faisal and Marzuq had provided. The burial ceremony was simple and soon completed. All remained to the end to honor Alric.

When the ceremony was over, many eyes were filled with sorrow. The villagers took it upon themselves to set up tables and serve food in the monastery garden. The abbot sat at the head of the table, flanked by Faisal and Marzuq. The villagers, sailors, and soldiers intermingled freely. There were no speeches, and the conversation was subdued and calm.

The daylight had gone when the last table was cleared. The soldiers and sailors bade their farewell to the villagers. Faisal and Marzuq led the procession to the ship, still in the berth where it had been since its arrival, but now it was ready for the sea again; the mast had been put into place and the timbers freshly caulked.

Bron and his archers formed an impromptu guard at the sides of the walkway to the ship, where Faisal and Marzuq gratefully thanked them. The next tide, they estimated, would be early in the morning, and they were anxious to get under way and head for home.

* * *

The horizon was tinged with red, and suddenly the sun appeared spreading its light on a new day. Faisal thought about the time that they had spent at Wearmouth. Alric had truly been a remarkable man.

When the wind had strengthened, the men hoisted sail and took the ship out to sea. For the first half hour, the ship rocked gently on the waves as they moved into the open waters. In the east, a white cloud rested on the horizon. Such was the dawn of this happy day.

Faisal stood at the deck rail as he gazed in silence toward the village and the green fields beyond. He had given himself a pleasant respite from the thoughts that troubled him.

He could see the first stirrings of life as the villagers emerged from their huts. He felt nostalgia for Alric and even more for his own home and family as he looked at the sunrise. He had sought out a new way to travel. Alric had taught him much about the world, and he would discover other interesting things in the years ahead. He even thought about a journey to the land that lay on the other side of the Western Ocean.

Alric had said, "You will not realize that you are walking a new road every day."

Faisal would continue to work with the books, donated to him by Alric. In fact, it seemed that Alric had disposed of a lot of his personal items before he had left Baghdad. It was as if . . . Faisal placed his hand on his forehead, as the thought suddenly occurred to him. "*Insha'allah*," he said quietly. "As God wills it." He heard a sound and turned to see Marzuq approaching with one of Alric's two large volumes in his hands.

"Cousin," Marzuq said quietly, "have you read these last pages of grandfather Alric's journal?"

"I have, Marzuq."

"What do you make of them?" Marzuq asked, bursting with curiosity. "At first I thought they were the ramblings of an old man, and then I reminded myself that Grandfather Alric was a scientist first and last. He would not make up such stories."

Marzuq took a breath before he went on. "But I am at a loss to explain his thoughts concerning his long-dead sister, Hilda, and Grandmother Bemia and the fact that they appeared to him night after night and engaged in conversation; it is difficult to believe."

"Those were my thoughts also, Marzuq. Until I remembered that Grandmother Bemia's blond hair was quite fine and waist length."

"What . . . ?" Marzuq started to exclaim.

Faisal held up his hand as he continued. "Grandfather's room was cleaned each morning."

"That is correct," Marzuq agreed.

"I cannot, for the life of me explain why these thoughts do trouble me," Faisal said quietly, "but I noticed hair on the chairs before we sat down in grandfather's room. The hairs were blonde and very long, like Grandmother Bemia's, as I last remember her. I know that none of the villagers had such long hair. And," he looked at Marzuq, "the room had the scent of rose water!"

"Then, can it be true . . . ?" Marzuq started to ask, and his eyes opened wide as recognition took hold. "I remember when we were children and we spent time with Grandmother Bemia, there was always the smell of rose water about her."

Faisal looked into Marzuq's eyes. "Did not Grandfather Alric know ahead of time of the deaths of our grandfathers Khalil and Ahmed?" Faisal asked rhetorically. "I think it is time to go home, cousin," he concluded.

Marzuq nodded in agreement.

* * *

INDEX OF CHARACTERS

Abal: *wild rose*; maidservant to Lady Amira; one of three who gives Alric a bath on his introduction to the house of Lord Jabir; see also Buhjah and Maha.

Abdul al-Warith: *Servant of the Supreme Inheritor*; First Minister to the Caliph, Harun al-Rashid.

Ahmed: *most highly adored, most praised*; variation of the name Muhammad; soldier and captain under Khalil; widowed and childless through acts of war.

Ali al-Maslawi: *Ali from Mosul*; former tribal leader; now one of the Caliph's trusted ministers.

Alim: *wise, learned*; Guardian of the Tablets of Nineveh to His Most Royal Personage the Caliph, Harun al-Rashid.

Alric: born ca. 775 A.D. in Wearmouth, located in Bernicia, the northern province of Northumbria; also known as Alric al-Biritaanya ibn Jabir.

Amira: princess; wife of Jabir; mother of Asad and Khalil; adoptive mother of Alric and Bemia.

Asad: *lion*; not to be confused with *As'ad,* which means *happy, fortunate*; brother to Khalil; Caliph's representative in Constantinople; also given the title Emir.

Bashir: *bringer of glad tidings*; captain of the prison guard and son of my Amira's niece, Durah.

Bron: *brown, dark*; a farmer and an archer; leader of the village archers who helped Marzuq defeat the sea raiders.

Buhjah: *joy, delight*; maidservant to Lady Amira; one of three who gives Alric a bath on his introduction to the house of Lord Jabir; see also Abal and Maha.

Bemia: *battle maiden*; born in Deira, the southern province of Northumbria, located to the south of Wearmouth; became Alric's wife.

Durah: *pearl*; Amira's niece; husband killed in a skirmish with infidels; mother of Bashir, captain of the palace guard.

Ecgfrith: an older monk who was skilled in the medical arts and who took Alric on as an apprentice.

Ethelbald: abbot of the monastery at Wearmouth at the time of the first raid of the sea raiders and at the time of Alric's capture.

Faisal: *decisive*; Khalil's oldest son; a man of more than forty summers; chosen to captain the ship that carried Alric back to Britain.

Fayyad: *generous*; father-in-law and business partner of Abdul al-Warith when he was a young man.

First Minister: Abdul al-Warith, *Servant of the Supreme Inheritor*, and chief adviser to the Caliph, Harun al-Rashid.

Gorm: father of Haldor.

Gunnarr: second-in-command to Haldor.

Haldor: captain and leader of the sea raiders.

Hana: *happiness*; a servant to Alric in his old age.

Harun al-Rashid: *Harun (Aaron) the Just, Harun the Rightness*; caliph of Baghdad.

Hilda: sister to Alric; killed by sea raiders saving Alric's life.

Jabir: *bringer of glad tidings*; palace guard; sergeant; son of Amira's niece, Durah; not to be confused with Jabir, husband of Amira.

Jabir: full name Jabir al-Hajjaj ibn Yusuf abu Asad abu Khalil, meaning Jabir the pilgrim, son of Yusuf, father of Asad and Khalil; not to be confused with the great-nephew of Amira.

Jawal: *generous*; one of Ali al-Maslawi's breakfast club friends; see Ma'mun and Mash'al

Kalila: *beloved*; wife of Abdul al-Warith, First Minister to the Caliph, Harun al-Rashid; daughter of a wealthy Baghdad merchant, Fayyad; her dowry added much to Abdul's wealth; met an untimely end when she discovered Abdul's illegal dealing.

Khalil al-Din: *good friend of the faith*; birth name: Khalil ibn Jabir; son of Jabir and Amira; younger brother of Asad; rescues Alric from the sea raiders; adoptive brother of Alric and Bemia.

Latif: *gentle, kind*; a soldier who showed an interest in Alric's writing on the way to Baghdad from Constantinople.

Maha: *has beautiful eyes*; maidservant to Lady Amira; one of three who gives Alric a bath on his introduction to the house of Lord Jabir; see also Abal and Buhjah.

Malik Lail: *Man-With-No-Face*; code name for the kidnapper of Bemia.

Ma'mun: *trustworthy*; one of Ali al-Maslawi's breakfast club friends; see also Jawal and Mash'al.

Maria: Spanish servant to the First Minister; a gift from the First Minister's Umayyad contact in Spain.

Ma'ruf: *well-known* or *good*; see also Rufus.

Marzuq: *blessed by God, fortunate*; second son of Ahmed; commander of the guards aboard the ship that carried Alric back to Britain.

Masarrah: *delight, joy*; wife of Alim.

Mash'al: *torch*; the hanger-on or interloper in Ali al-Maslawi's breakfast club; see also Jawal and Ma'mun.

Munib: *repentant*; Ahmed's cousin; owner of the caravansary in Mosul.

Nawal: *gift*; daughter of Alim and Masarrah.

Rafiq: *kind, friend*; Alric's contact on the way from Baghdad to Mosul.

Rasil: *messenger*; original name unknown; an assassin who is paid to kill Bemia; well-educated; lost his considerable inheritance through gambling and drinking; also known as the Messenger of Death.

Rufus: a servant from Brittany who helps Alric and Bemia in the laboratory; Celtic by birth; captured as a teenager during a raid and used as a slave; also called Ma'ruf, *well-known* or *good*.

Sakhr: *rock*; grandson of Ali al-Maslawi; captain of the guard who escorts Alric to the palace; after which Sakhr and his men become Alric's honor guard.

Sighard: sentry killed by the sea raiders during the first attack on Wearmouth.

Skardi: brother to Haldor and second-in-command; killed by Hilda.

Thawab: *reward*; valet to Alric on the journey back to Britain.

Thomas-One-Eye: a monk (Brother Thomas) so called by the villagers because of an accident cutting firewood that resulted in a flying piece of wood piercing his eye.

Toki: older half-brother of Gorm and uncle to Haldor; captain of the knar and drowned when the ship sank before the raid on Wearmouth.

Wahid: *unequalled*; Chief Steward in the house of Jabir; served as Khalil's guardian when he was young and Jabir was away on travel.

GLOSSARY

Abaya: overgarment worn by some women in Muslim cultures; traditional abayas are black and may be either a large square of fabric draped from the shoulders or head, or a long black caftan; the abaya should cover the whole body save face, feet, and hands; it can be worn with the *niqab,* a face veil covering all but the eyes; Saudi Arabia requires women to wear abayas in public; the *niqab* is optional; contemporary abayas are usually caftans, cut from light, flowing fabrics like crape, georgette, and chiffon. They are now made in colors other than black.

Abaya, Leila: a traditional woman's outer robe, usually worn over the head, and the front is kept closed by means of tassels on the left side; there is also a strap with snap buttons inside to hold the abaya in place and keep it from slipping to the sides.

Abd: *servant of, slave of,* used in Arabic names often in conjunction with one of the ninety-nine names of God.

Abu: *father of,* used in Arabic names.

Ali: a nephew and son-in-law of the Prophet Mohammed and one of the first converts to Islam.

Alim: Religiously learned man (pl: Ulema).

Allah: Arabic word for God.

Animal fat: when rendered down gives glycerin.

Aqua fortis: nitric acid.

Ayatollah: *sign of God*; modern title for a high-ranking Shiite leader.

Baraka: *blessing*.

Burqa: *Niqab* or face veil for Muslim women. This *burqa* has two layers of cloth covering the face—the inner layer (touching the skin) is made of cotton, while the outer layer is made of chiffon. There are two other layers of cloth—one to cover the head, and a flip-down flap that covers the eyes as well. This *niqab* has a band of cloth to tie around the head. In other countries, a *burqa* is also known as a *khimar* or chador.

Britannia: the Roman name for Britain.

Caliph: from the Arabic word *Khalifa*; supreme ruler of the early Islamic empires.

Caravansary: a medieval motel for caravans either in cities or in rural areas along caravan routes.

Emir: from the Arabic word *amir* meaning *prince*; a prince or army commander.

Fatwa: nonbinding legal opinion.

Galabia, variant of **djellaba:** a long, loose, hooded garment with full sleeves, worn especially in Muslim countries.

Glycerin (glycerol): produced when animal fat is rendered down.

Hadith: tradition relating to what the Prophet Mohammed said or did.

Hajj: pilgrimage to Mecca, one of the five pillars of Islam.

Hegira: Mohammed's emigration with his followers from Mecca to Medina in 622 that marks the beginning of the Muslim calendar.

Hijab: traditional head covering worn by Muslim women.

Houri: one of the beautiful dark-haired virgins who attend the faithful in Paradise; mentioned in the Qur'an.

House of Wisdom (*Bayt al-Hikma*) was a library and translation institute in Abbasid Baghdad; it was a major center of learning during the Islamic Golden Age.

Hummus bi tahinah: chickpeas with a sesame paste.

Ibn: *son of;* used in Arabic names.

Imam: leaders, specifically either (1) a prayer leader, or (2) for Shiites, the divinely guided political and religious leader of the community.

Iron oxide: used to prepare ointments to soothe the skin and cure the oozing and weeping of skin rashes.

Islam: *the Path;* from the Arabic for "submission" to the will of God.

Jilbab: a long, flowing, baggy overgarment worn by Muslim women to satisfy the need for modesty; covers the entire body except for hands, feet, face, and head—the head is then covered by a scarf or wrap.

Jubah: a loose-fitting garment; a cloak; a long, flowing Arabic robe, usually white.

Kaaba: square building in Mecca believed by Muslims to be the house Ibrahim erected for God and the focus of Muslim worship

Kaftan (caftan): a man's cotton or silk cloak buttoned down the front, with full sleeves, reaching to the ankles and worn with a sash; traditional wear in the eastern Mediterranean.

Kharijite: from the Arabic *seceder*, an early political sect of Islam.

Kibbi: a ground mixture of wheat and lamb.

Madhhab: legal school or rite.

Madrasa: theological college.

Maghrib: from the Arabic "west," the western Islamic lands, including Tunisia, Algeria, Morocco, and sometimes Spain.

Magnesia: an ore of magnesium used for preparing medicines to cure ailments of the stomach.

Mahr: dower; see also **Sadaq**.

Malachite: an ore of copper used to prepare an eye salve.

Mamluk: slave.

Mazza: hot and cold appetizers.

Mihrab: niche in the Mecca-facing wall of a mosque.

Mile: as used in this text, a unit of distance based on the Roman mile which denoted a distance of 1,000 paces (1 pace is 2 steps, 1,000 paces being, in Latin, *mille passus*) or 5,000 Roman feet; about 1,618 modern yards.

Minbar: pulpit.

Miraj: from the Arabic *ladder*; Mohammed's mystical journey to heaven.

Mosque: from the Arabic *masjid*; a place of Muslim worship.

Mu'al-alim: *teacher*.

Mufti: independent legal scholar who offers *fatwas,* or nonbinding legal opinions.

Muhammad: Mohammed.

Mujaddid: literally, *a renewer* (of the century); a religious reformer.

Mujtahid: a person who interprets the application of Islamic law.

Muslim: literally *one who submits himself* [to the will of God]; a follower of the religion of Islam.

Niqab: a face veil.

Qadi: judge.

Qibla: direction of prayer, at first toward Jerusalem and since 623 toward the Black Stone in the Kaaba at Mecca.

Qur'an: from the Arabic "recitation," God's word as revealed to the Prophet Mohammed.

Ramadan: ninth month of the Muslim year and the month of fasting during daylight hours.

Sadaq: dower; see also **Mahr.**

Shah: Persian word for *king*.

Shari: rules and regulations that govern the day-to-day lives of Muslims.

Shiite: from the Arabic *party*; one who believes that authority passed from the Prophet Mohammed to his lineal descendants.

Shukran: Thank you.

Sufi: from the Arabic word for *wool*; a mystic.

Sultan: from the Arabic word for *power*; a title given to a powerful political leader, such as a king or sovereign of a Muslim state.

Sunni: customary procedure for living, specifically the ways and customs of Mohammed.

Sunna: one who follows the ways and customs of Mohammed, specifically those who accept that authority was passed down through consensus of the Muslim community.

Tabbulah: a salad of onions, chopped tomatoes, radishes, parsley, and mint.

Thobe: a disdasha for men; a robe worn indoors.

Tus (Toos, Tous (Persia): a city where the remains of Harun al-Rashid are said to be buried; 300 miles east of the southernmost tip of the Caspian Sea.

Ulema: religiously learned men (singular: Alim).

Vizier: adviser to a ruler; government minister.

Waleemah: wedding reception.

Wali: guardian of the bride.

Zinc oxide: used to prepare ointments to soothe the skin and cure oozing and weeping skin rashes.

ABOUT THE AUTHOR

Elizabeth James is the pen name of a scientist and his wife, a teacher-calligrapher, who live in the Rocky Mountain region of the United States.

Both were born and grew up in County Durham, England, an area that has a rich and colorful history. They were educated in England before moving to Alberta, Canada. In 1980, they moved to the United States.

They are avid readers and students of history who were nurtured by teachers at school. Collecting antiquarian books and manuscripts has enriched their interest in history. It was one of the manuscripts that initiated their interest in writing their first novel.

They are currently working on their fourth novel, which revolves around the life and work of one of the Japanese American scientists who played a role in their second novel, *Across the Bridge*.

Printed in the United States
124386LV00004B/1-42/P